'Every decade must have a great story of how we fail, how our society comes apart. Joe Hill has just written ours – which makes us all refugees seeking a safe haven in the wreckage of a world made brutal and hostile. Ominously superb'

Nick Harkaway, author of *Tigerman*

'Joe Hill has always been good, but he's created something incandescent here, soaring and original. He's a master storyteller who writes with fire in his veins'

Lauren Beukes, author of *Broken Monsters*

'A terrific story; a *Lord of the Flies* for the Twitter generation: part post-apocalyptic fable, part social satire. It's clever, gripping and packs a hell of a punch'

Joanne Harris, author of *Chocolat*

'I devoured this book as if the pages themselves were on fire . . . an end of the world tale with a blazing heart of hope at its core. A contender for book of the year'

Sarah Pinborough, author of *13 Minutes*

'This is a book that starts with a bang and then relentlessly builds. Joe managed to make my skin crawl in the first chapter, turning what should be a time for celebration into something decidedly creepy. At the mid-point of a lengthy book it became near un-putdownable, in that horrifying "can't look away from a car crash" kind of way. Although the details are dark and even horrible, the narrative pull is relentless and unstoppable'

Mark Yon, *SFF World*

'Take the ideas, characters, and tone of *Station Eleven* (2014) and add a large helping of the action, villains, and unrelenting menace from *Doctor Sleep* (2013) and you have *The Fireman*, an excellent example of the very best that genre fiction has to offer readers today'

*Booklist*

**Also by Joe Hill from Gollancz**

Heart-Shaped Box

20th Century Ghosts

Horns

NOS4R2

In the Tall Grass (with Stephen King)

# THE FIREMAN

Joe Hill

GOLLANCZ
LONDON

# THE FIREMAN

A NOVEL

JOE HILL

GOLLANCZ
LONDON

Page 748 constitutes an extension of the copyright page

First published in Great Britain in 2016 by Gollancz
an imprint of The Orion Publishing Group Ltd
Carmelite House, 50 Victoria Embankment
London EC4Y 0DZ

An Hachette UK Company

1 3 5 7 9 10 8 6 4 2



A CIP catalogue record for this book is
available from the British Library.

ISBN (Hardback) 978 0 575 13071 5
ISBN (Export Trade Paperback) 978 0 575 13072 2

Printed and bound by CPI Group (UK) Ltd, Croydon, CR0 4YY

FSC
www.fsc.org
MIX
Paper from
responsible sources
FSC® C104740

www.joehillfiction.com
www.orionbooks.co.uk
www.gollancz.co.uk

For Ethan John King, who burns bright. Your dad loves you.

Inspiration:

J. K. Rowling, whose stories showed me how to write this one,

P. L. Travers, who had the medicine I needed,

Julie Andrews, who had a spoonful of sugar to help me swallow it,

Ray Bradbury, from whom I stole my title,

my father, from whom I stole all the rest,

and my mother, who introduced me to most of the mycology (and mythology) I relied on to write this story.

Although *Draco incendia trychophyton* is an invention, my ma would tell you that almost every feature of my fictional spore can actually be found in nature.

Outside the street's on fire
in a real death waltz . . .

—*"Jungleland," Bruce Springsteen*

Though I spends me time in the ashes and smoke
In this 'ole wide world there's no 'appier bloke.

—*"Chim Chim Cher-ee," Robert and Richard Sherman*

It was a pleasure to burn.

—Fahrenheit 451, *Ray Bradbury*

# THE FIREMAN

# Prologue

# Lit

Harper Grayson had seen lots of people burn on TV, everyone had, but the first person she saw burn for real was in the playground behind the school.

Schools were closed in Boston and some other parts of Massachusetts, but here in New Hampshire they were still open. There had been cases in New Hampshire, but only a few. Harper had heard that half a dozen patients were being held in a secure wing of Concord Hospital, looked after by a medical team outfitted in full-body protective gear, every nurse armed with a fire extinguisher.

Harper was holding a cold compress to the cheek of a first grader named Raymond Bly, who had caught a badminton racquet in the face. There was always one or two each spring when Coach Keillor broke out the badminton racquets. Without fail, he told the kids to walk it off, even when they were holding a handful of their own teeth. One of these days she wanted to be there to see him take a badminton racquet in the nuts, just so she could have the pleasure of telling *him* to walk it off.

Raymond had not been crying when he came in, but when he saw himself in the mirror he lost his composure briefly, his chin dimpling, the muscles in his face trembling with emotion. The eye was black and purple and almost sealed shut, and she knew the sight of his reflection was more frightening than the pain.

To distract him, she reached for the emergency candy stash. The emergency candy stash was a battered Mary Poppins lunch box, rusting at the hinges, containing a few dozen individually wrapped candy bars. There were also a large radish and a potato in there, items she reserved for managing the most serious cases of misery.

She peered inside, while Raymond held the compress to his cheek.

*"Hmm,"* Harper said. "I think I've got one more Twix bar in the candy box and I could really use one."

"Do *I* get candy?" Raymond asked in a congested voice.

"You get something better than candy. I have a big tasty radish, and if you can be *very* good, I'm going to let you have it, and I'll have the Twix bar." She showed him the inside of the lunch box so he could inspect the radish.

"Ugh. I don't want a radish."

"What about a big, sweet, tasty potato? This is Yukon Gold right here."

"*Ugh.* Let's arm wrestle for the Twix. I can beat my dad arm wrestling."

Harper whistled three bars of "My Favorite Things," pretending to think it over. She was prone to whistling bits from 1960s movie musicals and had secret fantasies of being joined in song by helpful blue jays and cheeky robins. "I don't know if you want to arm wrestle with me, Raymond Bly. I'm very fit."

She pretended she needed to look out the window to think it over—which was when she saw the man crossing the playground.

From where she stood, she had a direct view of the blacktop, a few hundred feet of tarmac marked up with the occasional hopscotch grid. Beyond that was an acre of mulch, with an elaborate play set planted in it: swings, slides, a climbing wall, and a row of steel pipes the kids could bang on to make musical gongs (privately Harper referred to these last as the Xylophone of the Damned).

It was first period and no kids were out now, the only time of the day there wasn't a flock of screaming, rioting, laughing, colliding children rushing about in sight of the health office. There was just the man, a guy in a baggy green army jacket and loose brown work pants, face in the shadow of a grimy baseball cap. He crossed the asphalt at a slant, coming around the back of the building. His head was down and he staggered, couldn't seem to hold to a straight line. Harper's initial thought was that he was drunk. Then she saw the smoke coming out of his sleeves. A fine, white smoke poured out of the jacket, around his hands, and up from under his collar into his long brown hair.

He lurched off the edge of the pavement and onto the mulch. He took three more steps and put his right hand on the wooden rung of a ladder leading up into the jungle gym. Even from this distance, Harper could see something on the back of his hand, a dark stripe, like a tattoo, but flecked with gold. The specks flashed, like motes of dust in a blinding ray of sunlight.

She had seen reports about it on the news, but still, in those first moments, she could hardly make sense of what she was looking at. Little candies began to fall out of the Mary Poppins lunch box, rattling on the floor. She didn't hear them, wasn't aware she was now holding the box at a crooked angle, dumping out miniature candy bars and Hershey's Kisses. Raymond watched the potato drop with a fleshy thud and roll out of sight under a counter.

The man who walked like a drunk began to sag. Then he arched his spine convulsively, throwing his head back, and flames licked up the front of his shirt. She had one brief glance at his gaunt, agonized face and then his head was a torch. He beat his left hand at his chest, but his right hand still held the wooden ladder. His right hand was burning, charring the pine. His head tipped farther and farther back and he opened his mouth to scream and black smoke gushed out instead.

Raymond saw the expression on Harper's face and started

to turn his head to look over his shoulder and out the window. Harper let go of the candy box and reached for him. She clamped one hand to the cold compress and put her other hand behind Raymond's head, forcibly turning his face from the window.

"Don't, dear," she said, surprised at the calm she heard in her own voice.

"What was that?" he asked.

She let go of the back of his head and found the cord for the blinds. Outside, the burning man sank to his knees. He bowed his head, like one praying to Mecca. He was engulfed in flames, a mound of rags pouring oily smoke into the bright, cold April afternoon.

The shade fell with a metallic crash, shutting out the whole scene—all except a feverish flicker of golden light, glimmering madly around the edges of the blinds.

# BOOK ONE

# CARRYING

# APRIL

## 1

She did not leave the school until an hour after the last child had gone home, but even so she was departing early. Most school days she was required to stay until five, for the fifty or so children who hung around for extended hours while their parents worked. Today, everyone was gone by three.

After she shut off the lights in the nurse's office, she stood at the window and looked out into the playground. There was a black spot by the jungle gym where the fire department had hosed away the charred bits that couldn't be scraped up. She had a premonition she would never return to her office and look out this window again, and she was right. School was suspended statewide that evening, with assurances they would reopen when the crisis passed. As it happened, it never passed.

Harper imagined she would have the house to herself, but when she got home, Jakob was already there. He had the TV on, turned low, and was on the phone with someone. From his tone—calm, steady, almost lazy—a person would never guess Jakob was in a state of excitement. You had to see him pacing to know he was keyed up.

"No, I didn't see it myself. Johnny Deepenau was down there in one of the town trucks, pushing the debris out of the road, and he sent us pictures from his cell phone. It looked like a bomb went off inside. It looked like terrorism, like . . . hang on. Harp just walked in." Her husband lowered the phone, pressed it to his chest, and said, "You came home the back way, didn't you? I know you didn't come through downtown. They've got the roads all sewed up from North Church to the library. The whole town is crawling with cops and National Guard. A bus exploded into flames and crashed into a telephone pole. It was full of Chinese people infected with that shit, the Dragonscale shit." He let out a long, unsteady breath and shook his head—as if it shocked him, the nerve of some people, igniting in the middle of Portsmouth on such a nice day—and turned from her, put the phone back to his ear. "She's fine. Didn't know a thing about it. She's home and we're going to have a good old shouting match if she thinks I'm letting her go back to work anytime soon."

Harper sat on the edge of the couch and looked at the TV. It was tuned to the local news. They were showing footage from last night's Celtic game, just like nothing was happening. Isaiah Thomas rose up on his toes, fell backward, and let go of the basketball, hit a shot from nearly half court. They didn't know it then, but by the end of the following week, the basketball season would be over. Come summer, most of the Celtics would be dead, by incineration or suicide.

Jakob paced in his rope sandals.

"What? No. No one got off," he said into the phone. "And it may sound harsh, but there's a part of me that's glad. No one to pass it on." He listened for a bit and then, unexpectedly, laughed and said, "Who ordered the flaming pupu platter, right?"

His pacing had taken him all the way across the room to the bookshelf, where there was nothing to do but circle around and come back. As he turned, his gaze drifted to Harper again and this time he saw something that stiffened his back.

"Hey, babygirl, are you all right?" he asked her.

She stared at him. She couldn't think how to reply. It was a curiously difficult question, one that required a certain amount of introspection.

"Hey, Danny? I have to go. I want to sit with Harper for a

minute. You did the right thing, going to pick up your kids." He paused, then added, "Yes, all right. I'll send you and Claudia the pictures, but you didn't get them from me. Love to you both."

He ended the call, lowered the phone, and looked at her. "What's wrong? Why are you home?"

"There was a man behind the school," Harper said, and then a wedge of something—an emotion like a physical mass—stuck in her throat.

He sat down with her and put a hand on her back.

"Okay," he said. "It's okay."

The pressure on her windpipe relaxed and she found her voice, was able to start again. "He was in the playground, staggering around like a drunk. Then he fell down and caught fire. He burned up like he was made of straw. Half the kids in school saw it. You can see into the playground from almost every classroom. I've been treating kids in shock all afternoon."

"You should've told me. You should've made me get off the phone."

She turned to him and rested her head on his chest while he held her.

"At one point I had forty kids in the gym, and a few teachers, and the principal, and some were crying, and some were shivering, and some were throwing up, and I felt like doing all three at the same time."

"But you didn't."

"No. I passed out juice boxes. Cutting-edge medical treatment, right there."

"You did what you could," he said. "You got who knows how many kids through the most awful thing they'll ever see in their lives. You know that, don't you? They're going to remember the way you looked after them the rest of their lives. And you did it and now it's behind you and you're here with me."

For a while she was quiet and motionless inside the circle of his arms, inhaling his particular odor of sandalwood cologne and coffee.

"When did it happen?" He let go of her, regarded her steadily with his almond-colored eyes.

"First period."

"It's going on three. Did you eat lunch?"

"Uhn-uh."

"Light-headed?"

"Uh-huh."

"Let's get some food into you. I don't know what's in the fridge. I can order us something, maybe."

*Who ordered the flaming pupu platter?* Harper thought, and the room tilted like the deck of a ship. She steadied herself on the back of the couch.

"Maybe just some water," she said.

"How about wine?"

"Even better."

He got up and crossed to the little six-bottle wine cooler on the shelf. As he looked at one bottle, then another—what kind of wine did you pair with a fatal contagion?—he said, "I thought this stuff was only in countries where the pollution is so thick you can't breathe the air and the rivers are open sewers. China. Russia. The Former Communist Republic of Turdistan."

"Rachel Maddow said there's almost a hundred cases in Detroit. She was talking about it last night."

"That's what I mean. I thought it was only in filthy places no one wants to go, like Chernobyl and Detroit." A cork popped. "I don't understand why someone carrying it would get on a bus. Or a plane."

"Maybe they were afraid of being quarantined. The idea of being kept from your loved ones is scarier than the sickness for a lot of people. No one wants to die alone."

"Yeah, that's right. Why die alone when you can have company? Nothing says 'I love you' like passing along a horrible fucking fatal infection to your nearest and dearest." He brought her a glass of golden wine, like a cup of distilled sunshine. "If

I had it I'd rather die than give it to you. Than put you at risk. I think it would actually be easier to end my own life, knowing I was doing it to keep other people safe. I can't imagine anything more irresponsible than going around with something like that." He gave her the glass, stroking one of her fingers as he passed it to her. He had a kind touch, a *knowing* touch; it was the best thing about him, his intuitive feel for just when to push a strand of her hair behind her ear, or smooth the fine down on the nape of her neck. "How easy is it to catch this stuff? It's transmitted like athlete's foot, isn't it? As long as you wash your hands and don't walk around the gym in bare feet, you're fine? Hey. *Hey*. You didn't go close to the dead guy, did you?"

"No." Harper did not bother to stick her nose in the glass and inhale the French bouquet as Jakob had taught her, when she was twenty-three and freshly laid and more drunk on him than she would ever be on wine. She polished off her sauvignon blanc in two swallows.

He sank down next to her with a sigh and shut his eyes. "Good. That's good. You have a horrible need to look after people, Harper, which is fine in ordinary circumstances, but in some situations a girl has to look after—"

But she wasn't listening. She had frozen, leaning forward to set her wineglass on the coffee table. On the TV, the program had cut away from hockey highlights to an old man in a gray suit, a newscaster with shy blue eyes behind his bifocals. The banner across the bottom of the screen said BREAKING NEWS SPACE NEEDLE ON FIRE.

"—going to Seattle," the anchor said. "Be warned, the footage is very graphic and upsetting. If there are children in the room they should not look."

Before he was done talking NECN cut to helicopter footage of the Needle, reaching up to jab at a bright, cold, blue sky. Black smoke filled the interior and boiled from the windows, so much that it obscured many of the other helicopters circling the scene.

"Oh my God," Jakob said.

A man in a white shirt and black pants leapt from one of the open windows. His hair was on fire. His arms pinwheeled as he dropped out of frame. He was followed seconds later by a woman in a dark skirt. When she jumped, she clasped her hands to her thighs, as if to keep her skirt from flapping up and showing her underwear.

Jakob took Harper's hand. She threaded her fingers through his and squeezed.

"What the fuck is happening, Harper?" he asked. "What the fuck *is* this?"

## MAY—JUNE

# 2

FOX said the Dragon had been set loose by ISIS, using spores that had been invented by the Russians in the 1980s. MSNBC said sources indicated the 'scale might've been created by engineers at Halliburton and stolen by culty Christian types fixated on the Book of Revelation. CNN reported both sides.

All throughout May and June, there were roundtable discussions on every channel, in between live reports from places that were in flames.

Then Glenn Beck burned to death on his Internet program, right in front of his chalkboard, burned so hot his glasses fused to his face, and after that most of the news was less about who did it and more about how not to catch it.

# JULY

## 3

There was a fireman causing trouble.

"Sir," said Nurse Lean. "Sir, you can't cut the line. You'll have your free examination when it's your turn."

The Fireman glanced over his shoulder at the line that stretched down the hall and around the corner. Then he looked back. His face was filthy and he wore the same yellow rubber jacket all the firemen wore and he had a child in his arms, a boy, hugging him around the neck.

"I'm not checking in. I'm dropping off," he said, and his accent made people look. You didn't expect a New Hampshire fireman to sound like he was from London. "And it's not about what they're here for. This isn't about the mold. My boy needs to see a doctor. He needs him *now,* not in two hours. This is an *emergency*. I don't see why I can't make anyone here in this so-called emergency room understand that."

Harper was passing along the line, handing out lollipops and paper cups of apple juice to the little kids. She also had a radish in one pocket and a potato in the other, for the most seriously unhappy children.

The sound of an English accent distracted her and lifted her spirits. She associated English accents with singing teapots, schools for witchcraft, and the science of deduction. This wasn't, she knew, terribly sophisticated of her, but she had no real guilt about it. She felt the English were themselves to blame for her feelings. They had spent a century relentlessly marketing their detectives and wizards and nannies, and they had to live with the results.

Her spirits needed lifting. She had spent the morning stowing charred corpses in body bags, their blackened, shriveled tissues still warm to the touch, still fuming. Because the hospital was running out of bags, she had to pack a pair of dead children into a sack together, which wasn't so hard. They had burned to death with their arms around one another, had fused into a single creature, a tangled cat's cradle of charred bones. It looked like death metal sculpture.

She hadn't been home since the last week in June and spent eighteen hours out of twenty-four in a full-body rubber suit that had been designed to repel Ebola. The gloves were so tight she had to lube her hands up with petroleum jelly to get them on. She stank like a prophylactic. Every time she inhaled her own fragrance of rubber and K-Y she thought of awkward college encounters in the dorms.

Harper made her way toward the head of the line, approaching the Fireman from behind. It was her job to keep the people who were waiting content, not Nurse Lean's, and Harper didn't want to wind up on Nurse Lean's bad side. Harper had only been working under her, at Portsmouth Hospital, for three weeks, and was a little afraid of her. All the volunteer nurses were.

"Sir," Nurse Lean said now, in a voice thin with impatience. "Everyone in this line is having an emergency. It's emergencies all the way back to the lobby. We take 'em in the order they come."

The Fireman peered over his shoulder at the line. A hundred and thirty-one of them (Harper had counted), weary and stained with Dragonscale and staring back at him with hollow-eyed resentment.

"Their emergencies can wait. This boy's cannot." He snapped back around to face Nurse Lean. "Let me try this another way."

His right arm hung at his side. He held a tool close against it, between his arm and body, a rusty iron bar, with hooks and prongs and hatchet blades bristling from either end. He opened his hand and let the bar slide down into full view, so that one end was almost touching the dirty linoleum. He waggled it but did not raise it.

"Either you let me through that door or I take this halligan and begin smashing things. I will start with a window and work my way up to a computer. Get a doctor, or let me by, but do not imagine I am going to wait in line while this nine-year-old boy dies in my arms."

Albert Holmes made his lazy way down the hall, coming from the double doors that led into the pre-quarantine exam rooms. He wore an Ebola suit, too. The only thing that marked Al out as different from the medical staff was that instead of a rubber hood, he had on a black riot helmet, the glass faceplate pulled down. He also wore his belt on the outside of his suit, his security badge and his walkie-talkie on one hip, his Teflon nightstick on the other.

Harper and Al closed in at the same time, from opposite directions.

"Let's settle down here," Al said. "Listen, bud, we can't have you in here with that—what'd you call it? The hooligan thing. Fire personnel have to leave their equipment outside."

"Sir? If you'll come with me, I'd be *glad* to talk to you about your son's complaint," Harper said.

"He's not my son," said the Fireman, "and I'm not his hysterical father. What I am is a man with a dangerously ill child and a heavy iron bar. If someone doesn't take the one, they're going to get the other. You want to talk to me? Talk where? Through those doors where the doctors are, or at the end of the line?"

She held his gaze, *willing* him to be good, promising him with her eyes that she would be good to him in return, she would listen and deal with him and his boy with warmth, humor, and patience. Telling him that she was trying to protect him, because if he didn't chill out he was going to wind up facedown on the floor with pepper spray in his eyes and a boot on his neck. Harper had been on staff for less than a month, but that was long enough to become accustomed to the sight of security drubbing unruly patients into better behavior.

"Come with me. I'll get him a lemon ice and you can tell me about whatever's wrong with him—"

"—at the end of the line. What I thought." He turned away from her and took a step toward the double doors.

Nurse Lean was still in his way. If anything, she looked more imposing than Albert Holmes. She was bigger, an immensity of breasts and gut, as formidable as any defensive tackle.

*"SIR,"* she said. "If you take one more step, we'll be treating you this afternoon for a variety of bruises and contusions." She swept her pale-eyed stare of death down the line. Her next statement was addressed to all of them. "*We will have order in this queue.* We will have it the easy way or we will have it the hard way, but *we will have it.* Does everyone understand me?"

There were low, embarrassed murmurs of assent up and down the line.

"I'm sorry." Sweat crawled at the Fireman's temples. "You don't understand. This boy—"

"What's wrong with him? Besides the same thing that is wrong with everyone else?" Nurse Lean said.

The boy was more or less the most beautiful child Harper had ever seen. His dark, curly hair was a delightful tangle above eyes the lucid pale green of an empty Coke bottle. He had on shorts and everyone could see the marks on the back of his calves: black, curving stripes, tattoolike, delicate and almost ornate.

Without any trace of concern in her voice, Nurse Lean added, "If you aren't infected, you shouldn't be holding him. Are you infected?"

"I'm not here about me," said the Fireman. It only came to Harper much later that this was a neat way of not answering. "He's not touching me."

It was true. The boy in his arms had his head turned and

his cheek plumped against the Fireman's turnout jacket. Still: if the Fireman wasn't sick, he was either idiotically fearless or just idiotic.

"What's wrong with him?"

"His stomach," the Fireman said. "There's something wrong with his stomach. He can barely stand—"

"It's very hot in here," Nurse Lean said. "I'm sure he's not the only child with a stomachache. Go to the end of the line and—"

"No. *No. Please.* This child recently lost his mother. She was in a building collapse a few days ago."

Nurse Lean's shoulders slumped and for a moment a kind of glum sympathy was visible on her features. For the first and only time she seemed to look not at the Fireman but at the boy curled in his arms.

"Ah. That's rotten. Listen, sweetheart, that's just rotten." If the boy was listening, though, he gave no sign. Nurse Lean lifted her gaze to the Fireman and was abruptly glaring again. "Something like that, who wouldn't have a stomachache?"

"Hang on, now. Let me finish. A building fell and killed her and he was there, he was right *there*—"

"There are trained counselors who can talk to this boy about what happened to him and maybe even get him something fizzy and sweet for his dyspepsia."

"Dyspepsia? Are you listening to me? He doesn't need a Coke and a smile, he needs a *doctor*."

"And he'll get one, when it's his turn."

"I picked him up an hour ago and he *screamed*. Does that sound like dyspepsia to you, you incurious twat?"

*"Hey,"* said Albert Holmes. "No one needs that mouth—"

Nurse Lean's face darkened to a scalding shade of red. She spread her arms out to either side, like a small child playing airplane.

*"YOU AND THAT BOY WILL GO TO THE BACK OF THE LINE, OR YOU WILL BE ADMITTED TO THE EMERGENCY ROOM WITH THAT STEEL ROD OF YOURS JAMMED UP*

*YOUR NARROW LIMEY ASS! DO YOU UNDERSTAND ME?"*

If Nurse Lean had shouted this way at Harper, she would've burst into tears. It was staggering—like walking into a gale. Children in line covered their ears, hid their faces against their mothers' legs.

The Englishman didn't so much as buckle. He glared. Harper was only faintly conscious of the fact that the boy didn't flinch either. In fact, he was staring at Harper, his eyes dreamy and damp, a little adrift. She assumed he was just faint from the heat, but it turned out there was more to it than that.

Harper tried again. "Sir? I'm *sure* I can help you. We can discuss the boy's symptoms at the back of the line and if he needs immediate attention, I'll bring a doctor right to him. If his stomach is bothering him, we don't want to upset him with a lot of yelling. Let's take this down the hall. Please. You and me . . . how 'bout it?"

All the anger went out of his face in an instant and he looked at her with the flicker of a weary smile. The boy might have lost his mother, but Harper saw then, for the first time, that the Fireman was in grief himself. She could see it in his eyes, a kind of exhausted glaze that she associated with loss.

"Do you fancy the Dire Straits too? A kid like you? You must've been chewing your blocks the last time they had a hit."

"I don't follow," she said.

"You and me . . . how 'bout it? Dire Straits?" he said, cocking his head and giving her an inquisitive look.

She didn't know what to say, wasn't sure what he was talking about. He stared for a half instant longer, then gave up. The Fireman squeezed the boy gently, then set him on his feet with great care, as if he were handling a fragile vase filled to the brim with water. "His name is Nick. Do you want to walk Nick to the back of the line?" he asked Harper. "And then I can carry on my conversation with this lot?"

"I think you should *both* come with me," she said to the Fireman, but she took the boy's hand. Her rubber glove squeaked softly.

She could see the child wasn't well. His face was waxy beneath his freckles and he swayed on his feet. Also she could feel a troubling heat in his soft, child-chubby fingers. But then a lot of people with the spore ran fevers, and the spore itself was often two to three degrees above body temperature. No sooner, though, had the Fireman set him down than the child bent at the waist with a pained grimace.

The Fireman crouched before the child and leaned his halligan against his shoulder. He did an odd thing then: he closed his hands into fists, showed them to the boy, then made an odd patting gesture, as if he were imitating a dog pawing at the air. The boy made the grimacing face and a funny teakettle sound, unlike anything Harper had ever heard from a child in distress; it sounded more like a squeak toy.

The Fireman craned his head to look back at Harper, but before he had a chance to speak, Albert Holmes moved, closed a hand around one end of the halligan.

"What the *hell* do you think you're doing?" the Fireman said. "Sir? Let go of the weapon."

The Fireman tugged on it. Al tugged back, harder, pulling him off balance, and then he had an arm around his throat. The Fireman's bootheels squealed on the tiles as he kicked for purchase, tried to get his feet under him.

Harper observed their wrestling match the way she might've glimpsed the passing scenery on an accelerating carousel. She was playing back what she had just seen—not only the odd way the Fireman had swatted at the air, but the way it looked as if the boy were straining to lift a weight beyond the limits of his strength.

"You're deaf," she said to the child, but of course she was really only talking to herself. Because he was deaf.

She had, at some point in nursing school, had a single day of instruction in American Sign Language, of which she remembered nothing. Or at least, she didn't *think* she remembered anything of what they had taught her. But then she found herself pointing her fingers at her ribs and twisting them, as if she were hand-screwing something into her own sides. She patted low on her abdomen. *Does it hurt here?*

Nick nodded uncertainly. But when she reached to feel beneath the hands cupped over his abdomen, he stumbled back a step, shaking his head frantically.

"It's all right," she said, enunciating slowly and with great care, on the off chance he could read lips. She had picked up, somewhere—maybe in that one-day class on ASL—that the very best lip-readers could only understand about 70 percent of what they saw, and the majority of deaf fell far short of that. "I'll be careful."

She reached once more, to probe his midsection, and he covered up again, backing away, a fresh sweat glowing on his upper lip. He keened softly. And then she knew. Then she was sure.

Al tightened his arm across the Fireman's windpipe, cutting off the air, choking him out. The same move had killed Eric Garner in New York City only a few years before, but it had never gone out of style. His other hand had pulled the halligan down and in, trapping it against the Fireman's chest.

If Harper had been able to focus, she might've found the Fireman's reaction peculiar. He didn't let go of the halligan, but he wasn't struggling to free himself from Albert's choke hold, either. Instead, he was biting the fingers of the black glove on his left hand. He was pulling the glove off with his teeth when Harper spoke, in a clear, ringing voice that caused them both to go still.

"Nurse Lean? We need a gurney to get this child into a CAT scan. We should prep for abdominal surgery. Maybe there's someone in pediatrics who can handle it?"

Nurse Lean looked past the Fireman, her face stony, her gaze distant and distracted. "What's your name? You're one of the new girls."

"Yes, ma'am. I was brought in three weeks ago. When they put out the call for volunteers. Harper. Harper Grayson."

"Nurse Grayson, this isn't the time or place—"

"It is. It has to be. He has either a burst appendix or one that is about to burst. Also, do we have a nurse who knows sign language? This child can't hear."

The Fireman was staring at her. Al was staring, too, gaping at her over the Fireman's shoulder. By then Al had relaxed his arm, letting the other man breathe. The Fireman rubbed his throat with his left hand—he had quit trying to pull his glove off—and beamed at her with a mix of appreciation and relief.

Nurse Lean's face had darkened again, but she seemed flustered. "You can't make that diagnosis without a CAT scan."

"I can't make that diagnosis at all," Harper said. "But I'm just—I'm sure. I used to be a school nurse and I had a boy with this last year. Look, do you see the way he's covering up?" She glanced at the Fireman, frowned, locked into something else he had been trying to tell them. "Building collapse—you said he was 'right there.' Did you mean he was *in* the building, with his mother, when it fell?"

"*Yes.* That is exactly what I was trying to explain. She was killed. He was struck by some debris. We pulled him out and at the time he seemed physically, *well,* a little battered, but nothing serious. And when he stopped eating and responding to people, we put that down to the shock. Then, this morning, he came up with sweats and couldn't sit up without pain."

"If he took a blow to the abdomen it could've damaged his appendix. When was his last bowel movement?"

"I can't say I keep track of when the kids go poo. I reckon I can ask, though, if this gentleman wanted to let me go."

Harper shifted her gaze to Albert, who stood there baffled, mouth hanging slightly open.

"Well," she said, and for the first time her voice was cross. "Let him go. Spit spot." *Spit spot* was a favorite of Mary Poppins, and Harper had, since childhood, liked to substitute Julie Andrews–isms for profanity whenever possible. It gave her a steely feeling of control and reminded her of her best self at the same time.

"Sorry, ma'am," Al mumbled, and not only removed his arm from the area of the Fireman's throat but carefully helped to steady him before stepping back.

"Lucky for me you let go when you did," the Fireman said to him, no anger or dislike in his voice at all. "Another minute and instead of dropping off a patient, I would've been one myself." The Fireman crouched down next to the boy, but paused to offer Harper another smile. "You're good. I like you. Spit spot!" He said it as if the words really meant *well done!*

He turned to face Nick, who was brushing tears away with his thumb. The Fireman moved his hands in a series of brisk gestures: closed fists, a pointed finger, a hand squeezed shut and another hand flying open from it. Harper thought of a man playing with a butterfly knife, or running through scales on some fantastic but invisible musical instrument.

Nick held out three fingers and pinched them together, as if he were grabbing for a fly in the air. Harper knew that one. Most people knew it. *No.* There was a little more after that she couldn't catch, his hands, arms, and face all in motion.

"He says he can't go to the bathroom. That he tried and it hurts. He hasn't gone to the bathroom since the accident."

Nurse Lean blew a hard puff of air, as if to remind everyone who was in charge. "Right. We'll have your son looked at . . . *spit spot.* Albert, will you radio for a gurney?"

"I told you already—he's not my son," the Fireman said. "I auditioned for the part, but the play was canceled."

"You aren't family, then," Nurse Lean said.

"No."

"That means I won't be able to let you go with him while he's examined. I'm—I'm very sorry," Nurse Lean said, sounding, for the first time all day, not just uncertain but also exhausted. "Family only."

"He'll be afraid. He can't understand you. He understands *me.* He can talk to *me.*"

"We'll find someone who can communicate with him," Nurse Lean said. "Besides. Once he goes through these doors he's in quarantine. The only people who go in there have Dragonscale or work for me. I can't make any exceptions on that, sir. You told us about the mother. Does he have any other family?"

"He has—" the Fireman began, paused, frowned, and shook his head. "No. There isn't anyone left. No one who could come and be with him."

"All right. Thanks—thank you for bringing him to our attention. We'll take care of him from here. We'll get him all sorted out."

"Give me a moment?" he asked her, and looked back at Nick, who was blinking at fresh tears. The Fireman seemed to salute him, then to milk an imaginary cow, and finished by pointing at the boy's chest. Nick's response required no translation. He leaned into the Fireman and let himself be hugged: gently, gently.

"I wish you wouldn't do that, sir," Nurse Lean said. "You don't want to get what he has."

The Fireman didn't reply—and he didn't let go until the double doors batted open and a nurse pushed a gurney into the hall.

"I'll be back to check on him." The Fireman lifted the boy in both arms and set him on the rolling cot.

Nurse Lean said, "You won't be able to see him anymore. Not once he's in quarantine."

"Just to inquire about his welfare at the front desk," the Fireman said. He offered Albert and Nurse Lean a sardonic but not ill-humored nod of appreciation and turned back to Harper. "I am in your debt. I take that very seriously. The next time you need someone to put out a fire, I hope I'm lucky enough to get the call."

Forty minutes later, the kid was under the gas, and Dr. Knab, the pediatric surgeon, was cutting him open to remove an inflamed appendix the size of an apricot. The boy was in recovery for three days. On the fourth day he was gone.

The nurses in recovery were sure he had not walked out of his room. The window was wide open and a theory made the rounds that he had jumped. But that was crazy—the recovery room was on the third floor. He would've shattered both legs in the fall.

"Maybe someone brought a ladder," Albert Holmes said, when the subject was being batted around over bowls of American chop suey in the staff room.

"There's no ladder that can reach to the third floor," Nurse Lean said in a huffy, aggrieved voice.

"There is on a fire truck," Al said around a mouthful of French roll.

# 4

In those stifling, overheated days of high summer, when a manageable crisis was teetering on the edge of an unmanageable disaster, the deaf child was not the only patient to vanish from Portsmouth Hospital. There was one other among the contaminated who escaped with her life, in the last days before everything went—not metaphorically, but literally—up in smoke.

All that month the wind blew from the north and a dismal brown fog settled over the coast of New Hampshire, swept down from the fires in Maine. Maine was burning from the Canadian border to Skowhegan, a hundred miles of blue spruce and fragrant pine. There was nowhere to go to escape the stink of it, a sweet-harsh odor of burnt evergreens.

The smell followed Harper into sleep, where every night she dreamt of campfires on the beach, roasting hot dogs with her brother, Connor. Sometimes it would turn out there were heads charring on the ends of their sticks instead of wieners. Occasionally, Harper woke shouting. Other times she woke to the sound of someone else crying out. The nurses slept in shifts, sharing a crash room in the basement, and they were all having bad dreams.

In the hospital, the infected were divided into two groups: "symptomatic normals" and "smolderers." Smolderers smoked on and off, always ready to ignite. Smoke curled from their hair, from their nostrils, and their eyes streamed with water. The stripes on their bodies got so hot they could melt latex gloves. They left char marks on their hospital johnnies, on their beds. They were dangerous, too. Understandably, perhaps, the smolderers were always wavering on the edge of hysteria. Although there was a chicken-and-egg aspect to it: Did they panic because their bodies were constantly smoking, or did they smoke because their minds were constantly in a state of panic? Harper wasn't sure. She only knew you had to be careful around them. They bit and they screamed. They made ingenious plans to grab the sun out of the sky. They decided they were actual dragons and tried to jump out the windows to fly. They came to believe their doctors were holding back limited quantities of a cure, and attempted to take them hostage. They formed armies, congresses, religions; plotted rebellions, fomented treasons, practiced heresies.

The rest of the patients were marked with 'scale, but were otherwise physically and emotionally normal, right until the moment they incinerated themselves. They were frightened and had no place to go and wanted to believe someone might develop a cure before their time ran out. A lot of them came to Portsmouth because even then there were rumors that the other local hospitals were simply trucking cases to the camp in Concord, a place that had turned back a Red Cross inspection team a few weeks before, and that had a tank parked by the gate.

The hospital filled every ward and the infected kept coming. The first-floor cafeteria was converted to an immense dormitory for the healthiest of the sick. That was where Harper met Renée Gilmonton, who stood out among all the others by virtue of being the only black person in a room of two hundred other patients. Renée said it was easier to spot a moose in New Hampshire than a black person. She said she was used to being stared at as if her head were on fire, people had been staring that way for years.

The cots made a kind of labyrinth, spread out across the entirety of the cafeteria, with Renée Gilmonton at the exact center. She was there before Harper came to work at the hospital at the end of June, had been there longer than anyone else walking around with the 'scale. She was fortyish, pleasantly rounded and bespectacled, gray showing in her neat cornrows, and she had not come alone: she had brought a potted mint with her, named Daniel, and a photo of her cat, Mr. Truffaut. When she had no one to talk to, she talked to them.

But Renée didn't often lack for human company. In a former life, she had been a professional do-gooder: organized a weekly pancake breakfast for a local orphanage, taught English to felons in the state prison, and managed an independent bookstore that lost money by the bucketload while hosting poetry slams. Old habits died hard. Not long after she came to the hospital, she organized two daily reading sessions for the littlest kids and a book group for the older patients. She had a dozen lightly toasted copies of *The Bridge of San Luis Rey* that had been widely passed around.

"Why *The Bridge of San Luis Rey*?" Harper asked.

"Partly because it's about why inexplicable tragedies occur," Renée said. "But also it's short. I feel like most folks want a book they feel like they have time to finish. You don't want to start *A Game of Thrones* when you might catch fire all of a sudden. There's something horribly unfair about dying in the middle of a good story, before you have a chance to see how it all comes out. Of course, I suppose everyone *always* dies in the middle of a good story, in a sense. Your own story. Or the story of your children. Or your grandchildren. Death is a raw deal for narrative junkies."

Around the cafeteria, Renée was known as Mrs. Asbestos, because she didn't have fevers, didn't smoke, and when someone went up in flames, Renée ran *toward* them to try and put them out, when most people ran *away*. Running toward the flames was, in fact, against doctors' advice, and she was often scolded for it. There was ample evidence that the simple stress of seeing one person ignite was enough to set off others. Chain reactions were a daily occurrence in Portsmouth Hospital.

Harper tried her best not to get attached. It was the only way to face the job at all, to keep working day after day. If she let herself care too much for any of them it would shatter her inside, the daily harvest of the dead. It would smash all the best parts of herself, her silliness and her sense of play and her belief that the kindnesses you showed others added up to something.

The full-body Tyvek protection suit wasn't the only armor she put on to do her job. She also dressed herself in an air of glassy, professional calm. Sometimes she pretended she was in an immersive simulation, the faceplate of her mask a virtual reality screen. It also helped not to learn anyone's name and to rotate from ward to ward, so she was always seeing different faces.

And even so, at the end of her shift she needed a half hour alone, in a stall in the women's room, to sob herself sick. She never lacked company. A lot of nurses had a post-shift cry penciled into their daily routine. The basement ladies' room, at 9 P.M., was a concrete box filled with grief, a vault that echoed with sniffles and shuddering breath.

But Harper fell for Renée. She couldn't help herself. Maybe because Renée gave herself permission to do all the things Harper couldn't. Renée learned everyone's name and spent all day getting attached. She let kids crawling with contamination and dribbling smoke sit in her lap while she read to them. And Renée worried over the nurses at least as much as any of the nurses worried about her.

"You won't do anyone any good if you drop dead of exhaustion," she said to Harper once.

*I won't do anyone any good if I don't,* Harper imagined saying back. *I'm not doing anyone any good, one way or another.* But she didn't say it. It would've been grief talking, and it was unfair to unload her sadness on someone who might not live to see another day.

Except Renée *did* live to see another day. And another. And another.

Also, she didn't try to hide her Dragonscale with gloves or scarves or long-sleeved shirts. She had a necklace of 'scale inked right onto her throat, pretty loops dusted with gold; bracelets of it up to the elbows. She did her nails in black with gold glitter to match.

"It could be so much worse," Renée said. "It could be a disease that involves pus or leaky privates. It could've been one of these things where your parts rot and fall off. There's nothing sexy about swine flu. I bet this is the most sexy pathogen ever. I think it makes me look like a tigress! A fat, frumpy tigress. Like if Catwoman got really out of shape."

"I don't think Catwoman has stripes," Harper said. She was sitting with Renée at the time, on the edge of Renée's cot. She nodded at the photo of Renée's cat. "Who's looking after that handsome fella?"

"Street is," Renée said. "I let him scamper before I brought myself in."

"I'm sorry."

"All the fires have smoked the mice out into the streets. I'm sure Truffaut is living high on the furry fat of the land. Do you think they'll survive after we're gone? The cats? Or will we take them with us?"

"The cats are going to make it and so are we," Harper said, in her best chin-up voice. "We're smart. We're going to figure this thing out."

Renée smiled wistfully. Her eyes were amused and a little pitying. She had gold flecks in her coffee-bean-colored irises. That might've been Dragonscale or it might've just been her eyes.

"Who says we're smart?" she asked, in a tone of playful contempt. "We never even mastered fire. We thought we did, but you see now, it has mastered us."

As if to punctuate this point, across the room, a teenage girl began to shriek. Harper turned her head and saw orderlies running to throw fireproof blankets on a girl struggling up out of her cot. She was shoved down and smothered. Flames belched from beneath the blankets.

Renée gazed sadly across the room at her and said, "And she just started *Clan of the Cave Bear.*"

Harper began to look for Renée whenever her duties brought her to the cafeteria. She sought her out to talk about books. It felt good to have that: some normal, pointless conversation in the morning, some talk that had nothing to do with the world catching fire. Harper made Renée a part of her day, knowing all the time it was a mistake, that when the older woman died, it would spoil something inside of her. After she recovered from the initial loss, Harper would be a harder person. And she didn't want to become a harder person. She wanted to stay the same Harper Grayson who could get wet-eyed at the sight of old people holding hands.

She knew Renée would be gone one day, and one day she was. Harper wheeled a trolley full of fresh sheets into the cafeteria and saw in a glance that Renée's mattress had been stripped bare and her personal items taken away. The sight of that empty bed was a wallop to the stomach, and Harper let go of the trolley and turned around, banging through the double doors, past the guards, and down the hall. She couldn't make it to the ladies' room in the basement for a cry, it was too far. She turned to face the wall, put a hand against it, and let go inside. Her shoulders shook and she sobbed and sobbed and sobbed.

One of the guards—Albert Holmes, as it happened—touched her shoulder.

"Ma'am?" he asked. "Oh my goodness. Ma'am? What's wrong?"

At first, Harper couldn't get a single word out. She was struggling for air, her whole body convulsively hitching. She fought it down. She was scaring him. He was a broad-shouldered and freckly kid who had been playing high school football not two years before, and the sight of a woman in tears was almost too much for him.

"Gilmonton," she said at last, half coughing it out.

"You didn't know?" Albert asked, his voice wondering and faint.

Harper shook her head.

"She left," Al said. "Walked right out past the morning boys."

Harper panted, her lungs aching, her throat full of tears. She thought maybe she was strong enough to get away now, get down to the bathroom, where she could find a stall and really let herself—

"What?" Harper said. "What did you say?"

"She took off!" Al told her. "Slipped right out of the hospital! With her little plant under one arm."

"Renée Gilmonton walked out?" Harper asked. "With her mint? And someone *let* her?"

Al stared at her with those wide, wondering eyes. "You should see the security footage. She was glowing! Like a lighthouse! You look at the tape. It's awesome. I mean 'awesome' the way they use that word in the Bible. The guys on duty ran for it. They thought she was going to explode. Like a human nuke. She was scared she was going to explode, too, which is why she ran outside. She ran outside and never came back. They don't know what happened to her. She wasn't even wearing shoes!"

Harper wanted to reach under her mask and wipe the tears off her face, but she couldn't. Wiping anything off her face was a nearly half-hour process. She couldn't remove her Tyvek until she had stood in a shower of bleach for five minutes. She blinked rapidly to clear her vision.

"That doesn't make sense. People with Dragonscale don't glow."

"*She* did," Al said. "She was reading to some little kids, right before breakfast, and the girl sitting in her lap jumped up because Mrs. Gilmonton was getting warm. Then people started to scream and scatter. She was lit up like a fuckin' Christmas tree. 'Scuse my French, ma'am. On the video her eyes look like death rays! She ran past two sets of guards, right out of the quarantine. The way she looked—hell, anyone would've ducked for cover."

Five minutes later, Harper watched the video herself, with four other nurses, at the reception desk down the hall. Everyone in the hospital was watching it. Harper saw it at least ten times before the day was done.

A fixed camera showed the wide corridor outside the entrance to the cafeteria, an expanse of antiseptic white tile. The door was flanked by security in their own combination of Tyvek suits and riot helmets. One of them leaned against the wall, leafing slowly through the pages of a clipboard. The other sat in a molded plastic chair, tossing his baton in the air and catching it.

The doors banged open and the hall flooded with brilliance, as if someone were pointing a spotlight into it. In the first moment, the glow was so intense it blew out the black-and-white image, filling the screen with a bluish glare. Then the light sensors in the security camera adjusted—a little. Renée remained a bright ghost, a wavering brilliance in the hourglass shape of a woman. The lit scrollwork of her Dragonscale obscured her features. Her eyes were blue-white rays of light and did, indeed, look a bit like death rays from a mid-fifties science-fiction film. She clutched her potted mint under her left arm.

The guard who had been tossing his baton twitched away from her. His nightstick dropped and clouted him on the shoulder and he fell out of his chair. The other guard tossed his clipboard in the air as if it had turned into a cobra. His heels shot out from under him and he sat down hard on the floor.

Renée looked from one to the other, seemed to lift a placating hand, and then hurried away.

Albert Holmes told Harper: "She said, 'Don't mind me, boys, I'm just going to go explode outside where no one will get hurt.'"

Dr. Ryall, the resident pathologist, was unimpressed. He had read about outlier cases, where the Dragonscale reached critical mass and then, for whatever reason, stalled without immediately causing a person to ignite. He assured anyone who would listen that Renée Gilmonton's remains would be found within a hundred paces of the hospital. But some orderlies swept the high grass in the field beyond the parking lot, looking for cooked bones, and didn't find any. Nor could they find any trace of which way she had gone: no singed brush or weeds. She seemed not to have exploded but *evaporated*, taking her potted mint with her.

The CDC had a team scheduled to visit Portsmouth Hospital in August, to review their quarantine procedures, and Dr. Ryall said he'd be sure to show them the video of the Gilmonton incident. He was confident they'd share his interpretation.

But the CDC team never got to look at it, because by the time August rolled around, Portsmouth Hospital was a hollowed-out chimney, gutted by fire, and Dr. Ryall was dead, along with Albert Holmes, Nurse Lean, and over five hundred patients.

# 5

She didn't know how long she stood there, watching Portsmouth Hospital burn. Thick black smoke, piled a thousand feet high, curdled above her, above all of them, a thunderhead that smothered the sky. The sun was a small red coin, glowing through that mass of smoke. One of the doctors said, "Anyone got marshmallows?" and laughed, but no one laughed with him.

They had lost the power, not five minutes after the fire alarm began its nerve-shredding *whoop*. Strobe lights throbbed in the darkness, smashing time into bright frozen slivers. Harper made her way out through those stammering shadows with her hands on the shoulders of the nurse in front of her, in a line of shuffling evacuees. The air on the first floor was smoky, grained with fine particulate matter, but the fire was somewhere above them. At first the shriek of the alarm was terrifying, but by the time Harper emerged into the day, she was almost bored, had been creeping along in the crowd for forty-five minutes. She didn't have any idea how bad it was until she cleared the building and could turn around.

Someone told her no one above the second floor had gotten out. Someone else said it started in the cafeteria; one person lit up, then another, then a third, like a string of firecrackers, and a guard panicked and bolted the door to keep anyone from getting out. Harper never found out if that was true.

The National Guard turned up in the early going and the troopers pushed the crowd back to the far edge of the parking lot. Beyond them, the Portsmouth Fire Department threw everything they had at the blaze, all six trucks . . . and anyone could see it wasn't going to make a lick of difference. Flame gushed from every shattered window. The firemen worked in the falling black ash with practiced professional indifference, blasting the great furnace of the hospital with thunderous jets of water that seemed to do nothing.

Harper had a dazed, almost concussed feeling, as if she had been struck very hard and knocked down and was waiting for her body to report the extent of her injuries. The sight of all that fire and all that smoke robbed her of thought.

At some point she registered a peculiar thing: a fireman, who was inexplicably standing on *her* side of the sawhorses, when he should've been down among the trucks with his brothers-in-arms. She only noticed him because he was staring at her. He wore his helmet and a filthy yellow jacket and he had a firefighting tool in one hand, a long iron pole with hooks and a hatchet bristling from it, and she thought she knew him. He was a wiry, gangly man in glasses, and his face was all sharp edges, and he regarded her with something like sorrow, while flakes of ash fell around them in soft black curls. Ash streaked her arms, feathered her hair. A wisp of ash broke on the tip of her nose and provoked a sneeze.

She tried to recall how she knew him, the mournful fireman. She probed her memory in the gentle, careful way she might probe a child's arm to make sure there was no fracture. A child, that was it: she knew him by way of his child, she thought. Only that was not quite right. She supposed she was being silly and she should just go over and ask him how they knew each other, but when she looked for him again he was gone.

Something collapsed inside the hospital. The roof, perhaps, pancaking in on the floor below it. Clouds of plaster and grime and ruddy smoke erupted from the windows on the top story. A National Guardsman wearing a paper mask over his mouth and blue latex gloves held his hands over his head as if he were surrendering to the enemy.

"Folks! We're going to move you back *again*! I'm going to ask all of you to take three steps back, for your own safety. This is me asking in my nice voice. You don't want to hear my not-so-nice voice."

Harper moved back one step, and another, and then swayed on her heels, feeling light-headed and parched. She was desperate for a cool drink of water to clear the grit out of her throat, and the only reasonable place to get one was home. She didn't have the car—it didn't make sense for her to have it, she never left the hospital—so she turned away to walk.

She went half a block before she realized she was weeping. She didn't know if she was crying because she was sad or because there was a lot of smoke in the air. The afternoon smelled like cookouts at summer camp, like charring hot dogs. It came to her that the hot dog smell was the odor of burning corpses. She thought, *I dreamed this.* Then she turned and vomited into the grass by the sidewalk.

There were clumps of people standing on the curb and in the road, but no one looked at her while she threw up. No one found her the least bit interesting, compared to the sight of the conflagration. People were entranced by flame and repelled by human suffering, and wasn't that some kind of design flaw? She wiped her mouth with the back of one hand and went on.

Harper did not look at the faces in the crowd and so she did not see Jakob standing among all the others until he caught her in his arms. The moment he was holding her, he was holding her up. The strength went out of her legs and she sagged into him.

"Oh God, you're all right," he said. "Oh God. I was so scared."

"I love you," she said, because it seemed to her that was what you said after walking away from an inferno, that was the only thing that mattered on a morning like this one.

"They've got roads shut down for blocks," he whispered. "I was so scared. I biked all the way here. I've got you. I've got you, babygirl."

He led her through the crowd, over to a telephone pole. His bike leaned against it, the one he had owned since college, a ten-speed with a basket between the handlebars. He pushed the bike with one hand, his other arm around her waist, and they went along that way, her head resting on his shoulder. They walked against the crowd, everyone else moving toward the hospital, in the direction of that greasy black column of smoke, into the falling ash.

"Every day is September eleventh," she said. "How are we supposed to live our lives when every day is September eleventh?"

"We live with it until we can't anymore," he said.

She didn't understand what that meant, but it sounded good, maybe even profound. He said it tenderly while dabbing at her mouth and cheek with a silvery-white square of silk. Jakob always carried a handkerchief with him, an Old World affectation that she found agonizingly adorable.

"What are you doing?" she asked.

"Getting the ash off you."

"Please," she said. "Please."

He stopped after a bit, and said, "All clean. All better." And kissed her cheek, and kissed her mouth. "I don't know why I did it, though. You were looking like a little Charles Dickens urchin for a moment. Grubby but scrumptious. Tell you what. I'll make it up to you. We'll go home and I'll make you spiritually filthy. How's that?"

She laughed. He had a somehow Gallic sense of the absurd; in college he had performed as a mime in a mime club. He could walk a tightrope, too—he was nimble in bed, nimble in life.

"That's fine," she said.

Jakob told her, "The whole world can burn down around us. I'll keep my arms around you until the end. No getting away from me."

She stood on her tiptoes and kissed his salty mouth. He had been crying, too, although he was smiling now. She rested her head on his chest.

"I'm so tired," she said. "Of being scared. Of not being able to help people."

He put his knuckle under her chin and gently forced her head up. "You have to let go of that. The idea that somehow it's your job to fix things. To run around . . . putting out all the fires." He looked meaningfully toward the smoke drifting above. "It's not your job to save the world."

That was so sensible, so reasonable, it made her ache a little with relief.

"You have to take care of yourself," he said. "And let me take care of you some. We've got such a short time to treat each other right. We're going to make it special. We're going to make it worth something, starting tonight."

She had to kiss him again, then. His mouth tasted of peppermint and tears, and he returned her kiss carefully, tentatively, as if discovering her for the first time, as if kissing were an entirely new, curious experience . . . an experiment. When he lifted his face up, his expression was serious.

"That was an important kiss," he said.

They made their shuffling way along the sidewalk, traveling a few paces more. She rested her head on his biceps and shut her eyes. A few steps later he tightened his arm around her. She had been drifting, half asleep on her feet, and stumbled.

"Hey," he said. "No more of that. Look. We have to get you home. Get on." He threw his leg over the saddle of the bike.

"Get on where?"

"The basket," he said.

"We can't. I can't."

"You can. You have before. I'll ride you home."

"It's a mile."

"It's downhill the whole way. Get on."

This was something they had done in college, goofing, her up on the basket on the front of his bike. She was a slip of a girl then and was not much more now, five foot six and 115 pounds. She looked at the basket, resting between his handlebars, then at the long hill, banking down away from the hospital and around a curve.

"You'll kill me," she said.

"No. Not today. Get on."

She couldn't resist him. There was a part of her that inclined naturally toward passivity, toward accommodation. She came around the front of the bike, put a leg over the wheel, and then scootched her butt up onto the basket.

And all at once they were off, the trees on her right beginning to glide dreamily by. The ash fell around them in enormous feathery flakes, falling in her hair and onto the brim of his baseball cap. In no time at all, they were going fast enough to be killed.

The spokes whirred. When she exhaled, the air was torn from her mouth.

People forgot that time and space were the same thing until they were moving quickly, until pine trees and telephone poles were snapping past them. Then, in the middle of all the rush, time expanded, so that the second it took to cross twenty feet lasted longer than other seconds. She felt that sense of acceleration in her temples and the pit of her stomach and she was glad for Jakob and glad to be away from the hospital and glad for speed. For a while she clutched the basket with both hands, but then, when the spokes began to hum—whirring so fast they made a kind of droning music—she let go, and held her arms out to either side, and soared, a gull sailing into the wind, while the world sped up, and sped up.

# 6

The night of the hospital fire, Jakob led her through the house, and she yawned over and over, like a child up past her bedtime. She felt lightly sedated, awake but thoughtless, so that she never knew what was going to happen to her next, even when what was going to happen next was entirely predictable. He walked her down to the bedroom, holding her little hand. That was all right. She was tired and the bedroom seemed like the right place to go. Then he peeled her out of her nurse greens while she stood there and let him. She had on pale pink old-lady underwear that came to her belly button. He tugged those down as well. She yawned hugely and put her hand over her mouth and he laughed because he had been leaning in to kiss her. She laughed, too. It was funny, yawning in his face that way.

The night of the hospital fire, he drew her a bath in the deep claw-footed tub that she loved so. She didn't know when he walked away from her to do it, because it seemed he never left her side, but when he led her in there, the tub was already full. The lights were off, but there were candles. She was happy to see the bath because she smelled like smoke and sweat and the hospital, but mostly smoke, and she had ash on her, and some of that ash was probably dead bodies.

The night of the hospital fire, Jakob laved water over her back with a washcloth. He scrubbed her neck and ears, and then collected her hair on the top of her head and dunked her. She came up laughing. Then he told her to get up, and she stood in the tub while he lathered her in soap. He soaped her breasts and the small of her back and her neck and then he smacked her bum and told her to get back into the tub and she obediently sat.

The night of the hospital fire, Jakob said, "It's so fucking cheap when people say *I love you.* It's a name to stick on a surge of hormones, with a little hint of loyalty thrown in. I've never liked saying it. Here's what I say: We're together, now and until the end. You have everything I need to be happy. You make me feel right."

He squeezed out the washcloth and hot water rained down her neck. She shut her eyes, but saw the red light of the candle flame through her eyelids.

He went on, "I don't know how much time we have left. Could be fifty years. Could be one more week. But I do know that we're not going to get cheated out of one second of being together. We're going to share everything and feel everything together. And I am going to let you know, in the way I touch you, and the way I kiss you"—as he said it, he touched her, and kissed her—"that you are the best thing in my life. And I'm a selfish man, and I want every inch of you, and every minute of your life I can have. There's no *my* life anymore. And no *your* life. Just *our* life, and we're going to have it our way. I want birthday cake every day and you naked in bed every night. And when it's time to be done, we'll have that our way, too. We'll open that bottle of wine we bought in France and listen to our favorite music and have some laughs and take some happy pills and go to sleep. Die pretty after the party is over, instead of going down screaming like those sad, desperate people who lined up to die in the hospital."

It was like hearing his wedding vows all over again, just as yearning and sweet and intense. So that was all right.

Except it wasn't, not entirely. There was something wrong about calling the people who came to the hospital *sad* and *desperate.* There was something immoral about mocking them. Renée Gilmonton had not been sad and desperate. Renée Gilmonton had organized story hour for the kids in the ward.

But Jakob had the gift of confession, could talk about how he wanted to touch her and be with her, with all the daring and athletic skill he brought to riding a unicycle or walking on a tightrope. He was small and compact and muscular, and also intellectually muscular, mentally something of an acrobat. Sometimes she felt that those intellectual acrobatics were a bit tiring; at those times she felt less as if they were feeling everything together, more as if she were simply his audience, someone to applaud his latest leap through the burning hoop of existentialism and his backflip onto the trampoline of nonconformity. But then she was opening her legs to him, because his hands knew how to do things she needed to feel. And anyway, all his talk just meant that he wanted her and she made him happy. She had to kiss him again, and she did, twisting in the bathtub and flattening her breasts against the cold porcelain, and holding the back of his head so he couldn't get away until she had a good long taste of him. Then she broke free and yawned once more and he laughed and that was all right.

The night of the hospital fire, she rose from the water, and he handed her a glass of red wine and then wrapped a hot towel around her. He helped her out of the tub. He walked her into the bedroom, where there were more candles burning. He dried her and guided her to the bed and she climbed across it on all fours, wanting him to pull off his clothes and push himself into her, but he put a hand on the small of her back and made her lie flat. He liked to make her wait; to be honest, she liked to be made to wait, liked him to be in charge. He had strawberry-scented cream and he rubbed it into her. He was naked beside her, his body dusky and fit in the low light, his chest matted with black fur.

And when he rolled her over and got inside her, she made a sobbing sound of pleasure, because it was so sudden, and he was so intent about it. He had hardly started when the condom slipped off. He stopped his motion for a moment, frowning, but she reached down and flung it aside, and then took his ass and pushed him down on her again. Her nurse greens were on the floor, stinking of smoke. She would never wear them again. A hundred square miles of French wine country were on fire and more than two million people had burned to death in Calcutta, and all she wanted was to feel him inside her. She wanted to see his face when he finished. She thought there was a good chance they'd be dead by the end of the year anyway, and he had never been inside her this way before.

On the night of the hospital fire, they made love by candlelight, and, later, a baby began.

# AUGUST

# 7

Harper was in the shower when she saw the stripe on the inside of her left leg.

She knew what the stripe meant in one look and her insides squirmed with fear, but she wiped cool water from her face and scolded herself. "Don't start with me, lady. That's a goddamn bruise."

It didn't look like a bruise, though. It looked like Dragonscale, a dark, almost inky line, dusted with a few oddly mineral flecks of gold. When she bent close, she saw another mark, on the back of her calf—same leg—and she jerked upright. She put a hand over her mouth because she was making little miserable sounds, almost sobs, and she didn't want Jakob to hear.

She climbed out, neglecting to turn off the shower. It didn't matter. It wasn't like she was wasting the hot water. There wasn't any. The power had been out for two days. She had gone in the shower to wash the sticky feeling off her. The air in the house was smothering, like being trapped under a pile of blankets all day long.

The part of her that was five years a nurse—the part that remained calm, almost aloof, even when the floor was sticky with blood and a patient was shrieking in pain—asserted itself. She choked down the little sobs she was making and composed herself. She decided she needed to dry off and have another look at it. It could be a bruise. She had always been someone who bruised easily, who would discover a great black mark on her hip or the back of her arm with no idea how she had injured herself.

She toweled herself almost dry and put her left foot up on the counter. She looked at the leg and then looked at it in the mirror. She felt the need to cry rising behind her eyes again. She knew what it was. They put down *Draco incendia trychophyton* on the death certificates, but even the surgeon general called it Dragonscale. Or he had, until he burned to death.

The band on the back of her leg was a delicate ray of black, blacker than any bruise, silted with grains of brightness. On closer inspection, the line on her thigh looked less like a stripe, more like a question mark or a sickle. Harper saw a shadow she didn't like, where her neck met her shoulder, and she brushed aside her hair. There was another dark line there, flaked with the mica-specks of Dragonscale.

She was trying to regulate her breathing, trying to exhale a feeling of wooziness, when Jakob opened the door.

"Hey, babe, they need me down to the Works. There's no—" he said, then fell silent, looking at her in the mirror.

At the sight of his face, she felt her composure going. She set her foot on the floor and turned to him. She wanted him to put his arms around her and squeeze her and she knew he couldn't touch her and she wasn't going to let him.

He staggered back a step and stared at her with blind, bright, scared eyes. "Oh, Harp. Oh, baby girl." Usually he said it as one word—*babygirl*—but this time it was distinctly two. "You've got it all over you. It's on your legs. It's on your back."

"No," she said, a helpless reaction. "No. No no *no*." It nauseated her, to imagine it streaked across her skin where she couldn't see.

"Just stay there," he said, holding a hand out, fingers spread, although she hadn't taken a step toward him. "Stay in the bathroom."

"Jakob," she said. "I want to look and see if there's any on you."

He stared at her without comprehension, a bright bewilderment in his gaze, and then he understood and something went out of his eyes. His shoulders sank. Beneath his tan he looked wan and gray and bloodless, as if he had been out in the cold for a long time.

"What's the point?" he asked.

"The point is to see if you've got it."

He shook his head. "Of course I have it. If you have it, I have it. We fucked. Just last night. And two days ago. If I'm not showing now, I will later."

"Jakob. I want to look at you. I didn't see any marks on me yesterday. Not before we made love. Not after. They don't understand everything about transmission, but a lot of doctors think a person isn't contagious until they're showing visible marks."

"It was dark. We were in candlelight. If either of us saw those marks on you, we would've thought it was a shadow," he said. He spoke in a leaden monotone. The terror she had seen on his face had been like a flicker of heat lightning, there and gone. In its place was something worse, a listless resignation.

"Take off your clothes," she said.

He stripped his T-shirt off over his head and dropped it on the floor. He regarded her steadily with eyes that were almost amber in the dimness of the room. He held out his arms to either side, stood there with his feet crossed and his chin lifted, unconsciously posing like Christ on the cross.

"Do you see any?"

She shook her head.

He turned, arms still outstretched, and looked back over his shoulder. "On my back?"

"No," she said. "Take off your pants."

He revolved again and unbuttoned his jeans. They faced each other, a yard of open space between them. There was a kind of cruel erotic fascination in the slow, patient way he stripped for her, pulling out his belt, pushing down the jeans and the underwear, too, all in one go. He never broke eye contact. His face was masklike, almost disinterested.

"Nothing," she said.

He turned. She took in his limber brown thighs, his pale backside, the sunken hollows in his hips.

"No," she said.

"Why don't you turn off the shower," he told her.

Harper shut off the water, picked up her towel, and went back to drying her hair. As long as she concentrated on breathing slowly and steadily, and did all the things she would normally do after a shower, she felt she could put off the urge to burst into tears again. Or to begin screaming. If she started to scream, she wasn't sure she could stop.

Harper wrapped the towel around her hair and walked back into the gloomy swelter of the bedroom.

Jakob sat on the edge of the bed, in his jeans again, but holding his T-shirt in his lap. His feet were bare. She had always loved his feet, tan and bony and almost architectural in their delicate, angular lines.

"I'm sorry I got sick," she said to him, and suddenly was struggling not to cry again. "I swear, I had a good look at myself yesterday, and I didn't see any of this. Maybe you don't have it. Maybe you're okay."

Harper almost choked on the last word. Her throat was clutching up convulsively, sobs forcing their way out from deep in her hitching lungs. Her thoughts were too awful to think, but she thought them anyway.

She was dead and so was he. She had gone and infected them both and they were going to burn to death like all the others. She knew it, and his face told her he knew it, too.

"You had to be Florence fucking Nightingale," he said.

"I'm sorry."

She wished he would cry with her. She wished she could see some feeling in his face, could see him struggling to restrain the kind of emotions she felt in herself. But there was only blankness, and the odd, clinical look in his gaze, and the way he sat there with his wrists hanging limply over his knees.

"Look on the bright side," he said, glancing at her stomach. "At least we don't have to figure out what to name it if it's a girl."

It was as bad as if he had struck her. She flinched, looked away. She was going to say she was sorry again, but what came out was a choked, hopeless sob.

They had known about the baby for just over a week. Jakob had smiled slightly when Harper showed him the blurred blue cross on the home pregnancy pee-stick, but when she'd asked him how he felt, he'd said, *Like I need time to get my head around it.*

The day after, the Verizon Arena burned to the ground in Manchester, twelve hundred homeless refugees inside—not one got out alive—and Jakob was loaned to the Public Works Department there, to help organize the clearing of the wreckage and the collection of bodies. He was gone thirteen hours a day, and when he came home, filthy with soot and quiet from the things he had seen, it seemed wrong to discuss the baby. When they slept, though, he would spoon her from behind and cup her stomach with one hand and she had hoped this meant there was some happiness—some sense of purpose—stirring inside him.

He pulled his T-shirt on, in no hurry now.

"Get dressed," he said. "It'll be easier to think if I don't have to look at it all over you."

She walked to her closet, crying hard. She felt she could not bear the lack of feeling in his voice. It was almost worse than the idea of being contaminated, of being poisoned.

It was going to be in the seventies today—it was already seventy in the bedroom and would soon be warmer, the bright day glowing around the edges of the shades—and she fumbled through the coat hangers for a sundress. She picked out the white dress, because she liked how she felt in it, liked how it made her feel clean and simple and fresh, and she wanted that now. Then it came to her that if she wore a dress, Jakob would still be able to see the stripe on the back of her leg, and she wanted to spare him. Shorts were out, too. She found a tatty old robe the color of cheap margarine.

"You have to go," she said, without turning to face him. "You have to get out of the house and away from me."

"I think it's too late for that."

"We don't know you're carrying." She belted the robe but didn't turn around. "Until we know for sure, we have to take precautions. You should pack some clothes and get out of the house."

"You touched all the clothes. You washed them in the sink. Then you hung them on the line across the deck. You folded them and put them away."

"Then go someplace and buy new things. Target might be open."

"Sure. Maybe I can give a hot little case of Dragonscale to the girl at the cash register while I'm there."

"I told you. They don't know if you can catch it from people before they're visibly marked up."

"That's right. *They* don't know. *They* don't know shit. Whoever *they* are. If anyone really understood how transmission works, we wouldn't be in this situation, would we, babygirl?"

She didn't like the wry, ironic way he said *babygirl*. That tone was very close to contempt.

"I was careful. I was really careful," she said.

She remembered—with a kind of exhausted resentment—boiling inside her full-body Tyvek outfit all day, the material sticking to her flushed, sweaty skin. It took twenty minutes to put it on, another twenty to take it off, following the required five-minute shower in a bleach solution. After, she remembered the way she'd stink of rubber, bleach, and sweat. She carried that stench on her the whole time she worked at Portsmouth Hospital, an odor like an industrial accident, and she got infected anyway, and it seemed like a real bad joke.

"Don't worry about it. I've got stuff in my gym bag I can wear," he said. "Stuff you haven't had your hands all over."

"Where will you go?"

"How the fuck do I know? Do you know what you've done?"

"I'm sorry."

"Well, that makes it better. I don't feel so bad about both of us burning to death now."

She decided if being angry made him feel less scared, then it was all right. She wanted him to be all right.

"Can you sleep at Public Works?" she asked. "Without coming in contact with the other guys?"

"No," he said. "But Johnny Deepenau is dead, and the keys to his little shitbox trailer are hanging up in his locker. I could stay there. You remember Johnny? He drove the number three Freightliner."

"I didn't know he was sick."

"He wasn't. His daughter got it and burned to death and he jumped off the Piscataqua Bridge."

"I didn't know."

"You were working. You were at the hospital. You never came home. It wasn't the kind of thing I was going to tell you in a text message." He was quiet. His head was down and his eyes were in shadow. "I sort of admire him. For understanding he had seen all the best his life was going to offer him and recognizing there was no point in hanging around for the last shitty little bit. Johnny Deepenau was a Budweiser-drinking, football-watching, Donald Trump–voting, stone-cold bozo who never read anything deeper than *Penthouse* magazine, but he understood that much. I think I have to throw up," he said, without changing his tone of voice, and he rose to his feet.

Harper followed him through the den and into the front hall. He didn't use the bathroom attached to their master bedroom, which Harper supposed was now off-limits, as she had recently occupied it. He went into the little bathroom under the stairs. She stood in the hall and listened to him retching through the closed door and she practiced not crying. She wanted to stop being weepy around him, didn't want to burden him with her emotions. At the same time, she wanted Jakob to say something kind to her, to look anguished for her.

The toilet flushed, and Harper backed away into the den to give him space. She stood beside his desk, where he sat to write in the evening. Jakob had wound up a deputy manager with the Portsmouth Department of Public Works almost by accident; he had intended to be a novelist. He had dropped out of college to write, had been working on the book ever since, six years now. He had 130 pages he had never let anyone read, not even Harper. It was called *Desolation's Plough.* Harper had never told him she hated the title.

He came out of the bathroom, came as far as the entrance to the den, and then held up there. At some point he had found his baseball cap, the one that said FREIGHTLINER on it, which she always thought he wore ironically, the way Brooklyn hipsters wore John Deere caps. If they still did that. If they had ever really done that.

The eyes below the brim were bloodshot and unfocused. She wondered if he had been crying in the bathroom. The idea that he had been weeping for her made her feel a little better.

"I want you to wait," he said.

She didn't understand, looked a question at him.

"How long until we'll know for sure if I have it?" he asked.

"Eight weeks," she said. "If you don't have anything by the end of October, you don't have anything."

"Okay. Eight weeks. I think it's a farce—we both know if *you* have it, *I* have it, too—but we'll wait eight weeks. If we both have it, we'll do it together, like we said." He was silent for a moment, staring down at his feet, and then he nodded. "If I don't have it, I'll be here for you when you do it."

"Do what?"

He looked up at her, real surprise in his face. "Kill ourselves. Jesus. We talked about this. About what we would do if we caught it. We agreed it's better to just—go to sleep. Than to wait around and burn to death."

She felt a hard constriction in her throat, wasn't sure she could force words past it, then found she could. "But I'm pregnant."

"You're never going to have the baby now."

Harper's own reaction surprised her; for the first time, Jakob's dull, angry certainty offended her.

"No, you've got that wrong," she said. "I'm not an expert, but I know more about the spore than you do. There are studies, *good* studies, that show it can't cross the placental barrier. It goes everywhere else, the brain, the lungs . . . everywhere but there."

"That's bullshit. There isn't any study that says that. Not one that's worth the paper it's printed on. The CDC in Atlanta is a pile of cinders. No one is studying this shit anymore. The time to do science is over. Now it's time to run for cover and hope the thing burns itself out before it burns us off the face of the planet." He laughed at this, a dry, humorless sound.

"They *are* studying it, though. Still. In Belgium. In Argentina. But fine, if you don't want to believe me, that's fine. But believe this. In July, at the hospital, we delivered a healthy infant to a woman who was contaminated. They had a party in the lounge off pediatrics. We ate half-melted cherry ice cream and we all took turns holding the baby." She did not say that the medical team had spent a lot more time with the baby than the mother had. The doctor wouldn't allow her to touch him, had carried the child out of the room while the mother screamed for him to come back, to let her have one more look.

Jakob's face wasn't such a blank now. His mouth was a pinched white line.

"So what? This shit—how long do people last? Best-case scenario? After the stripes show up?"

"It's different for everyone. There are a few long-term cases, people who have been around since the beginning. I might last—"

"Three months? Four? What's the average? I don't think the average is even *two* months. You only learned you're pregnant *ten days ago.*" He shook his head in disbelief. "What did you get to take care of us?"

"What do you mean?" She was having trouble keeping up with the run of his thoughts.

"What did you get to do it with? You said you were going to get that stuff—the stuff my dentist gave me after my root canal."

"Vicodin."

"And we can crush it up, right?"

Her robe had come unbelted and hung open, but it seemed like too much effort to fix it, and she had forgotten she wanted to spare him the sight of her infected body.

"Yes. That's probably one of the more painless ways to kill yourself. Twenty or so Vicodin, all crushed up."

"So that's how we'll do it. If we both have the 'scale."

"But I don't have any Vicodin. I never got it."

"Why? We talked. You said you would. You said you'd lift some from the hospital and if we got sick, we'd have wine and listen to some music and then take our pills and sail on."

"I forgot to grab some on my way out of the hospital. At the time, I was in a hurry not to burn alive." Although, she thought, given her current condition, she hadn't escaped anything.

"You brought home Dragonscale but couldn't bother to get us something so we could take care of each other. And then on top of it you get yourself pregnant. Christ, Harper. You've had yourself one hell of a month." He laughed, a short, breathless bark. After a moment he said, "Maybe I can get us something to do it with. A gun, if necessary. Deepenau had NRA stickers plastered all over his piece-of-shit pickup. He must have something."

"Jakob. I'm *not* going to kill myself," she said. "Whatever we talked about before I got pregnant doesn't matter now. I am carrying Dragonscale, but I am also carrying a baby, and that changes things. Can't you see it changes things?"

"Jesus fucking Christ. It isn't even a baby yet. It's a cluster of unthinking cells. Besides, I know you. If it had a defect, you'd get an abortion. You worked in a goddamn clinic once, for chrissake. You'd walk in every morning, past the people screaming you were a murderer, calling you a baby killer."

"The baby *doesn't* have a defect, and even if he *did* I wouldn't—that doesn't mean I'd—"

"I think cooking to death in the womb is kind of a defect. Don't you?"

He stood holding himself. She saw he was trembling.

"Let's wait. Let's give it some time and see if I've got this shit, too," he said at last. "Maybe at some point in the next eight weeks we'll find ourselves on the same page again. Maybe at some point here, you'll be seeing things a little less selfishly."

She had told him he needed to get out of the house, but she hadn't wanted him to go, not really. She had hoped he would offer to stay close, maybe sleep in the basement. It scared her, to imagine being all alone with her infection, and she had wanted his calm, his steadiness, even if she couldn't have his arms around her.

But something had changed in the last sixty seconds. Now she was ready for him to leave. She thought it would be better for *both* of them if he went, so she could have the dark, quiet house to herself for a while—to think, or not think, or be still, or cry, or do whatever she had to do—clear of his terror and angry disgust.

He said, "I'm going to ride my bicycle down to Public Works. Get the key to Johnny Deepenau's trailer out of his locker. I'll call you this afternoon."

"Don't worry if I don't pick up. I might turn my phone off so I can go back to bed." She laughed then, bitter, unhappy laughter. "Maybe I'll wake up and it'll all be a bad dream."

"Yeah. We can hope for that, babygirl. Except if it's a bad dream, we're both dreaming it." He smiled then—a small, nervous smile—and for a moment he was her Jake again, her old friend.

He was on his way to the door when she said, "Don't tell anyone."

He paused, a hand on the latch. "No. I won't."

"I'm not going to Concord. I've heard stories about the facility there."

"Yeah. That it's a death camp."

"You don't believe it?"

"Of course I believe it. Everyone who goes there is infected with this shit. They're all going to die. So of course it's a death camp. By definition." He opened the door onto the hot, smoky day. "I wouldn't send you there. You and me are in this together. I'm not giving you up to some faceless agency. We'll handle this ourselves."

Harper thought he meant this statement to be reassuring, yet, curiously, she was not reassured.

He walked down the steps and onto the curving path that took him out of sight in the direction of the garage. He left the door open, as if he expected her to come outside to watch him go. As if this were required of her. Maybe it was. She belted the robe, crossed the short length of the foyer, and stood in the doorway. He carried his bike out into the drive, hauling it over one shoulder. He didn't look back.

Harper lifted her head to peer into Portsmouth. A filthy sky lowered above the white steeple of North Church. Smoke had hovered over town all summer long. Harper had read somewhere that 12 percent of New Hampshire was on fire, but didn't see how that could be true. Of course that was pretty good compared to Maine. Maine was all the local news talked about. The blaze that had started in Canada had finally reached I-95, effectively cutting the state in two, a burning wasteland almost a hundred miles across at its widest point. They needed rain to put it out, but the last weather system to move that way had evaporated in the face of the heat. A meteorologist on NPR said the rain had fried like spit on the surface of a hot stove.

Coils of smoke rose here and there, brown, dirty loops climbing from the Strawbery Banke. There was always something burning: a house, a shop, a car, a person. It was surprising how much smoke a human body could throw when it was engulfed in flame.

From her spot on the front step, she could see down the road, toward South Street Cemetery. A car rolled slowly through the graveyard, along one of the narrow gravel lanes, trundling ahead the way a person will when trying to find an open space in a crowded parking lot. But the passenger-side window was down, and fire was gushing out. The interior was so filled with flames, Harper could not see the person who must've been sitting behind the wheel.

Harper watched the car roll off the road and into the grass, until it thunked gently to a stop against a headstone. Then she remembered she had come out to watch Jakob ride away. She looked around for him, but he was already gone.

# SEPTEMBER

# 8

Two days later her left arm was sheet music. Delicate black lines spooled around and around her forearm, bars as thin as the strands of a spiderweb, with what looked like golden notes scattered across them. She found herself pulling her sleeve back to look at it every few minutes. By the end of the following week, she was sketched in Dragonscale from wrist to shoulder.

One day she pulled her shirt off and glanced at herself in the mirror on the back of her armoire and saw a belt riding just above her hips, a tattoo in gold and black. When she got over feeling winded and sick, she had to admit to herself that it was curiously beautiful.

Sometimes she took off all her clothes except her underwear and examined her new illustrated skin by candlelight. She wasn't sleeping much, and these inspections usually took place a little after midnight. Much as it was possible to imagine a visage in a flickering fire, or a figure in the grain of a wooden surface, she thought she saw half-finished images scrawled in the 'scale.

That was usually when Jakob called, from the dead man's trailer. He wasn't sleeping, either.

"Thought I ought to check in," he said. "See what you did with yourself today."

"Puttered around the house. Ate the last of the pasta. Made an effort not to turn into a heap of coals. How are you?"

"Hot. It's hot here. It's always hot."

"Open a window. It's cool out. I've got them all open and I'm fine."

"I've got them all open, too, and I'm roasting. It's like trying to sleep in an oven."

She didn't like the angry way he talked about not being able to cool off or the way he fixated on it, like the heat was a personal affront.

Harper distracted him by talking about her condition in a languid, almost breezy tone. "I've got a swirl of 'scale on the inside of my left arm that looks like an open umbrella. An umbrella sailing away on the wind. Do you think the spore has an artistic impulse? Do you think it reacts to the stuff you've got in your subconscious and tries to ink your skin with pictures you might like?"

"I don't want to talk about the shit you've got on you. I get shaky thinking about it, about that disgusting shit all over you."

"That makes me feel nice. Thank you."

He let out a harsh, angry breath. "I'm sorry. I'm—I'm not unsympathetic."

She laughed—surprising not just him, but herself. Good old Jakob used such smart, picky words sometimes. *Unsympathetic.* Before he dropped out of college he had been a philosophy major, and he still had the habit of hunting through his vocabulary for exactly the right term, which, somehow, inexplicably, always made it the *wrong* term. He corrected her spelling sometimes, too.

Harper wondered, idly, why it took getting contaminated to notice the marriage itself was sick.

He tried again. "I'm sorry. I am. I'm boiling. It's hard to be—thoughtful."

A cross-breeze fanned through the room, cool on her bare tummy. She didn't know how he could possibly be hot, wherever he was.

"I was wondering if the Dragonscale started doodling Mary

Poppins's umbrella on my arm. You know how many times I've seen *Mary Poppins*?"

"The Dragonscale isn't reacting to your subconscious. *You* are. You're seeing the kinds of things you're already primed to see."

"That makes sense," she said. "But you know what? There was a gardener in the hospital who had swirls of this stuff up his legs that looked just like tattoos of crawling vines. You could see delicate individual leaves and everything. Everyone agreed it looked like ivy. Like the Dragonscale was making an artistic commentary on his life's work."

"That's just how it looks. Like strands of thorns. I don't want to talk about it."

"I guess it couldn't be in my brain yet, so it couldn't really know anything about me. It takes weeks to pass up the sinuses to the brain. We're still in the getting-to-know-each-other phase of the relationship."

"Christ," he said. "I'm burning alive over here."

"Boy, did you call the wrong person for sympathy," she said.

# 9

A couple of nights later she poured herself a glass of red wine and read the first page of Jakob's book. She told herself if his novel was any good at all, the next time she talked to him she would admit she had looked at some of it and tell him how much she loved it. He couldn't be angry at her for breaking her promise never to look at the manuscript without permission. She had a fatal illness. That had to change the rules.

But after one page she knew it wasn't going to be any good and she left it, feeling bad again, as if she had wronged him somehow.

A while later, after a second glass of wine—two weren't going to do any harm to the baby—she read thirty pages. She had to quit there. She couldn't go any further and still be in love with him. In truth, maybe thirty pages had been three too many.

The novel was about a former philosophy student, J., who has an unfulfilling job at the Department of Public Works and an unfulfilling marriage with a cheerfully shallow blonde who can't spell, reads YA novels because she lacks the mental rigor for mature fiction, and has no sense whatsoever of her husband's tortured inner life. To assuage his existential disappointment, J. engages in a series of casual affairs with women Harper had no trouble identifying: friends from college, teachers from the elementary, a former personal trainer. Harper decided these affairs were inventions . . . although the lies J. told his wife, about where he was and what he was doing when he was really with someone else, corresponded almost word for word with conversations Harper remembered having.

Somehow, though, the clinical reports of his affairs were not the worst of it. What she detested even more was the protagonist's contempt.

He hated the men who drove the trucks for Public Works. He hated their fat faces and their fat wives and their fat children. He hated the way they saved all year to buy tickets in nosebleed territory for a pro-football game. He hated how happy they were in the weeks after the game, and hated the way they would tell the story of the game over and over as if recounting the battle of Thermopylae.

He hated all of his wife's girlfriends—J. had no friends of his own—for not knowing Latin, drinking mass-produced beer instead of microbrews, and raising the next generation of overfed, overentertained human place-fillers. This did not stop him from fucking them, however.

He did not hate his wife, but felt for her the kind of affection a man usually reserves for an excitable puppy. Her immediate acceptance of his every opinion and observation was both disheartening and a little hilarious to him. There was not a single criticism he could offer that she would not immediately accept as true. He made a game out of it. If she worked all week to throw a dinner party, he would tell her everyone had hated it—even if it had been a wonderful time—and she would cry and agree he was right and immediately rush out to buy some books so she could learn to do a party right. No, he did not hate her. But he felt sorry for her and felt sorry for himself, because he was stuck with her. Also, she cried too easily, which suggested to him, paradoxically, a shallowness of feeling. A woman who got teary over commercials for the ASPCA could not be expected to wrestle with the deeper despair of being human in a crass age.

There was all this—his derisive rage and self-pity—and there was bad writing too. His paragraphs never ended. Neither did his sentences. Sometimes it could take him thirty words before he found his way to a verb. Every page or two he'd drop a line in Greek or French or German. The few times Harper was able to translate one of these bons mots, it always seemed like something he could've said just as well in English.

Harper thought, helplessly, of Bluebeard. She had gone and done it, she had looked in the forbidden room and seen what she was never supposed to see. She had discovered not corpses behind the locked door, but contempt. She thought hatred might've been easier to forgive. If you hated someone, she was at least worthy of your passion.

He had never told her what the book was about, not in any concrete terms, although sometimes he would say something airy-fairy like, "It's about the terror of an ordinary life" or "It's the story of a man shipwrecked in his own mind." But the two of them had shared long postcoital discussions about what their lives would be like after the novel came out. He had hoped it would make them enough money so they could get a pied-à-terre in Manhattan (Harper was unclear on how this was different from an apartment, but assumed there had to be something). She had eagerly and breathlessly talked about how great he'd be on the radio, funny and clever and self-deprecating; she had hoped they would have him on NPR. They talked about things they wanted to buy and famous people they wanted to meet, and remembering it now, it all seemed shabby and sad and deluded. It was bad enough that she had been so utterly convinced he had a brilliant mind, but much worse to discover he was convinced of it, too, and on such thin evidence.

It amazed her, as well, that he had written something so appalling and then left it in plain sight, *for years*. But then he had been sure she wouldn't read it, because he had told her not to, and he understood she was inclined to obedience. Her entire self-worth depended on doing and being just what he wanted her to do and be. He had been right about that, of course. The novel would not have been so awful if it did not contain within it a certain degree of truth. She had only looked at *Desolation's Plough* because she was dying.

Harper put the novel back on his desk, cornering the edges

of the manuscript so it stood in a neat, crisp pile. With its clean white title page and clean white edges, it looked as immaculate as a freshly made bed in a luxury hotel. People did all sorts of unspeakable things in hotel beds.

Almost as an afterthought, she put a box of kitchen matches on top of it as a paperweight. If her Dragonscale started to smoke and itch, she wanted to have them close at hand. If she had to burn, she felt it only fair that the fucking book burn first.

# 10

It was almost one in the morning the next time he called, but she was still up, working on a book of her own—her baby book. Her book began:

> *Hello! This is your mother, in book form. This is what I looked like before I was a book.*

She had taped a picture of herself directly beneath. It was a photograph her father had taken of her, when she was nineteen years old and teaching archery for the Exeter Rec. Department. The kid in the photograph was a gangly girl with pale hair, ears that stuck out, bony boyish knees, and scrapes on the insides of her arms from accidents with the bowstring. Pretty, though. In the photo, the sun was behind her, lighting her hair in a brilliant ring of gold. Jakob said it was her teen angel picture.

Below it she had taped a reflective silver square, something she had clipped out of a magazine ad. Beneath it she wrote: *Do we look alike?* She had a lot of ideas about what belonged in the book. Recipes. Instructions. At least one game. The lyrics of her favorite songs, which she would've sung to the baby if she'd had a chance: "Love Me Do," "My Favorite Things," "Raindrops Keep Fallin' on My Head."

There would be no girly-girly tragic stuff if she could help it. As a school nurse, she had always modeled herself on Mary Poppins, aiming for an air of good-tempered calm, self-assurance, a tolerance for play, but an expectation that the medicine would go down along with the spoonful of sugar. If the kids thought it was possible she might break into song and shoot fireworks from the tip of her umbrella, that was all right with her.

Such was the tone she was trying to nail in the baby book. The question was what a child wanted from his mother; her answer was Band-Aids for scrapes, a song at bedtime, kindness, something sweet to eat after school, someone to help with homework, someone to cuddle with. She hadn't figured out how to make the book cuddly yet, but she had stapled a dozen Band-Aids into the inside cover, along with four prepackaged alcohol swabs. She felt the book—*The Portable Mother*—was off to a roaring good start.

When the phone rang, she was in front of the TV. The TV was always on. It had not been off in six months, except in the occasional spells when there was no power. She had electric at the moment and was parked in front of the screen, although she was working on the book, not really paying attention.

There was nothing to watch anyway. FOX was still broadcasting, but from Boston, not New York. NBC was on the air, but from Orlando. CNN was on the air, too, in Atlanta, but the evening news anchor was a man named Jim Joe Carter, a Baptist preacher, and his reports were always about people who had been saved from the spore by Jesus. All the rest of the channels were HSB, the Homeland Security Broadcast, or local news programs, or static. The HSB was broadcast from Quantico, Virginia. Washington, D.C., was still burning. So was Manhattan. She had the TV tuned to FOX. The phone rang and she picked it up. She knew it was Jakob even before he spoke. His breath was strange and a little choked and he didn't say anything, not at first.

"Jakob," she said. "Jakob, talk to me. Say something."

"Do you have the TV on?"

She put down her pen. "What's wrong?"

Harper had not known how she would be with him, the next time they spoke. She worried she would not be able to keep the resentment out of her voice. If Jakob thought she sounded hostile, he would want to know why, and she would have to tell him.

She could never keep anything from him. And Harper didn't want to talk about his book. She didn't even want to think about it. She was pregnant and crawling with a flammable fungus and she had recently learned Venice was burning, so now she was never going to get to see it by gondola. With all that going on, it was a bit much to expect her to provide a literary critique of his shitty novel.

But he laughed—roughly and unhappily—and the sound of it rattled her and caused her to forget her resentment, at least for the moment. A part of her thought, calmly, clinically: *hysteria*. God knew she had seen enough of it in the last half a year.

"That's the funniest thing anyone has said since I have no idea," he said. "What's *wrong*? You mean besides the world catching fire? Besides fifty million human beings turning into balls of flame? Are you watching FOX?"

"I'm watching. What's wrong, Jakob? You're crying. Has something happened?" It was no wonder he held her in contempt. In ten seconds he had her worrying about him again, when five minutes ago she would've been glad not to hear from him for a month. It embarrassed her, that she couldn't hang on to her rage.

"You seeing this?"

She stared at the TV, jittery footage of a meadow somewhere. A few men in yellow rain slickers and elbow-high rubber gloves and gas masks, carrying Bushmaster assault rifles, were on the far side of the field. The tall yellow grass undulated in a soft rain. Beyond the men in the rain slickers was a line of trees. Off to the left was a highway. A car shushed over a rise and swept past, headlights glowing in the half dusk.

"—cell phone camera," said the newscaster. "We caution you, this footage is graphic." That was hardly worth mentioning. It was all graphic these days.

They were bringing people out of the woods. Kids, mostly, although there were some women with them. Some of the kids were naked. One of the women was naked, too, but clutching a dress to the front of her body.

"They've been showing this one all night," Jakob said. "The news loves this. Look. Look at the cars."

The field was in full view of the highway. Another car came over the rise, and then a pickup. Both vehicles slowed as they passed the field, then sped up again.

The women and children who had been marched out of the trees were bunched together into a tight group. The children were crying. From the distance, their voices, all together, sounded like the first keening wind of fall. One of the women took a small boy in her arms, lifted him up, and squeezed him to her. Watching it go down, Harper was struck with a brief but intense wave of déjà vu, the improbable certainty that she was watching herself, at some future point. She was seeing how she herself would die.

The woman who had been stripped, and who was clutching her dress, lunged toward one of the rain-slicker men. At a distance, her bare back looked as if it had been slashed, then stitched up with brilliant gold thread: the Dragonscale. She let go of her dress and careened, naked, toward an assault rifle.

"You can't," she howled. "Let us go! This is Ameri—"

The first gun might've gone off by accident. Harper wasn't sure. But then, they had brought them to the field to shoot them, so maybe it was wrong to think anyone was shot there by accident. *Prematurely* was, perhaps, the more accurate word for it. The muzzle of a gun flashed. The naked woman kept coming, one step, two, then tilted forward into the grass and disappeared.

There followed an instant—just enough time to draw a single breath—of surprised, baffled silence. Another car came over the rise and began to slow.

The other guns went off, all together, firecrackers on a July night. Muzzles flashed, like paparazzi snapping shots of George Clooney as he climbed out of his limousine. Although George Clooney was dead, had burned to death while on a humanitarian aid mission to New York City.

The car passing by on the highway slowed to a crawl, so the

driver could watch. The women and their children fell while the guns stuttered in the September rain. The car accelerated away.

The rain-slicker men had missed one person, a little girl, slipping, spritelike, across the field toward the hidden observer with the cell phone. She rushed across the meadow as fast as the shadow of a cloud. Harper watched, gripping her baby book in both hands, holding her breath, sending out a silent wish: *Let her go. Let her get away.* But then the girl folded in on herself and tumbled forward and collapsed and Harper realized it had never been a person at all. The thing racing across the field had been the dress that the naked woman had been holding. The wind had made it dance for a moment, that was all. Now the dance was over.

The program cut back to the studio. The newsman stood in front of a wide-screen TV, replaying the footage. He kept his back to it and spoke in a smooth, calm voice. Harper couldn't hear what he was saying. Jakob was talking, too, but she couldn't hear what he was saying, either.

She spoke over both of them. "Did you think she looked like me?"

Jakob said, "What are you talking about?"

"The woman who was hugging the little boy. I thought she looked like me."

The newscaster was saying, "—illustrates the dangers of people who have been infected and who don't seek—"

"I didn't notice," Jakob said. His voice was strangled with emotion.

"Jakob. Tell me what's wrong."

"I'm sick."

She felt as if she had stood up too quickly, although she hadn't moved. She perched on the edge of the couch, light-headed and a little faint.

"You've got a stripe?"

"I've got a fever."

"Okay. But do you have marks on you?"

"It's on my foot. I thought it was a bruise. I dropped a sandbag on my foot yesterday and I thought it was just a bruise." For a moment he sounded close to crying.

"Oh, Jakob. Send me a picture. I want to look at it."

"I don't need you to look at it."

"Please. For me."

"I know what it is."

"Please, Jake."

"I know what it is and I have a fever. I'm so fucking hot. I'm a hundred and one. I'm so hot and I can't sleep. I keep dreaming the blankets are on fire and I jump out of the bed. Are you having those dreams?"

No. Her dreams were much worse than that. They were so bad she had recently decided to quit sleeping. It was safer staying awake.

"What were you doing with a sandbag?" she asked, not because she cared, but because it might calm him to talk about something besides infection.

"I had to go back to work. I had to risk it. Risk contaminating other people. That's the position you've put me in."

"What are you talking about? I don't understand."

"If I just disappeared, people would wonder where I was. They might come by the house and find you. The price of your life is other lives. You've made a potential murderer out of me."

"No. Jakob, we've covered this. Until the 'scale is visible on your body you aren't infectious. Almost everyone agrees on that. And even then, you can only pass it through skin-on-skin contact. I don't think you're a mass murderer just yet. So what about the sandbag?"

"They had everyone in Public Works up on the Piscataqua Bridge the other day, taking orders from the National Guard. Building a gun emplacement to shoot any diseased motherfuckers who might try and drive through the new checkpoint. Why are we talking about the fucking bridge?"

"I need you to send me a picture of the mark on your foot," she said, and her tone was firmer now, her nurse voice.

"I think it's in my *head,* too. Sometimes it's like there are pins pricking in my brain. Like there are a hundred little needles in there."

That stopped her. It was the first thing he said that sounded not just hysterical but crazy.

When she went on, her voice was calm and certain: "No. Jakob, *no.* It does eventually coat the myelin in the brain and nerves, but it wouldn't happen until well after you had Dragonscale all over your body."

"I fucking *know.* I fucking *know* what you did to me. You killed the both of us, and our baby, too, to satisfy your ego."

"What are you talking about?"

"You *knew* it was dangerous to work in that hospital, but you wanted to feel important. You have this thing in you, Harper. You have this *need* to be hugged. You seek out chances to be with people who are hurting, so you can stick a Band-Aid on them and get some cheap, easy affection. That's why you became a school nurse. It's easy to squeeze a kiss out of a kid with a scraped knee. Kids will love anyone who gives them a penny lollipop and a Band-Aid for their boo-boo."

It left her breathless, the spoiled rage she heard in his voice. She had never heard him that way before.

"They were desperate," Harper said. "They needed every nurse they could get. The hospital was calling in retired nurses who were eighty-five years old. I couldn't just sit at home and watch people die on TV and not do anything."

"We have to decide," he said. Almost sobbed. "I do not want to fucking burn to death. Or be hunted down and butchered in a field, begging for my life."

"If you aren't sleeping, that could explain a high temperature. We don't know you're sick. Sometimes fever indicates onset of infection, but not always. Not even mostly. I didn't get a fever. Now I want you to send me a photo of your foot."

There was a clumsy knocking sound, muffled bumps, then a click, the sound of the camera app taking a still. Fifteen seconds passed with no other noise than his labored, miserable breathing.

A photo came through of his dark bare foot, stretched out on some industrial-looking carpet. The top of the foot was a single bloody abrasion.

"Jake," she said. "What is that?"

"I tried to scrape it off," he said. His voice was almost sullen. "I had a bad moment. I sandpapered it."

"Do you have any other stripes on you?"

"I know what it looked like before I went crazy," he said.

"You don't scrape at this stuff, Jake. That's like scraping a match on a matchbook. Leave it alone." She lowered her phone and looked at the photo again. "I want to see more stripes before you make up your mind you've got Dragonscale. In the early going, it can be difficult to tell the difference between a bruise and a stripe, but if you just leave it alone—"

"We have to decide," he said again.

"Decide what?"

"How we're going to die. How we're going to do it."

On the TV, they were showing a segment about the Dalmatians, crews of women and teenagers who made lunches and cupcakes for the volunteer fire crews.

"I'm not going to kill myself," Harper said. "I told you that already. I've got this baby in me. I mean to see it born. I can deliver by C-section next March."

"March? It's *September.* You'll be *cinders* by March. Or target practice for a cremation squad. You want to die like those people in the field?"

"No," Harper said quietly.

"I know what you did to me," he said. He drew a shuddering, effortful breath. "I *know.* I keep getting hot patches on my arms and legs. I loved that you made your work so socially conscious, that you were so connected to community, even if it was, always, just this thing you did to satisfy your own narcissism.

You needed to surround yourself with crying kids, because of the good feeling it gives you about yourself when you wipe away their tears. There are no unselfish acts. When people do something for someone else, it's always for their own personal psychological reasons. But I'm still a little sick to see how fixated you are on your own needs. You don't even care how many people you spread it to. As long as nothing uproots you from your delusion of saving one more child."

He was trying to get a fight out of her, wanted to push her into saying things she didn't want to say. She tacked in another direction. "These hot patches. I haven't heard of that. That's not a symptom of—"

"That's not *your* symptom. It's mine. Don't pretend you're a fucking doctor. A fucking master's in nursing and three years of working at an elementary school doesn't make you Dr. motherfucking House. You wipe a real doctor's sweat off his upper lip when he's performing surgery and shake his prick when he's done taking a leak."

"Maybe you should come home. I can examine you without touching you. Maybe I can reassure you."

"I am going to wait," he said. "Until I am sure. And *then* I am coming home. And you need to be there. Because you promised."

"Jakob," she said again, but he was gone.

# OCTOBER

# 11

The power went out again one hot, smoky morning, a few days after her last call from Jakob, and this time it didn't come back.

By then, Harper was down to the last cans from the back of the cupboard, the ones with dust on them that she couldn't remember buying. She hadn't been out of the house since the day before she found the first stripe on her leg. She didn't dare. Maybe she could cover up—she didn't have the 'scale on her face or hands—but her heart quailed at the thought of bumping into someone in the corner store and accidentally sentencing them to death.

One part of her wondered if she could eat Crisco. Another part of her knew she could and soon would. She had saved a little cocoa powder, hoping she could make it taste like chocolate pudding.

There was no single moment when she thought: *I am going*. There was no hour of steely-eyed decision, when she realized soon she would be out of food and have to start taking chances.

One day, though, she unstrung clothes from the line across the back deck and began to make a pile on the bed, next to *The Portable Mother*. At first it was just a collection of things she meant to put away: some T-shirts, a pair of jeans, her sweats. But it also looked like a stack of things she might take with her if she were packing the car to go elsewhere. When she opened the dresser, she found herself picking things out instead of putting them away.

There was no destination, no plan, almost no thought at all. She operated on no more than the half-formed notion that it might be smart to have some things in her old carpetbag, in case she had to leave the house in a hurry. Mostly she was zoned out, gliding along with no more intention or purpose than a leaf blown about by a restless fall breeze. She had the radio on, a violently pink Hello Kitty boom box that ran on D-cells, and she folded clothes to the classic-rock radio station, Tom Petty and Bob Seger supplying the sonic equivalent of wallpaper.

At some point, though, her consciousness settled back into the moment, and she realized the music had stopped. The DJ was belting out a monologue and had been at it for a while. She recognized his voice, a hoarsened, raspy bass that belonged to a former morning-show joker. Or had he been a right-wing radio host? She couldn't recall and she couldn't quite remember his real name, either. When he referred to himself—which he did frequently—it was as the Marlboro Man, on account of all the burners he had smoked. That was what he called people sick with Dragonscale: burners.

He boomed, with a certain crass authority, that the former president was blacker than he used to be, since he had cooked to death from Dragonscale. He said when he went off the air he would be out with a Cremation Crew, chasing burners out of their hidey-holes and lighting them up. Harper sat on the bed and listened with a repulsed fascination while he told a story about forcing three girls to take their shirts off, to prove they didn't have Dragonscale on their boobies.

"Healthy American boobies, that's what we're fighting for," he said. "That needs to be in the Constitution. Every man has a right to life, liberty, and germ-free titties. Learn the drill, girls. If we show up at your front door, be ready to do your patriotic duty and show us your freedom-loving, virus-free knockers."

The knocker crashed at the front door, and Harper jumped as if a Cremation Crew were kicking it in. The sound was, in a way, more startling than someone screaming in the street, or a fire siren. She heard people screaming every day and sirens every hour. She could not remember the last time someone had knocked on the door.

She padded down the hall and looked through the peephole. Tony the Tiger and Captain America stood together on the front step, holding wrinkled plastic bags. Beyond them, down at the end of the drive, a man sat with his back to the house, smoking a cigarette, a tendril of smoke rising from his head.

"Trick and treat," came a muffled voice. A girl's voice.

"Trick or . . ." Harper started, then stopped. "It's not Halloween."

"We're getting an early start!"

It offended her, some idiot sending his kids house to house in the middle of a plague. She had stern ideas about parenting, and such behavior fell well short of her standards. It riled up her inner English nanny and made her want to stab the offending grown-up in the eye with an umbrella.

Harper picked her Windbreaker off the hook and slipped it on to cover the pretty scrollwork of Dragonscale scrawled on her arms. She opened the door, but left it on the chain, and peered out through the six-inch gap.

The girl might've been as old as eighteen or as young as thirteen. With her face hidden behind her Captain America mask, it was impossible to tell. Her head was shaved and if Harper hadn't heard her voice, she would've taken her for a boy.

Her brother was possibly just half her age. The eyes that peered out through the holes in his Tony the Tiger mask were very pale—the light green of an empty Coke bottle.

"Trick and treat," Captain America said again. A gold locket, shaped like a hardcover book, hung outside her moth-eaten turtleneck.

"You shouldn't be knocking on doors for candy." She looked past them to the man smoking a cigarette on the curb with his back to the house. "Is that your father?"

"We aren't here to get a treat," Captain America told her. "We're here to give you one. And we've got tricks, too. You can have one of each. That's why it's trick *and* treat. We thought it would cheer people up."

"You still shouldn't be out. People are sick. If someone sick touches someone who isn't, they can give you the bad thing they've got." She raised her voice and yelled past them. "Hey, buddy! These kids shouldn't be out! There's a contagion on!"

"We're wearing gloves," Captain America told her. "And we won't touch you. No one is going to catch anything from anyone. I *promise*. Sanitation is our number-one priority! Don't you want to see your treat?" She jabbed the boy with her elbow.

The Tiger held open his bag. There was a bottle of sugared gummy vitamins in there—prenatal vitamins, she saw. Harper snapped her head up, eyeing one child and then the other.

"What *is* this?"

"They're like Sour Patch Kids," said Captain America. "But you can only take two a day. Are you all right?"

"What do you mean am I *all right*? Hang on a minute. Who *are* you? I think I want to talk to your father." She lifted herself on tiptoes and hollered over their heads. "I want to talk to you!"

The man sitting on the curb didn't look at her, just waved one hand in a sleepy, dismissive gesture. Or maybe he was fanning the smoke away from his face. He blew a trickle of smoke rings into the afternoon.

Captain America cast a casual glance over her shoulder at the man on the curb. "That's not our father. Our father isn't with us."

Harper dropped her gaze. The boy was still holding the bag open for her to inspect his offering. "These are prenatal vitamins. How do you know I'm pregnant? I don't look pregnant. Wait. *Do* I?"

Captain America said, "Not yet."

"Who sent you here? Who told you to give this to me?"

"Don't you *want* them? If you don't want them, you don't have to take them."

"It's not about whether I *want* them. You're very kind, and I *would,* but—"

"Take them, then."

The boy hung the bag on the doorknob and stepped back. After a moment, Harper reached through the gap and slipped the bag into the house.

"Now have a trick," the girl said and held her own bag open, so Harper could see what was inside.

Tony the Tiger didn't seem to have anything to say. He never made a sound.

Harper looked into the bag. There was a slide whistle in it, in plastic wrap.

"They're really loud," said Captain America. "You can hear it all the way from here to Wentworth by the Sea. A deaf person could hear it. Take it."

"There's nothing else in the bag," Harper said. "You don't have any other tricks to hand out."

"You're our last stop."

Harper wondered, for the first time, if she might be dreaming. It felt like the kind of conversation that occurred in a dream. The children in their masks seemed like *more* than children. They seemed like *symbols.* When the girl spoke, it felt like she was talking in a secret dream-code; a psychologist could spend hours trying to puzzle it out. And the boy. The boy just *stood* there staring at her. He never blinked. When Harper spoke, he stared at her lips like he wanted to kiss her.

She felt a brief but almost painful stab of hope. Maybe *all* of it was a dream. Maybe she had a bad case of flu, or something worse than flu, and everything that had happened in the last three months was a vision inspired by sickness. Wasn't this *exactly* the kind of thing a person would dream if she were on fire with a fever? Perhaps she was only *dreaming* Jakob had left her and that she was alone in an infected world, a world that was burning, and her only visitors in weeks were a pair of masked children who spoke in fortune-cookie messages.

*I will take the whistle,* Harper thought, *and if I blow it, if I blow hard, my fever will break, and I will wake up in bed, covered in sweat, with Jakob pressing a cool washcloth to my forehead.*

The girl hung her bag from the doorknob and stepped away. Harper took it, clutched the crinkling plastic to her chest.

"Are you sure you're *all right*?" the girl asked. "Do you *need* anything? I mean, besides your trick and your treat? You don't come outside anymore."

"How do you know I don't come outside anymore? How long have you been watching me? I don't know what you're up to, but I don't like games. Not unless I know who I'm playing with." She looked past them, elevated herself onto her tiptoes once more, and shouted at the man sitting on the curb with his back to her. "I don't like games, buddy boy!"

"You're all right," Captain America said, in a confident, assertive tone. "If you need anything, just call."

"Call?" Harper asked. "How am I supposed to call? I don't even know who you are."

"That's all right. We know who *you* are," Captain America said, and gripped the little boy by the shoulder, and turned him away.

They walked swiftly down the path toward the street. As they reached the curb, the man sitting there pushed himself to his feet, and for the first time Harper saw he wasn't smoking a cigarette, he was just smoking. He blew a last mouthful of cloud, which disintegrated into a hundred small butterflies of smoke. They scattered, flapping frantically away into the smoggy morning.

Harper slammed the door, yanked the chain off, threw the door open wide, took three reeling steps into the yard.

"Hey!" she shouted, her heart clouting against the inside of her chest, as if she had just run a few laps around the house.

The guy looked back over his shoulder at her and she saw he was wearing a Hillary Clinton mask. For the first time she noticed he was wearing slightly reflective yellow pants, like the sort firemen wore.

"Hey, come back here!" she yelled.

The man walked the children swiftly away down the sidewalk, disappearing behind a hedge. The boy was practically skipping.

Harper crossed the yellowing grass, still clutching the bag with the slide whistle in it. She reached the sidewalk and looked around for them, blinking in the haze that drifted perpetually along the street. It was thicker than usual today, a pale mass that gradually erased the road, so that she couldn't see to the end of the block. The smoke swallowed houses, lawns, telephone poles, and the sky itself. It had swallowed the man and his children, too. Harper stared after them, eyes watering.

When Harper was back in her house, she put the chain on the door again. If a Quarantine Patrol showed up, that chain might buy her enough time to get down into the basement, out the back door, and into the woods. With her carpetbag. And her slide whistle.

She was turning the whistle over in her hands, wondering how loud it was, when she realized the house had gone perfectly still. No music and no Marlboro Man. Somewhere in the last few minutes, the batteries had died in her Hello Kitty radio. The twenty-first century—like her masked visitors—had briskly and unapologetically slipped away from her, leaving her all on her own again.

*Trick and treat,* she thought.

# 12

When her cell phone was close to dead, she knew it was time to make the call she had been putting off—that if she waited one more day she might not be able to make the call at all. She had a glass of white wine to loosen herself up and she rang her brother. Her sister-in-law Lindy answered.

In her early twenties, Lindy had parlayed her hobby of fucking the bassists in second-string rock bands into a job at a recording studio in Woodstock, which was what she was doing when she met Connor. He was playing bass for a prog-metal band called Unbreakable. They weren't. Connor wound up with a bald spot the size of a tea saucer and a job installing hot tubs. Lindy became an instructor at an upscale gym, where she taught aerobic pole dancing to housewives, which she likened to being an animal trainer working with walruses: "You want to throw sardines at them just for turning in a complete circle without falling down." Not long afterward, Harper let her own gym membership lapse. She couldn't stop worrying about what the trainers said about her in private.

"How are you, Lindy?" Harper asked.

"I don't know. I have a three-year-old. I'm too tired to think about how I'm doing. Ask me again in twenty years, if any of us are still around then. You must want Con." She lowered the phone and screamed, "Con! The Sis!"

Connor picked up. "Hey! It's the Sis! What's up?"

"I've got big news," she said.

"Is it the monk? The monk in London?"

"No. What monk?"

"The one they shot trying to walk into the BBC. You don't know about the monk? Him and three others. They were all sick. Long-term sick—this monk has been walking around with the junk since February. They think he might've infected literally thousands. They think he wanted to infect the newsroom staff to make a political point. Terrorism by way of disease. Crazy motherfucker. He was glowing like a lightbulb when they cut him down."

"It's not a disease, you know. Not in the traditional sense. It's not a germ. It's a spore."

"Uh-huh. They talked to his followers when they rounded them up. He was telling them they could *learn* to control the infection and not to infect others. That they could go home, live among normal people. And if they did infect someone they loved, well, they could just teach them how not to be sick, too. He probably had a brain full of sickness. You had some patients like that in the hospital, didn't you? Crazies with spore all over their brain?"

"It gets all over the brain, but I don't know if that's why some people go crazy after they're infected. Hearing you could explode into flames at any second will put a lot of mental strain on a person. Maybe the real surprise is that anyone stays sane." She thought she would know pretty soon if the 'scale had any effect on a person's mental state. It was probably beginning to coat her brain right now.

"Is there something happening besides the terrorist monk?" Connor asked.

She said, "I'm pregnant."

"You're—" he said. "Ohmigod, Harpo! Oh my God! Lindy! Lindy! Harpo and Jake got pregnant!"

In the background, Harper heard Lindy say, "She's pregnant," in a flat tone that carried no note of celebration. Then she said something else, in a lower tone; it sounded like a question.

"Harpo!" Connor said. He was trying to sound joyous, but she heard the strain in his voice, and she knew Lindy was being unpleasant somehow. "I'm so, *so* happy for you. We didn't even know you were *trying*. We thought—"

In the background, but perfectly audible, Lindy said, "We thought you'd be crazy to get pregnant in the middle of a plague, after you spent months in constant contact with infectious people."

"Do Mom and Dad know?" Connor asked, his voice flustered. Then, before she could answer, he said, "Hang on."

She heard him press the phone to his chest to muffle it, something she had seen him do dozens of times. She waited for him to come back to her. Finally he did.

"Hey," he said, out of breath, as if he had just run up a flight of stairs. Maybe he had jogged upstairs to get away from Lindy. "Where were we? I'm so happy for you. Do you know the sex?"

"It's too early for that." She took a deep breath and said, "What would you think if I came to visit for a while?"

"I think I would try to talk you out of it. You don't want to go on the road the way things are now. You can't go thirty miles without hitting a roadblock, and that's the least of what's out there. If something happened to you, I'd never forgive myself."

"If I could come, though—speaking hypothetically—what would happen if I turned up on your doorstep tomorrow?"

"I would start with a hug and we'd go from there. Is Jakob on board with this plan? Does he know a guy with a private plane or something? Put him on, I want to say congratulations."

"I can't put him on. Jakob and I aren't living together anymore."

"What do you mean, you aren't—what happened?" Connor asked. He was silent for a moment. Then he said, "Oh Jesus. He's sick, isn't he? That's why you want to come. *Jesus,* I knew you were being weird, but I thought—well, you're pregnant, you're entitled."

"I don't know if *he's* sick," she said softly. "But *I* am. That's the bad news, Connor. I came down with it six weeks ago. If I turned up on your doorstep, the last thing you'd want to do is hug me."

"What do you mean?" His voice sounded small and frightened. "How?"

"I don't know. I was careful. It can't have happened in the hospital. They had us in rubber head to foot." She was again surprised at the calm she felt, staring the fact of her sickness in the face. "Connor. The womb isn't a good host for the spore. There's a strong chance the baby will be born healthy."

"Hang on. Hangonhangon. I mean. Oh *God*." He sounded like he was trying not to cry. "You're just a kid. Why'd you have to work in that hospital? Why'd you have to fucking go in there?"

"They needed nurses. That's what I am. *Connor.* I could live with this for months. *Months.* Long enough to have the baby by C-section. I want you and Lindy to have him after I'm gone." The thought of Lindy being mother to her unborn child was a bad one, but she forced herself not to think about it. Connor, at least, would be a good dad: loving, and patient, and funny, and a bit square. And her child would have *The Portable Mother* for the tough times.

"Harper. Harper. I'm sorry." His voice was strained and close to a whisper. "It's not fair. All you ever are is nice to people. It's just not fair."

"*Shh. Shh,* Connor. This baby is going to need you. And I'm going to need you."

"Yeah. No. I mean—wouldn't it be better if you went to a hospital?"

"I can't. I don't know what it's like in New York, but here in New Hampshire they're sending the sick to a quarantine camp in Concord. It's not a good place. There's no medical treatment there. Even if the baby lives, I don't know what they'll do with him. Where they'll place him. I want the baby to be with *you,* Connor. You and Lindy." Just saying Lindy's name was hard. "Besides. People with the spore, when they congregate, they sometimes set each other off. We know that now. We saw it in the hospital. Going to a camp crowded with other people who have this thing is a death sentence. For me and probably the baby, too."

"So what about *our* baby, Harper?" said Lindy, her voice sharp and loud in Harper's ear. She had picked up an extension. "I'm sorry. I am so fucking sorry I feel ill. I can't imagine what you're going through. But, Harper. We have a *three-year-old*. And you want us to *hide* you? You want us to take you *in* and risk you passing this infection to our *child*? To *us*?"

"I could stay in your garage," Harper whispered, but she doubted Lindy heard her.

"Even if you don't pass it to us, what happens if someone finds out? What happens to Connor? To me? They're locking people up, Harper. We're probably breaking six federal laws even *talking* about this," Lindy said.

Connor said, "Lindy, get off the phone. Let me talk to my sister."

"I am *not* getting off the phone. You are *not* making this decision without me. I am *not* going to let her talk you into risking all of our lives. You want to see our fucking little boy *burn* to death? No. *No. NOT* happening."

"Lindy. This is a private conversation," Connor said—whined, really. "This business is between me and Harp."

"When it comes to decisions that could affect the safety of our child, it stops being private business and starts being *Lindy* business," she said. "I would risk my life for either one of you, but I will not risk my son's life, and it isn't right to ask me to. Being a hero isn't an option anymore when you have a little kid. I know it, and Harper, you know it, too. If you didn't know it before you got pregnant, you know it now. You want your baby to be okay. I understand, *because I feel the same way about mine.* I am sorry, Harper. I am. But you made your choices. We have to make ours. They aren't heroic choices, but they'll keep our little boy alive until this is all over."

"Lindy," Connor pleaded, although what he was pleading for, Harper couldn't guess.

Because Lindy was awful, an awful person, someone who liked being a mother because it gave her a child and a husband to bully. Everything about her was horrible, from her pointy nose to her pointy little tits to her pointed, shrill voice . . . but she was right. Harper was a loaded gun now, and you didn't leave a loaded gun where a child could come upon it. The thought crossed Harper's mind, not for the first time, that choosing to try to live was, in some ways, a monstrous act, an act of towering, possibly homicidal selfishness. Her death was a certainty now and she felt everything depended on not taking anyone else with her, in not putting anyone at risk.

*But someone is* already *at risk. The baby is at risk.*

Harper shut her eyes. A pair of candles burned on the coffee table, and she could dimly apprehend their light through her eyelids, a sickly red glow.

"Connor," Harper said. "Lindy is right. I wasn't thinking. I'm just scared."

"Of course you are," Lindy said. "Oh, of course you are, Harper."

"It was wrong to ask. I've been knocking around by myself for too long—Jakob left last month, so he wouldn't get it, too. You spend too much time alone, you can talk yourself into some really rotten ideas."

"You ought to call your father," Lindy said. "Fill him in on what's happening."

"What?" Connor cried. "Jesus, Dad can't know about this! It'll kill him. He had a heart attack last year, Lindy. You want him to have another?"

"He's a smart man. He might have some ideas. Besides, your parents have a right to know. Harper ought to be the one to explain to them the situation she's put us all in."

Connor was sputtering. "If it doesn't stop his heart, it'll break it. Lindy, *Lindy.*"

"You might be right, Lindy," Harper said. "You're the most practical of any of us. I might have to call Mom and Dad at some point. But not tonight. I've only got three percent charge left on my phone, and I don't want to give them the bad news and then get disconnected. I want you to *promise* you'll let *me* tell them. I don't want them to hear it from you and not be able to get in touch with me. Besides, like you said: I made this situation, I'm the one who has to bear the responsibility."

Harper didn't have any intention of calling her parents and telling them she would likely be dead within a year. There would be no good in it. They were in their late sixties, stranded in God's waiting room, a.k.a. Florida. They couldn't help her from there and they couldn't come to her; all they could do was get an early start on mourning her, and Harper didn't see the point.

Nothing mollified Lindy faster than someone telling her she was right, however, and when she spoke again, a kind of hushed calm had come into her voice. "Of course I'll let you be the one to tell them. You speak to them when you can, and when you're ready. If they need someone to talk to, we'll do what we can to comfort them from our end." In a distraught, distracted voice, she added: "Maybe this is the thing that will finally bring your mother and me together."

There was a silver lining, Harper thought. Maybe she was going to burn to death, but at least it would give Lindy a chance to bond with her mother-in-law.

"Lindy? Connor? My phone is about to die and I don't know when I'll be able to call again. I haven't had power in the house for days. Can I say good night to Connor Jr.? It must almost be his bedtime."

"Ah, Harper," Connor said. "I don't know."

"Of *course* she can say good night to him," Lindy said, on Harper's side now.

"Harp, you aren't going to tell the little guy you're sick, are you?"

"Of *course* she won't," Lindy said.

"I—I don't think you should tell him about the baby, either. I don't want him to get the idea in his head that he's going to have a— Jesus, Harper. This is really hard." He sounded like he was trying not to cry. "I want to put my arms around you, Sis."

She said, "I love you, Con," because whatever Jakob believed about those three words, they still mattered to Harper. They were as close to an incantation as any she knew, had power other words lacked.

"I'll put Junior on," Lindy said, her voice gentle, hushed, as if she were speaking in a church. There was a plasticky clatter as she put her extension down.

Her brother said, "Don't be mad. Don't hate us, Harper." He was speaking in a whisper, too, his voice hitching with grief.

"I would never," she said to her brother. "You have to take care of each other. What Lindy said is just right. You're doing the right thing."

"Oh, Harp," Connor said. He inhaled deeply, a wet, choked breath, and said, "Here comes the kid."

There followed a moment of silence as he passed the phone over. Perhaps because it was so quiet, Harper caught a noise in the street, the gravelly rumble and crash of a big truck moving along the road. She was unused to hearing traffic after dark, these days. There was a curfew.

Connor Jr. said, "Hi, Harper," bringing her thoughts back to the world on the other end of the line.

"Hi, Connor Jr."

"Daddy is crying. He says he hit his head on sumpin'."

"You have to give him a kiss and make it better."

"Okay. Are you crying? Why are you crying, too? Did you hit *your* head?"

"Yes."

"Everyone is hitting their head!"

"It's that kind of night."

Something thumped. Connor Jr. cried, "I just hit *my* head!"

"Don't do that," Harper said.

Harper noticed, in a distracted, half-conscious way, that the big truck she had heard earlier was still out in the street, still rumbling.

The thump thumped again.

"I hit my head again!" Connor Jr. said happily. "We all hit our heads!"

"No more," Harper said. "You'll give yourself a headache."

"I did give myself a headache," he announced with great cheer.

She kissed the phone with a loud wet smack. "I kissed the phone. Did you feel it?"

"Uh-huh! I did. Thank you. I feel better already."

"Good," she said.

The knocker slammed on the front door. Harper came up off the couch, as startled as if she had heard a shot in the street.

"Did you just thump your head again?" Connor Jr. asked. "I heard you thump it real hard!"

Harper took a step toward the front hall. The thought was in her that she was walking in the wrong direction—she ought to be headed for the bedroom to get her carpetbag. She couldn't think of a single person who might be at the door this time of the evening that she would want to see.

"Do *you* want a kiss to make it better?" Connor Jr. said.

"Sure. A kiss to make it better and a kiss good night," she said.

She heard a damp smooch, and then, in a soft, almost shy tone, Connor Jr. said, "There. That should do it."

"It did."

"I have to go now. I got to brush my teeth. Then I get my story."

"Go have your story, Connor Jr.," she said. "Good night."

Out in the hall she heard a sound she didn't recognize: a rattling-rasping click-and-clack. A muted bang. She waited for Connor Jr. to say good night back to her, but he never did, and at last it came to her that there was something different about the silence on the other end of the line. When she lowered her phone she discovered it was dead, had lost the last of its charge. It was just a paperweight now.

The raspy *click-clack-bang* came once more.

Harper stepped into the front hall but held up, two yards from the door, listening to the stillness.

"Hello?" she asked.

The door opened four inches before the chain caught it with another loud rattly bang. Jakob peered through the open space into the hallway.

"Harper," he said. "Hey, wanna let me in? I want to talk."

# 13

She stood just beyond the entrance to the den, looking down the hall at the piece of Jakob she could see through the gap between door and frame. He had a four-day growth on his long, hollow-eyed face. They had talked, the way people do, about who would play them in the movie version of their lives (why anyone would want to make a movie about an elementary school nurse and a man who answered phones for the Public Works Department was another question). She had thought Jason Patric, or maybe young Johnny Depp for him, someone dark and wiry who looked like he could do a handstand and who might occasionally write poetry. Right now he looked like Jason Patric or Johnny Depp in a movie about heroin addiction. His face was damp with sweat, and his eyes glittered with a fever brightness. (Casting Harper had been easier—Julie Andrews, obviously, Julie Andrews at twenty-eight, not because they looked anything alike, but because Harper wouldn't consider anyone else for the part. If they couldn't get Julie Andrews at twenty-eight, then they'd just have to call the movie off.)

He had not come home on his bike. Beyond him, idling alongside the curb, was one of the town trucks, a pumpkin-colored 2.5-ton Freightliner with a big snow-wing plow on the front, battered and blackened from hard use. They had kept the plows running day and night, clearing wreckage out of the roads. There was always a car burning somewhere that had to be moved.

She started down the hallway, hugging herself. The air coming through the open slot of the door was cool and smelled of fall, that spicy-sweet odor of apples and crushed autumn leaves and distant smoke. Always smoke.

"You should've called," she said. "I didn't know you were coming over. I was going to sleep soon. I probably wouldn't have heard you."

"I would've got in somehow. Kicked a window in."

"I'm glad you didn't. There's no oil in the boiler. It's hard enough keeping this house warm without windows bashed in. It's getting cold out there."

"You aren't kidding. Want to let me in?"

She didn't much care to answer that question, not even to herself.

Harper wished he had come during the day. She could readily imagine unthreading the chain for him on a bright, sunny afternoon. But with the October darkness behind him, and the October chill coming through the gap between door and frame, it was impossible not to think about the last time they'd talked, and how he had made coming home sound like a threat.

She pushed out a deep breath and said, "How are you?"

"Better. A lot better, Harp. I'm sorry I freaked you out." He gave her a hangdog look from beneath his long, almost girlish eyelashes.

"What about the spore? You were worried you were infected. Have you seen any other marks on you?"

"No. Nope. I panicked. I lost it. No excuses. I'm all right—except for an incurable case of shame. You've got the Dragonscale, but I'm the one who has been acting like—like—" He looked away, back toward his Freightliner, then said, "*Shit*. Should I go? Come back tomorrow? I just—wanted to talk about stuff. I was overcome with a sudden late-night desire to convince my wife I'm not a hysterical piece of shit."

"I want to talk, too. I think we need to."

"Right?" he said. "About the baby? If we're going to do this thing—if we're going to have this kid—we're going to need a plan. Next March is a long way off. You want to unlock this gun, though? I'm cold."

"Hang on," she said. She pushed the door shut and put her hand on the chain. She slid it down the slot, to the open hole, then caught herself, playing back what he had just said. She had misheard him, she thought. Her ears had played a trick on her.

"Jakob," she said, holding the chain in place. "Did you say something about a gun?"

"What? No. *No*. I don't—would you let me in? I'm freezing my narrow little ass off out here."

She looked through the peephole. He stood very close to it, so she could only see his right ear, part of his face.

"Jakob," she said. "You're scaring me a little. Will you show me your hands?"

"Okay. I think you're the one being paranoid now, but okay. Now watch. Here are my hands." He took a step back from the door and held out his hands to either side of his body.

His left foot shot up and into the door. The chain flew loose. The door smashed her in the face and drove her stumbling back and down onto her ass.

His right hand came up with the gun, a small revolver, pulling it from one deep pocket of his track pants. He did not point it at her. He stepped in through the door and elbowed it shut behind him.

"I want things to be nice," he said. He held his free hand up, palm out, in a placating gesture.

She got up on all fours and started to scramble away, trying to stand.

"Stop," he said.

She didn't stop. She thought she could get around the corner and into the kitchen, make it down the stairs to the basement and out the back door. When she stood, though, he kicked the back of her left leg, behind the knee, and she went down again.

"Babygirl, stop," he said. "Don't."

She rolled onto her side. He stood over her with the gun, giving her a perplexed look.

*"Stop,"* he repeated. "I don't want it to be like this. I want things to be like we talked about. I want things to be nice."

She began to crawl again. When he took a step toward her, she grabbed at the side table, the one with the driftwood lamp on it, and twisted it, trying to throw it at him. He batted it aside, hardly glanced at it, his gaze fixed on her.

*"Please,"* he said. "I don't want to hurt you. The thought makes me sick."

He reached out with his left hand, offering to help her up. When she didn't take it, he bent forward and grabbed her upper arm and dragged her to her feet. She struggled to pull loose but he yanked her off balance so she fell against him, into his chest. Then he wrapped her in an embrace, holding her against him.

"Please," he said, rocking back and forth with her. "Please. I know you're scared. I'm scared, too. We have a right to be scared. We've both got this thing and we're dying." The gun was there, against the small of her back. Her shirt was hiked up and she could feel cold metal against her spine. "I want it to be like we talked about. I want it to be nice. I want it to be good and easy. I don't want to go out desperate and scared and crying, and I don't want you to die that way, either. I adore you too much for that."

"Don't touch me," she said. "We don't know if you're sick. I don't want to pass it to you."

"*I* know it. I *know* I have it. I know I'm going to die. We both are. It's just a matter of how."

He loosened his grip on her. He was kissing her—sweetly, devoutly. He kissed her hair. He kissed her forehead. When she shut her eyes, he kissed her eyelids, each one, and she shivered.

"You shouldn't kiss me," she whispered.

"How am I supposed to keep from kissing you? It was the sweetest thing I ever had."

She opened her eyes and looked into his face. "Jakob. I can feel you're hot, but I don't see any marks on you. How can you be sure you're infected?"

He shook his head. "My hip. It started yesterday and it's got worse and worse. My whole hip is on fire."

Jakob had his right arm loosely around her waist, the gun grazing her spine. He reached up with his other hand and drew his knuckles along her cheek in a gentle, smoothing gesture. She shivered helplessly.

"Let's go sit down. Let's have it like we talked about. Let's have it nice, just like we both wanted."

# 14

He steered her into the den, where, half a year before, they had sat together drinking white wine and watching people jump from the top of the Space Needle. He gripped her upper arm like he was preparing to disjoint it, twist it loose from her body the way a person might wrench a drumstick off a roast chicken. Then he seemed to realize he was hurting her and he let go and slipped his palm—gently, almost tenderly—along her biceps.

The shadows in the room shifted this way and that in the red candlelight.

"Let's sit," said the shadow beside her, one among the many. "Let's talk."

Jakob sank into his favorite chair, the Great Egg of Jakob . . . a chair made of wicker with an egg-shaped frame and a hole in the side, a cushion nestled within. He was a small man and he could cross his legs Buddha-style and still fit himself entirely within the wicker teardrop. He put the gun in his lap.

She perched on the edge of the coffee table to face him. "I want to look at your hip. I want to see the 'scale."

"You want to tell me I don't have it, but I know I have it."

"Will you show me your hip?"

He paused, then stretched one leg out through the egg, and rolled a little onto his side. Jakob pushed down the elastic waistband of his track pants, to show her the hollow of his right hip, which was a bloody, abraded mess. The flesh was yellowish-black beneath a cross-hatching of deep scratches. It appalled her to look at it.

"Oh, Jakob. What did you do? I told you, if you find a mark on you, leave it alone."

"I can't stand to look at it. I can't stand to have it on me. I don't know how you can bear it. I get a little nuts. I tried scraping it off with a razor." He made a choked, ragged noise that could not quite pass for laughter.

Harper narrowed her eyes, looking it over, "The 'scale calcifies into bright flecks. I don't see any flecks."

"It's yellow. All around the edges."

"That's bruise. That's just bruise. Jakob . . . is this the only mark on you?"

"On the inside of my knee. And an elbow. Don't ask to see them. I'm not here for a medical exam." He turned to sit properly and allowed the waistband of his track pants to snap back into place.

"Are they all like that?"

"I scratched them up the same. I got hysterical. I'm ashamed of that now, but it's true."

"I don't think that's Dragonscale. I've seen a lot of it, I should know. And Jakob: you've been out of this house six weeks. Almost seven. If you don't have it yet, that probably means—"

"It means you'll say anything to stop what happens next. I knew you'd try and tell me I wasn't sick. I could've scripted this entire conversation. You think I don't know what a burn feels like? It hurts all the time."

"It's infected, Jakob, but not with the *trychophyton*. It's infected because you clawed yourself up and it hasn't been treated or dressed. Jakob. Please. You're healthy. You should leave. You should go right now."

"Stop it. Stop bargaining and stop lying. I don't want to hate you right now, but every time you tell me another lie, to try and save yourself, I just want to shut you up."

"When was the last time you ate?"

"I don't know how you can even talk about food. Maybe I should just do it right now. This is awful. This isn't like we talked about. We talked about making love and having music and reading our favorite poems to each other. We talked about making it nice, a little party for two. But you're just scared, and if I didn't have this gun you'd run away. You'd run and let me die by myself. Without a shred of guilt about what you did to me. About passing it to me. That's the real reason you keep telling me I'm okay, I think. You're not just lying to me. You're lying to yourself. You can't face it. What you did."

His voice was serene, without the slightest trace of the hysteria she had heard when they talked on the phone. His gaze was serene, too. He watched her with the sort of glassy calm Harper associated with the mentally ill, people who sat on park benches chatting gaily with invisible friends.

His newfound calm did not entirely surprise her. Terror was a fire that held you trapped in the top floor of a burning building; the only way to escape it was to jump. He had been stoking himself up to this last leap for weeks. She had heard it in his voice, every time they talked on the phone, even if she didn't recognize it at the time. He had made his choice at last and it had brought him the peace he was looking for. He was ready to go out the window; he wanted only to be holding her hand on the way down.

What did surprise her was her *own* calm. She wondered at it. In the days before the Earth began to burn, she had carried anxiety with her to work every morning and brought it home with her every night; a nameless, inconsiderate companion that had a habit of poking her in the ribs whenever she was trying to relax. And yet in those days there was nothing really to be anxious about. Her head would spin at the thought of defaulting on her student loans, of getting into another yelling match with her neighbor about his dog's habit of tearing open garbage and spreading it all over her lawn. And now she had a baby in her, and sickness crawling on her skin, and Jakob was crazy, sitting there watching her with his gun, and there was only this quiet readiness, which she irrationally believed had been waiting for her all her life.

*At the end, I get to be the person I always wanted to be,* she thought.

"Is that really so terrible?" she asked. "Is it really so awful that I wanted to believe you didn't have it? I wanted you and the baby to make it. I wanted that more than I ever wanted anything, Jake."

Something seemed to dim in his eyes. His shoulders drooped.

"Well, that was stupid. No one is going to make it. The whole world is toast. Literally. The planet is going to be a cinder by the time we're done with it. Everyone is going to die. This is the last generation. I think we always knew that. Even before Dragonscale. We knew we were going to choke on our pollution and run out of food and air and all the rest of it."

He could not resist lecturing her, even in the last minutes of her life, and it came to her then that she hadn't been in love with him for years. He was a tiresome know-it-all. This was followed by a second, startling notion that she wasn't quite ready to process, which was that she hadn't gone to work in the hospital hoping to be Florence Nightingale, no matter what he said. She had gone to work there because she wasn't interested in her own life anymore. She had never felt she was putting anything of great value at risk.

This was followed by a slow throb of anger, which she felt as a hot prickle in her Dragonscale. *Jakob* had done that to her—plunged his philosophical syringe into her life and tried to suck all the simple happiness out of it. In a sense, he had been trying to kill her for years.

She felt herself getting ready. She didn't even know for what. She was gathering her courage for some act that was as yet unclear to her, but which she felt was coming, rushing toward her.

"I read your book," she said.

And there, she saw a flicker of something human, something besides his patient, beatific, dangerous calm. Behaviorists talked about micro-expressions, emotions that jumped to the surface, revealing all, in a flicker almost too fast to catch. For the briefest instant he regarded her with uncertainty and a blanch of discomfort. It was a wonder, how much information could pass between two people in a single glance, without a word being said. He had, after all, really cheated on her with any number of their friends. That momentary look of shame was as good as a confession.

"Pretty dirty, dude," she said. "I was getting hot flashes that don't have anything to do with Dragonscale."

"I asked you not to read it," he said.

"So shoot me."

He made a harsh barking sound. It took her a moment to identify this noise as laughter.

She exhaled again and threw her hands down and shook them, as if they were wet and she were air-drying them. "*Whoo.* All right. The world is going to have to burn out without us. I want something good before I go."

He gave her a dull, hopeless look.

"Please. I'll try," she said. "I'll try to make it nice."

"I don't know if it'll do any good. I'm not in the mood anymore. I think maybe I just want to get it over with."

"But *I'm* not ready. And you want it to feel right for *me*, don't you? Besides. I'm not going without getting laid once more." And she laughed and tried to smile. "You've got no one to blame but yourself, Jakob Grayson. Leaving a bored and lonely woman all alone with that pile of shameless filth." Gesturing with her head at the manuscript on the desk.

He smiled himself, although it looked forced. "Sex means more to you than it does to me. I know that turns the stereotype on its head. You really live in your body more than I do. It's one of the things I always found exciting about you. But now—at the moment, I suppose I regard the sexual act with a certain amount of disgust."

She turned and crossed to the Hello Kitty boom box on the shelf. She had brought it in here the other day after discovering fresh batteries in the basement.

"What are you doing?" Jakob asked.

"Music."

"I don't need music. I'd rather just talk."

"*I* need music. And a drink. You need a drink, too."

Finally, something got through to him. He said, "I'd *kill* for a drink." He made the harsh barking sound again, the one that seemed to stand for laughter.

He could've shot her already, if her death was all he wanted, but it wasn't. Part of him wanted more: a last kiss, a last fuck, a last drink, or maybe something deeper, forgiveness, absolution. Harper wasn't inclined to let him have any of it, but was happy to let him hope. It was keeping her alive. She turned on the FM. The classic-rock station was playing an oldie but a goodie. A lovestruck Romeo was getting ready to start the serenade, you and me, babe, how 'bout it, and for no reason at all, Harper thought of Hillary Clinton.

She stood in front of the sound box, moving her hips from side to side. She didn't doubt that Jakob currently regarded sex with disgust, but he wasn't the only one who had taken some psychology courses in college. She hadn't forgotten what lay just across the border from disgust.

She kept her back to him for maybe ten seconds, pretending to be lost in the music, then cast a slow look over her shoulder. His gaze was fixed raptly upon her.

"You hurt me," she said. "You threw me down."

"I'm sorry. That was across the line."

"Except in the bedroom," she said.

He narrowed his eyes, and she knew she had pushed it too far, had strained his credulity—she *never* talked that way about sex—but before he could speak, she said, "Our bottle!" As if she were just remembering. "I want to have that bottle of wine we brought back from France. Remember? You said it was the best you ever had and we should save it for something important." She gave him what she hoped was a wry look and said, "Is this important enough?"

The wines were all there in the study with them, the whites in the cooler that wasn't keeping them cool anymore, the reds in the cupboard. Whenever they went somewhere, they bought a bottle of wine, the way other people bought fridge magnets. They hadn't gone so many places, though, in the last few years. She grabbed for the honeymoon French Bordeaux, and her palm was so damp with sweat it almost slipped out of her grasp and flew across the room at him. She imagined him jumping in surprise and shooting her in the stomach, just out of reflex. Killing her *and* the baby in one shot, which, when she thought about it, would be perfectly in keeping with Jakob's character. He was parsimonious by nature, hated waste; he had often scolded her for using too much milk in her cereal.

She pinned the bottle between her body and her right arm, and took two wine goblets from where they hung under one of the bookshelves. The deep crystal glasses clinked musically together, while her hands trembled. She got the corkscrew.

Her plan was to use it to pull the cork, then ask him to pour the wine. And while he was pouring it, she would wiggle the cork off the screw and stab him in the face. Or, if she didn't have the stomach for that, she would at least try to impale him in the back of the hand that held the gun.

She sat down on the edge of the coffee table, facing him and the Great Egg. The gun rested on his knee, the barrel pointing at her, but without any particular intention. She had the corkscrew in her right hand, the twisted point sticking between her middle and ring fingers. He was a long way off—she would have to throw herself at him to get the corkscrew into his face. But maybe he would be closer when he poured the wine. Maybe.

Then she shifted her gaze to his eyes and saw him staring at her with icy speculation. His face was pale and still and nearly expressionless.

"Do you think if you get me drunk and fuck me, it'll change my mind about what has to happen?" he asked her.

She said, "I thought getting drunk and making love and having a good time was the whole idea. Doing it on our terms. Isn't that what you wanted?"

"It is. But I'm still not clear that's what *you* want. I don't know if that's what you *ever* wanted. Maybe in some vapid, Lifetime movie sense, you liked the idea of pulling a Romeo and Juliet, and dying side by side, but you were never really committed. You never thought it would happen. Now it's time, and you'll do anything to get out of it. Including whore yourself." He rocked back and forth and then said, "I know it's politically incorrect to say, but what the hell, we're both about to die: I've never thought much of the intelligence of women. I've never once met a woman who had any true intellectual rigor. There's a reason things like Facebook and airplanes and all the other great inventions of our time were made by men."

"Yeah," she said. "So they could get laid. Are we going to drink this wine or what?"

He made the barking sound again. "You're not even going to deny it?"

"Which part? The part about how women are stupid, or the part about how I don't really want to kill myself with you?"

"The part where you think you can shake your ass and make me forget what I came here to do. Because it's getting done. If nothing else, I have a moral obligation to stop you from going out in the world and infecting someone else like you infected me."

"Thought you said the world was going to end, so what would it matter? What would it—" But she couldn't talk anymore. Something awful was happening.

The cork wouldn't come out of the bottle.

It was a fat cork, sealed with dribbles of wax, and she had the bottle under her arm and was pulling at the corkscrew with the other hand, but the cork wouldn't give in the slightest, felt fixed in place.

He reached across the table with his left hand and caught the neck of the bottle and tugged it out from under her arm. His right hand continued to grip the gun.

"I told you these needed to be kept someplace dry," he said. "The cork swells. I told you it was a mistake to just stick the reds in the cabinet."

*I told you* had to be some kind of karmic opposite to the words *I love you.* He had always found it much easier to say "I told you." It would've been something to resent, if she didn't feel all the breath go out of her. Because now Jakob had the corkscrew. She had let him take it without a struggle, without an objection, the only weapon she had.

He squeezed the bottle between his thighs, hunched and pulled. His neck reddened and cords stood out in it. Those fat blobs of wax split and the cork began to move. She looked at the gun. He still held it with his free hand—but it shifted a titch, to point more toward the bookshelf behind her.

"Get your glass," he said. "It's coming."

She picked up her goblet and scootched forward, so her knees bumped his. Time began to move in small, careful increments. The cork moved another centimeter. And another. And came out with a perfect little pop. He exhaled and set the corkscrew down by his knee, where she couldn't reach it.

"Have a taste," he said, and spilled a trickle into her outstretched glass.

Jakob had taught her how to drink wine when they were in France, had instructed her in the subject with great enthusiasm. She stuck her nose into the cavern of the glass and inhaled, filled her nostrils with peppery fumes so strong it was possible to imagine getting drunk off them alone. It smelled good, but instead she flinched and frowned.

"Oh, damn it, does *everything* have to be wrong?" She lifted her gaze. "It went over. It's complete vinegar. Do we get another one? We've got that one from Napa. The one you said all the collectors want."

"What? It's not even ten years old. That doesn't seem right. Let me see." He bent toward her, coming halfway out of the Egg.

His eyes widened the instant before she moved. He was quick, almost quick enough to duck out of the way, but that little lean was all she needed.

She smashed the glass into his face. The goblet shattered with a pretty, tuneful sound, and glass fangs tore open the skin in bright red lines, carving across his cheekbone, the bridge of his nose, and his eyebrow. It looked like a tiger cub had swiped at his face.

He screamed and lifted the gun and it went off. The sound of it was a shattering slam, right next to her head.

A shelf of books behind her exploded and the air filled with a snowstorm of flying pages. Harper came to her feet, pitching herself to her left, toward the door to the bedroom. She smashed a knee against the edge of the coffee table, coming around it, registered the impact but felt no pain.

An awesome silence gathered around her, the only noise in it a high-pitched whining, the sound of a struck tuning fork. A torn sheet of paper, part of some book, floated down and caught against her chest, stuck there.

The recoil flipped the Great Egg straight back, with Jakob still in it. The bottle flew as he fell backward, sailed across the room, and clubbed her in the shoulder. She kept going, crossed the den in three steps, and reached the door to the bedroom. The doorframe exploded to the left of her ear, throwing white chunks of wood into her hair, into her face. The sound of the gun going off was so muffled, it was like hearing a car door slam in the street. Then she was through, into the bedroom.

She snatched thoughtlessly at the sheet of paper stuck to her chest, pulled it back, stared down at it, saw a handful of words:

> *his hands were the hands of some amazing conductor playing all the symphonies of blazing and burning to bring down the tatters and charcoal ruins of history.*

She flung it aside, behind her, back into the den, and slammed the door after it.

# 15

There was a lock on the door that she didn't bother with. No point. It was a button lock and he'd kick right through it. She wasn't even sure the door would stay shut, half the doorframe missing where a bullet had smashed into it.

She grabbed the wooden chair to the left of the door and flung it down, something to put in the way. Her carpetbag was at the foot of the bed, clothes stacked inside under *The Portable Mother.* She caught it by the leather handles and kept going, on to the window that looked over the backyard. She flicked the lock and shoved it up. Behind her, the chair shattered with a muffled crunch.

The hill behind the house dropped steeply, a long grade that led down to the trees. The bedroom appeared to be on the first floor, if you were looking at the house from the front. But when you came around back, it was possible to see the bedroom was really on the *second* floor: a finished, walk-in basement was beneath it. From the bedroom window, it was a fifteen-foot drop into darkness.

As she threw her legs over the sill, she looked down and saw she was pouring blood, the whole front of her white halter soaked with it. She couldn't feel where she had been hit. She couldn't take time to think about it. She jumped, dragging her bag. The window exploded outward behind her as Jakob put a bullet in it.

She fell and expected to hit the ground and didn't and fell some more. Her stomach flipped inside her. Then she hit, her right foot folding under her with a breathtaking flash of pain. She thought of pianos falling in silent movies, shattering on impact, ivory keys spilling over the sidewalk like so many scattered teeth.

Harper lunged off balance, fell forward, hit the dirt, rolled, and rolled, and rolled. She lost her grip on the carpetbag. It tumbled along with her, flinging its contents into the darkness. Her right ankle felt as if it had been shattered, but it couldn't be shattered, because if it were, Jakob would catch her and he would kill her.

She flopped to a halt two-thirds of the way down the steep slope, the smoke-filled night sky whirling overhead. At one edge of her vision, she could see her tall, narrow house looming over her. At the other, she could see the edge of the woods, the trees half shed of their leaves, skeletons in rags. All she wanted to do was lie there and wait for the world to stop moving.

But there wasn't time for that. It would take him all of twenty seconds to get down the stairs into the basement and out the back door.

She pushed herself up. The ground tilted precariously beneath her, felt as unsteady as a dock floating on a turbulent lake. She wondered if some of the dizziness was blood loss, looked at her soaked blouse, at the deep red stain down the front of it, and smelled wine. He had not put a bullet in her after all. It was the honeymoon Bordeaux; she was wearing it. All of France's wine country was nothing but ash now, which meant the stain on her blouse was probably worth a few thousand dollars on the black market. She had never worn anything so expensive.

Harper put her left hand on the ground to steady herself and planted it on some shirts and something wrapped in crinkly plastic. The slide whistle. God knew why she had packed it.

She shoved herself up and off the ground. Harper left her carpetbag and her scattered clothes and *The Portable Mother,* but she held on to the slide whistle. She took her first step toward the woods, and her right leg nearly folded underneath her. Something *grated,* and there was a flash of pain so intense her knees buckled. She might not be shot, but she had fractured something in her ankle, there was no doubt about it.

"Harper!" Jakob screamed from up the hill behind her. "Stop running, Harper, *you bitch*!"

The fractured bone in her ankle grated again, and a flash of pain, brilliant and white, went off behind her eyes. For a moment she was running blind and close to crumpling, passing out. In action movies, people dropped out of windows all the time and it was no big deal.

As she ran, she found herself pulling at the cellophane wrap on the slide whistle. It was thoughtless, automatic action, her hands operating of their own accord.

On her next step, she put too much weight on the right foot, and the ankle folded, and she screamed weakly, couldn't help it. A spoke of withering pain lanced straight from her ankle into her pelvis. She went down on one knee, behind some scrubby hemlocks.

She lifted the whistle and blew, pulling out the slide, so it made a shrill, out-of-place *carnival* sound in the forest. It was *loud*. That first gunshot had done something to her ears, bruised her eardrums and muffled her hearing, but the slide whistle cut right through it, loud as a bottle rocket whining away into the night.

"Harper, you bitch! My *face*! Look what you did to my face!" Jakob roared. He was closer now, almost to the woods.

Harper pushed herself up again. She staggered deeper in among the trees, holding a hand up in front of her to protect her face from branches. Every time she put weight on her right foot, it was like her ankle breaking all over again. Sweet crisp leaves crunched beneath her heels.

She was scared now, as scared as she could ever remember being in her life, and the sound of her fear was the *wheeeeeee-oooooop* of a pennywhistle, slicing through the night. She didn't know why she was blowing it again. It would lead Jakob right to her.

She loped jaggedly off course. No, that wasn't right; for her to wander off course, she needed to *have* a course, and she had no idea where she was going. The pennywhistle fell from her hand and she went on without looking back. She put her right foot in a soft depression, and wrenched her ankle again, and cried out softly, and fell to one knee.

"I'm coming, Harper!" Jakob yelled, and he made the barking sound of laughter. "Wait till you see what I'm going to do to *your* face!"

Harper reached out, blindly, to the right, for a tree trunk that remained stubbornly out of reach. She was in danger of falling onto her side. If that happened, she wouldn't be able to get up. She would be lying there, curled in the fetal position, gasping for breath, when Jakob found her and began pumping bullets into her.

Leaves crackled and someone took her hand. She opened her mouth to cry out and the sound caught in her throat. She stared up into Captain America's stoic, blank face.

"Come on," said Cap in a girl's voice, and she hauled Harper to her feet.

They hurried along the edge of the forest, holding hands, the bald girl showing Harper the way. Her feet hardly seemed to touch the ground, and Harper felt again what she had felt when they first met, that this wasn't happening, this was being dreamt.

The girl led Harper to an oak that had probably been old when Kennedy was shot. There were boards nailed into the trunk, leading up into the branches, remnant of some long-forgotten tree house. Harper thought of the Lost Boys, thought of Peter Pan.

"Up," the girl whispered. "Quick."

"Quick-*ly*," said the Fireman, as he came out of the bushes from Harper's right. His face was so filthy it was nearly black, and he was wearing his big fireman's helmet and sooty yellow coat, and the halligan swung from one hand. "Proper usage, Allie. Try not to distort my language with your horrible Americanisms." And he grinned.

"He's coming," Allie said.

"I'll send him on his way," said the Fireman.

Jakob cursed, from somewhere close by. Harper could hear him crashing through the brush.

She climbed into the tree, using her right knee instead of her foot. It wasn't easy, and the girl was close behind her, shoving at her ass with both hands.

"Will you *hurry up,*" Allie hissed.

"I busted my ankle," Harper said, reaching for a wide branch above her and pulling herself onto it.

She hitched her rear to one side, sliding out across the branch to make room for the girl. They were about twelve feet off the ground and Harper could see through the leaves of the oak to the small open area below. The Fireman did not go far—just a few steps in the direction of Jakob's crashing noises. Then he positioned himself behind a sumac and waited.

A breeze, smelling faintly of bonfires, lifted and tossed Harper's hair. She turned her face into it—and realized she could see her house through the trees. By daylight, she would have a good view of her own back deck and the windows into the kitchen from here.

Jakob spilled from the bushes, going past the Fireman without seeing him. Jakob's face was bleeding; the laceration below his left eye was particularly bad, a flap of skin wobbling and hanging down over his cheekbone. He had leaves in his hair and a fresh scrape on his chin. He carried the gun low, at his side, barrel pointed toward the forest floor.

"Oi!" said the Fireman. "Why are you running about with a gun? Someone could get hurt. I hope you have the safety on."

Jakob made a sound, a little cry of surprise that was also like a sharp, indrawn breath, and turned, lifting the revolver. The Fireman brought the halligan down, that long rusty bar, with tools bristling from either end. It whistled in the air and struck the barrel of the gun with a clang. The pistol dropped and thudded to the ground and went off and the flash lit the forest.

"No, I guess not," said the Fireman.

"Who the fuck are you?" Jakob asked. "You with Harper?"

The Fireman cocked his head to one side and seemed to consider this for a moment, his eyes puzzled. Then his face brightened, and he opened his mouth in a generous, toothy grin.

"Yes, I suppose I am," he said, and rocked back on his heels, as if this were something he had only just realized and found delightful. It came to Harper, then, that he was crazy—as crazy as Jakob. "Harper. Like Harper Lee, I imagine. I only knew her as Nurse Grayson. Harper. Wonderful name." He cleared his throat and added, "I suppose I'm also the man telling you to sod off. These woods don't belong to you."

"Who the fuck do you think they belong to?" Jakob asked.

"Me," said the Fireman. "I fucking think they fucking belong the fuck to me. I can swear, too, mate. I'm English. We swear without fear. The C-word? We say that too: cunt cunt cunty cunt cuntcunt." Without dropping the grin he said, "Go on, now. Get lost, you loudmouthed cunt."

Jakob stared at the Fireman warily, seemed genuinely not to know what to say or what to do. Then he turned and bent over, reaching for his gun.

The Fireman lashed out with the halligan, using it like a polo stick, striking the pistol and knocking it away into the ferns. Jakob did not hesitate, but pivoted and threw himself at the thin, wiry Englishman. The Fireman lifted the halligan, bringing it up between them, but then Jakob had his hands on it, and they were wrestling over it, and Jakob was the stronger man.

Stronger, and he had better balance . . . that sense of balance that carried him across tightropes and allowed him to perch comfortably on a unicycle. He set his feet and twisted at the waist, lifting the Fireman right off the ground, swinging him half a foot through the air and slamming him into the trunk of the very oak Harper sat in.

Harper felt the force of the impact shake the tree branch beneath her, felt the whole tree shudder.

Jakob pulled the bar back a few inches and slammed the

Fireman into the tree again. The Fireman grunted, and all the air shot out of him, a whistling exhalation through his nostrils.

"You motherfucker," Jakob was saying, almost chanting. "I'll kill you, motherfucker, I'll kill you, and I'll kill her, and I'll—" His voice trailed off; he had run out of people to kill.

He slammed the Fireman into the tree again, and the Fireman's helmet cracked loudly against the trunk. Harper flinched and caught a shout in her throat. Allie, though, had her hand on her knee, and she squeezed it.

"Watch," she whispered. She had pulled the mask down around her neck, and Harper saw a beauty: chocolate eyes that glittered with hilarity, tomboy freckles, and delicate features that seemed even sharper and clearer because her head was shaved smooth, to better show the hollows of her temples and her fine bones. "Look at his *hand*."

And Harper saw that the Fireman's bare left hand was boiling with gray smoke. The left hand had let go of the halligan bar and dropped to the Fireman's side. Harper flashed to a memory—the Fireman wrestling with Albert in the hallway off the emergency room, and trying to yank his glove off with his teeth.

Jakob pulled back on the halligan bar, meaning to drive the Fireman into the tree trunk again. But at that moment the Fireman reached over the bar and put his hand on Jakob's throat, and fire belched from his palm.

That flame was as blue as a blowtorch. The Fireman's hand wore a glove of radiant fire. The blaze roared like a rising wind and Jakob screamed and let go of the halligan and fell away. He screamed again, grabbing at his blackened throat. His feet got tangled and he went straight down on his ass and then he sprang up once more and ran, heaving himself blindly through the branches and brush.

The Fireman watched him go, his left hand a torch. Then he opened his filthy yellow turnout jacket, put his burning hand under it, and clapped the jacket shut, trapping his hand between the coat and his shirt.

He opened the jacket and shut it and opened it again, beating at his hand calmly—he looked rather like a child trying to use his armpit to make farts—and the third time he opened the jacket, the flame had gone out and the hand was spewing filthy black smoke. He waved the hand in the air, letting the smoke boil off it. In the distance, Harper could hear branches snapping and brush crackling, the sound of Jakob running away. In another moment the woods were quiet except for the alien chirp of night insects.

The Fireman held up his left hand, drew a deep breath, and blew away the last of the smoke. His palm was sketched with Dragonscale. Those fine, delicate black lines were ashed over now, the surface snow white, with a few sparks nested here and there, glowing faintly. The rest of the skin covering his hand was—fine. Clean and healthy and pink and impossibly unburnt.

Allie said, "I love it when he does that, but his best trick is when he makes a phoenix. It's better than fireworks."

"True enough!" said the Fireman, turning his head and grinning cheekily up at them. "I put the Fifth of November and the Fourth of July to shame. Who needs Roman candles when you've got me?"

# BOOK TWO

# LET YOUR DIM LIGHT SHINE

# 1

Allie was first out of the tree, grabbing the branch and swinging to the ground. Harper meant to go down by way of the rudimentary ladder nailed into the trunk, but as soon as she slid off the branch she had been sitting on, she dropped.

The Fireman was there to break her fall. He didn't exactly catch her. He just happened to be below her when she went down. She flattened him under her and they hit the dirt together. The back of her head smashed him in the nose. Her right heel bounced off the ground. The pain that shot through her ankle was exquisite.

They groaned in each other's arms, like lovers.

"Fuck," she said. "Fuck fuck *fuck*."

"Is that the best you can do?" the Fireman asked. He was holding his nose and blinking back tears. "Just a lot of 'fuck fuck fuck' over and over again? Can't you expand your range a little? Goddamn bloody arsefoam. Daddy drilling Mommy on the kitchen table. That sort of thing. Americans curse without any imagination at all."

Harper sat up, her shoulders hitching with her first sobs. Her legs were trembling and her ankle was broken and Jakob had nearly killed her, had wanted to kill her, and people were shooting guns and bursting into flame and she had fallen out of a tree, and the baby, the baby, and she couldn't help herself. The Fireman sat up next to her and put an arm around her and she rested her head on the slippery shoulder of his jacket.

"There, there," he said.

And he held her for a bit, while she had a good, unglamorous cry.

When her sobs had subsided to hiccups he said, "Let's get

you up. We should be going. We don't know what your deranged ex-husband might be up to. I wouldn't put it past him to call a Quarantine Patrol."

"He's not my ex. We're not divorced."

"You are now. By the power vested in me."

"What power vested in you?"

"You know how captains of ships can marry people? Little-known fact, firemen can divorce people as well. Come on, up with you."

The Fireman encircled her waist with his left arm and hoisted her to her feet. The hand on her hip was still warm, like fresh bread from the oven.

"You set your hand on fire," she said. "How did you do that?"

On the face of it, she already knew the answer. He had Dragonscale, same as her. His hand was still uncovered and she could see a black-and-gold scrawl tracing the lines of his palm, running in a coil around and around his wrist. A fine gray smoke trickled from the thicker lines.

She had seen at least a hundred people with Dragonscale ignite—ignite and begin to scream, blue fire racing over them, as if they were painted in kerosene, their hair erupting in a flash. It was not something anyone wanted or could do to themselves, and when it happened it was not controlled and it always ended in death.

But the Fireman had consciously lit himself up. And only part of himself, just his hand. Then he had calmly put himself back out again. And somehow he had not been hurt.

"I thought about offering a class once," the Fireman said. "But I couldn't figure out what I was teaching. Advanced Pyromancy? Spontaneous Combustion for Dummies? Arson 101? Besides, it's hard to get people to sign up for a course when failing a test means burning alive."

"That's a lie," Allie said. "He won't teach you. He won't teach anyone. Liar, liar, pants on fire."

"No, not tonight, Allie. This is my favorite pair of dungarees and I can't afford to burn them up just because you want me to show off."

"You've been spying on me," Harper said.

The Fireman glanced up into the branches of the oak, where she had been perched only a moment before. "There's an excellent view of your bedroom from up there. Isn't it odd, how people with something to hide will pull the curtains at the front of the house, but never think to cover the windows out back."

"You spend a lot of time wandering around in your underwear, reading *What to Expect When You're Expecting,*" Allie said. "Don't worry. He never peeped through your windows at you while you were getting dressed. Maybe I did once or twice, but not him. 'E's a proper English gen'lem'n is wot he is." Allie's faux English accent was at least as good as Dick Van Dyke's in *Mary Poppins*. If Harper had been a sixteen-year-old boy, she would've been mad for her. You could just tell she was the best kind of trouble.

"Why?" Harper asked the Fireman. "Why spy on me?"

"Allie," the Fireman said, as if he had not heard Harper's question. "Run on ahead to camp. Bring your grandfather and Ben Patchett. Oh, and find Renée. Tell Renée we have acquired her favorite nurse. She'll be so pleased."

Then Allie was gone, springing into leaves in a way that made Harper think of Peter Pan's shadow zinging around Wendy's bedroom. Harper had a head crammed full of children's books and could be quite compulsive about assigning people storybook roles.

When the girl was gone, the Fireman said, "Just as well to have you to myself for a moment, Nurse Grayson. I'd trust Allie Storey with my life, but there are some things I'd rather not say in front of her. Do you know the summer camp at the end of Little Harbor Road?"

"Camp Wyndham," Harper said. "Sure."

Dead leaves crunched underfoot and their smell sugared the air with autumn's perfume.

"That's where we're headed. There's a fellow there, Tom Storey, Allie's grandfather. They call him Father Storey. Once upon a time Tom was the program director at the camp. Now he has the place opened up as a shelter for folk with Dragonscale. He's got more than a hundred people hiding there, and they've banged together a decent little society. There's three meals a day—for now, anyway. I don't know how much longer *that* will last. There's no electric power, but they've got working showers if you can stand being pelted by ice water. They've got a school, and a kind of junior police force called the Lookouts, to keep watch for Quarantine Patrols and Cremation Crews. That's mostly teenagers—the Lookouts. Allie and her friends. Gives them something to do. They have all the religion you could possibly want, too. In some ways it isn't like any religion that's ever come before and in other ways, *well*. Fundamentalists are much the same wherever you go. That's one of the things I wanted to forewarn you about, while Allie ran on ahead. She's even more devout than most, and that's saying quite a lot."

There was a rending crack, a sliding, reverberating crash that shook the forest floor and caused Harper's pulse to leap. She stared back through the woods in the direction they had come from. She couldn't imagine what could possibly have made such an enormous, shattering noise.

The Fireman cast a brief, considering glance over his shoulder, then took her arm and began to move her along again, a little more briskly now. He continued as if there had been no interruption at all.

"You have to understand that most of the camp is between your age and Allie's. There are a few oldsters, but a lot more who ought to still be in school. Most of them have lost family, seen the people they love burn to death in front of them. They were in shock when they found their way to camp, refugees, deranged by grief, and just waiting around to burst into flame themselves. Then Father Storey and his daughter Carol—Allie's aunt—taught them they don't have to die. They've offered them hope when they had none and a very concrete form of salvation."

Harper slowed, in part to rest her sore ankle, in part to absorb what he was saying.

"What do you mean, they're teaching people they don't have to die? No one can teach someone with Dragonscale not to die. That's impossible. If there was a treatment, some pill—"

"You aren't required to swallow anything," the Fireman said. "*Not even their faith.* Remember that, Nurse Grayson."

"If there was anything that could prevent the Dragonscale from killing people, the government would know by now. If there was something that worked, *really* worked, something that could extend the lives of millions of sick people—"

"—people with a lethal and contagious spore on their skin? Nurse Grayson, no one wants us *extending* our lives. Nothing could be less desirable. *Shortening* them—that's what would best serve the public good. At least in the minds of the healthy population. One thing we know about people with Dragonscale: they don't burst into flame if you shoot them in the head. You don't have to worry about a corpse infecting you or your children . . . or starting a conflagration that might take out a city block." She opened her mouth to protest and he squeezed her shoulder. "There'll be time to argue this point later. Although I warn you, it's been argued before, most notably by poor Harold Cross. I feel his case largely settles the matter."

"Harold Cross?"

He shook his head. "Leave it for now. I only want you to understand that Tom and Carol have given these people more than food or shelter or even a way to suppress their illness. They've given them *belief* . . . in each other, in the future, and in the power they share as a flock. A flock isn't such a bad thing if you belong, but a few hundred starlings will tear an unlucky martin to feathers if it crosses their path. I think Camp Wyndham could be a very unfriendly place for an apostate. Tom, he's tolerant enough. He's your inclusive, modern, *thoughtful* religious type, an ethics professor by trade. But his daughter, Allie's aunt: she's barely more than a kid herself, and most of the other kids have made a kind of cult around her. She sings the songs, after all. You want to stay on her good side. She's kind enough, Carol is. Means well. But if she doesn't love you, then she's afraid of you, and she's dangerous when she's afraid. I am uneasy in my mind about what might happen if Carol ever felt seriously threatened."

"I'm not going to threaten anyone," Harper said.

He smiled. "No. You don't strike me as the type to make trouble, but to make peace. I still haven't forgotten the first time you crossed my path, Nurse Grayson. You saved his life, you know. Nick. And you saved my skull, while you were at it. I seem to remember it was just about to be kicked in when you intervened. I owe you."

"Not anymore," Harper said.

Ahead of them, in the dark, branches rustled and were pushed aside. A modest assembly emerged, Allie leading the way. The girl was breathing hard and had a pretty flush of color on her delicate features.

"What happened, John?" asked a man standing directly behind her. His voice was low and melodious and even before she saw Tom Storey's face, Harper liked him. At first, she could make out little more than his gold-rimmed spectacles flashing in the darkness. "Who do we have here?"

"Someone useful," the Fireman said, only now she knew his name: John. "A nurse, a Miss Grayson. Can you take her the rest of the way? I'm no doctor, but I think she fractured her ankle. If you'll help her along to the infirmary, I'd like to go back and collect her things while there's still time. My guess is there'll soon be police and a Quarantine Patrol swarming her place."

"Gee, can I help?" said one of the other members of the greeting party. He stepped forward, slipping easily between the Fireman and Harper, and put his arm around her waist.

Harper slung hers over his shoulders. He was a big man, maybe quarter of a century older than Harper, with sloping shoulders and pale silver hair beginning to thin up top. Harper thought of an aged and well-loved Paddington Bear. "Ben Patchett," he said. "Glad to meet you, ma'am."

There was a woman with them, too, short, squashy, her silver hair braided into cornrows. She smiled tentatively, perhaps unsure Harper would remember her. Of course there was no chance at all Harper could've forgotten the woman who fled Portsmouth Hospital, shimmering as brightly as a flare and just as sure to explode.

"Renée Gilmonton," Harper said. "I thought you ran away to die somewhere."

"That's what I thought, too. Father Storey had other ideas." Renée put an arm under Harper's armpits, helping to support her from the other side. "You took such good care of me for so long, Nurse Grayson. What a pleasure to have a chance to tend to you for a bit."

"How'd you bust your ankle?" Father Storey asked, lifting his chin so the dim light flashed on the lenses of his spectacles, and for the first time Harper could see his features, his long, skinny, deeply lined face and silver beard, and she thought: *Dumbledore*. The beard was actually less Dumbledore, more Hemingway, but the eyes behind the lenses of his glasses were a brilliant shade of blue that naturally suggested a man who could cast runes and speak to trees.

Harper found it hard to reply, didn't know yet how to speak of Jakob and what he had tried to do to her.

The Fireman seemed to see in a glance how the question defeated her, and answered himself. "Her husband came for her with a gun. I chased him off. That's all. Time is short, Tom."

"Isn't it always?" Father Storey replied.

The Fireman started to turn away—then pivoted back and pressed something into Harper's hand. "Oh, you dropped this, Nurse. Do keep it on you. If you ever need me again, just blow."

It was her pennywhistle. She had dropped it running from Jakob and forgotten all about it, and was absurdly grateful to have it returned.

"He doesn't slip everyone his slide whistle of love," Allie said. "You're *in*."

"Mind out of the gutter, Allie," the Fireman said. "What would your mother have said?"

"Something dirtier," Allie said. "Come on, let's go get the nurse's gear."

Allie dropped the Captain America mask back over her face and bounded into the trees. The Fireman cursed under his breath and began to hurry after her, using that great iron pole of his to swat aside the underbrush.

"Allie!" Father Storey cried. "Allie, please! Come back!"

But she was already gone.

"That girl has no business mixing herself up in John's work," said Ben Patchett.

"Try and stop her," Renée said.

"The Fireman—John—he lit himself on fire," Harper said. "His whole hand burst into flame. How'd he do that?"

"Fire is the devil's only friend," Ben Patchett said, and laughed. "Isn't that right, Father?"

"I don't know if he's a devil," said Father Storey. "But if he is, he's *our* devil. Still . . . I wish Allie wouldn't go with him. Does she *want* to get herself killed like her mother? Sometimes it almost seems she's daring the world to try."

"Oh, Father," said Renée. "You raised two teenage girls. If anyone understood Allie, I'd think it would be you." She looked off into the woods, in the direction Allie had disappeared in. "Of course she's daring the world to try."

# 2

It was barely a mile to Camp Wyndham, but it seemed to Harper they were tromping after Father Storey, through the weary, stifling darkness, for hours. They wallowed in drifts of leaves, wove in and around pine trees, clambered over a pile of rocks, always moving toward the briny scent of the Atlantic. Her ankle thrummed.

Harper did not ask where they were and Father Storey did not say. Not long after they started moving, he popped something into his mouth—it was the size of a blue jay's egg—and after that made no sound.

They emerged alongside Little Harbor Road, looking across the blacktop at the turnoff into Camp Wyndham: a lane of hard-packed white shell and sandy earth. The entrance was barred by a chain hung between a pair of tall standing boulders that would not have looked out of place at Stonehenge. Beyond, the land mounded up in green hills. Even at night, Harper could see the white steeple of a church, sticking up over the ridge a half mile away.

The burned-out and blackened hull of a bus was parked off the road, just past those totemic blocks of granite. It was up to its iron rims in weeds and had been baked down almost to the frame.

Before they crossed the road, Father Storey clapped twice. The four of them hobbled up out of the brush and crossed the blacktop to the sandy lane. A boy descended the steps of the bus to stand in the open doorway and watch them approach.

Father Storey removed the white egg from his mouth and glanced back at Harper and her human crutches.

"The bus may look like a wreck, but it isn't quite. The headlights work. If someone unknown were to come up our road, a boy in the bus would wait for our visitors to move out of sight, then flash a signal. Another boy, in the steeple of the church, keeps a lookout for it. The eye in the steeple sees all the people." He smiled at this, then added, "If necessary we can get into hiding in two minutes. We drill every day. Credit to Ben Patchett—this inspiration is his. My own ideas involved a fantastical system of bird whistles and the possible use of kites."

The boy in the bus had a beard that made Harper think of Vikings: a stiff coil of braided orange wires. But the face behind the beard was young and soft. Harper doubted he was any older than Allie. He lazily twirled a nightstick in one hand.

"I guess I misunderstood the plan, Father," the boy said. "I thought you were off to *bring* us a nurse, not someone who *needs* a nurse." His gaze shifted from one face to another and he smiled in a worried sort of way. "I don't see Allie."

"We heard a thunderous crash, a stupendous roar of mindless violence and senseless destruction," Father Storey told him. "Naturally, Allie ran straight toward it. Try not to worry, Michael. She has the Fireman with her."

Michael nodded, then dipped his head toward Harper in a way that was almost courtly. His eyes shone with the fevered innocence of someone who has been Saved. "Hello to you. We're all friends here, Nurse. This is where your life begins again."

She smiled back at him but couldn't think how to reply, and in another moment it was too late, Ben and Renée shuttling her along. When Harper looked back, the boy had vanished into the bus.

Father Storey was about to put the gumball back in his mouth, then saw Harper looking at it. "Ah. Bit of a compulsion of mine. Something I picked up reading Samuel Beckett. I stick a pebble in my mouth to remind myself to be quiet and listen now and then. I taught in a private school for decades, and with all these young people wandering about, the urge to deliver impromptu lectures is very strong."

They followed the winding lane through leafy darkness,

past a dry swimming pool and a riflery range where brass cartridges glittered dully amid dead leaves. All seemed long abandoned—an appearance maintained at some effort, Harper learned later.

At last they reached the top of the hill. A soccer pitch lay on the other side of the slope in a shallow, grassy cup below them. Children yelled and chased a ball that glowed a pale, eerie green, the color of a ghost. Beyond that, through the trees, loomed a long boathouse and the heaving blackness of the sea.

The chapel was on the right, set back from the road. It was placed on the far side of a sculpture garden of mossy dolmens and tall monoliths. The Monument Park was an odd, primitive sort of thing to find guarding the way to a perfectly modern-looking church with a tall steeple and bright red doors. The church might be a place of worship, but the sculpture garden looked more a place of sacrifice.

What caught Harper's attention in particular was a knot of six teenagers, sitting on logs, at one corner of a vast barn of a building that turned out to be the cafeteria. They were gathered around a campfire that burned a peculiar shade of ruby-gold, as if the flames were shining through red crystal.

A slim-shouldered beauty swayed in the undulating crimson light, strumming a ukulele. At first glance, she might've been Allie's twin. But no, she was older, mid-twenties maybe. Her head was shaved, too, although she had preserved a single black lock of hair, like a comma, on her brow. The aunt, Harper guessed.

She led the others on a sing-along, their voices lacing together like lovers' fingers. They sang an old U2 number, sang about how they were one but not the same, and how they would carry each other. As Harper went by, the woman with the uke lifted her gaze and smiled and her eyes were bright as gold coins, and that was when Harper saw there was no campfire at all. It was *them* making the light. They were all of them tattooed with loops and whorls of Dragonscale, which glowed like fluorescent paint under a black light, hallucinatory hues of cherry wine and blowtorch blue. When they opened their mouths to sing, Harper glimpsed light painting the insides of their throats, as if each of them were a kettle filled with embers.

Harper felt she had never seen anything so frightening or beautiful. She shivered and for a moment was conscious of her body beneath her clothes and a feeling like fingers gently tracing the lines of Dragonscale on her skin. She swayed with a sudden giddy light-headedness.

"They're shining," Harper muttered, a little thickly. Her head was filled with their song and it was hard to push a thought through it.

"You will, too," Ben Patchett promised her. "In time."

"Is it dangerous?" Harper breathed. "Can they catch fire doing that?"

Father Storey popped the stone out of his mouth and said, "The Dragonscale is like anything that makes fire, Nurse Grayson. You can use it to burn a place down . . . or light your way to something better. No one dies of spontaneous combustion in Camp Wyndham."

"You've beaten it?" Harper asked.

"Better," Father Storey said. "We've made friends with it."

# 3

Harper sprang shuddering to consciousness from an ugly dream, twisting in her bedsheets.

Carol Storey leaned over her, a hand on her wrist.

"You're all right. Breathe."

Harper nodded. She was woozy, her pulse rapping so hard it made her vision flash.

She wondered how long she had slept. She remembered being half carried up the steps into an infirmary, recalled Ben Patchett and Renée Gilmonton following her careful instructions as they set her ankle and bound it in rolls of gauze. She dimly remembered Renée bringing her lukewarm water and some gel tabs of acetaminophen, remembered the older woman's dry, cool hand on her forehead and worried, watching gaze.

"What were you dreaming?" Carol asked. "Do you remember?"

Carol Storey had enormous, wondering eyes with irises of chocolate, flecked with gold speckles of Dragonscale. Hoops of gold and ebony circled her wrists, and she wore a short T-shirt that rode up to show crossed belts of the 'scale above her hips. It gave her the look of a goth gunslinger. Where her skin was unmarked, it was pale almost to the point of translucency. She was so delicate it looked as though, if she stumbled and fell, she might shatter, like a ceramic vase.

Harper's breasts were sore, there was a dry spoke of heat in her fractured ankle, and her thoughts were muddled and slow with the dregs of a deep sleep. "My husband wrote a book. I dropped it. The pages went everywhere. And . . . I think I was trying to put it all back in order before he got home. I didn't want him to know I'd been reading it." There had been more—

more and worse—but it was already slipping away, dropping out of sight, like a stone kicked into deep water.

"I thought I'd better wake you," Carol said. "You were shivering and making these awful noises and—well—smoking a little."

"I was?" Harper asked. She realized she could smell a faint odor of char, as if someone had burned a few pine needles.

"Only a little." Carol gazed at her with a look of pained apology. "When you sighed, there'd be a blue puff. It's stress that does it. After you've learned to join the Bright, that won't happen anymore. Once you're really one of us—part of the group—the Dragonscale won't *ever* hurt you. It's hard to believe, but one day, you may even look at the 'scale as a blessing."

In Carol's voice, Harper heard the innocent and utter belief of the fanatic, and was dismayed by it. She had learned from Jakob to think of people who spoke of blessings and faith as simple and a little infirm. People who thought things happened for a reason were to be pitied. Such folk had given up their curiosity about the universe for a comforting children's story. Harper could understand the impulse. She was a fan of children's stories herself. But it was one thing to spend a rainy Saturday afternoon reading *Mary Poppins* and quite another to think she might actually turn up at your house to apply for the babysitting job.

She did her best to appear blandly interested, but her distress must've shown. Carol rocked back in her chair and laughed. "Was that a little too much, a little too fast? You're new here. I'll try and go easy on you. I warn you, though, in this joint, the lunatics really *are* running the asylum. What does the cat say to Alice in *Wonderland*?"

"'We're all mad here,'" Harper said, and smiled in spite of herself.

Carol nodded. "My father wanted me to take you around and show you the camp. Everyone wants to meet you. We're late for lunch, but Norma Heald, who runs the cafeteria, promised to keep the kitchen open until we ate."

Harper lifted her head and squinted out the windows into a darkness so complete she might've been underground. The infirmary's single wardroom had three cots, with curtains hung between them to create some privacy; she occupied the central bed. It had been dark when she dozed off and was dark now, and she had not the slightest notion what time it might be.

As if Harper had asked, Carol said, "About two A.M. You slept through the whole day . . . which is just as well. We all live like vampires here: up at sundown, back to the crypt at dawn. No one is drinking blood yet, but if we run out of canned goods, it's hard to say what will happen."

Harper sat up, wincing—just the fabric of her hoodie brushing against her sore, swollen breasts was enough to make them hurt—and discovered two things.

The first was that one of the curtains was pushed back and a boy sat on the next camp bed over, a boy she recognized . . . a boy with dark, curly hair and delicate, elfin features. The last she had seen him, he was suffering from acute appendicitis, his face greasy with sweat. No—that wasn't quite right. She supposed she had seen him more recently than that. It had surely been him at her door in the Tiger mask with Allie. Now he sat cross-legged, watching her with the intentness of a child in front of a favorite television show.

The second was that a radio was on, tuned to static. It sat on the counter, next to a plaster model of a human head, the skull removed to reveal the brain.

Harper remembered the boy was deaf and moved her hand in a slow wave. In response, he reached behind his back, found a sheet of paper, and handed it to her. On it was a drawing—a little boy's drawing, although it showed skill—of a large striped cat walking across green grass, tail in the air.

TEMPORARY CAT read the words beneath the stalking feline.

Harper gave him a quizzical look and a smile, but he was already sliding off the cot and trotting out.

"That's Nick, yes?" Harper asked.

"My nephew. Yes. Odd duck. It runs in the family."

"And John is his stepfather?"

"What?" Carol said, and it was impossible to miss the sudden edge in her voice. "No. Not at all. My sister and John Rookwood dated for a few months, in a very different world. Nick's actual father is dead, and John—well, he barely registers in the boy's life anymore."

It seemed to Harper this was a little unkind—not to mention unfair—considering the Fireman had carried Nick to the hospital in his arms and had been ready to fight security and everyone in line to get him treatment. Harper also knew when a topic was an unwelcome one. She left the subject of John Rookwood for another time and said, "Nick gave me a temporary cat. Why did he give me a temporary cat?"

"It's a thank-you note. You were the nurse at the hospital who saved his life. That was an awful week. That was the most awful week of my life. I lost my sister. I thought I was going to lose my nephew. I knew we were going to be best friends and I was going to be crazy for you, even *before* I met you, Harper. Because of what you did for Nick. I want us to have matching pajamas. *That's* how crazy I am for you. I wish *I* had a temporary cat to give you."

"If it's temporary, do I have to give it back?"

"No. It's only to tide you over until he can get you a *real* cat. He's hunting one. He's made some snares and complicated traps. He goes around with a net on a stick, like catching cats is the same as catching butterflies. He keeps bugging people to find him catnip. I'm not sure the one he's hunting is real. No one else has seen it. I'm starting to think it's like Snuffleupagus, Big Bird's friend? Just in his head."

Harper said, "But Snuffleupagus *was* real."

"That is the most wonderful sentence I have ever heard. I want that on my gravestone. *Snuffleupagus was real.* No more. Just that."

Harper couldn't put her weight on her right foot, but Carol got an arm around her and helped her stand. As they hobbled past the radio on the counter, Carol reached out—hesitated a moment—and moved the dial slowly through bands of static. That anatomical model of a human head gaped at them in amazement. It was a grotesque thing, skin peeled away from one half of the face to show the sinew and nerves beneath, one eyeball suspended in a fibrous red nest of exposed muscle.

"What?" Harper asked. "Are you listening for something in particular?"

"Snuffleupagus," Carol said, and laughed, and switched the radio off.

Harper waited for her to explain. She didn't.

# 4

The cafeteria was perched on top of the hill, overlooking the soccer pitch and the pebbly beach below. Moss and strands of yellowing dead grass grew on the shingled roof and the windows were boarded up, giving it a look of long disuse.

The impression of abandonment was dispelled the moment Carol pushed open the door and led them into the seating area, a dim, cavernous space with exposed beams of red pine. Plates clattered in the kitchen and the air was fragrant with the odor of marinara sauce and stewed pork.

Lunch appeared to be over and done, but they didn't have the place entirely to themselves. Renée Gilmonton sat at a table for two, across from an old fella in a Greek fisherman's cap, both of them hunched above steaming coffees. A boy sat alone at the next table over, the kid who looked like a Viking. Michael, Harper remembered. He was forking up noodles in red sauce and turning the pages of an ancient *Ranger Rick,* reading by the light of a candle in a jelly jar. The evening before, Michael had come across as maybe seventeen. Now, bent over an article on "Miami's Marvelous Manatees," his eyes wide with fascination, he looked like a ten-year-old in a fake beard.

Renée lifted her chin and caught Harper's eye. It was a pleasure and a relief to have a friend here, to not be completely alone among strangers. Harper flashed back to other lunches in other cafeterias, and the anxiety that came with not seeing a familiar face and not knowing where to sit. She suspected Renée had waited around in hopes of meeting up with Harper and helping her to settle in . . . a small act of consideration for which Harper was indecently grateful.

The serving counter was manned by Norma Heald, a mountainous pile of flesh with the broad, sloping shoulders of a silverback gorilla. The postmeal cleanup was under way—Harper saw a couple of teenage boys in the kitchen, plunging dishes into soapy water by the light of an oil lamp—but Norma had reserved some pasta in a steel warming pan and a couple of ladles of sauce. There was coffee and a can of condensed milk for cream.

"We had sugar for a while and it was full of ants. Ants in the coffee, ants in the muffins, ants in the peach cobbler," Carol said. "For a few weeks, ants were my primary source of protein. No sugar now, though! Just syrup. Sorry! Welcome to the Last Days!"

"The sugar is gone and the milk will follow," Norma said. "I put out two cans of milk for the coffee, but there's only one left."

"The other got used up?" Carol asked. "So quickly?"

"Nope. Stole."

"I'm sure no one stole a can of milk."

"Stole," Norma repeated, her tone of voice closer to satisfaction than outrage. She sat behind the counter, occupied with a pair of silver knitting needles that raced back and forth, clicking and clacking, all the time she spoke. She was working on a giant shapeless tube of black yarn that might've been a prophylactic for King Kong.

Harper and Carol made their way to Michael's table, Carol making a come-on-over gesture to Renée and the old fella. "Sit with us, you two. We can all share Harper! There's enough to go around."

They arranged themselves around the table, bumping knees. Harper lifted her hand for her fork, but Carol grasped her fingers before she could reach it.

"Before we eat, we go around the circle and say one thing we're glad for," Carol said, leaning into Harper and speaking in a confidential tone of voice. "Sometimes it's the best part of the meal. Which will make more sense after you've tried the food."

"We snacked already, but I don't mind bowing the head with you," said the old man, who hadn't yet been introduced.

Renée squeezed Harper's other hand and then they were all sitting in a ring, leaning in toward the light of the single candle, like a group assembled for a séance.

"I'll start us off," Carol said. "I'm glad for the woman sitting next to me, who saved my nephew when he had appendicitis. I'm glad she's here and I have a chance to show her how grateful I am. I'm glad for her baby, because babies are exciting! Like fat little sausages with faces!"

The old fella spoke with lowered head and half-shut eyes. "I'm glad for the nurse myself, because a hundred and twenty-four people need a lot of lookin' after, and I've been over my head for months. I'm all this camp's had for medical care since the end of August, and all I know is what I larnt in the navy. I don't want to say how long it's been since I studied as a hospital corpsman, but at the time they had only just phased out the use of leeches."

"Me, I guess I'm mostly just glad to be in a place where people love me," Michael told them. "People like Aunt Carol and Father Storey. I'd do anything for them, to keep this place safe. I lost one family. I'd rather die myself than lose another."

"I'm glad to have had a hot lunch," Renée said, "even if it was fried Spam in Ragú. I'm also glad this camp has an ace fisherman in Don Lewiston, and I'll be gladder still the next time it's my turn for fish." Nodding at the old fella. Then she looked sidelong at Harper and said, "And I'm *so* glad to see my friend from Portsmouth Hospital, who marched around eighteen hours a day, whistling Disney tunes and trying to keep up the spirits of a thousand sick and terrified patients. Every time she came in the room, it felt like a break in a month of clouds. She made me want to keep going when there wasn't any other reason."

Harper wasn't sure she'd be able to find her own voice, was

ambushed by unexpected emotion. In her days at Portsmouth Hospital, she had felt about as useful as Renée's potted mint, and it caught her unprepared to hear someone tell her different. Finally, she managed, "I'm just glad not to be alone anymore."

Carol squeezed her fingers. "I am so glad to be part of this circle. We are all voices in the same chorus and we sing our thanks."

And for a moment it was there again: Carol's eyes pulsed with brightness, her irises becoming rings of fey green light. Michael's eyes flashed as well, and Harper saw a prickle of red and gold flicker across the whorls of Dragonscale on his bare arms.

Harper let go of Carol's hand as if at a physical shock. But then the weird sheen was gone and Carol was eyeing her mischievously.

"Freaked you out, didn't I? Sorry. You'll get used to it, though. Eventually it'll happen to you, too."

"It's a little frightening," Harper said. "But also . . . well, like magic."

"It's not magic. It's a miracle," Carol said, like someone identifying the make of her new car: *It's a Miata.*

"What's happening when you shine like that?" Harper asked. Something came back to her then and she looked, almost accusingly, at Renée. "It's the same thing that happened to you in the hospital. You ran out covered in light. Everyone thought you were going to explode."

"So did I," Renée said. "I stumbled onto it by accident. They call it joining the Bright."

Michael said, "Or the Network. But I guess that's only people my age. A lot of my friends joke that it's just another social network. Only they're kind of not joking."

"You probably understand that the Dragonscale responds badly to stress," Carol said.

The old fella, Don Lewiston, laughed. "That's one way a puttin' it."

"That's because it feels what you feel," Carol continued. "That's such a powerful concept. I'm surprised more people haven't followed the thread of that idea to see where it goes. If you can create a feeling of security and well-being and acceptance, the Dragonscale will react in a very different way: by making you feel more alive than you've ever felt before. It will make colors deeper and tastes richer and emotions stronger. It's like being set on fire with *happiness*. And you don't just feel *your* happiness. You feel everyone *else's,* too. Everyone around you. Like we're all notes being played together in a single perfect chord."

"And you don't burn," Michael said, twisting the orange coil of his beard.

"And you don't burn," Carol repeated.

"It doesn't seem possible," Harper said. "How does it work?"

"Harmony," Carol said.

"Harmony?"

"Connection, anyway," Renée said. "Strong social connection. John has some interesting theories about it, if you can draw him out. He told me once—"

Carol's face darkened. An artery, squiggling in her right temple, thickened. "John Rookwood isn't here and he doesn't *want* to be here. He prefers to keep his distance. It's easier to maintain his own personal myth that way. I think he looks down on us, honestly."

"Do you really think that?" Renée asked. "I've never had that impression. I would've said he looks *out* for us. If he does have a condescending view of camp, he has a peculiar way of showing it. He's the person who led most of us here in the first place."

There was an uneasy silence. Renée gazed at Carol with an innocent curiosity. For her part, Carol would not meet her stare. Instead she took a long swallow of coffee, a benign, easygoing gesture that Harper saw through. For an instant, there had been hate in her face. John had made it clear the night before, in the woods, that he was no fan of Carol Storey; the feeling, it seemed, was mutual.

Michael was the first to speak and smooth over the awkward moment. "The easiest way to join the Bright is to sing. The whole mess of us, the entire camp, get together in church every day after breakfast and have a big sing and we always shine. You'll shine, too. It might not happen right away, but stick with it. When it comes over you, it's like someone plugged you in to a giant battery. It's like all the lights are turning on in your soul for the first time in your life." His eyes had a bright, hot look that made Harper want to check him for fever.

"I had no idea what was happening to me, the first time I went into the Bright," Renée said. "To say I was surprised doesn't do it justice, Mrs. Grayson."

"You better start calling me Harper," Harper said. She didn't add that she thought she was all done being Mrs. Grayson. That name belonged to Jakob, and she felt she had left everything of Jakob's behind in the woods. Her maiden name had been Willowes. She missed the way it rolled off her tongue, and the thought of having her old name returned to her felt like another escape—a far more satisfying and peaceful escape than her leap out the bedroom window.

"Harper," Renée said, trying it out. She smiled. "I don't know if I'll be able to get used to it, but I'll try. Well, *Harper.* I was reading to the children. We were working our way through *Charlie and the Chocolate Factory,* and I stopped to sing 'The Candy Man' song from the film. A few of them knew the words and sang along with me. It was such a nice, peaceful moment, I forgot we were all sick. I got that melty, tranced-out feeling that comes over you when you're in front of a fire and you've had a couple drinks. And suddenly the kids began screaming. Time began to run thick and slow. I remember one of the children knocked my potted mint off my little end table and it seemed like I had half an hour to reach out and catch it. And when I did, I realized my whole arm was splattered with light. I thought it was so glorious looking, I couldn't find it in me to be terrified. But then someone shrieked, *Get away from her, she's going to explode!* And right away, I thought, *I am! I'm going to go off like a grenade!* Sometimes I think people are a bit more suggestible when they enter that state. The Bright. So I ran for my life, with my potted mint. Straight past two sets of guards and half a dozen doctors and nurses, across the parking lot and into the meadow south of the hospital. I thought I would set the grass on fire when I waded into it, but I didn't. It took a while for the light to die out, and afterwards I was shivery and drunk."

"Drunk?"

"Oh, yuh," said Don Lewiston. "You wind up pretty pickled after you go into the Bright. Especially the first couple times. You forget your own name."

"You—what?"

Carol said, "A *lot* of people forget their own name the first time. I think that's the most beautiful part of it. All the stuff you think defines you—it peels off like Christmas wrapping. The Bright winnows you down to your truest, best self, the version of you that goes deeper than a name or what football team you root for. And you become aware of yourself as just one leaf on a tree, and everyone you know and love, they're all the other leaves."

*A willow,* Harper Willowes thought, and shivered.

"First time I ever joint the Chorus," Don Lewiston said, "I forgot the face of my father, the sound of my mother's voice, and the name of the ship I spent the last twenty years on. I wanted to kiss everyone I saw. Oh, and I got real goddamn generous. I remember this was in chapel, after a good hard sing. I was sittin' next to a couple young fellas, and I was just burstin' to tell 'em how much I loved 'em, and all I could think to do was take off my boots and try to give them away. One boot for each of them, so they'd always have somethin' to remember me by. They laughed at me, like grown-ups havin' a yuk at some kid who just drank his first beer."

"Why didn't you come back to the hospital?" Harper asked Renée. "After you . . . went Bright?"

"At first it never occurred to me. I was just too out of my right mind. I was still holding my mint and it came to me that it didn't belong in a pot, that it was *cruel* to keep it in a pot. I was ashamed of myself for all the months I had held it prisoner. I drifted deep into the woods and had myself a nice quiet planting ceremony. Then I sat with my mint, with my face turned up to the sun, feeling about as content as I've ever felt in my life. I believe I thought I was going to photosynthesize, along with my plant. At some point I heard a branch snap and opened my eyes and there was Captain America and Tony the Tiger. And you know what? I wasn't the least surprised to see them. A superhero and a tiger-boy just seemed like the next logical part of my day."

"Allie," Harper said. "And Nick. Nick! What about Nick? How can he join your sing-alongs and shine with the rest of you if he can't hear?"

The others looked at one another—and erupted into happy laughter, as if Harper had said something quite witty.

"Nick," Carol said, "is a natural. He could shine before *I* could. Why, though . . . *why* it's so easy for him to join the Bright . . . that's a question not one of us can answer. Nick says just because *he* can't hear music doesn't mean the *Dragonscale* can't. My dad says it's another miracle. He's a great believer in miracles. So am I, I guess. Come on, Harper, I want to show you the rest of the camp."

"If you want a crutch," Michael said, "I have a shoulder."

On their way out, they stopped to put their dishes in a bin of gray, soapy water, and Harper glanced at the two teenage boys working in the kitchen. They were drying glasses by hand while listening to a radio.

It was tuned to static.

# 5

The kids were chasing a soccer ball in the valley again, the eerie pale green ball racing this way and that, like a will-o'-the-wisp on crack.

"I don't know how we'll wear them out when it snows," Carol said.

"What happens when it snows?"

"Mr. Patchett says we'll have to be more careful about our movements outside," Michael told her. "If we leave tracks, someone could see them from the air. There isn't one part of winter I'm looking forward to."

"When did you come to camp, Michael?" Harper asked.

"After my sisters burned to death," he said, without any trace of distress. "They burned together. They were still holding each other after I put them out. That's a blessing, I think. They didn't die alone. They had each other for comfort. They're gone from this world, but I hear them whispering to me in the Bright."

Carol said, "Sometimes when I'm in the Bright, I would swear I feel my sister standing right next to me, close enough so I could lay my head on her shoulder, like I used to. When we shine, they all come back to us, you know. The light we make together shows everything that was ever lost to darkness."

Harper clamped down on a shudder. When they spoke of the Bright, they had all the uncomplicated happiness of pod people.

Carol led Harper into the garden of towering monoliths and pagan stone altars. "There's a rumor these rocks are thousands of years old and were placed here by an ancient tribe, with the help of alien technology. My father says they were hauled here from the quarry in Ogunquit, though, which is why it's better never to ask him about anything really interesting."

When Harper was in among the stones she could see brass plaques screwed into the towering pillars of granite. One listed the names of seventeen boys who had died in the mud of eastern France during the First World War. Another listed the names of thirty-four boys who had died on the beaches of western France during the Second. Harper thought all tombstones should be this size, that the small blocks to be found in most graveyards did not even begin to express the sickening enormity of losing a virgin son, thousands of miles away, in the muck and cold. You needed something so big you felt it might topple over and crush you.

"This is our church," Carol told her. "If you go up in the steeple on a clear day, you can see into Maine. Only you don't want to look at Maine. There's nothing up north except for black smoke and lightning. In the mornings we come to sing and share the Bright and usually my dad will say a few words. After, it serves as a schoolroom." Carol pointed at a path tunneling through sumac and firs. "I live back there, through the woods, in the little white house with the big black star on it. I stay with my dad. I feel guilty about that sometimes. I should probably stay with all the other women, in the girls' dorm—that's where we're going next. My dad says I can move out anytime if I want to be with the other women, but I know if I left he wouldn't ever sleep. He'd drink too much coffee and worry and pace around and worry more. He only sleeps about five hours as it is and I have to make him take a pill to do that. Come on! Let me show you where I keep my harem!"

Carol led her around to the back of the chapel, where four stone steps descended into a hole the rough size, shape, and depth of a grave. At the bottom of the pit was an old door on rusted hinges, half open to look into the cellar.

"You'll have to manage without us from here," Michael said, nodding to Don. "We're not allowed."

"It's no place for two strappin' young boys like us," Don

Lewiston said. “All them wimmen undressin’ you with their eyes, plottin’ ways to use you to satisfy their repress’t needs—it makes a decent man feel lucky to escape with his life and virginity intact.”

Michael lowered his head, a blush darkening his pale features. Don laughed.

Carol shook her head and clucked her tongue. “Michael Martin Lindqvist Jr., you are just too much fun to embarrass.”

Renée said to Harper, “If you don’t have any garter belts, you can borrow a few of mine. One of the rules of the girls’ dorm, no clothes allowed except for French underwear. Corsets and so on.”

“I am *not* listening to any of you,” Michael said. “I am saving myself for marriage.”

He foisted Harper off on Carol and marched briskly away, at something very close to a run. Don Lewiston strolled after him, hands in his pockets, whistling “Spanish Ladies.”

Carol helped Harper make her way below. There were more steps on the other side of the door, descending deeper into the hill.

The room beneath the chapel was a single enormous space, the ceiling supported by whitewashed brick pillars. Camp cots made a knee-high maze across the pitted cement floor. Close to thirty women were hanging around, sitting on their beds, or standing by a folding table set up against the back wall where there was a Mr. Coffee.

Michael and Don could, in fact, have safely descended the steps without fear of finding themselves in a silken garden of delights. The room had an unsexy smell of damp and mothballs and most of the girls had the waxen look of people who had not seen daylight for a long time. No garter belts in sight, but a lot of wet socks hung over pipes to steam-dry. The prevailing fashion was Salvation Army chic.

There was a double-sided chalkboard close to the foot of the steps, the sort of thing sandwich shops stood on the sidewalk to advertise the day's specials. Harper paused to see what was written on it, in bright chalk and girlish lettering:

HOUSE RULES

NO CELL PHONES EVER! YOUR CELL PHONE SHOULD'VE BEEN TURNED IN TO A LOOKOUT!

SEE SOMETHING, HEAR SOMETHING . . . SAY SOMETHING!

EVERYONE HAS A JOB TO DO! KNOW YOURS!

FOOD, BEVERAGES & MEDICAL SUPPLIES BELONG TO EVERYONE!! NO HOREDING!

NO GOING OUTSIDE IN THE DAYLIGHT!

LISTEN TO THE LOOKOUTS! IT COULD SAVE YOU'RE LIFE!!

DON'T LEAVE CAMP WITHOUT TALKING TO A LOOKOUT FIRST!

WEAPONS ARE STRICTLY FORBIDDEN!

SO ARE SECRETS!

SAFETY IS EVERYONE'S BUSINESS!!!

Act like everybody depends on you! They Do!!

"Quick," Carol said. "What's your favorite song, celebrity crush, and the name of your first pet?"

Harper said. "'You've Got a Friend in Me,' Ewan McGregor, mostly for *Moulin Rouge,* and my first pet was a schnauzer named Bert, because he was soot black and made me think of the chimney sweeps in *Mary Poppins.*"

Carol stood up on a chair and cleared her throat and waved an arm over her head to get the attention of the room. "Hey, everybody! This is Harper! She's our new nurse! 'You've Got a

Friend in Me,' Ewan McGregor, and a schnauzer named Bert! Let's have a big cheer for Nurse Harper!"

This was met by a mix of hooting, applause, and halloos. Allie Storey threw a bra at Harper's head. Someone else yelled, "Harper what?"

Carol opened her mouth to reply, but Harper spoke first.

"Willowes," she called out. "Harper Willowes!" And to herself, in a lower voice, she said, "Again. It seems."

Carol led Harper on a winding path among the beds, to a neatly made cot near the center of the room. Harper's carpetbag had been set upon the pillow.

Harper unbuckled it and peeked inside. Her clothes had been picked up and put in neat stacks. *The Portable Mother* rested on top of all. Harper folded her Temporary Cat and put it inside the cover. Her child's first pet.

"I should thank Mr. Rookwood for collecting my things," Harper said, remembering only after the words were out of her mouth that the Fireman seemed to be Carol Storey's least favorite subject. It was too late, though, so, in a casual, offhand tone, she finished: "Where would I find him?"

There was no look of contempt or anger this time. Instead, Carol regarded her with a mild, almost bland expression, then punched her softly on the arm. "Come on outside again. I'll show you."

Even with Carol's help, Harper's ankle was twanging painfully by the time they mounted the steps into the night. The temperature had dropped. The air had texture now, a thousand fine quivering grains of almost-rain blowing in off the ocean.

They stood alone, at the rear northeastern corner of the chapel. Carol pointed over the soccer field, the pines, and the boathouse below. Out in the surging blackness of the water was a darker blackness, a small island.

"He's out there," she said. "John Rookwood. He doesn't come to church. He doesn't eat with us. He keeps to himself."

"What's he doing there?"

"I don't know. It's a secret. It's his secret. He never leaves the island for long and no one knows why. You hear different stories. *She* died out there, you know. My sister. She burned to death and almost took Nick with her. Maybe John is out there mourning her. Maybe he's doing penance. Maybe he just likes being mysterious."

"Penance? Does he blame himself somehow?"

"I'm sure," Carol said, and although her face was carefully composed, Harper once again heard an edge, a razor wire of emotion. "Not that it's his fault. He wasn't on the island when it happened. No. My sister didn't need any help to kill herself. She managed that just fine on her own." Carol gave Harper a sidelong look and said, "But I'll tell you what. I won't let the kids go out there anymore: Nick and Allie. I think John understands. You might not want to make a habit of dropping in for social visits yourself. People who get too close to John have a way of going down in flames."

# 6

After a breakfast of soft, milky oatmeal and bitter coffee, it was time for services.

Ben Patchett was her crutch again and helped her along, out into the unseasonably warm October night. Dragonflies whisked through the perfumed dark. The buzz of excitement and pleasure, rising from the crowd around her, brought to mind small country carnivals, Ferris wheels, and fried dough.

They filed into the narrow, high-ceilinged chapel, beneath splintery exposed rafters. The nave was a long cabinet of shadows, windows boarded up against the night, the enormous space lit by just a few candles. Giant shadows twitched restlessly against the walls, more distinct than the people that threw them.

Harper had an arm across Ben Patchett's shoulder as he led her to a pew midway up the aisle. Another man squeezed in on her right side, a small, tubby fellow, a little older than Ben, with pink cheeks and the smooth complexion of an infant. Ben introduced him as Nelson Heinrich, who in a former life had owned a shop called Christmas-Mart, which perhaps explained why he was wearing a sweater with reindeer on it when it was just turning Halloween.

The merry chatter died as Father Storey stepped to the podium. He moved his spectacles up his nose and peered owlishly at his own songbook, then announced: "If you'll open to page 332, we begin tonight with a plain but honorable hymn, beloved by the Pilgrims in the early days of America."

This was met by a smattering of laughs, although Harper didn't understand why until Nelson opened the songbook to the right place. It was a camp songbook, for little boys and girls, not a true hymnal, and the song on page 332 turned out to be "Holly Holy" by Neil Diamond. Harper approved. If anyone could save her soul, it was probably him.

Carol rose from the bench behind the organ and came to the front of the stage. She lifted her ukulele to acknowledge a little flurry of applause.

Nelson bent toward Harper's ear and, rather loudly, said, "It's easy, you'll see! Nothing to it! Just lay back and enjoy it!" An unfortunate statement with unfortunate connotations, Harper thought.

Ben winced, then added, "It doesn't always come right away. Don't worry if nothing happens to you tonight. It would be amazing if anything did! Like bowling a strike the first time you pick up a—"

But he didn't have a chance to finish. Carol began to play, belting out that melody that sounded as much like a marching song as a gospel. When they all began to sing—over a hundred voices resonating in the gloom—a pigeon was startled off one of the rafters above.

Allie and Nick were in the row directly ahead of her and the first Harper knew anything was happening was when the boy turned his head and smiled at her and his normally aquamarine eyes were rings of gold light.

Wires of Dragonscale on the back of Ben Patchett's hand lit up, like fiber-optic threads filling with brightness.

A glow built from all directions, overpowering the dim red illumination of the candles. Harper thought of an atomic flash rising in a desert. The sound of the song mounted along with the light, until Harper could hear all those voices in her chest.

Onstage, Carol's belted white gown was rendered diaphanous, the body beneath painted with light. She didn't seem to mind or notice. Harper thought, helplessly, of the hallucinatory nudes who pirouetted through the credits of the James Bond movies.

Harper felt she was being swallowed by all their noise. The brightness was not beautiful but awful, like being caught in headlights hurtling madly toward her.

Ben had an arm around her waist and was unconsciously kneading her hip, a gesture she found revolting but could not seem to break away from. She glanced at Nelson and found him wearing a choker of light. When he opened his mouth to bellow out the next line, Harper saw his tongue glowing a toxic shade of green.

She wondered whether, if she began to scream, anyone would hear her over all the other voices. Not that she was going to scream—she had lost her breath, could not even sing. If not for her fractured ankle, she might've run.

The only thing that got her to the end of the song was Renée and Don Lewiston. They were across the aisle and a little closer to the stage, but Harper could see them through a gap in the crowd. Renée's head was turned to look back at her and she smiled sympathetically. The loops of 'scale around her neck shone, but it was a faded sort of glow, and the light had not reached her kind, clear eyes. More important, she was *still there,* still present, paying attention. And that was when Harper understood what so unnerved her about the others.

In some way Ben and Nelson, Allie and Nick, and all the rest of them had left the room, leaving behind lamps made of human skin. Thought had been replaced by light, and personality by harmony, but Renée at least was still there . . . and so was Don Lewiston, who sang dutifully, but did not glow at all. Later, Harper learned that Don was only sometimes able to shine with the others. When he turned on, he turned on intensely, but more often he was completely untouched by their song. Don said it was because he had a tin ear, but Harper was unconvinced. His rumbling, rough bass was perfectly in tune, and he sang with a casual, disinterested confidence.

Harper smiled weakly for Renée, but felt unsteady and sick. She had to close her eyes to withstand the assault of the last thunderous verse—her Dragonscale crawled unpleasantly, and the only thought she could manage was, *Stop, stop, stop*—and when it was over, and the room erupted into stamping feet and whistles and applause, it was all she could do not to cry.

Ben absently stroked her hip. She was sure he didn't know he was doing it. The threads of light on his exposed 'scale were fading, but a brassy sheen remained in his eyes. He regarded her with affection, but not much recognition.

*"Mmnothing?"* he asked. His voice had a drifting, musical quality, as if he had just woken from a restorative nap. "No luck? I wasn't paying attention. Kind of lost myself for a minute there."

"No luck," Harper said. "It might be my ankle. It's been achy all morning and it's a little distracting. Maybe I'll just sit for the next song and rest it."

And she did sit the next time. She sat and closed her eyes to shut out the bright glare that so felt like oncoming headlights.

She sat and waited to be run down.

# NOVEMBER

## 7

Harper woke the night of Thanksgiving from a dream about Jakob and *Desolation's Plough*. She smelled smoke and couldn't figure out what was burning and then she realized it was her.

Harper wasn't in flames, but the stripe across her throat had charred the collar of her Coldplay T-shirt, causing it to blacken and smoke. Beneath the shirt, she felt a sensation like bug spray on a scrape, only all over.

She threw aside her sheets with a cry and yanked off her shirt. The stripe marked her skin in inky lines flecked with grains of poisonous red light. The jellyfish sting intensified, made thought impossible.

The sound that went up all around her, from the other women stirring in their beds, made her think uncharitably of pigeons startled into flight: a nervous cooing. Then Allie was with her. Allie put her legs around Harper's waist and clasped her from behind. She sang, in a soft, barely audible whisper, lips close to Harper's ear. In the next moment Renée was beside her, holding her hand in the dark, lacing her fingers through Harper's.

Renée said, "You're not going to burn. No one burns here, that's one of the rules. You want to break the rules and get us all in trouble with Carol Storey? Deep breaths, Nurse Willowes. Big deep breaths. With me, now: *Innn*. Out. *Innnn*."

And Allie sang that old Oasis song. She sang that Harper was her Wonderwall, in a sweet, unafraid voice. She even did it in her Fireman voice, in a darling faux-snotty English accent of the sort best known as Mockney.

Harper didn't start to cry until the Dragonscale dimmed and went out and the pain began to pass. It left behind an achy, sunburnt feeling, all through the spore.

Allie stopped singing, but went on holding her. Her bony chin rested comfortably on Harper's shoulder. Renée rubbed her thumb over Harper's knuckles in a loving, motherly way.

Nick Storey stood in the dark, four paces from Harper's cot, watching her uneasily. Nick was the only boy who slept in the girls' dorm, splitting a cot with his big sister. He clutched a slide whistle to his chest with one hand. He couldn't hear it, but he knew he could blow through it and call the Fireman. And what good would that do? Maybe the Fireman would've brought a hose to douse her ashes.

"Attagirl," Renée said. "You're okay. All over. Could've been worse."

"Could've been better, too," Allie said. "You just missed a perfectly good opportunity to toast an awful Coldplay T-shirt. If I ever spontaneously combust, I hope I'm holding a whole stack of their CDs."

Harper made sounds that might've been laughter or might've been sobs; even she wasn't sure. Maybe a bit of both.

# 8

Harper filed into the night in her singed Coldplay shirt, moving along toward the cafeteria and breakfast with all the rest of them. She walked without seeing where she was going, letting the human tide carry her along.

A dream. A dream had almost killed her. She had never imagined that going to sleep might be as dangerous as a glass of wine with Jakob over a loaded gun.

In the dream, she was enormously pregnant, so huge it was both horrible and comic. She was trying to run, but the best she could manage was a tragic, hilarious waddle. She was clutching *Desolation's Plough* to her sore and swollen breasts and the pages were sticky with blood. There were bloody handprints all over it. She had the confused idea that she had beaten Jakob to death with it and now she had to hide the evidence.

She was running across the road to bury it, as if it were a corpse. An icy wind sheared up the highway, caught the manuscript, and dashed it to the blacktop.

Harper got down on the frozen asphalt, grabbing pages and trying to collect the manuscript there in the dark and the cold. In the logic of the dream it was necessary not to lose a single page. She had gathered up about a third when a pair of headlights snapped on, three hundred feet down the road. A two-ton Freightliner with a plow the size of an airplane wing was parked along the curb.

"Oh, you bitch," Jakob called from behind the wheel. "Do you know how hard I worked on that? Where is your respect for literature?"

The gears ground. The Freightliner began to roll. Jakob flicked the beams to high, pinning her to the road with a blinding blue light. He accelerated, crunched up into second gear, the noise of the engine rising to a diesel scream, and the headlights were piercing her right through, the headlights were hot on her skin, the headlights were *cooking* her—

Just remembering it made her Dragonscale prickle with an unwholesome heat.

She walked with her head down, so lost in her hopeless, dismal thoughts that she was startled when someone planted a cold, gentle kiss on her cheek. She looked up in time to be kissed again, on her right eyelid.

It was snowing. Great fat white flakes as big as feathers floated aimlessly down from the darkness, so soft and light they barely seemed to be descending at all. She closed her eyes. Opened her mouth. Tasted a snowdrop.

The cafeteria was steamy and smelled of seared Spam and white gravy. Harper shuffled through a din of shouts, laughter, and clattering utensils.

The children had made paper place mats shaped like turkeys and colored them in. All the kids were working as waiters that evening, and wore Pilgrim hats made out of construction paper.

Renée steered Harper to one of the long tables and they sat down together. Ben Patchett glided in from the other side, bumping Harper's hip with his own as he settled on the bench.

"Did you want to sit with us, Ben?" Renée asked, although he had already plopped himself down.

In the last three weeks, Ben had developed a habit of hovering. When Harper walked toward a door, it seemed like he was always there to hold it open for her. If she was limping, he slipped up against her, unasked, to put an arm around her waist and serve as her crutch. His fat, warm hands reminded her of yeasty, uncooked dough. He was harmless and he was trying to be useful and she wanted to be grateful, but instead she often found herself wearied by the sight of him.

"You okay, Harper?" Ben narrowed his eyes at her. "You look flushed. Drink something."

"I'm fine. I already had some water and you wouldn't believe how much I'm peeing these days."

"I said *drink*." He pushed a paper cup of cranberry juice at her. "Dr. Ben's orders."

She took the cup and drank, mostly to shut him up. She knew he was kidding, trying to have fun with her in his clumsy way, but she found herself even more irritable with him than usual. It was no problem for *him* to join the Bright. Ben Patchett always lit right up in chapel, from the first chords Carol played on the pipe organ. He was never going to wake up burning. He didn't have to be afraid of going to sleep.

Harper's bad dreams of being run down in the road didn't surprise her in the least. She felt trapped in the path of oncoming headlights at least once a day, when all the rest of them sang. More and more, she dreaded entering the chapel for services. She had been in camp all month and had not been able to join the Bright, not a single time. In chapel, she was the one dead bulb on the Christmas tree. She clenched her fists in her lap throughout each day's ceremony, a white-knuckled flier gritting her teeth through a battering stretch of turbulence.

Recently, even Ben had stopped reassuring her it was just a matter of time before she *connected,* before she *plugged in, joined up* . . . all those phrases that made it sound like a matter of getting online with some modem of the soul. When services were over, and they all filed out, Harper saw people avoiding eye contact with her. Those who did meet her gaze did so with small, cramped, pitying smiles.

There was a stir of commotion halfway across the room as Carol helped Father Storey up onto a chair. He raised both hands for quiet, smiling down at the almost full room and blinking through his gold-rimmed bifocals.

"I—" he began, in a mumbly, muffled sort of way, and then he reached into his mouth and plucked out a white stone. His audience responded with a rumble of adoring laughter.

Someone—it sounded like Don Lewiston—shouted, "Hey,

Fadder, is that what's for dinner? *Christ,* the food in this joint is bad."

Norma Heald glowered in the direction of whoever had been yelling, then called out, "No snacking before meals, Father."

Father Storey smiled and said, "I thought this being the day of Thanksgiving, I should say something before we dig in. You can put your hands together if you want, or hold hands with whoever is next to you, or tune me out and listen to the wind, as it suits you."

Throats cleared and chair legs thumped. Ben Patchett took Harper's hand in his, his palm moist and doughy. Renée gave Harper a sidelong glance that was full of sardonic sympathy—*Look who has a boyfriend! Lucky you!*—and took the other hand.

"All of us together are a chorus of praise, saved by song and light," Father Storey began. "We are grateful to have this chance to come together in harmony, saved by our love for each other. We have so much to be thankful for. I know I am thankful for biscuits and white gravy. It smells great. We all sing our thanks for Norma Heald, who busted her butt making this amazing Thanksgiving dinner with very limited supplies. We sing our thanks for the girls who sweated puddles assisting her in the kitchen. We sing for Renée Gilmonton, who helped the kids with their Pilgrim hats and taught them how to be an ace waitstaff. We sing for John Rookwood, who isn't here tonight, but who miraculously provided us with the cocoa and marshmallows I'm not supposed to mention, because we don't want the kids to get excited."

A shriek of happiness went up around the room, followed by an indulgent murmur of adult laughter. Father Storey smiled, then shut his eyes. His brow furrowed in thought.

"When we sing together, we sing for all the people who loved us but who aren't here tonight. We sing in memory of every minute we got to have with them. I lost a daughter—a beautiful, smart, funny, combative, difficult, inspiring daughter—

and I couldn't miss her any more than I do. I know other people here feel just the same about the ones they lost. I sing for what I had with my Sarah. And when we raise our voices in harmony, I feel her still. I find her spirit in the Bright. I hear *her* singing for *me,* as I sing for her."

The wind shrilled beneath the eaves. Someone took a choked breath. Harper could feel the silence in her nerve endings, a sweet, painful throb.

Father Storey opened his wet eyes and swept a grateful, affectionate look across the room. "The rest of us, we're still here, and it feels pretty good. One more night on Earth, with a little music and some fresh biscuits and some good conversation. That's about all I ever wanted. I don't know about anyone else. And now I think everyone would just about sing with joy if I'd shut up so we can get to eating."

A cheer went up, a loud yell of pleasure, followed by applause. Don Lewiston stood. Then others were standing with him, pushing back their benches and chairs, so they could clap for the old man, who told them it was all right to still sometimes be happy, even now. As Father Storey came down out of his chair, they rose from theirs, whistling and clapping, and Harper whistled and clapped with them, glad for him. For one moment, anyway, she was not sick at heart about waking up to the smell of smoke.

They ate: greasy cubes of Spam, half drowned in gravy, on top of floury, buttery biscuits. Harper didn't have any appetite at all and ate mechanically, and she was surprised when it was all gone and she was scraping the plate for the last of the gravy. *She* might not be hungry, but the baby was always in the mood for a little something. She looked at the half biscuit on Renée's plate a moment too long, and the older woman smiled and used a plastic fork to shove it onto Harper's dish.

"No," Harper said, "Don't. I don't want it."

"That would be more convincing if I didn't see you picking crumbs off the tablecloth and eating them."

"Oh, God," Harper said. "I'm such a pig. It must be like sitting next to a fucking swine at the trough."

Ben twitched and looked away. Harper was not a big one for swearing, but around him she couldn't help herself. Ben avoided profanity like a cat avoided getting wet, said *heck* for *hell, crap* for *shit,* and *frick* for *fuck,* a habit Harper found unpleasantly prissy. When she herself swore, it never failed to make him flinch. Sometimes, Harper thought he was more of an old lady than Norma Heald.

She supposed she had been looking to pay him back ever since he decided to play Daddy and make her drink her cranberry juice. No sooner had she done it, though, than she felt guilty. It was a lousy thing to do, set out to offend a guy who had never been anything but decent to her.

He put his fork down and stood up. Harper felt a flash of horror, wondered if she had so offended him he was about to flee. But no; he was making his own announcement, climbing up onto the bench, putting two fingers in his mouth, and blowing an earsplitting whistle.

"I don't have a rock in my mouth," Ben said, "but by the time I'm done talking, some of you will probably wish I did." He smiled at this, but no one was quite sure whether to laugh or not, and the room remained silent except for a low, uneasy rustle of back-chatter. "The snow may be pretty, but it's going to make our lives a whole lot harder. Up until now we've had the freedom to go about camp as we like and the kids have had plenty of room to run and play. I am sorry, but now all that has to change. Tonight the Lookouts will be setting out planks to create walkways between buildings. When you're passing between buildings, you *must* stay on the planks. If a Quarantine Patrol comes through here, and they find the snow all churned up with footprints, they are going to know people are hiding here. I want the Lookouts to meet me in Monument Park after tonight's chapel. We need to practice getting the boards up and out of sight. I want to be able to make them disappear inside of two minutes. We can do this, but it isn't going to come easy, so expect to be out there for a while, and dress accordingly."

This was met by groans, but Harper thought they were less than entirely heartfelt. The teenagers who had signed up to be Lookouts loved hustling in the cold, pretending they were marines on a black op. Most of them had been preparing for postapocalyptic stealth missions since they were old enough to pick up an Xbox controller.

"Father Storey mentioned that Norma Heald just about killed herself pulling together today's meal. It wasn't easy, given what she has to work with. Which brings me to some unfortunate news. Norma and Carol and myself spent six hours in the kitchen yesterday, going over our supplies. I won't kid you. We're in a corner and we've had to make some tough decisions. So starting on Monday next week, everyone between the ages of thirteen and sixty, who isn't infirm or pregnant"—Ben glanced down at Harper and winked—"will draw a ticket out of a hat, just before lunch. If your ticket has an X on it we'll ask you to skip that meal. On an average night, probably thirty people will miss out on their lunch. If you happen to lose in the hunger games—" He paused, smiling, expecting laughter. When he didn't get any, his face darkened, and he hurried on. "You can skip drawing a ticket at the next lunch. I'm sorry. It's simple math. This camp was outfitted with enough dry and canned goods to keep a couple hundred kids fed for a few months. We've had over a hundred people here since July, and more turning up every week. The barrels are low and there isn't going to be any more anytime soon."

No one mock-groaned this time. Instead, Harper heard nervous whispers and saw people casting worried looks back and forth. Allie, who was two tables away, turned to Michael, sitting beside her, raised a hand to cover her mouth, and began to hiss furiously into his ear.

"Anyone who draws a losing ticket will still be offered coffee or tea, and as a thank you . . . well, Norma has discovered some sugar. A large can of it. It doesn't even have ants in it. So if you pull a bad ticket you can also have a teaspoon of sugar for whatever you're drinking. *One*. Teaspoon. It's not much, but it's something. It's the best we can do to show our gratitude." Ben's voice hardened, and he went on. "On the subject of low supplies and missing meals: someone is taking cans of condensed milk. Some of the Spam has gone missing, too, and we don't have any to spare. That has to stop. It's not a joke. You are literally stealing food out of the mouths of children. And if someone took Emily Waterman's big teacup yesterday, I would be grateful if you would just put it back on her bed at some point. You don't have to explain yourself. Just do it. It's a very, very large teacup, about the size of a soup bowl, with stars printed in the bottom. It's her lucky cup of stars and she's had it since she was tiny and it means a lot to her. That's all. Thank you."

He waited to see if anyone would applaud for him but no one did, and finally Harper reached up and held his hot, damp hand while he climbed down. She wasn't annoyed with him anymore. Conversation returned to the room, but it was subdued and troubled.

He sat poking his plastic fork at some smears of gravy on his plate. Renée leaned forward to look around Harper and said, "Are you all right, Ben?"

"It was bad enough being the guy who took away the cell phones," Ben said. "Now I'm the guy who took away lunch. Aw, frick it."

He pulled himself up off the bench, took his plate to the counter, and dumped it in a bin full of gray, soapy water.

"I don't care if *I* miss lunches." Renée watched Ben turn up his collar and exit the cafeteria without a look back. "They were pretty terrible anyway, and I was hoping to lose ten pounds. Of course, he's got it all wrong. People weren't angry at him when he took away the cell phones. They were glad! They were relieved someone was thinking about how to keep us all safe.

They don't hold one single thing he's done against him. Not even what he did to Harold Cross. The only person who blames Ben Patchett for what happened to Harold is Ben Patchett."

"Harold Cross," Harper said. "I've heard that name before. Who's Harold Cross and what did Ben do to him?"

Renée blinked, staring at Harper in surprise. "Shot him. You didn't know that? Shot him right in the throat."

# 9

There were little triangles of coconut custard pie on a graham cracker crust for dessert, the best and sweetest thing Harper had eaten since she came to camp. She closed her eyes after each spoonful, to better concentrate on the creamy taste of it. It was so good she felt a little like crying, or at least writing Norma Heald a sincere thank-you card.

Renée was gone for a bit, helping to prepare cocoa for the children, and when she returned she had two mugs of black coffee, and Don Lewiston and Allie Storey in tow. Nick Storey was there, too, trailing along in his big sister's wake. He carried a mug of hot chocolate before him, with a kind of reverence, not unlike a child bearing the wedding rings at a marriage.

"Are you all right?" Renée asked. "You're making a face."

"That's my orgasm face," Harper said, around her last bite of pie.

"I don't think it's any accident that a slice of pie comes in the exact same shape as a slice of pussy," Allie said.

"Do you girls want to talk amongst yourselves?" Don asked. "I could come back another time. This conversation is headin' in a direction what might be upsettin' to the ears of an innocent like myself."

"You can sit down," Renée said, "and tell what happened to Harold Cross. I think Harper ought to know about it, and the both of you can tell it better than I can. Don, you worked with him. Allie, you knew him better than most. And you were both there at the end."

"I wouldn't say I knew him all that well. It got to a point where I couldn't even stand to be in the same room with him," Allie said.

"But you tried," Renée said. "You made an effort. There aren't many other people here who can say that."

Nick perched on the bench to Allie's left. He looked from Allie to Renée and back, then moved his hands in the air, asking something of his sister. Allie furrowed her brow and began to make minute gestures with her fingers.

"My mom was a lot better at sign," Allie said. "I'm only really confident about my finger-spelling. He wants to know what we're talking about. One good thing about the little guy being deaf. We don't have to worry about him overhearing the really rotten bits and getting sad."

"And he doesn't read lips at all?" Harper asked.

"That's only in movies."

Don sipped at his coffee and grimaced. "Tell you what, nothing will cure a case of feeling good faster than a sip of this coffee. Except maybe for talkin' about Harold Cross." He set his mug down. "Harold was pretty much always alone. Kind of a fat kid no one liked. Too smart for his own good, y'unnerstand? Smarter than everyone else and happy to let you know it. If you were diggin' a latrine, he'd tell you a better, more scientific way to do it . . . but he wouldn't pick up a shovel himself. Would say his back hurt or summin'. You know the type."

"He wore this striped T-shirt and a pair of black denim shorts and I never saw him wear anything else. He had a booger on that shirt once that was there for three days. Swear to Jesus," Allie said.

"I remember that booger!" Don said. "He had that thing on his shirt so long he shoulda given it a name!"

Nick was still watching, and now he asked Allie something else, in a few slow, careful gestures. Allie's reply was faster this time, and involved a knuckle screwed into her nose, miming the act of digging for boogers. Nick grinned. He dug a stub of pencil out of his jeans and wrote something on his turkey-shaped place mat. He pushed the mat across the table to Harper.

*He'd get smoky sometimes, too. Not bad, but like if you throw a lot of wet moss on a campfire. Just a little nasty smoke coming out from under his shorts. Allie said it was coming from his butt-chimney.*

When Harper looked back, Nick had a hand clamped over his mouth and was making a thin, quavering whistle. He might lack the power of speech, but the giggles, it seemed, remained available even to the mute.

Renée said, "He was a former med student, and when I came to camp, he was in charge of the infirmary. I'd guess he was twenty-four years old, maybe twenty-five. He went around with a little reporter's notebook and sometimes he'd sit on a rock and start scribbling in it. I think that worried some people. You felt like he was taking notes on you."

Allie said, "Now and then one of the girls would try to snatch his notebook away, to see what he was writing. That would get his Dragonscale acting up and he'd storm off in a haze. *Literally* fuming, you know?"

"From the butt-chimney," Don Lewiston said, and this time they all laughed, *except* for Nick, who had lost the thread, and could only smile quizzically.

"The first time he joined the Bright, he lit up fast," Allie said. "Some people get it right away and some people don't. In Harold's case, it maybe came over him *too* quickly. He fell into the Bright so fast and hard it scared him. He screamed and dropped to the floor and rolled around like he was burning. Later he said he didn't like how it felt, having other people in his head. Which doesn't *really* happen. It *isn't* telepathy. No one gets inside your head. It's just a good feeling, coming off the people around you. It's like being held. Like the perfect hug. After that first time, Harold just about never lit up. He kept himself at a distance from the rest of us. He wasn't participating—he was just watching us."

"Yuh. That's right," Don agreed. "Then, one day, after he'd been in camp about two weeks, he stood up at the end of services and said he'd like to address the room. Kinda dumbstruck everyone. As a rule, if there's any talkin' to do in chapel, Father Storey or Carol are the ones to do it. It was like watchin' a TV show and suddenly one a the extras decides to deliver a speech ain't in the script."

"Father Storey," Renée added, "God love that man, he just poked his thinking rock in his mouth and sat down to listen, like a student settling in for a lecture on his favorite subject."

Allie rasped a hand over the bristly curve of her head. "Harold told us we had a moral obligation to let the world know about our 'discovery.' He said we didn't belong in hiding. He said we ought to be on cable news, that we ought to go public about what we could do. He said our process of subduing the Dragonscale was of scientific interest and there were lots of people who wanted to know more about us. Aunt Carol said, 'Harold, darling, what do you mean, *lots* of people want to know about us?' And Harold said he had been texting with a doctor in Berkeley who thought our community might represent a real breakthrough. There was another doctor in Argentina who wanted Harold to take blood samples of people when they were in The Bright. Harold said all this like it was no big deal. He didn't seem to have any idea what he had done."

"Oh, Harper, it was bad," Renée said. "That was a bad night."

"Mr. Patchett jumped up and asked how many people he'd been texting with and if he'd been texting from inside camp. Mr. Patchett said tracing the location of a smartphone was the easiest thing in the world and for all Harold knew he was drawing a big X on a map for the local Quarantine Patrols. People started crying, grabbing their kids. We were like people on an airplane who have just heard from the pilot that there's a terrorist in the cockpit." Allie's gaze came unfocused. She wasn't seeing Harper anymore, but was looking back into a summer night of alarm and commotion. "Mr. Patchett made him give up his cell. He spent three minutes scrolling through Harold's texts. It turned out he had been in contact with thirty different people, all over the country. All over the world! Sending them photos, too, stuff that would make it easy to identify where we were hiding."

"Harold wanted the camp to have a vote," Don Lewiston put

in. "Well. He got one all right. Ben led a vote to confiscate every cell phone in camp, had Allie 'n' Mikey collect 'em all in a great trash bag."

"I didn't like what happened to Harold after that," Renée said. "If we ever did him wrong, it was then."

Allie nodded. "After the phones got taken away, it was like Harold was a poisonous bug, and the whole camp wanted to keep him under a jar, where he couldn't sting anyone. Little kids started calling him Horrid instead of Harold. No one would sit with him in the cafeteria, except for Granddad, who can get along with anyone. Then, one day, one of the girls chucked a Frisbee right in Harold's face and smashed his glasses. She pretended it was an accident, like she meant for him to catch it, but it was really shitty, and I told her it was shitty. I felt like someone had to *try* and stick up for him. I felt like it was bad for all of us, not to care about him. So I helped fix his glasses and I started sitting with him and Granddad at lunch. I signed up for chores with him, so he wouldn't have to work alone. I had this whole idea I was going to unearth the *real* Harold. Only I did and it was as nasty as the rest of him. We were doing dishes together for Mrs. Heald in the cafeteria one day, and all of a sudden he stuck his hand down my shorts. When I asked him what the fuck he was doing, he said there was no reason for me to be picky about who I screwed, since the whole human race was going down the toilet anyway. I shoved him so hard his glasses fell off and broke again. So that was Harold."

Nick was looking from face to face with great, fascinated eyes. His cocoa was mostly gone, and there was a smear of chocolate around his mouth, and he was the most Norman Rockwell thing Harper had ever seen. He showed Allie something he had written on his place mat. She borrowed his pencil to reply. Nick nodded, then bent, wrote something more, and pushed it across to Harper.

*I tried to warn Allie she couldn't trust him. He used to make his nastiest butt-smoke whenever he was around her. Deaf people can smell things most peeple can't, and I could smell the evil in it.*

Harper turned the place mat so Renée could read it. Renée looked at it and looked up at Harper and the two of them erupted into laughter. Harper quaked, surprised at the force of her own jollity; she felt unaccountably close to tears. Nick watched them with bewilderment.

She had a swallow from her mug to calm herself down, then felt a bubble of hilarity rising in her again, and almost coughed coffee up her nostrils. Renée pounded her on the back until her choking fit had passed.

Don read what Nick had written and one corner of his mouth lifted in a wry smile. "Funny, that. I never smelt evil on him. But I smelt somethin' *else* on him, once . . . and in a way, that was the first domino in the chain that led to him gettin' kilt. Harold took a job workin' under my direction, diggin' up bloodworms for bait. It was funny, him volunteerin' for a physical job. Kinda like the queen offerin' to scrub out toilets. No one else wanted him, though, so I took him on my crew. He tolt me he knew a spot south of camp, a marshy flat where the bloodworms were easy to find. He knowed what he was talking about, too. Lots of days he'd come back with more bait than any of the other boys I sent out diggin'. But then other days he'd show up with maybe two worms in his bucket and just shrug and say his luck was bad. Well, I figured on those days he was goin' off to nap somewheres, and didn't worry myself too much about it. Till one day, middle a August, he shows up with nothin', and as he's puttin' down his empty pail, he lets a burp slip, and goddamn if I don't smell pizza on his fackin' breath. That didn't sit easy with me. You may have noticed, pizza ain't on the menu here in Camp Wyndham. I slept an uneasy sleep, and the next day, I decided I had to pass a word along to Ben Patchett. Ben wasn't no more happy about it than I was. He got real stiff and pale and sat rubbin' his mouth awhile, and finally said he was glad I spoke up. Then he asked me if I'd mind making Michael a part of my bait team for a week. I knew what Mikey was goin' to be diggin' for, and it wasn't worms, but we had to find out what Cross was up to, so I said ayuh. Well, Mikey took to trailin' him at a distance.

The first few days, the worst thing he seen Harold do was take a dump and use the pages from one of the camp library books for toilet paper."

Renée winced. "It turned out to be *The Heart Is a Lonely Hunter*. Our only copy. If I had known what he was going to do with it, I would've given him a copy of *Atlas Shrugged*."

"On the fourth day, though, our boy Mike followed Harold to an abandoned summer cottage a half mile away, place with a generator and Internet. The boy is in there on a laptop, typin' e-mails with one hand and crammin' down a pepperoni Hot Pocket with the other. Not only was Harold right back to the same tricks, spillin' our secrets to the same people, but he had a whole deep freezer full a chow he was keepin' to his own self."

Don passed the job of telling the story to Allie with a sidelong look. She nodded and went on, "I was there when Mike showed up. This was over at the House of the Black Star, where my aunt lives with Granddad. This wasn't so long after my mom passed away." Allie spoke quietly, neither hiding her pain nor making a display of it. "Aunt Carol had some of Mom's things and she asked me to look through them and see if there was anything I wanted for Nick and myself. There wasn't anything, really, except this." She touched a finger to the book-shaped gold locket at her throat. "When Mike came in and said what he had seen, we stopped what we were doing, and Granddad sent me to find Mr. Patchett. By the time I got back with Ben, Aunt Carol was sitting in a chair with her face in her hands and she had gray threads of smoke coming off her. She was *so* stressed.

"She said we needed to force Harold out of camp. But Mr. Patchett said that would be the worst thing we could do. If we sent Harold away and he got picked up by a Quarantine Patrol, they'd make him tell everything he knew about us. Mr. Patchett wanted to lock Harold up somewhere, but Granddad said it would be enough to make Harold promise to remain on camp grounds and stop contacting outsiders. Carol and Mr. Patchett gave each other this look, like: Which of us is going to tell him that's the most senile thing he's ever said? But the thing about my granddad is . . . it's kind of hard to convince him people won't just do the right thing. You hate to say anything that sounds hostile or untrusting or small-hearted around him. You feel like he'd be disappointed in you. Mr. Patchett gave in. He got Granddad to agree to keep Harold under close watch and that was it."

Allie put her elbows on the table and rested her chin in the cradle of her hands. She wasn't looking at any of them now, had lowered her gaze to stare disconsolately inward. Harper felt they had just about come to it, now. The end of Harold Cross's story . . . which also happened to be the end of Harold Cross.

At last she went on, "After Mr. Patchett confronted Harold about what he had been up to, Harold came down with stomach pains and took himself to the infirmary. Mr. Patchett made sure there was always a Lookout stationed there, day and night, to guarantee Harold didn't wander off. If they weren't stationed right in the ward with him, they were in the waiting room. When it happened, it was on *my* shift, during the day, when the whole camp was asleep. At some point near the end of my watch, around dusk, I had to pee, and the only way to get to the bathroom is to walk across the ward. I crept through on tiptoe, real careful, trying not to wake Harold up. He was in one of the partitioned-off sleeping areas. I could just see him under his sheets, through a crack between the hanging curtains. I had almost made it to the bathroom when my hip bumped a bedpan and it fell with a loud bang. Harold didn't even roll over. Suddenly I got a cold sick feeling and I pulled aside the curtain to have a closer look at him. It was just pillows under the sheets." She looked up and met Harper's eyes, and her gaze was wounded and ashamed. "See . . . I was asleep most of the afternoon, while I was supposed to be on guard in the waiting room. I told myself it wasn't hurting anyone. I figured if Harold tried to sneak out past me, I'd hear him. I thought I was too light a sleeper for him to get by me. Some light sleeper. I must've been in a low-grade coma. Maybe Norma Heald slipped a roofie into my tea, hoping to get lucky with me." The corner of her mouth tweaked up in a little smile, but her chin trembled.

Don put a leathery hand on the back of her neck and gave her a gentle, awkward sort of pat. "You ever think if you woke up when he was trying to sneak out, he might a belted you one? He was goin' out that door, one way or t'other."

"Harold couldn't fight his way past Nick," Allie said, brushing roughly at her eyes with the back of one hand.

"Who says he would a fought? He might a called you into the ward and then socked you with a wrench. No, ma'am. He was goin' to depart our company, by hook or by crook. It was mad to think we could hold him prisoner without lockin' him up. I'd fistfight sharks for your grandpap, but he was wrong about how t'handle Harold, and Ben Patchett was right."

Nick had noticed Allie rubbing at her eyes. He scribbled something on the place mat. Allie read it and shook her head.

"No, I don't want your last marshmallow."

He wrote something else, then stuck a spoon in his mug and dredged out part of a melted marshmallow. Allie sighed and opened her mouth and let him feed her.

"He says it's medicine for misery," Allie told them in a muffled sort of way, chewing gummy marshmallow. A bright tear skipped down one cheek. "It does make me feel better, actually."

Don Lewiston leaned in, elbows on the table. "I can tell the rest, I s'pose, quick enough. Allie got Mike, and Mikey ran for Ben Patchett. My cot is next to Ben's, and all their whisperin' woke me up. When I heard they were all settin' out to see if they could bring Harold back, I offered to go with 'em. Maybe I felt like I *had* to go. Harold had been part of my crew. My lack of supervision is what gave him the chance to get back in contact with the outside world. I don't remember who went and got a rifle from the range, but I think it was on all our minds Harold might not come back of his own free will. I remember this one"—he patted Allie's shoulder—"was tolt to stay here. As you might guess, that did about as much good as shoutin' at clouds. We covered probably three miles of hard trail in twenty minutes, makin' a beeline for Harold's little hideout, and Allie was out in front the whole way. And it was still a damn'd close thing. When we got there, it was pretty much the worst-case scenario. Maybe some a the people Harold had been e-mailing with were who they said they were. Maybe *most* of 'em were. But one of 'em wasn't. When we got to the cabin, there was a van parked out front and men with guns. Not a state-run Quarantine Patrol. Cremation fellas. We saw the whole thing from behind this old stone wall that was out behind the cabin. They had Bushmaster rifles and were thumpin' Harold with the butts. Shovin' him around. Havin' fun. Harold was down in the dirt, clutchin' his laptop, and beggin' them not to kill him. He was sayin' he wasn't dangerous, that he could control his infection. He was tellin' em he could lead 'em to a hidin' place where there were lots of people who could control the Dragonscale. That was when Ben asked Mikey if the rifle was loaded."

"I thought we were going to fight for Harold," Allie said. "Like on a TV show. Four of us against twelve of them. Pretty stupid, huh?" Her voice was rough and strained, and Harper was conscious of Allie trying to hold back her tears.

"Mikey's hands were shaking so hard he spilled bullets all over the ground, but Ben—he turned into a different man altogether. He was a cop in his former life, you know. You could see the cop in his face. He went calm, but he also went *hard*. He said, 'You better let me do this, son,' and took the rifle out of Mikey's hands. He put the first one in Harold's throat. He put the second in the laptop. The Cremation Crew hit the dirt and for all I know they're lying there still, because we got up and ran like hell and never looked back." His coffee was gone. He rolled his mug between his palms. "Ben Patchett looked icy enough out in the woods, but when he got back, he cried his eyes out. Sat on one of the pews with Father Storey holdin' him like a child. Father Storey shushed him and told him if it was anyone's fault it was his own, not Ben's."

Nick was frowning, writing on the place mat again. He

pushed it to Allie, who read it, then turned it toward Renée and Harper so they could read it.

*Mr. Patchett shouldn't have sent someone to get a rifle. He should've sent someone to get JOHN. He could've saved Harold.*

"Maybe so," Don said, who was reading the place mat upside down. "We were in a helluva rush, though. And it was a good thing we moved fast, as it turned out. If we were even two minutes slower, Harold might've coughed it all up. Then instead of one dead kid, we'd have a camp full dead kids, and dead grown-ups, too." He set his mug down on the table with a glassy clink. People were up on their feet, filling the room with a lot of loud, happy conversation. It was time for chapel. Harper felt the familiar bunched knot of dread tightening in her stomach. Another song was coming, another harmony she wouldn't be able to join, another overwhelming blast of noise and light.

"I guess that's all of it," Renée said. "The sad ballad of Harold Cross."

Harper didn't want to go, and so when she spoke, it was more to stall for time than anything else. "Maybe not quite all. There is one thing I'm wondering about. What was in his notebook? Did anyone ever find out?"

"I've wondered that myself," Don said, getting to his feet. "It never turned up. Maybe he had it on him when he was kilt. If so, it didn't reveal the location of camp, or this whole place would be burnt to the ground by now." He clucked his tongue, shook his head. "I don't expect we'll ever know. Some mysteries ain't ever gonna be solved."

## DECEMBER

# 10

Two sisters, Gail and Gillian Neighbors, were having a spat.

They shared a single bottle of red nail polish, which had gone missing, and each accused the other of losing it or maybe hoarding it. They were twins and barbaric with each other by nature. Gillian already had a twisted nipple, and when Harper separated them, Gail was clutching a dirty sock to a bloody nose. Gillian had jammed her thumb at least an inch up one nostril.

Harper patrolled the dorm, asking around. It felt good to think about someone else's problems. Better than worrying about lights-out, when she would lie in her cot, desperate to sleep and sick at the thought of what might happen when she did.

She figured Allie would know who, if anyone, might've helped themselves to the nail polish (the shade was called "Incendiary," which the Neighbors twins didn't seem to realize was funny). Allie and another girl were playing rummy on a stack of suitcases. Harper wandered over and stood behind this other girl, Jamie Close, and waited to be noticed.

"I'm glad *I'm* not sleeping next to her," Jamie Close was saying to Allie.

Jamie was one of the older Lookouts, nineteen going on twenty. She had close-set eyes and an upturned nose, which conspired together to give her an unfortunate swinish mien.

"Sleeping next to who?" Allie asked absentmindedly over her cards.

"You know: Nurse Sunshine." Jamie went on, "She woke up coughing smoke last night. Did you hear her? I'm, like, *burn* already, so some of us can sleep. I'm, like—"

Allie stepped on Jamie's foot, hard. A child might've imagined it was an accident; a very small, very naive child. Jamie stiffened and went silent.

After a moment, Allie's gaze drifted up and she appeared to see Harper for the first time. "Hey! What's going on, Nurse Willowes?"

"The Neighbors twins lost a bottle of nail polish. Just asking around to see if either of you might have seen it."

Jamie Close sat rigidly on an upturned bucket. Her T-shirt was hiked up to show the tramp stamp on the small of her back: a tattoo of the Confederate flag, above the word REBEL. She didn't have the nerve to look back at Harper. "Sorry, ma'am. I don't do nothin' with my nails but chew on 'em."

Allie looked like she wanted to say something—her eyes were apologetic and worried—but she just opened her mouth and closed it and shook her head.

Harper smiled effortfully, thanked them, and walked off. Her Dragonscale pulsed with a disagreeable warmth, in a way that made her think of someone breathing on coals.

# 11

She dreamt she wore a gown of wasps and woke when they began to sting.

The basement was stuffy and dim in the late morning and she lay motionless, still feeling wasp-stung: on her collarbone, on the inside of her left thigh, between two of her toes.

Harper pressed her chin into her chest, looking down, and saw a red spot burning through her T-shirt above her left breast, as if someone were pressing the tip of a cigarette into the cotton . . . from the *inside*. A silky thread of white smoke trickled up from the growing burn. Harper watched, in a state of horrible lassitude, as the hole expanded, the edges a bright orange lacework. At last she rubbed it out with her thumb and brushed the sparks off her chest.

Her body throbbed from nearly a dozen of those wasp-sting burns. She flapped back her blanket, to see if her clothes were burning anywhere else, and a gush of black smoke drifted toward the ceiling. She was reminded of her childhood fascination with smoke signals. What would this message translate to? Probably: *Help, I am going to be burned alive.*

*Enough,* she thought.

She sat up, very carefully, iron bedsprings creaking. She did not want to wake anyone, did not want to cause any trouble. In those first moments, she was not clear about what she meant to do, only that she didn't want to have to talk to anyone about it. That *enough* indicated some kind of decision, but it was not immediately clear to her what she had decided.

In the next bed, Renée slept on her side, deep in her own dreams, smiling at some imagined event. Harper half had an urge to lean over and kiss her forehead, to have one final moment of physical contact. *Final moment?* Harper found she couldn't look at Renée for long. *Enough* represented some kind of betrayal of their friendship. *Enough* was going to hurt Renée, would leave her—what? *Bereft* was the word that came to mind. *Bereft* and *enough* went together like bride and groom.

Harper considered packing *The Portable Mother* and her clothes into her carpetbag, but *enough* was a destination that required no baggage. *Enough* was a reverberation deep inside her, a kind of ringing emptiness, as if she were a steeple in which a bell had been solemnly struck. Ask not for whom it tolls.

She rose and paced across the cool, dusty concrete. Harper paused at the bottom of the steps for a look back at the maze of cots, a labyrinth of sleeping women. In that moment she loved them all, even awful Jamie Close with her ugly mouth and upturned nose. Harper had always wanted a tough friend like Jamie, someone rude and mouthy, who would cut a bitch for talking smack. She loved Renée and the Neighbors girls and little Emily Waterman and Allie and Nick. Nick most of all, with his bottle-glass-green eyes and articulate hands, which drew words on the air like a boy wizard sketching spells.

She climbed three steps to the door, eased the latch up with a click, and slipped out. She blinked at the watery sunlight. She hadn't seen any in a while and it hurt her eyes.

The sky was high and pale, like the dingy canvas roof of a circus tent. She went up more steps, trailing wisps of smoke behind her. The 'scale had burned holes in her sweats, holes all through her *Rent* T-shirt. She had seen *Rent* with Jakob and he had held her hand while she wept at the end. She was surprised to find herself longing for Jakob now, for the wiry strength of his arms when he held her around the waist. It didn't seem to matter that the last time she had seen him he had been waving a gun at her.

She supposed Jakob had been right. It would've been much easier to do things his way. He had known how awful it would be to burn to death. He had only wanted to spare her. For that she had carved open his face with a broken glass and wasted their special bottle of wine.

Harper had told herself she was staying alive for the baby, but the baby never had anything to do with it, not really. She was holding on because she could not bear to say good-bye to her life and every good thing in it. She had selfishly wanted more. She had wanted to hold her father again and smell his Eight & Bob cologne, which always made her think of sea-soaked rope. She had wanted to sit by a swimming pool somewhere, with the sun glowing on her mostly bare skin, drifting half awake while her mother gabbed on and on about all the funny things Stephen Colbert had said on TV the night before. She had wanted to read her favorite books again and revisit her best friends one more time: Harry and Ron, Bilbo and Gandalf, Hazel and Bigwig, Mary and Bert. She had wanted another good hard lonely cry and another pee-your-pants laughing fit. She had wanted a whole bunch more sex, although, looking back, most of her sexual history involved sleeping with men she didn't much like.

She had told herself she was going on with her life because she wanted her son (she was curiously certain it was a boy, had been almost since the beginning) to experience some of those good things, too; so he could meet her parents, read some good books, have a girl. But in reality, her son was never going to do any of those things. He was going to die before he was even born. He was going to roast in her womb. She had lived on only to murder him. She wanted to apologize to the baby for ever conceiving him. She felt like she had already failed to keep the only promise she had ever made him.

When Harper reached the top of the steps, she realized she had forgotten her shoes. But it didn't matter. The thin crust of the first snow had melted away, except for a few lumps under the pines. The wind lashed the high tangles of dead grass and ruffled the sea into sharp-edged wavelets.

Harper wasn't sure she could bear the wind off the water for long, not in her thin, raggedy things, but for a few moments, anyway, she thought she could use a blast of sea air. She wasn't supposed to be out in the daytime—Ben Patchett would be upset if he knew—but Camp Wyndham was sere and cold and empty, and no one was around to see.

Harper set out for the shoreline, tramping across damp, rotten grass. She paused once, to inspect a white rock the size of a baby's skull, streaked with black, mica-flecked seams in a way that made her think of Dragonscale. With some effort, she was able to force the large stone into one pocket of her sweats.

She made her way through a band of evergreens, past the boathouse, collecting a few more interesting-looking rocks as she descended to the waterfront.

Harper crooned to herself disconsolately, chanting the words to a song she had overheard some of the smaller kids shouting at each other. She wondered if they even knew the tune it was parodying, "Hey Jude." Probably not.

*'ey* ***yooooou,***
*don't start to* ***cry***
*if you* ***fry*** *now*
*it will be* ***shiiiiity,***
*A* ***pity!***
*If you turn into a* ***heap!***
*Cos it's my turn to* ***sweep!***
*And take out the ashes.*

She smiled without any pleasure at all.

She had wanted to believe in Aunt Carol's miracle, had wanted so badly to believe she could sing her way out of trouble. It worked for all the others, kept them safe and filled them with contentment, and it should have worked for her, too, but it didn't, and she couldn't help it: she resented them for doing what she couldn't. She resented them for pitying her.

Out here, alone in the bitterly cold clear light of the morning, she could admit to herself that she found them repugnant when they all lit up in church. To stand among them when their eyes shone and their Dragonscale pulsed was almost as awful as being fondled in a crowd by a strange hand. Of all the things she wanted over, she wanted an end to morning chapel, to the sound and the fury, the song and the light.

Harper padded to the splintery expanse of the dock. Here at the open ocean, the salty air came at her in battering, cleansing strokes. The boards, worn soft by a decade of spray and damp, felt good under her feet. She walked to the end and sat down. The stones in her pockets clunked on the pine.

Harper stared out at the Fireman's island, her toes trailing over the water. She dipped a big toe in and gasped, the water so cold it made the knuckles in her feet throb with pain.

Someone had left a length of fraying green twine wrapped around one of the posts. She began, almost idly, to unwind it. She felt it was important not to think too closely about what she was out on the dock to do. If she looked at it straight on, she might lose her nerve.

On some half-conscious level, though, she knew the cold of the ocean would be almost as unbearable as the wasp-sting sensation of the Dragonscale going hot, and instinct would drive her back to the shore. But if she tied her wrists, she wouldn't be able to swim, and the cold would ease from pain to dullness soon enough. She thought she would open her eyes while she was underwater. She had always liked the blurred darkness of the aquatic world.

The overcast haze thinned to the east and she could see a streak of pale blue. She felt as clear and open as that blue sky. She felt all right. She began to loop the twine around her wrists.

The breeze carried a distant cry.

She hesitated and cocked her head to listen.

At one end of the little island was the ruin of a single-room cottage. Only two walls still stood. The other two had collapsed along with the roof. Charred beams crisscrossed within.

A second, smaller building, some kind of windowless shed—painted green with a white door—had been built on the crescent of sand that faced Camp Wyndham. It had a turf roof, and a dune had blown into a high drift against the far wall, so it half resembled a hobbit hole burrowed into the side of a hill. A tin chimney pipe vented a trickle of smoke all day and all night, but as far as Harper knew it had never drawn any attention from the outside world. You could not scan the shoreline without seeing a dozen little coils of smoke just like it.

Now, though, the chimney carried the echo of a strained, small, faraway voice.

*"No! No, you won't! You can't!"* the Fireman shouted. *"You don't get to give up!"*

Her heart sprang like a trap. For one alarming moment, she was sure he was speaking to her.

But of course he couldn't see her from inside his shed. He didn't have any idea she was there.

*"Haven't I done everything you wanted?"* he cried, the wind catching his voice and carrying it to her clearly by some perverse trick of acoustics. *"Haven't I done everything you asked? Don't you think I want to quit? But I'm still here. If I don't get to go, you don't."*

She felt she should run—she had no right to be hearing any of this—but couldn't move. The fury she heard in his voice ran through her like a pole, holding her in place.

A great iron clang crashed inside the shed. The door shook in its frame. She waited, helplessly, to see what would come next, hoping with all her heart he was not about to step outside and see her.

He didn't and there was no more. Smoke trickled peacefully from the chimney, thinning quickly as it rose into the general haze. The wind thrashed the wiry tufts of sea grass on the island.

Harper listened and waited and watched until she realized she was shivering from the cold. She dropped the twine she had been winding around her wrists. A gust snatched it, floated it into the air, flipped it into the sea. Harper drew her knees to her chest, hugging them for warmth. The stone like a baby's skull was digging painfully into her hip, so she worked it out of her pocket and set it on the edge of the dock.

Too close to the edge. The stone toppled over the side. *Bloosh,* went the sea, as it swallowed the rock.

It was such an agreeable sound, Harper dropped in all the other stones she had collected, one by one, just to hear that sound again and again.

Norma Heald said there were ghosts out there, ghosts made of smoke. Maybe John had been yelling at one of them. Maybe he was yelling at shadows. Or at himself.

Ghosts carried messages from beyond, but they didn't seem like they would be terribly good listeners. John sounded so wretched and hurt, Harper thought *someone* ought to listen to him. If the ghosts wouldn't, she would.

Besides, Jakob had always thought he knew what was better for her than she did, and if she killed herself, it would be admitting he was right. That alone was reason to persist—just to stick it to him. Now that she was more awake, she was feeling less forgiving about the gun.

No one heard Harper letting herself back into the basement of the chapel. Her blankets smelled like a campfire, but they were so cozy she was asleep in minutes . . . and this time there were no dreams.

# 12

On the night of the first lottery to see who would eat and who wouldn't, Harper pulled kitchen duty. Norma planted Harper just beyond the serving window, behind a folding table set with thermoses and mugs and a big rectangular tin of sugar.

"You can sweeten the coffee for the losers. One spoonful each, no more. And let 'em see that belly of yours, remind 'em what they're skippin' lunch for: your precious little miracle," Norma said.

This did not make Harper feel better. It made Harper feel fat, entitled, and lonesome. Of course she wasn't fat, not really. Yes, all right, she could no longer button the top of her jeans, a fact she hid by wearing loose hoodies. But it wasn't like the furniture shook when she crossed the room.

Lunch was watery porridge with a side of peaches, dished out from yet another can. It fell to Nelson Heinrich to dispense the lottery tickets, and he turned up to do the job wearing one of his Christmas sweaters: dark green with gingerbread men dancing across it. He wore a Santa cap, too, an obscene touch in Harper's opinion; as if he were handing out candy canes and not taking away meals.

The tickets were piled in a woman's brown leather purse. The losing tickets had black X's marked on them. Harper thought that purse was some kind of karmic opposite to the Sorting Hat. Instead of being sent to Slytherin or Gryffindor, you were sent off to go hungry with a cup of sweet coffee. You wouldn't even be allowed to stay in the cafeteria with the others.

*I don't think that would be a good idea,* Ben Patchett had explained. *If we let the losers stay, folks will take pity and start sharing. Normally I'm all for share and share alike, but in this case, it would defeat the whole purpose of the lottery. There's so little to split, if people begin dividing their portions, it'll be like no one's getting fed at all.*

Then he said there would only be twenty-nine losing tickets in the purse. He had decided to take the thirtieth, to show he wasn't asking anyone to do anything he wasn't ready to do himself.

At 2:00 A.M.—their normal lunchtime—Norma slid back the bolt on the cafeteria doors and stood aside as people began to push in, snow dusting their caps and shoulders. It was coming down again, in a fast, light, powdery flurry.

Don Lewiston was at the head of the line and he made his way up to Nelson Heinrich. Nelson blinked at him in surprise. "Don, you're sixty-three! You don't need to draw a ticket! I didn't and I'm only sixty! Go on and get your peaches. I already had mine. Gosh, they were yummy!"

"I'll draw a ticket, same as any t'others here, thank you, Nelson. I've never been a big eater anyway and would almost rather a cup of coffee with some sugar."

Before Don could stick his hand in the purse, Allie slipped up alongside him and grabbed his wrist.

"Mr. Lewiston, I'm sorry, if you could just wait a minute. We've got a mess of Lookouts who have been out in the cold all night, sweeping off the boards between houses. Father Storey said it would be all right if they drew first," Allie said.

She looked away from Don, down along the line, and gestured with her head. Teenagers began to shuffle toward the front.

Someone shouted: "Hey, what's with the cutting in line? Everyone here is hoping to get some lunch."

Allie ignored him. So did Michael, and the kids coming along behind him. Michael eased around Don Lewiston with a nod, reached into the purse—and came up with a white stone, the size of a robin's egg.

"Huh," he said. "Look at that. I think I drew a loser!"

He popped the stone in his mouth and walked past the line

of serving windows, on to the coffee bar. There he silently poured a cup of coffee for himself and held out his ceramic mug so Harper could dump in his sugar.

Nelson Heinrich stared after him, mouth lolling open in a rather witless way. He looked down into the purse, trying to figure out where the stone had come from.

Allie began to whistle a jaunty little tune.

Gillian Neighbors drew next. Another stone.

"Just my luck!" she said happily, and plopped the stone in her mouth. She walked on to Harper, poured a coffee, and waited for her sugar.

Behind her, her sister, Gail, was reaching into the purse, and this time Harper could see she already had the stone in her palm, even before she began to dig around among the tickets.

Harper wanted to laugh. She wanted to clap. She felt like a girl filled with helium, so light she might've come free from the floor and bumped up against the ceiling like a balloon. She ached with happiness—a fierce, bright happiness of a sort she had not felt in all the time she had been sick with Dragonscale.

She wanted to start grabbing the kids, the Lookouts, Allie's friends, and squeezing them. And not only because of what they were doing: forgoing the lottery and simply volunteering to do without, taking it upon themselves to skip lunch so others could eat. It was just as much what Allie was *whistling,* a song Harper recognized from the first three bars: a melody so sweet she felt it might break her in two, just as a glass can be shattered by certain musical tones.

Allie was whistling "A Spoonful of Sugar," the very best song from the very best movie ever.

Gail Neighbors drew the white stone, made a clucking sound, and walked on to get her coffee. All of the kids were doing it: Allie's kids. All the teenage girls who had shaved their heads to look like her and all the teenage boys who had signed up for Lookout duty just to be around her.

Don Lewiston pushed back his Greek fisherman's cap and scratched his forehead with his thumb and began to whistle himself. He nodded as each Lookout walked past to collect a stone and skip lunch.

Father Storey was whistling, too. Harper had not seen him enter, but there he was, standing to one side of the door, smiling enormously, but blinking at tears. Aunt Carol stood beside him, her head resting on his shoulder, whistling with the rest of them, and her eyes were gold coins. Almost a dozen people were whistling the song now, the melody as lovely as the first warm perfumed breath of spring, and their eyes shone like lamps. Burning gently on the inside. Burning with song, with the Bright.

Gail Neighbors held out her mug for sugar. As Harper dumped it in, she began to sing.

*"Just a spoonful of sugar,"* Harper sang, her voice thick with emotion, *"makes the medicine go down, makes the medicine go dow-own . . ."*

She sang and for a moment forgot all about being pregnant, being fat, being lonely, being covered in some kind of flammable spore that was ready to ignite. She sang and forgot Jakob's awful book and Jakob's awful gun. She forgot the world was on fire.

A spoke of heat flashed up from the base of her spine and spread over the ribbons of Dragonscale on her skin, in a sweet, shiver-inducing rush. She swayed on her heels without being aware of it. The world possessed a new, liquid quality. She was conscious of a tidal rocking in her blood, as if she were afloat in a pool of warmth and light, as if she were an embryo herself, not the carrier of one.

The next time she poured sugar, the glittering grains seemed to fall in slow motion: a cascade of riches. Brightness cascaded along the Dragonscale around her wrists and throat, a silvery-white trill. She was a kite, filled and rising with song instead of wind. She was as warm as a kite in the sun, too, her skin blazing—not painfully, but with a flush of pleasure. Her hand wore a glove of light.

The Lookouts came and nodded to her and took their coffee or tea and went on and they all shone; they were all lit up like ghosts. She was glad for each of them, in love with each of them, although she could not remember who any of them were. She could not remember anything that had come before the song. She could not think of anything that mattered more than the melody. She did not believe that any spoonful of sugar, no matter how sweet, could be as fine as the melting sweetness running through her then.

Father Storey was the last to come up for coffee. He had drawn a stone himself, of course. He hadn't put it in his mouth yet, was just holding it.

"There is Miss Willowes!" he cried. "Happy at last. Happy and looking well!"

"Miss . . . Willowes?" she asked, her voice as slow and dreamy as sugar spilling from a spoon. "Who's Miss Willowes?"

"It'll come back to you," he promised.

# 13

It did, too. Her name returned to her just before dawn, came back to her almost as soon as she stopped trying to remember it. Her subconscious coughed it up without any warning, in much the way it would sometimes supply her with the answer to a question in a crossword that had been stumping her.

She did not wake coughing smoke again. There were no more hot flashes burning up her T-shirts in the night. At the next chapel, Carol sat at the pipe organ to play "Spirit in the Sky," and the congregation rose to sing. They roared and stamped like drunk sailors in a Melville story, full of grog and scaring the seagulls with their sea chanteys, and Harper bellowed with them, bellowed till her throat ached.

And they shone, all of them together, Harper, too. Her eyes blazed like lamps, her skin hummed with warmth and pleasure, her thoughts soared away from her like a kestrel rising on a hot summer updraft, and for a few weeks everything was almost all right.

# BOOK THREE

# SPEAK OF THE DEVIL

# JANUARY

## 1

She woke on the second day of January, not from a nightmare, but to a sensation of something shifting inside her, pushing out against the muscles of her abdomen.

Harper lay awake in the darkness, eyes open wide, her hands spread across the taut gourd of her stomach.

A bony protrusion, about the size of a thumb knuckle, pressed up from within, rising against her right palm.

"Hey, you," she whispered.

# 2

The night the locket went missing, Renée and Harper were listening to the Marlboro Man on a battery-powered radio.

"I don't understand how you can stand that man." Norma Heald was passing by their cots and had paused to hear what they had on. "Every word is a drop of poison in your ears."

Renée said, "He's the closest thing to local news left."

"More importantly," Harper told her, "we're awful women and his awfulness excites us. The more awful, the better."

"Yes," Renée said. "That, too."

Harper was planting kisses on squares of parchment paper, trying out various shades of lipstick. After a kiss, she would wipe her mouth clean and try another. Renée had collected different lipsticks from everyone in the basement.

When Harper made a pleasant lipstick print, she would hand it off to Renée, who would roll it around a cinnamon stick, or a fragrant piece of shriveled lemon peel, and tuck it into a little glass bottle and cork it up. These were emergency kisses. Harper was stocking the Portable Mother with them so that when her son needed a kiss, he would have plenty to choose from. The Portable Mother was no longer a book, but a package, a whole collection of potentially useful items, which had swelled to occupy Harper's entire carpetbag.

Nick was underfoot, playing Yahtzee against himself. Dice rattled and crashed inside the plastic cup. The basement was crowded, loud with conversation, argument, laughter, creaking bedsprings, everyone trapped in close quarters while it snowed heavily outside.

On the radio, the Marlboro Man said, "You think a girl with Dragonscale can blow smoke rings with her vajayjay? Friend,

I always wondered about that myself. Well, this weekend the Marlboro Man was on the loose in Portsmouth with the Seacoast Incinerators and had a chance to find out. I'll tell you all about it in a minute, but first, here's a story from Concord. Governor Ian Judd-Skiller said members of the National Guard were only defending themselves when they shot and killed eleven burners yesterday on the Canadian border. The mob charged the barricade with sticks—not white flags, as has been reported elsewhere—and the besieged soldiers opened fire to disperse . . ."

"He's a murderer," Norma said and sniffed. "That DJ you're listening to. He's killed people like us. And he *boasts* about it. Hemlock in your ears—that's what he is."

"Yes," Renée said. "He's very stupid, you know. That's another reason to listen. The more we know about *him,* the less likely he'll ever know anything about *us*. People call in with tips and this bozo airs them live. If anyone ever mentions Camp Wyndham or points him in our direction, we'll have a head start. And even if they don't call in, I've learned all kinds of things about the Cremation Crew he runs with, just by paying attention to his program. I've learned it's made up of eight men and women, and that two are former military and were able to supply some heavy ordnance. A fifty-caliber something? I gather that's a pretty big gun. I know they travel in two vehicles, a van and a big orange truck. I know they have a police scanner, and most of the time, local law enforcement is happy to—"

"Orange truck?" Harper asked. "You mean like a town truck?"

Across the room, Allie screamed, "*No, NO*!" and flipped her cot with an echoing bang.

Every head turned—except for Nick's, of course, since he had heard nothing.

Allie kicked over a battered suitcase, dumping filthy laundry on the floor.

"Fuck!" she screamed. "Fuck! Fuck *fuck* fuck *fuck* FUCK!"

Conversations petered out. Emily Waterman, barely eleven, a girl who had outlived her entire family and who had pretty feathers of Dragonscale on the backs of her freckled arms, climbed under her cot and covered her ears.

Renée was the first to move, her round, pleasant face remaining entirely calm. Harper was two steps behind her.

Renée slowed as she approached Allie, moving toward her in much the same way she might've attempted to get near a feral cat. Harper sank to her knees to look under Emily Waterman's bed.

"Emily? Everything is okay," Harper said, reaching out for her. In a whisper, she added, "Allie is being a fusspot."

But Emily shook her head and shrank from Harper's hand. Harper wished she had her *Mary Poppins* lunch box, with its individually wrapped candies and emergency radish.

"Allie," Renée said. "What's wrong?"

"It's gone, it's *fucking* gone—"

"What's gone? What did you lose?"

"I didn't *lose* anything. My locket was under my pillow and now it isn't because one of you *bitches* took it." She glared around the basement.

Emily made a thin squeal of terror and turned her face from Harper's outstretched hand. Harper considered trying to pull her out for a hug, decided that might be too alarming, and settled for reaching under to stroke her back.

Renée said, "Allie, I know you're upset, but you need to lower your voice—"

"I don't need to do shit."

"—because you're frightening the little ones. Why don't you ask Nick—"

"I asked him, don't you think I *asked* him when I started *looking* for it, fifteen minutes ago?"

A tendril of pale smoke trickled from under one pant leg of Emily Waterman's baggy overalls.

"Allie!" Harper said. "Stop it. You're giving Emily the smokes!"

"Please, Allie," Renée said, putting a hand on Allie's shoulder. "We've all been under so much pressure, you wouldn't be human if you didn't sometimes want to scream. But if you'll sit down with me—"

"Will you stop *touching* me?" Allie cried. She shrugged off Renée's hand. "You don't know anything about me. You aren't my mother. My mother *burned* to death. You are *no* one to me. You are not my mother and you are not my friend. You're a *pain* vulture who circles around and around, looking for someone to feed off. That's why you spend all your free time reading to the kids. You love their wounded little hearts. You feed off their loneliness just like a vampire. You love kids with no parents, because they *need* someone. It's easy to read them a story to make yourself feel special. But you aren't special. Stop feeding off us all."

A stunned silence fell upon the basement.

Harper wanted to say something but had lost the trick of speech. She was not sure if she had been silenced by her horror—she had never imagined Allie, who was so daring, so clever, so beautiful, and so funny, could be so cruel—or by a crippling wave of déjà vu. For when Allie insisted altruism was really selfishness, and kindness a form of manipulation, she sounded just like Jakob. She had all his savage powers of logic. It made a person feel naive and childish for imagining there could be any good in the world at all.

For herself, Renée had lifted an arm to protect her face, as if she expected to be struck. She studied Allie with a mute, wounded fascination.

The room was still waiting for her to reply—to defend herself—when Nick charged across the basement, inserting himself between Allie and Renée. He held up his Yahtzee scorecard, turned over to the back, where he had written:

*TWO YAHTZEES IN A ROW*!!

Allie stared at this message with blank incomprehension. Then she took the sheet of paper from his hands, balled it up, and threw it in his face. It bounced off his forehead and onto the floor.

Nick staggered backward, as if he had been shoved. His shoulder thumped into Renée's breast. Harper did not think she had ever seen so much naked hurt in a face before.

He ran. Before anyone could catch him, he flew to the stairs. He hesitated at the bottom of the steps for one last look at his older sister, and for a moment he fixed her with a glare of contempt as fierce as anything Allie herself could produce. Like their elfin good looks, a gift for hate was, perhaps, something that ran in the family.

Harper called his name, called for him to wait. But of course Nick didn't—*couldn't*—hear her. Harper rose to go after him, but he had already dashed up the stairs, banged through the door at the top, and launched himself into the falling snow.

She turned a frustrated look upon Allie.

"What? *What?* You got something to say, Nurse Nobody?" Allie asked her.

"Yes," Harper said, summoning up all the Julie Andrews she had in her heart. "A *bad* show, Allie. A very bad show. He also lost his mother, you know, and you are *all* he has left. For shame. After he threw two Yahtzees!"

Allie's response to this shocked Harper more than anything else. Her face crumpled and she began to sob. She sat down hard, with her back against the springs of her overturned bed.

At this sudden display of defeat, the Neighbors twins, Jamie Close, and all the other members of Allie's unofficial, unnamed sorority—that society of orphan girls with shaved heads—flocked to her side. Even Emily Waterman scuttled out from under her cot and ran over to throw her arms around Allie's neck. Girls took her hands and sat beside her, whispering soothingly and fussing over her. Gail Neighbors began to quietly pick up her things. One entering the room would've imagined Allie was the person who had just been bullied and humiliated, not Renée or Nick.

Harper returned to her cot, which was at a right angle to Renée's. Renée was already sitting on the edge of her mattress by then, looking as worn and disheartened as Harper felt.

"Should one of us go after Nick?" Renée asked.

"I don't think so. He won't go far in this snow. The Lookouts will yell if he so much as steps off the planks. One of them will bring him back eventually."

The Marlboro Man was still chattering, saying something about a woman who had smelled like a wet cat when she burned. He seemed offended that she had the bad grace to stink when she died. Talk radio was enough to make Harper think the end of the world wasn't so bad after all.

"I can't take anymore," Renée said, and Harper thought she was speaking of life in the camp, but she only meant the DJ. Renée reached out and, with an irritated flick, switched the radio to AM and began to skip through bands of static.

Harper said, "What are you doing? Why are people in this camp always listening to static? What are all of you listening *for*?"

"Martha Quinn," Renée said.

"Martha *Quinn*? Martha Quinn, who used to be on MTV a thousand years ago?"

"She's out there . . . somewhere."

"Lies," Norma Heald murmured. "All lies. That's a pipe dream."

Renée ignored her. "You know what the kids say."

"I have *no* idea what the kids say. What do they say?"

"She came back from the eighties to save mankind. Martha Quinn is our only hope."

# 3

"I've never heard the broadcast myself, but supposedly she's transmitting from off the coast of Maine." Renée struggled into a bulky orange parka.

It was later. Women milled around the bottom of the basement steps, picking coats and hats out of cardboard boxes, readying themselves for the three-hundred-foot march through the snow to the cafeteria and supper. Outside, the wind screamed.

"From a boat?"

"From an island. They've got a little town and their own research lab, backed by the federal government. What's left of the federal government, anyway. They're testing experimental treatments."

Jamie Close grinned, showing snaggled teeth, two incisors missing from the lower part of her mouth. "They've got a serum they give to you in eighteen shots. Like for rabies. It suppresses the Dragonscale, but they need to give it to you *every day*. Bend over, drop your pants, and bite on this stick, because you're getting it right in the ass. I say no thank you to that. If I wanted someone poking painful things in my ass every day, I've got an uncle I could look up."

Harper had a scarf over her mouth, wound around and around the lower part of her face, and she felt this gave her permission not to reply. She squeezed into the crowd of women making their way up the steps, out into the darkness and the shrieking gale.

"It's not as bad as that," murmured Gail Neighbors. At least Harper thought it was Gail Neighbors. It would've been difficult to tell the twins apart under any circumstances, but with a hat pulled to the girl's eyebrows and the puffy collar of her parka up around her ears, Harper could hardly see any of her face. "Apparently they're doing great things with medical marijuana. Everyone gets an allowance, seven joints a week. Government-bred weed, so it's really clean, really mellow."

"Also, the legal drinking age there is sixteen," said the one Harper thought was Gillian. They had both turned sixteen, Harper recalled, just after Thanksgiving.

The pressure of the crowd behind Harper ejected her out of the stairwell and into the night. A pair of planks ran alongside each other, across the snow, dwindling off into the darkness. The salty gale battered at Harper, caused her to stagger. She wasn't as steady on her pins as she had been a couple months ago. Her center of gravity was shifting. She steadied herself against a boulder wearing a white cap of snow.

The Neighbors girls passed her, went on ahead. Emily Waterman skipped along behind them, and Harper heard her saying, "They have ice cream on Fridays! Homemade ice cream! Three flavors, strawberry, vanilla, and I think coffee. Coffee is my favorite."

"Ice cream every day!" promised one of the Neighbors girls.

"Ice cream for breakfast!" said the other, and then they were gone into the night.

Allie took Harper's elbow, helped her to stand straight.

"Think Nick went to the cafeteria?" Allie asked in a low, dispirited voice. He hadn't returned to the dorm, hadn't been seen since running out.

"I don't know," Harper said. "Probably."

"Think Renée will ever talk to me again?"

"I think you'll feel better as soon as you apologize."

"Don Lewiston knows where it is."

"Where what is?"

"The island. Martha Quinn's island. At least he *thinks* he knows. He showed me on a map once. He says based on all the information, it's probably Free Wolf Island, off Machias."

"So he's heard the broadcast?"

"No."

"Have you?"

"No."

"Has *any*one heard Martha Quinn?"

*"No,"* said Carol Storey, before Allie could reply.

They had reached an intersection, beyond Monument Park, where the path from the chapel met a series of planks extending from the woods. Carol emerged from the snow, which was whipping almost sideways, her father behind her. She led him as if he were a child, holding his mittened hand.

"You ask everyone in camp," Carol Storey said. "It's always someone else who has heard it. And if it makes them feel better to have a perfect safe haven to daydream about, what's wrong with that? I've caught myself going through the AM band sometimes, too. But I'll tell you what. Even if she's out there, Martha Quinn doesn't have anything we need. We've already got everything we need right here."

Harper stamped into the cafeteria, snow falling off her boots in wet white clumps. Father Storey flapped his coat and a small blizzard fell around his legs. She cast her gaze around for Nick and didn't see him.

They collected trays and moved along the line to be served.

Father Storey said, "I always had a bit of a crush on Martha Quinn, in her bright vests and skinny ties. There's something about a woman in a tie. You just want to grab it and pull her over for a squeeze." He winked. Norma Heald dished him a scoop of ravioli. The sauce had the consistency of mud. "Norma, this looks delightful. Is it your own recipe?"

"It's Chef Boyardee," Norma said.

"Wonderful!" he cried, and shuffled along to get himself some Ritz crackers.

Norma rolled her eyes to watch him go, then looked back to Harper. She collected another scoop of ravioli, but instead of dumping it into Harper's bowl, she waved the big serving spoon at her. "I remember when she was on TV. Martha Quinn. Teaching little girls to dress like tiny whores. Her and Madonna and the one with the hair like cotton candy, Cyndi

Lauper. People like Martha Quinn are the reason this world is being scourged by fire. You ask yourself if God would let such a woman live, and make her His voice, calling His people to safety? Look in your heart. You know He wouldn't. She is gone and Madonna is gone and every moneylender in Jew York City who got rich turning little girls into prostitutes is gone. You know it and I know it." The ravioli fell from the spoon into Harper's bowl with a thick wet *schlopp.*

"I doubt very much that God harbors anti-Semitic views toward New York City or anywhere else, Norma," Harper told her. "Seeing as he called the Jews his own chosen people, that seems highly unlikely. Have you seen Nick? Did he come in for dinner?"

Norma Heald gave her a glazed, dull, unfriendly look. "Haven't seen him. Why don't you go outside and yell for him?"

"He's deaf," Harper said.

"Don't let that stop you," Norma said.

# 4

Michael brought Nick back a few minutes before dawn. Nick was soaked through and shivering from his night out, his dark hair matted into tangles, his eyes sunk in deep hollows. Harper thought he looked feral, as if he had been raised by wolves.

The boy walked swiftly past Allie's bed, without so much as a glance at his sleeping sister, and went straight to Harper's cot. He wrote on a sticky pad: *I don't want to sleep with her anymore. can I sleep here?*

Harper took his pad and wrote: *teach me how to say "time for bed" in sign language and it's a deal.*

That was how Nick Storey came to sleep with Harper instead of Allie, and how Harper renewed her education in American Sign Language; they settled on one new word or phrase a night as the price of admission to her bed. She was a good student, she liked practicing with him, and she was glad to have the distraction.

Although maybe she was *too* distracted: when the thief got around to stealing the Portable Mother, Harper didn't even know it was gone until Renée Gilmonton asked what had happened to it.

# 5

Harper had never seen the Fireman in chapel before—no one had—and she was as surprised as the rest of them when he turned up the night after the Portable Mother was stolen. He did not come all the way into the building, but remained in the narthex, just beyond the inner set of doors. His presence contributed to a low but steady sense of anticipation that had been building all night. Word had passed that Father Storey was going to make an announcement about the thefts in the girls' dorm. He was going to do something.

"I think we should send the bitch away," Allie said over breakfast. "Find out who she is and pack her shit. No excuses, no apologies."

Harper said, "What if the thief gets picked up by a Cremation Crew? Not only would they kill her, they'd force her to tell them about camp."

"She isn't going to tell them anything. Not if we yank her fucking tongue out before she goes. And break her fingers so she can't write."

"Oh, Allie. I don't think you mean that."

Allie only stared back with an expression of glassy, indifferent serenity. Like all the Lookouts, she had been skipping lunches for over a month now. Her cheekbones protruded in a way that made a person quite aware of the skull under her skin.

For herself, Harper didn't want Father Storey, or anyone else, to worry about what she had lost. Everyone had lost something: homes, families, hope. Put alongside these things, the Portable Mother seemed no very great loss.

Which was not to say it meant nothing. She had found no end of things to squeeze into the carpetbag for the baby. There was a wooden sword with a rope handle for when he needed to practice his sword fighting. There was a mini audio player on which Harper had recorded lullabies, bedtime stories, and a few poems. There was an umbrella for rainy days, slippers for lazy ones. Most of all, there was the notebook that had started it all and which she had filled up with facts (*your grandfather—my father—worked at NASA for thirty years . . . he made honest-to-God spaceships!!*), advice (*you can put anything in a salad—slices of apple, hot peppers, nuts, raisins, chicken, anything—and it will all taste good together*), affection (*I haven't said I love you anywhere on this page, so here's a reminder: I love you*) and lots of capital letters and exclamation points (*I LOVE YOU!!!*).

Others had made contributions as well. Allie Storey put in a plastic Iron Man mask for when he was on secret missions and needed a disguise. Renée Gilmonton had appropriated eighteen short books from the camp library, one that would be right for each year of her son's life, starting with *Wheels on the Bus* and ending with *Of Mice and Men*. Don Lewiston had made a present of a ship in a bottle. Carol Storey offered Harper a View-Master full of pictures of historic places that were all gone now. These days, the Eiffel Tower was a blackened spear puncturing a sky of smoke. The Strip in downtown Las Vegas was a charred wasteland. But in the View-Master, the neon lights and spouting fountains would be bright forever.

When the last stragglers had filed into the chapel, Father Storey climbed the steps to the podium, took his thinking pebble out of his mouth, and said, "I thought I would reverse the usual order of things tonight and get my blab out of the way before we sing and join the Bright. I apologize in advance. Much as I do love to hear myself talk, I know the songs are *my* favorite part of the night. I imagine you feel the same way. Sometimes I think with half the world on fire—with so much dying and so much pain—it's a special kind of sin to sing and feel good. But then I think, well, even before Dragonscale, most human lives were unfair, brutal, full of loss and grief and confusion. Most human lives were and are too short. Most people have lived out their days hungry and barefoot, on the run from this war and that famine, a plague here and a flood there. But people have to sing anyway. Even a baby that hasn't been fed in days will stop crying and look around when they hear someone singing in joy. You sing and it's like giving a thirsty person water. It's a kindness. It makes you shine. The proof that you matter is in your song and in the way you light up for one another. Other folks may fall and burn—*will* fall and burn. There isn't one of us who hasn't seen it happen. But here no one burns. We *shine*. A frightened, faithless soul is perfect kindling—"

"Amen," someone murmured.

"—and selfishness is as bad as kerosene. When someone is cold and you share your blanket, you're both warmer than you would've been alone. You offer the sick your medicine and their happiness will be *your* medicine. Someone probably a lot smarter than me said hell is other people. I say you're in hell when you don't give to someone who needs, because you can't bear to have less. What you are giving away then is your own soul. You have to care for each other or you walk on cinders, a matchstick ready to be struck. That's what I believe, anyway. Do you believe it?"

"I do," Ben Patchett said from Harper's right. Others said it with him. Harper herself.

Sitting there in the pews, she felt as in love as she had ever been with Jakob in their happiest hours . . . or more so. Not with any one man or woman but with all of them, the whole church full of believers. All her fellow travelers in the Bright. There had been moments in the last few weeks when it seemed to her she was discovering what it was like to be in love for the very first time.

Jakob had told her that all acts of altruism were secretly acts of selfishness, that you were really only doing for others to please yourself. And he was right, without ever really understanding what he was right about. He thought altruism was worthless if it brought you happiness—that it wasn't really altruism at all—without seeing that it was all right to feel good about making other people feel good. When you gave your happiness away, it came back twofold. It kept coming and coming, like the loaves and fishes. Its impossible increase was, maybe, the one miracle that would never be disproved by science. It was the last wonder allowed to religion. To live for others was to live fully; to live only for yourself, a cold kind of death. The sugar was sweeter when you gave it to someone else to taste.

She had not thought she was a religious person, but in the church at Camp Wyndham, she had discovered *everyone* was religious. If you had it in you to sing, you had it in you to believe and be saved.

With the possible exception of the Fireman, perhaps. The Fireman was watching Father Storey with an expression of calm detachment, and blowing smoke rings. He wasn't smoking a cigarette. He was just making the rings from somewhere in his throat, fat cloudy circles that rose in rippling hoops. He caught Harper watching and grinned. Show-off.

Father Storey slipped his glasses off, polished them on his sweater, and put them back on. "I guess someone doesn't believe it, though. About two months ago someone started helping themselves to items from the kitchen. Nothing much—a little milk, some potted meat. Hardly worth mentioning. When you think about it, stealing a few cans of Spam might even be looked upon as doing us all a kindness. Then some other things went missing from the girls' dorm. Emily Waterman had a teacup taken, her lucky cup of stars. A bottle of nail polish was swiped from the Neighbors girls. Five days ago, someone stole my granddaughter's locket from under her pillow. I'm not sure it matters that it was gold, but it had a picture of her mother in it, all Allie had left of her, and it broke her heart to lose it. Then, yesterday, the thief helped herself to Nurse Willowes's care package for her unborn child. I believe most of you know about her care package, what she's been calling the Portable Mother."

Father Storey put his hands in his pockets and rocked from

the hips and for a moment his glasses flashed, reflecting the candle on the podium, becoming circles of red flame.

"I am sure whoever took the things from the girls' dorm must feel very ashamed and frightened. There isn't a person in this room who hasn't suffered terribly since finding themselves marked with the 'scale, and under a strain like that, it can be easy to act impulsively, to take from someone else, without thinking how you would hurt them. I say to the person who took these things, and who sits among us now: you have nothing to fear by coming forward."

"Don't bet on it," Allie whispered, and the Neighbors twins stifled nervous laughter. There was no amusement on Allie's face, though.

"It would take bravery of the deepest kind to use your voice and speak up and admit what you did. But if you tell us the truth—if you raise your voice to give back—everyone in this room will shine for you. The happiness we all feel when we sing will be nothing compared to it. I *know* it. It will be sweeter than any song, and every heart here will give you something better than the things you took. They'll give you forgiveness. I believe in these people and their goodness and I want you to know the same things about them that *I* know. That they can love you even after this. Everyone here knows what makes the Dragonscale glow. Not music—if it was just the music, my deaf grandson wouldn't glow with us. It's *harmony*—harmony with one another. No one will shame you or ostracize you"—he lowered his chin and gave the room an almost-stern look over his glasses—"and if they do I will set them right. In this place we raise our voice in song, not in contempt, and I believe whoever took these things could no more help themselves than my grandson can help being deaf. Believe in us and I promise: it will be *all right*." And he smiled so sweetly Harper's heart broke a little. He was like a child, gazing into a July night and waiting on fireworks.

No one moved.

A floorboard creaked. Someone cleared their throat.

The small candle wavered on the lectern.

Harper discovered she was holding her breath. She dreaded the thought that no one would speak and that they would disappoint Father Storey, would erase that smile. He was the last innocent man in the world and she could not bear for that to change. The thought—ludicrous but intense—came to her that she ought to say *she* had stolen the things, but of course no one would believe that, and she hadn't stolen them, so she couldn't return them.

The Neighbors sisters gave each other anxious looks, each of them squeezing the other's hand. Michael stroked Allie's back until she shrugged him off. Ben Patchett exhaled—a thin, tense, unhappy breath. Onstage, Carol Storey hugged herself tightly as if to ward off a chill. In the whole room, perhaps the only person immune to the tension was Nick. He was no lipreader under the best of conditions, and certainly not by candlelight, from fifty feet away. He was doodling gravestones in the back of a songbook. The dearly departed included the famous I. M. DUNFORE, HARRY PITTS, and BARRY D. BODIE. One tombstone read HERE LIES A THIEF, KILLED WITHOUT GREEF . . . so then again, maybe he was following along just fine.

When Father Storey looked up at last, he was still smiling. He showed not the slightest sign of regret.

"Ah," he said. "It was too much to ask, I suppose. I imagine whoever took the things from the kitchen and the girls' dorm must feel terribly pressured. I only meant to show you that everyone here wishes you well. You are one of us. Your voice belongs with ours. The things you took must be an awful weight on you and I'm sure you'd like to be out from under it. Simply leave the things you took somewhere they can easily be found and drop a note to tell me where to look. Or have a private word with me. I won't judge you and have no interest in punishment. When all of us are walking with a death sentence inscribed right on our skin, what need is there of punishment? We have all been found guilty of being human. There are worse crimes." He looked back at Carol and said, "What are we singing tonight, joy?"

Carol opened her mouth, but before she could reply, someone shouted, "What if she *doesn't* come forward?"

Harper glanced around: Allie. She was quivering—with fury, but also, maybe, with nervousness—and at the same time, her jaw was set in a look that was perfectly stubborn, perfectly hostile, and perfectly Allie. Somehow Harper wasn't surprised. Allie was the only person in camp who wasn't in awe of the old man.

"What if the thief just keeps taking more stuff?" Allie asked.

Father Storey lifted an eyebrow. "Then I imagine we'll make do with less."

"It's not fair," whispered Gillian Neighbors. Her voice was low, pitched to just above a whisper, but in the great echoing space of the chapel, everyone could hear.

Carol stepped forward, to the edge of the stage, looking at her feet. When she lifted her chin, her eyes were red, as if she had been crying or was about to start.

"I don't feel like singing especially," she said. "I feel like something important slipped away tonight. Something special. Maybe our trust in each other. Allie, my niece, doesn't want to stay with the other girls anymore, knowing there's a thief there. She doesn't have any other pictures of her mother, my sister. No way to remember her. Just what was in the locket. That locket will never mean to anyone what it means to her and her brother. I don't understand how anyone could hurt her that way and then come in here and sing like she cares about other people. It makes the whole thing feel phony. I'll play a song you all know, and you can sing if you want, or you can be silent with me. Whatever feels right to you. A part of me feels like if we can't all be honest with each other, silence might be better. Maybe we should all hold one of Father Storey's stones in our mouth for a bit, and consider what really matters."

That sounded a little schoolmarmish in Harper's opinion,

but she saw people nodding. She also saw Allie brushing away an angry tear with one finger, then twisting her head and turning to furiously whisper something to Gail and Gillian Neighbors.

Then Carol began to play, picking at the strings of her ukulele, not strumming. Notes rang out, like little hammers striking silver chimes. It took only a moment for Harper to recognize "Silent Night." No one sang. There was, instead, a reverential hush, the room utterly silent aside from Carol's playing.

Harper wasn't sure who lit up first. At some point, though, she became aware of a faint luminescence in the cavernous dim. Eyes shone the blue-green color of lightning bugs flashing in a summer night. Dragonscale became scribbles of dim fluorescence. Harper thought of those fish that lived in the deepest basins of the ocean, illuminating the depths with their own glow-in-the-dark organs. It was a cold, alien light, different from the usual almost-blinding intensity of the Bright. Harper had not imagined they could create harmony without a sound, that they could join in a silent chorus of disapproval rather than song.

Only about half the room turned on, and Harper was not among them. For the first time in weeks she was unable to join, to *connect*. Over the last few weeks, she had come to look forward to chapel, and slipped into the Bright as she would've slipped into a warm bath. Now, though, the water was cold. She couldn't understand how any of the others could stand it.

The last note hung in the air like a snowflake that refused to fall. As it died away, this new, ill-hued Bright died away with it, and the darkness around them returned.

Carol blinked at tears. Father Storey put his arms around her from behind and hugged her to his chest. Maybe the thief had stolen that locket from four people, after all: the dead woman had been Carol's sister and Tom Storey's daughter, as well as Allie and Nick's mother.

Father Storey peered over Carol's shoulder into the chapel and smiled. "Well. That was very beautiful, but I hope we won't make a habit of it. I like hearing all of you. We will be rearranging the pews for morning reading and—ah! John! I almost forgot you. Thank you for coming tonight. Is there something you wanted to say to us?"

The Fireman grinned from the back of the room.

"I've found two men in need of shelter. With permission, I'd like to bring them into the camp. I can't vouch for them, Father—I haven't been able to get close enough to talk to them yet. They've painted themselves into a bit of a corner. I can get them out and I can make a distraction to cover their escape, but I'll need some others to lead them back to camp."

Father Storey frowned. "Of course. Anyone who needs our help. I'm surprised you'd even ask. Is there some special reason for concern?"

"Judging by the orange suits they're wearing," the Fireman said, "the ones that say 'Brentwood County Court' on the back, they might be even more in need of salvation than the average member of your flock, Father."

# 6

When Father Storey asked the Fireman who he'd need, Harper didn't expect to be on his list, but she was the only person he mentioned by name.

"Two or three men and Nurse Willowes, if you please, Father. I don't know what kind of state they'll be in. At the very least they've spent twenty-four hours in a cramped hiding place, in temperatures barely above freezing, so they'll be suffering from exposure. It might make sense to have medical assistance on hand. What say we group up in Monument Park in twenty minutes? I'd like to get under way."

The service was over. Everyone crowded into the aisles, all of them yammering at once. Harper pushed her way through the close press of bodies and the noise. Ben Patchett was saying something—*Harper, you're pregnant, he's out of his mind if*—but she pretended not to hear. In another moment she was through the enormous red doors and out into a cold so dry and sharp it stung the eyes.

Alone in the infirmary, she flung open cabinets, collecting anything that might be useful and dumping it in a small nylon knapsack. In her haste, her elbow struck the big anatomical model of a human head. It tipped off the counter and smashed on the floor.

She cursed, turned to kick the shards out of sight—was in too much of a hurry to sweep—then hesitated.

The head had busted into several large pieces. One half of the face gaped up at her with an idiotic astonishment. A stenographer's notebook, rolled into a tube and bound up with thick rubber bands, lay among the shards.

Harper picked it out of the shattered pieces, undid the rubber bands, and looked at the cover.

PRIVATE NOTEBOOK OF HAROLD CROSS
MEDICAL OBSERVATIONS AND PERSONAL INSIGHTS
WITH SOME OCCASIONAL POETRY

She considered what to do with it, thought there might be quite a few people in camp who would want to know what Harold had written about in the weeks before his death. Finally she decided not to decide. There wasn't time. She tossed it in a drawer and got out of there.

Captain America was waiting on the steps of the infirmary.

"I've got some other masks if you want one," Allie said, leading the way along the wobbling planks set out between buildings. "I've got Hulk, Optimus Prime, and Sarah Palin."

"Is it important to disguise our identity?"

"I don't think so. But it does make you feel more badass. Like when guys rob a bank and they're all wearing scary clown masks? I have a *huge* girl boner for scary clown masks."

"Unless you have Mary Poppins, I think I'll go as I am. But thank you for asking."

Allie led her through the looming pagan rocks of Monument Park, to a stone altar that would've been the perfect place to sacrifice Aslan. Father Storey stood behind it, with the Fireman on his right, and Michael and Ben on his left—an image that Harper thought oddly recalled *The Last Supper.* Michael even had Judas's stringy red beard, if none of his malice or fear.

"Allie?" Father Storey raised one hand, palm out, as if in benediction. "I promised your aunt you'd have no part in this. Head down to the bus—you're watching the gate tonight."

"I swapped with Mindy Skilling," Allie said. "Mindy didn't mind."

"And I'm sure she won't mind if you swap back."

Allie shot a questioning, hostile look at the Fireman. "I *al-*

*ways* go. Since when do I not get to go? *Mike* is going. He's only a year older than me. I started the Lookouts, not him. I was the first."

"The last time you went running around with John, your aunt Carol sat staring out the window, clutching one of your sweaters and praying," said Father Storey. "She wasn't praying to God, Allie. She was praying to your *mother* to keep you safe. Don't put her through another night like that. Have mercy on her. And have mercy on me."

Allie went on staring at the Fireman. "You going along with this bullshit?"

"You heard him," the Fireman said. "Run along, Allie, and don't give me one of your sixteen-year-old death stares. If you want to have a row with me, it'll have to be later."

She glared at him for a moment longer—eyeing him as if trying to decide how best to get even. Then she looked at Michael, opened her mouth as if to plead with *him*. Mike half turned away, though, scratching his back with his rosewood nightstick, and pretended not to see her staring.

"Fuck you," Allie said, her voice shaking with anger. "Fuck all of you."

In the next instant she bolted into the trees. Harper had been able to move like that once; she remembered being sixteen quite vividly.

Father Storey smiled in a way that looked awfully like a wince. "In her own soft-spoken, gentle fashion, she *does* manage to get her point across, doesn't she? I would add that compared to her mother, Allie Storey is the very model of restraint."

"Shoot," Ben Patchett said. "I forgot to grab a flashlight."

"No worries, Ben," the Fireman said, stripping off his left glove. "I brought a light."

His hand ignited in a gout of blue flame, with a soft whoosh, illuminating a circle ten feet in diameter. The boulders threw monstrous shadows halfway down the hill.

Ben Patchett swallowed heavily as Harper fell in beside him. "I'll never get used to that," he said.

# 7

They followed the Fireman away from the church and in under the pines, where there were no boards to walk on. But the snow was brittle here, frozen and glassy on the surface, and for the most part they could make their way downhill without leaving any tracks.

Downhill? They seemed to be heading toward the water. Harper was surprised, had expected them to pile into a car.

Harper's foot went through the polished surface of the snow and she lurched into Ben's side. He steadied her, then looped his arm through hers.

"Let me help you," he said. He cast a hooded look at the Fireman's back and muttered, "Crazy bringing you along."

A weight and ill-shaped mass in his pocket pressed against her arm and she frowned. She pushed her fingers into his coat pocket and found a revolver: hatched walnut grip, cold steel hammer.

She slipped her arm free.

He glanced at her, half smiling. "You're supposed to ask if that's a gun in my pocket or if I'm just happy to see you."

"Why do you need that?"

"You have to ask?"

"Sorry," she said. "I thought we're off to help people, not shoot them."

"*You're* off to help people. I'm on this trip to make sure my favorite nurse gets back to camp in one piece. We don't know anything about these two men. We don't know what they were locked up for. Maybe John Rookwood is all right risking your life for a couple outlaws, but I'm not." His face flushed and he looked down and away. "You ought to know by now how much I care about you, Harp. If something happened—sheesh."

She put her hand on the back of his arm and squeezed. She hoped he read that squeeze as *Thank you for caring* and not *God, I'm horny, we should really screw sometime.* In her experience it was very difficult to offer a man affection and kindness without giving him the impression you were also offering a lay.

He smiled. "Besides. Departmental regulations require any officer transporting a prisoner to carry his firearm at all times. You can give up the badge, but it's hard to give up the mind-set. Not that I ever *really* gave up the badge."

"You still have it?"

"I keep it with my secret decoder ring and the fake mustache I used for undercover work." He bumped her affectionately with his shoulder.

The snow was the color of blue steel, of gunmetal, in the moonlight.

He mused, "Sometimes I think I ought to put it back on."

"The fake mustache?" She peered into his features. "I guess you could pull one off without looking too sleazy. You have a good face for a mustache."

"*No.* My badge. Sometimes I think this community could use some law. Or at least some justice. Think about this gal who's running around, helping herself to grub and jewelry. If she comes forward and admits what she did—or if we find her out—is that *really* going to be the end of it? We're all just going to hug it out on Father Storey's say-so?"

"Maybe she could peel potatoes for a week or something."

"Or we could lock her up for three months, teach her a lesson. I even know where I'd do it. There's a meat locker below the cafeteria, just about the size of a cell at the county jail. Bring in a cot and—"

"Ben!" she cried.

"What? She wouldn't freeze. It's probably warmer in there than in the basement of the church. There hasn't been any electric for months."

"That's disgusting. Solitary confinement in a room that smells like rotten meat. Over a couple cans of milk?"

"And the Portable Mother."

"Fuck the Portable Mother."

He flinched.

Father Storey and Michael Lindqvist ambled along ahead of them, Father Storey saying something, a hand on Mike's back. Mike walked with his nightstick stuck out to one side, rapping it against the occasional tree trunk, like a boy running a stick over the boards of a fence. Ben watched them for a bit, then shook his head and snorted.

"If I was Mike, I'd be relieved to get out of camp and I don't know if I'd hurry back. He might be in more danger here."

"From who?" Harper asked.

"From Allie. That girl has a temper. I wouldn't want to cross her."

"You think she's mad Michael didn't come to her defense?"

"Especially after what they were up to before chapel. I saw the two of them ducked behind a pine at the edge of the woods, making out like they were never going to see each other again. If I was her father, I would've—but I'm not, and I guess neither of them are exactly kids anymore."

"I didn't know they were a going thing."

Ben waggled his hand. "On again, off again. Apparently on again." He smiled at this. When he spoke once more, his voice was pitched low and soft. "Putting the thief in the meat locker might be a kindness. You don't see that, because you think everyone is as warmhearted as you. Father Storey doesn't see it either. You and he are two sides of the same coin in that way."

"How is it a kindness?"

"It would keep her from getting killed. It's less a punishment, more like protective custody."

Harper opened her mouth to disagree, then recalled Allie's talk of finding the thief and yanking out her tongue. She closed her mouth and said nothing.

Three canoes were tied alongside the dock, bobbing in the

sea. The Fireman lowered his burning left hand, put it under one flap of his turnout jacket, and smothered the flame.

"It'll be safer and faster to go the rest of the way by water." He settled into the canoe at the far end of the dock, slid his halligan into the bottom.

Ben frowned. "Um—John? Am I counting wrong, or are we at least a boat short? We're rescuing two men, aren't we? So . . . where are we going to put them?"

"You'll have room for them. I'm not coming back by boat. I've arranged for other transportation." The Fireman undid a rope and pushed the canoe into the Atlantic. It rode low in the water and Harper wondered how heavy a halligan bar really was.

Ben gestured at one of the other canoes. "Harper, I don't know much about boats. Do you want to steer and I'll—"

"Actually," Father Storey said, "I have a private medical matter to discuss with Nurse Willowes. Do you mind?"

Ben *did* mind—for a moment the disappointment on his face was so bald it was almost funny. But he nodded, and climbed down into one of the other canoes. "We'll see you when we get where we're going, then. Watch out for icebergs."

Harper untied them while Father Storey carefully climbed into the front of their canoe. As they pushed out into the water, Harper shut her eyes and inhaled deeply. The air was so clean and smelled so richly of the sea, it made her briefly dizzy.

"I like it out on the ocean. Always have," Father Storey said, speaking over his shoulder. "You know, the camp has a nearly forty-foot sailboat stashed on John's island. Big enough to—oh, will you look at that!" He pointed across the water with a dripping paddle.

Allie was in the front of the Fireman's canoe with a paddle. She had sat up as soon as they were fifty feet from the dock.

"Do you remember what John said to her, back on shore? 'If you want to have a row with me, it'll have to be later.' " Father Storey did a voice that was a little like Paul McCartney in *Yellow Submarine*. Not a bad imitation of the Fireman at that. He said it again—" 'A row!' "—the British way, so it rhymed with *cow*, then repeated it once more, but in the American fashion, so it rhymed with *low*. "Ha! He was telling her we were taking the canoes, so she could run ahead and wait for us. Well. She comes by her go-screw-yourself streak honestly. I could never tell her mother, Sarah, a thing, either."

The shoreline, bristling with firs, scrolled by on either side of them as they made their way out of the little harbor.

"What's bothering you, Father? You said you're not feeling well?"

"I believe I said I had a private medical matter. I don't think I said it was anything to do with me. I guess I'm all right. A little sick at heart. You don't treat for that, do you?"

"Sure. Take two chocolates and call me in the morning. I think Norma Heald has a few Hershey's Kisses in the kitchen. Tell her I wrote you a prescription."

He didn't laugh. "I think I'm going to have to send someone away. I've been trying to figure out how to protect someone no one will forgive. It seems to me that sending her away is the only hope for her. If she stays here, I'm afraid of what the camp might do to her." He cast a glance back at Harper and smiled a little. "Every time I see them sing and shine together I always wonder what would happen if they formed a lynch mob. Do you think the Dragonscale would like a lynch mob as well as a chorus? I do."

# 8

*He knows who the thief is,* Harper thought. The idea was a sharp jolt, the mental equivalent of stepping on a tack.

"Why are you telling me this?" Harper asked.

He stared out over the prow of the boat. "The person of whom I speak would never leave willingly. Could you—if you had to—administer something? To pacify a person if she was—hysterical? Dangerous? To herself or . . . or others?"

Whatever Harper had been expecting to talk about, it wasn't this.

"I don't have anything strong enough in my supplies. To be honest, Father—"

"I wish you wouldn't call me that," he said, with a sudden bitterness. "I've never been ordained, not by any church. The only person who ought to call me Father is Carol. I never should've let that get started, but it satisfied my ego. I taught ethics and the history of Christianity at a prep school in Massachusetts. I've gone from old-fuddy-duddy-in-the-ivory-tower to high pope–Dalai Lama of the New Faith in five months. You show me someone who could resist that, I'll show you a *real* saint."

"Now, *Father.* If I heard someone sneering at you like that, I'd break something over their head. Don't you know you give all these people hope? You give *me* hope, and that's as magic as a whole church full of people glowing like Christmas lights. I've started to believe I might live to see my child born, and that's because of *you,* and the songs, and all these wonderful people who have gathered around you."

"Ah. That's big-hearted of you, Harper. You just remember: I didn't do anything to make all of you wonderful. You were that way when I found you."

They swung out and around a headland into open water. The bank was forty feet away, a steep hill rising through scrawny bare trees and boulders.

"To return to your question, I don't have sedatives of any strength whatsoever. God help us if I ever have to perform a surgery. The most powerful drug in the camp medicine cabinet is Advil. But even if I did have something stronger, I wouldn't like to sedate someone as a punitive measure. I don't do that. I help sick people."

"This person—she *is* sick. And before you ask, no, I don't want to say who I have in mind. Not until I've absolutely settled on what steps to take."

"I wasn't going to ask." She had already noticed the way he was trying to avoid naming names.

He paused, considering for a time, then said: "What do you think of Martha Quinn's island?"

"I think I'd feel a lot better about it if I knew someone who has actually heard the broadcast."

Father Storey said, "Harold Cross claimed to have heard it. Once. And he was texting with someone in Lubec, which has been operating as the capital of Maine ever since Augusta burned to the ground."

"Harold was texting with someone who *said* they were in Lubec," Harper said. "I never knew him, but by the sound of it, Harold was a little too trusting."

"I couldn't agree more," Father Storey said, and again there was that caustic, nasty tone of bitterness that was so unlike him.

Harper could feel the ocean under the boat, the dreamy pull of it. If they stopped paddling, the current would catch the canoe and draw it to the east. In half an hour they would be far enough out to see all the lights of Portsmouth; in an hour, far enough perhaps to see all the lights on the New Hampshire coast. An hour after that they would be too far out to see any lights at all.

"We're going to have to send someone away, I'm afraid. Force a woman from camp," Father Storey said. "When that happens . . .

well, I wouldn't send someone, no matter how deluded, into exile, all alone. Sooner or later a Cremation Crew would catch her. No. I think I will go with her. Perhaps in the big sailboat out on John's island. Myself and Don Lewiston. I'd like to go looking for Martha Quinn."

"Who'll take care of camp?"

"It would have to be John. He's the only one I'm certain is up to the job."

They swung around the headland to a narrow inlet, not more than eighty feet across, with houses on either side and decks built right over the water. Directly ahead was a short bridge, spanning the entrance to the small bay beyond.

She didn't recognize where they were until they were gliding under the bridge itself, where their breath produced metallic echoes, ringing off the rusting iron gridwork above them. South Mill Pond opened up before her, a gourd-shaped body of water between a park . . . and the Portsmouth Police Department.

Most of the buildings around the pond were dark, but the police department and the parking lot alongside it were lit up like a football stadium on game night. From where she sat, Harper could see two big hills of waste burning in the lot. Each pile was almost twenty feet high. Harper wondered what they were destroying—contaminated clothing? A few fire trucks were parked nearby, the fire department managing the blaze. Harper spied men in helmets and fire jackets moving here and there about the bonfires. The burning mounds produced an evil-looking smoke that climbed into the night, blanking out the stars.

The Fireman began to paddle toward the police station.

"Oh, John," Father Storey sighed. "I hope you know what you're doing."

The pond was no bigger than a soccer pitch and bisected by a causeway, which lay directly ahead of them. There was no crossing the causeway to the water on the other side without portaging the canoes. Harper wasn't sure where the Fireman intended to beach them, but one way or another, they'd be on shore soon.

Harper leaned forward and hissed, "We'll talk more when we get back to camp. Of course, though, I'll do what I can to help you. If I had the proper drugs, I'd be willing to sedate the thief, after you confront her . . . but only as a last resort. I can't believe it would come to that. If you and Carol approach this person together, privately, and show her the kind of empathy and understanding you were talking about in chapel—well, I can't imagine anyone in camp who wouldn't respond to that."

Tom Storey turned his head to look back at her, his brow furrowed in puzzlement, a question in his eyes, forming on his lips . . . as if she had posed a very baffling riddle. Harper wondered at it. She felt she could not have been more direct or clear. She wanted to ask him what he didn't understand, but there was no time. The Fireman was bringing them into shore, close to the causeway. Harper pointed with her paddle, and Father Storey nodded and turned away. *Later,* she thought, not imagining that there wouldn't be a later.

Not for Father Storey.

# 9

The embankment was made of rough-hewn granite blocks, rising from a ribbon of sand. The canoe made an agonizingly loud crunch as it came into the shallows. Ben was already waiting to pull their boat up alongside the other two.

The Fireman squeezed Allie's shoulder and pointed toward the causeway. He murmured something into her ear and Allie nodded and began picking her way along the little ledge of sand, staying low.

"Where's she going, John?" Harper asked in a whisper.

"The men we came here to rescue are on the other side of the causeway, and the only way to get to them without being seen is through *that*."

He pointed again and this time Harper saw one end of a drainage pipe beneath the causeway. At high tide the opening would be underwater, but right now it was nearly dry. Allie crouched and began clearing away the dead branches and rusted beer cans that choked the entrance.

"You're sending a sixteen-year-old girl to talk to a pair of felons?" Ben asked. "What happens when one of them grabs her by the hair and pulls her out of the pipe?"

"She doesn't have any hair to grab, Ben, and she knows her business. This isn't the first time she's helped someone out of a tight spot," the Fireman said.

He reached back into his canoe. Steel chimed. He rose with his halligan.

"I trust you, John," said Father Storey. "As long as you can promise me Allie will be safe."

"I couldn't promise that even if she stayed behind to knit with Norma Heald, Tom. But I'm not afraid of the two men hiding on the other side of the causeway. They want to get away, not get caught."

Michael said, "That pipe looks pretty small. You sure they'll be able to follow her back through?"

Allie was wrestling with a rusted shopping cart that partially blocked the entrance.

"I'm sure they won't," the Fireman said. "One is as tall as Boris Karloff and the other is roughly the size of a water buffalo. If they tried to follow her through, they'd be even more stuck than they are now. No, they'll have to go over the causeway, as soon as it's safe to cross without being seen. Ben, Michael, Father: you just be ready to help them. I don't know how well they'll be able to walk."

"What do you *mean,* they'll have to go over the causeway?" Ben asked. "When will it be safe for them to go?"

The Fireman clambered up the steep pitch of the embankment, using the halligan's pick end to hoist himself along. He glanced back and whispered, "When the screaming starts."

He reached the top of the wall, stood for a moment at the edge of the parking lot with the bronze glow of the firelight shifting over his features, then leaned his halligan against one shoulder and walked away whistling.

"Does he make you feel dumb?" Ben asked no one in particular. "He always makes me feel dumb."

"What now?" Harper asked.

"I guess we hunker down," Ben said. "And wait to see if anything goes wrong."

The Fireman had been gone not a moment—the strong, carrying sound of his whistle had only just faded away—when Allie reared back from the drainage pipe with a mewling cry of horror, stumbled, and sat down in the water.

"That was fast," Michael said.

# 10

Harper was the first to get to Allie, helping her to stand.

"What?" Harper whispered. "What is it?"

Allie shook her head, her eyes bright spots in the holes of her Captain America mask.

Harper went around her and crouched at the entrance to the drainage pipe. A mound of mud and sticks and leaves was wedged in there, a brushy, thorny mass, just beyond arm's reach.

The mass of leaves rose, shifted, and turned sideways.

It was an animal. There was a fucking animal in the pipe, a porcupine the size of a Welsh corgi.

Harper spied a stick, two feet long and forked at one end. She had an idea she could reach the stick past the porcupine and pull him toward her, drag him out into the open. Instead, the forked end of the stick jabbed the porcupine in the side. Quills bristled. The porcupine grunted and crept farther into the pipe.

She looked back for Allie. Michael had scrambled over to her and put his jacket around her. Her jeans were soaked from her spill into the water and she was shivering steadily. Shivering . . . and regarding the drainage pipe with a bleak look of alarm. Harper had never before seen the slightest trace of fear in Allie Storey, and in a way it was a kind of relief to know *something* could get to her.

Harper didn't blame her. The idea of squeezing into a three-foot-wide pipe with a fat, pissed-off porcupine was appalling, nearly unthinkable.

So she didn't think. Harper got down on all fours and put

her face into the pipe. She smelled rotting garbage and a warm mammalian reek.

"The hell you thinking?" Ben asked. "Aw, Harper. Aw, don't do that. Don't go in there. Let me—"

But when he reached for her, she twitched her arm away and pushed her shoulders into the pipe. Ben was six feet tall and over two hundred pounds and had as much chance of getting through the drainage pipe as the rusted shopping cart Allie had tossed into the shallows.

Harper, though, was only a little taller than Allie, maybe fifteen pounds heavier, and she knew if any of them were able to squirm through the pipe, it was her. It was going to be tight, though. She could feel that already, the walls forcing her shoulders in close to her body.

She remembered then that she was in her second trimester and probably *thirty* pounds heavier than Allie. She wondered if she had fattened up enough to get jammed in here. She considered going back, then squirmed forward another foot.

The porcupine had stopped waddling and turned sideways to watch her approach. She jabbed him with the stick again and the eye that faced her seemed to flash with outrage. It was the color of blood frozen in a drop of amber. The porcupine hissed and shuffled onward.

She followed him, crawling on hands and knees across corkscrew corrugations. She had gone perhaps a third of the distance when her hips caught.

Harper heaved forward to free herself, but didn't go anywhere. Instead, she felt the walls clamp tighter around her. She tried to go back, and couldn't, and flashed to an image of a cork stuck in a wine bottle, that last night with Jakob.

The porcupine hesitated and seemed to give her a look of unfriendly speculation: *What? Something wrong? A little stuck? Maybe you need a friendly poke from a stick to get you moving again?*

The water trickling between her hands was icy and the stainless steel walls were rimed with frost, but suddenly Harper was hot. Heat prickled up her sides and in the cup made by her collarbones. It was not the ordinary flush of warmth a person sometimes felt in a moment of anxiety. She knew *this* sensation well, a feeling like bug spray on abraded skin. She drew another sharp breath and smelled smoke, a sickly sweet stink, like maple-flavored bacon burning in the pan.

*That's you,* she thought, and when she looked down, she saw a pale fluff of smoke coming off the tracery of Dragonscale on the backs of her hands.

*I told you,* the porcupine whispered, in Jakob's voice. *We should've died together, the way we planned. Wouldn't that have been better than burning to death like this, in a dark hole? You could've just gone to sleep in my arms, no fuss, no pain. Instead you're going to roast here and when you begin to shriek, it will draw the police, and they'll get Allie, and Father Storey, and Ben, and Michael, and make them kneel on the sand, and put bullets in their brains, and it will be your fault.*

She pulled again. The pipe held her fast.

She blinked, eyes tearing from the smoke. It wasn't the fire that killed you, she understood then. It was terror, or maybe surrender. It was the moment when, with horror and shame, you realized you had got yourself stuck someplace and you were too weak to pull yourself free. The Dragonscale was the bullet, but fear was the finger that pulled the trigger.

Her breath screamed in her throat. She poked the porcupine with the stick before he could get any ideas, and stabbed a choked little squeal out of the thing. He began to hustle away, moving along even faster than before.

She couldn't see the other end of the pipe anymore through the smoke rising from her. She didn't know why she wasn't choking on it. She inhaled deeply, preparing to cough, and thought, *Sing*. Sing it away.

*"Dum dilly dilly, um dilly die,"* she whispered, in a cracked, hoarsened voice, and immediately stopped.

It was bad enough to be stuck in a pipe with a porcupine,

worse to be in there with a lunatic, even if the lunatic happened to be herself. The desperation she heard in her own voice unnerved her.

A fresh wave of chemical heat prickled over her body. Worms of heat crawled on her scalp. She could smell her hair frizzing and cooking and she thought if she got out of the pipe she would let Allie shave her head, but she wasn't going to get out of the pipe, because it was all a lie, the idea that singing could save you. British children sang to each other during the Blitz and the roof still caved in on them. Her own voice had never mattered. Tom Storey's faith was a prayer to an empty cupboard.

Smoke burned in her throat. White clouds spurted from her nostrils. She hated every moment of hope she had ever allowed herself to feel. Hated herself for singing along, singing with the others, singing *to* the others, singing—

*Singing* to *the others,* she thought. Singing in harmony. Father Storey said it was not the *song* but *harmony* itself that mattered. And you couldn't create harmony alone.

She blinked at the smoke, eyes watering, tears sticky on her face, and in a soft, uneven voice, sang again, her mind turned inward, to the life knotted like a fist in her womb.

*"I'll be your candle on the water,"* she sang. Not Julie Andrews this time, but Helen Reddy. It was the first song that came to mind, and at the sound of it, echoing faintly in the pipe, she felt the sudden, half-hysterical urge to laugh. *"My love for you will always burn."*

She was badly off-key, her voice warbling with emotion, but at almost the first word, her Dragonscale pulsed and shone with a soft golden light, and that sensation of her skin crawling with chemical heat began to abate. At the same time the baby seemed to subtly shift inside her, rotating like a screw, and she thought, *He's showing you what to do. He is in harmony.* A ludicrous idea, except then she swiveled her hips, following the twisting corrugations of the pipe, and eased forward. She came loose so suddenly she banged her head with a hollow gong.

Harper crawled into a funnel of smoke. Her lungs strained

to find oxygen that wasn't there, yet her head did not swim and she did not feel faint. Indeed, she had enough air to continue singing to the baby in an exhausted, whispered chant.

She lowered her head, blinking tears out of her eyes, and when she blearily looked back up, the porcupine was right in front of her, so close she almost put a hand down on him. His cloak of needles bristled.

She banged the stick against the side of the pipe, drew it back, and lanced it at the porcupine.

"I'll be a candle right up your ass, you don't keep waddling, fat boy," she half sang, half choked.

He began to trundle away from her again, but Harper had had enough of the porcupine and enough of the drainage pipe. She scooped the stick right under his rear end and shoved him along ahead of her. She felt this had the makings of a new Olympic sport: porcupine curling.

The rodent broke into what passed for a run with his species. He did not hesitate when he reached the end of the pipe, but dropped down and out through the opening. In the flickering orange firelight that illuminated the evening, Harper could see the porcupine was not so large after all. Jammed into the pipe, he had looked to be the size of a puppy. Out in the throbbing glow of the bonfires, he was no more than a hamster with quills. He glared back at her with a single, reproachful eye before continuing on. For a moment Harper felt almost guilty about the way she had treated him. She had also been driven from her home and felt she could relate.

She heard a startled whisper from outside the pipe and to the left. "The fuck is that?" Someone threw a rock at the porcupine and it scampered away into brush, the poor, persecuted thing.

Harper pulled herself forward a few inches, almost to the lip of the pipe.

"Hello out there," she said in a low voice.

The end of the pipe darkened and filled, the night sky eclipsed by the head and shoulders of a large man.

Harper was no longer smoldering and no longer singing,

and at some point in the last few moments, the gold flecks of Dragonscale had ceased to shine. Her arms and back, inked with the fine, delicate tracery of the spore, felt tender and sore, but not entirely unpleasant.

"Who is that?" asked the big man peering into the pipe.

Even scuffed, filthy, and ash-streaked, his carrot-colored jumpsuit was lurid in the shadows, as bright as neon. His build was bearish, his face blocky, acne-scarred . . . but his yellowish eyes struck Harper as almost professorial. Those eyes were, in fact, nearly the exact same color as the porcupine's eyes.

"I'm Harper Willowes. I'm a nurse. I'm here to help you get away. There are two of you, yes?"

"Yeah, but—he already tried squeezing in the pipe and he couldn't get in. And I'm even bigger'n he is."

"You aren't going to come through the pipe. You're going to walk straight across the causeway. There are friends waiting on the other side with boats. They'll take you to safety."

"Lady, we been hidin' in a culvert for twenty hours. Ain't neither of us up to sprinting across that road. My pard here can barely stand. I thank you for thinking of us. I sincerely do. But it's not happening. It doesn't matter if your boats are only a hundred feet away. They might as well be on the moon. There's fifty men up in that parking lot, most of 'em armed. If we break cover and make a dash for it—and a hobble would be more like it—they *will* shoot first and ask questions never."

"You aren't going to run," she said, remembering what the Fireman had said. "You're going to walk. And you won't be seen. There'll be a distraction."

"What distraction?"

"You'll know it when you see it," she said, because that sounded better than admitting she had no idea.

He grinned to show a gold tooth in the back of his mouth. He was what her father would've called an ugly cuss. "Why don't you come out here? Come on out and sit with us, darlin'."

"I have to get back. Just be ready," she said.

"You aren't gonna back all the way down that pipe, are you?

Wouldn't it be better to crawl out and get yourself turned around?"

She hadn't thought about going back until now—ridiculous but true—and didn't know how to reply. He was right, of course. She could no more get out of the pipe by crawling in reverse then she could by turning to smoke and vanishing; in fact, turning to smoke was a far more likely possibility.

If she went forward, though, even a foot, she imagined the bearish man snatching a handful of her hair, his smile going away and his eyes going dead. He and his friend could do whatever they wanted to her; she wasn't going to scream, bring down the law on them, give up the location of her friends. The Fireman had said they wanted to get away, not get caught, and that was true. But it was also true that they were convicts and she was a pregnant woman who couldn't call for help. It was entirely possible, she saw now, for them to have their cake and rape and murder it, too.

She was stuck again, maybe worse than she had been when she was halfway through the pipe. She could not see a way back and she didn't dare go forward. *Why don't you sing him something from one of your favorite musicals?* she thought, and almost laughed.

But as it happened there was nothing to figure out; it was a problem that never required solving. The big man was distracted by something up on the causeway. His eyes—reflecting the firelight—were bewildered and glassy with fright.

*"Haaaaa—"* he sighed. "Holy . . . *holy* . . ."

She assumed he was trying to say *Holy shit,* but he never got out anything more than that first word. And later it occurred to her that maybe he had said exactly what he meant: that what was happening up on the road was a kind of holy manifestation, as unlikely as a burning bush or a night sky full of angels, twinkling over Bethlehem.

Although *holy* wasn't the word that came to her mind when she saw what was happening up on the road.

*Infernal* was more like it.

# 11

The light dimmed. It was as if a great black curtain had been dropped between the water and the bonfires up in the parking lot.

The prisoner's eyes widened by degrees.

"What?" she asked.

He didn't reply, only gave his head a short, distracted shake. He put a hand on his knee and pushed, rising to his full height with some effort. She could see his legs were hurting. He stepped to her left, out of sight. She heard him whispering to someone, a low groan of pain, and the scuffle of shoes on rock. Then nothing.

No: not nothing. From a distance, she heard yells, startled cries.

It was as if all light were being swallowed, were being drowned. She could not for the life of her imagine what could smother the night that way.

She darted her head out of the pipe for a look, meaning to scuttle straight back if she saw the man in orange. But there was no one waiting for her. To her left was another sloped, six-foot-high wall of irregular granite blocks. A wide, concrete-lined culvert was set into it, sunk beneath the parking lot above. There was room for perhaps two men to crouch out of sight, under the concrete soffit, but rusted bars blocked the way into the darkened passage beyond. That was where they had hidden . . . jammed into that cramped space, huddled together for warmth against the wrought-iron bars.

Harper craned her neck to see up onto the causeway, but she was still most of the way in the pipe and from that angle couldn't make out much. What she *could* see was smoke: a bubbling black cloud, pouring into the sky, spreading across the road and the parking lot.

She slid forward on her knees, freed herself from the pipe, stood up, and gazed dumbly at the top of the embankment.

The devil stood in that immense cloud: a devil that towered two stories high, a broad-shouldered demon with a vast rack of horns. He was a flickering apparition of flame, buried deep in that boiling thunderhead of smoke. In one hand he held a hammer and he raised an arm as thick as a telephone pole and brought it down on a burning red anvil. Steel clanged—she heard it quite distinctly. Sparks flew from somewhere in the black cloud. The devil's tail—a slender, twelve-foot whip braided from fire—lashed behind him.

The black cloud was so immense, Harper could no longer see the police station or the parking lot or the bonfires. The smoke spread over the causeway, an impenetrable bank of toxic fog.

Men screamed, hollered, ran about on the other side of the smoke.

The devil brought the hammer down again and again, each time with another ringing *clang!* He tossed his burning head back, his eyes two red, delighted coals. In profile, it was impossible not to recognize him as the Fireman.

The devil finished his work, set aside his hammer, and lifted his new-forged instrument: a lance of fire, a pitchfork fashioned from pure flame, as long as his own body.

Someone on the other side of the smoke wailed. Harper had never heard a voice raised in such despair. It was the cry of a man afraid for his own soul.

Several ideas occurred to her in rapid succession, a string of firecrackers rattling off.

First: It was a shadow show. She didn't know how he was doing it, but she was sure that what she was seeing was no different than a little boy shining a flashlight at his hand and conjuring the shadow of an elephant on his bedroom wall.

Second: If she was going to go, she had to go *now*. This couldn't possibly last.

Third: John needed to go himself. To end his performance and slip away. He had made more than enough smoke and chaos to allow the prisoners to limp across the causeway unseen.

Fourth and last: Maybe he didn't care if he got away or not. Maybe he had never cared. Maybe the possibility of his own capture and death was not a concern but an enticement.

Harper climbed the slope on all fours, digging her fingers into the mossy gaps between stone blocks.

She struggled to her feet and stood up in that dense black cloud of smoke. She knew not to inhale, but her throat and nostrils began to burn anyway. It was a little better if she sank low, but only a little.

Harper advanced into the cloud. She could see the asphalt directly beneath her feet, but no more. The smoke was too dense to see any farther than that.

From the far side of the smoke bank, she heard a new noise—a chorus of organized, authoritative shouts—the sound of several men calling to one another as they worked in unison.

The blast of water hit the smoke bank, aimed at the devil's burning chest. Satan flickered, lifted his arms to protect his face, and for a moment the pitchfork quivered and took on the shape of an enormous halligan bar.

The Fireman shouted somewhere in the smoke, a surprised yell. Steel banged and clattered.

Satan staggered, wheeled about, and dropped his flickering pitchfork. He closed his wings around his body, hiding within, shrank into himself, and vanished.

The men holding the fire hose continued blasting water into the cloud. Spray rained past Harper. It hissed in the hot smoke, and the cloud changed in color and texture, going from polluted and black to humid and pale, not so much smoke as steam.

She knew what had happened. They got him, that was what.

The battering ram of water had knocked the Fireman right off his feet.

Without thinking, Harper ran deeper into the smoke, plunging toward where she thought she had heard his voice.

More yells, closer now. Some of them were moving into the cloud, coming toward her. No—coming toward the Fireman.

Her foot caught on something, a metal bar that clanged across the blacktop, and she stumbled, steadied herself. The halligan. Something moved nearby in the mist. Someone retched.

The Fireman rose unsteadily up onto all fours. His helmet had been blown off and his hair was drenched. His shoulders hitched. He gagged and vomited water.

"John?" she asked.

He lifted his head. His eyes were bewildered, unhappy.

"The fuck are you doing here?" he asked.

He rose to his knees, swaying, and opened his mouth to say something more. Before he could, a shape reared up in the clouds to his left, drawing his attention.

A thing—a bug-faced monstrosity—lurched out of the smoke. Its slick, glistening eyes were bright in the drifting mist, and it had a bulbous, grotesque mouth. Otherwise it resembled a man dressed in a fireman's turnout jacket and knee-high boots. It put one of those black boots between the Fireman's shoulder blades and shoved, and John was slammed down onto his face.

"You fuck," said the monstrosity—a fireman, a *real* fireman, in a gas mask. The Gasmask Man said, "You goddamn fuck, I got you now."

John started to rise onto all fours. The Gasmask Man cocked back one boot and drove it into his ribs, knocked his hands and knees out from under him.

"Fuck you, you little fuck," the Gasmask Man said. "You fucking fuck . . . guys! *Guys,* I got him! I *got* the fucking fuck!"

He booted the Fireman again, in the side this time, half turning him over.

Harper saw quite clearly that in moments John would be overrun, kicked to death by the Gasmask Man and his pals.

She bent and grabbed the halligan—

—and screamed in surprise and pain and dropped it. She looked at her hand in shock. Blisters were already forming on her reddened palm. The halligan was *hot,* nearly as hot as the business end of a branding iron.

Her cry caught the Gasmask Man's attention. He fixed her with his blind, terrible stare and pointed one gloved hand.

"You! Get the fuck on the fucking ground! Tits down, hands behind your fucking head! *Do* it, do it right the fuck—"

John rose with an angry shout, got his arms around the Gasmask Man's waist, and tried to throw him down. All he was able to do was back the guy up a few steps before the Gasmask Man—six inches taller and a hundred pounds heavier than John Rookwood—started shoving him the other way.

They grappled, turning in circles. The Gasmask Man closed his hands on John's right arm and twisted. A joint made a sickening, oddly wet pop. John went down on one knee and the Gasmask Man brought his knee up under his chin, snapped his head back. John toppled onto his back. The Gasmask Man stepped forward and put his boot on the Englishman's chest and stomped. Bones cracked.

Harper slipped off her coat, wrapped it around her burnt right hand, and scooped up the halligan bar again. Even through a fistful of fabric she could feel its heat, could smell it liquefying the nylon.

Harper lifted the halligan. The Gasmask Man turned, took his foot off John's chest, and came at her, arms spread. She slashed the halligan and the bar caught him across the helmet with a steely *thwang!* He took one more step and folded, diving face-first into the ground. His helmet sailed off, slicing Frisbee-like through the mist. It clattered to the blacktop, a grotesque dent creasing one side.

The sight of that dent sickened her. She felt bile rising in her chest, tasted it in the back of her throat. The sight of that dent was somehow worse than seeing a smashed-in head.

She didn't know what had made her do it. She had wanted to scare him away with the halligan, not crush his head in. She dropped the halligan in revulsion. It fell into the great dirty puddle spreading across the blacktop and hissed.

More yells. She saw another fireman sprint through the drifting white cloud of smoke and vapor off to her left. He raced past without seeing them.

The Fireman—her Fireman—had her by the elbow. His other arm, the right, hung at a strange angle at his side and he was half bent over, grimacing, a runner trying to catch his breath.

"You all right?" he asked.

She stared at him as if he were speaking in a foreign language. "John! I—I hit him with your halligan."

"Ooh, you did, too! Sounded like someone playing a steel drum." He grinned with admiration.

Someone yelled from what seemed only a few feet away. He glanced back over his shoulder, and when he looked at her again, the smile was almost gone. He gripped her shoulder.

"Come along," he said. "We have to go. Help me get his coat."

When she wouldn't go any closer to the dead body he let go of her and waded into the smoke. He bent with some effort—through her shock, she registered his face tightening with pain—and picked up the dented helmet. When he looked back at her, she still hadn't moved.

"His coat, Willowes!" he called to her. "Quickly now."

She shook her head. She couldn't. She couldn't even look at him. She had killed a man, smashed his brains in, and it was all she could do not to cry, not to fall on her knees.

"Never mind," he said, and for the first time he seemed impatient with her, even angry. He removed his own coat—it took a great deal of care for him to slip it gently off his dangling right arm—and when he got to her, he hung it over her shoulders. Beneath he wore a black shirt made of some kind of elastic material and bright yellow suspenders.

He went to put the dented helmet on her own head and she flinched, backed away. He followed her gaze to the body slumped on the ground and finally seemed to understand.

"Oh, for heaven's sake," he said. "You didn't kill him. Look—"

He stuck his boot behind the Gasmask Man's ear and gave a gentle nudge. The Gasmask Man made a small, unhappy shriek.

"There's no blood on it and no brains either, so put it on and *help me,*" he said, and this time she allowed him to set the helmet on her head. He stepped back and looked at her and grinned again. "Well! Aren't you the perfect little firewoman!"

And then his legs gave out.

# 12

She caught him before he could fall to his knees and got her hands around his waist. He sagged against her. He hummed a disconcertingly sunny tune, as they went around in a drunken circle.

"What is that?"

"The Hooters! *And we danced!"* He almost sang. "A lost treasure from a better time, the days of acid-washed jeans and fun hair. Do you like eighties music, Nurse Willowes?"

"Can we discuss the oldies another time?"

"What? *What?* The oldies? I've already had a man kicking in my ribs, and now you pull out my heart."

"Hey!" someone yelled at them, coming through the smoke. Harper looked past John and saw another Gasmask Man heading toward them, even bigger than the last. "You okay?"

Harper realized that in the shifting clouds, he believed they were firemen, too.

"He got away! The guy! The fucking fuck who made the smoke!" John shouted, and his voice carried no trace of an accent at all. "He clobbered us and went that way!" John pointed past her, through the streaming vapor.

"This fucking guy . . . this fucking guy *again,"* said the second Gasmask Man.

"We've got a fucking man down!" John cried, pointing back at the first Gasmask Man, sprawled on the ground. "Fucking fuck fuck!" Harper wanted to elbow him in the side, but his ribs couldn't take it.

"Go on, get the fuck out of here," said the second Gasmask Man. "Both of you. Get clear of the fucking smoke. I got him."

She had to help John walk, her arm around his waist, his

over her shoulders. They limped a few steps away and then the second Gasmask Man yelled at their backs.

"Hey! Wait!"

She forced herself to glance back, eyes lowered.

The second Gasmask Man extended the dropped halligan.

"Take it. There's a lot of fucking guys running around. I don't want someone falling down and taking a fucking hatchet to the knee."

"Right. Thanks," she said, then added, *"Fuck,"* for good measure.

The metal was still warm—her palm tingled painfully as she took hold of it—but the cold water on the ground had lowered its temperature enough so she could hold it without wrapping her hands first. She took hold of it and tugged, but for an instant the second Gasmask Man didn't let go of his end. Through the lenses of his mask, she saw his brow knot up. He was looking at the both of them, really *looking* at them, maybe for the first time. Just possibly he was thinking that fire*women* were few and far between, so few that he knew all of them by name and had suddenly recognized she didn't belong. In a moment he would jerk the halligan back out of her hand and come at them with it.

The damp white smoke eddied around them, sketching ghosts.

The second Gasmask Man let go of the halligan and turned away, shaking his head. He sank to one knee next to the man on the ground.

"Nurse Willowes," John murmured, and she realized it was safe to go.

She walked him through the smoke. Men ran past them, going the other way, calling to each other.

"He said 'this guy *again*,'" she said, leaning in to speak quietly into the cup of his ear. "Do you spend a lot of nights keeping the fire department in hysterics with creative acts of arson?"

"Everyone needs a hobby," he said.

Then they were through the smoke and into the parking lot, the Portsmouth Police Department not a hundred steps away on their left. The smoke was a towering wall of white cloud that masked the causeway and all of South Mill Pond behind them.

They had come out close to one of the two bonfires. It seethed, a sound it was impossible not to associate with rage, and she wondered, for the first time, if flame could hate . . . an absurd, childish notion that she could not quite set aside.

Lawmen milled about just beyond the double glass doors leading into the police department. Harper and John had emerged from the smoke right next to a cop with a round, freckled, innocent face, dressed in a black poncho and black rubber gloves. He didn't look at them, only goggled at the smoke. Harper thought she saw his lips moving in a soundless prayer. Was it any surprise, really? The whole world was burning and tonight they had seen the devil, come to claim his kingdom of fire at last.

Harper looked over at the first bonfire and saw they were not burning piles of clothes after all. Or, rather, they *were* burning piles of clothes—it was just that people were still wearing them. The bonfire to the left was a heap of desiccated bodies, blackened and shriveled corpses. In the flames, they snapped and whistled and crackled noisily, just like any kindling.

She glimpsed a dead woman, holding a dead child of about eight, the boy's face buried in her breast. She did not flinch from the sight. She had seen enough of the dead in Portsmouth Hospital. If she felt anything, it was simply that she was glad the two of them—mother and child—had died together, holding each other. To be held by your mother, or to be able to hold your child at the end, struck her as a kind of blessing.

"Keep your head down," John murmured. "He might see."

"Who?"

"The ex."

She looked past the first bonfire to the great orange town

truck on the far side. The tailgate was down, the rear end raised, as if to dump a heap of sand. Four or five bodies remained in the back end, had for some reason not slid out. Maybe they were frozen to the metal.

Jakob sat in the open passenger-side door, elbows on his knees, smoking a Gauloise. He was flushed, oiled with sweat from the heat of the bonfire, and hadn't shaved in a while. He had lost weight, and it showed in his face, in his sunken cheeks and the deep hollows around his eyes.

As if he felt her gaze—like a light touch on his scarred cheek—Jakob turned his head and stared back at her. His wounds had healed badly, shiny white slashes carved across the side of his face. Worse still was the black mark on his neck, a hideous burn in the shape of a man's hand.

She looked down, walked on. She counted to ten and risked another glance back. He had returned his stare to the causeway, peering dully into the smoke. He hadn't known her. That was maybe not such a surprise. Although she had recognized him right off, in some obscure way she felt she didn't know him, either.

"He isn't sick," Harper said.

"Not with Dragonscale."

Harper and John made their slow way across the parking lot, leaving the police station behind. The crowd thinned as they moved away from the lights. Although the other end of the parking lot was not entirely in darkness. The second bonfire cast a pulsing red glow into the gloom. The smell revolted her, a stink like they were burning wet carpet. She didn't want to look and couldn't help herself.

Dogs. They were burning dogs. Black ash drifted down out of the night.

"Look at all that ash," the Fireman said, blowing a flake away from his nose. "Idiots. Some of these men will be on our side of this battle in a few weeks. *You* may not have infected your husband, Nurse Willowes, but he may get lucky yet."

She gave him a questioning look, but he didn't seem inclined to explain himself.

"Why are they burning dogs?" she asked. "Dogs don't carry the 'scale, do they?"

"There are two infections running rampant. One is the Dragonscale, and the other is panic."

"It always surprises me when you do that."

"Do what?"

"Say something smart."

His laughter turned to a thin, anguished wheeze and they had to pause while he tottered in place, clutching his sides.

"My chest is full of broken glass," he said.

"We need to get you off your feet. How much farther?"

"There," he said, nodding into the darkness.

There were some other cars and pickups parked at the far end of the lot, and sitting among them was an antique fire truck—it had to be almost eighty years old—with a pair of headlamps set close together over a tall grille.

When John tried to lift himself up behind the wheel, he almost lost his footing and fell off the running board. She put her hands on his hips, caught and steadied him. He hung off the side of the truck, gasping. His eyes strained from his head, as if the simple act of breathing was work that required will and concentration.

When he had recovered himself, he tried again, hitching himself up into the old black leather seat. A copper bell hung from a metal brace, attached to the side of the windscreen. An *actual* bell, with a heavy iron clapper inside.

She went around to the other side of the truck and pulled herself in beside him. A pair of rusting steel brackets had been mounted behind the seats; the halligan fit neatly into them.

The engine, when it started, produced a pleasant series of throat-clearing sounds that made Harper think not of a truck, but of clothes tumbling in a dryer.

"Nurse Willowes, would you be a dear and wiggle the stick forward and to the right?"

He had his right arm crooked in his lap, left hand on the wheel. She didn't like the way his right wrist was turned.

"You better let me look at that arm," she said.

"Perhaps when we are at leisure," he said. "The stick."

She shifted it into reverse while he worked the clutch.

John eased the truck out from under the shadow of a great oak and onto the road, then asked her to put it into first for him. As they drove past the police department and out of the lot, he reached through the window and rang the bell, *ding-ding*. She thought of old film clips of San Francisco trolleys.

Perhaps as many as fifty people watched them go, and not a single one of them appeared to give them a second thought. One police officer even lifted his cap to them. Harper looked again for Jakob, but he wasn't sitting in the Freightliner anymore, and she couldn't spot him in the milling crowd.

"You have your own fire truck," she said.

"In a world with a fire burning on every corner, it's a surprisingly inconspicuous ride. Also you can't imagine how often a sixty-foot ladder comes in handy."

"I *can* imagine. You never know when you'll need to help a child escape from the third floor of a hospital."

He nodded. "Or change a reeee-alllly high lightbulb. Pull the gearstick back again? Into second—ah, lovely."

They left the bonfires, the smoke, the smell of burning man and dog, in a sudden rush of speed.

It had been a crisp wintry night down on the water. In the fire truck, moving at thirty miles an hour, it was arctic.

He ran the wipers and smeared gray ribbons of ash across the windscreen.

*"Ach,"* he said. "Look at all of that. We could infect most of Rhode Island with what we've got on the windshield."

They fled through the night.

"The ash," she said. "It's in the ash. That's why I didn't get Jakob sick. It doesn't transfer through any kind of touch. You have to come in contact with the ash."

"It's a surprisingly common way for fungus to propagate.

Third gear, please. Thank you. Farmers in South America will burn an infected crop and the airstream will carry fungal spores in the ash halfway around the world to New Zealand. *Draco incendia trychophyton* isn't any different. You inhale it along with the ash that protects it and prepares it for reproduction and soon it's colonizing real estate in your lungs. Could you shift us into fourth—yes, perfect." He smiled wanly and added, "I was there when you were infected, you know. The day the hospital burned. I saw you all breathing it in, but I was too late to warn anyone."

They banged a pothole—the truck didn't seem to have anything in the way of shocks, and they felt every rut, crack, divot, and seam—and he groaned.

"You're not too late to warn the rest of the world."

"What? You think I'm the first person to realize it spreads through the ash? I'm a lowly mycologist at a state college. Or was. I'm sure the process is well understood in the places where study of the Dragonscale is an active concern. Wherever that may be."

"No. If they understood transmission, they'd be warning people."

"Maybe they are . . . in the parts of the country that haven't fallen into chaos and been given up for dead. But you see, we're downwind. Of *every*one. The North American jetstream sweeps everything our way. Those who don't have it today will have it tomorrow, or next year. I believe it can wait in the ash for a host for a very long time. Thousands of years. Possibly millions."

The fire truck drifted off to the left-hand margin of the road. The edge of the hood clipped a mailbox, sent it flying. Harper grabbed the wheel and helped John bring the truck back into the humped middle of the lane.

John shivered weakly, touched his dry lips with his tongue. He didn't seem to be steering the truck so much as it was steering him, and he was hanging onto the wheel for dear life.

"It's really an ingenious cycle when you consider it. The ash infects a host who eventually burns alive, creating more ash to infect new hosts. Right now there's the sick and the well. But in a few years it'll just be the sick and the dead. There will only be those who learned to live with Dragonscale and those who were burned up . . . by their own terror and ignorance."

He reached out into the darkness and began to strike the bell, ringing it so loudly that it hurt Harper's ears, made her teeth ache. They were coming up on the turnoff. She wanted him to slow down, was trying to say it—*slow down, John, please*—when he grimaced and wrenched at the wheel, veering off Little Harbor Road.

The fire truck slung itself onto the snowbound lane that led to camp and sailed between the towering stones that flanked the entrance. Harper glimpsed a lean girl of perhaps twenty, standing to one side of the dirt track, the kid who had been assigned watch duty in the bus. She had heard John ringing his bell and known to drop the chain and let them through.

"Take us back down to third gear, Nurse Willowes—brilliant."

John swayed from side to side as the fire truck ran up the hill, slowing as it went. Harper began to go over in her mind what had to be done when she got him into the infirmary. She would need medical tape, gauze, Advil, scissors, a sling for his arm, compression bandages, a plastic splint. Beyond the Advil and the tape, she wasn't sure how much of that they had. They crested the hill—

—and continued on down the lane. The chapel flashed by on the left. The tires churned up a glittering spray of icy snow.

"You missed the turn to the infirmary," she said.

"We're not going to the infirmary. I can't be away from home all night. My fire will go out."

"So what? Mr. Rookwood, you're not making any sense. You have smashed ribs and a dislocated or broken wrist—with possibly a fracture to the forearm or the elbow as well—and you need to turn this thing around."

"I am long past the point where I could turn anything around, 'm'afraid, Nurse Willowes."

The truck continued to slow, thudding and rocking from side to side, as it passed through a gap in a thick band of fir trees and came out by the boathouse. He effortfully pulled at the wheel, braking as they rolled inside, past shelves of kayaks and canoes, and parked the truck in the center of the bare concrete apron.

He turned the key and they sat in cold, silent darkness. John sank forward until his forehead rested on the steering wheel.

"I have to get across the water, Nurse Willowes," he said, without looking at her. "I *have* to. Please. You said you want to help me. If you meant it, you'll get me back onto my island where I belong."

She climbed out and went around the truck to help him down.

He got his good arm over her shoulders and she lowered him, laboriously, first to the running board, then to the ground. His face was so pale it shone in the dark. His eyes widened with sudden wonder. Harper had seen that often enough in her days as a nurse. When the hurt came in full, it often left the injured as amazed as if they had seen a magician levitate.

They hobbled together over the glassy white surface of the snow, clinging to each other and creeping along in the mincing steps of the elderly.

A rowboat sat on the bank, oars stood up inside it. No canoes and no sign of Father Storey and the others. But then they wouldn't be back for at least an hour. It had been about that long getting to South Mill Pond in the boats, and they hadn't had to contend with fog.

A mist had come up and was piled atop the water, blanketing the horizon. John's little island was no more than three hundred feet offshore (at low tide it was almost possible to walk to it) but now Harper could see no sign of it.

"I hope they can find their way home in this," Harper said. "And that they'll figure out I went with you."

"Father Storey knows the way," John said. "He's been taking kids paddling along this shore since you were a kid yourself. Probably longer. And he knows I wouldn't have left you behind, either." Ignoring, Harper thought, that if it weren't for her, *he* would've been left behind.

John lowered himself gingerly into the bow and Harper shoved the rowboat off the bank, then clambered into the stern. She settled on the thwart and took the oars.

"Row," he said. "Take us across the River Lethe, ferryman. Ferrygirl. Ferrybabe." He laughed. *"Allons-y!"*

He reached for an oil lamp, set on the floor between the seats, raised the glass chimney, and stroked the wick with his finger. It ignited: a hot lick of blue flame. He glanced at her to make sure she was watching. Even hurt as he was, he loved the attention.

The oars clanked in their locks. She had a sensation of gliding out, not across the sea, but into the sky, across an impossibly buoyant acre of cloud. The mist parted before them, curling from the bow in luminous feathers.

Harper was still peering into the pale, cool, billowing fog, looking for the island, when they struck ground, jarred to a hard stop.

"Going to be a bit sloppy when we step out, but I don't imagine either of us will drown in the mud," he said. "Follow me and step where I step."

He got one leg over the side of the boat before she could get to him, and then fell sideways. He was holding the lamp and it flew from his hand, shattered somewhere in the dark, and went out. He shouted in pain, then laughed—a bad, drunken cackle that both frightened and irritated her.

She sprang from the boat and sank past her ankles into the tidal mud. It was like stepping into icy, sticky pudding. Harper lost a boot, struggling through the rank muck to his side. She lost the other boot as she helped him to higher ground. It was sucked off her foot with a wet smack of suction and she tromped on without it.

They made their unsteady way up onto damp, firm sand, through the cool wet. Harper spied the shed, a dim green wall with a white door set in it, and steered them toward it.

"You'll have to come back and drag the boat up." John lifted the latch and put his shoulder to the door. "The tide will come in and it will drift off if you don't."

Her eyes needed a moment to adjust to the gloom. She saw a cot; clothes hanging from a line; stacks of paperbacks that looked as if they had been soaked and dried many times, and were now swollen out of shape. A silvery fog-glow came through a pair of skylights, the only windows in the room.

In the back of the single-room workshop—that was the word that best described the place—was a big cast-iron barrel, turned on its side and raised off the floor on metal legs. Her father had a similar sort of thing in Florida, in his backyard; he used it to slow-roast BBQ pork shoulder. A chimney pipe was welded to one end, and bent away to disappear through the back wall.

The barrel had a sliding hatch in the side. Driftwood and heaps of sea grass were set in neat piles next to the homemade furnace. John let go of her and lurched unsteadily across the floor of narrow wooden planks, stopping before it. He peered in at a flame that burned in weird hues of green and blue.

"I'm here, darling," he said to the coals. "I'm home."

He found a few dry planks of driftwood and pushed them in the fire, his hands extending into the flame up to the wrists. Then he retreated, holding his sides. His eyes were glazed and blank and he never looked away from the furnace. He backed all the way to the narrow cot. When his calves struck it, he sat down.

Harper reached him, helped him lie back, and began to unbutton his shirt. He looked past her at his barrel full of fire. It seemed to hold him fascinated.

"Close the hatch," he whispered.

She ignored him, loosened his suspenders. "I want this shirt off."

"Please," he said and laughed weakly. "She might see us and get the wrong idea."

Harper put her palm to the side of his face. She didn't much care for the feverish heat she felt in his cheek. Harper tugged his shirt up, began to work it off him. It was no trouble to free his left arm, but when she began to wiggle it down the length of his right arm, he made a quick, gasping sound, somewhere between a sob and a laugh.

His right elbow was swollen, an ugly shade of purple mottled with darker, almost black spots.

"Can you bend it?" she asked.

The Fireman cried out when she lifted the arm gently, flexing the elbow, and moved her thumbs carefully over the knobs of bone. Nothing broken, but the soft tissues had gone fat and knotty, ligaments pulled into ragged threads. The wrist was worse than the elbow, already as thick around as his calf, with a deep blue bruise under the skin.

She took his right hand in one of hers and gripped his forearm with the other hand. She rotated the wrist, this way and that, looking for subluxation. A lump of bone—the lunate—had popped free from the others, come completely out of place.

"Is it bad?" he asked.

"Nothing serious," she said. She was going to have to realign it, the sooner the better. She crossed her thumbs over his wrist. His pale, almost colorless face was dewy with sweat.

"Say," he said. "You aren't about to do something awful to me, are you?"

She smiled apologetically and *squeezed*. The lunate squirted back into place between the other bones with a wet little *sock!* He shivered violently and shut his eyes.

Harper looked past his arm at his right side, discolored with a grotesque patchwork of bruises. She traced her fingers along his ribs. Fracture there. Fracture here. Another. A fourth.

"Harper," he breathed, gently. "I think I might pass out."

"It's all right if you do."

But he didn't. Not yet. He hunched on the edge of his mattress, shivering helplessly, battered arm clutched to his abused right side.

Harper wanted a sling for him. She shoved herself to her feet, began to sort through the clutter close to the bed. She found a box of dirty Frisbees, tennis balls, croquet hoops and mallets. Everything anyone would want for an afternoon of quiet fooling around outdoors. Tucked in behind the box was a camp longbow that had seen better days and—*there.* A canvas quiver with a few sad-looking, largely de-feathered arrows stuck in it. She dumped them clattering onto the floor. Another minute of hunting and she was able to turn up a pair of garden shears.

She snipped the quiver open from one end to the other, making a canvas trough. Harper loosened the strap that would've held the quiver to an archer's back. When she returned to the bed, John had dropped onto his left side across the mattress. He was still shivering, but in weak little pulses now. His eyelids drooped.

Harper fitted his right arm into her better-than-nothing makeshift sling, working with patient, deliberate care not to unduly jostle his wrist or elbow. He took a few short gasping breaths, but otherwise endured without a sound. When the arm was settled into place, she picked up his feet and flopped them on the mattress, then arranged a blanket over him.

She thought he had drifted off to sleep while she was tucking him in, but he whispered, "Now the hatch, please. To conserve heat. It'll keep the fire from burning down too quickly."

Harper pushed a curl of brown hair back from his sweaty temple and whispered, "All right, John."

She crossed to the furnace, but hesitated before clapping the hatch shut, her gaze drawn by the weird, vibrant hues of the blaze within: she saw flashes of jade and rose. She watched in a kind of peaceful trance for almost half a minute, and was just about to close the panel . . . when she saw her.

For a moment there was a face in the fire: a woman's face, with wide, startled eyes set far apart, and the smooth features of classical statuary, a face very like Allie's, but fuller and older and sadder. Her lips were parted as if she were about to speak. It was not a hallucination; not imagined; not a trick of the dancing firelight. The face in the flames stared at her for a full count of five.

Harper was trying to scream, but could not find the wind. By the time she was finally able to inhale, the woman she had glimpsed in the fire was gone.

# 13

Harper retreated, watching the flames for further wonders. Any thoughts of closing the hatch had been startled out of mind. She looked around for John, to ask him what she had just seen—to ask him what the *hell* was in the furnace—and saw he was asleep. His breath came in a thin, strained whistle.

She felt her own exhaustion deeply. Weariness was a dry, bitter ache in every joint. She settled in a soft chair with threadbare linen cushions, in a good position to watch the fire, to keep an eye on it in case it did anything else.

The flames rippled and flowed, casting their ancient hypnotic spell, draining the will and thought out of her head. It cast a blaze of heat, too, that was as agreeable as a comfortable old quilt. A part of her was afraid the woman would part those incarnadine curtains of fire and peer out at her once more. Another part of her longed to see her again.

She might've closed her eyes for a while.

A cry jolted her upright—a small sob of pain or terror. She wasn't sure how much time had passed, a minute or an hour, and didn't know if the cry had been real or imagined. She listened intently, but heard nothing more.

The flames had burned down some and she recollected at last that John had wanted her to close the hatch. It took all of her energy to get up and shut the sliding steel door. After she sat again and for a long while she floated, untethered, in the peaceful gray zone between sleep and wakefulness. She was as free and adrift as an empty boat on an empty sea, a good way to feel, but a bad thing to think, and suddenly she sprang all the way awake. The boat. John had warned her it had to be pulled farther up on the beach or they would be stranded.

The thought of losing the boat startled her out of the chair and onto her feet. The rest of her mental cobwebs were blasted away the instant she stepped outside into an abrasive, salty gust of wind.

It was near dawn and the fog was pearly and silken in the first light. The breeze was scattering it, pulling it to silvery scarves, and through a great rent in the fabric of the mist, Harper could see to the opposite shore.

Three canoes had been hauled up onto the snow. Everyone had come back alive, then. Nick was on the beach, dragging one of the canoes across the sand. Harper wondered who would've sent a little boy, all by himself, to haul the boats back into the boathouse. This close to morning, he belonged in bed.

She waved. The instant he saw her, he gave up on what he was doing with the canoe and began waving himself, frantically, flailing both arms over his head in the universal gesture of distress. And at last she registered the wrongness of the moment. Nick was not dressed for the weather, wore only a light black fleece and his slippers. And the canoe—he had not been dragging it *toward* the boathouse, but down into the water. No one had sent him to stow the canoes. He had come to find her.

In two steps she was up to her ankles in the brackish, stinking muck once again. Her boots were in that slop somewhere. She didn't look for them, just ran the rowboat into the water and stepped in.

By the time she pulled up alongside the dock, Nick was waiting with a mossy length of rope. He wound it around a cleat at the end of the boat, then seized her arm. She believed if he had been big enough he would've flung her up onto the pine boards, like a fisherman hauling in his catch.

He wanted to run but he didn't want to let go of her, either, yanking her arm as they climbed the steep slope. Nick's breath screamed in his throat. She couldn't go as fast as he wanted, crunching along in the granular snow in her bare feet.

"Stop," she said, and made him hold up with her, pretending

she needed to catch her breath when really she intended for him to catch his. "Can you write? What's happened, Nick?"

Harper slipped her arm out of his to mime the act of writing, scribbling an invisible pen on the foolscap of the milky air. But he shook his head, desperately, miserably, and ran on, not bothering to try and drag her anymore.

The mist rolled down through the trunks of the red pines, flowing like the ghost of a great flood, pouring over the ground, back toward the sea, in slow motion.

She followed him—pursued him, really—to the infirmary, where he had at last stopped to wait for her at the bottom of the steps. His aunt was beside him, dressed in thin flannel pajamas and barefoot herself.

"My father—" Carol said, her voice coming in savage bursts between sobs for air, as if she and not Harper were the one who had just charged half a mile up the hill through the snow. "It's my father. I prayed, I *prayed* you'd come back and you're here and you have to say you'll save him, you have to *say*."

"I'll do whatever I can," Harper said, taking Carol by the elbow, turning her toward the infirmary. "What happened?"

"He's crying blood," Carol said. "And he's talking to God. When I left him he was begging God to forgive the person who murdered him."

# 14

There were too many people in the ward. Carol and Harper squeezed through a crowd that included Allie and the Neighbors girls and Michael and a few other Lookouts. Some of them were holding hands. Mike had stripped to the waist and a red slick—blood and sweat—glistened on his chest. With his head bowed and his eyes closed and his lips moving in silent prayer, he looked like an Age of Aquarius seeker in a sweat lodge. A girl sat on the floor hugging her knees to her chest and sobbing helplessly.

Candles crowded the counters and bristled around the sink, yet the room was still only dimly lit. Tom Storey was stretched out in one of the camp beds. In the shadows he could've been a discarded overcoat lying on top of the sheets. Don Lewiston stood at the head of the cot.

"Young people," Harper said, as if she were decades older than Allie and Michael, and not a twenty-six-year-old who had finished school only four years ago. "Thank you. Thank you so much for everything you've done." She had no idea if they had done anything, but it didn't matter. It would be easier to steer them if they felt their important contributions had been recognized, if they believed they had made all the difference. "I have to ask everyone to leave now. We need air and quiet in this room."

Allie had been crying. Her cheeks were flushed, but hot white lines traced the passage of tears. Her Captain America mask, grimy and battered, hung around her neck. She gave Harper a small, frightened nod and squeezed Michael's hand. The two of them began to herd the others back into the waiting room, all without speaking.

Harper caught Michael's upper arm, drew him back. In a low voice she said, "Take Carol, too. Please. Tell her you want to sing with her. Tell her Nick is upset and needs his aunt. Tell her whatever you like, but *get her out of this room*. She can't be in here."

Michael moved his head in the slightest gesture of assent, then called back, "Miss Carol? Will you come sing with us? Will you help us sing for Father Storey?"

"No," Carol said. "I need to be with my father now. He needs me. I want him to know I'm here."

"He will," Michael said. "We'll sing together and call him to the Bright with us. If you want him to feel you close, that's how to do it. If you draw him into the Bright, he'll know you're with him, and he won't be scared or in pain. Nothing hurts there. It's the one thing we can do for him now."

Carol trembled in nervous bursts. Harper wondered if she was in shock.

"Yes. Yes, Michael, I think you're right. I think—"

Father Storey called out to them, in a voice that was good-humored but strained, as if he had been talking for a long time and his throat was worn out.

"Oh, Carol! When you sing I feel so in love with you my heart could crack." He laughed, sarcastic, un-Tom-like laughter. "After that last song, my heart is cracked just like a window! And a good thing, too! It's hard to see anything through stained glass."

Carol stood transfixed, staring toward him, a fixed look of pain and astonishment on her face, as if someone had stuck a knife into her.

Don Lewiston cupped Father Storey's skull, holding white cotton padding to his wound. Michael's shirt was wadded up on the pillow, the flannel already stiffening with blood.

Father Storey's eyes were open wide, each one looking in a different direction. One stared down and to the left. The other was pointed at the toes of his boots. He smiled with a certain low cunning.

"A thousand prayers every minute everywhere and what does God ever say back? Nothing! Because silence never lies. Silence is God's final advantage. Silence is the purest form of harmony. Everyone ought to try it. Put a stone in your mouth instead of a lie. Put a rock on your tongue instead of gossip. Bury the liars and the wicked under stones until they say no more. More weight, hallelujah." He took another little sip of air, and then whispered, "The devil is loose. I saw him tonight. I saw him come from the smoke. Then my head caved in and now it's full of rocks. More weight, amen! Better watch out, Carol. This camp belongs to the devil, not to you. And he isn't alone, either. Many serve him."

Carol stared at her father with a horror-struck fascination. Father Storey licked his lips.

"I brought this on myself. I called weakness kindness and told lies when I should've kept a stone in my mouth. I did the worst thing a father can do. I had a favorite. I am so sorry, Carol. Please forgive me. I always loved Sarah best. It is right and proper that I should go to her now. Give me another stone. More weight. I've said enough, amen."

He exhaled a long, dreamy breath and was silent.

Harper caught Carol's eye. "He doesn't mean it. He's suffering from a subdural hematoma. If he's talking nonsense, it's because of the pressure on his brain."

Carol looked back at her with a strange lack of recognition, as if they had never met before. "It isn't nonsense. It's a revelation! He's doing what he's always done. He's showing us the way." Carol reached out, blindly grasping backward, and took Michael's hand. She squeezed his fingers. "We'll sing. We'll sing and call him to the Bright. We'll give him all the light he needs to find his way back to us. And if he can't come back to us—if he has to go—" Her voice choked. She coughed, and her shoulders shook spasmodically, and she went on: "—if he has to go, he'll have our song to guide him and give him comfort."

"Yes," Harper said. "I think that's just right. Go and sing for him now. He needs your strength. And sing for me, because I need your strength, too. I'm going to try and help him, but I'm scared. It would mean the world to me if you could raise your voices for both of us."

Carol gave her a last, wondering look, then stood on her tiptoes and kissed her on the cheek. It was perhaps the last kindness she ever showed Harper. A moment later she brushed through the curtain and was gone, taking the others with her.

Don Lewiston was getting ready to walk out, too, pulling his sleeves down to button them.

"Not you, Don," Harper said. "You stay. I'll need you."

She circled behind the cot, taking Don Lewiston's place behind Father Storey's head. She gently lifted his skull in both hands. His silver hair was drenched in blood. She could feel the place behind his right ear where he had been struck, a warm wet lump, and another place, higher up, where there might've been a second blow.

"How did this happen?" she asked.

"I don't know," Don said. "I didn't get the whole tale. Mikey carried him into the camp, found him fackin' half dead in the woods. I guess it was one of the convicts. That's the early word. Ben is working on them right now."

Working on them? What did that mean? Didn't matter. Not now.

"And Father Storey couldn't say anything about what happened?"

"Not that made sense. He said it was a judgment. He said it was what he had coming to him for protecting the wicked."

"That's the pressure on his brain. He doesn't have any idea what he's saying."

"I know't."

She looked at Father Storey's pupils, sniffed his lips, and caught an unsurprising whiff of vomit. She thought about what she had to do and felt nauseated herself. Not the notion of doing it—it had been a long time since she had been squeamish about blood—but at the thought of getting it wrong.

In the waiting room, she heard voices warming up, heard the Lookouts humming together, trying to find the same note.

"I need a razor to shave away the hair back here," Harper said.

"Yes'm. I'll get'cha one," he said, and took a step toward the door.

"Don?"

"Yes'm?"

"Can you get your hands on a drill? Maybe from the wood shop? A power drill would be ideal, but I don't imagine you'll find one that has any charge. I'll settle for one I can crank by hand."

Don looked from her to Tom Storey—his white hair shampooed in red froth—and back.

"Oh, Jesus. Anything else?"

"Just hot water to sterilize the drill bit, please. Thank you."

When he didn't reply, she looked up to tell him that was all and that he should go, but he was already gone.

In the next room they began to sing.

# 15

Harper wiped Father Storey's face clean with a cool, damp kitchen towel, taking off soot and blood in long swaths to reveal the lean, curiously lupine face beneath. Now and then his left eye would well with another drop of blood. It would trickle down into his ear and she would wipe him clean again.

He seemed attentive, listening to the voices in the next room. They were singing the same song Harper had heard the night she first came to camp. They sang they were one blood and they sang they were one life. Harper was sure she would not be drawn into the Bright herself—she could not afford to drift away into that shimmering brilliance, where everything was easier and better. Her place was here, with the dying man. She wondered, though, if Father Storey might not be carried away, and if it might not be a real help to him after all, a replacement for the sedatives and the plasma she didn't have.

His Dragonscale, though, remained cold, dark swirls and scrawls on his old, loose flesh.

"God is a good story," he told her, all of a sudden. "I like that one and I also like frying pan and Wendy. We read that one together, Sarah, when you were little."

In her mind's eye, Harper glimpsed a serene, lovely face shaped in flame. She squeezed his hand.

"I'm not Sarah, Father Storey," Harper said. "I'm your friend, Nurse Willowes."

"Good. Nurse Willowes, I have a private medical blather to insult you with. I'm afraid someone has been playing us like a ukulele. Someone has been singing new words to old songs. It's important to act now. These savings won't last."

She said, "First we have to fix your head. Then we can worry about the thief."

"I would not put a thief in my mouth to steal my brains," he said. "Anyway, stones taste better. I think I hit my head on something and knocked my shadow off. Are you going to stick it back on, or did it get away?"

"All I need is a little needle and thread and we'll have you right as rain."

"Or at least right in my brain," he said. "I'm going down the drain. You know my little Sarah was an awful thief, too. She stole away from me—stole away from all of us. Even the Fireman. Poor John Rookwood. He tried not to kill her. I guess he's going to try not to kill you now. Probably he's in love with you, which is tough luck. Out of the frying pan and into the Fireman."

"Of course he tried not to kill her, Father Storey. He *didn't* kill her. I heard he wasn't even on the island when Sarah—"

"Oh! No. Of course not. He was an innocent grandstander. So was Nick. You can't blame the boy. They were both her unwilling accomplices. What she couldn't get from one she got from the other. She was a very accompliced woman. I know John blames himself, but he shouldn't. He's been incinerated for a crime he didn't commit. The bride died and we all cried. Not that they were married. They never would've married. All firemen are wedded to cinders, in the end. You ever ear that old hopscotch? John and Sarah, sitting in a tree, B-U-R-N-I-N-G." He paused, then his left eye fixed on something beyond her shoulder. "There's my shadow! Quick! Stitch it back on."

She looked. A dark form bobbed its head on the other side of the green curtain between the ward and the waiting room. Don Lewiston pushed through it, holding a steel pail of steaming water in one hand and a paper bag in the other.

"H'ain't gonna believe our fackin' luck," Don said. "I came up with a fackin' power drill, battery in it, still good. There's a old cuss what pull't in camp this week, had it in his pickup. I got the bit in the hot water right now."

"Do you have a razor? Scissors?"

"Yes'm."

"Good. Come over here. Father Storey? Tom?"

Tom Storey said, "Missed will owes?"

"Tom, I'm just going to give you a nice little haircut. Bear with me."

"What kind of beer? I'm not shally much a drinker but I ad go fuh a beer. I'm sull shirty."

Don Lewiston said, "You followin' any a this?"

"Don, I hardly follow you most of the time. Lift his head."

In the next room the song ended on a last deep note of harmony. Carol murmured to her small attentive flock. Carol and her faithful were deep in the Bright now, casting enough light to make the green curtain in the doorway glow an irradiated shade of lime.

Don held Father Storey's head between his crooked fingers while Harper clipped hunks of bloody hair away from the spot behind his ear where he had been struck. The scalp beneath was purplish-black, like eggplant.

In the waiting room their voices rose again. The Beatles now. The sun was coming, the long, lonely winter was over.

Father Storey stiffened and began to kick his heels.

"He's having a grand mal," she said.

"He's goin' t'choke on his tongue," said Don Lewiston.

"Anatomically impossible."

"We're losin' him."

Yes, Harper thought. If this wasn't a final convulsion, it was close to it. Foam dribbled from the corner of his mouth. His left hand grabbed fistfuls of the sheets, let them go, grabbed again. He couldn't do anything with the right hand. Harper was holding his right wrist, monitoring his erratic, racing pulse.

The song in the next room rose to a high, sweet, perfect note and Father Storey's eyes sprang open again and his irises were rings of gold light.

His back had been arched right off the mattress, so only his head and heels touched, but now he relaxed onto his bedsheets.

His heartbeat began to slow. Squiggles of dull red light pulsed in his Dragonscale, faded, pulsed again.

He almost seemed to smile, the corners of his mouth rising just slightly, and his eyelids sank shut.

"He's out," Don said. "B'God, it helped. They sang him outta the worst of it."

"Yes, I think they did. Put the bit in for me, will you, Don?"

"Are we doin' this?"

"He doesn't have much strength left. If it's not now, there won't be another chance later."

She shaved the rest of the hair off the back of Father Storey's head, to reveal the outraged flesh. It was no good giving herself time to think. It wouldn't help to dwell on maybe killing him, or lobotomizing him, slipping and driving the drill in deep enough to throw curds of brain.

Don stuck his hand in the nearly boiling water without any sign of distress—Harper thought those hands were just slightly more sensitive than a pair of canvas gloves—and brought up the dripping bit. He clicked it into a Black & Decker power drill straight from Home Depot and gave the trigger a squeeze. It whirred to life with a sound that made her think of eggbeaters and cake frosting.

He looked at the blackening bruise on Father Storey's scalp and swallowed.

"You aren't goin' ta ask me—" he began, then caught himself, and swallowed again. "I don't know how many fish I've put an end to, gutted and cleaned, but—a person—*Tommy*—I don't think I can—"

"No. I won't ask you to do it. It better be me, Mr. Lewiston."

" 'Course. You've done't before."

It was not quite a question, the way he put it, and she didn't think he required an answer. She held out her hand for the drill. The bit steamed.

"I will need you to hold his head. Do not let it move in any way while I'm operating, Mr. Lewiston," she said, in a tone of cold command that hardly seemed identifiable as her own voice.

"Yes'm."

He spidered his fingers over Father Storey's head, lifting it off the pillow.

She examined the drill, found the dial that controlled the power settings, and turned it up as far as it would go. She gave the trigger a test squeeze. It startled her, the bit spinning up to a chrome blur, the vibration shooting down her arm.

"I wish we had better fackin' light," Don said.

"I wish we had a better fackin' doctor," she said, and bent and located the tip of the drill two inches to one side of Father Storey's right ear, where the bruise was ugliest.

She pressed the trigger.

The bit chewed up the thin layer of skin in an instant, turning it to what looked like flakes of wet cooked oatmeal. The bone smoked and whined as the drill worked down into it. She applied pressure slowly, determinedly. Sweat sprang up on her face but Don was occupied holding the head still and she could not ask him to wipe her brow. A single drop of sweat caught in an eyelash and when she blinked, the eye began to burn.

Blood welled from the hole in the skull and raced up the grooves of the bit. She thought, obscenely, of a child sucking red Kool-Aid up through a Krazy Straw.

Without opening his eyes, Father Storey said, "Better, Harper. Thank you."

Then he was silent, and he did not speak again for two months.

# BOOK FOUR

# MARLBORO MAN

# 1

From the diary of Harold Cross:

**JUNE 18TH:**

THE GIRLS IN THIS CAMP ARE A PACK OF LESBIAN BITCHES AND IF THEY ALL BURNED TOMORROW I WOULDN'T GIVE A SMOKY FART.

THE WORD FROM SF IS THEY'VE GOT 2500 PEOPLE ALIVE IN THE PRESIDIO WHO HAVE THE 'SCALE AND NONE OF THEM ARE BURNING. FUCK THIS BULLSHIT. I'M GOING TO MAKE AN ANNOUNCEMENT IN CHURCH TOMORROW. SOMEONE NEEDS TO TELL THESE IGNORAMUSES YOU DON'T HAVE TO WORSHIP IN THE HOLY CHURCH OF CAROL STOREY'S SACRED PUSSY HAIRS TO LIVE. ANY RELEASE OF OXYTOCIN WILL TELL THE 'SCALE IT'S FOUND A SAFE HOST.

IF I HEAR ONE MORE ROUND OF "SPIRIT IN THE SKY" OR "HOLLY HOLY" I'M GONNA PUKE. WE COULD SHUT DOWN THE SPORE JUST AS EASY WITH ONE BIG CIRCLE JERK. A GIANT COMMUNAL CIRCLE JERK, AND CAROL'S PRETTY LITTLE HAND RIGHT ON THE ROD. HER DADDY CAN FRIG HER WHILE SHE FRIGS ME, THAT'S WHAT SHE REALLY WANTS ANYWAY.

I HAVEN'T WRITTEN A NEW POEM IN DAYS. I HATE THIS PLACE.

# 2

Harper read just the one page in Harold's notebook, picked at random, then flipped through some others. She glimpsed doodles of boobs and bush, saw some words in dark block lettering: SLUTS WHORES BITCHES CUNTS. Harper had never met him, but felt she understood Harold Cross pretty well. She thought a collection of Mr. Cross's poetry would probably go nicely alongside a copy of *Desolation's Plough*.

She turned back to the entry from June 18th and let her gaze linger on that one sentence: ANY RELEASE OF OXYTOCIN WILL TELL THE 'SCALE IT'S FOUND A SAFE HOST. She folded the notebook shut, slapped it against her thigh, and put it in one of the drawers . . . then, after a moment, took it out again.

The drop ceiling was made of big white squares of particleboard. She had to stand on a chair to reach them. Harper lifted one ceiling tile and pushed the notebook up and out of sight. Not as good as hiding it inside an anatomical model of the human head, but it would do for now.

She could not have said who she was hiding it from. Perhaps it was only that Harold had been hiding it himself, which meant he thought there was someone who would take it away if he or she had a chance.

As she was pushing the chair back where she found it, she noticed blood on her knuckles, staining the fingers of her right hand. Tom Storey's blood. She washed it off in icy water, watched pink swirls chase one another down the drain in candy-cane stripes.

Father Storey slept on his back, the top of his head bandaged in a cap of clean white gauze. The dusty windows above let in milky rays of sunshine. Like Father Storey himself, the daylight seemed tired out, hardly there. But the sheet was tucked under his chin, not pulled over his face. He had lasted the night. That was no small triumph.

Harper was woozy with exhaustion, but the baby wasn't going to let her sleep. The baby was hungry. What the baby wanted was a deep, warm, buttery bowl of Cream of Wheat, drowned in maple syrup. Food first, sleep after.

As she walked over the snow along a path of wobbling pine boards, through knee-high mist, she tried to remember what she knew about oxytocin. It had a nickname, "the cuddle hormone," because it was released when a mother held her baby—released in mother and child alike. Harper thought about crawling through that smoke-filled drainpipe and singing to the infant she hadn't seen yet and how it had shut down the 'scale.

Your brain gave you a fix of oxytocin when you hugged, when you received a round of applause, when you sang in harmony with someone and the singing was good. Strong communal experiences produced it like nothing else. You could get a dose from a good experience on Twitter or Facebook, too. When lots of people retweeted something you said or favorited a photo, they were throwing the switch for another squirt of oxytocin. Why not call it the social-networking hormone, then? That was better than "cuddle hormone," because—because—

She couldn't remember. There was something else about oxytocin, something important, but it had been too long since she had done the reading. For some reason, though, when she shut her eyes, she was picturing soldiers in desert fatigues and jackboots, cradling M16s. Why that? Why did oxytocin also make her think of crosses burning in the Mississippi night?

The cafeteria was padlocked from the outside and there was plywood nailed up in the windows. The place looked shut for the winter. But Harper had helped out enough in the kitchen to know where the key was hidden, hanging on a nail under the steps.

She let herself into the spacious, dusty dimness. The chairs and benches were all turned upside down on tables. The kitchen was gloomy, everything put away.

Harper found a tray of biscuits in the oven, covered with Saran Wrap. She took a tub of peanut butter from one of the cupboards, and was crossing the room to fetch a butter knife, when she almost stepped through an open trapdoor into the cellar. A slanted wooden ladder led down into a darkness that smelled of earth and rodents.

She was frowning at the open hole when she heard a curse from below, followed by a soft thud, as if someone had dropped a flour sack. A man groaned. Harper stuck a biscuit in her mouth and started down.

The basement was crowded with a lot of cheap steel shelving, plastic jugs of vegetable oil and sacks of flour packed onto them. Set into one wall was a walk-in freezer, the thick metal door open about half a foot and light shining out. She called "Hello," but didn't manage much more than a croak, had a throat full of dry biscuit. Harper crept to the massive door and poked her head inside.

The convicts were on tiptoes against the far wall. They were handcuffed together, the chain looped over a length of pipe located almost seven feet off the floor, so they had to stand there, each with an arm raised, like students trying to get teacher's attention.

She had seen one of the prisoners before—the big man with the queer yellow eyes—but the other was new to her. The second man could've been as young as thirty or as old as fifty, rangy and awkwardly built, with a high forehead that brought to mind Frankenstein's monster and a close-cropped cap of black hair, threaded with strands of silver. Both men wore thick woolen socks and the school-bus-colored jumpsuits.

The man Harper had met the night before grinned to show pink teeth. His upper lip was split open in a nasty gash and still drooling blood. The room had a rank stink of meat gone bad. Pools of gore had dried on the concrete, beneath rusted chains that had once suspended sides of beef.

Ben Patchett sat in a straight-backed wooden chair, his head between his knees. He looked like someone trying not to be sick. A battery-powered lamp sat on the floor next to a lumpy dish towel.

"What's going on here?" Harper asked.

Ben lifted his head and stared at her as if he had never seen her before.

"What are you doing here? You ought to be tucked into bed."

"But here I am." She was surprised at the mixture of aloofness and calm she heard in her own voice. It was not a tone she used with friends, but the one she reserved for irksome patients. "These men are suffering from exposure. Hanging them from a pipe wouldn't be my recommended course of treatment."

"Oh, Harp. Harper, you have no idea what—*this* guy. This guy here—" Ben said and gestured with his gun. Harper hadn't noticed until now he was holding it.

*"Me?"* said the prisoner with the bloody mouth. "Oh, yeah, *me*. I might as well 'fess up. I got sick and tired of dangling from this fuckin' pipe while shithead here shouts at me. I let my bad mood get the better of me and tried to attack his gun with my face. It's a shame you had to interrupt us. I was just getting ready to assault his boot with my nuts."

Ben glared. "I didn't do a thing to you wasn't self-defense." He looked at Harper. "He kicked me to the ground. Tried to stomp my head in, too."

"Self-defense, huh? Is that why you brought the towel full of rocks down here? You anticipated you'd have to defend yourself with 'em and your thirty-eight wasn't good enough?" said the bleeding man.

Ben blushed. Harper had never seen a grown man blush so hard.

She sank to one knee, folded back a corner of the towel on the floor. It was full of white rocks. She looked up, but Ben wouldn't meet her eyes. She peered over at the man with the busted mouth.

"What's your name?"

"Mazzucchelli. Mark Mazzucchelli. Lot of guys call me the Mazz. Lady, no offense, but if I had known this was what you meant when you said you were going to rescue us, I think I would've said thanks but no thanks. I was dying just fine where I was."

"I'm sorry. None of this should've happened."

"You got that right, Harper," Ben said. "Starting with the moment this fella decided to bash in Father Storey's head and run. Couple of guys found him trying to boost one of our cars, blood all over him."

"*Old* blood. Christ, it was *old* blood. Anyone could see it was old blood. Why would I attack this Father of yours anyway? Dude just saved my life. What would I get out of killing him?"

*"His boots,"* Ben said. "The ones you had on when we caught you running. His boots and his coat."

The Mazz looked at Harper with aggrieved, pleading eyes. "The guy, this Father of yours, he *gave* me his boots when he saw I didn't have any. Coat, too. He gave 'em to me because I couldn't feel my feet what for the cold. Is that the kind of guy you pay back with a rock to the head? Look, I've been tellin' this dude, I told him. The holy Father and I came back ahead of the other two boats. He was nothing but good to me. He gave me his boots and coat, 'cause he saw I couldn't stop shivering. When we got to shore, he led me into the woods. We walked, I don't know, couple hundred feet. Then he pointed at the church steeple and said stay on the path and in another minute or two I'd come to the chapel and there would be people to help me. He said he wanted to go back and make sure everyone else got to shore okay. I offered to give him his boots back but he wouldn't take them. And . . . all right. Look. I don't *know* none of you. I saw the chapel, but I also saw a perfectly good Buick parked around behind it, and I thought, *Shit, maybe I ought to go someplace where I* do *know people*. I didn't mean anything by it. I didn't know the car belonged to anyone."

"That's right. You didn't know it belonged to anyone. And

the world is just full of free cars. They're like picking daisies at the side of the road," Ben said.

"The world is fulla free cars *now,*" said the Mazz. "On account of a person relinquishes ownership of their wheels after goin' up in fuckin' smoke. There's probably a thousand cars in this state ain't no one ever gonna claim."

Harper stepped toward the convicts. Ben leaped up and caught her wrist.

"Don't. I don't want you near him. Stay behind me. This guy—"

"Is in need of medical treatment. My arm, please, Mr. Patchett."

He seemed almost to flinch from the formal use of his name. Or maybe he was flinching from her tone: calm, patient, but impersonal, quietly in charge. He let go of her arm, and if there was unhappy surprise in his face, perhaps it was because he understood he was letting go of his control over the situation as well. He could argue with Harper, but not with Nurse Willowes.

He looked past her to the prisoners. "You touch her—either one of you—I won't be using the *butt* of the gun on you, understand?"

Harper came close enough to the Mazz to smell his breath: a metallic odor of fresh blood. She leaned in to inspect his pink teeth.

"You won't need stitches," she said. "But I'd like to get a cold compress against your mouth. How are your feet?"

"Been a while since I could feel them. Gilbert is worse. Gil can hardly stand." He gestured with his head toward the other convict, who had not spoken yet. "And my hands . . . the cuffs . . . I got no circulation."

"We'll get those right off. Mr. Patchett?"

"No. They stay on."

"You can cuff them to something else if you think it's necessary, but you can't keep them like this, in a stress position. That has to stop. Whatever you think they've done, it doesn't justify abuse."

"I'll tell you about abuse!" cried the Mazz. "Keepin' us strung up here is the least of it! You ought to hear how I wound up with a busted mouth. See, I could take being locked up with my arm coming out of the socket, and I could take no food, nothing to drink, and no rest. What made me lose my composure is the feeling like maybe I need to have a crap. This one says he'd be glad to help me with that, soon as I start answering his questions the way he wants 'em answered. He said the next thing to come out of my mouth better be something good. I didn't want to disappoint him, so I spat in his fat cop face. Then he smashes me one. He would've hit me again, but I put my knee in his stomach and dropped him on the floor, which just goes to show I can whip his ass with one hand cuffed behind my back. *Literally.*"

Ben said, "Why don't you shut up before—"

"Before you give a handcuffed man another pistol whipping, Mr. Patchett?" Harper asked quietly.

Ben shot a startled, embarrassed glance at Harper, an expression that made her think of a sixth grader caught looking at a dirty picture.

"Shoot," he whispered. It was obvious he didn't want the convicts to hear him, but the acoustics of the bare metal room made a private conversation impossible. "Now, Harper. Come on. It wasn't anything like that. I cuffed 'em there because it was the easiest place, not to cause suffering. The towel full of rocks—that was just to scare them. And this guy tried to stomp my head in, same as he stomped in Father Storey's skull. I was lucky to get clear. I can't believe you'd take his word over mine. I have to think that's hormones talking."

"I don't care which of you is telling the truth," she said. It was an effort to keep the anger out of her voice. *Hormones.* "My concern is medical. This man is injured and can't remain hung up like he is. Get him down."

"I'll let him down. But he can wear the cuffs right into the crapper."

The Mazz said, "Fine by me. Long as you promise to wipe

my ass when I'm finished. And I better warn you, brother, this one feels like it's going to be wet."

"That's not helpful," Harper said.

"Copy that. Sorry, ma'am." The Mazz cast his gaze downward, but a smile teased the corners of his mouth.

"What about you?" Harper asked, turning to the man who hadn't spoken. "Gilbert. Do you need to use the facilities?"

"No, thank you, ma'am. I'm fairly constipated. I've been buttoned up for several days now."

This was met by a moment of silence and then Harper laughed. She couldn't help it. She could not even say why it was so funny.

"Gilbert. What's your last name?"

"Cline, but you can call me Gil. I don't need the bathroom, but I'd commit any number of crimes for a bite to eat."

"Don't worry," said Renée Gilmonton. "We won't let you go hungry, Mr. Cline. No felonies required."

Harper wheeled and saw Renée standing in the open locker door. Renée went on, "I don't know how you can maintain an appetite in here, though. *Whoo,* it smells bad. Is this the best we can do for them?"

"Jesus," Ben muttered. "First her, now you. I'm sorry the frickin' Hilton didn't have any rooms available for an attempted murderer and his accomplice. What the heck are you doing here? You ought to be asleep. No one should be out during the daytime. We have rules for a reason."

"The girls wanted an update on Father Storey and when I checked the infirmary, Harper wasn't there. I figured the cafeteria was the next best bet. Anything I can do to help?"

"No," Ben said.

"Yes," Harper told her. "This man needs a cold compress for his face, a cup of hot tea, and a visit to the bathroom, although probably not in that order. Both of them ought to have breakfast. And you're right, this is a filthy place for them. There's two unused beds in the infirmary. We ought to—"

"Out of the question," Ben said. "They stay here."

"Both of them? Right. I was meaning to get to that. You said Mr. Mazzucchelli assaulted Father Storey. I'm not clear why Mr. Cline is also locked up."

"Because they're in it together, these two. They already partnered up to break out of one place."

"But I take it Mr. Cline was nowhere near the scene of the attack on Father Storey?"

Ben's eyes were dull, expressionless. "No. He was in the boat with me. Father Storey and Mazzucchelli arrived back at camp first. Then Allie and Mike. Cline and me got lost paddling around in the mist and for a while I couldn't find the bay. Finally I spotted a flashing light and we rowed toward it. It was Allie, signaling us from the beach. She stayed on the beach to be sure we found our way back, while Michael went on ahead. We had barely pulled the canoe onto shore when we heard Mike screaming for help. We proceeded to the scene"—Harper noted the way Ben had unconsciously begun to tell the story as if he were giving a deposition to a hostile lawyer—"and found Mike sitting in the snow with Father Storey and blood everywhere. Mike said someone had killed him. But when Allie checked his pulse, we determined he was still with us. Michael carried Father Storey into camp, which was where we found a few men holding Mr. Mazzucchelli. Allie observed that Mazzucchelli was wearing Father Storey's boots and coat. After that the situation turned hostile. Both these men are lucky they weren't killed."

"That still doesn't explain why Mr. Cline is being treated as a threat," Renée said.

Gilbert said, "When things turned ugly, my partner shouted for help. I gave it."

"He broke three fingers in Frank Pendergrast's right hand," Ben said. "And punched Jamie Close in the throat so hard I thought he crushed her windpipe. Jamie is nineteen, by the way, barely more than a kid."

"A kid who was holding a broken bottle," Gilbert said, almost apologetically.

"I'll need to see them both," Harper said. "I should've seen Mr. Pendergrast before now."

"He didn't want to distract you from Father Storey," Ben said. "Don bandaged him up pretty good with some rags we had laying around."

"Goddamn it," she said.

The injuries she couldn't adequately treat because she didn't have the supplies kept piling up: subdural hematoma, facial contusion, advanced exposure, John's sprains and smashed ribs and dislocations, now a badly shattered hand. She had iodine, Band-Aids, and Alka-Seltzer. She had sealed the hole in Father Storey's skull with cork and candle wax, like a doctor from the seventeenth century. It *was* the seventeenth century out here in the woods.

Ben went on, "Whatever Cline did and whyever he did it, let's be clear. We all knew who bashed in Father Storey's head, Cline as well as us. He chose his side."

"He chose not to watch his friend be killed by a lynch mob," Renée said. "That's understandable."

Ben looked at Gilbert Cline and said, "What I understand is he ought to pick better friends. His buddy nearly killed a man. Cline knew it. He could've stayed out of it. He chose to commit some life-endangering assaults of his own. You want to dispute any part of this story, Cline, you go on and speak right up."

"No, sir," Gilbert Cline said, but he was looking at Renée. "That's how it happened. The Mazz is the only reason I didn't die in the lockup. And I never would've made it through the smoke and down to the canoes if not for him. I could barely move my legs. He just about carried me. I felt obliged not to stand back and watch him get killed."

"And did you think he bashed in Father Storey's head?" Ben asked.

Cline looked at Mazzucchelli and back to Ben. His face was a calm, composed blank. "It didn't cross my mind it mattered one way or another. I owed him."

Harper had, until now, been concerned with injury and exposure. She had not paused to think about what it meant if Mark Mazzucchelli had really done it . . . really taken a rock to the back of Father Storey's head, all for a pair of boots.

The rock.

"Was the weapon on Mr. Mazzucchelli when you discovered him trying to get away?" Harper asked.

"No," the Mazz said. " 'Cause it's all bullshit. I never had no weapon."

"We haven't found what he used to crush Father Storey's head in," Ben said, his voice stiff. "Not so far. We may turn it up yet."

"So what you have is an assault with no witnesses, no weapon, and a man who professes his innocence even after you hung him up in a stress position and struck him with your gun."

"It wasn't even a little like—"

Harper held up a hand. "You're not in court and I'm not a judge. I don't have any authority to go casting judgments. *And neither do you.* As far as I'm concerned, you don't have proof of *anything,* and until you do, these men ought to be treated as well as anyone in camp."

Renée continued, "And without any evidence of wrongdoing, I'm curious how long you plan to keep them locked up and on what basis. There needs to be some kind of fair process. They have a right to a defense. They have a right to *rights.*"

"I'd love to take that dump now," said the Mazz, but no one listened to him.

"I don't know if you heard, Renée," Ben said, "but the Constitution went up in flames, along with the rest of Washington D.C. The people in this camp would like very much not to wind up in cinders as well, Ms. ACLU."

"I used to donate to them every year, in fact," Renée said. "Never mind that, though. I'm trying to make a point. We don't just need to decide whether or not this man tried to kill Tom Storey. We need to decide *how* we decide, and *who* does the deciding. And if Mr. Mazzucchelli here *is* found guilty, we have to make a choice, as a community, about what to do with him . . . about what we can live with. That's the hard part."

"I don't think it's that hard. I think this community has already made a choice. You would know that if you'd been there when they started throwing rocks. I don't know what you were doing all night, but you missed all kinds of fun."

"Maybe I spent my night hiding in the woods," Renée said, "waiting for a chance to kill Father Storey."

Ben stared, his mouth open and his brow furrowed, as if she had just posed a particularly irritating riddle. He shook his head.

"You shouldn't make cracks. You don't have any idea what Carol and Allie and that crowd would do to you if they thought . . ." His voice trailed off, and then he started again, with a hard smile on his face. "Thing about you, Renée, you're a good-intentions person. With your tea and your books and your story sessions for the kids, you're just as harmless as they come. And like most really harmless people, you don't have the faintest idea what other people are capable of doing."

"But don't you see, Ben? That's precisely my point. We *don't* know what other people are capable of doing. None of us does. Who could say for certain Father Storey wasn't surprised by someone in this camp who wants to do him harm? For all you know, *I* might have a reason to want him dead, and it *might've* been me waiting in the trees with a rock. It could've been *anyone,* and without certainty we can't publicly execute a man. We ought not to even lock him up indefinitely."

"That's where you're wrong, Renée. That's where you talk yourself into a corner. See, Mark Mazzucchelli here, he had a motive *and* he had an opportunity. Which is bad. But what's worse, I can't think of one other person in this whole camp would wish harm on the sweet old man who took us all in, who gave us shelter, and who taught us how to protect ourselves from the Dragonscale. It's that simple. I can't think of one reason why anyone else would want Father Storey dead."

Which was when Harper remembered what Tom Storey had told her in the canoe.

*I'm going to have to send someone away,* he had said. *Someone who has done . . . unforgivable things.*

"Oh," Harper said, "I can think of a reason."

# 3

From the diary of Harold Cross:

**JUNE 19TH**

THE SHITTERS. THE LOATHSOME IGNORANT SHITTERS.

**JUNE 19TH, LATER:**

OFFICER CATSHITT TOOK MY PHONE. AND BEFORE HE SWITCHED IT OFF HE WIPED IT, RIGHT IN FRONT OF MY EYES. EVERY TEXT, EVERY MAIL, EVERY NOTE.

THEY DIDN'T UNDERSTAND ANYTHING. THEY DIDN'T EVEN TRY TO UNDERSTAND. AS SOON AS I TOLD THEM I HAD BEEN COMMUNICATING WITH PEOPLE ON THE OUTSIDE THEY WENT INTO HYSTERICS. IF THEY HAD THE JIM JONES KOOL-AID ON HAND THEY ALL WOULD'VE BEEN LINED UP FOR A CUP. NOW THAT I'VE CALMED DOWN, I WONDER IF I SHOULD HAVE ANTICIPATED THIS.

THE MOST UNIQUE CHARACTERISTIC OF THE FUNGUS IS THE WAY IT BONDS WITH THE MIND. DOCTOR SOLZHENITSYN IN NOVOSIBIRSK HAS SHOWN THE SPORE IS DENDRITIC IN NATURE AND COMPATIBLE WITH THE ARCHITECTURE OF THE BRAIN. OXYTOCIN TELLS DRACO INCENDIA TRYCHOPHYTON IT HAS FOUND A SAFE ENVIRONMENT. THE FUNGUS, IN TURN, STIMULATES FLOCK BEHAVIOR TO PRESERVE ITS OWN WELL-BEING, THE SAME GROUP-THINK THAT MAKES A CROWD OF SPARROWS TURN ON A DIME. THE 'SCALE IS SO OVERPOWERING, IT CAN TEMPORARILY ERASE EVEN FUNDAMENTAL NOTIONS OF PERSONAL IDENTITY. OTHER PEOPLE'S IDEAS SEEM LIKE YOUR OWN, OTHER'S PEOPLE'S NEEDS SEEM MORE IM-

PORTANT THAN YOURS, ETC. WE REALLY ARE LIVING IN THE ZOMBIE APOCALYPSE, IT'S JUST THE ZOMBIES ARE US.

ALL THIS MAKES SENSE, GIVEN THE NATURE OF OYXTOCIN, WHICH BRINGS COMFORT TO THOSE WHO PARTICIPATE IN TRIBAL BEHAVIOR. I'M NOT PART OF THIS STUPID CHRISTING TRIBE WHICH IS WHY I'M SMOKING ALL THE TIME AND GETTING NO CHEMICAL BENEFIT FROM THEIR IDIOTIC DAILY SINGALONGS. IT ALSO EXPLAINS WHY EVERYONE WAS SO EAGER TO TURN IN THEIR CELL PHONES (YES, FUCKFACE TOOK ALL OF THEM, NOT JUST MINE). THE 'SCALE HAS THEM ALL ADDICTED TO SOCIAL APPROVAL.

I WOULD LOVE TO KNOW WHY THE FIREMAN CAN STEER THE 'SCALE INSTEAD OF BEING STEERED BY IT. NO ONE IS MORE ALOOF THAN HIM. I WOULD KILL TO KNOW HOW HE CAN SET FIRE TO PARTS OF HIMSELF AND NOT BE HURT.

I'M NOT THE ONLY ONE WHO WANTS TO KNOW WHAT HE KNOWS, EITHER. I WAS DOWN ON THE BEACH THREE DAYS AGO AND HEARD THEM OVER ON THEIR ISLAND, YELLING AT EACH OTHER. WHATEVER HE KNOWS, HE WON'T TELL SARAH STOREY, AND BOY OH BOY IS SHE PISSED.

IF SHE TEARS HIM A NEW ASSHOLE, IT'S TOUGH SHIT FOR MR. ROOKWOOD. THIS INFIRMARY IS ALL OUT OF ASSHOLE PATCHES. AND EVERYTHING ELSE.

# 4

She swatted her thigh with the notebook and looked out the window. Goosedown flakes of snow floated about, couldn't decide if they wanted to fall or rise. Camp was a snow globe and some God-child had given it a shake.

Harper had been awake for fifteen minutes and still wasn't sure if it was morning or afternoon. The light was diffuse and gray, as if the whole world were hidden under a bedsheet. She sat on the edge of Father Storey's cot. Every once in a while he would draw a sudden, startled-sounding breath, as if he had just read something terrible in the newspaper. The obituary of a friend, maybe. His own obituary.

One thing that had been true in the summer of Harold Cross was even more true now. The infirmary was out of asshole patches and everything else. She had disinfected Father Storey's trepanation with a splash of port and had treated John Rookwood's mauled arm with a weak dose of good intentions. She wasn't sure good intentions always paved the road to hell, but they for sure weren't the highest standard of medical care.

She stood on the chair and reached up to put Harold's notebook behind the ceiling panel. Some little movement or gesture at the edge of her vision caught her attention. She looked around and discovered she and Father Storey had company that morning.

Nick was in the cot closest to the door, sheets pulled to his chest. His hair was a pretty black tousle. He gazed at her as if he had forgotten how to blink. He must've crept in while she was asleep and quietly settled into the first empty bed.

She pushed the notebook up out of sight, deciding to act as if this were a perfectly normal thing to do. When the ceiling tile was back in place she climbed down off the chair and stood at the foot of Nick's cot. Harper moved her hands carefully, using what he had taught her so far to ask why he was here.

He reached for the notepad and pen he carried with him everywhere he went, and wrote: *My stomach hurts. Allie walked me over. She had to come to the infirmery anyway because she's stashioned here today.* Harper sat beside him on the cot, took his notepad, and wrote: *Have you been vomiting? Diarrhea?*

He shook his head. She suspected anxiety for Father Storey, not food poisoning.

*What do you mean, Allie is stationed here?* Harper wrote and passed him his pad and pen.

*She's in the other room,* Nick scrawled.

Harper raised her shoulders in an exaggerated shrug, hands out, palms turned up: *Why?*

*Allie's here for protecshun. Aunt Carol wants to make shure granddad is safe. What did you just stick in the ceiling?* Before she could formulate a reply, he added, *I promise if you tell me I won't SAY A WORD.* She had to smile at that. Of course he wouldn't.

*Just some notes I'm keeping,* she said, which was true, even if it was leaving out a detail or two.

*Notes on what?*

*If you don't ask about that,* she wrote, *I won't ask if you really have a stomachache.*

He smacked the heel of his hand into his forehead, a gesture he must've picked up from television. She didn't judge. Harper sometimes felt she spent half her life playing Julie Andrews in the movie version of her life. The problem with role models is they teach you roles.

Harper used her finger-spelling to say *S-L-E-E-P.*

He nodded and said, "You too, right?" Speaking in silence, hands moving precisely through the air, as if he were adjusting the gears of an invisible machine.

"I go," she said with her own, less fluent hands. "Be soon back."

"Be careful," said Nick's hands.

Allie was in the waiting room, curled on the couch. Not asleep, not reading—just lying there with the knuckles of one hand pressed to her lips. She blinked and glanced up. For a moment her eyes were unfocused and she seemed to look upon Harper without recognition.

"Nick says you've been stationed here."

"Looks like. You've got Ben and Aunt Carol thinking someone in camp might be out to kill Granddad. I think that's nuts—everyone knows it was that guy the Mazz—but I don't call the shots."

"And Ben does?"

"He's just doing what Aunt Carol wants. And she wants Granddad safe. You can't blame her. Someone *did* try to kill him. Aunt Carol wants you to stay here from now on, too. So there's always medical staff on hand, in case he has a seizure or whatever."

"Am I going to start eating here, too?"

Harper was joking, but Allie said, "Yeah. She was really upset when she heard you wandered off yesterday to get something to snack on and left him all alone. His heart could've stopped. Or someone could've walked in and put a pillow over his face."

"I can't stay here. Not full-time. As a matter of fact, I have to step out right now. John's pretty banged up. I want to head over to his island and get a compression bandage and a brace on him."

Harper was not carrying either item but was counting on Allie not to notice, and she didn't.

"Can't," Allie said. "Even if you were allowed to leave the infirmary, it's the middle of the day. No one goes out during the day."

"What do you mean, even if I was allowed? Is that from Carol? Who put her in charge?"

"We did."

*"Who?"*

"All of us. We voted. You weren't there. You were sleeping.

We gathered in the church and we sang for Father Storey. We sang to everyone we've ever lost to show us what to do. I swear I could hear them singing with us. There were only a hundred and forty people in church, but it was like a thousand people singing all at once." Allie's bare arms pebbled with goose bumps at the memory of it. She hugged herself. "It felt like being *rescued* . . . from every bad feeling you ever had. I think it was just what we needed. Afterward, we settled down, and held hands, and talked. We talked about the things we were still glad for. We said thanks. Like you do before a meal. And we made plans. That was when we voted to give Ben final authority on all security matters. And we voted to make Aunt Carol head of the chapel services and daily planning, which is what Father Storey used to do. At first she didn't want to. She said she couldn't take on any more work. She said she needed to look after her dad. So we took another vote and everyone voted for Carol all over again. So then she said we were making a mistake. She said she wasn't strong like her father. That he was better than her in every way. Kinder and more thoughtful and patient. But we took a *third* vote and she won that one, too, unanimously. It was funny. It was so funny. Even Carol laughed. She was kind of crying-laughing."

Harper thought of something in Harold's diary—**THE FUNGUS STIMULATES FLOCK BEHAVIOR TO PRESERVE ITS OWN WELL-BEING, THE SAME GROUP-THINK THAT MAKES A CROWD OF SPARROWS TURN ON A DIME**—but she didn't like where that thought led her and pushed it aside.

Allie said, "I don't think I ought to let you go. The last time I was on duty in the infirmary and didn't do my job, a kid got killed." She gave Harper a crooked smile that had no real happiness in it.

"What are you going to do to me if I walk out? You going to tackle a pregnant woman?"

"No," Allie said. "I'd probably just shoot you in the leg or something."

She was smirking when she said it and Harper almost laughed. Then she saw the Winchester leaning in one corner of the room.

"Why in God's name do you have a *gun*?" she cried.

"Mr. Patchett decided the Lookouts on guard should have rifles," Allie said. "He said we should've passed out the guns a long time ago. If a Cremation Crew turns up, a little bit of shooting would—"

"—would get a lot more people killed, is what it would do. None of you ought to be carrying rifles. Allie, some of the Lookouts are all of fourteen years old." Harper did not mention that Allie herself was not yet seventeen. The idea of the kids stalking around in the snow with loaded guns agitated her, made her want to give Ben Patchett a hard poke in his soft gut.

"It's only the older kids," Allie said, but for the first time she sounded defensive.

"I'm going," Harper said.

"No. *Don't.* Please? Let's wait until dark and we can talk to Carol. Going out in the daytime is pretty much the most important rule in camp. It'll be dark soon."

"In this snow it might as well be dark already."

"We pulled the boards up. You'd leave tracks."

"Not for long. It's snowing now. My tracks will fill in. *Allie.* Would you let anyone tell *you* that you couldn't go?"

She had her there.

Allie stared into a blue dimness silted with a billion diamond flecks of flying snow. The muscles at the corners of her jaw bunched up.

"Shit," she said, at last. "This is so stupid. I shouldn't."

"Thank you," Harper said.

"You need to be back in two hours or less. If you're not back in two hours, I'm going to feed you to the wolves."

"If I'm not back in two hours, you ought to get Don Lewiston anyway, just to check on Father Storey's condition, see how he's doing."

Allie glared at Harper. "You have no idea how fucked this is. All us Lookouts met after chapel. Ben Patchett said too many people have been putting themselves ahead of the well-being of camp, doing what they like. He said we need to make some *examples* out of people who can't follow our rules. We all voted. We agreed. We made a *pact*."

"Mr. Patchett can worry about the well-being of the camp," Harper said. "I need to worry about the well-being of my patients. If he finds out, you tell him you tried to make me stay and you couldn't stop me. But he's not going to find out, because I'll be back before you know it."

"Go if you're going to go, then. Before I change my mind."

Harper had her hand on the latch when Allie spoke again.

"I'm glad he likes you," Allie said. "John is the loneliest person I know."

She glanced back, but Allie wasn't looking at her anymore. She was flopped on her side, curling up on the couch once more.

Harper thought the gentle blessings of children were often as unprovoked, unexpected, and uncalled for as their cruelties. Camp Wyndham that winter was neither Hogwarts nor the island in *Lord of the Flies*, after all, but a place of wandering, damaged orphans, kids who were willing to forgo eating lunch so there was enough food for others.

"I'll be back soon," Harper said, and when she said it, she believed it.

But she did not return until long, long after dark fell, and by then everything in camp had changed again.

# 5

The trees were ghosts of themselves in a smokeworld of low clouds and falling snow. The dying afternoon smelled like pinecones burned in an ashtray.

Harper meant every word of what she had promised Allie: that she was going to paddle over to the Fireman's island, check his condition, and come back. She had left out the part about needing to go home first because the infirmary cupboard was all but bare and she was going to have to hunt through her personal supplies for the things John needed. If Allie knew about *that,* she might've knocked her down and sat on her chest to keep her from going.

She thought she might have a good poke around while she was home. See what else she could find that might be of use in Camp Wyndham. Shampoos and books and socks.

But when she got there she discovered there wasn't as much to poke around in as she expected. She stopped at the edge of the woods, looking at what was left of her house with a feeling of shock so intense, it approached awe.

The side of the house facing the street had collapsed in on itself, the entire face swept away. Some great force had dragged the living room couch out into the yard and tossed it all the way to the edge of the driveway. Snow had mounded up on it, but Harper could still see the armrests. She guessed there was some more junk scattered across the lawn, but they were just lumps under the snow now. It looked like her house had been brushed by a tornado.

She caught her breath and thought back to the night she left. She remembered a rending crack, so loud it shook the ground. Jakob had climbed into his Freightliner and sideswiped the snowplow through the front of the house, dropped the roof in on what remained of their life together.

Papers hung impaled from bare tree branches, scattered all along the edge of the woods. Harper pulled one down: a page from *Desolation's Plough.* She read the first words—`despair is no more than a synonym for consciousness, and demolition much the same as art`—and let the fretful breeze tug the sheet out of her hand. It flapped away in the wind.

Harper was so dazed, she almost forgot her plan and drifted out of the woods into the yard, leaving footprints all the way. But a car shushed past on the road, making a sound like an admonition to be silent, and reminded her to take care. She worked her way around the house to the south side of the ruin, where trees crowded close to the wall. A single red spruce hung a wet and glistening limb over the snow, reaching out to almost touch the vinyl siding.

In a doctor's office of the mind, Nurse Willowes—dressed in crisp medical whites—addressed Miss Willowes, six months pregnant, sitting on the exam-room table in a paper gown. *Oh, yes, Miss Willowes, I hope you will continue at the gym. It's important to stay healthy and active for as long as you can do so comfortably!*

Harper wrapped both hands around the branch, which was about four feet off the ground, inhaled deeply, and *swung.* She pendulumed across two yards of snow and reached down with her feet, and her toes found purchase in the icy gravel that bordered the house. She felt herself sliding back, was in danger of letting go and falling onto the frozen ground. She pedaled her feet at the loose rock, lunged, and let go of the branch. Harper fell against the wall, the rubbery lump of her belly bouncing gently off the siding. A little extra cushioning, it turned out, came in handy.

She followed the narrow strip of gravel under the eaves around to the back of the house. The door into the basement was locked, but she did the combination jiggle-*kick*-shoulder-

*thump* Jakob had taught her and it opened up. She stepped into cold, stale air and pulled the door shut behind her.

When they first moved in they had remodeled the basement into an "entertaining area," complete with bar and pool table, but it had never really stopped feeling like a cellar. Cheap nubby carpet over cement floor. An odor of copper pipes and cobwebs.

The collapse of the house above had led to much more radical redecorating. The fridge had dropped through the ceiling from the kitchen and toppled over onto its side. The door hung open to show the condiments and salad dressings still nestled on the shelves. Wires dangled from the hole overhead.

The pool table remained curiously undamaged in the center of the room. Harper had never learned how to play. Jakob, on the other hand, could not only run the table, but could balance a pool stick on a single finger and a plate on the end of the cue, another of his circus tricks. In retrospect, Harper supposed it did not pay to be too impressed with a man just because he could ride a unicycle.

The camping supplies—tent, portable gas stove, oil lamp—were in the bank of cupboards against the back wall, and the first aid kit was packed in there with them. They had always liked backpacking. That was one thing she could look back on with fondness: they had both been crazy for sex in the woods.

She had badly twisted an ankle when they were hiking in Montana, and Jakob had cheerfully carried her piggyback the last mile to the Granite Park Chalet. She had bought the first aid kit as soon as they got home, to be prepared for the next time one of them banged themselves up on a hike, but there was no next time, and after a few more years there was no more hiking.

The kit was better stocked than she remembered. It contained a stack of compression bandages alongside ice packs and burn cream. But the real prize was shoved in next to the first aid supplies, and was the thing she had wanted most, her central reason for returning: a black elastic elbow brace, left over from two years before. Jakob had wiped out, playing her in racquetball, and sprained his arm. They hadn't ever played after that. Jakob claimed the elbow still sometimes gave him a twinge and said he didn't want to risk straining it again, but she had sometimes imagined he quit racquetball for far less understandable reasons. She had been shutting him out at the time he smashed his elbow into the wall. It wasn't so much that he hated losing. It was just that he hated losing *to her.* In their relationship, he was the coordinated one, and Harper was comically, adorably clumsy. He took it personally when she stepped out of character.

She rooted around in the other cupboards and found a long box of Gauloises, shoved back on a high shelf, the cellophane peeled off and a few packs missing. Jakob had announced, a year before—a million years before—that he had quit smoking cold turkey and felt sorry for people who didn't have the willpower to do the same. For once she was glad he was full of shit. As in any guerrilla economy, there was no underestimating the value of cigarettes these days. People had been wrong to hoard gold for the collapse of civilization. They would've been better served to stock up on Camels.

She went around behind the bar to see what they had for booze. Facing the counter, at her back, was a smoked-glass door that opened into an empty hole where they had planned to put a stereo someday. Hadn't got around to it. Jakob had insisted on a Bang & Olufsen system that cost almost ten thousand dollars and any plan to save for it had remained strictly hypothetical.

She crouched for a look in the liquor cabinet and found a bottle of thirty-year-old Balvenie that would taste like smoke and fill a person with angel's breath. There was also a bottle of cheap, banana-flavored rum that would be just fine if you wanted to get sick. Harper wondered what John Rookwood might tell her about Dragonscale after a Balvenie on the rocks or three.

She was still hunched down behind the bar when someone wiggle-*kick*-shoulder-*thumped* the basement door.

"Grayson!" cried a hoarse, wheezing, loud, somehow familiar voice, and Harper choked on a cry. Didn't reply, didn't move. Hunched there frozen, waiting for whoever it was to tell her what to do.

"Grayson!" the man shouted again, and Harper realized he was not outside shouting *in,* but inside shouting *out.* "It worked! We're in."

"I wanted to get that lock fixed. I was always worried someone was going to come in and steal the good whiskey and rape my wife," Jakob said. "I had very protective feelings toward the whiskey."

His voice was a knife, a thing she felt in the abdomen as much as heard.

Harper opened the tinted glass door into that hole where they had planned to stack a stereo. It was as deep as the footwell under a large office desk, nothing in it except some dangling cables. She climbed in with the first aid kit and the brace and the cigarettes, squeezing herself tight around the beach ball of her stomach. Three days ago she had climbed through a smoke-filled drainpipe with this stomach. She didn't think she would be able to do it now. She eased the glass door shut behind her.

"Right," said the first man, in a voice that made Harper think of a fat guy wheezing over a plate of scrambled eggs and a double order of bacon. "I get that. You don't want some reprehensible scumbag drinking up your stash of expensive booze. Unfortunately for you, you led me right to it." He laughed: a sound like someone squeezing a broken toy accordion, a kind of musical gasp. "Why don't you head upstairs and have a poke around? See if she's been here. We'll secure the basement. And by 'secure' I mean drink your whiskey, play pool, and look for dirty home movies."

"She hasn't been here. I come out here now and then, you know. Keeping an eye on the place. I figured she'd come back, sooner or later. For her books or her favorite pajamas or her old

Pooh Bear. I swear, sometimes I felt like a child molester, sleeping with her. We had to watch *Mary Poppins* every Christmas. As soon as we were done opening presents."

"Christ," said the one with the fat man's voice, and at last Harper knew why he was familiar to her. She had heard the Marlboro Man often enough on the radio. "And you waited until she got sick to try and kill her?" He bawled with laughter at his own joke. Another man—not Jakob—confirmed the cleverness of this bon mot with a shrill titter.

"You can see no one has been here from the snow. No footprints," Jakob said.

"You're probably right. But we'll look anyway. Just to be sure. You know about me and the secret broadcast? I ever told you about that? The radio in my head? No? When I was twelve, I could put my hand on a silent radio and close my eyes and I could *hear* the DJ introducing 'Walk This Way.' I could hear him *in my mind.* Like I was the antenna, pulling the signal right into my brain. I'd tell my buddies, I'll bet every one of you that if we turn on the radio, it'll be playing 'Walk This Way.' Everyone would pitch in a buck. I'd turn on the radio, and Steven Tyler would be right there, braggin' how his girl is a real good bleeder. Or, like, when I was old enough to drive. I'd be sitting in my friend's crap Trans Am, the car turned off, waiting for him to come out of a corner store with a six-pack of Schlitz. And suddenly I'd know Mo Vaughn had just slugged a home run. I'd *know.* My pal would come out, turn the keys—and all of Fenway would be cheering for the big hit, Joe Castiglione shouting about how far Mo smashed it. For a long time I thought maybe I was picking signals up on my fillings somehow. But ever since the plague days started, I've been hearing *new* signals. Sometimes I'll hear my *own* voice on the secret broadcast, reading a news report. I'll hear myself talking about how a dozen burners were discovered hiding in the basement of Portsmouth Library, and they were shot dead by a heroic Cremation Crew. So I'll get the gang together and we'll go down there, and sure enough—burners, hiding in the cellar. Remember that, Marty? Remember the time I said we ought to go down to Portsmouth Library and check things out? We killed every one of those motherfuckers. It all went down just exactly the way I heard it on my telepathic news report."

"That's true!" cried the third man, his voice piping and obsequious. "You *knew* they were going to be there, Marlboro Man! You knew before *any* of us."

"So that's why we had to come over here today? You had a psychic tickle that my wife might've come home?" Jakob asked. He didn't sound like a believer.

"Maybe. Maybe I heard a little voice that said why not run by and have a look. Then again, maybe I just remembered you saying you had some good Scotch and I wanted a taste. Why don't you have a peek around and we'll find out which it is."

"Sure," Jakob said. "Check behind the bar. See what's left."

A door opened across the room. Sheetrock and shattered lath tumbled out with a crash. Jakob cursed. The one named Marty made hyena sounds that approximated laughter. Jakob clambered away over sliding, tumbling, clattering debris.

Someone approached the bar. Harper could dimly see a man in snow pants through the tinted glass. A skinny guy with a bushy Afro of reddish wiry hair bent over, opened the liquor cabinet, pulled out the Balvenie.

"Is this stuff good?"

"Fuckin' A. Hand it over. Let me have a look." Silence. "Goddamn, this costs more than I used to make in a week. You think his wife is half as nice as his pool table and his whiskey?" said the Marlboro Man.

"Don't matter," Marty said. "She's got the skeeve. You ain't gonna fuck that."

"True. Speaking of skeeve, see if there are some glasses. I don't want your backwash in the bottle."

The skinny guy bent and dug around and came up with tumblers.

"You want music? Based on his pool table and his whiskey, I bet he's got a sweet fuckin' sound system," Marty said. He turned toward the stereo cabinet and pressed the magnetic catch. The glass door sprang open half an inch. Harper shut her eyes and thought, *Despair is no more than a synonym for consciousness.*

"No power, asshole," said the Marlboro Man. "A Porsche is just a half ton of worthless iron if there's no gas in the tank."

"Ah, fuck. Good point, Marlboro Man! I wasn't thinking!" He pushed the cabinet door shut without looking in.

"There's some breaking news."

Neither of them spoke for a few moments. She heard the gurgle of whiskey splashing into the glass, swallowing, and reverential sighs.

When Marty spoke again, his voice was pitched low. "He's kinda scary, don'cha think?"

"Who? Public Works?"

"Yeah. Jakob. With that burn on his neck. That black hand—cooked right in the skin. And his eyes, you know? Like dusty old glass. Like doll's eyes."

"Listen to you. You're practically Lord Byron, with the similes."

"Tell you what. I think he'd rather find the Fireman here than his wife. I think he's got a bigger hard-on for him than he does for the runaway bride."

"There ain't no Fireman."

There was an uneasy silence.

"Well," Marty said. "Marlboro Man . . . *someone* burned his neck. And the other night? Eighty guys saw the devil, two stories high, down by the police station. *Eighty guys.* And Arlo Granger, in the fire department, he wrestled with some dude in the smoke. Some dude with a British accent, dressed up in a fire helmet and everything. Arlo would've kicked his head in, except the Fireman had friends, like five friends, and they ganged up on him . . ."

"I know Arlo Granger, and that guy is a fuckin' liar. He told me once that he got backstage at a Rush concert and snorted coke with Neil Peart. I *wish* the guys in Rush snorted coke. Maybe it would amp 'em up and they'd try playing some real rock and roll for once, instead of that limp-dick prog-rock bullshit."

"My cousin is in the National Guard. Amy Castigan, you've hung out with Amy—"

"Amy . . . your cousin Amy . . . maybe. Yeah, I think she sucked my dick once."

"Yeah, yeah, me, too, but listen, *listen,* Marlboro Man. Amy was manning the checkpoint on the Piscataqua Bridge back in September, middle of the night . . . and she sees this red blaze coming up the river. Like someone shot a rocket at them. Her and the other guys hit the deck and just in time, too. This giant fuckin' bird of flame, thirty feet from wing tip to wing tip, dive-bombed 'em. It dived so close the sandbags caught fire! And while Amy and the guys in her unit were duckin' for cover, a car ran the checkpoint and some burners escaped into Maine. That was him, too! That's what he does! He's figured out how to weaponize Dragonscale, man."

"That's one possibility," the Marlboro Man said. "The other possibility is your cousin is the biggest fuckin' ho-bag on the East Coast, and someone ran the checkpoint while she was treating her entire unit to the Amy Castigan blow-job special. There ain't no Fireman. And Satan didn't turn up at the police department last night. People see things in flame. Freaky faces and stuff. That's all."

Harper thought, inevitably, of the girl in John's furnace: Sarah Storey, she was sure. The Marlboro Man could believe what he liked, but sometimes the face in the fire really *was* someone looking back at you.

Boards and plaster sheeting slid and thumped in the stairwell.

"Nothing," Jakob said. "Nothing and no one. I told you. If someone had been here, there'd be tracks. She's six months pregnant. I doubt she can go a hundred paces without running out of breath."

"That is a fair point, squire," said the Marlboro Man. "My ex, when she was pregnant, if she wanted anything—cigarettes, beer, ice cream, anything—she'd make me get it, even if it was only in the next room.

"Sorry the psychic flash didn't work out. But at least you found the Balvenie. We can take it with us. That's five hundred dollars a bottle, so drink it slow."

"What's the hurry? Have a couple drinks and I'll polish you off in a game of pool."

"I'd need more than a couple before that would happen," Jakob said.

"Want to wager on it?"

"With what? Money isn't what it used to be."

"I win, you have to go upstairs and find me a pair of your wife's panties," said the Marlboro Man.

"If *I* win, you have to wear them," Jakob said.

"Hey, what if *I* win?" Marty asked.

"What if you invent a cure for fuckin' Dragonscale? What if you didn't laugh like a thirteen-year-old girl with the hiccups?"

Marty laughed like a thirteen-year-old girl with the hiccups.

"Who breaks?" Jakob said.

There was a loud crack as one ball struck a dozen.

"Is this single elimination?" Marty asked. "Or best of three?"

"Whatever," said the Marlboro Man. "I don't have anyplace to be."

# 6

A powdery snow granulated the night. She drifted through a frozen darkness, her nostrils stinging from the cold. The light had been failing when she entered her house. Now, six games of pool later, it was who knew when—nine? ten?—and her legs were cramped from the hours she had spent balled up in the cupboard space behind the tinted glass door.

Jakob had been better at pool but the Marlboro Man was superior at holding his drink. The fat man—from his voice alone, Harper felt sure he was at least three hundred pounds—had left with a pair of her undies in his coat pocket, whistling "Centerfold." She waited at least thirty minutes to crawl out of her hiding place, half believing Jakob and his new friends would still be there, silently waiting for her. They had left the empty bottle of Balvenie upside down in one of the side pockets.

She should've been wretched, choking on sobs, or quaking helplessly in shock. Instead, Harper felt buzzed, as if she had just skied a slope at the very edge of her ability, taking turns faster than she had ever taken them before. She had heard of adrenaline highs, but wasn't sure if she had ever had one before. She was hardly aware of her legs carrying her forward.

Harper didn't know where she was going until she got there. She wandered right past the entrance to Camp Wyndham—past the chain hung between the stone monoliths, past the burned-out wreckage of the bus—and followed Little Harbor Lane until it switched to gravel. In another hundred feet it turned into a boat ramp, angling down into the lapping foam of the Atlantic.

And there was the Fireman's island. A quick clamber over

a stone breakwater, a two-minute walk along the shingle, and she came in sight of Camp Wyndham's dock.

She had promised Allie she would be back in two hours. It had been maybe twice that. Harper dreaded facing Allie, who was likely in trouble by now, and who almost certainly had spent the evening sick with worry. Harper decided solemnly to do whatever was necessary to make amends.

But Allie would have to worry a little longer. Harper had left John Rookwood on his island all alone for three days, with smashed ribs, a sprained elbow, and a wrist that had been seriously dislocated. He was her whole reason for slipping out of the infirmary. It would be a poor joke to head back without seeing him.

Besides. For all Allie's talk about how they were going to start making examples out of people who broke the rules, Harper couldn't take any of it too seriously. To Harper, it was elementary school all over again. There were rules, of course, and consequences for breaking them . . . but rules and consequences alike were applied by the grown-ups to the kids, and Harper was a grown-up. A student might get a demerit slip for running in the hall, but if someone on staff broke into a jog, presumably there was a good reason. Ben might be annoyed with her, but she would talk to him and smooth everything over. She was no more threatened by his authority (or Carol's) than she would've felt threatened by a teacher. It was not, after all, like anyone was going to make her write *I will not leave camp without a permission slip* a hundred times on the chalkboard.

She rowed across a heaving liquid darkness. She felt a kind of slow tidal rocking inside her as well, as if she herself contained a smaller sea.

Harper knocked on the doorframe of the Fireman's shed.

"Who's that, then?"

"Harper."

"Ah! Finally. I warn you, I'm not dressed."

"I'll give you a minute."

She took a deep breath of damp, salted, frozen air, let it out in a trickle of white fog. She had never looked around his island, not really, and tramped up the great central dune to see the view from the highest point.

It wasn't much of a rock. A couple acres long, shaped like an eye. One central ridge ran along the island lengthwise, with the Fireman's little shed built into one side of it. At the southern tip was the ruin of a guesthouse, a collapsed rectangle of carbonized beams poking out of a layer of snow no deeper than a bedsheet. She was momentarily surprised by the sight of the boat: it stood just above the pebbly shingle on the eastern face of the island, a thirty-five-foot-long sailboat resting in a stainless steel carriage, the deck covered by a taut white tarp. But then Father Storey had mentioned a boat out here, had talked about taking it on a search for Martha Quinn. If the snow kept falling, soon it would just look like a part of the landscape, one vast white dune to tower over the others.

The cold was making her cheeks numb. She tracked back down the sand and let herself into the Fireman's shed without knocking. She came in stamping her boots and rubbing her hands, shaking off snow.

"Willowes! I've never been so glad to see another human face! It feels like a car is parked on my chest. I haven't been in so much pain since Guns N' Roses broke up."

"Sorry," she said. She dropped the cloth shopping bag she had brought with her. "Busy day."

She opened her mouth to tell him about Jakob and the Marlboro Man and almost being discovered, then caught herself.

He was sitting on his cot, and he still wasn't wearing a stitch, except for the sling she had made out of a canvas quiver. His only gesture to modesty was the bedsheet bunched up in his lap and pooled around his hips. His skin was scrawled all over with the devil's handwriting in black and gold. The bruises beneath the 'scale had darkened to shades of blackberry and pomegranate. It hurt her in her own chest just to look at them.

"You still aren't dressed," she said.

*"Well,"* he said. "I wasn't sure I should bother. Aren't you going to examine me? Seemed a lot of effort to go to, just to take it all off again. And where have you been? I've been stranded on this muddy blob of sand for *days,* with no one to talk to but myself."

"At least you were having conversations with someone who thinks you're clever."

He fixed the cloth shopping bag with a rapacious glare. "There better be morphine in there. And cigarettes. And fresh-ground coffee."

"I *wish* I had morphine. In fact, we'll have to talk about that."

*"Cigarettes?"*

"I don't have any cigarettes for you right this instant, Mr. Rookwood," she said, choosing her words with care. This was not a lie—but it was also not strictly honest. Harper was becoming practiced at such evasions. "Look at it as an opportunity to quit before the smokes kill you."

"You think smoking is going to kill *me*? When *I* smoke, Nurse Willowes, it's other people who need to worry about their health. There better be fresh coffee, then."

"I brought you some wonderful loose teas—"

"*Tea!* You think I want tea?"

"Why not? You're English."

"And so you think I drink *tea*? What, do you imagine I used to wander around in the London fog in a deerstalker cap, talking to my mates in iambic pentameter? We *have* Starbucks, woman."

"Oh, good. Because I also have a few packets of Starbucks instant."

"Why didn't you say so?"

"Because you're such an amusing man to disappoint. How about I put on the kettle and you at least put on some pants? I don't recall any below-the-waist injuries that require a medical opinion."

He swept a foggy gaze around the floor, reached with one bony foot for his fireman pants.

She took a deep breath to tell him about going home—and then sidetracked herself again, saying, "Did you always want to be a fireman? How long have you been dressing like one? Since childhood?" That was the adrenaline talking. She wondered if this was how people felt after skydiving. Her hands had a tremor.

"Not at all. I wanted to be a rock star. I wanted to wear leather pants and spend weekends in bed with stoned fashion models and write songs full of pretentious riddles."

"I didn't know you were musical. What instrument did you play?"

"Oh, I never got around to learning an instrument. Seemed like too much work. Also, as my mother was deaf and my father a bully, musical education wasn't a priority in my family. The closest I ever got to the rock-star life was selling drugs."

"You were a drug dealer? I don't think I like that. What drugs?"

"Hallucinogenic mushrooms. Seemed a sensible way to turn a profit on my degree in botany. Mycology had always been my field of study. I sold a form of psilocybin called Smurfpecker that was quite blue, quite popular, and quite delicious with eggs. Do you want to split a Smurfpecker omelet with me sometime, Nurse Willowes?"

She turned her back on him, to give him privacy so he could pull on his pants. "The Dragonscale—that's a kind of spore. A fungus. You must know a lot about it."

He didn't reply. She glanced back and his face was composed into a look of benign innocence. He wasn't even trying to pick up his pants. They were still snarled around his feet. It irritated her that he wouldn't get dressed. It made him more of a creep than she had hoped he would be. She looked away once more.

"Is that why you can control it? Use it? Keep from burning alive like you're coated in asbestos? Is it because you understand something about it other people don't understand?"

He made a soft humming sound and said, "I'm not sure I understand the 'scale so much as I've helped it to understand *me*. The pans are in the box under the furnace."

"Why do I need a pan?"

"Aren't you going to make us eggs?"

"You have eggs?"

"No. Don't you? In that grocery bag of yours? For God's sake, Nurse Willowes, you must've brought me *some* goodies!"

"I am sorry to say I did not bring you eggs or French roast or morphine. Instead I hiked three miles and nearly walked right into a Cremation Crew to get a brace for your elbow and tape for your wrist. My ex-husband among them." She felt an unexpected prickle in the back of her eyes that she refused to let become anything more. "I also brought you some great loose tea because I'm nice and I thought it would cheer you up and I haven't even asked for thanks. All I've asked is for you to put on your pants, but you won't even do that, because I assume you get off on being naked and seeing if it rattles me."

"I can't."

"Can't *what*? Can't say thanks? Can't apologize? Can't show basic human courtesy?"

"I can't put on my pants. I can't bend over and pick them up. It hurts too much. And you've been very kind and of course I should've said thanks. I'm saying it now. Thank you, Nurse Willowes."

The contrition in his voice deflated her in some way. She was coming down off her adrenaline buzz now, a tide receding to reveal the fatigue beneath.

"I'm sorry. It has been a long couple of days. And I just got through the worst part of it. I went back home to salvage some supplies and Jakob turned up, with a crowd of new friends. One of them was that bully on the radio, the Marlboro Man, the one who's always bragging about all the burners he's executed. I had to hide. For a *long* time."

"You went home? Alone? Why didn't you send someone?"

"Who? The Lookouts are all kids. Starved, overtired kids. I didn't feel like putting one of them at risk. I couldn't send you, not with your ribs like they are. Besides, I knew where to look for the things I wanted. It just seemed to make more sense to go myself. You didn't tell me what happened to my house."

"That your ex decided to remodel with a two-ton snowplow? I felt like you had lost enough for one week. Why pile on? Are you all right?"

"I was . . . scared. I heard them talking about me. They talked about you, too."

"You don't say!" he said. He sounded pleased.

"Yes. They talked about a man with weaponized Dragonscale, someone who can throw flame, and who goes around dressed as a fireman. They couldn't decide if you were real or an urban legend."

"Ah! Halfway to being a rock star at last!"

"Mostly they talked about things they've done to people who are sick. The Marlboro Man keeps track of the numbers for the whole Cremation Crew, was talking about who's killed the most overall, who's murdered the most in one day, who killed the ugliest girl, who killed the hottest girl. It was like he was talking about the stats for his fantasy baseball team."

The Marlboro Man had praised Jakob for "busting his nut" on New Year's Day. It was several minutes before Harper realized the Marlboro Man was not talking about sex, but murder. Jakob had used his Freightliner to T-bone a Nissan with a sick family in it, a man, a woman, and their two children. The car had been pancaked. The bodies came squeezing out of the wreckage like toothpaste, or so the Marlboro Man said. Jakob had accepted the Marlboro Man's praise without comment, expressing neither pride nor horror.

What a curious thing: to think the man she had married, a man she had loved and been devoted to, had gone on to commit murders. Had killed and meant to kill again. Eighteen months ago, they had spent their nights cuddled on the couch, watching *Master of None*.

"I was scared I'd start shaking and they'd hear me. They'd hear my teeth chattering. Then they left, and when I knew

I was okay—that I was going to leave the house alive—I—I felt—like someone threw a grenade at me and then for some reason it didn't explode. I walked out of there with my head full of cotton fluff and my legs all rubber. Aren't you going to give me a talking-to?"

"For being an idiot and blithely walking right into trouble?"

"Yes."

"Naw. I can't think of two qualities I admire more in a person. Glad you came back, though. I haven't had coffee in days."

When she turned around, the Fireman was yawning, a fist covering his mouth and his eyes squeezed shut, and the sheet had dropped to show the line of his hip. Harper was surprised by her own reaction to the sight of his scrawny, hairy self, the dense pelt of hair on his sunken and battered chest. She felt an immediate twitch of physical want, florid and absurd, where there had been none a minute before.

She marched to the bed, feeling there was safety in briskness. "Raise your legs."

He lifted his feet. She tugged his fireman pants up to the knees, then sat down beside him and slipped an arm under his armpits.

"On three, lift your skinny ass." But she did most of the lifting and when she scooped him up, she heard it: the whistling inhalation, the shuddering start of a gasp, quickly bitten off. What little color was in his face drained away.

"The worst bit isn't the pain when I move. It's the itch in my chest. After every breath. Can't sleep the way it itches."

"Itch is good. We like itch, Mr. Rookwood. Bones itch when they're knitting back together."

"I suppose it will feel better after you tape up my chest."

"Mm, no, I'm sorry, that isn't done anymore. We don't want to constrict lungs that need to breathe. But I would like to strap up that wrist of yours and slip this brace on your elbow."

She inched the elastic brace up his forearm, shifted it into place, then went to work on his swollen, hideously bruised wrist. Harper pressed cotton pads to either side of the wrist, then wound medical tape around and around, up the wrist and down it, creating an almost stiff but comfortable cast around the joint. After, she lifted the right arm for a look at his discolored side. Harper traced her fingers over his ribs, carefully seeking out each fracture. She tried not to take any pleasure at all in the knuckles of his spine or the scrollwork of Dragonscale on his skin. He looked like an illustrated man from a carnival. There was no guessing how many people the Dragonscale had killed, but for all that, she could not help thinking it was very beautiful. Of course she was desperately horny. That didn't help.

"You might be in for worse than a tongue-lashing from Ben Patchett," the Fireman said. "And you might receive a very unhappy look and some great sad sighs from Tom Storey. Nothing makes a person feel more low and ashamed than disappointing the old man. It's like telling a department-store Santa you know his beard is fake."

"I don't think I'll be in trouble with Father Storey."

He gave her a sharp, searching look and all the humor dropped from his expression. "Better let me have it, then."

She told him about trepanning Father Storey's skull with a power drill and disinfecting it with port. She told him about Ben in the meat locker and the handcuffed prisoners and the dish towel full of rocks. Then she had to go back in time to tell him about her last talk with Father Storey, in the canoe.

The Fireman did not ask many questions . . . not until she recounted her final conversation with the old man.

"He was going to exile some poor girl for stealing a teacup and cans of Spam?"

"And a locket. And the Portable Mother."

He shook his head. "Still. That doesn't seem like Tom."

"He wasn't going to exile her because she stole. He was going to exile her because she was *dangerous*."

"And he knew this because he had confronted her over her thefts and she—what? Threatened him?"

"Something like that," Harper said.

But she frowned. It was hard to remember now precisely what Tom had said and how he had said it. It seemed like a conversation that had happened months, not days, ago. She found it maddeningly difficult to recall what he had told her about the thief; there were moments when it seemed to her he had never mentioned theft at all.

"And for some reason he decided he needed to go into exile *with* this thief?"

"To look after her. He was going to search for Martha Quinn's island."

"Ah, Martha Quinn's island. I like to imagine it's crowded with refugees from the eighties, wandering about in spandex and leopard fur. I hope Tawny Kitaen is there. She was at the center of all my earliest sexual fantasies. Who was Tom going to leave in charge of camp?"

"You."

"Me!" He laughed. "Are you sure he didn't say all this *after* getting conked in the head? I can't imagine anyone worse for the job."

"How about Carol?"

He had been smiling, but at this his look became unhappy again. "I like Carol for high holy priest about as much as I'd like another kick in the ribs."

"You don't think she means well?"

"I'm *certain* she means well. When your government was waterboarding poor sods to find bin Laden, *they* meant well. Carol's father was a moderating influence on her, a calming force on a brittle personality. Without him, *well.* Carol has Quarantine Patrols, the police, and Cremation Crews threatening her from the outside. She has the thief and those two prisoners to create pressure from the inside. Fear does not incline people to be moderate in their use of extreme tactics. Especially not people like Carol."

"I don't know. She didn't even want the job. She turned it down three times before she accepted."

"So did Caesar. I only wish Sarah—" He broke off and cast a frustrated look toward the furnace. Then he dropped his gaze and tried again. "It's not that Sarah would've kept Carol in check, or tried to wrest the camp from her, or any of that. But she would've tried to throw her little sister a line if she saw her drowning. That's what I'm worried about, you know. Bad enough that Carol might drown in her own paranoia. But what's worse is that drowning victims will pull others down with them, and right now she has her arms around the entire camp."

A knot snapped in the furnace with a dry, roasted crack.

"What was Sarah like? Not like Carol, I guess. More like Tom?"

"She had Tom's sense of humor. She also had more steel than anyone I've ever met. She threw herself at things like a bowling ball. You see some of that in Allie, you know. Sarah always made me feel like one of the ten pins." He cast a long, slow, considering look at the flames leaping in the furnace . . . then turned his head and gave Harper a sweet, almost boyish smile. "Which I guess is a fairly accurate description of a certain kind of love, innit?"

# 7

"What is there to say about Sarah before she met me? Pregnant at seventeen by her piano instructor, an angelically beautiful Lithuanian only a few years older than her. Cast out of the private academy where her father was a professor. Tom, her best friend in the entire world, and the most forgiving man she knows, says terrible things to her and sends her off to live with relatives. Finishes her senior year in disgrace at a public high school, baby bump under her sweaters. She gets married in a town office the day after she accepts her diploma. Her Lithuanian, humiliated and unable to get a job teaching, returns to private lessons, which is when Sarah discovers that screwing his students is one of his nervous tics. No matter—she stays married because if she left him she'd have to go home, and she's promised herself she'll never ask her father for another single thing in her life. Instead she decides the only way to save the relationship is to have another baby. Am I going too quickly? I promise we'll get to the interesting part in a moment."

"Which part is that?" Harper asked.

"The part where I come into the story. Nick is born. Nick is deaf. The father suggests putting him up for adoption, since he can never have a relationship with a defective brat who can't appreciate his music. Sarah suggests her husband find a new place to live and throws him out. He kicks through the screen door at four A.M. one October night and threatens the whole family with a badminton racquet. Sarah has a restraining order leveled against him. He responds by showing up at Allie's elementary school, supposedly to take his daughter to a dental appointment, and promptly disappears with the kid."

"Jesus."

"He was arrested four *long* days later, in a motel near the Canadian border, where he was trying to figure out how to reach Toronto without a passport for his daughter. I gather he had notions of getting to the Lithuanian embassy and trying to scuttle back to Europe with her. He was out on bail when he hung himself."

"Sounds like Sarah and me both picked our husbands in the same shop," Harper said.

"There was one good thing to come out of the piano tutor's last waltz. In those terrible days when Sarah didn't know where Allie was, her father showed up on her doorstep to do what he could for her. He made sure Sarah ate and slept, held her when she cried, saw to Nick's needs. It was his chance, you see—to be the father she wanted, the father Sarah had believed he was before he so completely, colossally failed her. I know Tom, and I doubt he ever completely forgave himself for turning away from her when she was a frightened pregnant kid.

"Tom stayed with her for months. Later Sarah moved closer to home, and he helped with the kids while she returned to school to study social work. Outreach to the disabled, that was her field.

"Now, as it happens, Tom Storey had supervised worship at Camp Wyndham since the 1980s, and was made camp director a decade later. The spring that Nick turned seven, Sarah suggested the camp host a two-week program for the deaf, and Tom made it happen.

"They went looking for counselors who knew how to sign, and I fit the bill. I learned sign language as a lad from my deaf Irish mother . . . which, I add, charmed quite a few of the kids, who liked to say my hands had an Irish accent. I was in the States to collect a master's degree and was glad to get a decent-paying summer job. A man just *can't* earn a living wage selling Smurfpecker in this blighted nation. I have to tell you, heroin dealers and meth slingers have made your country a wretched place to be a simple, honest drug dealer who wants to give his customers a lovingly curated experience.

"Tom hired me to teach outdoorsy stuff—what berries you could eat, what leaves not to wipe with, how to make fire without matches. I was always especially good at that last trick. On arrival we were each assigned a cute name. I was dubbed Woody John. Sarah got to be Ranger Sarah.

"We had a few days of orientation and training before the kids arrived, and I wasn't there long before I could see being named Woody was going to be a problem. On the very first day, Sarah greeted me by saying, 'Morning, Wood,' with a darling look of sweet innocence on her face. The other counselors heard her and fell all over the place laughing. Pretty soon everyone was saying it. 'Who's got Wood?' 'Hey, guys, don't be so hard on Wood.' 'I've been walking around all morning with Wood.' You get the idea.

"Well, the night before the kids were due to show up, we were all having some beers together, and I told her maybe one day if she was lucky and played her cards right, she might wake up with Wood. That got some laughs. She said it would be more like waking up with a splinter in an awkward place, and that got more.

"I asked her how come she got to be Ranger Sarah, and she said since she was program director she was allowed to pick her own name. So I announced by ancient English law I had the right to challenge her authority with trial by combat. I told her we'd settle it on the dartboard. We'd each get one throw. If I hit closer to the center, I could rename both her and myself. And I warned her ahead of time that I would be choosing Bushmaster for me and the Camp Beaver for her. She said I was going to lose, and she'd let me know my new name after the game, and that soon enough I'd be longing for the days when I was plain old Woody.

"By now everyone was deadly serious. And by 'deadly serious' I mean 'crying on the ground.' Of course I liked my odds. When I was an undergrad I spent more time in pubs throwing darts than I did in classrooms taking notes. I stood well back and nearly hit bull's-eye without so much as a warm-up.

Suddenly everyone went completely silent. Awestruck by my powers.

"Sarah didn't so much as blink. She pulled this little hatchet out of her belt, walked to the line, and chucked it. She didn't just hit bull's-eye, she split the board in half. She told me, 'You never said I had to throw a dart.' Well, that was how I became Tosser John. On account of how well I could toss a dart.

"And I suppose that's where it started—the feeling like we belonged together.

"At the time camp officially got going, Allie and her mother were hardly speaking. Allie, who was all of fourteen, had been dropped by her third therapist after throwing a paperweight at his balls. She had wrecked her mother's car after taking some boys for a spin in it. Older boys. I couldn't tell you how much of her behavior was a result of being kidnapped by a parent when she was in third grade, but certainly her anger went well beyond the ordinary teenage stuff. She hated her mother for exerting any control over her at all, and was furious she had been forced to work as a counselor-in-training. Those first few days were ugly. Allie would wander away from the kids to do things with her cell phone. If she didn't like what they were serving in the cafeteria, she'd walk out of camp and hitch a ride into town to meet up with friends. And so on.

"Sarah decided Allie was going to join her on an overnight backpacking trip to the Jade Well—a pool of icy water beneath an eighteen-foot cliff. Perhaps she had decided to strangle her and figured it would be easiest to hide the body out in the deep dark woods. They needed a third grown-up and drafted me. Off we went with twelve little kids on a ten-mile hike, walking in a cloud of mosquitoes. All I can say is thank God the children were deaf. Allie and Sarah cursed each other the whole way. When Allie glanced at her phone once, Sarah confiscated it. Allie would let branches snap back into her mother's face. The kids knew something was wrong and were getting more and more rattled.

"By the time we reached the Jade Well, the two of them were

screaming at each other. Everyone was sunburnt and chewed to pieces. Sarah was furious at Allie for forgetting the bug spray back at the bus, and Allie was angry at Sarah for blaming the mistake on her, and I was ready to quit. They were standing near the edge of the cliff and I just couldn't help myself. I took them both by the arm and dropped them over the side, right in their boots. And do you know what? They both came up laughing . . . laughing and spitting water at each other.

"The two of them were after me the rest of the hike. When they served out hot dogs they passed me a nice fresh tampon in a roll. They opened the roof of my tent at two A.M. and doused me with cold water. They spritzed me with hair spray instead of suntan lotion. And you know what? It was good. The hike out was as happy as the hike in had been miserable. The kids took to protecting me from Ranger Sarah and Muskrat-in-Training Allie. Nick especially. I think Nick decided it was his special responsibility to protect me from the madwomen in his family. He was my bodyguard for the rest of the summer.

"There was one more overnight hike on the last weekend of camp. That was the night Sarah unzipped my tent. She only said one thing. 'Did I play my cards right?'

"We had almost exactly a year together as a couple after that. She wanted to swim the Great Barrier Reef. I wish we had gone. I wish we had read books to each other. We had one weekend of sexy-times in New York City while her father looked after the kids. I wish we'd had more. I wish we'd walked more. I wish we hadn't sat in front of the TV so much. It was nice, we cuddled, we laughed at Stephen Colbert and Seth Meyers, but it didn't make much in the way of memories. We did such ordinary, banal things. Ordered pizza and played Trivial Pursuit with her sister and her dad. Helped the kids with homework. We did dishes together more than we ever made love. What kind of life is that?"

"Real life," Harper said.

He had not looked at her once while he recounted the story

of his courtship. Instead he stared at his own shadow, which rose and fell in an almost tidal motion as the firelight pulsed in the open furnace. "I spend more time thinking about the things I wish we had done than I do thinking about the things we *did* do. It was like we opened the perfect bottle of wine and each shared a sip . . . and then a clumsy waiter knocked the bottle to the floor before we got to have any more.

"The first time I saw the spore was at a luncheon presentation at the Boston Mycology Society, three months before Seattle." He didn't need to explain what he meant by *Seattle*. She knew he was talking about the Space Needle. "A fellow named Hawkins who'd just returned from Russia gave a forty-minute PowerPoint on it. I don't know what scared me more, the photos or Hawkins himself. His mouth kept drying out. He drank half a pitcher of water while he was standing behind the podium. And he spoke in such a low voice you had to strain to hear what he was saying. We were all just catching little bits: 'disease vectors,' 'contagion points,' 'cellular combustion.' Meanwhile he's flashing these horror-movie pictures of charred corpses, all teeth and blackened meat. I can tell you, no one went back to the buffet for seconds, but the bar sure was busy. This guy, Hawkins, said in closing that while there were only seventy-six known deaths in Kamchatka as a direct result of the spore, this had resulted in wildfires that had ended the lives of 530 other people. There had been almost eighty million dollars of damage to urban areas and the Russians had lost forty-three hundred acres of the richest timberland in the world. Hawkins said that three recent cases in Alaska suggested the pathogen might have a mode of transmission different than traditional viruses and that further study was urgently required. Based on his math, a quarter million sick in the United States would easily lead to the deaths of more than twenty million people and would turn over six million acres into an ashtray."

"How much is that?"

"About the size of Massachusetts. I have to say, he scared

the hell out of us at the time, but in retrospect, he was far too conservative. I suppose his calculations didn't consider a social breakdown so severe there would be no one left to fight the fires.

"But, you know . . . by dinnertime, I had mostly quit thinking about it. It didn't take long to feel like just one more of this century's possible but unlikely apocalypses, like an epidemic of bird flu wiping out billions or an asteroid cracking the planet in half. You can't do anything about it, and it's happening to poor people on the other side of the world, and the kids need help with homework, so you just stop thinking about it.

"As much as I *could* stop. It was in the subject header of every e-mail and the top thirty threads on every message board in the mycology community. There were webinars and conferences and a presidential committee. There was a report to the Senate. For a while I followed along out of academic interest. Also, you know me, Nurse Willowes, how I do like to show off. What I learned about the spore gave me great cachet at backyard barbecues. I don't think it hit me, on a human level, that this thing was ever going to reach *our* backyard until Manitoba started burning and no one could put it out. That was about a month before the first Boston cases.

"But what good was it knowing? If it was a plague like other plagues, you'd hide. Head for the woods. Take the people you love, hole up somewhere, bolt the door, and wait for the infection to burn itself out. *This,* though. One person carrying the spore could start a fire that would wipe out half a state. Hiding in the woods would be like hiding in a match factory. At least cities have fire departments.

"I can tell you exactly when and how I caught it. I can tell you where we *all* were when we caught it, because of course we were together. We had a little party for Carol's thirtieth birthday at the very beginning of May. Sarah and I had just moved in together. We had a little pool, though it was so cold no one wanted to go in except Sarah. It wasn't much of a party, just

Tom and the kids and Sarah and Carol and myself and a gluten-free cake for the birthday girl.

"Sarah and I often had late-night debates as to whether or not Carol had ever been laid. She had been engaged, as a younger woman, for five years, to a very devout young man who everyone knew was a homosexual except, apparently, Carol. He was, I think, one of these decent, haunted young queers who are drawn to religion because they're hoping to pray the gay away. Sarah told me she didn't believe they had ever slept together, although they exchanged some very passionate e-mails. Carol dropped in on her fiancé by surprise, while the boy was doing a residency at a theological institute in New York, and discovered him in bed with a nineteen-year-old Cuban dance student.

"I asked Sarah once if she thought Carol *herself* might be gay, and she frowned about it for a long time and finally said she thought Carol mostly just hated the idea of sex itself. She hated the idea of mess. Carol wanted love to be like a bar of soap: a purifying, hygienic scrub. She also said that Carol had full possession of their father and that was the only man who had ever really mattered to her.

"Carol and Sarah could be quite wary of each other. When Sarah was teenage and pregnant, Carol sent her a scolding letter about breaking their father's heart and promised never to speak to her again. And she did, in fact, stop talking to her until Nick was born. Sarah made a place for her little sister back in her life, but things were always uneasy between them. Carol could compete for attention in a way that was so childish it was sort of funny. If Sarah was winning at Scrabble, Carol would put on a coughing fit, say she had come in contact with an allergen, and make her father drive her to the hospital. If Sarah and Tom started talking about Victor Hugo, Carol would insist Sarah couldn't really appreciate his novels because she hadn't read them in the original French. Sarah just laughed that sort of thing off. I think she felt too sorry for Carol to compete with her and went out of her way to do nice things for her. Like the birthday party.

"I was just building up the energy to go inside and get another beer when there was a big thud—like something heavy falling off a truck a long way off, something so heavy it made the water shudder in the pool. Everyone glanced around—even Nick, who felt the vibration through his feet.

"Sarah stood in the shallow end, looking goose-bumpy and blue in the lips and very pretty, listening to hear if there was going to be something more. Nick saw it first—a black, oily tower of smoke, coming from the end of the block. There was another thud and another and then several close together, loud enough to shake the windows and make the silverware jump.

"Sirens wailed. Sarah said she thought it was the CVS drugstore on the corner and asked if I would look down the street and see.

"A lot of the neighbors had come out onto the sidewalks and were standing under the trees. The breeze turned and blew the smoke down the street. Oh, it stank. Like roasting tires and foul eggs.

"I made my way down the block until I could see the CVS. One side was a roiling wall of red flame. A woman wept on the curb, using her T-shirt to mop up her tears. I had a hanky, so I handed it to her and asked if she was all right. She said she had never seen anyone die before. She told me a guy on a motorcycle had slid into the wire cabinet outside the drugstore, the one full of propane cans. They went off like a string of the world's largest firecrackers. Someone said it was a hell of an accident, and she said it wasn't *just* an accident. She said the guy was on fire even *before* he hit the propane tanks. She said it was like *Ghost Rider.* She said his helmet visor was up and there was a burning skull in there—flame and grinning teeth.

"I went back home, meaning to tell them all to go inside. Not for any clear reason. Just some . . . vague apprehension. They were right where I left them, staring up at the smoke. They were standing there together in the snow. It had begun to snow, you see. Big goosefeather flakes of ash. Falling in everyone's hair. Falling in the birthday cake.

"A couple weeks later, Nick woke Sarah and me up to show us the stripe across his wrist. He didn't even ask what it was. He already knew. I found my first mark later that afternoon. Within four days we were all scrawled with Dragonscale . . . all of us except Sarah."

# 8

"All except Sarah?" Harper asked.

"Story for another night, I think."

"You must miss her very much."

His voice had tailed off and he stared across the room, into the open furnace, with blank, tranced eyes. He roused himself slowly, looked around, and smiled. "She's still with me."

Harper's pulse whumped in her throat. "What?"

"I talk to her almost every day." He narrowed his eyes to slits, peering intently into the flickering gloom, as if picturing her somewhere over there on the other side of the shed. "I can always imagine just what she'd say to take the piss out of me. When I ask myself a question, it's her voice that answers. We are taught to think of personality as a singular, private possession. All the ideas and beliefs and attitudes that make you *you*—we are raised to believe them a set of files stored in the lockbox of the brain. Most people have no idea how much of themselves they store *off*-site. Your personality is not just a matter of what you know about yourself, but what others know about you. You are one person with your mother, and another with your lover, and yet another with your child. Those other people *create* you—finish you—as much as *you* create you. When you're gone, the ones you've left behind get to keep the same part of you they always had."

She pursed her lips, exhaled a whistling breath. He was talking about memories, not ghosts.

His gaze drifted back to the open hatch in the side of the furnace, and she thought, *Ask him about what you saw—ask him about the face.* Some instinct for caution prevented her. She thought if she pressed him now, he would play dumb, pretend he didn't know what she was talking about. And there were, after all, other, more important matters to press him on.

"You hardly touched your coffee," she said. "It's gone cold."

"That is easily remedied," he said, and lifted his tin mug in his left hand.

The gold hieroglyphics marking his Dragonscale brightened and flashed. His hand became a chalice of flame. He rotated the mug slowly in his fingers and the brew within began to steam.

"I wish there was a way to treat you for being such a shameless attention hog," she said.

"What, you think I'm showing off? This is nothing. Yesterday, stuck in my bed, dying as much from boredom as from my staved-in chest, I taught myself to fart smoke rings in three different colors. Now *that* was impressive."

"I'm glad someone is having fun with the end of the world."

"What makes you think the world is ending?" He sounded genuinely surprised.

"Sure looks like the end of the world to me. Fifteen million people are infected. Maine is like Mordor now—a belt of ash and poison a hundred miles wide. Southern California is even worse. Last I heard, SoCal was on fire from Escondido to Santa Maria."

"Shit. I knew I shouldn't have put off going to Universal Studios."

"What part of the end of the world is funny to you?"

"All of it. Especially the arrogant notion that the world will end just because humans might not make it through this century. We were never properly grateful for making it through the last century, as far as I'm concerned. Humanity is worse than flies. If even one dried nugget of offal survives the flames, we'll be swarming all over it. Fighting about who owns it and selling the most fragrant chunks to the wealthy and the gullible. You're afraid it's the End Times because we're surrounded by death and ruin. Nurse Willowes, don't you know? Death and ruin is man's *preferred* ecosystem. Did you ever read about the bacterium that thrives in volcanoes, right on the edge of boiling rock? That's us. Humanity is a germ that thrives on the very edge of catastrophe."

"Who do you make these speeches to when I'm not around?"

He barked with laughter, then hunched over and grimaced. "The idea of dying while laughing is more romantic in concept than reality."

She turned to face him, and crossed her legs like one preparing to meditate. "Teach me to do what you can do."

"What? No. I can't. It's no good asking me how I do it. I don't understand it myself. I can't teach you because there's nothing to teach."

"God, you're a *terrible* liar."

He put his bowl of oatmeal on the floor. "That was dreadful. Like eating paste. I would've been better scraping bugs off the bottom of rocks. What do you have in that bag of yours for painkillers? I need something powerful to knock me out. I haven't slept longer than ten minutes at a time in the last three days."

She rose and dug through the cloth shopping bag on the floor. She returned with two slippery plastic pouches of Advil. "All I can spare for you. Wait at least six hours before you take the second—"

"What in the name of the holy pussydrill is this?" he cried. "*Advil?* Just *Advil*? You're not a nurse. You're a third-world torturer."

"I'm *desperate* is what I am, Mr. Rookwood. See that little grocery bag? There's a first aid kit in there. It contains over half of all the medical supplies I have to look after a hundred and fifty people, including an elderly coma patient with a quarter-inch hole in his skull."

He gave her a haggard, exhausted look. "You need provisions."

"You have no idea. Plaster. Morphine. Antibiotics. A shitload of second-skin burn pads. Antihistamines. Heart-start paddles. Norma Heald has rheumatoid arthritis and on a cold morning can hardly open her hands. She needs Plaquenil. Michael is diabetic and ten days from running out of insulin. Nelson Heinrich has high blood pressure and—"

"Yes, yes, all right. I get the idea. Someone needs to rob a drugstore."

"Someone needs to rob an *ambulance*."

"Yes, I suppose that would do, wouldn't it?" He gingerly touched his side. "I'll need four or five days before I'm ready. No, better make it a week. I'm too sore and tired to do what needs doing right now."

"You won't be ready to go anywhere for two to four weeks. I doubt you could walk as far as the chapel, in your current state."

"Oh, I'm not going. I'll send my Phoenix. Now listen. There's a house—"

"What does that mean, send a phoenix?" As she spoke, Harper remembered the Marlboro Man's pal Marty, half babbling: *This giant fuckin' bird of flame, thirty feet from wing tip to wing tip, dive-bombed 'em. It dived so close the sandbags caught fire!*

"Oh, another of my little goofs. A bit of fireworks to impress the natives and fortunately something I can manage from long range. You and a few reliable hands will want to find a side street well away from camp. Verdun Avenue would be fine, that's across from the graveyard, and I happen to know number ten is empty. Park in the driveway there and—"

"How do you know number ten is empty?"

"Sarah and I used to live there. One week from tonight, I want you to call 911. Use a cell phone, I think Ben held on to a collection of them. Tell emergency services your dear old dad is having a heart attack. When they ask, promise them you don't have Dragonscale. Tell them you need an ambulance and wait."

"They won't send an ambulance without a police escort."

"Yes, but don't worry about that. That's what the Phoenix is for—my little light show. When they pull up out front, I'll see that everyone is chased away and you can scarper with all the supplies you need. I wish you could simply drive off with the ambulance, but—"

"It'll have LoJack. Or some other way to trace it."

"That's right."

"I don't want anyone hurt. The people in the ambulance are risking their lives to take care of others."

"No one will be hurt. I'll scare the pants off them, but that's all."

"I hate asking you for help. You always do this. You make things mysterious that don't have to be mysterious, because you like to keep everyone wondering about you. It's a cheap high."

"Don't deny me my little pleasures. You're going to get everything you want. There's no reason I can't have a little of what I want, too."

"I'm not getting *every*thing. If I could do what you can do, I wouldn't *need* to beg for your help. Please—John. Can't you at least *try* to teach me?"

His gaze shifted past her to the furnace and back. "Might as well ask a fish to teach you how to breathe underwater. Now go away. My sides hurt and I need to get some sleep. Don't come back without cigarettes."

"Did you try and teach *her*? Sarah?"

He seemed to shrink from her. For an instant, there was so much shock and hurt in his eyes it was as if she had slugged him in the ribs. "No. Not me." Which was, she thought later, an odd sort of denial. He stretched out, turning onto his good side, so she was looking at the bony curve of his back. "Don't you have other people to look after? Give someone else the soothing balm of your bedside manner, Nurse Willowes. I've had all I can take."

She rose and put her shoes on. Zipped herself into her parka. Collected her bag. She stopped with her hand on the latch.

"I spent three hours hiding in a cupboard today, with my ex not a dozen feet from me. I had three hours to listen to him talk about the things he's done to the sick. Him and his new friends. Three hours to listen to him talk about things he'd do to me if he had half a chance. From their point of view, *we're* the bad guys in this story. If he sees me again he'll kill me. If he had the opportunity, he'd kill everyone in camp. And after he did it, he'd feel he had done a good day's work. In his mind he's that guy in the cowboy hat from *The Walking Dead,* wiping out the zombies."

To this, the Fireman said nothing.

She continued, "You saved me once. I will owe you for that the rest of my life, however long that happens to be. But if I die in the next couple of months, and you could've taught me how to be like you—how to protect myself? It'll be just the same as if you hid in the woods that night and let Jakob kill me."

Bedsprings creaked uneasily.

"I'm going to live to have this baby. If God can help me make it through the next three months, I'll pray. If Carol Storey can keep me alive, I'll sing 'Kumbaya' with her till my throat is hoarse. And if you can teach me something useful, Mr. Rookwood, I will even put up with your superior attitude and lack of manners and half-baked philosophy lectures. But don't imagine for a minute I'm going to drop it. You've got some keep-alive medicine. I want it." She opened the door. The wind wailed in a tone that was at once both terrifying and melodic. "One other thing. I didn't say I don't have any cigarettes. I said I don't have any cigarettes *for you*. And I *won't* . . . until you put your teacher hat on and give me my first class in surviving spontaneous combustion. Until that day, my Gauloises will stay in my shopping bag."

As she shut the door, he began to yell. Harper learned a few new obscenities on her way back to the boat. *Cunt-swill* was a good one. She would have to save that one for a special occasion.

# 9

Harper didn't know anyone was waiting for her on the dock until the boat bumped up against it and someone reached down to take the bow.

"Help you out there, Nurse?" Jamie Close offered a hand.

It was as if the darkness itself were speaking. Harper could hardly make out Jamie's squat, chunky figure against the black swaying pines and the black turmoil of black clouds in a black sky. Someone else was with her, cleating the front of the boat. Allie. Harper knew her by her lithe, boyish frame and quick grace.

Harper took Jamie's hand, then hesitated. The cloth sack of supplies was pushed in under the bench on which she sat, a canvas shopping tote containing the rum, cigarettes, instant coffee, and tea, among other things. What was hers belonged to all, according to the old rules of camp—but she was writing her own rules now. If liquor and smokes could buy the Fireman's secrets, then camp would have to do without.

Harper reached under the seat and plucked the first aid kit from the top of the sack. She rose, leaving the rest behind.

She looked past Jamie, trying to catch Allie's eye, but the girl had already stood up from the cleat and turned her back. She was trembling—from rage, Harper thought, not the cold. She had her rifle over her shoulder. So did Jamie.

"I'm sorry I didn't get back sooner, Allie. I understand if you're mad at me. If you're in any kind of trouble at all, I'll talk to Ben or Carol or whoever, and make them understand you bear no responsibility. But I don't see why you should be in trouble. I said I was going to check on the Fireman and come back and that's what I did. More or less."

"You left out the part about goin' home first, though, din'cha, Nurse?" Jamie said.

So they knew she had taken a detour on her way to the Fireman's island. She had kept to the trees as she headed out of camp, but had looked back once and wondered if Michael, up in the church tower, was peering down at her. The eye in the steeple sees all the people.

"The infirmary was short on some critical supplies. Fortunately I knew I could get what I needed from my own basement."

The two fell in on either side of her. Harper was reminded of a police escort walking a prisoner into court.

Jamie said, "That was all kinds of fortunate. You know what else was fortunate? You weren't clubbed to death with pool sticks. We *was* fortunate, too. We was fortunate they didn't follow your tracks, into the woods and all the way back to camp. Oh, yeah. We seen 'em. The Cremation Crew that turned up right after you went in. We both had our rifles but Allie told me I'd have to be the one to shoot you. She couldn't bear the thought of doing it herself. We hid in the woods watchin' till we lost the daylight. Then there wasn't no point."

Harper and her escorts came out of the firs and up alongside the soccer pitch, a snowy basket filled with moonglow. Harper couldn't tell if the thudding pain in her abdomen was a cramp of tension or the baby driving a heel into her.

"Allie," Harper said, "I'm sorry I scared you. I shouldn't have put you through any of that. But you have to understand, I can't bear the thought of sending a kid into danger when it's something I can do myself. And you're a kid. All of you Lookouts are kids."

"See, but you *did* put us in danger. You put the whole *camp* in danger," Jamie told her.

"I was careful. They wouldn't have found my tracks."

"They didn't need to find any tracks. They only needed to find *you*. Maybe you think you wouldn'ta said nothing, but it's funny how a pool cue up the snatch will loosen someone's lips.

You shouldn'ta gone. You *knew* you shouldn'ta gone. And what tore Allie up the worst was knowing she shouldn'ta let you. We made promises to keep people safe. To keep well-meaning dipshits like yourself in camp, under watch. All the Lookouts promised Mother Carol—"

"Mother *WHO?* She's *no one's* mother, Jamie." Harper thought Mother Carol and the Lookouts sounded like a band that might've been playing Lilith Fair in 1996.

"We promised her and we promised each other and we blew it. Carol was sick to death when she heard you were gone. Like she hasn't been through enough already."

"Fine. You've said what you had to say. Tell Carol you delivered her message, and next time if I feel like a breath of fresh air, I'll be sure to try and drop her a note. And Allie, you can quit the silent treatment. I'm a little too old to be impressed by that one. Got something to say? Do me a favor and spit it out."

Allie turned her head and glared at Harper with wet, accusing eyes. Jamie snorted.

"What?" Harper asked.

"You think *you're* in trouble. Ain't nothing compared to the hill of shit Allie is under for lettin' you go. Allie is doin' penance for it now. She asked for a chance to make amends and Mama Storey gave it to her."

"How? Did she take a vow of silence?"

"Not exactly. You remember what Father Storey used to do? That thing about suckin' on a stone when he needed to think?"

Snow squealed underfoot as they climbed the hill. Harper needed to the count of three to figure it out. It had been a long night.

"You have to be shitting me."

"I shit thee not. Allie is carrying a stone in her mouth to think over her mistakes and refocus on her obligations. The last time we let down our guard, someone took a stone and used it to crush Father Storey's head in. We all carry rocks now, to remember." Jamie removed one hand from her pocket and showed Harper a stone as big as a golf ball.

"Oh, for Christ's sake. So how long are you going to walk around sucking on that thing, Allie?" Harper asked her, as if there were any hope of an answer.

Allie looked like she wanted to spit the rock into Harper's face.

"That all depends on you, see?" Jamie asked. "Now, you weren't at the meeting when we agreed there needed to be consequences for people who think they're above the rules. No one is too pissed at you. Mikey saw you row out to the Fireman's island, so we've known you were safe for a while. Ben and Mother Storey had a talk and agreed it wouldn't be fair to make a big deal out of you leaving safe territory. At the same time, Carol was worried the rest of the camp would get ugly if you were held to looser standards'n everyone else. So they come to a decision and Allie agreed. Allie only has to carry the stone in her mouth until *you* take it from her. And *you* only have to carry it in your mouth for—"

"Jamie, I appreciate you being so direct with me. But you need to know, no matter what you think you all decided, that I am not ever going to suck on a stone in some medieval act of penance. If you think I will, then Allie isn't the only one with rocks in her head."

They emerged at the southeastern corner of the chapel, near the steps down into the women's dorm in the basement. Three Lookouts sat on logs, singing a rustic and curiously brutal hymn, "They Hung Him on a Cross." Their eyes were bright as brass coins, and the Dragonscale on their exposed hands was lit like burning lace, bathing the snow in crimson light. Their breath unspooled from their lips in threads of red steam. All of them were starved-looking, bones showing in their faces. Thin hands, thin necks, sunken temples, concentration-camp haircuts. A random, disassociated notion occurred to Harper: *When your stomach is empty, so is your head.*

"Well, I hope you change your mind, Nurse. 'Cause Allie's contrition doesn't end until yours begins."

"Allie," Harper said, "I take responsibility for my fuckup.

*Full* responsibility. Which means if you want to play martyr, that's up to you. I'm not making you do it." She cast a sidelong look at Jamie, and added, "And no one is making *me* do it, either. It's degrading and infantile. If someone wants me to peel potatoes or scrub pans, I'm not afraid to get my hands dirty. But I'm going to pass on this particular grotesque act of self-abasement, thank you."

"Allie is ready to do what it takes to make things right. People look up to you, Nurse—sure would be nice if you'd do the same. Allie is glad to serve as an example, for however long it takes."

"Or until dinner."

"Nope. Wrong on that. If you won't take the stone from her and carry it yourself, it stays in, breakfast, lunch, and dinner . . . although you might recall we Lookouts gave up *our* lunch a while back, so the likes of *you* could eat. I guess Allie'll have to take it out and put it under her pillow when she sleeps, but that's it."

"I don't know which of you is worse. Her with her mouthful of stone, or you with your mouthful of nonsense." Harper stopped walking, turned her back on Jamie Close, and spoke to Allie with her hands.

"Stop this," she said, in the language of silence that Nick had taught her.

Allie met Harper's gaze with cold, hating eyes. She had only ever learned how to finger-spell, and so her reply came in a slow trickle that Harper had to sound out in her mind:

Y-O-U

K-N-O-W

H-O-W

T-O

M-A-K-E

M-E.

The last part of this statement involved the use of Allie's middle finger and was widely known even to people who hadn't studied sign language.

# BOOK FIVE
# PRISONERS

# 1

From the diary of Harold Cross:

**JUNE 30TH**

BACK FROM THE CABIN. SHOULDN'T HAVE HAD THAT THIRD HOT POCKET. AM HALF-SICK FROM IT AND EVEN MY SMOKY DAMN FARTS SMELL LIKE PEPPERONI.

INTERESTING NEWS FROM CORDOBA. TWO HUNDRED INFECTED KILLED AT THE JESUIT MONASTERY IN ALTA GRACIA, BODIES BULLDOZED INTO A PIT BY THE MILITARY. DR. BÁ WAS ABLE TO RECOVER FOUR CORPSES, INCLUDING THE BODY OF EL HORNO DE CAMINAR, WHO SINGLE-HANDEDLY HELD OFF THE MILITARY'S ASSAULT FOR MOST OF AN HOUR BY CREATING SOME KIND OF FLAMING TORNADO, AN ACT THAT ALLOWED ALMOST A THOUSAND PEOPLE WITH DRAGONSCALE TO ESCAPE INTO THE JUNGLE. SOUND LIKE ANYONE WE KNOW? TRANSLATED INTO ENGLISH, EL HORNO DE CAMINAR MEANS "THE WALKING FURNACE."

DR. BÁ HAD A CHANCE TO WORK ON THE RECOVERED BODIES AND E-MAILED ME THE PRELIMINARY FINDINGS. INTERESTING STUFF. HE AUTOPSIED THE BRAIN OF A RECENTLY INFECTED CHILD AND IT SHOWED ONLY A DUSTING OF THE SPORE IN HIS SINUSES AND ON THE MEMBRANE SHEATH AROUND THE CEREBRAL CORTEX. BUT THE ARGENTINEAN FIREMAN HAD BEEN INFECTED FOR MUCH LONGER AND THE DRACO INCENDIA TRYCHOPHYTON HAD PENETRATED DEEP INTO HIS SUPERIOR TEMPORAL GYRUS.

EL HORNO DE CAMINAR GAVE AN INTERVIEW TO AN ALTERNATIVE MEDICINE BLOG, IN THE EARLY DAYS OF THE PLAGUE, AND EXPLAINED HOW HE WAS ABLE TO CONTROL FIRE WITHOUT EVER BEING HURT BY IT. "YOU CAN ASK THE SPORE TO KEEP YOU SAFE,

BUT YOU MUST FORGET YOUR OWN VOICE FIRST. YOU CAN ASK IT TO FIGHT FOR YOU, BUT YOU MUST COME TO IT AS A SUPPLICANT WITHOUT LANGUAGE." PROBABLY A CRAP TRANSLATION, BUT IT STRUCK ME AS INTERESTING. THE SUPERIOR TEMPORAL GYRUS HARBORS WERNICKE'S AREA, ONE OF THE SEATS OF SPEECH. I FEEL HE HAS EXPLAINED EVERYTHING AND YET I UNDERSTAND NOTHING.

# 2

Harper read the notebook in the bathroom, with the door locked, to prevent someone from walking in on her and finding her with it. She felt vaguely like an adolescent, privately examining a work of pornography with a dry mouth and a tripping heart.

When she finally stepped back into the wardroom and the milky glow of dawn, she discovered a white rock on the foot of her cot, a sheet of paper under it. WHEN WILL YOU TAKE YOUR MEDICINE? someone had written.

Father Storey drowsed in one bed, Nick in the other. With both of them asleep in the same pose, and with the same frowning look of concentration on their faces, it was impossible not to see the close familial resemblance. The child was still inside Father Storey somewhere, as a fly remains perfectly preserved in a bead of amber. The old man waited for Nick, a baggy overcoat that he would be ready to slip on in six decades.

Harper glanced at the curtain into the waiting room, to be sure she was unobserved, and put the notebook back in the ceiling. Then she picked up the stone and ducked into the next room.

Mindy Skilling, a pretty, waifish girl of about twenty, was on watch. Harper had treated her last month for a urinary tract infection. Mindy gave Harper a dewy, pitying look. She had a lovely, expressive face—bright eyes and long curling lashes—and Harper remembered that in a former life Mindy had studied acting.

"Did you put this on my bed?" Harper held out the stone.

Mindy shook her head.

"Who did?"

"Wouldn't you feel better," Mindy asked, "if you just got your punishment over with? I know Allie would feel better." Her eyes widened in sudden inspiration. She scooted to the edge of the couch. "What if you just put the rock in your mouth for five minutes? I'd tell everyone it was a whole half hour."

"Not five seconds," Harper said. "Oh, and Mindy? Next time you've got an infected bladder?"

Mindy stared at her with apprehensive, ready-to-be hurt eyes.

*You can piss off,* Harper said in her mind, but in real life she only sighed and said, "Forget it," and slipped back into the ward.

She really didn't have the right temperament for vicious comments. The few times in her life she had said truly nasty things to people, it had left her with a bad flavor in her mouth. A stone couldn't taste any worse.

# 3

Harper got it again—and she got it worse—the next evening, at first meal.

There was already a line, wrapped halfway around the inside of the cafeteria, when she came in out of the dark, snow melting in her hair. She had half run from the infirmary, with a shrieking wind at her back the whole way. She couldn't feel her ears and was desperately hungry from the first whiff of maple syrup and oats.

Half the camp was already seated, and the room was loud with conversation and spoons scraping in bowls. It was so loud Harper didn't hear Gail Neighbors at first, didn't know someone was talking to her until Gillian Neighbors poked her in the ribs to get her attention.

The Neighbors twins were right behind her, side by side. They wore matching red turtlenecks, an unfortunate wardrobe choice that suggested a resemblance to Thing One and Thing Two from the Dr. Seuss book.

"Allie didn't eat all day yesterday," Gail said. Harper was pretty sure it was Gail doing the talking—she was the one with the pointy chin.

Harper turned her back on them. "If she doesn't want to eat, that's up to her. No one is making her starve."

One of the sisters yanked on her sleeve and Harper had to glance back.

Gillian looked a lot less friendly than Gail. Her lips were a thin white line. She hadn't shaved her head recently and her scalp was blue with five o'clock shadow.

"Is it true it would only cost you half an hour with the stone to make amends?" Gillian asked.

"That and my dignity."

The two sisters did not reply. Harper turned her back on them once more. The line edged slowly forward.

"You're a real stuck-up bitch," one of them said softly.

This time, Harper did not glance back.

"You know, some people think—" said the other, and was shushed by the first.

Harper did not care what some people thought and did not dignify this comment with a response.

She didn't know Allie was on mess duty, dishing out scoops of oatmeal, until she reached the counter. Allie still had the rock in her mouth, Harper could tell by the way she pursed her lips.

Allie lifted her gaze and stared at Harper with watery, loathing eyes. Then she reached under the counter, found a smooth, egg-shaped lump of granite, put it in a bowl, and held it out to her.

Harper set down her tray and walked away, the Neighbors sisters shrieking with laughter.

# 4

Late at night—or early in the morning, depending on how you cared to look at it—Nick gave lessons in how to speak without words, and Harper was his attentive pupil, in the lonely classroom of the infirmary.

If anyone had asked why Nick was staying in the infirmary, instead of with his sister in the girls' dorm, or with the men in the boys' dorm, Harper would've said she wanted to keep him under observation. She would've claimed she was worried about a late-developing inguinal hernia as a result of his appendectomy in the summer. The word *inguinal* would be frightening enough to shut down any further questions. But there were no questions, and Harper suspected that few people gave any thought at all to where Nick slept. When you had no voice, you had no identity. Most people took no more notice of the profoundly deaf than they did of their own shadows.

They sat across from each other on Nick's cot, in their pajamas. Harper kept three buttons undone below her breasts to show the ripe pink globe of her belly, and when they were finished practicing sign for the night, Nick popped the cap off a Sharpie and drew a smiley face on it.

*What are you going to name her?* Nick asked. He tried to ask in sign language, but she lost the thread and he had to write it down.

"A boy," she said with her hands.

He pressed both palms on the bulging gourd of her stomach, closed his eyes, and inhaled gently. Then he signed, "Smells like a girl."

"How girls smell?" she asked, her hands finding the words automatically—a fact that produced a small flush of pride.

He gave her a confounded look and wrote: *like sugar & spice & everything nice, duh.*

*You can't really smell if it's a girl,* she wrote back.

*People who have lost 1 sense,* he scrawled, *become stronger in the others. Don't you know that? I smell LOTS of things other peeple don't.*

*Like what?*

*Like there's still something rong inside Father Storey.* Now his gaze was solemn and unblinking. *He smells sick. He smells . . . too sweet. Like flowers when they rot.*

Harper didn't like that. She had known a doctor in nursing school who claimed he could smell death, that the ruination of the body had a particular fragrance. He insisted you could smell it in someone's blood: a whiff of things spoiling.

The moss-colored sheet between the ward and the waiting room twitched, and Renée Gilmonton ducked through, holding a bowl covered in tinfoil.

"Norma sent me over with a glop of oatmeal for the sick ol' kid," Renée said, crossing to Nick's bed and sinking down on the mattress, directly across from Harper. Renée mined one pocket of her parka and came up with something else wrapped in tinfoil. "I figured he wasn't the only little guy who might be in the mood for a snack." Nodding at Harper's distended belly.

Harper half expected to peel back the foil and find a rock inside. *Eat that, bitch,* Renée would tell her, *and then get on your knees and repent for Mother Carol.* But of course it wasn't a rock, she could tell even before she unwrapped it, just from the weight. Renée had brought her a biscuit with an improbable smear of honey in the middle.

"Allie ought to be ashamed," Renée went on. "Giving you a rock instead of breakfast. You're well into your second trimester. You can't be skipping meals. I don't care what she thinks you did."

"I let her down. She trusted me not to do something stupid and I screwed her."

"You were trying to get medical supplies to care for your patients. You were trying to collect them from *your home*. No one can forbid you to go home. No one can take your rights away from you."

"I don't know about that. The camp voted to put Ben and Carol in charge of things. That's democracy, not tyranny."

"My. Black. Ass. That wasn't any real election. They took a vote after an hour of singing and everyone was spaced out in the Bright. Most of the camp were so blitzed they would've voted for a top hat and believed they were electing Abraham Lincoln."

"The rules—"

Renée shook her head. "This isn't about rules. Don't you know that? This is about control. You went home to get medical supplies—to *help* people. To help Carol's own father! Your real crime wasn't breaking a rule about leaving camp. Your *real* crime was deciding for yourself what would be best for the people in your care. Only Carol and Ben get to decide what's best for the people in Camp Wyndham now. Carol says we speak with one voice. What she doesn't say is that voice belongs to *her*. There's only one song to sing these days—Carol's song—and if you aren't in harmony, you can stick a stone in your mouth and shut the hell up."

Harper looked sidelong at Nick, who was bent to his bowl of oatmeal, paying them no mind, and for the moment showing no sign at all of the tummyache that had brought him to the infirmary.

"That would sound better if a Cremation Crew didn't turn up while I was home," Harper said. "If they had found me, they would've made me talk before they killed me. My husband was with them. My ex. *He* would've made me talk. I can see it in my head. I can picture him asking me questions in a very calm, reasonable voice, while he uses a pair of garden shears to take off my fingers."

"Yeah. Well. That part is—I don't know what to make of that part. I mean, what are the odds they'd show up at your house when you were there? That's like being struck by lightning."

Harper considered telling Renée about the Marlboro Man and his secret broadcast—the radio station he claimed to hear in his thoughts, his psychic transmission from the future—then decided she didn't want to think about it. She ate her biscuit instead. In the honey, she tasted jasmine, molasses, and summer. Her stomach rumbled, a sound as loud as someone sliding furniture across the floor, and the two women traded looks of comic surprise.

"I wish I could do something to tell Allie I'm sorry," Harper said.

"Did you try *telling* her you're sorry?"

"Yes."

"Then that's over and done. That should be enough. She's—she's not herself, Harp. Allie and I never got along all that well, but now she's like someone I don't even know."

Harper would've replied but for the moment was swiftly tucking away the last of the biscuit. It had looked big in her palm but had vanished with disappointing haste.

"Things are going bad here," Renée said. Harper half thought she was kidding and was caught off guard by the unease she saw in the other woman's eyes. Renée offered her a tired, crooked smile and went on: "You missed a good scene in the school this morning. I give the kids a twenty-minute recess after our little history class. They can't go outside, but we block off half the chapel with pews to give them some space to run wild. I noticed Emily Waterman and Janet Cursory whispering together in one corner. Once or twice Ogden Leavitt wandered toward them and the two girls shooed him away. Well, I brought everyone together after recess for storytime, but I could tell Ogden was feeling blue, trying not to cry. He's only seven and he saw his parents die—killed trying to run from a Quarantine Patrol. He only recently started talking again. I had him in my lap and I asked him what was wrong, and he said Emily and Janet were superheroes and he wanted to be a superhero, too, but they wouldn't tell him the magic rhyme and he thought secrets were against the rules. Janet was angry and called him a tattletale, but Emily went pale. I told Ogden I knew a rhyme for superpowers: *Be-bop-a-loo-loo, You have superpowers, too!* He cheered right up and said now he could fly and I thought, *Good job, Renée Gilmonton, you've saved the day again!* I tried to steer things back to story time, but then Emily stood up and asked if she could carry a stone in her mouth to make up for keeping secrets. I said that rule was only for *serious* secrets, *grown-up* secrets, but Emily looked ill and said if she didn't atone, she wouldn't be able to sing along in chapel, and if you didn't sing and join the Bright you could catch fire. That scared Janet, who started begging for a stone, too.

"I tried to reassure them. I told them they hadn't done anything they needed to atone for. Harper—they were just being *kids.* But then Chuck Cargill heard the commotion and wandered over. He's one of Allie's friends, about Allie's age. In the Lookouts, of course. And he said it was really cool they wanted to do penance like big kids and if they each had a stone in their mouths for ten minutes, it would clean the slate. He got them both stones and they sucked on them all through storytime, looking like Cargill gave each of them a lollipop.

"You want to know the worst part, Harp? As soon as story time was over, Ogden ran over to Chuck Cargill and announced he had been hiding comic books under his bed and asked if he could do penance, too. By the end of school half the kids had stones in their mouths . . . and Harp. They were *shining.* Their eyes were shining. Just like they were all singing together."

"Oxytocin," Harper muttered.

"Oxy*Contin*? Isn't that a pain medicine?"

"What? No. Nothing. Forget it."

"You missed morning chapel today," Renée said.

"I was rigging up a feeding line for Father Storey." She nodded back at the old man. A plastic pouch of apple juice hung from the armature of a floor lamp next to the cot. The tubing did two loop-de-loops before disappearing up his nostril.

Renée said, "It's different now, without Father Storey."

"Different how?"

"Before, when everyone joined the Bright, it was like—well, everyone compares it to being a little drunk, right? Like having a few swallows of a really good red wine. Now it's like the congregation is throwing down jars of cheap, filthy moonshine. They sing themselves hoarse and then after they just . . . *hum* for a while. Stand there swaying and humming, with their eyes burning."

"Humming?" Harper asked.

"Like bees in a hive. Or—or like flies around roadkill." Renée shuddered.

"This happens to you, too?"

"No," Renée said. "I've had trouble joining in. Don Lewiston, too. And a few others. I don't know why."

But Harper thought *she* did. When she had first read Harold Cross's notes about oxytocin she had thought, randomly, of soldiers in the desert and burning crosses in the night. She hadn't seen the connection then, but she did now. Oxytocin was the drug the body used to reward people for winning the approval of their tribe . . . even if their tribe was the KKK, or a squad of marines humiliating prisoners in Abu Ghraib. If you weren't part of the tribe, you didn't get the payoff. Camp was dividing itself, organically, naturally, into those who were *in*—and those who were threats.

Renée gazed disconsolately across the room, and in a drifting, absentminded voice, said, "Sometimes I think it would be better if one of these days we just . . ."

Her voice trailed off.

"We just—what?" Harper asked.

"Just helped ourselves to one of the cars and some supplies and took off. Gather up the last few sensible people in camp and run. Ben Patchett has all the car keys hidden somewhere, but we wouldn't have to worry about that. We'd have Gil, and he can—" She caught herself, went silent.

"Gil?"

"Gilbert. Mr. Cline."

Her face was a studied, falsely innocent blank. Harper

wasn't fooled for a moment. Something teased her memory, a terrible tickling in the mind, and then it came back to her. In the summer, when Renée Gilmonton was a patient at Portsmouth Hospital, she had told Harper about volunteering at the state prison, where she had organized and led a reading group.

"Do you two know each other?" Harper asked, but the answer was in Renée's bright, startled eyes.

Renée glanced at Nick, who sat now with the empty bowl in his lap, watching them both attentively.

"He doesn't read lips," Harper said. "Not really."

Renée smiled at Nick and mussed his hair and said, "Glad to see he's recovering from that stomachache." She lifted her chin, met Harper's stare, and said, "Yes, I knew him straightaway, the moment I saw him. Well, New Hampshire is a small state. It would be a shock if some of us didn't know each other from our former lives. He was part of the book club I led, up in Concord. I'm sure most of the men there joined the reading group just for a chance to talk to a woman. Standards drop after you've been locked up awhile, and even someone almost fifty and built like Mr. Potato Head starts to look good."

"Oh, Renée!"

Renée laughed and added, "But Gil cared about the stories. I know he did. He made me nervous at first, because he kept a notebook and wrote down everything I said. But eventually we got comfortable with each other."

"What do you mean comfortable? Did you have *him* sitting in your lap for story time?"

"Don't be awful!" Renée cried, with a look on her face that suggested such awfulness was, in fact, delightful. "It was literary talk, not pillow talk. He was hard to draw out—shy, you know—but I thought he had fine insights and told him so. I had encouraged him to seek a degree in English from UNH. I believe he had just enrolled in an online course when the first cases of Dragonscale began to appear in New England." Renée looked down at her boots and said, in an offhand tone: "We appear to be reconvening the book club, as a matter of fact. I have

Ben's permission to visit the prisoners. He even let me set up a corner of the basement with some ratty chairs and a scrap of carpet. Once a night, the prisoners are allowed out of that awful meat locker, to have a cup of tea and sit down with me. Under guard, of course, although whoever is watching us usually sits on the basement stairs to give us some privacy. We're reading *Watership Down* together. Initially Mr. Mazzucchelli was opposed to reading a story about rabbits, but I think I've brought him around. And Gil—Mr. Cline—well, I think he's just glad to have someone to talk to." Renée hesitated, then added, "I'm glad to have someone to talk to, too."

"Good," Harper said.

"I understand Gil has a quote by Graham Greene on his chest," Renée said. She was studying a bit of wet snow as it slid off the tip of one boot. Her voice was calculatedly indifferent. "Something about the nature of imprisonment. But of course I've never seen it."

"Ah!" Harper said. "Nice. If Ben comes in on the two of you and you've got Gil half out of his clothes, tell him it's a matter of urgent literary research, and ask him to come back later . . . after you're done consulting Gil's Longfellow."

Renée quaked with barely contained mirth. Harper half expected smoke to begin coming out of her ears, and in those days of burning and plague, this was not an entirely unrealistic possibility. It felt good to see Renée laughing over a little innocent filth. It felt like normal life again.

"Uh-oh. The hens are clucking over something." Ben Patchett brushed through the curtain into the ward and offered them an uncertain smile. "Should I be worried?"

# 5

"Speak of the devil," Renée said, wiping at her eyes with one thumb.

*The hens are clucking.* Harper thought it would be a toss-up, which term for women she hated more: bitch or hen. A hen was something you kept in a cage, and her sole worth was in her eggs. A bitch, at least, had teeth.

If there was irritation on her face, Ben didn't see it or didn't want to. He paced halfway to Father Storey's cot, considering the tube filled with amber-colored juice, the mostly empty plastic bag hanging from the lamp by the bed.

"Is that ideal?" Ben asked.

"Feeding him out of a Ziploc bag? Or the hole in his skull that I sealed with a cork and candle wax? Totally ideal. Just like they'd do it at the Mayo Clinic."

"Okay, okay. You don't need to snip at me. I'm not snipping at you. I'm a fan, Harper! You've done amazing things here." He sat on the edge of Father Storey's bed, across from her. Springs creaked. He looked at the old man's grave, resting face. "I wish he had told you more about this woman he planned to send into exile. He didn't say anything except he thought he was going to have to send her away and maybe he'd go with her?"

"No. He did say one other thing."

"What?"

"He said if he left he wanted John to be in charge of the camp."

"John. The Fireman." His voice flat.

"Yes."

"That's a fascinating piece of information to be hearing at this late date. Why would—the Fireman's not even part of the camp. That's ridiculous. Why not Carol? Why wouldn't he want his own daughter for the job?"

"Maybe because he knew she was the type of nervous paranoid who would think it's a good idea to hand out rifles to children," Harper said.

Ben glanced quickly at the curtain into the waiting room, as if worried someone might be standing just on the other side, eavesdropping on them.

"*I'm* the one who decided to distribute the firearms, and no one under the age of sixteen got one. And I'll tell you something else. I require the Lookouts to walk around with the bolt open at all times, to prove their rifle is unloaded. I ever see the bolt closed on any of those guns, they'll be sucking on a rock until . . ." His voice trailed off and he left the sentence unfinished. A rose hue suffused his cheeks. "And you might not want to run around camp calling Carol 'paranoid.' You're in enough trouble as it is. In fact, that's why I'm here. You strayed from camp two days ago, went home, and nearly walked right into a Cremation Crew. Then, after slipping away—thank God—instead of returning to your post you went across to see the Fireman and stayed there most of the night."

"My post?"

"Mother Carol made it clear she expects you to remain by her father's side, night and day, until the crisis passes. One way or another."

"The immediate crisis *did* pass, and I have other patients."

"Not as far as Mother Carol is concerned." Ben lowered his head, thought a moment, then looked up. "Is that when the Fireman plans to make his move? When his busted ribs are healed up?"

"Make what move? Move where?"

"Here. To take over."

"He doesn't want to take anything over." It crossed Harper's mind that she might've made a tactical mistake, telling Carol's first lieutenant that Father Storey had wanted someone else for Carol's job. Then she thought, *Fuck it.* If the notion of a power struggle with the Fireman made Ben squirm, all to the good. Let *him* feel harassed and threatened for once. "But I suppose he'll do whatever is best for the camp in the end. John always has."

Renée coughed in a way that seemed to mean *Shut up.*

Ben took a moment to compose himself. He laced his fingers together in his lap and looked down into the bowl made of his palms. "Let's go back to when you wandered out of camp. I've been trying to figure out what to do about that. I think I know how to fix it."

"What do you mean—fix it? There's nothing to fix. I went, I came back, everything is fine, and it's over."

"It's not that simple, Harper. We're trying to protect a hundred and sixty-three people here. A hundred and sixty-four if we count that baby you've got on the way. We *have* to take steps to keep people safe. If people do things that aren't safe, well, there have to be consequences. If people steal. If they hoard. If they go wandering and potentially get themselves captured by the people who want to kill us. Harp, I *know* why you went back. I know you had the best intentions. But every kid who ever went to Sunday school knows where good intentions get you. You weren't just risking *your* life and the life of that precious cargo you're carrying—"

Harper could not say why the phrase *precious cargo* made her feel ill. It wasn't the *precious* part, it was the *cargo* bit. Possibly it was also an aversion to cliché. When it came to speaking in clichés, Ben Patchett left no stone unturned.

"—but you were also risking Father Storey's life and the life of everyone in camp. It was dangerous and thoughtless and violated rules that exist for good reason and it can't go without consequences. Not even for you. And believe me: there do have to be consequences for unsafe behavior. There has to be a way to keep order. *Everyone* wants that. They won't stay without it.

They want to know we're taking steps to keep this shelter safe. People *need* law. They need to know someone is looking out for them. They may even feel better if they know a few hard-asses are in charge. Strength breeds confidence. Father Storey, God bless him"—casting a halfhearted look over his shoulder at the sleepless sleeper behind him—"never seemed to understand that. His answer to everything was to hug it out. His reaction to someone stealing was to say possessions are overrated. Things were going to hell even before we brought the convicts back to camp. So."

"So," Harper said.

He lifted his shoulders and then dropped them in a great sigh. "So we at least have to make a show of punishing you. And that's what we're going to do. Carol wants to see you tomorrow, to get an update on her father. I'll take you over and we'll stick around, have tea with her. When we come back, I'll pass the word you made amends at the House of the Black Star, that you spent most of the time there with a stone in your mouth. In a lot of ways, that's the fairest way to handle the situation. In my field, we say ignorance of the law is no excuse—"

*"Ignorantia juris non excusat,"* Renée said. "But considering punishments in this camp are handed out on the spot, without an opportunity to appeal to an impartial judge or present a fair—"

"Renée," Ben said wearily. "Just because you've read a couple of John Grisham novels doesn't make you a Supreme Court justice. I'm giving Harper a way out, so will you lay off my ass?"

"Ben, thank you," Harper said softly.

He was silent for a moment, then lifted his gaze and offered her a tentative, wan smile.

"Don't mention it. If anyone in this camp deserves a little slack—" he began.

"But there's no fucking way," Harper said.

He stared at her, his mouth partly open. It took him a while to come up with a response, and when he did, his voice was thin and hoarse. "What?"

"No," Harper said. "I'm not going to put a stone in my mouth in some moronic self-abasing act of contrition when I don't have anything to feel contrite about. And I'm also not going to let you lie to people and tell them I went along with this hysterical bullshit, either."

"Will you stop swearing at me?" he asked.

"Why, is swearing against the rules, too? Will it get me another hour with a stone in my mouth? Ben: no. I say *no.* Absolutely *no.* I am a fucking nurse, and it is my job to say when something is sick, and this is sick."

"I'm trying to make things easier here, for cripes' sake."

"Easier for who? Me? Or *you*? Or maybe Carol? Is she worried it might undermine her authority if I don't bow and scrape with the rest of you? If I don't play along, maybe other people will make trouble, is that it?"

"Ben," Renée said, "isn't keeping secrets also against one of the rules? You aren't going to get in trouble for plotting to get Harper out of a punishment, are you? I'd hate to see our head of security walking around with a rock in his mouth. That might cost him something in terms of respect."

"Jeeeshus," he said. "Jeeesum Crow. Listen to you two. Harper—they're gonna *make* you—you can't just—I can't *protect* you if you won't let me."

"Your impulse to protect me conflicts with my need to protect my self-respect. Sorry. Besides. I have this vaguely uneasy feeling you're offering to protect *me* from *you*. That's not doing me a kindness—that's coercion."

He sat there for a time. At last, in a wooden, stilted tone, he said, "Carol still needs to see you tomorrow."

"Good, because *I* need to see *her*. Going to my house to get a first aid kit was a decent start to restocking the infirmary, but it isn't nearly enough, and next time I go hunting for supplies, I *will* need help. Yours, and maybe a few other men. I'm sure

Carol will want to weigh in. I appreciate you making the arrangements for my audience with her eminence."

Ben stood, twisting his wool cap in his hands. Muscles bunched and unbunched in his jaw.

"I tried," he said.

He almost tore the curtain down on his way out.

# 6

From the diary of Harold Cross:

**JULY 13TH:**

THERE WAS NOTHING LEFT OF SARAH STOREY BUT A BAKED SKULL AND THE THIGH BONES. THE DEAFMUTE WAS IN THE COTTAGE WITH HER WHEN THE PLACE WENT UP BUT HE WASN'T EVEN SINGED. HE MIGHT'VE BEEN UNHURT IF THE ROOF HADN'T CAVED IN FROM THE HEAT. I'M MONITORING HIM FOR SIGNS OF INTERNAL INJURIES BUT THERE'S NOT MUCH I CAN DO FOR HIM IF HE'S GOT A RUPTURED INTESTINE. HE'D HAVE TO GO TO PORTSMOUTH HOSPITAL AND THAT'D BE THE END FOR HIM. ONCE YOU GO INTO PORTSMOUTH HOSPITAL, YOU NEVER COME OUT.

NO ONE WILL SAY SO IN FATHER STOREY'S HEARING, BUT I KNOW A LOT OF PEOPLE THINK SARAH WOULDN'T HAVE DIED IF SHE SPENT MORE TIME IN CAMP, SINGING IN CHAPEL WITH THE REST OF US. I'M LESS CONVINCED. I WISH I KNEW MORE ABOUT WHAT SHE WAS DOING OVER THERE WITH THE FIREMAN AND HER LITTLE BOY. I'M ALSO, FRANKLY, STUNNED: SHE CONTRACTED DRAGONSCALE LESS THAN TWO WEEKS AGO. FOR THE LONGEST TIME SHE WAS THE ONLY "HEALTHY" IN CAMP. I'VE NEVER HEARD OF ANYONE BURNING SO QUICKLY AFTER INFECTION. WILL HAVE TO SNEAK BACK TO THE CABIN SOON AND GET ONLINE, SO I CAN PASS THE DETAILS OF HER CASE ON TO THE RIGHT PEOPLE.

THE FIREMAN HASN'T LEFT THE ISLAND, NOT SINCE THE ACCIDENT. THE DEAF BOY IS HERE IN THE INFIRMARY WITH ME, SO I CAN MONITOR HIS CONDITION. AND ALLIE IS STAYING WITH HER AUNT AND GRANDFATHER. SHE DRIFTS AROUND LOOKING LIKE SHE'S

DOSED UP ON A HEAVY NARCOTIC. SHE'S THE ZOMBIE VERSION OF HERSELF, PASTY AND DEAD-EYED.

IS IT WRONG TO BE THINKING ABOUT HOW GRIEF IS A FAMOUS APHRODISIAC? IF SHE'S LOOKING FOR COMFORT, MR. HAROLD CROSS'S SHOULDER IS A FINE PLACE FOR HER TO SHED HER TEARS.

OH I AM A BAD BAD BAD MAN.

A THOUGHT, INSPIRED BY FILET AU STOREY: SARAH STOREY HAS TURNED TO ASH, AND HER ASH CONTAINS THE ACTIVE SPORE, WAITING FOR A NEW HOST. WHICH MEANS THE SPORE IS PREPARED FOR REPRODUCTION BY HEAT, BUT NOT DESTROYED BY IT. AN ENZYME MUST PROTECT IT FROM DAMAGE. ENOUGH OF THAT ENZYME COULD—THEORETICALLY—ALSO COAT THE SKIN AND ACT AS A FIRE RETARDANT. SO, MY THEORY: THE FIREMAN CAN TRICK THE ENZYME INTO PROTECTING THE HOST. SARAH STOREY COULDN'T AND IS NOW FLAMBÉ. BUT WHAT IS THE ENZYME TRIGGER? SOMETHING ELSE TO DISCUSS WITH THE GUYS ONLINE.

NICK STOREY ISN'T A COMPLETE MUTE. RIGHT NOW HE'S GROANING LIKE HE CAN'T TAKE A TURD. FML. I'M NEVER GOING TO GET TO SLEEP.

# 7

Harper woke with a jolt, as if her bed were a boat that had struck a rock, the hull grinding off stone. She blinked into the darkness, not sure if a minute had passed or a day. The boat shivered off the rocks again. Ben stood at the foot of it, nudging the bed frame with his knee.

She had slept from dawn to dusk and another evening had come.

"Nurse," Ben said. Only it was not the same Ben who had pleaded with her the night before. This was Officer Patchett, his soft, pleasant, round face gone blank and formal. He was even in his police uniform: dark blue trousers, pressed blue shirt, dark blue coat with a white fleece lining and the words PORTSMOUTH PD printed on the back in bold yellow letters.

"Yes?"

"Mother Carol is hoping for an update on Father Storey," Ben told her. "As soon as you're ready, Jamie and I will walk over with you."

Jamie Close stood in the doorway to the waiting room, passing a white rock from hand to hand.

"Before I update her on the patient's progress, I'd like to update myself. And take a minute to get ready. If you'll wait in the other room?"

Ben nodded and cast a casual look toward Nick, who was sitting up in bed, watching with wide, fascinated eyes. Ben threw him a wink, but Nick did not smile.

The police officer ducked through the curtain, but Jamie Close lingered.

"You like dishin' out the medicine," Jamie said. "We'll see how you like takin' it."

Harper was trying to think of a brave, clever reply when Jamie followed her superior back into the waiting room.

Nick signed, "Don't go."

"Have to," she said with her hands.

"Don't," Nick told her silently. "They're going to do something bad."

She grabbed the pad of paper and wrote, *Don't get yourself worked up. You might give yourself a stomachache.*

Harper was combing out her hair in the bathroom when there was a little knock.

"Yes? Come in."

Michael nudged the door inward three inches. His freckled, boyish face was very pale behind his coppery twist of a beard. "Insulin shot?"

"Go ahead. I'm dressed."

He removed the lid on the back of the toilet and fished out a plastic bag with a few disposable sticks of insulin left in it. It wasn't the most hygienic place to store medical supplies, but it kept them cold. He lifted his shirt to reveal a bony edge of fish-belly white hipbone, and dabbed at it with an antiseptic wipe.

"Ma'am," he said, not looking at her. "You need to be careful tonight. People ain't right. They aren't thinking right. Allie isn't thinking right."

"Will you be here keeping an eye on the infirmary while I'm visiting with Carol?" Harper asked.

"Yes, ma'am."

"Good. Nick will be glad to have a pal around."

"Ma'am? Do you hear what I'm saying? About people not thinking right? I tried to talk to Allie at breakfast. I don't know what's come over her. She hasn't eaten in days and she wasn't in any shape to be missing meals to begin with. Someone's got to do something. I'm scared—"

"Michael Lindqvist! She can take that stone out of her mouth and have breakfast anytime she likes. I'm sorry if you want me to give her an easy out, but I am not going to encourage more of this barbaric nonsense by going *along* with it. If you came in here to see if you could bully me or guilt me—"

"No, ma'am, *no!*" he cried with real anguish. "That's not what I'm trying to do at all! You're not doing anything wrong. That's not what's worrying me. What's worrying me is the way Carol and Ben and all Allie's friends are cheering her on while she starves herself. You're in the infirmary all day and all night, so you don't see that part. You don't see the Neighbors sisters whispering to her that she can't give in, that the whole camp believes in her. Or the way all her friends sit with after she's missed another meal and chant her name until her eyes start glowing and she's in the Bright. It's almost like she needs them to be proud of her more than she needs to eat. And none of 'em care how thin she is or how fragile she's getting. I'm scared she's going to go hypoglycemic and crash. Pass out and maybe swallow that stone! Christ, it's enough—it's enough to make a person think about just grabbing her and—you know—throwing some stuff in a suitcase."

He was the second person in twenty-four hours to admit he had given thought to scarpering off. Harper wondered how many others were about sung out and if Carol knew how dangerously slippery her grip on the camp really was. Maybe she did. Maybe that explained everything.

Michael swallowed heavily. In a steadier, lower voice, he finished: "You do what you think is right. Just don't get hurt, ma'am. Allie may hate your guts right now, but she'd hate herself more if you got hurt on her account." He took a shaky breath, and then added, "I love Carol as much as I ever loved my own mother, you know that? I do! I'd die for her in a heartbeat." His eyes were damp and pleading and an unspoken *but* hovered in the air between them.

There was more to say, but no time to say it. Ben and Jamie Close were waiting.

# 8

Ben led the way. They walked on a bridge of pine planks set end to end across the snow. There seemed to be no light in all the world except for the white disk of Ben's flashlight. Jamie Close followed behind. She had her rifle over her left shoulder and a broom handle in her right hand, cut short, one end wrapped in tape. She whistled while she swung it back and forth.

They came out from beneath the firs and proceeded to the House of the Black Star, the cottage where Carol had wintered with her father. It was a tidy one-floor place—gingerbread shingles and black shutters—named for the enormous iron barn star that hung on its north-facing side between a pair of windows. Harper thought it was a fine bit of decoration, ideal for any inquisitor's dungeon or torturer's crypt. Two Lookouts sat on the single stone step, though they jumped to their feet when Ben came out of the trees. Ben didn't acknowledge them, but only stepped past them and rapped on the door. Carol called them in.

Carol sat in an aged mission chair covered in cracked, glossy leather. The chair had surely belonged to her father: it was a place to read Milton, smoke a pipe, and think wise, kindly, Dumbledorish thoughts. There was a matching love seat with creamy pale leather cushions, but no one was seated there. Carol had a pair of Lookouts with her, but they sat on the floor, at her feet. One of them was Mindy Skilling, damp-eyed and adoring before Mother Carol. The other was a girlish male, with close-cropped pale hair, feminine lips, and a big knife on his skinny belt. Almost everyone in camp called him Bowie, but Harper wasn't sure if that was because of the knife or because of his resemblance to Ziggy Stardust. He watched them enter from beneath pink, drooping lids.

Harper didn't expect to see Gilbert Cline there, too, but he was seated on the low stone ledge in front of the fire. Red worms twisted in the heaped coals, and the warmth didn't reach far. Frost had turned the panes of glass to brilliant squares of diamond and made Harper feel as if she had entered a cave behind a frozen waterfall.

Jamie Close banged the door shut and leaned against it. Ben heaved himself down on the love seat with a great sigh, as if he had just come in from hauling armfuls of wood. He patted the space beside him, but Harper pretended not to see. She didn't want to sit with him, and she didn't care to appear as a supplicant at Carol's feet. She remained close to the wall, her back to a window, winter breathing on the nape of her neck.

Carol's gaze drifted to Harper, her eyes glassy and feverish and bloodshot. With her shaved head and starved, wasted face, she had the look of an aged cancer patient, responding poorly to chemotherapy.

"It's good to see you, Nurse Willowes. I'm grateful you could come by. I know you've been busy. We were just hearing from Mr. Cline about how he came to be hiding by South Mill Pond, not a hundred yards from the police department. Some tea? Some breakfast?"

"Yes. Thank you."

Mindy Skilling rose without being spoken to and padded away into the darkened kitchenette.

"It seems Mr. Cline couldn't plausibly have had anything to do with what happened to my father," Carol went on. "And I've been interested to know something about who my dad risked his life for. Maybe *gave* his life for. You don't mind, do you, Nurse Willowes? He was just starting to tell us the story of his escape."

"No. I don't mind," Harper said. Mindy was already back,

handing her a little china cup of hot tea and a plate with a thin slice of fragrant, nutty coffee cake on it. Harper's stomach rumbled noisily. Coffee cake? It seemed only slightly less luxurious than a foaming hot tub.

"Go on. Please continue, Mr. Cline. You were saying where you and Mr. Mazzucchelli met?"

"This was in Brentwood, at the county lockup." Cline gave Harper a lingering, curious look—*What are you here for?*—before turning to face Carol. "They've got a facility there to hold maybe forty prisoners. And they had a hundred of us there.

"There were ten cells, each about ten feet long, with ten men packed in each. They put a TV in a hall and played *Bedknobs and Broomsticks* and *Pete's Dragon* so we'd have something to watch. All they had was kid videos they keep around for family visits. There was one guy who lost his mind down the hall. Sometimes he'd start screaming *'I'll be your candle on the water!'* until guys started hitting him to shut him up. After a while I started to think they were running those two videos to torture us."

It jarred her, to hear about someone trapped and going mad with panic while singing that particular song. Gilbert Cline was, in some ways, describing Harper herself, when she got stuck in the storm drain.

"None of us were supposed to be down there longer than a few days. There's only a couple reasons you wind up in Brentwood. Most of the men there were awaiting trial. In my case, I was down from the prison in Concord to provide testimony in an ongoing case, not my own. The Mazz had been brought in from the state prison in Berlin to appeal his conviction."

"What was he in jail for?" Carol asked.

"He looks like a rough customer," Gil said, "but they locked him up for perjury. I can't tell you whether he hurt your father or not, ma'am. But the Mazz isn't the sort of guy who buys himself trouble with his hands. His mouth has always been his problem. Can't help himself. He doesn't know how to tell a story without smearing a thick layer of bullshit on top."

"One more reason to hear about your escape from Brentwood from you instead of him," Carol said.

"And you can spare us the potty mouth while you're at it, mister," Ben said. "There's ladies present."

Harper almost choked on her last mouthful of coffee cake. She could not have explained to anyone quite why the phrase *potty mouth* bothered her more than the word *bullshit*.

She cleared her throat and morosely considered her empty saucer. She had meant to eat her slice of cake slowly, but there was only a little bit of it, and after the first soft dissolving mouthful of sugar and nutmeg she hadn't been able to help herself. Now it was horribly, tragically, impossibly all gone. She put the saucer on an end table so she wouldn't be tempted to lick it.

Gil continued: "I was only supposed to be in Brentwood until I testified. But they shut the court down. I waited for them to pack us up and send us back, but they never did. They just kept shoveling in more prisoners. A young man in my cell once approached the bars to say he wanted to lodge a complaint and meet with his lawyer. A state trooper walked over and popped him right in the mouth with his nightstick. Knocked in three teeth with one slug. 'Your complaint has been noted. Speak right up if there's anything else bothering you,' this cop said, and then gave us all a look to see if anyone else was dissatisfied with their treatment."

"That didn't happen," Ben said. "In my twenty years of police work, I've heard a thousand reports of police brutality, and only about three I thought held water. The rest was just sorry drug addicts, drunks, and thieves, looking to get even with the person who locked them up."

"It happened, all right," Gilbert said, in a calm, untroubled tone. "Things are different now. Law ain't law anymore. Without someone higher to answer to, the law is just whoever's holding the nightstick. A nightstick—or a dish towel full of rocks."

Ben bristled. His chest swelled, threatening to pop a button. Carol held up one hand, palm outward, and Ben closed his mouth without speaking.

"Let him continue. I want to hear this. I want to know who we brought to our camp. What they've seen, what they've done, and what they've been through. Go on, Mr. Cline."

Gil lowered his gaze, like a man trying to remember some lines of verse from a poem he had memorized years before, for a long-ago English class, perhaps. At last, he looked back up, meeting Carol's stare without fear, and he told them how it had been.

# 9

"They weren't all bad cops in Brentwood. I don't want to give that idea. There were folks who made sure we had food and drink and toilet paper and other necessities. But the longer we were in there, the harder it was to find a friendly face. There were a lot of angry cops who didn't want to be looking after us. And when people started to get the 'scale, they weren't just angry. They were scared, too.

"Anyone could see what was going to happen, the way we were all crowded in together. One morning, a guy came down with Dragonscale, in a cell at the end of the block. The other prisoners panicked. I understand why they did what they did. I like to think I wouldn't have gone along with them, but it is hard to say. His cellmates forced the infected boy into a corner, not touching him, just driving him back with pillows and such. Then they clubbed him to death."

"Jesus," Ben whispered.

"He didn't die easy, either. They were banging his head off the walls and the floor and the side of the toilet for twenty minutes, all while this one lunatic in another cell sang 'Candle on the Water' and laughed about it. Eventually the infected prisoner began to smolder and char. He never completely caught fire, but he made plenty of smoke before he died. It was like being in an Indian sweat lodge. Men were crying from all the smoke and coughing on the ash.

"Well, after they beat this poor kid to death, the staties dragged the corpse out of the cell with rubber gloves and disposed of him. But we all knew it was going to spread. The whole place was a concrete petri dish. Pretty soon it was on a couple guys in a completely different cell. Then it was on three boys in *another* unit. I have no idea how or why it could hop around like that."

Harper could've told him, but it was no matter now. The Fireman had said the world was divided into the healthy and the sick, but soon it would be down to the sick and the dead. For everyone in the room, the subject of how Dragonscale spread was now of academic interest only.

"The state cops didn't know what to do. There wasn't a facility for dealing with felons coated with Dragonscale, and they didn't want to release any of the prisoners into the civilian population. The cops got dressed in riot gear and rubber gloves and herded all the men who had Dragonscale into one cell, all together, while they tried to figure out what to do.

"Then, one morning, this guy starts screaming, 'I'm hot! I think I'm dying! I got fire ants crawling all over me!' Then he was screaming smoke. It was coming out of his throat before the rest of him started to burn. That's going full dragon, I've heard, when you breathe fire before you die. You do it because the tissues in your lungs have ignited, so you're burning from the inside out. He was running around screaming and smoke pouring out of his mouth like someone in an old cartoon who accidentally drank hot sauce. All the men in the cell with him were pressed flat against the cinder blocks to keep from catching fire themselves.

"Well, the cops came running, led by the head bull, a fella named Miller. The bunch of them stared into this cell at the burning man for a few seconds and then they started shooting." He waited to see if Ben would object. Ben sat very still, his arms draped over his knees, staring at Gilbert steadily in the wavering red light of the fire. "They pumped, I don't know, three hundred rounds in there? They killed everyone. They killed the guy who was burning and they killed all the men around him.

"After the shooting stopped, this head bull, Miller, he hitches up his belt like he just finished a big breakfast of pancakes and bacon and tells us he saved our lives. Stopped a chain reaction before it could get started. If they didn't shoot the whole bunch, the jail block would've turned into an inferno. The other cops stood around looking shocked, staring at the guns in their hands, like they couldn't fathom how they had all gone off.

"They had a few of us put on rubber cleaning gloves and carry the bodies out. I volunteered myself to get some fresh air. I was in Brentwood for three, four months and they never got the smell of burned hair and gunsmoke out of the jail block. Oh, and that empty cell? That filled back up, too. There weren't any trials happening. No one was getting processed. But cops were still arresting folks for looting and such and they had to put them somewhere.

"They fed us on corned beef and lime Jell-O for the first couple months. Then the food situation got a little dicey. One day we had canned peaches for lunch. Another day, three cops busted open a concession machine and passed out candy bars. We had rice eight meals straight. One day they announced they were going to discontinue breakfast. That was when I started to believe I was going to die in Brentwood. Sooner or later they'd discontinue lunch. Then one day the cops wouldn't come down to the cellblock at all."

His voice was a rasp that made Harper think of someone running a knife across a leather strop. She stepped into the kitchenette without asking for permission, found a cup, and poured him some tap water. She brought it back and offered it to him and he took it with a look of surprise and gratitude. He drank it off in three swallows.

When it was gone, he licked his lips and said, "Like I say. Some of the cops were all right. There was a guy named Devon. A dainty little fellow. Most of the guys called him a homo behind his back, which maybe he was, but I'll tell you what. He never shot anyone and one day he brought two shopping bags full of beer down for us. He said it was his birthday and he wanted to celebrate. So he poured us plastic cups of warm beer and handed out cupcakes and we all sang 'Happy Birthday' to him. And that was the best birthday I've ever been to. Stale supermarket cupcakes and room-temperature Bud to wash it down." He glanced at Ben and said, "See, there are some good cops in this story."

Ben grunted.

Carol said, "There's always a little decency in the worst places . . . and always a little secret selfishness in the best."

Harper wondered if Carol was taking a veiled swipe at her. If so, it was a clumsy, ineffectual sort of swipe—after all, Harper wasn't the one with coffee cake in the cupboard while the rest of the camp made do with canned beets. She supposed a small quantity of supplies were still trickling into camp now and then, one way or another, carried in by the occasional new arrival. And she imagined the best pickings wound up here, courtesy of Ben and the Lookouts: treats to help Mother Carol keep up her strength in her time of trial.

"Yeah, well, that wasn't the only decent thing Devon did for us. In the end, he did a little more for us than hand out plastic cups of suds. We'll get back to him in a minute.

"The mortar between the cement blocks in the walls was crumbly. Not so crumbly you could chip it away and escape—never in ten thousand years—but you could get a kind of chalk residue on your fingers if you rubbed at it. The Mazz figured out if you mixed it with spit, you could make a white paste. That's what he used to cover the Dragonscale when he came down with it, and that's what I used, too. A couple black guys in our cell got the 'scale, but they scraped themselves up, then claimed they had a fight. A cop threw in a roll of bandages for them, and they used that to cover the marks. By the end of the week, everyone in our cell was carrying Dragonscale and covering it up one way or another. See, all of us were afraid of Miller and the others coming down and shooting up another cell.

"It was in other cells, too. I don't know if every man in the block had it by January, but I think by New Year's Day, more had it than didn't. Some were good at hiding it. Some weren't. The cops knew after a while. You could tell because they began delivering food wearing elbow-length gloves and riot helmets, in case anyone tried to spit on them. You could tell because they looked so goddamn scared behind the plastic faceplates.

"Well, one morning Miller came downstairs with twelve other cops, all of them in their riot gear and carrying shields. Miller announced he had some good news. He told us there was a transport waiting outside. Anyone who was sick with Dragonscale was eligible for transfer to a camp in Concord, where they'd get the best medical treatment available and three squares a day. Miller read from a sheet of paper that they were having ham and pineapple that evening. Rice pilaf and steamed carrots. No beer, but cold whole milk. The cells opened up and Miller told everyone with Dragonscale to come out. A short black guy with a frill of Dragonscale running right up onto his left cheek stepped out first. It looked like a tattoo of a fern. Most people don't get it on their faces, but he did, and I guess he saw no reason to pretend he wasn't carrying it. Another guy came out after him, and then a few more, and then some guys I didn't even know had it. Pretty soon about half of the block had emptied into the corridor that ran between cells. I was going to go myself. It was the thing about cold milk that got me. You know how good a cup of cold whole milk is, when you haven't had one in a long time? My throat hurt thinking about it. I even took a step forward, but the Mazz caught my arm and just gave his head a little shake. So I stayed.

"Most of the guys in our cell went, though. One guy who was in with us, Junot Gomez, he shot me a confused look and muttered, 'I'll think of you when I'm eatin' breakfast tomorrow.'" Gilbert lifted his glass to his lips before he remembered it was empty. Harper offered to get him more water, but he shook his head.

"What happened?" Carol asked.

"Is it really that obvious they didn't ever get their ham and rice pilaf? I guess so, huh? They led 'em upstairs and outside and they shot them all. The guns went off loud enough to shake the walls, and they thundered away for almost half a minute. Not pistols. We were hearing fully automatic bursts of fire. I thought it was never going to stop. You couldn't hear anything else, not shouts, not screams . . . just guns going, like someone feeding logs into a wood chipper.

"After the shooting stopped, everyone was real quiet. The cellblock hadn't ever been so quiet, not even in the middle of the night, when people were supposed to be sleeping.

"A while later Miller and the others came down. You could smell homicide on them. Gunsmoke and blood. They brought their M16s and Miller stuck the barrel through the bars at us and I thought, *Well, now it's our turn.* Damned if we went and damned if we stayed. I felt sick about it, but I didn't fall on my knees and start to beg."

"Good," Harper said. "Good for you."

"He says, 'I want ten men for a cleanup crew. You do good, you can have a soda after.'

"And the Mazz says, 'What about a glass of cold milk?' Needling him, you know. Only Miller didn't get the joke. He just said, 'Sure, if we have any.'"

"The Mazz asks, 'What happened out there?' Like we didn't know already.

"Miller says, 'They tried to escape. Tried to seize the truck.'

"And the Mazz, he just laughs.

"Miller blinks at him and says, 'They were all dead anyhow. It's better this way. We did 'em a favor. We made it quick. Better than burning alive.'

"The Mazz says, 'That's you, Miller. Always thinking about how to help your fellow man. You're the picture of empathy.' I told you—the Mazz just has an instinct for running his mouth when anyone else would know to shut up. I thought for sure he'd get shot, but you know what? I think Miller was in shock, too. Maybe his ears were still ringing and he couldn't hear the Mazz too good. All I know is he just nodded, like he was agreeing with him.

"He opened the cell and the Mazz and I came out. Some other men drifted from the other cells. Guards had us sit down and take off our shoes and leave them behind, so we wouldn't try and run. When there were ten of us, we went upstairs, flanked by men in body armor. They walked us down a long concrete corridor and out through a pair of double fire doors into the parking lot.

"It was a cold, bright morning, so bright I couldn't see at first. The whole world was just a white blur for at least a minute. I've thought about that a lot in the time since. The men they gunned down—they must've been staggering around blind while they got shot.

"When my vision cleared I could see the brick wall was shot to shit. Most of the bodies were up against it, but a few had tried to run. At least one guy made it twenty feet across the lot before his head got blown off.

"They had a town truck backed up to the rear of the building. They handed us rubber gloves and told us to get working. They wanted to get the bodies off to Portsmouth for 'disposal.' The guy I told you about, Devon, the birthday boy who brought us beers that time? He was out there, too, with a clipboard. He checked us off as we collected our gloves and would have to check us off again when we went back to our cells. He looked like a different man. He looked like he had had ten birthdays in the last month, not one.

"At first it was easy throwing the bodies into the back of the truck, but after a bit, the Mazz and I had to climb up to arrange them and make room for more. Cold as it was, they were already going stiff. It was more like moving deadfall than you might think. I turned over Junot Gomez, who died with his mouth open, like he was going to ask someone a question. Maybe he was going to ask them what they were serving in Concord for breakfast." Gilbert Cline laughed at that, a single, harsh sound that was more jarring than a sob would've been. "We had about forty of the corpses piled in the truck when the Mazz grabbed my elbow and pulled me down with him. He drug Junot's body over the both of us. Just like that. No discussion. Like we planned it. It never even occurred to me to have second thoughts.

"Well. I don't know that there was anything to think about. The guards thought we were healthy for the moment, and they wouldn't figure on two healthy men squirming in with a pile of infected corpses. And it wasn't like it was safer to stay. Sooner or later they'd shoot the rest of us, for one reason or another. They'd shoot us and tell themselves it was the right thing to do, that they saved us from starvation, or burning alive, or whatever. The people in charge can always justify doing terrible things in the name of the greater good. A slaughter here, a little torture there. It becomes moral to do things that would be immoral if an ordinary individual did 'em.

"Anyway. There isn't much more to tell. We hid under bodies while the other prisoners kept throwing more in. No one seemed to notice we were missing. Then, just as they were finishing, I heard someone jump into the truck and start wandering around. Bootheels clanging on metal. The bodies didn't fully cover us and I could see between them and suddenly I was looking up at Devon and his clipboard, and damn if he wasn't looking right back at me. We stared at each other for the longest second in the history of recorded time. Then he nodded, just a little. He got down out of the truck and banged the tailgate shut and it started up. One guard shouted to Devon and asked if everyone was accounted for and Devon said yes they were. He lied for us. He knew we were in the truck and he lied so we could slip away. Someday this is all going to be over and I'm going to find that guy and buy him a beer. No one ever deserved one more."

The fire whistled and seethed.

"Then?" Carol asked.

"The driver threw it into first gear and hauled out of there. Half an hour later we pulled into the big lot in Portsmouth where they were burning the dead. The Mazz and I got out of the truck without being seen, but we only made it as far as a culvert on the edge of that pond there. And then we were stuck. We couldn't get across the pond and we couldn't get across the lot. I'm not sure what would've happened if the Fireman didn't show up. I guess we either would've frozen to death or given ourselves up and been shot. I hope I get a chance to thank him. It must feel pretty good to have him on your side. You almost feel sorry for anyone who goes up against him."

A prolonged, awkward silence followed.

"Thank you, Mr. Cline," Carol said. "Thank you for sharing your story. You must be tired after all that talk. Jamie, will you take him back to the lockup?"

"The handcuffs, Jamie," Ben said.

Jamie stepped forward and Mindy rose to her feet and they moved in on Gil, one on each side of him. Gil looked from Carol to Ben, his gray eyes weary and hooded. He stood and put his hands behind him. The handcuffs made a ratcheting sound as Jamie snapped them onto his wrists.

"I was going to ask if there's a chance I might be transferred out of the meat locker and in with the other men," Gil said. "But I guess not."

Carol said, "I'm very grateful to you for how forthright you've been. Grateful—and happy. Happy you are with us. Happy you don't have to fear being hauled out into a parking lot and gunned down. But Mr. Cline, after what Mr. Mazzucchelli did for you, I am not sure it's in the interest of this community to let you out. He helped you escape and you seem like a loyal soul. How could you not want to help do the same for him? No. Back to the lockup, Jamie. It may seem like horrible treatment, but you understand why it's necessary, Mr. Cline. As you said yourself, the people in charge can always justify doing terrible things in the name of the greater good. I think I know pretty well what you were implying when you said it. I think we all knew you were taking a dig at *me*."

The corners of Gil's mouth went up in a little smile.

"Ma'am," Cline said, "I hid under dead bodies less cold than you." He glanced at Harper and gave her a short nod. "Thanks for the water, Nurse. See you around."

Jamie thumped him in the small of the back with her broom handle. "Come on, sexy. Let's get you back to the honeymoon suite."

When she opened the door, the wind blew snow in halfway across the room. Mindy and Jamie escorted Gilbert out, the door thudding shut behind them. The house creaked in the gale.

"Your turn, Harper," Carol said.

# 10

"Tell me about my father," Carol said. "Is he dying?"

"His condition is stable right now."

"But he won't wake up."

"I'm hopeful."

"Ben says he should've woken up by now."

"Yes. If it was a subdural hematoma with no complications."

"So why hasn't he?"

"There must've been complications."

"Like what? What kind of thing is a 'complication'?"

"I couldn't say with any certainty. I'm a nurse, not a neurologist. A piece of bone in his brain? Or just a deep bruise on the brain. Or maybe he had a stroke while we were operating. I don't have any of the diagnostic equipment I'd need to figure it out."

"If he wakes up"—Carol began, and her breath seemed to hitch before she could go on, although her face remained slack, expressionless—"how retarded will he be?"

They didn't use the word *retarded* to discuss brain damage, but Harper didn't think it was the time or place to correct her. "He may suffer no impairment at all or he may be severely damaged. At this point I'd just be guessing."

"Would you agree, though," Carol said, "that he should've recovered by now? This is an unexpected outcome, isn't it?"

"I was hoping for better."

Carol nodded, slowly, almost dreamily. "Is there anything you can do for him?"

"With what I have on hand? Not much. I rigged up a way to pass him fluids—watered-down apple juice—but that will only sustain him for so long. If the infirmary was better stocked, though, it would open up a range of options to improve his care. It would give me more flexibility with other patients, too. That's what I was hoping to talk to you about. I spoke with John—"

"Yes," Carol said. "So I heard."

Harper continued as if there had been no interruption. "—and he has a plan to get us the supplies—"

This time Ben broke in.

"Didn't I tell you?" Ben asked Carol. "Didn't I say we could trust the Fireman to have a plan for us?" He spoke in a flat, almost bored tone, but beneath that there was an edge in his voice.

Harper tried again. "John thinks he can help us get what I'd need to look after your father and see to his long-term care, if he remains incapacitated. I think it ought to be considered."

"Tell me," Carol said.

Harper laid out the Fireman's plan: how he wanted them to take Ben's police cruiser to Verdun Avenue, use one of the camp cell phones to call an ambulance, wait for them to show up, and then—

"—then John says he'll send a phoenix to chase away the EMTs and any police who come along with them," Harper finished. She felt this was a rather lame way to wrap up and was, briefly, nettled with John and John's perverse theatrical impulses. "I'm not sure what he means by that, but he hasn't let us down in the past."

"It'll be another of his stunts," Carol said. "One of his distractions. He does like his distractions."

Ben said, "I don't see why we need his help. We can take down an ambulance without him. We have enough guns."

"To get how many people killed?" Harper asked.

"Oh, it won't come to that. We'll put it to them like this: either you give us what's in the ambulance or you wind up riding in one. Most people are pretty cooperative when they've got a rifle poking them in the eye."

"They'll have guns, too. They'll have a police escort."

"Sure. But when we meet them, I'll be in my uniform and driving my police cruiser. They won't be on guard. We'll have the drop on them before they know what's up," Ben told her.

"Why go it alone?" Harper asked. "Why not do it John's way?"

"The last time we did things John's way, someone nearly murdered my father," Carol said.

"What happened to your father happened *here,* back on our ground. John's plan *worked.*"

"Yes. It worked out all right for *him.*"

"Now what does that mean?"

Instead of answering, Carol said, "When was John planning to give us the benefit of his help?"

"Three nights from now."

"We can't wait that long. It'll have to be tomorrow. Ben, I'm trusting you to do this without any violence unless you absolutely have no other way."

Ben said, "Right. Well. There'll be four of them—two responders in the ambulance, two in the police cruiser—so there better be five of us. Jamie is the best shot in camp after me. Nelson Heinrich used to have his own NRA Facebook page and is apparently good with a rifle. That girl Mindy Skilling who just walked out of here could place the 911 call for us. She's old enough, so I wouldn't feel irresponsible about taking her along, and she's dramatic. Went to Emerson, I think? I figure—"

"Wait. *Wait,*" Harper interrupted. "Carol, there's no reason we can't hold off for three nights. Your father—"

"—is nearly seventy years old. Would you wait three nights if it was your father? If you could do something now?"

It was in Harper to say, *My father wouldn't want people getting shot for him,* but she couldn't get the words out of her mouth. In truth, she thought Carol was right. If it were her father, she would've begged the Fireman to do whatever he could, as soon as possible. Begging wasn't the sort of thing Julie Andrews did, but Harper wasn't above it.

"All right. I'll talk to John. See if he can move things up to tomorrow night."

Carol fussed with the black curl of hair that fell across her forehead. "John John John John John John John John. If John is in no hurry to help my father, I'd feel awful about rushing him."

"He isn't delaying for no reason. His ribs are knocked in, Carol."

Carol nodded sympathetically. "Yes. Yes, of course, John *must* be allowed to rest. I don't want him disturbed. We don't need him. Nurse Willowes, Ben will require a list detailing everything you need to give my father the very *best* care."

"That won't work. I have to go with them."

"Oh, no. No, you couldn't. You are so brave and kind to want to go, but I need you at my father's side. We can't risk you."

"You're going to have to. Ben is only going to have a few minutes in the ambulance. Do you really want him picking through two hundred bottles, trying to make sense of pharmacological abbreviations? Personally, I wouldn't take a chance on it, if it were my father." Turning it around to see how Carol liked it.

Carol gave her a baleful look.

"My father needs more than good medicine. He needs a good nurse," Carol said. "One is no good without the other. Be sure you come back."

Harper didn't know what to say to that. The whole conversation had been confounding, full of hints she didn't understand and implications she didn't like.

Carol said, "Ben, I want to talk over the plan with you. I want to know everything. Who you're taking with you. What Verdun Avenue is like. Everything. Nurse—" She flicked her glance at Harper. "You can find your own way back to the infirmary, I hope."

It surprised Harper that they would just let her walk out unsupervised. To a degree, she thought herself as much a prisoner as Gilbert Cline, only with a nicer cell. They had brought her to the House of the Black Star under guard, and she had expected to leave the same way.

A part of her wanted to walk out the door right away, before Carol changed her mind and decided to send her back with Bowie or one of the Lookouts hanging around outside. She already had in mind a modest detour on her way back to the infirmary. But she forced herself to wait, fingering the black buttons on her overcoat. There was, after all, still one other matter to address.

"Carol . . . I was hoping we could talk about Allie. She's been walking around with a rock in her mouth for days, because she believes she has something to atone for. I think she's doing it, partly, because she looks up to you. She wants to impress you. She wants everyone to know how devoted she is to camp. Can't you make her stop?"

"I can't," Carol said. "But you can."

"Of *course* you can make her stop. Tell her she's punished herself enough. You're her aunt and she loves you. She'll listen. You're almost all she has. You're *responsible* for her. You need to step in before she has a collapse."

"But we're *all* responsible to *each other,*" Carol said, her face assuming a maddening serenity. "We're a house of cards. If even a single card stops supporting its share of the weight, the whole camp will collapse. That is what Allie is trying to tell *you*. She carries *your* stone in her mouth. Only you can pluck it out."

"She's a child and she's acting like one. It's your job to be the adult."

"It's my job to look after more than a hundred and fifty desperate people. To keep them safe. To keep them from burning alive. In a way, I am a nurse, too. I have to protect this camp from the infection of despair and selfishness. I have to protect us from secrets, which can be like cancer. From disloyalty and disaffection, which run like fevers." As she spoke, she straightened in her chair, and her wet eyes glittered with a sick heat. "Since my father fell, I have tried to be what all these people need. What they deserve. My father wanted Camp Wyndham to be a *nice* place for people who had no other place to go. And that's all I want. I just want it to be a *nice* place . . . and I think it's nicest when we all look out for each other. My dad thought so, too." She clenched her hands together and then squeezed them between her knees. "We're stronger together, Harper. And if you're not with us, you're all alone. These days, alone is no way to be." Her look, Harper thought, was almost pitying. "Don't you see that?"

# 11

Harper followed a barely discernible path beneath an obscure sky.

Whichever way she turned her face, snow blew into it. The wind gusted. A tree cracked. Boards wobbled and flexed underfoot, requiring her to proceed slowly to keep her balance.

When the House of the Black Star was out of sight behind her, she held up in the frozen, pine-scented dark. In another two hundred steps, she would cross the trail that wound down through the trees to the shingle and the dock. She could be across the water in ten minutes, tell John they were going after the ambulance tomorrow, tell him—

A child ran through the pines to her right, a flickering shadow shape, and she turned her head to look and saw that it wasn't a child at all, only a skein of snow, fleeing through the trees.

Whack!

A snowball hit her in the side of her head, but she didn't know it until she had gone another two steps. It took that long to register. She was not aware of reeling to one side or her right knee giving out under her until she found herself kneeling in the snow.

Harper saw a blur of motion from the corner of her eye and raised an elbow in time to block the next snowball. The impact deadened her arm. A ringing shock jolted from elbow to hand. The snowball shattered the moment it struck her. The speckled white stone that had been packed in its center rolled out onto the snow in front of her.

Girl shapes jumped from behind trees on either side of her, breathless with laughter. Harper thought she saw a snowball sailing at her stomach and dropped her arms to cover it, and it hit the side of her neck instead, a sharp sting, followed by numbness.

They circled.

The water in her eyes wanted to turn to ice, freeze there. The faces surrounding her were stiff and white and inexpressive, as if she were being attacked by department-store mannequins.

One of them charged at her back and shoved her. She toppled onto her side.

"Please be careful, girls," she said. "I'm pregnant. I'm not fighting you."

"Whitewash, whitewash!" sang someone who sounded horribly like Emily Waterman.

Someone grabbed her hair in one gloved hand, picked up a fistful of snow in the other, and scrubbed her face with it. A girl shrieked with laughter.

When Harper blinked away the snow, Tyrion Lannister from *Game of Thrones* was crouched before her. He looked at her with a blank-eyed incredulity: a cheap plastic mask. He—no, *she,* it was a girl behind that mask—held out a hand, palm up. A flat white stone rested in it.

"Eat it," came the voice from behind the mask. "Eat it, bitch."

"Make her eat it," another girl said.

"Eat it, eat it, eat it," girls chanted.

Harper was on her side in the snow, one arm covering the ripe swell of her belly, the other arm trapped under her body. The girl holding her hair yanked. Then she yanked harder.

Harper opened her mouth and held it open like a child letting a doctor look at her tonsils. Tyrion Lannister forced in the stone: a cool, flat weight.

Captain America watched from between two pines, five paces away. Harper stared at Allie until her eyes blurred with tears and her vision doubled, trebled.

There was a sound like someone ripping a bedsheet in half. The hand clutching her hair yanked, pulling Harper's chin up, forcing her head back. Another hand slapped her in the mouth, hard. A thumb moved back and forth, pressing a strip of duct tape flat across her lips.

"Half an hour," said the girl who had her by the hair. "It stays in for half an hour. Now get up. Get on your knees."

Harper was lifted onto her knees. The girls pulled her arms behind her and there was another ripping sound, while one of them tore off a fresh length of duct tape and bound her wrists together.

*"Mbeby,"* Harper said, meaning be careful of the *baby*. She had no idea if anyone understood her.

Two girls danced together, holding hands, twisting and spinning each other: one wore an Obama mask, the other a Donald Trump face. In all this time, Captain America didn't move, but remained between two firs, as motionless and unblinking as an owl.

Flashlights played across the pines, a swarm of bright gold lights. Harper had to look again before she realized none of the girls were holding flashlights. It was the girls themselves, leaping about, laughing, kicking snow at her. They were lit up, like in church when they sang together. They shone for each other, the 'scale throbbing, intense enough to cast a brightness from under their jackets, up around their open collars.

So there were other ways to enter the exalted state of the Bright, then. A chorus or a firing squad: either would serve to satisfy the 'scale. A gang rape was as good as a gospel.

Harper heard the snicker-snack of scissors. Her gold hair began to fall in the snow.

"Ha ha! Ha ha!" said the smallest of her attackers, the girl she was sure was Emily Waterman. "Cut it off cut it off *cudidauff!*" Her voice was a drunk bray.

The wind sighed, reluctantly, like a lover who realizes it's time to go. Her hair fell around her while the scissors went *snickety-snack*.

"How's that rock taste?" one of the girls asked. "I bet not as good as the Fireman's prick."

The girl who had been clipping her hair said, "Isn't it sexy?

The way the scissors sound?" She opened and closed them next to Harper's ear. "Gives me shivers. I like cutting your hair so much I'm sorry there's not more of it. I'm sorry I have to stop. Maybe next time I'll cut something else. You need to decide if you're with us or against us. If you're going to shine with us or not shine at all. You want *my* medical advice? I prescribe a change in your bitchy attitude."

Yes, they were all shining . . . all except for Allie. Allie took a step toward her and made a small choked sound of grief, but when Harper turned her gaze upon her, she faltered and froze in place. She even lifted one hand, palm outward, as if somehow Harper could leap up, free her hands, and strike her.

Harper thought there was a chance that soon one of them would haul back and kick her belly like a football, just for the fun of it. They didn't know what they were doing anymore. Maybe they had already gone much further than they had intended. Maybe they had just meant to pelt her with snowballs and run. They had forgotten who they were. They had forgotten their own names, the voices of their mothers, the faces of their fathers. She thought it was very possible they would kill her here in the snow without meaning to. Use that pair of scissors to open her throat. When you were in the Bright, everything felt good, everything felt *right*. You didn't walk. You danced. The world pulsed with secret song and you were the star of your own Technicolor musical. The blood leaping from her carotid artery would be as beautiful to them as a sparkler throwing a burning red shower of phosphorus.

The girl who had been standing behind her all this time pushed her onto her side in the snow. A bubble of some powerful, dangerous emotion quivered inside her and Harper remained very still so it would not burst. She did not want to find out what it was . . . whether it was grief, terror, or, worst of all, surrender.

Each of the girls took turns dancing up to her and kicking snow in her face, and Harper closed her eyes.

The girls stood over her, whispering. Harper couldn't bear to look at them, to see that circle of masked faces gathered around her. They talked on and on, in soft, hissing, unintelligible voices. Harper shivered violently. Her jeans were soaked and her wrists hurt and her face was raw and burnt from all the snow that had been thrown in it.

At last she opened her eyes at a squint. The whispering continued, but the girls were gone. The only thing talking was the wind, shushing the pines.

She wriggled and twisted her wrists. The tape was on her gloves, not her skin, and in a while she was able to squirm one hand free. Harper pulled off the other glove and tossed them both aside, still stuck together with duct tape. She did not hesitate, did not give herself time to think, but found the edge of the duct tape over her mouth and ripped it off. She tore away some of her upper lip with it.

Harper spat the stone into the snow. It was pink with blood.

She got so light-headed when she stood up, she had to put a hand against a pine to steady herself. She made her way from trunk to trunk, like a wobbly toddler taking her first steps and using the furniture to steady herself. She found the turning to the waterfront and started down the hill. She got perhaps twelve steps when someone called out to her.

"Nurse Willowes?" Nelson Heinrich shouted. "Where are you going? The path to the infirmary is up here."

He stood on the boards with Jamie Close. Jamie was dressed in the same clothes she had been wearing the last time Harper saw her, the blaze orange snow pants and the puffy slate-colored parka. The only thing different was that she had taken off her Tyrion Lannister mask.

"That snow is up to your neck. Why don't you come back here before you're buried alive?" Nelson's face was scrubbed red from the cold and he grinned to show his two front teeth.

Harper's breath steamed. When she licked her upper lip she tasted blood.

It took her almost five minutes to trudge the twenty steps back to the boards, wading waist-deep in the snow, powder getting inside her boots.

"Jamie and I were just off to relieve the Lookouts at Mother Carol's! Good thing we showed up when we did. You were all turned around." He reached out with both hands to help her up onto the planks. He frowned, but his eyes were gay with amusement. "But look at all these tracks! We have rules, you know! No wandering off the paths! We can move the boards, but we can't make tracks disappear. What if a hunter wanders by? By God, if we were discovered, they'd ship us all off to Concord! If they didn't just shoot us here! Wandering puts the whole camp in peril! Mr. Patchett and Mother Carol have been very clear about that. One hour with a stone should remind you of your responsibilities."

Jamie Close stepped around him, holding out a white stone in her palm. She grinned to show a chipped tooth.

Harper took the rock and obediently put it in her mouth.

# 12

She was walked, like a prisoner, through the trees, Nelson leading her back to camp, Jamie behind her with her rifle and her sawed-off broomstick. Harper was surprised to find she didn't mind the stone as much as she thought she would. She believed with time she might even start to find it a comfort. The stone invited calm, meditation. It insisted on silence—inner silence as well as actual silence.

It demanded her entire attention, which was a relief because so much of what she normally thought about twisted her up inside: if she could keep Father Storey alive, if she could keep herself alive, what she would do if the baby had Dragonscale like her, what would happen if stress brought on premature labor.

The stone forced it all away and at first she thought if she had known how easy it was to live with a rock in her mouth, she wouldn't have resisted so furiously. Then she thought she had always known, deep down. She had always understood that obedience would be a great comfort to her, and that was in fact exactly why she resisted. She had sensed if she gave in once, just once, the next time would be easy.

They emerged from the woods close to the chapel. The double doors to church were open and people were looking out at her. She felt sure most of them knew what she was walking away from.

Harper turned her stare on them, cold, remote, unashamed, and was pleased to see some of them shrink back into the shadows. Most of the kids, however, held their ground. The punishment of others was a matter of great interest to children, a source of tremendous gratification.

Allie paced at the bottom of the chapel steps, but when she saw Harper she went still.

"Keep that ass of yours moving, Nurse," Jamie said.

Allie waited until Harper had gone past, then couldn't keep herself in check. She broke and sprinted across the snow to intercept them.

"Allie," Nelson Heinrich said, "you're supposed to be Lookout in the steeple tonight. Go back to your post."

Allie ignored him. "Harper. I want you to know, I never meant for—"

But Harper had quietly dropped the stone from her mouth into her hand. She hawked up a mouthful of phlegm and spat it on Allie's cheek. Allie flinched as if slapped.

Jamie thumped her in the back of the head, with a fist or the stick, Harper wasn't sure.

"That stone belongs in your mouth!" Nelson squawked. "And you can keep it in there until sunup now!"

Harper never broke eye contact with Allie, whose face was wrinkling with shock and misery, her startled eyes beginning to spill over. Harper watched until Allie's first sob. Then she put the rock back into her mouth and continued on into the infirmary.

# BOOK SIX
# PHOENIX

# FEBRUARY

# 1

From the diary of Harold Cross:

**AUGUST 10TH:**

THEY LOVE SINGING THOSE OLD-TIME HYMNS IN THIS CAMP. WE GET "AMAZING GRACE" ALMOST EVERY SINGLE NIGHT, CAROL STROKING THE KEYS OF THE ORGAN LIKE SHE THINKS SHE'S RAY CHARLES. LET ME TELL YOU SOMETHING, THERE'S NO GRACE AND THERE'S NO GOD AND I'M THE PROOF. IF THERE WAS A KIND, BENEVOLENT MASTER SPIRIT WATCHING OVER US, I WOULD NOT BE A VIRGIN AT TWENTY-FIVE. I AM PERHAPS THE ONLY WHITE AMERICAN MALE OVER THE AGE OF EIGHTEEN WHO HAS NOT MANAGED TO USE THE APOCALYPSE TO GET HIMSELF SOME PUSSY.

ALLIE STOREY SPENT TWO WEEKS COMING ON TO ME—PRACTICALLY HUMPING MY LEG. SITTING WITH ME IN CHAPEL. ASKING ME TO "HELP OUT" IN THE KITCHEN WHEN THE PLACE IS DEAD EMPTY, SO WE COULD BE ALONE TOGETHER. FLICKING WATER ON ME SO I'D FLICK WATER ON HER, SO SHE COULD LET ME HAVE A LOOK AT THE TWINS UNDER HER WET T-SHIRT. I THOUGHT MAYBE SHE WAS FEELING NEEDY BECAUSE HER MOTHER DIED. AS I NOTED EARLIER, ALLIE'S LOSS SUGGESTED MY POSSIBLE GAIN: THE DEATH OF A LOVED ONE IS A NATURAL APHRODISIAC. IT WAS LOGICAL TO HOPE SHE'D SEE MY COCK AS A POTENTIAL COPING MECHANISM.

BUT I THINK NOW SHE WAS PLAYING SOME FUCKING GAME WITH ME. MAYBE SHE PRETENDED TO LIKE ME TO ENTERTAIN THE OTHER

GIRLS—MAYBE THEY DARED HER TO SEE HOW MANY DAYS SHE COULD STRING ME ALONG, HOW MANY TIMES SHE COULD GIVE ME BLUE BALLS AND THEN LEAVE ME HANGING. FINALLY AFTER WEEKS OF WAVING IT IN MY FACE, I MAKE A MOVE ON HER, AND SHE ACTS LIKE IT WAS ATTEMPTED RAPE.

"JESUS, YOU SHITHEAD, CAN'T YOU LET ANYONE JUST BE YOUR FRIEND?" SHE SAYS.

"YEAH," I SAY. "LET'S BE FRIENDS. LET MY DICK BE FRIENDS WITH YOUR FUN HOLE."

SHE SHOVES ME SO HARD MY GODDAMN GLASSES HIT THE FLOOR AND SHE GRINDS HER HEEL ON 'EM ON THE WAY OUT AND NOW I'M JUST ABOUT BLIND.

I WISH SHE WAS IN THE COTTAGE WHEN HER MOTHER BURNED. I WISH THEY BURNED TOGETHER. I WISH THIS WHOLE PLACE BURNED.

THIS PLACE IS A HOT, DUSTY PRISON CAMP, AND EVERYONE IS WATCHING ME ALL THE TIME, BUT A LATE-BLOOMING FRIENDSHIP WITH JR HAS MADE IT POSSIBLE FOR ME TO SLIP OUT OF CAMP ON AN ALMOST DAILY BASIS. THE MAN IS A MAGICIAN. EVERY TIME I VISIT THE CABIN, I ASK MYSELF WHY THE HELL I STAY AT CAMP WYNDHAM. NOT ONLY DO I HAVE A GENERATOR AND INTERNET THERE, I HAVE HOT POCKETS. EVERY BITE IS EXTRA DELICIOUS KNOWING NO ONE ELSE IN CAMP GETS ANY.

HAD AN E-MAIL FROM SAN FRANCISCO: BIG BREAKTHROUGH ON STUDIES OF THE INFECTED LUNG THERE. THEY'VE GOT TWO THOUSAND PEOPLE IN THE PRESIDIO WHO HAVE HAD DRACO INCENDIA TRYCHOPHYTON FOR THREE MONTHS OR LONGER, AND NINE OF THEM SHOW EVIDENCE OF THE SAME SKILLS THE FIREMAN HAS DEMONSTRATED: LIMITED IMMUNITY FROM BURNS, AN ABILITY TO SELECTIVELY LIGHT THEMSELVES ON FIRE, CONTROLLED PROJECTION OF FLAME. IN THE MEDICAL COMMUNITY, THESE PEOPLE ARE CALLED PYROMANCERS. NOW THERE'S A SUGGESTION THAT ALL OF THE PYROMANCERS, AND MANY OF THE OTHER LONG-TERM CASES, CAN ENDURE LEVELS OF SMOKE THAT WOULD KILL MOST PEOPLE.

OF COURSE WE'VE KNOWN FOR A LONG TIME THAT THE SPORE "EATS" CARBON DIOXIDE AND EXUDES OXYGEN. BUT IN THE LONG-

TERM SICK, THE SPORE EVENTUALLY COATS THE PARTS OF THE BRAIN THAT CONTROL RESPIRATION (THE PONS AND MEDULLA OBLONGATA). A PRELIMINARY THEORY HOLDS THAT WHEN THE HOST BEGINS TO SUFFER FROM SMOKE INHALATION, THE BRAIN TELLS THE DRAGONSCALE IN THE LUNGS TO GO INTO OVERDRIVE, EATING THE TOXINS, AND PRODUCING CLEAN BREATHABLE AIR. A BETTER NAME FOR DRAGONSCALE WOULD BE THE NIETZSCHE VIRUS—IF IT DOESN'T KILL YOU, IT MAKES YOU STRONGER.

WORKING ON A NEW POEM:

ALLIE STOREY IS A DIRTY WHORE,
MUCH LESS BEAUTIFUL THAN THE SPORE,
THAT PROTECTS HER LUNGS FROM SMOKE,
EVEN WHEN SHE DESERVES TO CHOKE

NO, I KNOW. NOT VERY GOOD.

THANK GOD I'VE GOT MY CABIN AND THE INTERNET AND THERE'S STILL A LITTLE PORN LEFT. THERE'S EVEN DRAGONSCALE PORN NOW! IT'S SURPRISINGLY HOT. HA HA. GET IT? GET IT?

# 2

The Dodge Challenger punched itself into the night with an effortless force that brought to mind a jet accelerating toward the end of the runway. It was Harper's first time in a police cruiser. She was sitting in the back, where they put the people under arrest. That made a certain amount of sense, she thought.

She was sandwiched between Nelson Heinrich and Mindy Skilling. Mindy stared at Harper and Harper's new haircut with damp, sympathetic eyes. Harper ignored her. Now and then Nelson whistled a few bars of "I'd Like to Buy the World a Coke." She was doing her best to ignore him too.

Ben was up front, driving. Jamie Close sat in the passenger seat, with a Bushmaster across her knees. The Bushmaster had come out of the trunk, along with a .410 shotgun, which Ben had handed to Nelson. Nelson had it between his knees now, the barrel pointing straight up beneath his chin. Every time the Challenger banged over a pothole, Harper had the nauseating image of the gun going off with a deafening blam and flinging Nelson's brains on the roof.

Of all of them she was the only one who didn't have a gun. She wasn't terribly surprised they hadn't offered. Maybe they weren't sure who she might decide to use it on.

"What if the cops who show up with the ambulance are people you know?" Nelson asked. "You were with Portsmouth PD all that time, you must know the whole team!"

"I'm sure it *will* be people I know," Ben replied.

"So . . . what if they won't give up the ambulance? If it's guys you used to be friendly with—guys you used to go drinking with—wouldn't they expect you *not* to shoot?"

"If it's guys who know me, then they'll know I never bluff."

Nelson sat back and nodded placidly. "Not worth worrying about, I guess. They won't be friends of *mine*. If you have any qualms at all, you know you can count on me to do what has to be done." He whistled a little more of "I'd Like to Buy the World a Coke."

"Now hold on," Ben said, but then Jamie Close spoke up.

"Isn't that Verdun Avenue on the left, Mr. Patchett? Don't want to miss our turn."

"Right," Ben said. "Everything looks different with all the lights out."

They had traveled two miles from Camp Wyndham and not seen another car the whole way. Snow lay undisturbed in the road. Gas-lamp-style streetlamps stood along the sidewalks, but cast no light. The only illumination at all was the blue sheen of moonglow on snow.

As they swung onto Verdun, they glided past the burned-out ruin of a CVS, a dismal concrete box lined with rectangular holes where the plate-glass windows had been. Harper looked upon the place almost as a crime scene. It had burned and the ash from the blaze fell in a poisoned snow on everyone downwind, and who knew how many were dead now as a result.

Verdun Avenue was a short side street of stately Colonials mixed, seemingly at random, with modest ranches that looked like they might date from the sixties. They slowed before a cottage with cedar shakes and a chest-high hedge bordering the lawn. Ben wheeled the car around to face back the way they had come and slugged it into park.

He reached across Jamie Close's knees, opened the glove box, and then sat up with what looked, at first glance, like an oversized snow globe. Ben set it on the dash and turned it on: a red-and-blue strobe that lit the street in pinball-machine flashes.

Ben turned halfway around, to look into the backseat. "Nelson? I'm going to place you over there, behind that hedge. Keep low. After Mindy makes the call, her and the nurse are going to tuck themselves down in the backseat. Jamie? You and I are out front, to greet whoever turns up. You stand on the passenger side of the car and try to look like a cop. I'll be in the road. They'll see my flashing lights and they'll get out to see what's going on. I'll tell them to get on the ground with their hands behind their heads. That's your cue to stand up, Nelson. Give them a whistle, let them know we've got them covered from both sides. We won't have any trouble out of them once they see they're surrounded. There's two duffel bags in the trunk and a Styrofoam cooler packed with ice for anything we need to keep cold. Mindy and Harper will load up while the rest of us cover the responders." Ben looked from Nelson to Jamie, carefully making eye contact with each. "We treat them with respect and understanding. No screaming. No swearing. No 'Get your effing butt on the ground or I'll blow your effing head off.' Understand me? If we stay calm, they'll stay calm." Ben peered at Mindy. "Are you ready? Do you know what you're going to say?"

Mindy nodded, as solemn as a child being entrusted with a secret. "I'm ready."

Heavy-duty wire grating separated the front seat from the back, but Ben was able to pass a cell phone through a narrow slot in the center. Mindy turned it on. The screen filled the rear of the car with all the brilliance of a small spotlight. Once, Harper had thought that smooth bright glass face looked like the Future. Now she thought no other object in the entire world more fully embodied the Past.

Mindy inhaled deeply, preparing herself. Her face tightened and her chin dimpled with emotion, perhaps at some keenly remembered grief. She dialed 911.

"Yes? *Yes?* My name is Mindy Skilling," she panted, breath hitching as she struggled not to sob. "I am at ten Verdun Avenue. *Ten. Verdun.* Please, I need you to send an ambulance. I think my father is having a heart attack." A tear spilled out of her eye, a trickle of brightness. "I'm on my cell. We haven't had a landline that worked in weeks. He's sixty-seven. He's lying down. He's on the living room floor right now. He threw up a few minutes ago." Another desperate silence. "No, I'm not with him. I had to run outside to get a signal on my phone. Is someone coming? Is there an ambulance coming? Please send someone."

Distantly, Harper could hear the voice on the other end of the line, a *squonk-squonk* like grown-ups talking in a Charlie Brown cartoon.

"No. Neither of us have Dragonscale. We're normal. Dad doesn't let anyone near us. He doesn't let me go out either. That's what we were fighting about when—oh Jesus. I was bitching at him. He was trying to walk away from me and I was following him around bitching at him and he was holding his neck. Oh, oh, I'm so stupid."

Harper noticed Nelson blinking at tears, watching raptly.

"Please come. Please hurry. Don't let my daddy die. Ten Verdun. Please please pl—" Mindy abruptly pressed the END CALL button.

She wiped her thumb under one eye, then the other, smearing away tears. She sniffed—a wet, congested sound—although her expression had reverted to a look of sweet vacancy. She passed the phone back into the front seat.

"I've always been good at crying on cue," Mindy said. "It's amazing how much work you can get if you can weep on command. Insurance commercials. Allergy commercials. Mother's Day promotions."

"You were great." Nelson's voice was thick with emotion. "I almost started crying myself."

Mindy sniffled, wiped her hands down her pink, wet cheeks. "Thank you."

Ben nodded at Jamie. "Now it's our turn onstage. Come on, let's do this."

Ben and Jamie climbed out of the front, and Jamie opened the door so Nelson could slide out of the back. When Nelson was standing next to the car, Jamie slammed the door shut again. If they were all killed in the next few minutes, Harper and Mindy Skilling would be trapped in the police car. Mindy, at least, had a gun, a little silver-plated .22. If she could play a gun moll as well as she could play a grieving daughter, Harper thought they'd have a chance.

"Crying is easy," Mindy continued. Harper didn't think she was talking to her. Instead, she seemed to be addressing the empty car, as if she hadn't noticed the others had left. "At least for me. I think it's harder to appear genuinely happy—to laugh like you mean it. And then, hardest of all, is dying in front of a crowd. I had to do a death scene as Ophelia . . . worst five minutes I've ever had onstage. I could hear people sniggering at me. By the time the scene was over, I wished I really *had* died."

Harper tracked Ben and Jamie with her gaze as they made their way to the front of the car to stand in the headlights, where they would be backlit. Ten Verdun Avenue was behind a thick wall of snow-dusted hedge that came to Nelson Heinrich's chest. Ben waved a hand, *A little more to your right, a little more,* positioning him about midway along the hedge.

She looked past Nelson, at the house where once the Fireman had dwelt with Allie and Nick and the dead woman. Around one side of the cottage she could see a plank fence, the gate open just slightly to show the corner of an empty swimming pool.

Harper tried to imagine John and the others crowded around a picnic table back there. She pictured Nick squirting some mustard on a hot dog, Allie pawing in a bag of chips, the plastic crinkling noisily. She visualized Tom and Carol Storey sitting across from each other with a Scrabble board between them, heard the click of tiles as Tom played a word. It was not hard to conjure up the smell of burgers charring on the grill, the odor mixing with the sharp chlorinated scent of the pool. And then, what's that? The first thuds as propane tanks begin to explode at the CVS, and John turning from the grill with his spatula in one hand and Sarah coming out of the water to stand stiff and alert in the shallow end of the pool and—Harper caught herself there, thinking about Sarah Storey in the pool. Thinking about chlorine.

"Now, this, *this* is exciting," Mindy said, leaning forward, big damp eyes glittering in the dark.

"Is it?"

"Yes," Mindy said. "I've always wanted to play a heist scene."

Harper heard the yowl of an approaching siren. Blue and silver lights made the street corner into a wintry discothèque. A police cruiser swung around the corner, in no great hurry, and glided toward them.

Ben walked forward, one hand raised in greeting, while the driver of the police car pulled himself out from behind the wheel. The interior of the cruiser was fully lit. A second police officer, a thickset woman, remained in the passenger seat with a laptop open across her knees,.

The cop who had been driving stepped into the headlights, raising a palm to shield his eyes and see Ben more clearly. He was a short little guy, his hair gray bristles like shavings of dull steel, a pair of gold-rimmed spectacles resting on the end of his nose. Harper's first impression was that he looked more like an accountant than a police officer.

"Ben Patchett?" He smiled a puzzled smile. "Hey, I don't think I've seen you in—"

A shocked realization clicked into place behind his eyes. The dumpy police officer turned and began to run back to the car, handcuffs jingle-jangling on his belt.

"Bethann! Bethann, radio back—" he was shouting.

Jamie Close reached between the Challenger's headlights for her Bushmaster. It had been propped against the grille, half hidden behind her.

Ben lowered his head and took four hustling steps toward the police cruiser—not moving toward the officer who looked like a CPA, but crossing in front of the hood, moving around toward the passenger side of the car.

"Hey!" Jamie shouted. "Hey, fucker, stop running or someone is—"

The shotgun went off from behind the hedge with a heart-freezing clap of sound. The little gray-haired police officer stumbled and his gold-rimmed spectacles fell into the road and Harper thought, *He's been shot, Nelson just shot him.* But then the little man steadied himself and stood still, holding his open hands out to either side of his body.

"Don't shoot!" he screamed. "For God's sake, don't shoot!"

The female police officer inside the car had twisted her head around, so her chin was pressed to her collarbone. She had one hand on a mic attached to her shoulder, was squeezing the button. Ben stood over her, pointing his pistol at her temple through the window.

"It's all clear," Ben said. "All clear! Possible heart attack, that's a code twenty-four, code twenty-four. Let them know, Bethann."

Bethann stared at him from the corners of her eyes, then repeated, "Code twenty-four, code twenty-four at ten Verdun Avenue, officers on scene, awaiting ambulance."

She released the mic without being told, closed her laptop, and rested her hands on top of it.

Jamie walked down the center of the road, the butt of the Bushmaster socked into her shoulder, sighting down the barrel at the little police officer in the street.

"Get on your knees," she said. "On your knees, cop. We aren't looking to hurt no one."

"Bethann, if you'd step out of the car and lay facedown on the sidewalk, I think we can get through this without any ugliness," Ben said.

Harper heard another siren now, deeper in tenor, rising in volume to make the cold air reverberate in a way she could feel on her skin. Mindy glanced at Harper, her eyes shining with excitement.

"I wish we were filming this," she whispered.

"Ben," called the gray-haired cop, as he lowered himself to his knees. Jamie stood over him, pointing the Bushmaster at the back of his head. "You got the shit, don't you? You got that shit all over you. You're sick with it."

"I'm carrying Dragonscale, but I don't know you'd rightly

call me sick, Peter. By my way of thinking, I'm better than I ever was." Ben stepped back, keeping his gun leveled on Bethann, who opened her door and got out with her hands raised. Without looking away from her, Ben called, "Nelson, didn't I tell you to keep your finger off the trigger? Why did you discharge your weapon?"

Nelson stood behind the hedge, holding the .410 so it pointed into the sky. "It stopped him running, didn't it?"

Ben said, "While you were blazing away, Bethann was speaking into an open mic."

"Oops!"

"What's that mean?" Jamie asked.

"It means if you're smart you'll get out of here while you still have time to run," Bethann said. "There's a good chance they heard the shot over the radio and are already sending additional officers."

"Oh, I don't think so," Ben said. "Around the time I had to stop going to work, we were already stretched so thin it could take upwards of half an hour to get any kind of backup. And that was months ago. Everyone knows things have only gotten worse. Even if dispatch was listening, they're not going to send the cavalry because they might've heard something irregular in the background."

"Yes, that's true!" Peter agreed, on his knees in the road, hands stretched out to either side. "But it isn't just dispatch listening these days. You don't know *who's* on the radio anymore."

"Now what the heck is that supposed to mean?" Ben asked, but if Peter answered, Harper couldn't hear it. His voice was drowned out by the caterwaul of the ambulance turning onto Verdun off Sagamore.

Jamie was the first to move, stepping around Peter, on his knees, and striding toward the ambulance as it pulled in behind the police cruiser. She pointed the Bushmaster through the windshield, calling out as she came forward:

"Hey there! Take your hands off the wheel—"

Nelson's shotgun went off with a thunderous slam. The ambulance leapt forward, like a person jumping in surprise. Jamie sprang aside to get out of the way and even still was clipped by the driver's-side mirror. The Bushmaster was knocked out of her hands and would've hit the road if she hadn't been wearing the strap around her neck.

The cop named Peter got up on one foot, the other knee still touching the road, and the shotgun blammed again. Peter's head snapped back. His wispy gray combover flipped up. He began to sink backward as if he were performing some sort of advanced yoga pose.

*"Stop shooting!"* someone screamed. Harper never knew who. For all she knew, she was hearing herself.

The ambulance began to back up. Its bent front bumper was tangled in the police cruiser's rear fender, and it dragged Peter and Bethann's car along with it, through a cloud of smoke. Ben watched the ambulance dragging the cruiser away in a kind of gaping bafflement, as if he himself had been shot.

When Bethann took off, she did not try to grab for Ben's gun and she did not try to draw her own. Instead she pushed herself off the sidewalk and gave Ben a kind of comical shove, one hand in his face, the other on his breastbone. He reeled. She turned, took one step, then a second. Ben's right foot plunged over the curb. He pitched backward toward the street. His pistol cracked. Bethann buckled, pushing her chest out, arching her back. Then she straightened and ran another half dozen steps, her hand falling to the butt of her Glock, before she suddenly fell face-first onto the icy, unshoveled sidewalk.

The tires of the ambulance smoked and spun. Jamie got her hands back on the Bushmaster and lifted it to her shoulder, hollering something Harper couldn't hear. There was a wrenching clang of tortured steel. The rear fender of Peter and Bethann's cruiser fell in the road. The ambulance, free, shot backward, straight into a telephone pole, banged to a stop once more.

The tires screamed and it jolted forward, veering straight toward Jamie. The Bushmaster went off in a series of pops.

The shotgun sounded with a clap. Ben stepped into the road, leveled his pistol, and fired one shot after another.

The windshield of the ambulance exploded. The siren choked, made a dismal, dying wail, and went silent. A headlight exploded with a bright snap.

Jamie backpedaled, moving aside, then stood there, watching dumbly as the ambulance glided sedately past, no longer gaining speed, but moving at a surreal creep like a zombie in a horror movie. They watched as it rolled over Peter the cop's body. Peter's spine snapped like a tree branch. The ambulance trundled on another five yards before thumping to a stop against the curb, the fuming, bullet-riddled grille less than twenty feet away from the front of Ben's Challenger.

# 3

Ben Patchett stood at the ready, like a shooter taking target practice at the gun range. He had swiveled around to follow the passage of the ambulance as it rolled by him, firing the whole time. At last, he lowered the gun and looked around at the broken glass and the blood in the street with a sort of stunned amazement.

They were all shining—all of them. Even Harper was lit up, could feel the tingling thrill of the Dragonscale racing over her skin. Nothing created a sense of harmony, it seemed, like a communal act of homicide.

"Whoa!" Nelson cried, a kind of ragged excitement—maybe even euphoria—in his voice. "Anyone hurt?"

"Is anyone *hurt*?" Ben shouted, almost screamed. "Is anyone *HURT*, you jackass?" Harper had never heard him say anything so profane. "What's it look like? We got four corpses here. Why in God's name did you start shooting?"

"I shot the back tire out," Nelson said. "So they couldn't get away. The guys in the ambulance. They were backing up. Didn't you see?"

"They didn't start backing up until you started shooting!" A vein stood up in the center of Ben's forehead, an ugly red twig pulsing across his brow.

"No. No! I swear, they were making a run for it. Seriously! Jamie, you were standing right there. Weren't they making a run for it?"

Jamie stood over Peter the cop, pointing her Bushmaster at the corpse, as if he might get up and start running again. Peter, however, was bent over backward and grotesquely squashed, a red tread mark printed across his flattened chest. Some of his guts had been forced up and out his mouth in a bluish-red mass of slick tissue.

"What?" Jamie lifted her head, and looked from Norman to Ben, her face bewildered. She put a finger behind her right ear. "What'd you say? I can't hear anything."

"Look. Maybe if we had instant replay, we could go back and see what really happened. I don't know. I thought they were trying to drive away. Someone had to do something, so I shot out a tire." Nelson shrugged. "Maybe I made a rookie mistake. If you want to lay all the blame on someone, go ahead! Pile it on! I don't mind being the scapegoat here."

Ben looked as if he had been knifed, mouth open, eyes wide and unblinking. He went to put his pistol back in his holster, and missed on the first two attempts.

Jamie came around to Harper's side of the car and let her out of the backseat.

"Come on," Jamie said. "Let's go." Moving around to open the trunk and collect the duffel bags.

Harper felt short of breath, as if she had stepped into shockingly cold water. Her legs wobbled. A high-pitched drone rang in her ears.

She walked to the ambulance, glass crunching underfoot, and looked in. The driver was a young black woman who had dyed her close-cropped hair a ripe banana yellow. Her mouth was open as if to call out. Her eyes were wide and startled. Her lap was filled with blue safety glass.

Harper couldn't see a bullet hole and didn't know what had killed her. She had no doubt the driver was dead—she could see it in her face—but she pulled open the door and put two fingers on her neck to feel for a pulse. When she did, the driver's head slid over to rest on her right shoulder, leaving a smear on the vinyl headrest. A single bullet had entered her open mouth and exited through the base of her skull.

The woman in the passenger seat—a tiny, small-boned woman zipped into a blue EMT jumpsuit—groaned. She had dropped onto her side, facedown across the front seat.

Harper left the driver, made her way around to the passenger side. She opened the door and climbed onto the step.

There was blood on the passenger seat and blood soaking the passenger's right shoulder. Harper suspected a bullet had pulverized her scapula on the way through . . . painful, but hardly fatal. Someone she could help. She felt a relief so intense it left her weak.

"Can you hear me?" Harper asked. "You have a wound in your shoulder. Do you think you can move?"

But even as Harper spoke to her, she had the growing sense there was more wrong than a smashed shoulder. It was the way the small woman was breathing. Her inhalations required a sobbing effort; her exhalations were worse, made a strenuous gurgling sound.

Harper put one knee up in the footwell, leaning into the ambulance and taking the woman by the hip, lifting and rolling her slightly. The EMT had another bullet wound, dead in the center of her chest. Blood drenched the front of her jumpsuit. Bubbles frothed in the wound when she exhaled.

The woman's eyes strained from her head in pain. She stared up at Harper and Harper stared back and then recoiled in surprise, bumping her head on the dash. Harper *knew* her. She had crossed paths with her a few times in the summer, when they were both working at Portsmouth Hospital. The EMT was pretty, in a freckled, boyish way: upturned nose, pixie cut.

"Charity," Harper said, remembering her name and saying it aloud in the same moment. "We worked at the hospital together. I don't know if you remember me. I'm going to take care of you. You have a collapsed lung. I'm going to step away and get the gurney and put you on it. You need a chest compress and oxygen. You're going to be all right. Do you understand me? I'll be right back and we'll make you more comfortable."

Charity gripped Harper's hand and squeezed. Her fingers were warm and sticky with her own blood.

"I remember you," Charity said. "You're little Mary Poppins. You're the one who was always humming that song 'Spoonful of Sugar.' "

Harper smiled in spite of the blood and the stink of gunsmoke. "That's me."

"Want to know something, little Mary Poppins?" Charity asked. Harper nodded. "You and your friends just murdered two EMTs. I'm going to die and you aren't going to save me. Eat a spoonful of sugar with that, bitch." She shut her eyes and turned her face away.

Harper flinched, bumped her head again, as she retreated. "You aren't going to die tonight. Hang on, Charity. I'll be right back." Harper was aware her own voice was an octave too high, uneven and unconvincing.

Harper hopped down from the cockpit. She was halfway around to the rear of the ambulance when Ben gently took hold of her upper arm.

He said, "You can't do anything for her, you know. I wish to God you could, but you can't."

"Get your hand off me." Harper twisted her biceps free from his grip.

Mindy walked past her, an empty duffel bag in each hand, deliberately not looking at the squashed police officer in the road. Red and blue lights chopped the night into a series of frozen moments, little slices of time captured in stained glass.

"We have to get what we came for and go," Ben said. "There'll be more police soon. We *can't* be here when they arrive, Harper."

"You should've thought of that before you shot up the street, you assholes. You stupid assholes."

"If they get even one of us, they get us all. If you love Nick and Renée and Father Storey and the Fireman, you'll get what we came for and roll."

*I'm going to die and you aren't going to save me. Eat a spoonful of sugar with that, bitch.* Harper heard it again in her head and felt a frustration—a rage—so intense it was like nausea. She wanted to hit Ben, to scream at him. She wanted to hit him over and over while she wept.

Instead, she spoke in a soft voice that wavered with emotion and which she hardly recognized. She was unused to hearing herself plead.

"Please, Ben. *Please.* Just a chest compress. She *doesn't* have to die. I can *save* her. I can make sure she'll still be alive when the next police car gets here."

"Pack what we need for camp and we'll see if there's time," he said, and she understood she would not be allowed even to apply the chest compress.

She lowered her head and went to the rear of the ambulance.

Mindy was already standing in the brightly lit interior with its stainless steel surfaces, its rolling gurney, its drawers and cabinets. Already Harper's sense of sickened frustration was congealing into a rancid form of grief. They had done the killing; now it was time for the looting. On some level she felt the plan had *always* been to murder and steal, and she had not only gone along with it, she had all but engineered it.

She packed without thought. She filled the cooler with plasma and fluids and sent Mindy away with it. She packed the first duffel, then the second, collecting the items every respectable health clinic would stock and that her own infirmary lacked: reels of gauze, bottles of painkillers, ampoules of antibiotics, sterile thread and sterile tools, a bundle of second-skin burn gel pads. By the time Mindy got back, Harper was on her knees, packing adult diapers into the second bag—she was using them to insulate and cushion little glass bottles of epinephrine and atropine—and wondering if she could squeeze in an oxygen tank.

Jamie banged her fist on the steel door.

"Time. We got to move."

"No! Two more minutes. Mindy, I want that cervical collar and I want—"

"It's *time,*" Jamie said and she reached in for the duffel that was already full and slid it out on the ground.

"Go on," Mindy said. "I'll get the cervical collar, Ms. Willowes."

Harper cast an unhappy, half-desperate look around at open cupboards and drawers hanging open. Her gaze found the heart-start paddles, the kit no bigger than the briefcase for a laptop.

"Nelson!" Harper cried.

He appeared at the rear of the ambulance, eyes goggling in that strangely smooth, unlined, pink face that always made her think of a fat baby.

"The heart-start paddles," Harper said. "I want them."

She jumped out of the back, duffel in one hand and a compression bandage in the other. She brushed past Nelson and walked quickly to the front of the ambulance.

"I came as soon as I—"

Charity was no longer breathing in that strenuous way—or in any other way. Harper rolled her onto her back and wrenched down the zipper at the front of the jumpsuit. When it stuck, she tore the jumpsuit open. The bullet hole was just below her right breast. Harper touched Charity's wrist to take her pulse. Nothing. She felt sure there had been nothing for a long time now.

"Nursey," Jamie said. "You can't help *her,* but there's people back at camp you can. Come on. Let's go home." Her voice was not unkind.

Harper let Jamie draw her by the elbow out of the ambulance. She got turned around, back toward Ben's Challenger. Harper reached out blindly and found the straps of her duffel.

"I'll gather up the others. See you at the car," Jamie said.

Harper walked around to the open trunk of Ben's car, moving in a daze. She heaved the duffel into the back, next to the cooler, and then looked up the street.

At the end of Verdun Avenue there was that blackened, burned-out concrete shell that had once been a CVS drugstore. Out past the CVS, right at the intersection of Verdun and Sagamore, a white windowless van idled. Call letters were painted on the side, words dragging cartoonish streamers of flame: WKLL

• HOME OF THE MARLBORO MAN. At a distance, Harper could hear another vehicle coming down Sagamore, something heavy and slow: her ear caught the soft blasting hiss of air brakes and the diesel whine of a heavy engine. It sounded like a school bus.

The passenger-side window of the WKLL van was down. A man leaned out of it with a spotlight and flipped the switch. A blinding beam of light, as dazzling as a fresh-cut diamond, struck Nelson Heinrich, nailing him to the spot in the middle of the road. Nelson had just climbed out of the ambulance with the heart-start paddle kit in both hands. He squinted into the brightness.

A low squall of feedback whined from a brace of speakers on the roof of the van.

Harper felt blood beginning to rush inside of her, her internal chemical carousel getting up to speed.

The voice that followed boomed like the voice of God. It was the hoarse, roughened voice of a man who has screamed his way through an entire Metallica concert. Harper had heard the voice live only a few days before, in her own house. Before that, she had listened to him often enough on the radio, narrating the apocalypse and providing the end of the world with a sound track that was heavy on seventies cock rock.

"What are we doing tonight, folks? Lootin' an ambulance? There weren't some nuns needed raping or an orphanage to burn down? Well, tell you what. I got good news, and I got better news. I'm the Marlboro Man, here tonight with the Seacoast Incinerators, and if you're looking for medicine, *boy,* have you come to the right place. We got just the thing for treating you infected bags of meat. The even better news is there's an ambulance right here, so after we're done with you thieving and killing fucks, we won't have to go very far to find the body bags."

"Get under cover!" Ben screamed.

The side door of the WKLL van slid open. Harper had never seen anything like the gun mounted there outside of a movie. She did not know the make or caliber—did not know she was looking at an M2 Browning .50 caliber—only that it was the type of gun you usually saw bolted on top of tanks or inside combat helicopters. She could see it was belt-fed. A chain of bullets hung down into an open metal case.

A man sat on a low stool behind it, wearing a pair of bright yellow ear defenders. She had two thoughts before the night was crushed into fragments of sound and white flame.

The first was, absurdly, that such a gun could not possibly be legal.

The second was that the other vehicle, the one rolling into sight just past the ruin of the CVS, was not a school bus, of course, but an orange Freightliner with a plow the size of an airplane wing across the front, and Jakob behind the wheel.

# 4

The Browning went off in a series of deep concussions that could not be thought of merely as sound. Harper felt those stammering blasts through her entire body, in her teeth, in her eyeballs.

The ambulance shuddered. Pulverized tar leapt up from the street as the Browning strafed from left to right. Bullets passed through Nelson Heinrich's legs, tearing them apart and throwing red smoke: blood turned to a cloud of vapor. His right leg folded backward at the knee, like the leg of a praying mantis. The portable defibrillator dropped a shower of white sparks. Nelson jittered like a man at a tent revival show getting a dose of the Holy Spirit.

Harper went down on her hands and knees, dropping behind the rear of Ben's Challenger. From around the tire she saw Ben in Peter and Bethann's cruiser. He knelt in the driver's seat, leaning out with his automatic pistol. She saw the gun muzzle flash, but couldn't hear the report over the merciless thudding of the .50 caliber.

Then Ben jerked his head back into the car and shrank down. In the next instant Peter and Bethann's police cruiser was rocking from side to side, as if in a gale. Windows erupted. Bullets whanged into steel, blew out tires, sheared off the open driver's-side door—it fell with a bang into the street—sprang open the trunk, smashed taillights.

Jamie had retreated behind the front of the ambulance, sunk into a crouch, Bushmaster between her legs. The Dodge

Challenger was only a dozen steps from where she was taking shelter, but it might as well have been in a different county. Trying to cross that distance made about as much sense as diving headfirst into a wood chipper.

Then the shooting was over. Distantly, Harper heard the jingle-jangle of empty cartridges falling into the road. The air throbbed with reverberations.

"Whoa, whoa, whoa!" shouted the Marlboro Man. "I saw AC/DC with Bon Scott in '79 and they sounded like pussies compared to our noise. You all lay still unless you want to hear our encore. Let me tell you what's going to happen now. You're all going to—"

A gun popped from the rear of the ambulance. After the racket of the Browning, Mindy Skilling's little silver pistol sounded like a party cracker.

"Run for it, Mr. Patchett!" Mindy shrieked. "I'll cover you! Run, run, everyone run! My life for Mother Carol! My life for the Bright!" The gun popped again and again. Mindy was no longer in the ambulance, but crouched on the sidewalk, behind the ambulance's rear end.

"Mindy!" Ben shouted. "Mindy, *don't*—"

The Freightliner ground into first gear and lurched forward with a raggedy diesel roar. It crashed over a curb, wrenching a holly bush out of the ground and flinging it aside in a shower of dirt. The truck found second gear with a steely crunch and third a moment later. Filthy smoke gushed from the exhaust pipe behind the cab. Mindy's little gun popped and popped, bullets spanging musically off the plow. At the last moment Jamie Close dropped her Bushmaster and scrambled away from the ambulance, clambering on all fours across the sidewalk, to take shelter behind a telephone pole.

The Freightliner hit the ambulance, picked it up off the asphalt, and tossed it across the yard of 10 Verdun Avenue. Mindy Skilling was still behind it and she went along for the ride, was under it when it rolled on top of her and slid across the lawn. The ruin of the ambulance wrenched up grass and earth, left a wide, smoking skid mark behind it. One of Mindy Skilling's boots was squashed deep into the dirt, but the rest of her was beneath the deformed wreck. She had said it was hard to die in front of an audience, but in the end she had made it look easy.

"Who else wants to be a hero?" the Marlboro Man's voice boomed from the loudspeakers. "We got all night, plenty of ammo, and the next best thing to a tank. You can come on out with your hands up and play Let's Make a Deal, or you can try and fight it out. But let me tell you, if you decide to make a scrap of it, not one of you will live to see the light of day. Does everyone understand me?"

No one spoke. Harper couldn't find her own voice. She had thought nothing could be louder than the sound of the .50 caliber, lighting up the street, but the Freightliner crashing into the ambulance had been like a seventy-five-gun broadside from a ship of the line. She felt incapable of even beginning a thought, let alone completing one. One moment ticked by, and then another, and finally it was the Marlboro Man who spoke up yet again—only this time there was a distracted uncertainty in his voice.

"The fuck is that?" he said, his voice muted. Harper wasn't sure he meant to broadcast that one.

The street brightened as if the sun had, impossibly, jumped into the sky. A rushing gold light flared and lit the road with a perfect noontime clarity. Or almost perfect. That unseen sun was *moving*, swooping straight up the lane. A hot summer gale rocked the cars, blasting them with the smell of the Fourth of July: a perfume of cherry bombs, campfires, hot tarmac. Then it was gone and the darkness dropped back over Verdun Avenue.

The Marlboro Man chuckled nervously. "You wanna tell me the fuck that was? Someone shoot a flare gun at us?"

The light began to build again: a bronze burning glow that

made the spotlight shining from the van as unnecessary as a penlight at high noon in July. Harper rose to one knee and twisted her head to look over the roof of the Challenger . . . just in time to see a teardrop of flame, the size of a private jet, plunging out of the night above.

# 5

In the first instant of seeing it, the light was so intense, Harper was half blinded and could not make out any features of what was falling upon them. It was simply a blaze of red glare, plunging toward the stretch of road between the WKLL van and the Dodge Challenger.

It was thirty feet above the road and still dropping when the bolt of flame opened wings to reveal the blazing, monstrous bird within. The heat deformed the air around it—Harper saw it through a blur of tears. At the sight, she was struck through with wonder, with terror. The people who had witnessed the mushroom cloud rising from Hiroshima could've felt no less. It was twenty-four feet across from burning wing tip to burning wing tip. Its open beak was large enough to swallow a child. Feathers of blue and green flame, yards long, rippled from its tail. It made no sound at all, aside from a rushing roar that reminded Harper of a train passing through a subway tunnel.

Time snagged in place. The bird hovered less than a dozen feet above the road. The blacktop beneath it began to smoke and stink. Every window on the street reflected the bonfire light of the Phoenix.

Then it was moving—and so was Harper.

Its wings lashed at the air, and it was like someone had thrown open the hatch to a great furnace. A withering billow of chemical heat rolled down the road, and the Dodge Challenger shook in the gale. Harper was crawling around to the driver's-side door.

The Phoenix launched itself at the white van. One wing stroked a hedge and the brush ignited, became a wall of flame. The Phoenix flew into the open side door of the van. Harper had a glimpse of the gunman behind the Browning shrieking and raising his arms in front of his face. The front doors were flung open. The driver and the passenger toppled into the street.

The massive bird of flame hit the van so hard it went up on two tires, tilting toward the driver's side, threatening to overturn, before crashing back onto all four wheels. The interior boiled with fire, with threshing wings of flame. A bullet went off with a metallic *spow!* Then another. Then .50-caliber ammunition was exploding like kernels of popcorn, blam-blam-blamming inside the white van, flashing as the shells went off, bullets bonging off the roof, the walls, deforming the vehicle from the inside.

Harper hoisted herself behind the wheel of Ben's Challenger, sat on broken glass. The keys were in the ignition. She stayed low, just peeking over the dash, while she started the car.

Up the road, the Freightliner turned in a slow circle, tires chewing up the snow and dirt in front of 10 Verdun.

Harper threw the cruiser into drive and stamped on the gas. She only went a short distance, though—less than five yards—before slamming one foot on the brake. The Challenger shrieked to a stop, close to where Jamie was crouched behind a telephone pole. Jamie broke and ran, crossed the open blacktop, and dived into the passenger seat. She was saying something, shouting something, but Harper didn't hear and didn't care.

Up the road, the Phoenix emerged from the side door of the van, stretching its head out on a comically long neck as if to scream triumphantly into the night. The van continued to shake and jump on its springs while the ammo popcorned inside the wreck. The windshield exploded. Someone was screaming.

Harper launched the Challenger up the street, swerving across half-melted rubble to pull alongside the shot-up police cruiser. Ben flung himself out, hobbled across the space between the two cars, and tumbled into the backseat facedown, his legs hanging out the door. The air reeked of burning tires.

The Freightliner roared and leapt up the street at the van and the Phoenix. The plow struck the side of the Econoline with a shattering clang and tossed it aside as if it were an empty shoebox. The van rolled, spraying blue sparks, the roof collapsing. The Freightliner charged after it, hitting it again, flipping it to the far side of the cross street, Sagamore Avenue. The Phoenix exploded from the gaping windshield and streaked into the sky—much diminished, Harper saw. Minutes earlier, it had been the size of a Learjet. Now it was smaller than a hang glider.

Her foot found the gas pedal. The Challenger jumped forward hard enough to shove her all the way back into her seat. Ben's legs were still hanging out the rear door. He had wrapped seat belts around his hands to keep from being tossed out, was kicking his feet to try and pull himself farther into the car.

She looked out as they launched themselves past Nelson Heinrich on his back in the street, legs splintered and smashed, folded at improbable angles. The defibrillator sat on the dead man's chest, the plastic black with scorch marks, a bullet hole the size of a fist in the center of it. At least she thought he was dead. It was only after they were well past him that Harper wondered if Nelson had turned his head to watch them go.

The Freightliner filled the road before them. Harper swerved toward the parking lot in front of the burned-out CVS. The Challenger jumped the curb. Harper felt herself lift weightlessly off the seat. The car hit the lot with a spray of sparks and Ben howled, still hanging on.

They slewed onto Sagamore Avenue and Harper gave it all the gas it would take. A bronze light lit their way from above. The Phoenix escorted them for a quarter of a mile, a brassy blaze that made headlights all but unnecessary—and then it soared out and ahead of them. For a few moments it was gliding this way and that in front of the car, a vast kite of bright fire. At last, with a final dip of its wings, it left them, rose in a sputtering rush into the night, and was gone, disappearing over trees to the east.

An especially hard piece of glass or steel was jabbing Harper in the butt, and she reached under her to get rid of it. It turned out to be the cell phone Mindy Skilling had used to call 911. Without really considering it, she pushed it into the pocket of her snow jacket.

No one saw.

# 6

Harper was unprepared to get back and find the infirmary full of people, lamps burning in every corner, and the air humid from the close press of bodies. She knew before anyone spoke to her, just from the way they looked at her, that they were in a panic, and she wondered how they already knew about the massacre on Verdun Avenue.

The waiting room was crammed with Lookouts: Michael Lindqvist, the Neighbors twins, Chuck Cargill, Bowie, a few others Harper didn't know by name. Allie was there, too, and looked so afraid, so pale and distraught and starved, Harper couldn't feel any anger toward her. Norma Heald sat in the corner, a quaking mound of white flesh in a flower-print dress.

What surprised Harper most was to find Carol there, bundled into a threadbare pink and yellow robe that was so old the colors had taken on an exhausted, thin hue. Those words—*exhausted, thin*—applied as much to Carol herself. Her skin was stretched tight over the skull beneath, her eyes burning dangerously hot in their sockets.

Harper had an arm around Ben's waist, helping him stumble-skip along. His left cheek, his left forearm, his left hand, and his left buttock were cactused with glass needles. Jamie was right behind them, lugging the Styrofoam cooler full of plasma. They had spilled far more blood than they had brought home.

"What?" Harper asked. "Why are you all—"

"Seizure," Carol said. "My father had a seizure. While you were out there and he was here alone. His heart stopped. He died."

# 7

Later, Nick told Harper everything, using a combination of sign language and notes. He was there for the whole thing. He was holding Father Storey's hand when the old man stopped breathing.

Nick had been in a nervous state when Harper left with Ben to hit the ambulance. Somehow he had worked out what was up and was sure someone was going to die. Michael Lindqvist had tried to settle him down. They had beans and tea and played Battleship. The second time Nick yawned, Michael said it was time for a nap, and even though Nick said he wasn't tired, he was asleep in the cot next to his grandfather inside of five minutes.

He had a dream of light falling in the darkness, a torch dropping from a sky of midnight blue. The torch plummeted behind some hills and there was a red flash and the world began to shiver and rattle, as if some hidden scaffolding beneath the green grass were coming apart. Nick jumped awake, but the clattering sound continued.

Which was when he saw it: Father Storey's head snapping from side to side and foam running from the corners of his mouth. Father Storey's whole bed jittered and shook. Nick ran into the waiting room, where Michael was on watch, flipping through a *Ranger Rick* that was older than Nick himself. He dragged Michael off the couch and propelled him into the ward, hauled him along to Father Storey's bedside. Michael froze at the foot of the cot, rigid with shock.

Nick ran around his cot to his little satchel of clothes and books and dug out the most valuable item in all the world that night: his slide whistle. He shoved up a window and began to blow.

It was not the Fireman who answered the call, but Allie, and half a dozen Lookouts. By the time they got there, Father Storey had gone still. His chest had ceased its labored rise and fall. His eyelids had a gray, sickly pallor. Nick held his cold, gaunt hand, the skin loose on the bones, while Michael wept with the savagery of a small, bereft child.

Allie brushed past them both. She used a finger to scoop the foam and vomit out of Father Storey's mouth, put her lips over his, and exhaled into his lungs. She braided her fingers together and began to thrust against the center of his chest. She had learned CPR two summers before, when she was a counselor-in-training at Camp Wyndham, had received her instruction and certification from John Rookwood. So: in some ways the Fireman had answered the whistle after all.

She was at it for close to five minutes, a long, desperate, silent, timeless time, driving her hands down onto his chest and breathing into his mouth in front of a steadily growing audience. But it wasn't until Carol arrived—until she shoved through the curtain and screamed, "Dad!"—that Father Storey coughed, gagged, and with a weary sigh, began to breathe on his own again.

*Aunt Carol called him back from the dead,* Nick wrote Harper.

*Your sister called him back,* Harper scribbled in reply, but she had the unpleasant notion that most people would think the same as Nick and would credit Carol with a kind of miracle. After all, she already drove back death by leading them in song every day. Was this really so different? Once again she had confronted death, armed only with her voice, and once again the doomed had been saved.

Harper spent an hour at Father Storey's side, removing the feeding tube she had run down his nostril, getting him on a clean drip, changing his diaper and the pillowcase, which was stained with an acrid-smelling mix of vomit and blood. His pulse was strong but erratic, speeding along for a few beats, slowing, then staggering back into a hurry. His whiskery face was gray, almost colorless, and his eyelids were open on slits to show the whites of his eyes.

A stroke, she thought. He was stroking out, a little at a time. Whatever she had hoped or believed up until then, she thought now it was very unlikely the good old man would ever open his eyes or give her a smile again.

She dug up tweezers, sterile thread, a needle, bandages, and iodine, and went looking for Ben Patchett. By then it was early morning, the light watery and dismal, which perfectly mirrored how she felt.

She found Ben with Carol in the waiting room. He sat with one cheek of his ass on the edge of the coffee table, keeping his weight off the other cheek. He had been methodically picking the largest pieces of glass out of his face and arm and making a pile of them: a glistening heap of bright shards and shiny red needles.

Most of the rest had left, though Michael and Allie remained. They sat on the couch, holding hands. Michael had stopped crying, but there were white lines etched on his cheeks, tracing the path of his tears. Jamie leaned against the door. The side of her face was swollen in a ripe red bruise.

Carol said, "He's dying."

"He's stable. He's getting fluids. I think he's fine for now. You're tired, Carol. You should go home. Try and rest. Your father needs you to be strong."

"Yes. I will be. I intend exactly that. To be strong." Carol fixed Harper with a fevered, unblinking stare. "Here is a thought for you. If my father *had* died, someone in this camp—maybe a *few* someones—would be glad. Whoever bashed in his head is *praying* for him to die. You want sickness? There are people in this place who wish my father dead with all their hearts. Who probably wish *me* dead. I don't know why. I can't make sense of it. I only want us all to be safe . . . safe and good to each other. But there are some who want my father gone, who want *me* gone, who want to tear us apart and turn us against each other. *That's* sickness, Nurse Willowes, and nothing you brought back from the ambulance can cure it. It can't be cured. It can only be cut out."

Harper thought Carol sounded overtired and overwrought and didn't think this was worth replying to. She shifted her gaze to Allie. Harper wanted to thank her for saving Father Storey's life, but when she opened her mouth, she remembered how Allie had stood there and watched while the other girls kicked snow on her and cut off her hair. The words died before they made it to her lips.

Instead, she spoke to Ben. "Come into the ward and get those pants off. I want to clean your wounds."

Before Ben could rise to his feet, Carol spoke again. "You walked away from my father once and you were almost captured. You walked away a second time and my father had a fit and almost died. He *did* die. And was called back. You aren't walking away again. You will stay here in the infirmary until he recovers."

"Carol," Harper said, struggling with all her heart for tenderness, "I can't promise you he *will* recover. I don't want to deceive you about his chances."

"I don't want to deceive you about yours, either," Carol said. "You may think letting him die will make room for you and the Fireman—"

*"What?"* Harper asked.

"—but when my father's time in this camp is over, so is yours, Ms. Willowes. If he dies, you're *done* here. I want you to understand the stakes. You said yourself it is time for me to be strong. I agree. I need to be strong enough to hold people to account, and that is what I mean to do."

The Dragonscale scrawled on Harper's chest prickled painfully, heating up against her sweater.

"I will do everything I can," Harper said, struggling to keep her voice even. "I love your father. So does John. He doesn't have any interest in taking over or running the show. Neither do I! Carol, I just want a safe place to see this baby into the world. That's it. I'm not looking to undermine anyone or anything. But you need to understand—if he does die—despite my best efforts—"

"If that happens you go," Carol said. There was, suddenly, a new calm in her voice. She was sitting straighter, her pose almost regal. "And so I trust you will not let it happen."

Harper's breath was fast and short. For the second time in one night, she felt like she was pinned down, trapped by lethal fire. "I *can't* promise I can keep him alive, Carol. No one could promise that. He's been grievously injured, and his age makes a full recovery . . . very unlikely." She paused, then said, "You don't mean what you're saying. Sending me away would put the whole camp at risk. What if I was picked up by the sort of people who tried to kill us tonight? They'd force me to tell everything I know—that's what Ben says."

"Not if your baby was here with us," Carol said. "You'd keep quiet then, no matter what they did to you. Of course I wouldn't send you away until after you gave birth, no matter what happens to my father. And of course I wouldn't punish the infant by sending him away with you. That's no way to treat a child. No. If my father dies, you go, but the baby will stay here with us to ensure your silence. I'd look after him myself."

# 8

Harper drew the black thread through Ben's cheek. He shut his eyes, screwing his face up in pain. She gave the line a sharp yank to make him look at her.

"Did you hear her?" Harper whispered. Her heart was still whacking away in her chest. "*Ben*. Did you hear the crazy coming out of her?"

Ben sat on her cot. They were in the ward, away from the others, no one else in immediate earshot except Father Storey and Nick, and neither of them was listening.

Outside the windows, ranks of icicles dripped bright water in the milky glow of the sun. Ben drew a thin, whistling breath.

"Nurse? Do you think you could please leave my face on my skull? I'm kind of attached to it."

She hissed: "I can't promise *anyone* I can keep Father Storey alive. I can't promise to save him. I want to know what you're going to do if he dies. Are you going to be the one who pulls my baby out of my arms?"

"No! No. I wouldn't take your kid from you, Harper," he whispered back. "But I'm sure there are plenty of people who would, if Carol told them it had to be done. Jamie Close. Norma Heald."

"And you'd just stand by and let it happen?"

A shadow moved across the curtain between the ward and the waiting room. Carol? Allie?

Ben took a deep breath and when he spoke again, his voice was raised so he could be heard in the next room, and probably halfway to the cafeteria. "Almost everyone in this camp has been taken from someone. Almost everyone is an orphan in some way. Your baby would fit right in. I wouldn't like to see it happen, but there's a lot of things I've had to live with that I didn't like. I'm sure I could manage one more. What I won't do is bargain in secret with you, or be part of a whispering campaign against Mother Carol. People who are whispering aren't in harmony with the rest of the camp, and the only way we'll survive is if we all speak with one—"

"Oh, give it a fucking rest," Harper told him and poked him in the face with the needle to give him a stitch he didn't really need.

# 9

It was close to a week before she turned on the phone.

For all that time she kept it on her in the pocket of her sweats. Several times a day she would put her hand on it, to reassure herself it was still there. It comforted her to move her thumb along its glassy face and smooth steel curves.

She didn't dare attempt to use it. For those first days after they returned from the raid, she was uncomfortably aware of being under watch. There was always a Lookout in the waiting room—supposedly to protect Father Storey—and her guards had a habit of yanking the curtain aside at random moments and sticking a head into the ward on one pretense or another. Harper didn't even have the courage to try and hide it in the ceiling with Harold's notebook. She felt there was too great a chance of someone walking in on her while she was standing on the chair, reaching to move a drop ceiling panel.

Harper settled on a date to risk making a call. Her father's birthday was the nineteenth. He would be sixty-one, if he was alive. Only her self-restraint didn't hold out until then.

She woke early on the morning of the seventeenth with contractions, sharp enough to make her gasp. Her insides were raw dough in the hands of a burly baker who was tediously, methodically, brutally intent on kneading every centimeter of tissue. It was a sensation not unlike being overcome with the cramps of diarrhea, and a sweat prickled on her face while she waited it out.

The nurse inside her identified this rhythmic clenching-up as Braxton-Hicks contractions, just a little practice for the oncoming main event. The mother-to-be entertained sickening notions of premature birth. She was at twenty-eight weeks.

Such a thing was not impossible, especially for a woman who had been exposed to all manner of stress, gunfights, and slaughter. The idea that she might be going into labor—that the baby might be coming *right this instant*—made her feel as if she were in an elevator that had begun to fall, the cables giving way.

But before she could get too worked up, the contractions subsided, leaving her insides as fizzy as if she had chugged a cold Coca-Cola. Blood boomed in her ears. And the thought occurred to her that she ought to make that call today, now, and let her father know she was hoping to give him a grandchild for his birthday. It was incredible to think her parents didn't know she was pregnant . . . let alone that she was still alive. Her mother would scream, actually scream.

Nick was asleep on his side in the next cot, one hand curled beneath his cheek. She had no fears of waking him. He would sleep on even if she made the call right next to his bed. The floor was so cold it hurt to walk across it on bare feet. She shifted aside the curtain for a peek into the waiting room. The boy out there, a kid named Hud Loory who often drew fishing duty with Don Lewiston, dozed on the couch, his rifle on the floor. That boy would be eating a rock for breakfast if Ben Patchett stopped by on a spot inspection.

Harper let herself into the bathroom and locked the door. She sat on the lid of the toilet and turned on the phone. It had less than a quarter power and only a single bar. She stared at the flat, glassy, impossibly brilliant screen for ten seconds, then typed in her mother's cell from memory and pressed SEND.

The phone produced a grainy hiss that lasted for three seconds. A recording played of a woman with an aggrieved, accusatory voice: "The number you have dialed is not in service. Please check the listing and try again."

She tried her father's line next. The phone made a series of rapid beeps, like someone telegraphing a message in Morse code. This was followed by a hideous angry blatting and she had to hang up.

Her next thought was e-mail. She pulled up the Web browser on the phone to sign into her Gmail account. She waited, breathing shallowly, for the log in page to appear. It never did.

Instead, she was redirected to the Google main page. Only it was different now. Instead of a big blank white page with the word

Google

in the center, she arrived at a page with the word

Goodby

on it instead. Beneath was the search box, and the two familiar buttons. When she had last visited Google, one of those buttons read Google Search and the other said I'm Feeling Lucky. Now, the button on the left read

Our Search Is Over.

The button on the right read

We Were So Lucky.

For some reason—maybe because she was still emotionally jangled from her intense bout of contractions—it made Harper damp-palmed and anxious to see the Google page defaced in such a way. She had a feeling that nothing good would come from attempting a search, but she typed in *Google Mail* in the search box anyway and hit RETURN.

Instead of bringing up her results, the words she had typed

into the search box hissed, blackened, and crumbled to pixelated ash. Black trails of digital smoke wavered up from a pile of burnt crumbs.

It was ludicrous to cry because there was no more Google, but for a moment Harper felt very close to weeping. The idea that Google could collapse and be gone was as hard to imagine as the fall of the Twin Towers. It had seemed at least as permanent a part of the cultural landscape.

Maybe it was not just Google she felt like crying for, but all of it, all of the good, smart, clever creations that were sliding away now, sinking into the past. She missed texting and TV and Instagram and microwaves and warm showers and retail therapy and quality peanut butter. She wondered if there was anyone even growing peanuts anymore and felt very blue, and when she swallowed she tasted tears. She missed it all, but most of all she missed her mother and father and brother, and for the first time she allowed herself to consider the real possibility that she would never hear from any of them again.

Harper did not want to wake the Lookout in the waiting room with a sudden sob. She clutched the phone between both hands and pressed her knuckles to her mouth and waited out her grief. Finally, when she was sure she had herself under control, she planted a wet kiss on the screen of the phone, said, "Happy birthday, Dad," and turned it off.

When she returned to the ward, she hid the phone in the ceiling with the notebook. She slipped back under her sheets and had a nice little cry into her pillow.

Soon enough she was done with tears and feeling sleepy and comfortable. The baby pressed a tentative hand against the stiff, fibrous wall of his cell, fingers spread—she could feel them, she was sure—and seemed to give her a clumsy comforting pat. She pressed her hand to his, less than half an inch of tissue between them.

"Just you and me now, kid," she said, but of course it had been just the two of them for months.

# 10

That night, she dreamt of Jakob again, for the first time in months. She dreamt of Jakob and the Freightliner, of the headlights rushing toward her and the engine screaming in a way that seemed to express more hate than any human voice could manage.

But Jakob wasn't riding alone anymore.

In the dream—how curious!—Nelson Heinrich was riding with him.

# 11

Four days after she put the phone away, where it would trouble her no more, Michael Lindqvist pulled guard duty in the infirmary. He came to see her as soon as his shift began.

"Ma'am?" he said, sticking his face between the curtain and the doorframe in a way that reminded Harper of Kermit the Frog, nervously studying the evening's audience. "Can I see you about a thing?"

"Of course," Harper said. "No appointments necessary. All forms of health insurance accepted."

He sat on her cot and she pulled a pale green curtain between them and Nick for privacy. She wondered if he was going to ask her about prophylactics.

Instead he wiggled a sheet of paper out of his pocket and offered it to her. "Just thought you'd want to look at this in private. You never know when Mr. Patchett might pop by to make sure everyone is being good boys and girls."

She opened the note and began to read.

*Dear Ms. Willowes,*

*What happened to you that night in the woods was all my fault. I could've stopped it at any time and I didn't. I don't expect you to forgive me, but I hope someday I can earn back your respect, or at least your trust. I would apologize to your face but lately I've been pissing everyone off and I'm confined to the dorm, so I have to tell you this way. I'm sorry, Ms. Willowes. I never wanted you to get hurt. I never wanted anyone to get hurt. I'm such an asshole.*

*If there's anything I can do to help you, just tell Mike. I would like so badly to make it up to you. You deserve everything and anything. And also: thank you for being a substitute, part-time, all-purpose mom to my brother. You've been better family to him than I have. Please tell him I'm thinking about him and I miss him. While you're at it, give my grandpa a kiss for me.*

*Please please please be careful.*

*Hopefully someday your friend again,*
*Allie*

Michael sat with his fingers laced together, hands squeezed between his knees. He looked pasty and couldn't stop jiggling one leg.

"Thank you for bringing this to me. I know you could get in a lot of trouble, carrying secret messages."

He shrugged. "It wasn't any big thing."

"It is, though." Harper felt as lovely and free as a ten-year-old girl on her first day of summer vacation. She had already forgiven Allie everything. She had that in her—could forgive easily and lightly, with the best feeling in the world. Harper looked at the letter again and frowned. "What does she mean, she's confined to the dorm?"

Michael's eyes widened in comic surprise. He had the least guarded face of anyone Harper had ever met. "You don't know? No. No, course you don't. You almost never get out of this place. The night you robbed the ambulance, Allie went to see the Fireman and tell him what was going down. She's the reason he knew he had to send a Phoenix to make sure you all got back safe. Allie has been in a world of shit ever since. Carol had her removed from the Lookouts and made her carry a stone in her mouth for three days. The way Carol sees it, Allie chose sides against her and made her look bad in the process. Now she's only ever allowed out of the dorm to do kitchen chores and visit the chapel. And she isn't glowing anymore when we all sing!

She just stands there with her head down, not looking at anyone."

"That girl saved Tom Storey's life," Harper said. "How can Carol punish Allie after she saved Tom's life?"

"Um," Michael said.

"What?"

"The story in camp is that Allie gave *up* on trying to save Father Storey and was just standing there crying when Carol came in and called him back by shouting his name. She called Father Storey back from the deep Bright, which is where you go when you're dead."

"Allie didn't—she wasn't—what nonsense! *You* were there, haven't you told—didn't someone explain what really—"

Michael's head sank between his shoulders and his face assumed a hangdog look.

"You want to be careful the kind of stories you tell these days. Carol and Ben have their version of what happened. There isn't room for any other versions. When Allie said it wasn't true—and she did—Ben gave her a stone again for disrespecting authority. The people in this camp these days, well . . . you might've heard we only speak with one voice now." His head sank still lower. He dropped his gaze. "I hate it, you know. All of it. Not just what's happening to Allie, but also how Carol is. She's so suspicious and strained and ready to lash out. She has patrols circling her cabin because one night she thought she saw shadows moving in the trees. Emily Waterman came out of the cafeteria laughing about something, and Carol decided she must've been laughing at *her,* and gave her a stone. Emily cried and cried. She's just a kid."

He swung one foot. The laces of his boot were undone and they swooped back and forth and clicked against the underside of the bed frame. After a moment he asked: "Can I tell you somethin' kind of personal, ma'am?"

"Of course."

"A lot of people don't know I tried to kill myself once. Right after my sisters burned to death. I was hiding in what was left of my house, which was half burnt down. My parents were gone. My sisters were . . . these girl-shaped mounds of ash in the wreckage of the living room. I just wanted it all to go away. I didn't want to smell smoke anymore. I didn't want to be lonely. I had a little Honda scooter I used to deliver pizzas on. I started it up in the garage and waited for the exhaust to kill me. First I got a headache, then I threw up. Eventually I passed out. I was unconscious for about forty minutes before the scooter ran out of gas, and then I woke up. I don't think the garage was very airtight.

"A few days after that I went wandering. I had an idea maybe I'd find my way to the ocean, and walk in to clean the stink off me."

Harper remembered her own desolate morning walk to the ocean, not so long after she first came to camp. She wondered if Michael had gone to the water for the same reason as her, seeking a final cold plunge into quiet darkness and no more worry, no more loneliness.

"Instead I heard some girls singing. They were singing really nice, in sweet, clear voices. I—I was so out of it, I thought maybe it was my sisters, calling to me. I found my way out of the trees and into Monument Park and saw it wasn't my sisters at all. It was Allie and Carol and Sarah Storey and the Fireman and a few others. They were singing a real old song, that one where the guy says he doesn't know much about history. Sam Cooke, I think? They were singing and they were all lit up, soft and blue and peaceful. They looked at me like they had been waiting all day for me to get there. I sat down to watch and listen and at some point Carol sat beside me with a wet towel and began wiping the grime off my face. She said, 'Oh, look! There's a boy under there!' And I started crying and she just laughed at me and said, 'That's another way to get the dirt off.' I had been walking barefoot and she got down and wiped the blood and the dirt off my feet. It would kill me to do anything to hurt her. I thought I'd never be loved like my mom and my sisters loved me and then I found my way here."

He paused, fidgeting, and then sighed, and when he spoke again, it was in a lower voice. "But that stuff Carol said about taking your baby away from you: I don't know why she'd even *think* something like that. We can't do that. And then there's the way she treats Allie. Seems like Allie has a stone in her mouth all day, every day, and she won't ever spit it out, because that would be like admitting defeat. Allie would rather starve first. You know how she is. And then . . . and then sometimes after chapel, after we've been singing our hardest, I come back to myself, and my head is ringing like after I tried to kill myself in the garage. Sometimes I think the way we give ourselves over to the Bright now, those are *also* like little suicides." He sniffled and Harper realized he was close to tears. "It used to be better. It used to be really good here. Anyway. Like Allie said in her letter. You aren't all alone. You've got us. Allie 'n' me."

"Thank you, Michael."

"Is there anything I can do for you?"

"Yes. There is. But if it's too much, you must say no. Don't feel you have to do anything that would put you at more risk than is safe."

"Uh-oh," he said. "I was thinking maybe you'd want me to sneak you some creamers for your coffee. I guess you're thinking bigger."

"Is there any way I can get out of here for an hour to see the Fireman? And if I did, could you keep a close eye on Father Storey while I'm gone?"

He blanched.

"I'm sorry. I shouldn't have asked."

"No," he said. "It's okay. I could cover for you if Mr. Patchett showed up, I guess. I could pull the curtain across your bed, put some pillows under your sheets, and tell him you're napping. Just—if I sneak you out—if I get you together with him . . .

do you promise you'll come back? You aren't going to jump in a car with the Fireman and take off tonight, are you?"

Of all the things he could've said or asked, she had not seen that one coming.

"Oh, Michael, of course I wouldn't. I wouldn't abandon Father Storey in his condition."

"Good. Because you *can't* leave camp," he said and sat forward and gripped her wrist. "Not without taking Allie and me."

# 12

Harper descended the hill through a bitter cold that stung her nostrils and hurt her lungs. Her breath smoked, as if she were going full dragon, burning from the inside out.

It was coldest on the shale, alongside the water, numbing the exposed parts of her face. A thread of smoke rose from the tin chimney on the Fireman's shed, the only sign of life in the entire ice-locked world. She hated walking out on the dock, felt exposed, half expected someone to shout. But no one saw her, and the dock itself was hidden from the church steeple by a band of tall evergreens. She lowered herself into the rowboat and cast off the line. Once she was on the water she might be visible (the eye in the steeple sees all the people) but it was moonless and starless and she thought in the deep dark she might go unobserved.

This time she was able to walk to the shed without losing her boots in the mud. The muck was frozen to the hardness of tile. Harper knocked on the doorframe. When no one replied, she knocked again. From within she smelled woodsmoke and sickness.

" 'S'unlocked," the Fireman said.

She eased into the little room, into stifling heat and golden light from the open furnace.

He was in bed, with the sheet snarled around his waist and legs, arm in his filthy sling. The room had an odor of phlegm and his breathing was strenuous.

She dragged a chair to the side of his bed and sat down. Then she leaned forward and put her cheek to his bare chest. His skin blazed and smelled of sandalwood and sweat. The

Dragonscale decorated his breast in patterns that brought to mind Persian carpets.

"Breathe normally," she said. "I didn't bring a stethoscope."

"I *was* getting better."

"Shut up. I'm listening."

His inhalations crackled faintly, like someone rolling up plastic wrap.

"Shit," she said. "You've developed an atelectasis. I don't have a thermometer, but I can tell you're feverish. Shit, shit. I don't understand."

"I think *Atelectasis* was an early album by Genesis. One of the ones they recorded before Phil Collins took over singing and they turned to middlebrow MTV crap."

"It's a smarty-pants word for a certain kind of pneumonia. You see this as a complication with fractured ribs, but I wouldn't expect it in a man your age. Have you been smoking?"

"No. You know I don't have cigarettes."

"Have you had any fresh air?"

"A great deal."

She narrowed her eyes at him. "How long is a great deal?"

"Er, eighteen hours? Give or take a couple?"

"Why were you outside for *eighteen* hours?"

"I didn't mean to be. I passed out. I always pass out when I send a Phoenix somewhere." He gave her an apologetic smile. "I was too weak, I think. Not ready to create one. It took too much out of me. Although it's a good thing I sent one. As if their machine gun wasn't bad enough, that plow your ex is driving around is as bad as a Panzer—"

"Wait a minute. Go back. How do you know my ex showed up at Verdun Avenue? Who told you?"

"No one told me. I was there with you."

"What do you mean you were *there* with me?"

He sighed, winced, pressed his good hand to his bad side. "You hid behind Ben's police cruiser when the shooting started. Nelson was the first one to die—he was torn apart in the street. Then the town truck hit the ambulance and Mindy Skilling was mashed beneath it. After, you tore out of there like one of your American NASCAR blokes. I recall everything right up to the moment your ex smashed the van and nearly crushed me flat. Nearly crushed the Phoenix flat, I mean."

Harper couldn't wrap her head around it. Up until now she had assumed the Phoenix was a glorious pyrotechnic display that could somehow be operated from a distance, rather like a remote-control airplane. A puppet of flame, with John Rookwood tugging the strings from here on his island.

Yet he could recount the confrontation with Jakob and the Marlboro Man as if he had fought it out with them in person, a concept Harper found perplexing and also irritating, because John so clearly loved being impressive and mysterious.

"That's impossible. You can't have seen all that."

"Oh, let's not get carried away. It's only improbable. And besides. I didn't *say* I saw it. I *didn't* see it. But I *remember* it." He saw her getting ready to interrupt and held a hand up, palm out, to forestall questions. "You know that the Dragonscale, over time, saturates the human brain. It listens in to your thoughts and feelings and reacts to them. It's dendritic in nature and it bonds with the mind."

"Yes. That's why people catch fire when they're afraid or under stress. Panic releases cortisol. The Dragonscale reacts to cortisol by assuming the host is no longer safe. It erupts into flame, producing lots of ash, enabling it to depart for better real estate."

He looked at her with admiration. "Yes. That's the mechanism exactly. Who have you been talking to?"

"Harold Cross," Harper said, pleased to surprise him for once.

The Fireman took this in, then lifted one corner of his mouth in a smile. "You found his notebook. I'd love to see it sometime."

"Maybe after I'm done with it," she said. "Cortisol kicks off spontaneous combustion. But oxytocin—the social-networking hormone—puts the Dragonscale at ease. Anytime you feel the pleasure of group approval, you increase the Dragonscale's sense of security and make it less likely to burn you to death later. That I understand. I *can't* understand how you could be here in your cabin, while also seeing things that were happening two miles away."

"But I told you, I didn't *see* them. I *remember* them, and that's the difference. The Phoenix has a cloud of Dragonscale burning at its core. That Dragonscale contains a crude copy of my thoughts, my feelings, my responses. It's an outboard brain. Eventually it returned to me, came back to the nest, where it died out, having done its job. The ash fell on me like snow while I was unconscious on the beach, and in the hours that followed, I *dreamt* everything the bird did and saw. It all came back to me, fragmentary at first, but eventually the entire awful scene."

Harper weighed this notion in her mind. Ash that could think and flame that lived and a spore that could swap impulses and memories with the human mind. It was, she thought, just exactly the sort of fantastical nonsense that evolution was always going in for. Nature was a grand one for sleight of hand and magic tricks.

When she spoke again, it concerned the Dragonscale not at all. "You need a course of antibiotics. As it happens, I have some. I'll send Michael over with a bottle of azithromycin. He should be able to slip over during the changing of the watch at dawn. Come on, Mr. Rookwood, let's have a look at your arm."

"I take it you won't be available to bring my medicine yourself?"

She declined to meet his gaze. Instead she gently loosened the sling and unbent his elbow. He grimaced, but she thought it was more from the anticipation of pain than any actual suffering.

"Things are going sour here, John. I'm confined to the infirmary, on house arrest and forbidden to leave Father Storey's side. I'm only here tonight because Michael drew watch, and Mike isn't playing by Carol's rules anymore. Neither is Allie, who is on permanent house arrest in the girls' dorm. Michael was afraid if he let me go see you, I might not come back. He doesn't want me driving off without him." She considered for a moment. "It's only a matter of time before a couple dozen defectors try to make a run for it. Fill some cars with supplies and light out. Renée has already talked about leaving with Don and the prisoners and a few others."

"Where would you go?"

"Oh, I don't know that I'd head out with them, whatever Michael thinks. While there's still a chance for Father Storey, it wouldn't be right to abandon him."

The Fireman did a strange thing then. He glanced past her at the furnace—then leaned in and spoke in a soft voice, as if he didn't want to be overheard. "I admire a good bit of foolishness more than anyone, Harper, but in this case it won't do. Your first obligation is to yourself and that baby, not to Tom Storey. He had the biggest heart of any man I ever knew and I'm sure he wouldn't want you to stay for him. He's been under for—how long? Six weeks? Seven? After a crushing blow to the head? At the age of seventy? He's gone. He's not coming back."

"Men have recovered from worse," she said, although as she spoke, Harper found herself wondering if she even still knew the difference between a diagnosis and a denial. "Besides. *John*. I'm close. Nine weeks? Eight? I need somewhere to have this baby. The infirmary is a good place. I don't know if I can find better. Don could deliver the child. He's reeled in plenty of fish—I'm sure he can manage one more. Right now, so close to my due date, I wouldn't leave camp unless there was no other choice." She did not mention that if Father Storey died, she really would have no other choice. She would run with the baby or be sent into exile without it. But she did not want to distress John by telling him about Carol's threats, not now. John was sick; he was beat up and feverish and his lungs were full of filthy damp. Her job was to give sympathy and care, not elicit it.

She got up, went through some drawers beneath what had once been a worktable, and came back with some scissors. Harper snipped the filthy tape away from his wrist. It was still swollen and grotesquely discolored but it was only a little stiff when she asked him to rotate it, and she decided it didn't need to be re-bound.

"I think we can be done with the sling as well. But keep the brace on your elbow until you can bend the arm without sharp pain. And *try* to rest it. Until you've had a little more time to heal, you better limit yourself to intellectual masturbation only. We don't want to put any undue strain on this wrist."

For once he had nothing to say.

She sat back and said, "You know, Michael won't leave camp without Allie. And I'm sure Allie won't run without Nick. It scares the shit out of me to imagine them ditching camp and taking their chances out in the wild. What about *you*? They'd be safe if they went with you. You could look after them: Allie and Nick."

His gaze shifted briefly to the furnace behind her, then dropped. "And do you really think I'm in any condition to go anywhere?"

"Maybe not now. But we'll make you better. *I'll* make you better."

"Let's not get ahead of ourselves. There isn't even a plan yet. Just a lot of loose talk."

Harper cast a slow and uneasy glance at the open furnace herself. She saw no one looking back at her from the flames: not a mystery woman and not Sirius Black. She thought of how John had glanced at the fire before leaning close to speak in a soft voice, as if he did not want to be overheard. Something else occurred to her, almost randomly, something he had said about the Phoenix: *It's an outboard brain*. The thought raised a chill on the nape of her neck.

"No," she said. "But we better get working on one. I think we should try to meet here. *All* of us. Even the prisoners, if it can be managed. We don't need to work out just how we're going to leave, but also where we're going to go and how we intend to survive." She steeled herself and added, gently, "You say Father Storey wouldn't want me to risk my life or the baby's life by staying. I say Sarah wouldn't want *you* to risk your life by staying."

"Oh, I don't know," he said. "It wouldn't be so bad: to be buried here. Why not? In some ways I feel like this is where my real life started. Here in Camp Wyndham, where I met Sarah, and where we all returned after we came down with Dragonscale. There would be a certain narrative elegance in my life ending here as well."

"Fuck narrative elegance. How *did* you all wind up deciding to hide out here?"

"Nowhere else to go. That simple, really."

"You can do better than that," Harper said.

"If you insist," he told her.

# 13

"We were all marked. The first lines appeared on Nick's arm and back. Three days later we looked like we had all gone to the same tattoo parlor in hell. Except for Sarah. In the space of seventy-two hours, Sarah had to face the idea of losing her son, her daughter, her sister, her father, and her boyfriend. You'd expect a person to quit functioning.

"But she didn't quit. Her children still needed her, and as long as they could feel and think and be comforted, she was set on being whatever they wanted her to be. Besides, for a couple of weeks she assumed she had the infection, too, and just wasn't symptomatic. I think when she finally realized she didn't have it, she was more upset and shocked than she would've been if she *did*. How could every one of us have it except her? She got mad at me a couple times, as if it were *my* fault she wasn't crawling with Dragonscale. *Why all of you and not me?* That's what she kept asking."

"She was in the pool," Harper murmured.

"Figured it out, did you? Yes. The poisoned ash fell from the sky and we all got it on us, but Sarah had gone swimming. The chlorine killed the spore, or at least created a barrier against it. In any random slaughter, the difference between living and dying rarely has anything to do with willpower or wisdom or pluck. It's just a matter of where you're standing. Two inches to the right and the bus hits you. If your office is on the ninety-second floor instead of the ninetieth, you don't make it out in time.

"Sarah put off grief. She put off a nervous collapse. I don't know how she bore up, but she did. The only time I saw her nearly hysterical was when her father said we should all book ourselves into the federal quarantine in Concord. The thought of her children being taken from her was like being prodded with hot sticks. We had to back off. I think we were all afraid of what she might do to herself if we created a situation where Allie or Nick might be yanked from her life and never seen again.

"For a few days Allie stayed curled up in a ball, just crying. Then one morning she came out of the bathroom with her head shaved and announced she was all done being sad. That night her mother and Allie did 'shrooms together. The next night, Sarah and Allie snuck out and stole a car. They were deranged but happy. They looted a costume store. Sarah came home as Hillary Clinton. Allie took a Captain America mask because she liked the big 'A' on it. They thoughtfully brought a Tony the Tiger mask for Nick. I said I always wanted to be a fireman and next time I hoped they'd think of me. Two nights later they stole an antique fire truck from the parking lot of a museum full of classic cars and all the fireman gear that was inside it. They had to park it in the boathouse at Camp Wyndham, just to have a place to stick it. Allie was determined to raise some hell before she died and Sarah felt it was important for a mother to support her daughter's goals in life.

"I didn't think Carol would last long. I remember that. She dropped ten pounds she didn't have to lose. She stopped sleeping. She'd watch TV, half naked, for twelve hours straight, as insensible as someone who has had a lobotomy. She smelled like a lit match and was always seeping smoke. The only thing that could bring her out of her miasma was her father, who made sure she ate and slept, and otherwise tended to her needs.

"Then one morning I heard banging doors and screaming in the street. It was early and I was the only one up. I crept down the walk and looked out over the hedge. They had a lorry pulled up in front of a house down the street, a police van that had been pressed into service by Quarantine Patrol. Some SWAT types in gas masks were wrestling a woman into it. They had a doctor with them, in a mask and gloves, carrying a clipboard, and telling her this was for the protection of her own children. Telling her they would contact an appropriate relative to come and collect the kids. A boy of about four was sobbing his eyes out, trying to follow them. Another member of the Quarantine Patrol kept taking him by the shoulder and turning him around. Somewhere inside the house I could hear a baby shrieking. Just before they shoved the woman into the truck, she turned her head and I saw her face. It was the same lady who had been weeping on the curb the day the drugstore went up in flames.

"That afternoon, we had a family conference around the dining room table and I filled them in on what I had seen. Allie said we needed a plan, in case they came back and knocked on *our* door. Tom said if such a thing happened, the best thing we could do was not be there to answer it. He said he had spent every summer for the last forty years at Camp Wyndham and saw no reason to change his plans now, and never mind summer camp had been canceled. He said he had been over to camp with Carol once already and there were enough dry goods on hand to feed an army for a decade. He was only off by nine years.

"He settled into the house that had always been his, supposedly with Carol to look after him, although it was really the other way around. Sarah and I claimed a cabin close to the boathouse, because Nick liked to play fireman on our stolen fire truck. Would it sound strange to say those were lovely days? We had fresh eggs then, waffles, and coffee. We had swims at dawn and campfires at dusk. Sarah dusted off the organ in the church and played Billy Joel and Paul McCartney. She tried to get her sister to play with her, but Carol stayed in the House of the Black Star, her 'scale smoking and fuming. Waiting to die.

"One morning Sarah went into Portsmouth to get news and groceries. She could shop for us, she wasn't sick. She came back with the Neighbors girls. Two days later, Norma Heald showed up on her own. She had worked in the cafeteria in summers past and thought it would be safer to look for food here than in a supermarket. That was the beginning of Tom's people.

"A few days after Norma showed up in camp, Carol came flying out of the House of the Black Star, looking wild, almost incoherent with terror, found Sarah, and said it was happening. She said to come quick. She said Tom and Nick were lighting up—that both of them were about to burst into flame.

"We ran so hard and fast we left Carol behind. We ran sick and scared. You can't imagine what it's like to run so hard toward something you don't want to see. Like running toward your own firing squad. I was sure we'd find both of them withered and blackened, the house afire.

"Sarah burst through the front door and then stopped so suddenly I ran into her and knocked her down. Allie was right behind me and tripped over the both of us. We were all tangled together on the floor when I saw them.

"The dishwasher in that house has to be older than you, Harper. It had seen almost three decades of service, and thumped and shook when it was turned on. The beat, if you can imagine it, is very like that old song 'Wooly Bully.' You know that one? Tom sat with his back to the machine and Nick in his lap and that Wooly Bully thump going through the both of them. Tom had his fingers laced through Nick's and he was singing and the both of them were *shining*. Tom had his sleeves rolled back to show the 'scale on his forearms, and it was as brilliant as swirls of glow-in-the-dark paint.

"It didn't bother him at all, watching us crash in through the doors like the Keystone Kops. He gave us a laughing sort of look and went right on singing. Sarah said, 'Oh, Dad, oh, God, what's happening to you?'

"And he said, 'I'm not sure, but I think the Dragonscale likes Sam the Sham. Come and sing with us and see if you don't like the way it makes you feel.'

"By the time Carol came through the door we were all sitting together in a circle by the thumping dishwasher, singing garage rock and lit up like a carnival. As soon as the Dragonscale started to warm up and glow you knew you were all right. That you weren't going to burn. Well, you know what it's like in the Bright.

"We sang until the dishwasher finished its cycle, and as soon as the machine quit thumping, our Dragonscale began to cool and go dim. We were all so high. I couldn't remember which of Tom's daughters I was dating, so I kissed both of them. Sarah had a laugh at that. Allie kept counting her toes, because she couldn't remember how many she had. I guess you'd have to say we were good and baked. Baked! Ha! Isn't that clever? Isn't it—no? Ah. Well.

"We gathered the others in the chapel that evening. Sarah sat at the organ and Carol tuned her ukulele and they played 'Bridge over Troubled Water' and 'Let It Be' and we lit up like sparks blowing from a bonfire. Their voices were so smoky and sweet. I have never been so drunk or so happy. I could feel myself letting go of my identity, the way you might put down a heavy suitcase you no longer need carry. It was, I imagine, how bees feel. Not like an individual at all, but like one humming note in a whole world of perfect, useful music.

"After we were all sung out, Tom spoke to us. That seemed natural. He told us things we knew but needed to hear. He told us we were lucky for every minute we had together, and I knew it was true. He told us it was a blessing, to be able to feel each other's love and happiness so intensely, right on our skin, and I said amen, and so did all the rest of us. He told us that in the darkest moments of history, kindness was the only light you had to find your way to safety, and I know I cried to hear him say it. I feel a little like crying now, just remembering it. It's easy to dismiss religion as bloody, cruel, and tribal. I've done it myself. But it isn't religion that's wired that way—it's man himself. At bottom every faith is a form of instruction in common decency. Different textbooks in the same class. Don't they all teach that to do for others feels better than to do for yourself? That someone else's happiness need not mean less happiness for you?

"Only Sarah did not shine, because only Sarah did not have the Dragonscale. But she knew as well as the rest of us that we had solved something. That we had found a working cure. We didn't need a spoonful of sugar to make the medicine go down. The sugar *was* the medicine. Sarah sang with us, and watched us turn on, and kept her own counsel. I had been with her long enough by then that I should've seen what was coming. What she would do.

"But I didn't see what was coming because I was drunk most of the time. Not drunk on booze, you understand. Drunk on that rush of light and pleasure that came over me when we all sang together. Allie began to go out at night in her Captain America mask, to spy on friends, kids she knew from school. If she saw they were sick with the 'scale, she'd recruit them and their families. Tell them there was a way to stay alive. That the infection didn't have to be a death sentence. We had a dozen new people coming in every week.

"Sarah sent me along with Allie to make sure she got back to camp in one piece. I took to dressing as a fireman, because I discovered that in a world full of things burning up, no one looks at a fireman twice. I couldn't even remember my own name for most of June, I was so drunk on the Bright. I was just . . . just the Fireman." He coughed, weakly. A fragrant puff of smoke blew from his mouth, turned into the ghost of a toy-sized fire truck, and dissolved.

"Show-off," Harper said. "What happened next?"

"Sarah died," he said, and bent forward and surprised Harper by kissing her nose. "The end."

# BOOK SEVEN

# NO STRAIGHT ARROW

# MARCH

# 1

From the diary of Harold Cross:

**AUGUST 28TH:**

MARTHA QUINN IS REAL.

HAS A WEBSITE, MARTHAQUINNINMAINE. THEY PROCESS YOU IN MACHIAS, CLEAN YOU UP, GIVE YOU FRESH CLOTHES AND A SQUARE MEAL, AND TAKE YOU OVER ON A LOBSTER BOAT. THEY'VE GOT WHAT'S LEFT OF THE CDC THERE WORKING ON A CURE.

I'M GOING. TOMORROW OR THE DAY AFTER. IF I STAY HERE, SOONER OR LATER, I'LL BURN TO DEATH. THE OTHERS ARE GETTING THE BENEFIT OF SOCIAL CONNECTION, BUT I'M NOT, AND WITHOUT REGULAR DOSES OF OXYTOCIN, MY BIOCHEMICAL FUSE IS STILL HISSING.

I WON'T BE ASKING ANYONE'S PERMISSION. I KNOW I WON'T GET IT. CAROL HAS ME UNDER PRETTY TIGHT WATCH. THE ONLY THING I'VE GOT GOING FOR ME IS JR. HE'S ARRANGED TO SLIP ME OUT OF HERE SO I CAN GET TO THE CABIN TONIGHT AND SEND MY LAST E-MAILS.

NOT SURE HOW I'LL MAKE IT SO FAR NORTH WHAT WITH ALL OF SOUTHERN MAINE ON FIRE BUT JR SAYS MAYBE A BOAT. I CAN'T WAIT TO SAY GOOD-BYE TO THIS SHITHOLE FOREVER.

# 2

Her first thought was: *It can't be that easy.*

She turned the page, hoping for more, but that was it. After that, the notebook was blank.

Rain fell. It hammered on the tin roof in a continuous rattle and crash. The rain had been falling ten hours straight. Sometimes trees fell, too. Harper had woken to the sound of one going over somewhere close by, with a great creak and a floor-shaking smash. The wind struck the infirmary again and again, one battering rush after another. It was like the end of the world out there. But then every day was like the end of the world now, come rain or shine.

Harper had not imagined there was anything left in the diary to learn, let alone shock her. Martha Quinn was real. The island was a real place.

Nick was watching her carefully: no surprise there. Harper had long since quit trying to keep the notebook secret from him. It was, in the narrow confines of the ward, impossible anyway. She met his intense, unwavering, curious gaze. He did not ask if she had read something important. He *knew.*

It was a Lookout named Chuck Cargill in the waiting room that night. He had walked in on Harper two hours ago, when she had her sweater off and was rubbing lotion on the pink curve of her stupendous belly. She had a bra on, but Cargill was nevertheless so alarmed to find her in a state of undress he had dropped the breakfast tray he was carrying on the counter with a clatter, as if it had suddenly become too hot to handle. He reeled backward, stammering some sort of incoherent apology, and ducked back out through the curtain. Ever since, he had been careful to clear his throat, knock on the doorframe, and ask for permission to come in. Harper thought he might never be able to make eye contact with her again.

She also thought if she wanted to get the phone down out of the ceiling, he probably wouldn't walk in on her while she was using it. No one else would, either. Even Ben Patchett wasn't going to do spot inspections on a night like tonight.

Harper turned the straight-backed chair around and climbed unsteadily onto it. She reached into the ceiling, found the cell phone, and climbed back down. Nick stared at her—at *it*—with wide, fascinated, wondering eyes. She gestured with her head: *Come over here.*

They walked to the far end of the ward, putting as much distance as they could between themselves and the curtain into the waiting area. Harper and Nick sat down side by side on the edge of Father Storey's cot, with their backs to the doorway into the next room. If Cargill *did* suddenly walk in, the phone would be concealed by their bodies and she might have time to shut it down and stick it under the mattress.

She squeezed the power button. The screen flashed gray, then a deep obsidian black. The battery life was a whopping 9 percent.

Harper pulled up the browser and loaded marthaquinninmaine.

# 3

Music played, tinny and flat through the little iPhone speakers, barely audible over the rain, but no less lovely for all of that. It was a song Harper used to perform herself when she was eight years old, using a wooden spoon as the microphone, sliding across the kitchen linoleum in her Miss Piggy slippers. Ric Ocasek sang that this one girl was just what he needed, over a melody that sproing-sproinged along like a Slinky walking down a staircase.

Photos loaded, but slowly.

The first showed a vast gradual slope of waist-high grass, yellowing in the autumn. The ocean was a sheet of battered steel in the background. Martha Quinn stood in the center of a long line of children, five on either side of her, her arms around the waists of the two closest. She was as bony as ever and even at nearly sixty, her face was impish and kind, her eyes narrowed in a way that suggested she had a good joke she wanted to tell. The wind blew her platinum hair back from her high brow. Her sleeves were rolled up to show the Dragonscale on her forearms, a black-and-gold scrollwork that brought to mind ancient writings in Kanji.

As the song faded, a second photograph loaded. A doctor in a white lab coat, a pretty Asian woman with a clipboard in one hand, crouched to be at eye level with a scrumptious nine-year-old girl. The little girl clutched a stuffed raccoon doll to her chest and her nose was wrinkled in a shriek of laughter. Her bare, chubby arms were lightly scribbled over with 'scale. They were in the white, clean, sterile hall of a hospital unit somewhere. There was a sign on the wall in the background, blurred, almost out of focus. It wasn't an important part of the image and so Harper saw it without really noticing it . . . then narrowed her eyes and looked again. When she registered what it said, the intensity of her emotions drove all the air out of her. Just two words:

- *Pediatrics*
- *Maternity*

The third photo began to load as the song faded out. A voice began to speak—a voice Harper knew only from 1980s retrospectives on VH1 and MTV. The volume was already so low, Harper could barely hear Martha Quinn over the furious tinny drumming of rain on the ceiling, but out of caution she turned it down still more and bent close to listen.

"Whoo, hello, was that just what *you* needed? It was just what *I* needed. Well, it was *one* of the things I needed. It's a pretty long list. I NEED to know that Michael Fassbender is still alive, because, HELLO! That man was right in so many ways. He was setting ladies on fire way before the spore got loose, you know what I mean? I NEED new episodes of *Doctor Who,* but I'm not holding my breath, because I bet everyone who made that show is dead or hiding. Is there still an England out there? I hope you didn't burn up, British Isles! Where would the world be without your epic contributions to culture: Duran Duran, Idris Elba, and *Love Actually*? Drop me an e-mail, England, let me know you're still hanging in there!"

The next image showed a large tent with some folding tables set up in it. A processing center. The tables were manned by the sort of broad-shouldered, blue-haired old ladies that worked high school cafeterias . . . although they wore the bright yellow spacesuits that were standard for anyone who might come in contact with Ebola, anthrax, or Dragonscale. One of the stout old ladies was offering a stack of blankets, pajamas, and forms to a kind of family: an old man with bushy gray eyebrows, a fatigued-looking woman of maybe thirty, and two little boys with bright coppery hair.

"I need peach pie. BAD. I am sorry to say there is no peach pie here on Free Wolf Island, but we do have our own apple orchard, and boy, I can't wait until it's apple-picking season and I can go out and get myself a basket of Granny Smiths, Cortlands, Honeycrisps, Honey Boo Boos, Honey Grahams, Graham Nortons, Ed Nortons . . . all that good stuff. No bad apples here! I wish there was a fruit named after me. I wonder what a Quinn would taste like. Probably it would taste like 1987. The best thing about radio is you can imagine me just like I looked in 1987, every man's fantasy. And by 'every man,' I mean shy thirteen-year-olds who liked to read comics and listen to the Cure. ANYHOO! I need more solar panels. I only have four lousy solar panels! It's okay, that's better than none. But as you know, I can only broadcast for three hours a day and then our transponder transpires to expire. A heads-up: you are probably not hearing me live, but on a recorded loop. We upload a new loop every day, around eleven A.M., give or take twenty-four hours."

Nick couldn't hear Martha Quinn, but he could see the images loading on the screen, and he bent forward, eyes as wide as one who has been mesmerized.

"What else do I need? I need *you* to get your butt up to Machias and come on over, because we got cocoa! And barrels of walnuts! And a former TV weather anchor who makes amazing fresh bread in a wood-fired stove! Do you know what I'm talking about? I'm talking about Free Wolf Island, located seventeen miles off the coast of Maine, a place where you can safely settle if *you*—yes, *you!*—happen to be the lucky winner of a case of Dragonscale. We've got a bed for you. And that's not all! We've got a federally operated medical facility, where you can receive cutting-edge experimental treatments for your condition. As I speak to you, I myself, Martha Quinn, am lubed up in a cutting-edge experimental salve that smells and looks exactly like sheep shit, and guess what! I have not burned alive all day! I haven't even had a hot flash! My last hot flash was in 2009, and that was before the infection even got started."

Now a photo of an island seen from off the coast: a ridge of green, a beach of blue stone, a scattering of New England–style cottages along a single dirt road. The sun was just coming up or just setting and it cast a gold flare upon the dark water.

"No one is saying the word *cure*. Do not even whisper the word *cure*. There are six hundred sick people on this island, and what they are mostly sick of—besides the *Draco tryptowhatever*—is getting their hopes up over the latest treatment. But I *will* say that our last death by fire was almost twelve weeks ago. That's right: six hundred infected and just one dead in the last three months."

A final image showed a smiling elderly pair with a child. The man was gangly, weathered, with high, almost patrician cheekbones and a weary relief in his eyes. His wife was small, round, the corners of her eyes deeply grooved with laugh lines. The man had a five-year-old boy up on one shoulder. They wore fall clothes: flannel shirts, jeans, knit hats. The woman had Dragonscale scrawled all over the backs of her hands. The caption read: *Sally, Neal, and George Wannamaker arrive at the Machias Processing Center and prepare to depart for Free Wolf Island. Do YOU have friends and family on the island?* ***Click*** *for a photo gallery of the*—and here a counter showed the number 602—*people to receive shelter and comfort in the Free Wolf Island Quarantine and Research Zone.*

"When you get to Machias—and you *will* get here, you have to believe that; I got here and so will you—you will be directed to a processing tent. They'll take care of you. They'll give you a pillow, a blanket, a pair of cute paper slippers, and a hot meal. They'll put you on a boat and send you right over to us, where you will be fed, clothed, and housed. All that, plus the opportunity to rub elbows with incredible celebrities like myself! And a guy who did the weather for a channel in Augusta, Maine! What are you waiting for? Pack your stuff and get your little butt here. Your bed is made. Time to sleep in it.

"I'm going to spin another song, and then I'll be back with a list of the latest safe routes from Canada . . ."

Nick pointed to the picture of the island, and then asked Harper, in sign, "Is this a real place?"

"You bet," she said in gestures. "A good place for sick people."

"When do we go?" Nick's hands asked.

"Soon," Harper said, unconsciously speaking aloud while saying it with a gesture at the same time.

In the bed behind her, Father Storey sighed heavily and in a voice of quiet, gentle encouragement, said, "Soon."

# 4

When Harper's pulse had settled down, she checked Father Storey's—holding his thin wrist in her fingers and monitoring the thump of the blood in his arteries. His heartbeat was slight and not altogether steady, but she thought it had a little more zip than the day before. When she stroked a fingernail up his bare foot he curled his toes and made a soft snort of amusement. When she had tested him that way last week, she might as well have been tickling a loaf of bread.

She couldn't ask Nick if he had heard Father Storey speak, of course—the only time his deafness had ever frustrated her. She wanted desperately for someone, *anyone,* to have heard him. She considered sending for Carol. Perhaps Tom would respond to his daughter's voice. By some accounts, he had before. Even if he didn't stir again, Carol had a right to know her father had spoken today.

But after turning the thought over, she rejected it. Carol would rejoice to hear her father was recovering—but the rejoicing could wait. Harper wanted to talk to him before anyone else did. She wanted to see what he remembered, if anything, about the night he had been clubbed in the head. And she wanted to warn him about what the strain of the last months had done to Carol, how the winter had left her ravaged and feverish and mistrustful. He needed to know about the slaughter on Verdun Avenue, and children marching around camp with rifles, and people forced to carry stones in their mouths to shut them up.

No: in truth, *Tom* didn't need to know those things. *Harper* needed him to know those things. She wanted the old man back to make things right again. How she had missed him.

She sat with him the rest of the night, his hand in hers,

stroking his knuckles. She spoke to him sometimes. "You hibernated through the whole winter, just like a bear, Tom Storey. The icicles are dripping. The snow is almost all gone. Time to wake up and crawl out of your cave. Nick and Allie and Carol and John are waiting for you. I'm waiting, too."

But he did not speak again, and at some point close to dawn, she dozed off with his hand in her lap.

Nick woke her an hour later. The rising sun shot through the mist outside, turned it shades of lemon and meringue, sweet as pie.

"He looked at me," Nick told her with his hands. "He looked at me and smiled. He even winked before he went to sleep again. He's coming back."

Yes, Harper thought. Like Aslan, he was coming back and he was bringing the spring with him.

*Just in time,* she thought. *He's coming back just in time and everything is going to be okay.*

Later, she would remember thinking that and laugh. It was either that or cry.

# 5

Harper needed to clear her head, needed to do some quality thinking, so she walked out of the infirmary into the bitter chill. No one stopped her. They were all in the chapel together. Harper could hear them singing, could see their mystery lights flickering around the edges of the closed red doors.

The funny thing was that they were all singing "Chim Chim Cher-ee," which didn't seem like the kind of rag they'd go for in chapel. Almost everyone in the congregation had seen someone they loved devoured by fire, lived in fear of burning themselves. But now their voices rose together in hopeful praise of ashes and soot, voices that quivered with a kind of hysterical delight. She left them behind.

The air was clean and sharp and the walking was easy. Harper had left her big belly, and the baby inside of it, back at the infirmary, needed a break from being pregnant. It felt good to be thin again. She let her thoughts wander and in no time at all found she had reached the place where the dirt track from camp joined Little Harbor Road. That was farther than she had meant to go, farther than was necessarily safe. She glanced at the rusting, battered blue school bus, expecting to be yelled at by whoever was on watch. A gaunt, dark figure slumped behind the steering wheel. She guessed whoever it was had to be dozing.

She was going to turn around and walk back when she saw the man in the road.

There was a guy right in the middle of Little Harbor Road, not a hundred feet away, pulling himself arm over arm, like a soldier wriggling under barbed wire on a battlefield. Or, no:

really, he was pulling himself along like someone whose legs didn't work. If anyone came along in a hurry, he was going to get run over. Aside from that, it was awful, watching him struggle along across the icy tarmac.

"Hey!" Harper called. "Hey, you!"

She lifted the chain draped across the entrance to Camp Wyndham and started briskly toward him. It was important to get this done—deal with the man in the road—and get back out of sight before a car turned up. She shouted at him once more. He lifted his head, but the only streetlight was behind him, so his face remained in shadow: a round, fleshy, fat face, hair thinning on top. Harper hurried the last few steps to him and knelt down.

"Do you need medical attention?" she asked. "Can you stand up? I'm a nurse. If you think you can stand up, give me your hand, and I'll walk you to my infirmary."

Nelson Heinrich lifted his head and gave her a sunny smile. His teeth were red with blood and someone had removed his nose, leaving a pair of red slots in the ragged flesh. "Oh, that's all right, Harper. I've made it this far. I can lead them the rest of the way without your help."

Harper recoiled, fell back into the road, sitting down hard. "Nelson. Oh, God, Nelson, what happened to you?"

"What do you think?" Nelson said. "Your husband happened to me. And now he's going to happen to you."

The headlights came on down the street, flashing over both of them. The Freightliner awoke with a boom of combustion and a grinding of gears.

Nelson said, "Go on, Harper. Go back." He winked. "I'll see you soon."

She held her hands up over her face to shield her eyes from the light and when she lowered them she was awake, sitting up on her elbows in bed in the infirmary and having another contraction.

"These are dreams about the baby coming," Harper said to

herself, in a low voice. "Not about Nelson Heinrich leading a Cremation Crew to camp. Nelson Heinrich is dead. He was torn apart by machine-gun fire. You saw him dead in the road. You *saw* him."

It was funny how the more she said it to herself, the less she believed it.

# 6

It was five days before Father Storey spoke again.

"Michael?" the old man muttered, in a muzzy tone of bemusement and curiosity, and a moment later Mike Lindqvist pushed the curtain back and ducked into the ward.

"Did you call for me, ma'am?" he asked Harper.

The sound of Father Storey's voice jackknifed Harper's pulse, made her blood strum with surprise. She opened her mouth to tell Michael that it had been the old man, then thought better of it. Michael would carry the news to Allie and who knew where that would lead.

"I did," Harper said. "I need your help. I need you to carry a note to Allie."

"That's no trouble," he said.

"I'm afraid I require a bit more than that. I want to get together with the Fireman again. And I want Allie to go with me. Allie and Renée and Don Lewiston. You should be there, too, if it can be managed. And—if at all possible—Gil Cline and the Mazz. Is there a way . . . *any* way . . . such a thing could be done?"

Michael paled. He rested one cheek of his ass against the edge of the counter and lowered his head and plucked at the copper wires of his little goatee. Finally he looked up.

"What's this meeting about?"

"The possibility of leaving. The possibility of staying. It's past time for some of us to make plans about our future. Father Storey is stable for the moment. But if his condition changes suddenly, we'll want to be ready."

"For the worst?"

"For whatever."

Michael said, "If Carol finds you all out on the island together, making secret plans with the Fireman, she'll lock every one of you up. Or worse."

"We could face worse even if we do nothing."

Michael swiped one hand across his freckled forehead and bowed his head in thought again. At last he nodded, uneasily.

"I know how to do it. It isn't exactly like breaking them out of San Quentin. Renée visits the prisoners for lunch every day . . . that's when they meet for their little book club. That's the only time those boys ever come out of the meat locker. Renée tidied up a far corner of the basement, put down carpet and some easy chairs, so they'd have a nice place to read and talk. While they're meeting, whoever is on guard steps into the meat locker to clean up. Empty the bucket they pee in during the day. Gather up the dirty clothes. That sort of thing. So maybe while he's in there, the Mazz comes back, says, 'Oops, I forgot my book.' And then on his way out closes the meat-locker door. The guard is stuck in there for the whole hour. He can kick and shout all he wants. That meat locker is pretty soundproof with the door clapped shut. They'll never hear him during a noisy lunch, not with the trapdoor closed.

"But Renée and the men would have to walk out past all the people in the cafeteria."

Michael shook his head. "There's another way out of the basement. There's some steps that lead up to the parking lot out back. I guess that's where the trucks brought in supplies. Those doors are locked from the outside with two padlocks, but I could make sure they were unlocked. Renée and Gil and the Mazz would have to be back by one A.M., when their little book club wraps up for the day. Renée lets the guard out, says, 'Sorry! We didn't know you were stuck in here, couldn't hear you over all the noise from people above us.' Whoever pulls meat-locker duty will be some pissed, but I bet they won't even tell Ben Patchett. Too embarrassed. Also, who wants to wind up sucking a rock for two days, when no one got hurt and everything turned out fine?"

Nick sat watching them both, his knees drawn up under his chin. He couldn't know what they were talking about, didn't read lips, but his face was as ill as if he were watching the two of them handle sticks of TNT.

"Good, Michael. That's good," Harper said. "It's simple. With this kind of thing, the simpler the better, don't you think?"

He ran his thumb along the tight twists of his beard. "I think it's just great . . . as long as the prisoners don't decide to knock Renée down and run for it as soon as they're out of the basement."

"They wouldn't *need* to knock her down," Harper said. "If they decided to run, Renée would run with them. But I think . . . I think she can convince them they have a better chance of long-term survival if they ally themselves with the Fireman. They don't just want to escape, they want to last." She had not forgotten about the way Gil spoke of the Fireman, with a mix of quiet admiration and something approaching reverence.

"Yeah, well. Maybe. But maybe when they get out of the basement, it would be best if Allie was waiting for them out in the parking lot, with a rifle over her shoulder. She doesn't have to point it at them. It's enough just for her to have it on her. When Allie isn't confined to the girls' dorm, she's usually doing one punishment assignment or another. I could arrange it so she has to scrub pans that night. Ben Patchett works out the daily punishment details, but he lets *me* hand them out. So Allie collects all the pans from the kitchen and goes outside and finds the gun I've left for her. She's waiting by the basement doors when Renée comes out with the prisoners. She'd have to be back by one A.M., too."

Anxiety tickled Harper's stomach. It seemed like there was a lot that could go wrong.

"What about Don Lewiston?" Harper said.

"He's easy. He spends most of the night down along the water, tending to his fishing poles. No one minds him. He's not under observation. He can meet you at the dock, row you across."

"And *you*?" Harper asked. "Will *you* come, Michael? I'd like it if you were there. I think Allie would, too."

He showed her a small, apologetic smile and gave his head a curt shake. "Nope. Better not. I'll make sure I've been assigned guard duty here in the infirmary, so I can slip you out and cover for you while you're gone. I don't need to be a part of your conference, anyway. Allie can fill me in later." He looked sidelong at Nick and said, "Take the kid, too. Bet he'd love to see his sister. And John."

Harper said, "I'm fighting the urge to hug you very, very hard, Michael Lindqvist."

"Why fight it?" he asked.

# 7

But in the end Nick didn't want to go.

When the hour came, he was sitting in the worn-out chair beside Father Storey's cot, reading a comic book: a man made of flame did battle with an enormous yellow-and-orange robot that resembled a walking Freightliner, headlights for eyes and shovels for hands. He said he wanted to stay with Tom.

"What if he wakes up and we're gone?" Nick asked her in sign. "There ought to be someone here if he opens his eyes."

"Michael will be here," Harper said.

Nick shook his head, his face solemn. "That's not the same." Then he added, "Grandfather's been moving a lot. He could wake up anytime."

It was true. Sometimes Tom Storey took a deep breath and heaved a great, satisfied-sounding sigh . . . or he would produce a sudden humming noise, as if he had just had a quite surprising thought. Other times his right hand would drift up to rub his breastbone for a moment or two before falling back to his side. What Harper liked best was the way, sometimes, Tom would lift one finger to his lips, in the *shh* gesture, and smile. It was an expression that made Harper think of one child inviting another to share a hiding place during a game of hide-and-seek. Tom had been in his hiding place for months but maybe was almost ready to reveal himself.

Harper nodded, smoothed down Nick's hair, and left him to the company of his comic book and the silent old man. Michael was in the waiting room . . . and Don Lewiston was with him, had turned up to escort Harper down to the water. Don wore a plaid winter coat and a cap with earflaps, and his nose was pink from the cold. He stood in the half-open door. Michael was on his feet, too, didn't seem able to sit down, but instead paced the waiting area, twisting a *Ranger Rick* in his hands. The magazine was rolled into a tight, crooked tube.

"Nick's not coming," Harper said. "Maybe it's just as well. If Ben Patchett comes by on a spot inspection, he won't think anything of it if you tell him I'm napping. Us pregnant ladies sleep whenever they can. But if he doesn't see any sign of me *or* Nick, that's going to make him suspicious." When she mentioned the possibility of a spot inspection, Michael seemed to visibly sicken, so much color leaving his face that even his lips looked gray. She wondered if he was having second thoughts, now that the moment had come. She asked, "How we doing?"

She was asking about Michael's state of mind, but Don answered instead as if she had inquired about the evening's acts of subterfuge. "The others are already on their way to the island. I met Allie and Renée in the woods with the prisoners. Chuck Cargill is shut into the meat locker. He hollered his head off and kicked the door a bunch of times, but Renée says after you get halfway across the basement, it just blends with the noise from upstairs in the cafeteria."

"Go if you're going," Michael said. "I've got things covered here. You don't have to worry, Ms. Willowes, and *you* don't have to rush. I can cover for *you* until the shift change, just before the sun comes up. But those others don't have much time. If the prisoners aren't back across the water in forty-five minutes, we're all cooked."

Harper stepped toward Michael and put her hands on his, to make him stop twisting his *Ranger Rick*. She leaned in and kissed his cold, dry brow.

"You are very brave, Michael," Harper said. "You are one of the bravest people I know. Thank you."

Some of the tension went out of his shoulders. "Don't overrate me, ma'am. I don't see I have a lot of choice. If you love someone, you have to do what you can to keep 'em safe. I wouldn't want to look back later and think I could've been of use, I could've helped, but I was too scared."

Harper cupped his pink cheek. Michael couldn't meet her eyes. "You ever tell Allie this? That you love her?"

He shuffled his feet. "Not in so many words, ma'am." He risked a glance into Harper's face. "You aren't going to say anything to her, are you? I'd appreciate it if you'd kind of keep what I said between you and me."

"Of course I won't say anything," Harper said. "But don't leave it too long, Mike. These days, I'm not sure it's ever a good idea to leave anything important for tomorrow."

Don held the door for her and she stepped out into the dark and sharp, stinging cold. Every star stood out with a bitter clarity, a needle-tip brightness. Pine boards still zigzagged between buildings, providing walkways, but the snow was gone, and now the planks crossed a humped wasteland of mud.

They stepped off the boards to make their way down the hill, through the trees. There was no chance of leaving tracks. At that arctic hour, the earth was frozen solid, a billion flecks of opalescent ice gleaming in the dirt. Don Lewiston offered her his arm and she took it, and they made their way like an old married couple over the frozen ground.

Halfway to the beach, they paused. A girl was singing, from the steeple of the church, her voice sweet and sure. Harper thought it might be one of the Neighbors twins. They both had sung a cappella in high school. Her song carried on the cold, clear air, and the melody was so innocent and sweet it raised gooseflesh on Harper's arms. It was an early Taylor Swift tune, a bit of fluff about Romeo and Juliet . . . which reminded Harper of another, older song about those unhappy, luckless lovers.

"There are a lot of good people in this camp," Harper said to Don. "Maybe they've gone along with some bad ideas, but only because they're scared."

Don narrowed his eyes, squinted toward the steeple. "She has a lovely voice, sure. I could listen to that all night. But I wonder if you'd still think so well of this camp if you had heard everyone singin' together in chapel a couple hours ago. Or at least, it was singin' when they started out. But after a while everyone was just hummin', this one long idiot note. You feel like you're inside of the world's biggest beehive and everyone around you looks like they're burnin' from the inside. Their eyes just fackin' . . . *blaze*. They don't smoke, but they throw heat, so much heat you could just about pass out from it. Sometimes they all get hummin' so loud I feel like my skull is vibratin' and I just about have to stick a fist in my mouth to keep from screamin'."

They resumed walking, the stones and dirt crunching under their feet.

"And you can't join in? You don't shine with them?"

"Once or twice. But it ain't treated me right. It's not how hard it hits you—though when I come up out of it, my skull is always ringin' so fackin' hard it's like I slammed down a quart of Jack. The worst part isn't forgettin' who I am, either. That's bad, though . . . but thinking I might be Carol is worse. It's like your own thoughts are a faraway radio station, and Carol's station is closer, broadcasting her music right over yours. Hers gets louder and clearer and yours gets fainter and thinner. You start thinkin' Father Storey is your *own* dear dad lyin' in the infirmary with his head mashed in, and the idea that whoever done it hasn't been punished will make you so sick and angry you feel like you're boilin'. You'll wonder if someone is goin' to come bash *your* head in next, if there are secret forces and whatnot workin' against you. What you feel in your heart is that if you have to die, you want to die singin', with the whole camp around you. Everyone holdin' hands. You almost *hope* it will happen . . . that a Cremation Crew will come. 'Cause it'd be a relief to get it over with, and you aren't scared of the end, because you'll be burnin' up with all the people you love right close beside you."

Harper shuddered and leaned into Don for warmth.

They made their way out onto the dock and Don helped Harper into the rowboat. She was glad to have his hand clutching her arm and she stepped down from the dock. She had made the trip across the water often enough over the last few months, but now, for the first time, she felt unsteady on her legs and uncertain of her own balance.

In a few deep, steady strokes, they had left the beach behind. Don sat on the thwart between the oars, leaning into each pull and rocking back, his whole body extending into a straight line. He was old, but like beef jerky: knotty and tough.

Would the eye in the steeple (which sees all the people) observe them now? Don had mentioned to Ben that he might take the boat out to fish tonight. Hopefully their movements on the water this evening would be accepted as Don Lewiston paddling around, looking for flounder . . . if they were spotted at all.

Without any prompting, Don seemed to pick up where he had left off a few minutes before.

"It's bad, having a head full of Carol. It's bad not knowin' my own name, not knowin' my mother's name. But I'll tell you. A month back, we all had a big hard sing, like we do. And then Carol gave a kind of sermon, about how there is no history before we got Dragonscale. That a new history started for each of us when we got sick. That the only life that matters is the life we have now, together, as a community, not the life we had before. And then we sang again and we all lit up—even me—and we hummed real hard, and afterward we staggered out of there like drunk sailors on New Year's Eve. And I forgot"—his breath hitched as he leaned forward to pull against the oars once more—"I forgot my mate, Bill Ellroy, what fished with me for thirty years. He was snatched right out of my head. Not just for hours. For days. I had the best years of my life out on the boat with Billy. It's hard to tell you how good they were. We'd fish three weeks hard, come back and unload our catch in Portsmouth, then take the boat out to the Harbor Islands, drop anchor, and drink beer. I'd hate goin' home. I liked every minute of bein' with Billy. I liked who I was when I was by his side." He had stopped rowing for a moment. The boat rocked in the swell. "Bein' with him was like havin' the whole ocean under you. We didn't talk much, you know. We didn't need to.

You don't talk to an ocean and it don't talk back. You just . . . let it carry you." He began to stroke the oars again. "Well. When I suddenly realized I had lost him for a while—that he had been wiped out—that was when I decided I had enough of this place. No one gets to take Bill Ellroy from me. Nobody. Not for no reason. No one gets to take our friendship. There was a thief workin' in this camp last fall, and if Carol had ever caught her, she would've fed her piece by bloody piece to wild dogs. I'll tell you what, though. The things that are stolen from us every night, when we all sing together, those are a lot more important than most of what the thief took. And we know who's takin' 'em, and instead of lockin' her up, we elected her head of camp."

He fell silent. He had taken the extra precaution of rowing them around the northern tip of the island, to the far side of the rock, so he could beach the rowboat where it couldn't be seen from shore by the casual observer. Harper spied two canoes already pulled up on the gravel. Beyond, set back from the water, was the thirty-three-foot cruising sloop, sitting in its steel carriage and covered by its taut white tarp.

"What do you think happened to the thief, anyway?" Harper asked. "I don't think there's been a theft all winter."

"Maybe she ran out of things to steal," Don said. "Or maybe she just finally got what she wanted."

Harper watched Don lean and pull, lean and pull, and thought the power of the Bright couldn't compete with being close to someone you loved with all your heart. One took away; the other gave you access to your best, happiest self. *I liked who I was when I was by his side,* Don Lewiston said, and Harper wondered if there had ever been anyone in her life who made her feel that way about herself, and at that moment the boat ground onto the sand with a wet crunch, and Don said, "Let's go see the Fireman, huh?"

# 8

Before she climbed out, Harper reached into the bin under the thwart and found her hidden grocery sack, which still contained a bottle of cheap banana-flavored rum and the carton of Gauloises. Don waited for her halfway up the shale, under the bow of the long white sloop. He had a hand on the hull when she caught up to him.

"Can you sail it?" she asked.

He lifted an eyebrow, gave her an amused, sidelong glance. "All the way around the Horn and on to exotic Shanghai if I had to."

"I was thinking just a ways up the coast."

"Yuh," he said. "Well. That would be easier."

They went on arm in arm, through the dunes, up the narrow, weedy trail, over the hill, and on to the Fireman's shed. Don lifted the latch and eased the door open onto laughter and warmth and shifting golden light.

Renée stood at the furnace, wearing oven mitts and hanging the kettle on its hook over the coals. Gilbert Cline had settled near her, sitting in a straight-backed chair against the wall. He had his gaze on the door when it opened—ready to move if he didn't care for the company, Harper thought.

The Mazz sat at one end of John Rookwood's cot and John at the other, both of them quivering with laughter. The Mazz's wide, ugly face was suffused a deep shade of red and he was blinking at tears. All of them—all except for Gil—had their eyes on Allie, who stood over a pail, pretending she was a man taking a piss. She wore John's fireman helmet and held a plastic lighter at her crotch.

"And this is only the *second* coolest thing I know how to do with my dick!" Allie announced in her intentionally atrocious English accent. She flicked the lighter, so her pretend cock spurted flame. "I'll have your campfire going in no time, but if you're really in a hurry to bake your hot dogs, I'll just bend over, and you can . . ."

Allie saw Harper in the doorway and her voice trailed off. Her grin faltered. She let the lighter go out.

John, however, continued to tremble with amusement. He gestured to the Mazz and said: "What she just demonstrated, that *did* happen to me once. But this was years before Dragonscale, and a little penicillin cleared it right up."

The Mazz bellowed with laughter, was so raucous it was impossible not to be entertained. The ghost of a smile even briefly reappeared on Allie's lips—but only for a moment.

"Wow," Allie said. "Ms. Willowes, you got huge."

"I'm glad to hear your voice, Allie. It's been a while. I've missed it."

"I don't know why you would. Mostly when I *do* open my mouth, it seems like people just get hurt."

Her gaze dropped. Her face wrinkled with emotion. It was difficult to watch her trying not to cry, all the muscles in her face struggling at once with the strain to hold it in. Harper reached out and took Allie's hands, and when she did, Allie lost the fight and began to weep.

"I feel so bad," Allie said. "I think we were supposed to be really good friends and I fucked it all up and I'm so sorry."

"Oh, Allie," Harper said, and tried to squeeze her. Her stomach made squeezing people tricky, and instead of a hug, she wound up giving Allie a rubbery bump with her belly. Allie made a strangled sound that was part sob, part laugh. "We *are* really good friends. And to be honest, I had wanted to try a shorter haircut for years."

This time Harper was certain the sound Allie made was a laugh, although it was choked and half muffled; Allie had her face buried against Harper's chest.

At last, Allie stepped back, wiping her hands down her wet

cheeks. "I know everything in camp is going bad. I know everyone is batshit crazy, my aunt especially. It's scary. *She's* scary. Threatening to take your baby away if Granddad dies, when you've already done everything anyone could do—that's so fucked up and sick."

John sat forward, his smile fading. "What's this?"

"You were unwell," Harper said, not looking directly at him, but speaking over her shoulder. "I didn't want to bring it up. You look better now, by the way."

"Yes," John said. "Antibiotics and Dragonscale have a lot in common. One is a mold that cooks bacteria, and the other is a mold that cooks us. I wish there was a pill we could take to cure us of Carol Storey. She's out of her good goddamn mind. She can't have meant it. Take your baby? What is this rubbish?"

Harper said, "Carol told me . . . she told me if Tom died, she'd hold me personally responsible, and send me away. She'd keep the baby, so that if I'm captured by a Quarantine Patrol or a Cremation Crew, I won't be tempted to give away any information about Camp Wyndham."

"It's not just that. She really would want the baby to be safe. She wants to protect us. *All* of us," Allie said. She cast her gaze around the room, looking at each of them, and her voice was almost pleading. "I know she's awful. I know she does terrible things now. Thing is, my aunt Carol would *die* for the people in this camp. Without a second thought. She really *does* love everyone . . . at least everyone she isn't suspicious about. And I remember before Granddad got his head bashed in. She was *good* then. When she knew she could help people by singing and playing music and showing them how to join the Bright, she was the best person in the world to have as your friend. I could always go cry to her if I had a fight with my mom. She made me tea and peanut butter sandwiches. So I know you guys all hate her, and I know we have to do something. But you also have to know I still love her. She's a fuck-up, but so am I. I guess it runs in the family."

John relaxed, leaned back against the wall. "*Decency* runs in your family, Allie. And a really unsettling streak of personal daring. And charisma. All the rest of us flutter around you Storeys like moths around candles."

Harper thought automatically of how the romance between a moth and a candle usually ended: with the moth spinning to its death, wings smoking. It didn't seem like a thought worth sharing at that particular moment.

Gilbert Cline spoke up from over by the furnace. When Harper glanced at him, she noticed Gil had one hand around Renée's waist. "It sure is a relief to be out of that meat locker for a while. Next time I step out for a breath of fresh air, I'd just as soon not have to go back. Right now, though, we've got half an hour. If we've got things to figure, we better figure 'em now."

The Mazz lifted his chin, was looking down the length of his bulbous nose at Harper's grocery bag. "I don't know about anyone else, but I always do my best figuring over a drink. Looks like the nurse brought just what the doctor ordered."

Harper lifted out the bottle of banana rum. "Don, would you find us cups?"

She dashed a little rum into a collection of chipped coffee cups, tin mugs, and ugly tumblers and Don passed them around. The last cup Harper offered to Allie.

"Really?" Allie asked.

"It tastes better than a rock."

Allie tossed back the quarter inch Harper had given her in a single swallow, then made a face. "Oh, God. No it doesn't. This is piss. Like drinking gasoline after someone stirred it with a Butterfinger. Or like a banana smoothie that went rotten. Horrible."

"You want another slosh, then?" Harper asked.

"Yes, please," Allie said.

"Well, too bad," Harper told her. "You're a minor and one sip is all you get."

"I used to eat sardines out of the can and drink the oil afterward," Don said. "It was a gruesome thing to do. That oil always had little fish tails and fish eyes and fackin' fish guts and little black rubbery strings of fish shit, and I drank it anyway. Just couldn't help myself."

Gil said, "Saw a movie where a fella said he'd eaten dogs and lived like one. I never ate a dog, but there was men that caught and ate mice in Brentwood. They called 'em basement chickens."

"Worst thing I ever ate?" the Mazz speculated. "I wouldn't like to go into the details in polite company, but her name was Ramona."

"That's lovely, Mazz. Very tasteful," Renée said.

"Actually, it wasn't even a little tasteful," the Mazz told her.

"This reminds me: Are you going to eat the placenta?" Renée asked Harper. "I understand that's a thing now. We stocked a pregnancy guide at the bookstore with a whole chapter of placenta recipes in the back. Omelets and pasta sauces and so on."

"No, I don't think so," Harper said. "Dining on the placenta smacks of cannibalism, and I was hoping for a more dignified apocalypse."

"Rabbit mothers eat their own babies," the Mazz said. "I found that out reading *Watership Down*. Apparently the mamas chow on their newborns all the time. Pop them down just like little meat Skittles."

"The worst part," Allie said, "is that you've all only had one drink."

Don said, "So who's the captain of this ship? Who's settin' our course?"

"You're so adorable when you're nautical," John Rookwood said to him.

"He's right, though," Renée said. "That's the first order of business, isn't it? We need to hold the election."

"Election?" Harper asked. She was vaguely aware that she was the only person in the circle who didn't have a knowing smile on her face—a fact she found mildly irritating.

"We need to settle on an evil mastermind," Renée told her. "Someone to set the agenda when we have meetings. Someone to call a vote. Someone to make on-the-spot decisions when there isn't time to vote. Someone to boss around the minions."

"That's silly. There's just seven of us. Eight, if you count Nick."

Don Lewiston lifted his eyebrows and turned an expectant expression toward Renée Gilmonton.

"You're off by fifteen," Renée said.

"Make it seventeen," Don said. "The McLee brothers are with us too."

"There are . . . what . . . twenty-five people ready to . . . strike out on their own?" Harper asked. *Dumbledore's army,* she thought. *The Fellowship.*

"Or strike out at Ben and Carol," Don said, "and take back the damn camp." He saw Allie blanch and added, "Strike out gently, I mean. Politely. You know. With good manners."

"We can do some things by way of a vote," Renée said. "But working in secret as we are, a lot of choices will require an executive decision. It's a necessary job, but I don't think it's likely to be a terribly rewarding one . . . or particularly safe. You want to think about what might happen to whoever we put in charge, if we're discovered."

"I don't *need* to think about it," Allie said. "I know. When my aunt talks about slicing the rottenness out of camp, she's not playing with words. She's talking about cutting a bitch. She'd have people killed. She'd have to set an example." Allie smiled at them, but looked wan. "I read in history that public executions used to be popular events. I'm sure if Aunt Carol announced one, Mrs. Heald would make sure there was popcorn for everyone."

The fire cracked and hissed. A coal popped.

"You really think it could go that far?" Gil asked, his voice suggesting only mild curiosity. "Public executions?"

"Boy," the Mazz said. "After the shit we seen go down in Brentwood, I'm surprised you got to ask. Myself, I can't get too worried about the consequences. I've already decided I'll do *whatever* I have to, to get out of that basement meat locker . . . one way or another. On my feet or on a slab."

"Same," Gil said.

Harper said, "But we *can't* vote tonight. Not if there are fifteen—seventeen—other people who want to throw in with us. How would we manage such a thing?"

Don and Renée and Allie traded looks and Harper felt once again that they were ahead of her by a step.

"Harper," Renée said. "We've *already* managed it. Everyone has already cast their vote, except for the seven of us in this room, and maybe the McLee brothers."

"Nope," Don said. "They made their wishes known, too."

"So it's down to just us. And let me tell you, it was hard work getting us this far. It isn't so easy to hold an election for the head of a secret society. Because I wouldn't tell anyone who was in and who wasn't. I don't like to be paranoid. But I couldn't discount the possibility that some of the people who told me they want to leave Camp Wyndham are feeding information back to Carol. For example, I never heard a single vote for Michael Lindqvist. I'm sure most people would be *shocked* to hear he's with us. He's always been Ben Patchett's right hand. No . . . most of the voting condensed around the two or three really obvious candidates."

"What makes someone an obvious candidate?"

"Anyone who isn't a part of the Bright anymore. Anyone who isn't singing Carol's song. Basically: the people in this room tonight. Not only do we all still have to cast our vote, we're also all the leading candidates." She reached into a worn, striped shoulder bag she had brought with her, and came up with a tablet of yellow lined paper. She placed it facedown on an end table. "After we fill out our own ballots, I'll let you know how everyone else voted." Renée reached into the shoulder bag again and came up with a pad of red sticky notes. She peeled squares off, one at a time, and handed them around. Don found a chipped mug with pens stuck into it and passed them out.

"Do we have an official title for the man or woman who wins this thing?" Gil asked, frowning at his own blank square.

"I like 'Master Conspirator,'" said the Fireman. "That has a nice ring. A touch of poetry and darkness to it. If you could get killed for having the job, you should at least have the pleasures of an official title with some sex appeal."

"So it shall be," Renée said. "Cast your vote for Master Conspirator."

There was a fidgety silence and the sounds of pens scratching on paper. When they had each finished, Renée was waiting with her tablet in hand.

"Of the fifteen people I spoke to," Renée began, and cleared her throat, and went on. "We had two votes for Don and two votes for Allie."

"What?" Allie cried, sounding genuinely surprised.

"Three for the Fireman," Renée said, "four votes for Harper, and four for me."

Harper flushed. Her Dragonscale prickled—not unpleasantly.

Don said, "When I spoke to the McLee boys, they made their intentions clear enough. They both picked Allie."

"No, no, no, NO," Allie said. "I don't want the fucking job. I'm sixteen. If I won this thing, my first act as head honcho would be to burst into tears. Besides, Robert McLee only voted for me because he has a weird crush. A muscle twitches under one eye whenever he talks to me. And the other one just does what Robert tells him. Besides, they shouldn't get a vote! Does Chris McLee even have pubic hair yet?"

"I agree," the Fireman said. "No pubes, no vote. And since I'm against child sacrifice, I'm in favor of allowing Allie to *un*-nominate herself. Did anyone who voted for Allie have a backup choice?"

"As it happens," Renée said, peering at her pad, "they do. One person chose John as an alternate. The other selected Don."

"Fack," Don said.

"Did the McLee brothers have a backup choice?" Renée asked.

"It wouldn't matter if they did," Don said, "since we agree they're too young to vote." Which was how Harper knew they had also picked Don as a backup.

"That's three for Don, and four for Harper, John, and myself."

"Better make it five for you, Renée," Gil said, unfolding his sticky and setting it on the table before him. "You did most of the planning and thinking that took us this far. I don't see any reason to change horses now."

Renée leaned toward him and lightly kissed his cheek. "You're such a kind and sweet man, Gil, I will ignore that you just called me a horse."

The Mazz said, "And five for the Fireman." Raising his own sticky so the rest of the room could have a look. "I seen him literally bring hell down on the Portsmouth PD. That makes him the man in my book."

Don unfolded his own sticky and said, "Me, myself, I voted Harper. I seen the way she handled the infirmary when Father Storey was brought in and I seen the way she drilled into his head." He lifted his rheumy blue eyes and met Harper's gaze. "The worse things get—the more people are screamin' and cryin' and carryin' on—the calmer you get, Nurse Willowes. I couldn't stop shakin', and your hand was as steady as a board. I want you for it."

"We still have a three-way tie for the lead."

"Not anymore. Make it six for Harper," Allie said. "I think it ought to be her, too. Because I know no matter how bad I fuck up, she won't ever stick a stone in my mouth and make me feel like Judas. Even though after what I did, God knows she'd have every right."

"Oh, Allie," Harper said. "You apologized once. I don't expect you to do it over and over."

"It's not an apology. It's a vote," Allie said, meeting Harper's gaze almost with defiance.

"Yes, it is," Renée said. "And my vote is for Harper, too. It is awfully good of some people to have asked me to take the job, but I'd rather read about a grand escape than plan one. Besides, I'm terrible at keeping secrets and I hate to scheme against people. It seems rude. I don't deal with guilt well and I'm worried we might hurt some feelings in the process of defending ourselves. Also, I'm juggling a couple of books. Being a full-time conspirator would take away from my reading time. So it'll have to be Harper."

"Hey!" Harper said. "I've got books to read, too, lady!"

"It also crossed my mind that you *are* very pregnant, and I think that makes it much, much less likely they'll hang you if we're caught," Renée said. "And Harp, I hate to break it to you, but I think this puts you in charge. By my count you just won the vote, five to seven."

"Make it six to seven," Harper said. "Because I voted for John."

"What a coincidence." The Fireman opened his mouth in a toothy grin that made him look just mildly deranged. "So did I." Opening his vote and turning it to show what he had written there, a single word: *myself.*

# 9

Ten minutes later the others were gone. Only Harper and the Fireman remained behind.

"Tell Michael I'll be along in a few hours and not to worry," Harper told Don Lewiston.

Renée leaned in from outside, through the half-open door, her hand on the latch.

"Don't forget to come back, Harper," Renée said, her eyes glittering from the cold or from delight, it was hard to say.

"Go on, you," Harper said. "Hurry. Don't you know the first rule of running a conspiracy? Don't get caught."

The door closed. Harper and the Fireman heard whispers, choked laughter, Allie singing a line of "Love Shack," and then the crunch of boots moving away. Finally it was just the two of them again, in a taut but agreeable silence, the kind of silence that precedes a first kiss.

They didn't kiss, though. Harper was aware of the open furnace at her back, the heat cast by the shifting flames, and wondered who was watching. He had gotten up twice to feed driftwood to the fire, and each time she thought, *If we abandon Camp Wyndham, he won't be with us. He has to stay here and tend his private flames.*

"It was a setup," she said. "You guys counted the votes ahead of time."

"*Well.* I wouldn't go that far. Let's just say the outcome was not entirely unforeseen. Why do you think Michael made a special point to let you know there was no rush to return tonight?"

There had been time, when they were all together, to sketch two different plans in broad outline. One imagined what they would do if they had to leave in a hurry. The other plotted a method to (gently) wrest control of camp away from Carol. It had been left to John and Harper to work out the details for both eventualities.

"I'm ready to hatch schemes if you are," he said.

"I need sugar for my best scheming," she said, found her canvas tote, and tugged out a Mary Poppins lunch box. "Nothing gets me in a conspiratorial mood like an illicit candy bar, even if they are a year old."

His brow knotted. "I warn you. Claiming to have candy bars when you don't would be a gross violation of your Hippocratic oath never to inflict needless suffering."

"I have news for you, Rookwood. I'm a nurse. We don't take the Hippocratic oath. That's just doctors. Nurses only swear to one thing—the patient will take his medicine."

"Sometimes you say something just a bit menacing and it gives me a happy little shiver," he said. And then, without any change of tone or hesitation, he added, "I'd burn Camp Wyndham to the ground before I'd let Carol and her sycophants take your baby from you. There'd be nothing left of this place but charred sticks. I hope you know that."

"Wouldn't be very fair to the rest of them, would it?" Harper asked. "They're not bad people, most of them. All they want is to be safe."

"Isn't that always a permission slip for ugliness and cruelty? All they want is to be safe, and they don't care who they have to destroy to stay that way. And the people who want to kill us, the Cremation Crews, all they want is safety, too! And the man I killed with the Phoenix the other night—the man behind the .50 caliber. I felt I had to do it. I had to cook him down to the bones. It was the only way I could know for sure you'd get back to me."

He looked at her with a curious mix of bemusement and grief. She wanted to take his hand. Instead she gave him a miniature Snickers and took a tiny Mounds bar for herself.

"Are *we* going to have to kill people to be safe?" Her voice was very quiet. "Do you think it will come to that? With Ben? With Carol? Because if you do, I think maybe I should row back to shore now. I don't want to make a plan to murder anyone."

"If you row back to shore now," he said, "it might murder *me*. So I guess you'll have to stay."

"I guess so," she said, and poured them each a little more rum.

# 10

He said the candy bar was awful and he needed another one to get the taste out of his mouth. She gave him a cigarette instead and another splash of rum. He lit up with his thumb.

Harper wasn't so sure about the escape plan. It had too many moving parts. She had a list going, beginning with the letter *A* (Father Storey is responsive), continuing on through *E* (create a distraction by dropping the bell in the steeple), and finishing with *Q* (Don leads the other boats north). That was way too much of the alphabet.

The Fireman, on the other hand, loved the plan. Of course he did. He had the starring role. Harper kept trying to subtract letters, and he kept trying to add them.

"I wish we had time to dig a tunnel," the Fireman said.

"To *where*?"

"It doesn't matter. You can't have a decent prison break without a tunnel. The aspiring novelist in me wants a secret tunnel hidden behind a false wall, or a poster of a famous movie star, or possibly in the back of a wardrobe. We could call it Operation Narnia! Don't tell me you wouldn't like that."

"I wouldn't like if you turned into a novelist. I might have to tear off half your face. That's what I did with the last wannabe writer to cross my path."

He swished the dregs of his banana liquor around his paper cup and then tossed the last of it back. "I forgot your husband was an aspiring novelist."

"Sometimes I think *every* man wants to be a writer. They want to invent a world with the perfect imaginary woman, someone they can boss around and undress at will. They can work out their own aggression with a few fictional rape scenes.

Then they can send their fictional surrogate in to save her, a white knight—or a fireman! Someone with all the power and all the agency. Real women, on the other hand, have all these tiresome interests of their own, and won't follow an outline." A glumness settled upon her. It crossed her mind that she had never been Jakob's friend or wife or lover, but only his subject, only *material*. Writers were as parasitic, she supposed, as the spore itself.

"I am in one hundred percent agreement on the subject of outlines. Any writer who works by outline should be burned at the stake. Possibly with their own outline and notecards used as kindling. That's what I dislike most about our plan. It's an outline. Life doesn't work by outline. If I were writing this scene, I wouldn't even bother describing our plan, not in any detail. I already know it won't work out the way we're hoping. It would just be wasting the reader's time." He saw the look on her face and kicked her foot. "Oh, come on. We have candy bars and smokes and booze and evil plans. Don't get morose on me. What else is in that lunch box of yours?"

She took out a deformed, tumorous potato and set it on the bed.

The Fireman recoiled. "Aa! What the awful, bearded Christ is that?"

"That? That's Yukon Gold, Chumley," she said.

"Ah, well," he said. "I suppose we've had enough chocolate. How about a baked potato?"

He picked it up and clasped it between his hands. Smoke began to rise from between his fingers and with it, the smell of roasting spuds. The smell cheered Harper up. She couldn't help it.

"I love a man who knows how to cook," Harper said.

# 11

He had salt and a little tumbler of olive oil and they split the potato. The fragrant mineral smell of it filled the shed. It was so good, it made Harper feel a bit teary, and when it was gone she licked oil and salt off her hands.

"You know what I miss?" she said.

"If you say Facebook, you'll ruin a perfectly lovely evening."

"I miss Coca-Cola. That would've been so good with a Coke. You know, we might've fucked up the planet, sucking out all the oil, melting ice caps, allowing ska music to flourish, but we made Coca-Cola, so goddamn it, people weren't all bad."

"As a species, we might not live to regret melting the ice caps. That's where it comes from, you know: the spore. I'm eighty percent sure. That's why all the earliest cases were along the Arctic Circle. It was under the glaciers. I think it's happened before, too. Everyone believed the dinosaurs were wiped out by a meteor strike, but I figure it was the spore. It hides under the ice until the world warms up enough to let it back into the air. Then it burns everything until the world is so blanketed in smoke the planet freezes over again. The mold dies out, except for a little bit that is preserved once more under the ice. There have been six extinction events in the life of this planet. I bet every one of them was the spore."

"You're saying it's a planetary T cell. It attacks any infection that throws the environment out of whack. Like us."

He nodded.

"That's the third-best theory I've ever heard. I like the idea that the Russians bred a superfungus back in the seventies, out on this island for testing biological weapons. Rebirth Island, I think it was called. They had to abandon the site in 2000 after the spore got loose. But the island was in a lake that dried up and animals crossed back and forth, carrying the ash in their fur. All the early cases were in Russia."

"You said *third*-best theory. Is there something better than Arctic melt or a Russian island of pure evil?"

"I also like the idea that God is punishing us with killer athlete's foot for wearing Crocs." She gave herself another tipple of banana liquor. In her medical opinion, another sip wouldn't give the baby a deformed brain. "Now that the world is over, what do you most regret not getting to do?"

"Julianne Moore," he said. "And Gillian Anderson. At the same time or separately, it really would've made no difference."

"I mean what did you want to do that *actually might've happened.*"

"I wish I had discovered a new kind of mold I could've named after Sarah."

"Wow. You romantic son of a bitch."

"What about Harper Willowes? What did *you* always want to do?"

"Me? Julianne Moore, same as you. That hot little bitch had one fine ass."

The Fireman went and got a dish towel and apologized over and over for spitting his banana rum on her, while he patted her shirt dry.

# 12

He got up to stir the fire and came back holding the longbow that had sat in the corner all winter long. He stretched out on his cot, holding the bow as if it were a guitar and thwanging its one atonal string.

"Do you think Keith Richards is still alive?" he asked.

"Sure. Nothing can kill him. He'll outlast us all."

"Beatles or Stones?" he asked.

She sang the opening lines of "Love Me Do."

"Is that a vote for the Beatles?"

"Of course I pick the Beatles. It's a stupid question. It's like asking what you like better: silk or pubic hair?"

"Ah, that's disappointing."

"Of *course* you'd pick the Stones. Anyone who'd walk around pretending he's a fireman when he isn't—"

"What does *that* have to do with anything?"

"Men who love the Stones are fixated on cock. I'm sorry, but that's the only word. And a firehose is a symbolic fantasy cock. It's pathetic. Male Stones fans are frozen at eighteen months old, just discovering the thrill of yanking on the rubber band of their own phallus. Female Stones fans are even *worse*. Mick Jagger has a weird gross mouth that makes him look like a cod, and this turns them on. They're sexually aroused by fish-men. They're deviants."

"So what are Beatles fans fixated on? The glory of pussy?"

"Exactly. Strawberry Fields is not just a place in Liverpool, Mr. Rookwood." She held out her hand. "Give me that. Every time you twang the cable you're putting unnecessary torque on the cams."

"You talk like an auto mechanic when you're drunk. Did you know that?"

"I'm not drunk. You're drunk. I'm a former archery instructor. Now give it."

He gave her the bow. She stood it upright, ran her fingers down the slick of the cable.

"An archery instructor?"

"When I was in high school. For the town rec department."

"What inspired you? Jennifer Lawrence? Did you have Catsass Everdame fantasies? Jennifer Lawrence was a corker. I hope she didn't burn to death."

"No, this was pre–*Hunger Games*. I went on this whole Robin Hood jag when I was nine years old. I started saying *thy* and *thou* and when my parents asked me to do a chore I'd drop to one knee and bow. At the peak of my obsession I wore a Robin Hood costume to school."

"For Halloween?"

"No. Just because I liked the way it made me feel."

"Oh God. And your parents let you? I didn't know you were neglected as a child. That gives me a sad feeling in my"—he paused, to try and figure out where his sad feelings were located—"emotions."

"My parents are sturdy, practical people who own several ratlike dogs. They were very good to me and I miss them very much."

"I'm sorry for your loss."

"I don't think they're dead. But they are in Florida."

"The first stage of decline." He nodded sadly. "I suppose they dress their dogs in sweaters."

"Sometimes, if it's cold. But how did you know?"

"They let you cavort about in public wearing a Robin Hood outfit, to what I can only assume was a deluge of cruel taunts from your peers. It's easy enough to guess how they'll treat their pets."

"Oh, no. They didn't know about my Robin Hood outfit. I had it in my backpack and changed into it in the bathroom at school. But you're right about the taunts. That was a dark day for Harper Frances Willowes."

"Frances! Lovely. May I call you Frannie?"

"No. You may call me Harper." She rested her chin on the top of the bow. "My dad got me my first bow for Christmas, when I was ten. But he took it away before New Year's."

"Did you shoot someone?"

"He caught me soaking arrows in lighter fluid. I just really, really wanted to shoot a flaming arrow at something. It didn't matter what. Still do. I feel like that would complete me: to see a burning arrow go *thwock* into something and set it afire. I suppose it's how men feel when they imagine sinking balls-deep into the perfect piece of ass. I just want one sexy little *thwock*."

John choked on another mouthful of banana rum. She had to pound him between the shoulders to get him breathing again.

"I am certain you are drunk," he said.

"No," she said. "I've limited myself to a very responsible two cups of banana-flavored dog vomit. I'm pregnant."

He gasped, began to cough once more.

"Come on," she said. "Let's go shoot flaming arrows. Want to? The fresh air will do you good. You need to get out of this hole more often."

He gave her a look through watering eyes. "What are we going to shoot?"

"The moon."

"Ah," he said. "A nice fat target. Do I get to shoot, too?"

"Sure," she said, and pushed back her chair. "I'll get the arrows. All you have to do is bring the fire."

# 13

The cold was so sharp after the banana-scented heat of the Fireman's shed, it drove the breath out of her and stung her cheeks like a slap.

She led him around the shed, up through the high sea grass, and down the dune to the ocean-facing side of the island, out of sight from shore. When he struggled in the sand, she reached back and took his hand to help him along.

They stopped at one corner of the big cruising sloop, sitting in its steel carriage. From here, Harper could see the name written across the stern in sparkling gold cursive: THE BOBBI SHAW. *The Bobbi Shaw* featured prominently in their plans, appearing in steps *F, H,* and *M–Q*.

The Fireman looked around, wearing his rubber fireman's jacket like a cape and clutching himself inside of it. Finally he found what he was hunting for—the moon, an ice-colored button pinned to the black cape of the sky.

"There it is. Kill it so we can go back inside where it's warm."

She had the bow in one hand, a clutch of arrows in the other. She dropped all but one of the arrows onto the blue shale, held the last out to him, point first.

"Got a light?"

He closed his fist around the black carbon of the arrow and slid his hand along it. Blue fire followed, as if the arrow were soaked in gasoline and he had touched a match to it.

She nocked the arrow and sighted along the burning shaft. Fire lashed off it in a red banner. She aimed for the moon and let go.

A blazing red comet sliced through the darkness. The arrow climbed two hundred feet, hooked hard to the right, and dropped in a shower of embers.

She held the bow over her head, feeling joyously savage.

"Isn't that beautiful!" he said.

She turned his hand over and looked at his palm. "And it didn't hurt?"

"Not even a little. It isn't so hard to understand. Not really. The Dragonscale will burn a host to the ground if it has to, but it won't destroy itself. I taught it to stop thinking of me as a host. I hacked the code and reprogrammed it to forget there's any difference between *me* and *it*."

"I hate when you explain things. By the time you're done explaining something, I always feel like I know less than I did before you started talking."

"Look at it this way, Willowes. You know it's in your brain. You know it *feels,* just not in words. Feed it stress and panic, it'll read that as a threat, and will burst into flame to start its reproductive cycle and escape. Feed it harmony and contentment and a sense of belonging, and it will read that as security. It doesn't just sense your pleasure, but *amplifies* it. It provides you with pleasurable feedback, gives you the world's cheapest high. But in both cases, it's not *acting,* it's *re*acting. What Nick taught me—"

"What?" Harper said. "Nick? What *Nick* taught you?"

He blinked at her, flustered, losing his way. "Yes, *well,* Nick—Nick won't—doesn't—I mean, obviously not anymore, not after—" He shook his head, waved a dismissive hand in the air. "Why are you bringing Nick into this, anyway? You're throwing me off."

*I didn't bring Nick into it,* she was going to say. *You did.* She even got as far as opening her mouth. Then she shut it again and let him go on.

"When you're all together in church, you *sing* to it. It *likes* that. That's how you pacify it. But you're still mucking about with words and it doesn't care about words. There was some writer who said language is no way to communicate, and the Dragonscale couldn't agree more. All those words in your head are constant reminders that *you're a host.* You have to think about what you want the Dragonscale to do for you *without* words. Imagine what it must be like to be deaf, to think deaf thoughts, with sign as your first and primary language."

"Like Nick," Harper murmured.

"Yes, if you like," he said, waving a hand in the air again, as if brushing off an irritating midge. "Nick can feel the thump of a drumbeat in his bones, and if you teach him the lyrics to a song, he will sing to himself, but in the wordless words of the deaf. If you can sing to the Dragonscale *without* words, then, *then* you're speaking *its* language. Then it no longer looks at you as *separate,* but as the same. That's all I did. That's all I ever do. I sing it one of my favorite songs, but without words. I sing for my coat of flame and my sword of fire, and the Dragonscale produces them."

"And Nick taught you how? Nick can do it too? Cast flame, like you?"

He gave her a bleary, baffled, miserable look. Then, in a voice so soft she hardly heard, he said, "Quite a bit better than me, actually."

She nodded. "But not anymore?"

The Fireman shook his head. She absorbed that, decided they could return to it later.

"What song do you sing to it?"

"Ah. You don't know it." Waving the hand again and looking away. She thought, though, he was relieved to be off the subject of Nick. "Although I thought when I met you—well, one of the first things you said to me was a line from the song. For a half moment I thought I had encountered someone who loved Dire Straits as much as myself."

She stepped back from him. Swayed in the frozen air. Shut her eyes, inhaled deeply, and began to sing, in a soft, low-pitched, tuneful hush.

"A lovestruck Romeo
sings the streets a serenade
laying everybody low
with a love song that he made
finds a streetlight
steps out of the shade
says summin' like:
'You and me, babe—
how 'bout it?' "

She opened her eyes. He stared at her with his mouth hanging open, eyes bright and watery, as if he might start crying.

"You're *glowing*," he said. "You're singing my favorite song in the world and you're glowing like a diamond on an engagement ring."

She looked down and noticed it was true. Her throat was a collar of coral light. She was shining through her sweater.

He leaned toward her and kissed her then—a warm, affectionate kiss that tasted of rum and coffee and butter and pecans and cigarettes and Englishman. He drew back, looked at her uncertainly.

"I'm sorry," he said.

"I hope not."

"You taste like a candy bar."

"A spoonful of sugar, I understand, *does* make the medicine go down."

"Is it medicine?"

"An important part of your recovery. Take two and call me in the morning."

"Two?"

She kissed him again, then pulled back and laughed at his expression. "Come on now, John. Your turn to shoot. You'll be good at it. You're English. You have the blood of Robin Hood coursing in your veins. Here."

She gave him the bow. Showed him where to put his hands, kicked at his feet to make him spread his legs.

"You pull the cable to the corner of your mouth, like this," she said, miming it for him. "Practice without an arrow for a moment."

He practiced, swaying in the bitter cold, his nostrils red and the rest of his face the color of pale wax.

"How's that? Do I look like Errol Flynn?"

"You are a dashing motherfucker," she told him.

She picked an arrow off the rocks, held it in one fist, closed her eyes, and frowned in concentration.

"What are you doing there?"

She didn't look at him, but felt his gaze upon her and was glad. In that moment she knew she was going to do it. It was like knowing you were going to hit a bull's-eye before the arrow left the bow.

Harper saw it in her head, the way she would move her hands in sequence to say *you and me, babe, how 'bout it,* without using any words at all. She saw it all and in that moment she knew how easy it was. You didn't have to do anything to connect with the Dragonscale. In that way it was just like being pregnant. She felt the song in her tendons and nerve endings, felt it flow like blood, without a sound, without words, without even the memory of words. You and me, babe, how 'bout it?

She lit up. Harper opened her eyes to see the cup of her hand spurt a heatless flame—a blue, mystic flame—all around the arrow, and she cried out in shock and dropped it.

The Fireman snatched at her arm and clapped her hand under his turnout jacket to extinguish the blaze. Red freckles appeared high in his cheeks. His eyes strained behind his glasses.

"What are you *doing*?"

"Nothing," she said.

"What in God's name do you think you're doing? Do you want to die?"

"I—I just wanted to see—"

But he had turned away, his coat flapping, and began to lurch back up the dune.

She caught up to him at the top of the ridge, the highest point of the island. The shed was below, built right into the side of the slope. Moss and sea grass carpeted the roof. She tried to take his shoulder, but he spun around, throwing her hand off him.

He gave her a bewildered, bookish look, eyes straining behind his square glasses. "Is that what this was all about? Get me drunk and make out with me to see if you can *trick* me into teaching you how to burn yourself to death?"

"No. John. *No.* I kissed you because I felt like kissing you."

"Do you know what happened to the last person who decided she wanted to pull a burning rabbit out of a hat?"

"I know what happened."

"No, you don't. You have no idea. She turned to cinders." As he spoke he was backing unsteadily away from her.

"I know she died. I know it was terrible."

"Shut up. You don't know anything except I have something you want and you'll do whatever you need to get it: booze me up, flounce around, fuck me if necessary."

*"No,"* she said. She felt she was caught in nettles. She couldn't struggle free and everything she said was another step deeper into the thorny tangle. "John. *Please.*"

"You don't know *what* happened to her. You don't know what's *still* happening to her. You don't understand a thing about us." He threw the bow over the side of the roof, which was when she realized he had retreated out onto the top of his shed. He reeled back another step.

"Get away from me. And never do what you just did again." He held out his hands. Golden light throbbed in his Dragonscale. His palms became shallow dishes, brimming with flame. "Unless you want to burn like this forever."

"John, stop it, stop moving. Just stay where you are and—"

He wasn't listening. He took another step back and spread his arms. Wings of brightest fire spread in a cape from his hands, down to his sides. Black smoke gushed from his nostrils.

"Unless you want to be in hell for the rest of your life," he said. "Like m-m-muh-muh—"

His eyes widened with surprise. He began to whirl his arms around and around for balance, drawing flaming hoops in the air. His right foot slid out from under him and down the roof. He dropped to one knee, lunged, and grabbed a fistful of grass. For one moment of perfect stillness he hung at a crooked angle. The long tough grass turned to threads of copper and burnt away in his hot hand.

"John!" she cried.

He dropped, banged down the tin roof, off the edge and into the night. She heard him hit the dune with a thud, a thump, a gasp, a soft whump.

Silence.

"Nothing broken!" he called. "Don't worry! I'm all right!"

He was quiet again.

"Except maybe my wrist," he said, in a suddenly disconsolate voice.

Harper closed her eyes and exhaled with relief.

"Ow," the Fireman said.

# 14

After she popped the lunate back into place—it went in with a meaty *thwack!* and a shrill cry—and retaped the wrist, she made him drink two ladles of frosty water and swallow four Advil. She forced him to lie down and then spooned against him in his cot for one, her arm around his waist.

"You asshole," she said. "You're lucky you didn't smash in those ribs again."

He put his injured hand over hers.

"I'm sorry," he said. "About what I said."

"Do you want to tell me about it? About what happened to her?"

"No," he said. "Yes. Do you really want to hear?"

She thought she already knew much of it, but she squeezed his thumb between her fingers, to let him know she was ready to listen. He sighed—a weary, haggard sound.

"Now and then Sarah and I would paddle out here, you know . . . to the cottage on this little island, to be away from the others. Allie didn't come with us—she had become almost completely nocturnal by then and slept most of the day, storing up energy for her night runs. Nick tagged along, but usually he'd nod off after a picnic out on the dunes. There were beds in the cottage, but he liked to sleep in the rowboat. He enjoyed the rock of the tide and the way the boat knocked against the pylons. There was a little dock then, out alongside the cottage. Well, that was all right. Sarah and I could have some wine and some fresh air and do what grown-ups like in the cottage.

"We had a sleepy romp in the sheets one day after a meal of cold chicken and some kind of salad with raisins in it. Just as Sarah was dozing off, she asked me if I would check on Nick.

I went out in my bare feet and jeans—and saw a little gusher of flame spout up from the boat. I'm sure I would've screamed, only I was too scared to get any air. I staggered out onto the dock, trying to shout Nick's name, as if he could've heard. All that would come out was a thin wheeze. I was sure I'd find him ablaze.

"But he wasn't *on* fire, he was *breathing* fire. Every time the boat knocked against the pylons, he'd cough a mushroom cloud of red flame and then laugh a dozy little giggle. I don't think he was all the way awake or really knew what he was doing. I know he wasn't aware of me watching. After all, he couldn't hear me, and he wasn't looking my way, his entire drowsing attention focused on his work with the flame. By then I had dropped to my knees. My legs had gone all weak. I watched him for two or three minutes. He'd blow rings of fire and then wave his fingers and dash off a dart of flame to jump through the hoops.

"Finally I was able to get back to my feet, although my knees were still shaking. I made my unsteady way back to the cottage. My tongue was stuck to the roof of my mouth and I needed a drink of water before I was able to speak. I woke Sarah gently and told her I needed to show her something and not to be afraid. I said it was about Nick and that he was all right, but she needed to see what he was doing. And I led her out.

"When she saw flame spurting from the boat, she got wobbly herself and I needed to hold her arm to support her. But she didn't shout for him, didn't cry out. She let me lead her to him, trusting me that there was no reason to panic.

"We stood over him and watched him play with fire for most of five minutes before she was overcome and sank to her knees and reached into the boat to touch him. She stroked her hand over his hair and he snapped out of the trance he was in and for a moment was coughing black smoke and blinking blearily. He jumped up on a gunwale, looking embarrassed, as if we had found him flipping through a girlie magazine.

"She climbed into the boat, her whole body trembling, and took him into her arms. I descended after her. For a long time we sat together in silent conference. He told his mother no, he wasn't hurt, it hadn't caused him any pain at all. He told us he had been doing it for days and that it never hurt. He said he always did it in the boat, because something about the sway of the ocean helped him get going. He enumerated his many accomplishments. He could breathe smoke, blow streams of fire, and light one hand like a torch. He told us he had made little sparrows of flame and set them flying and that sometimes it seemed to him he was flying with them, sometimes it seemed to him he was a sparrow himself. I asked him to show us and he said he couldn't, not right then. He said after he lit himself on fire it sometimes took him a while to recharge. He said after throwing sparrows—that was how he described it in sign language—sometimes it was hard to get warm, that he'd have the shivers and feel like he was coming down with flu.

"I wanted to know how he was doing it. He did his best to explain, but he is only a little boy, and we didn't learn much, not that day. He said you could put the Dragonscale to sleep by rocking it gently and singing to it like you'd sing to a baby. Except of course Nick is deaf and doesn't have any idea what singing sounds like. He told us that he thought music was like the tide or breath: something that flowed in and back out again in a kind of soothing rhythm. He said he'd get that flow going in his mind and then the Dragonscale would dream whatever he wanted it to dream. It would make rings of fire or sparrows of flame or whatever he liked. I said I didn't understand and asked him if he could show me. He looked at his mother and Sarah nodded and said it was all right, he could try to teach me how to do it . . . but if either of us ever hurt ourselves, we had to stop, right away.

"The next morning my lessons began. After three days I could light a candle. In a week I was throwing ropes of fire like a walking flamethrower. I began to show off. I couldn't help myself. When Allie and I went on one of our rescue missions, I would make a wall of smoke to create an impressive getaway. And once when we were chased by a Cremation Crew, I turned on them and ignited, made myself into a great burning demon with wings to scare them off. They ran wailing!

"How I loved having my own legend. Being stared at and whispered about. There is no drug in all the world as addictive as celebrity. I boasted to Sarah that getting Dragonscale was the best thing that had ever happened to me. That if someone came up with a cure, I'd refuse to take it. That the 'scale wasn't a plague. It was evolution.

"We often discussed my ideas about Dragonscale: how it was transmitted, how it bonded with the mind, how it produced enzymes to protect Nick and me from burns. I say we discussed my ideas. What I really mean is I lectured her, and she listened. Oh, I did like having an audience for all my insights and theories. That's what should be on her death certificate, you know. Sarah Storey—talked to death by John Rookwood. In a sense that's what happened to her.

"I remember the day after I first turned into a devil and scared off a crowd of armed men. I took Sarah out to the island for a picnic and a celebratory screw. She was quiet, off in her own head, but I was too full of my own greatness to really notice. We made love, and after I lay in bed, feeling like a rock star. A rock star at last. She got up and found her jeans and dug a bottle out of a pocket, a bottle full of white grime. I asked her what she had there. She said it was infected ash. Then, in front of me, she dumped it on the kitchen counter and snorted it. She poisoned herself intentionally. She did it before I had time to scream. She knew all about how to infect herself, of course, because I had told her just how the spore spread.

"Three days later the first marks appeared across her back. It looked as if the devil had lashed her with a burning whip. I was right about the method of transmission, but for once there wasn't any pleasure in saying 'I knew it.' She was dead less than four weeks later."

# 15

He grimaced, holding his right wrist in his left hand. "How's your pain?" she asked.

"It's not as hard to talk about as I thought. It feels good to remember her, even the bad stuff at the end. Sometimes I think I've spent the last nine months lighting fires because it feels so good to burn things down. Like: if Sarah burned, then so can the rest of the world. Arson is almost as good as Prozac." He went silent, thinking. "Shit. You weren't asking about psychological pain, were you?"

"Yeah, I was asking about your wrist."

"Oh. Uh. Quite hurty actually. Is that normal?"

"After popping the bones of the wrist out of place for a second time? Yes." He twined the fingers of his good hand through hers. He stared across the room at the furnace, the hatch open on a square of yellow leaping flame.

"I hate a little that this feels good," he said.

"We're just holding each other. We're not even undressed."

"I shouldn't have kissed you outside."

"We were drunk. We were having fun."

"I'm still in love with her, Harper."

"That's okay, John. This isn't anything."

"It *is,* though. It's something to me."

"Okay. It's something to me, too. But we aren't going to do anything you have to feel bad about. You haven't been held since she died, and people need that. People need closeness."

Firewood whistled and snapped.

"But she *isn't* dead. She isn't alive, but she isn't dead, either. She's . . . stuck."

"I know."

The Fireman turned his head to look back at her, his gaunt features drawn in alarm and surprise.

"I've known for a while," Harper said. "I saw her once. In the fire. I know there's *something* there, anyway, something in the furnace that you're keeping alive. But whatever that is, it *can't* be a person. It can't be aware. Flame can't have a consciousness."

"The *spore* can. That's how the Phoenix seems alive. It *is*. It's a part of me. Like a hand. Sarah's body burned, but the girl in the fire remains. As long as I keep the fire going, some incombustible part of her survives."

"You should sleep."

"I don't think I can. Not with my wrist throbbing like it is. Besides. Maybe I don't just need to tell. Maybe you need to hear. Before you go any further down the road you're on and wind up killing yourself like she did."

# 16

"She took to the Bright straight off. I've never seen anyone get it faster. Four days after she developed visible marks, she was lighting up with us in chapel, brimming with brightness and joy. You know how the 'scale can be peculiarly beautiful? Comparing Sarah to the others was like comparing lightning to the lightning bug. It was exciting, and a little scary. She had more power than any of us. She'd play the organ, and after, no one could remember their own name—they could only remember hers. For hours after we joined together in the Bright, people would drift around, talking like her, walking like her."

"Carol has that effect on people now." Harper considered for a moment, then said, "Allie does, too, I think. To a lesser degree."

"Sarah wanted me to show her how to light herself up, how to cast flame. She wanted to know how to send her consciousness out into fire. By then I was incorporating the Phoenix into rescue attempts, and Nick was making flocks of burning sparrows to hunt for the infected. I wouldn't teach her, though. I was angry. I was so angry. Angry and scared. It was one thing to be contaminated by accident, and another to contaminate yourself on purpose. She wouldn't let me off the hook, either. She threw every boast, every know-it-all lecture, every smug certainty back in my face. If casting fire was safe for her deaf nine-year-old and safe for her lover, it was safe for her. I had told her I wouldn't trade the 'scale for anything, that I was *glad* to be a carrier. Didn't we *all* say, in chapel, every day, how lucky we were? How blessed? She had seen us reeling with pleasure, with delight. How could I want that for myself and deny it to her? She had seen me fight for the sick and wanted to fight by my side. How could I refuse her?

"The more she talked, the more pigheaded I became. I hated her, myself, the world. I was ill with it, sick with malice. There was so much I didn't know. Only two people could throw fire without hurting themselves, Nick and myself. I held back on trying to teach Allie, although she had nagged me often enough. I had sound reasons for reluctance. Consider this, for example: What if full mastery of the Dragonscale is only possible for those with a Y chromosome? I'm sure that sounds sexist, but nature has never had any great interest in gender equality. What if you need a certain blood type to make it work? What if it's a quirk of DNA, like those who are immune to HIV because of a mutation that strips of them of the receptor the virus needs to infect them?

"So I wouldn't teach Sarah. In the last weeks I was hardly talking to her. We shouted, we screamed at each other, but that wasn't what I would call talking. I thought if I didn't teach her, at least she wouldn't be any worse off than anyone else in camp. At least she would be kept safe by joining the Bright. I thought I could protect her by shutting her out. Putting a wall up between us."

If Harper listened very intently, she could hear the coals whistling softly in the furnace.

"So she turned to Nick," she said.

"Yes," he replied, in a listless tone. "Nick told me later that she very quickly learned to light candles with her fingertips, which was how I started. He said he thought if she could do that much, it meant it would be okay to teach her more. But he also said the first time she lit a candle she yelped like it burned, although she told him she only cried out because she was startled. Later he noticed she would always keep a glass of cold water on hand, and after lighting candles would grip it tightly, as if her fingertips were sore. Sometimes she even dipped her fingers into it. All this was done without my knowledge. They practiced at night, out in the cottage, when I was off with Allie, rescuing the sick and polishing my personal legend.

"Sarah wanted to learn how to push her consciousness into puppets of flame, as I did with the Phoenix and Nick did with his flocks of flaming sparrows. Nick thought that was like skipping basic addition and going right to fractions. He wanted her to try making her hand into a torch first, or practice throwing balls of flame. But she teased and kidded and gamed him into it. Nick never had a chance. So he explained the general principles, just the basic ideas. He didn't think she'd really—he assumed she was just curious—and—"

He fell silent again, staring at the furnace, its orange glow shifting over his features like a gentle touch.

"I was just back from one of my expeditions with Allie. We had returned to camp with a few refugees . . . poor Nelson Heinrich among them, I believe. I was already on my way out to the island when I saw the smoke, coming from the cottage. It was all over long before anyone in camp realized what was happening.

"I paddled to the dock at the southern end of the island—the dock that isn't there anymore. As I pulled myself onto the planks, the roof of the cottage fell in. I flung myself in through the back door and a moment later the chimney collapsed on the dock behind me, crushed most of it into the water. The whole first floor had old, exposed beams. One of them had dropped onto Nick. He was unconscious, but I could see him breathing. Heat billowed, distorting the air. Everything was smoke and sparks. I saw him—and I saw *her.* What was left of her. Bones and ash and—and—" He swallowed, shook his head, pushed the memory aside. "I am sure if Nick weren't there I would've dropped. I was hysterical. In shock. But he *was* there and I needed to get him out. I tried to lift the beam, but I couldn't. It had to weigh near on four hundred pounds. I strained against it, not budging it, screaming at God, screaming at Sarah, just screaming.

"Then she was there with me. On the other side of the beam, beside her son." The Fireman spoke now in a hush, staring into the furnace with what was either awe or dread. "I shuddered to see her. In the middle of all that blazing heat, I shuddered like someone in a freezing rain. She was so lovely. She was the most lovely thing. She was walking flame, as blue as a blowtorch, her hair flowing ribbons of red and gold fire. She made a hatchet out of thin air—a hatchet of fire, you understand—and swept it through one end of the beam. Snapped it in two in one stroke. That hatchet was so hot it would've sliced through the beam even if it had been an iron girder. I tossed the big piece of lumber off Nick and got the hell out of there with him. I only looked back once, at the door. She was still standing there, watching me go with him. She *knew* me. I could see recognition in her features. Her face was beautiful and—sad. Confused. I *knew* she was self-aware. She had been a woman one moment. In the next she was an elemental of fire."

"The house fell in on itself. The fire burned low. I never left the island. I sat in the dunes and watched. People came to me to offer food or comfort. I paid them no mind. Allie sat with me for hours. The sun rose up hot and dry and baked the island beneath it and I didn't move. The house was still burning when the sun set again, although by then it was mostly smoldering coals. I dozed off for a while. When I woke she was standing in what remained of the ruin, a ghost of pale golden flame. She vanished again almost as soon as I saw her, but by then I knew for sure. What remained of her consciousness was threaded in the coals, spread across a billion microscopic particles of Dragonscale that wouldn't and couldn't be destroyed. She was ash and flame. I have been on the island ever since and I have never let that first fire burn out. It's still going, in the furnace. She's still there. She's still with me. I believe her consciousness is held in place by the energy produced by the fire and will only break apart if the flames die for good.

"And I suppose that's all of it. Few people in camp have any idea what Nick can do. He doesn't cast flame anymore. You can understand why. He holds himself responsible for the death of his mother. Can you imagine being nine years old and having that thought in your head? He doesn't know she's still with us, and I haven't dared show him. I'm scared of what it would do to him. What if he thinks she's suffering and it's his fault?" He shifted about uncomfortably and his gaze drifted from the furnace to the door. He stiffened. "My God. You've been here for hours. You have to get back to the infirmary before sunrise. You've already stayed too long."

"A minute more," she told him. "Michael promised he could cover for me all night if he had to."

He rolled halfway over to look into her face. "You have to take care of yourself, Harper. There's a boy who loves you very much. You're the one thing that keeps him going." It took her a moment to realize he was talking about Nick, not himself. "He's still got all that guilt on him. He's trapped under it, as badly as he was ever trapped under the beam."

"Look who's talking," she said.

For a moment he couldn't meet her gaze. "You *see* why I don't want you doing anything ever again like what you did with the arrow. I've already lost one woman I care about. You don't get to burn yourself up like her, Nurse Willowes. I can't lose you, too."

She held him a moment longer, then kissed his whiskery cheek, and climbed from the bed. She arranged his sheets over him, tucked him in. Harper stood above him, looking down into his lean, tired face.

She said, "What happened to Sarah Storey isn't your fault, you know. Or Nick's. Neither of you has any right to blame yourself for her death. Harold Cross could've explained why. I love you, John Rookwood"—she had never said this to him before, but she said it now, firmly and calmly, and continued without giving him a chance to reply—"but you are *not* a doctor and you do *not* understand the nature of this infection. Sarah Storey didn't die because Nick taught her badly. She didn't die because she lacks a Y chromosome. Or because she was missing some necessary mutation. Or any other random reason you can think of. In between his horrible poetry and stomach-turning misogyny, Harold filled a notebook with solid research. The spore only penetrates the human brain very slowly. It takes about six weeks to reach Broca's region, the area that processes communication. Even in the deaf. You said she had only been infected for—what? Two weeks? Three? She rushed it. That simple."

He gazed at her in bewilderment. "You can't know that. Not for sure."

"But I *do,* John. You have every right to grieve, but I'm afraid your guilt is undeserved. So are your fears about my safety. I've been covered in Dragonscale for almost nine months. It's in every cell of my body. There is nothing you know how to do that I can't learn. You should've talked to Harold."

The Fireman let out a long sighing breath and all at once seemed smaller, hollowed out.

"I—I didn't have much to do with Harold in the last weeks before the poor boy died. He was grotesque to Allie and I was out here on the island in mourning. I hardly saw him. Actively avoided him, in fact."

"What are you talking about? You're the one who snuck him out of the infirmary. He said so in his journal."

The Fireman shot her a surprised, wondering look. "Either you're mistaken or he was keeping a diary of daydreams. In which case I'm not sure we ought to place much confidence in his medical information, either. I didn't help him slip out of the infirmary. Not once. You can't imagine what an odious little troll he was."

Harper gazed at him blankly, feeling wrong-footed and mixed up. She had looked through the diary plenty of times and was sure Harold had said John Rookwood had been his one ally in the last days.

"Enough of this," he said and nodded at the door. "You have to go. Keep your head down and hurry right back to the infirmary. We'll figure it out later. There'll be another night for this."

But there never was.

# 17

Harper returned in darkness, the air curiously warm and aromatic with the smell of pines and rich black loam. When she ducked into the infirmary, there was a thin line of milk-colored light drawing a pale gleam along the far eastern edge of the Atlantic. She found Michael sprawled on the couch in the waiting room with a *Ranger Rick* spread across his chest and his eyes closed. When she shut the door he stirred, stretched, rubbed at his soft boy's face.

"Any trouble?" Harper asked him.

"Bad," he said, and lifted the *Ranger Rick*. "I'm stuck halfway through the word find, which is pretty pathetic when you think this is for kids." He showed her a big, sleepy, innocent smile and said, "Way I heard it, the prisoners got back fine, and no one the wiser. I guess Chuck Cargill was pretty huffy about spending an hour shut into the meat locker. He told 'em he'd take scalps if any of them said anything about it to Ben Patchett and got him in trouble."

"One of these nights, Michael, I'd like to set up a transfusion, and run some of your blood into me. I could use a dose of your courage."

"I'm just glad you got a couple hours with your guy. If anyone in this camp deserves one night of TLC, it's you."

Harper wanted to tell him that the Fireman wasn't exactly her guy, but found when she tried to reply that her throat was choked up and there was an uncomfortable burning in her face that had nothing to do with Dragonscale. A different sort of boy might've laughed at her embarrassment, but Michael only politely redirected his gaze to his word find. "My two sisters would've finished this thing hours ago, and they weren't either of 'em even ten years old. I guess I'll get it tomorrow. I arranged with Ben to watch the infirmary all week. In case you needed more time to work things out with Mr. Rookwood, or to pass messages to the others, or whatnot."

"I could kiss you on the mouth, Michael."

Michael turned scarlet, all the way back to his ears, and Harper laughed.

She thought she would find Nick asleep when she came in, and she did . . . but he wasn't in his bed, or in hers. He was stretched out alongside his grandfather. Nick's arm was across Tom Storey's chest, his pudgy hand resting over Tom's heart. That chest rose, caught in place for an unnerving length of time, and then sank, in a slow, weary cycle that made Harper think of a rusting oil derrick about ready to grind to a halt.

A pale slash of dawn fell across Nick's cheek, bringing out the pink, healthy warmth in his impossibly flawless complexion. It touched some curls of his tousled black hair and turned their tips to brass and copper. She could not help herself. When she came around the side of the bed to check Father Storey's IV, she reached out and lightly mussed Nick's hair, delighting in the boy-silk of it.

He slowly opened his eyes and yawned enormously.

"Sorry," she said, with her hands. "Back to sleep."

He ignored her and replied in sign: "He was awake again."

"How long?"

"Just a few minutes. He said my name. With his mouth, not with sign language, but I could tell."

"Did he say anything else?"

Nick's face clouded over. "He asked where my mom was. He didn't remember that part—that she died. I couldn't tell him. I said I didn't know where she was." He turned his face away, stared out the window into the blood glow of morning light.

The Dragonscale could rework the biology of a person's lungs so he could breathe even in suffocating smoke. But it couldn't do anything about your shame, couldn't make you breathe any easier when you had a four-hundred-pound beam of guilt across your chest. She wanted to tell him that he didn't get anyone killed. That blaming himself for what happened to his mother was as silly as blaming gravity when someone stepped out of a window and fell ten stories. Nor was there any sense in blaming his mother—when Sarah Storey stepped out the window she had honestly believed with all her heart she could fly. Death by plague was, after all, not a punishment for moral failings. Men and women were firewood, and in a time of contagion the righteous and the wicked were fed to the blaze in turn, without any discrimination between them.

"Some will come back to him," Harper said to Nick.

"And some of it won't?"

"Some won't."

"Like who tried to kill him?"

"Give time," she told him. "With time, he may remember big lot."

Nick frowned, then said, "He told me he wants to talk to you. He said he just needs a little more sleep."

Harper grinned. "Did he say how much more?"

"Just till tonight."

"Is that what he said?" Harper asked.

Nick nodded solemnly.

"Okay," Harper said. "But try no be disappointed if he no wake tonight. This will be long slow get well time."

"He'll be ready," Nick said. "What about you?"

# 18

In an unexpected turn of events, Father Storey—completely recovered and wearing an immaculate surplice—told Harper to go unto the old school bus, at the gates of Camp Wyndham, and keep a watch on the road. He even used the word *unto,* like someone quoting verse from the Bible. He issued this command from a throne of bleak white rock, at the center of the Memorial Circle, while his flock emerged from the vast red doors of the chapel behind him. The people of Camp Wyndham were in gay spirits, laughing and chattering animatedly, while some of the children sang "Burning Down the House" in their high piping voices. Harper was troubled to observe some of the adults lugging big red cans of gasoline.

"What's going on?"

"It was foretold we should have a cookout," Father Storey informed her. "For we expect friends to come upon us tonight, bearing happy tidings. I say unto you, arise and go along the road and keep your watch. We will prepare the cookfire, and roast s'mores in the name of the Bright." He winked at her. "Don't take too long and I'll save you one."

She wanted to ask who had done all the foretelling, but time skipped before she could find out, and then she was walking along the road, beneath a dark and starless sky. In the distance, she could hear the congregation roaring the Talking Heads, bellowing about the sweet release of burning it all down. She hurried. She didn't want to miss s'mores. She wondered who had brought them chocolate and marshmallows. Probably the same person who had been foretelling things.

She was in such a hurry she almost stumbled over the man in the road. She took a wild lurch into high, wet grass to avoid stepping on him. She had not yet reached the bus, which was farther down the hill.

Nelson Heinrich lifted his head and looked up at her. She knew it was Nelson by his ugly Christmas sweater, even though half his face had been flayed off, to show the red bunching muscles beneath. His foggy, good-humored eyes peered out from that glistening crimson mask. He looked almost exactly like the anatomical bust that had once been on the counter in the infirmary.

"I told you I'd get here!" Nelson said. "I hope there are enough s'mores for everyone! I brought friends!"

The Freightliner rumbled at the bottom of the hill, filthy smoke coming unstrung from the exhaust pipe behind the cab.

Nelson pulled himself another half a foot, arm over arm. His guts—long ropes of intestine—dragged in the dirt behind him. *"Come on, guys!"* he shouted. *"I told you I could show you where to find them! Let's go get something sweet! A spoonful of sugar for everyone!"*

Harper fled. She didn't flee as well as she used to. At eight months pregnant, she ran with all the agility and grace of a woman carrying a large stuffed chair.

But she was still faster than Nelson, and the Freightliner wasn't moving just yet, and she crested the hill ahead of both of them and came into the light of the great fire. An enormous bonfire blazed, a mountain of coals as big as a cottage, great tongues of flame lapping at the overcast night. Instead of stars, the night was filled with whirling constellations of dying sparks. Harper opened her mouth to scream but there was no one to hear, no one standing around the fire with marshmallows on sticks, no knots of adults drinking cider, no children chasing one another and singing. They had not gathered to enjoy the fire; they *were* the fire. It was a great sagging hill of black corpses, flames squirting through the eye sockets of charred skulls, the heat whistling through baked rib cages. The fire made a quite cheerful sound, knots popping, bodies seething. Nick sat on the very top of the bonfire. She could tell it was Nick, because even though he was a cooked and withered corpse, he was staring back at her with his burning eyes, gesturing frantically with his hands: *Behind you behind you* ***behind you.***

She whirled just as Jakob pulled the air horn of the Freightliner in a shrill, heartrending blast. The truck idled, headlights off, twenty feet away, her ex-husband no more than a dark figure behind the steering wheel.

"Here I am, darlin'!" he shouted. "You and me, babe! How 'bout it?"

And there was a great crash as he threw the big orange truck into gear and the headlights snapped on, so much light, so much—

# 19

—light shining into her face. She blinked and sat up, one hand lifted to shield her eyes from the glare. Bile stewed in her throat.

She peered past the beam of the flashlight. Nick stood behind it, his eyes wide in his small, handsome face, his hair a delightful mess. He lifted one finger to his mouth—*shh*—and then pointed to Father Storey.

Whose eyes were open and who was smiling at her, showing her his old, soft, kindly, Dumbledore smile. His gaze was perfectly clear and alert.

Harper sat up and turned to face him, hanging her legs off the side of her cot. A candle guttered in a shallow dish at his bedside.

In a quiet, fragile voice, Father Storey said, "From time to time my friend John Rookwood has teased me by saying the study of theology is as pointless as a hole in the head. I understand from Nick you saved my life with a quarter-inch drill bit through the back of my skull. I think that puts me one up on John. We'll have to let him know." His eyes glittered. "He also liked to tell me that religious people are closed-minded. Who has the open mind now, eh?"

"Do you remember who I am, Father?" she said to him.

"I do! The nurse. I'm quite confident we were friends, although I'm afraid I'm having trouble recalling your name just now. You cut your hair, and I think that's throwing me off. Is it... Juliet Andrews? No. That's . . . that's wrong."

"Harper," she said.

"Ah!" he said. "Yes! Harper . . ." He frowned. "Harper Gallows?"

"Close! Willowes." She touched his wrist, took his pulse. It was strong, steady, slow. "How's your head?"

"Not as bad as my left foot," he said.

"What's wrong with your left foot?"

"It feels ant-bit."

She went to the end of his cot and looked at the foot. In between the big toe and the second toe was an infected lump, where it did indeed look like he might've been bitten by a spider. There were other, older red marks where he had been bitten other times, and all of it was encircled by a yellowing bruise.

"Mhm," she said. "*Something* got you. Sorry about that. I was probably preoccupied with looking after that hole in your coconut. You suffered a serious subdural hematoma. You nearly died."

"How long have I been out?" he asked.

"A little over two months. You've been in and out of consciousness the last few days. After your head injury, there were . . . serious complications. You suffered at least two seizures, several weeks apart. At one time I doubted you'd recover."

"Strokes?"

She sat on the edge of his bed. In sign language, she asked Nick to get her "heart-ear-listen-to-him thing" and he went to the counter to find her stethoscope.

"Are you talking to my grandson in sign language?" Father Storey asked.

"Nick is a good teacher."

He smiled at that. Then his brow furrowed in thought. "If I had a stroke, how come my speech isn't slurred?"

"That doesn't always happen. Likewise, partial paralysis. But you have feeling in both hands, your feet? Your face isn't numb?"

He stroked his beard, pinched his nose. "No."

"That's good," she said in a slow voice, thinking it over. Seeing in her mind the swollen red spider bite between his toes, then dismissing it.

Nick brought her the stethoscope. She listened to Father Storey's heart (strong) and lungs (clear). She tested his vision, asking him to follow the head of a Q-tip with his gaze, moving it in toward his nose and then out.

"Will I slip back into coma?" he asked.

"I don't think so."

"Where did the IV come from?" he asked, looking over at it.

"That's a long story. A lot has changed in the last few months."

His eyes brightened with excitement. "Is there a cure? For the 'scale?"

"No," she said.

"No. Of course not. Or we wouldn't still be hiding at Camp Wyndham and you wouldn't be treating me in the infirmary." He studied her face and his smile became something sad and worried. "Carol? What has she done?"

"Let's keep the focus on you for now. Would you like to try a sip of water?"

"I would. I would also like to have my question answered. I believe I could manage both at the same time."

She did not ask Nick to get the water, but went and poured some herself. Wanted the time to think. When she came back to the bed, she held the cup and waited while Father Storey struggled to get his head off the pillow to take a sip. When he was done he slumped back and smacked his lips.

"I think it would be best for Carol to speak to you herself," Harper said. "She'll be relieved to know you're awake. She's been—at her wit's end without you. Although she's had the support of Ben Patchett and his team of Lookouts, and that's meant a lot. They've kept things going, anyway." She thought that was a politic way to put it.

Father Storey wasn't smiling anymore. His complexion was pale and sickly and he was starting to sweat. "No, I better see John first, Ms. Willowes. Before my daughter is notified I'm awake. Can you bring him to me? There are matters that won't wait." He paused and then his gaze met hers. "What was done with the person who attacked me?"

"We don't *know* who attacked you. Some think it was one of the prisoners, a man named Mark Mazzuchelli. But he insists that you split up in the woods and when he left you, you were fine. I raised the possibility you might've been assaulted by the camp's thief, who wanted to shut you up before you could—"

"Expose them over a few cans of Spam?" Father Storey asked. "Anyway, what do I know about the thief?"

"You told me you knew who it was."

"Did I? I don't . . . I don't *think* I did. Although I suppose I might've and forgot. There are several things I don't recall, *including* who decided to thump me in the head." He pursed his lips and his brow furrowed, and then he shook his head. "No. I don't think I ever figured out who the thief was."

"You told me in the canoe that someone would have to leave camp. Do you remember that conversation?" Harper asked. "The night we rowed to South Mill Pond together?"

"Not really," Father Storey said. "But I'm sure I wasn't talking about the thief."

"Who do you think we were talking about, then?" Harper asked.

"I imagine we were discussing my daughter," Father Storey said, as if it should be obvious. "Carol. She called a Cremation Crew on Harold Cross. She set him up—arranged the whole thing, so when Ben Patchett shot the poor boy, it would look like he *had* to, to protect the camp and keep Harold from giving information to our enemies."

# 20

Harper had a sidelong look at Nick. He had settled on the foot of her cot, hands folded together under his chin, to watch his grandfather. His face was a serene blank. The room was very dark, with only the low flame of that single candle to cast any light, and she had no sense Nick had any idea what Father Storey had just told her. She reminded herself that he wasn't much of a lip-reader even in the best light.

"How do you know this?" Harper asked.

"Carol told me so herself. You will recall, the last time I spoke to the congregation, I discussed the need to find it in our hearts to forgive the thief. Later, when we were alone, Carol and I fought over that. She said I was weak and that people in camp would abandon us if we didn't show strength. She told me I should've made an example out of Harold Cross. I remarked that a very terrible example *had* been made out of Harold Cross, one I was sure pleased her. I was being nasty and exaggerating, but she got confused and said, in a flat voice, 'So you know.' I felt all icy through my chest and said, 'What do you mean?' And she said, 'That I used him to set an example.'

"Of course I only meant that Harold had disobeyed and got himself killed, but Carol misunderstood me and thought I was confronting her over what she had done. She said it was just as well she called a Cremation Crew on him. If she hadn't done it, Harold would've been discovered eventually anyway, only there might not have been anyone close to keep him from being captured alive. She said she wasn't ashamed of herself. She had saved me, and my grandchildren, and the entire camp. She was flushed and looked—*triumphal*. I said I didn't believe Ben Patchett would be part of such a scheme and she laughed as if

I had made a very good joke. She said I had no idea how hard it was, to carry on the pretense that everyone was as good and kind as I hoped they'd be, to perpetuate my childish fantasies of everyday decency and abundant forgiveness. I didn't know what to say. I couldn't think. She said in a lot of ways I was as responsible for Harold's death as she was, that I had forced us all into a position where he *had* to be shot. She told me if there had been more severe punishments right at the beginning—if, for example, we'd kept him in leg irons or taken a birch to him in public—he wouldn't have continued to put everyone at risk by sneaking out of camp. Well, before I could come up with a response, Ben Patchett was hammering at the door, saying it was time to go. Honestly, I didn't dare try to answer her arguments, not with Ben and Carol both there. I know my daughter wouldn't hurt me, but I wasn't sure what Ben might—"

"How sure?" Harper asked. "If she was rattled, if she thought she might be exiled, don't you think she could've been the one who clubbed you in the head?"

"Not for an instant. My daughter would never, *ever* try to have me killed. I am as sure of that as I am of my own name. No. I abjure the notion entirely. Tell me—while I was unconscious, did she seem in any way ambivalent about my recovery?"

Harper inhaled deeply, remembering. "No. In fact, she threatened to have me driven from the camp and my baby taken from me if you died."

Father Storey blanched.

"She was—she has been—hysterical at the thought you might die," Harper added and then gave her head a little shake. She was remembering what the Fireman had told her, that Carol had always been desperate to have her father all to herself, that he was, in a sense, the one true passion in her life. Love could turn to murder, of course. Harper understood that better than most, perhaps. But somehow . . . no. It didn't feel right. Not really. Carol might set a death warrant upon Harold Cross, but not her father. Never her father.

Father Storey seemed to see this exact conclusion in Harper's frowning expression. "You mustn't imagine Carol felt I represented any kind of threat to her. Nor was she ashamed of what she had done. She was proud! She sensed, of course, that if the entire camp knew, it might crack us all apart, that there was a need for secrecy. But not a need for shame. No, I can't believe my own daughter would conclude she needed to kill me to preserve my silence. It is impossible to imagine. I am sure she hoped I would come around to her way of thinking with time, accept that a little murder was necessary to protect the camp. At the very least, she hoped I would continue to be the loving, decent, charitable face of our nightly chapel services, and leave her to see to the 'dirty details' of looking after the community. Those were her exact words."

It maddened Harper that she couldn't put together what had happened to Father Storey in the woods. She felt it was all right there, everything she needed to know, but it was like meeting an acquaintance and not being able to remember the person's name. No matter how she strained, she couldn't see it.

*So leave it,* she thought. Didn't matter. She didn't need to figure it out. Not right now.

"Bring John," Father Storey said gently. "Then we'll talk with Carol. And Allie. And Nick. I'd like my family around me, now. If there are difficult things to say, we'll get through them together. That's what we've done in the past and it hasn't failed us yet." He narrowed his eyes. "Do you think—people will understand what Carol did to Mr. Cross? Do you think they'll forgive her?"

Harper wondered how many people would forgive Father Storey for exposing her, but didn't say so. He saw her doubts in her face, anyway.

"You think it will be the end of our camp?" he said.

After a moment, she replied . . . not with an answer, but with a question of her own. "Do you remember all the talk about Martha Quinn's island?"

"Yes."

"It's real. We know where it is. I'd like to go there. There's a medical facility where I can safely deliver my baby. I know some others would like to go as well. I think . . . after it gets around about Harold Cross . . . and that you've recovered . . . I think, yes, camp might break up. The night you were attacked, you told me someone was going to have to be exiled from camp. Sent away for good. I didn't know you meant Carol. I suppose"—she drew a deep, steadying lungful of air. She was about to suggest an idea she found perfectly loathsome—"she could come with me. With us. Those who will leave, if we're allowed to go."

"Of course you would be allowed to go," he said. "And perhaps it might be better to keep Carol here after all. In some form of confinement. I would stay behind as well, to look after her. To help her back to her best self, if at all possible."

"Father," Harper said.

"Tom."

"*Tom.* Maybe we should wait for another day to talk to your daughter. You're very weak right now. I think you should rest."

He said, "I'll rest better when I've seen my granddaughter and John. And yes, my daughter. I love Carol very dearly. I understand if you can't—if you hate her. But know at least that whatever she's guilty of, whatever her crimes, she always believed she was doing it in the name of caring for the people she loves."

Harper thought Carol had a sick need to make others conform—to yield—that had nothing to do with love at all, but Tom Storey could no more see that in his daughter than Nick could hear.

She didn't bother to say so, though. If Tom really meant to deal with her tonight, there was plenty of unpleasantness to come, and she didn't care to add to it. So: John first. Send word for Allie. Allie would bring Carol. Whatever Father Storey had to face, he wouldn't face it alone.

She turned to Nick and spoke with her hands. "I am going to get the Fireman. Keep Papa company. He needs you. He can have sips of water, small, not many. Do you see? Is my words right?"

Nick nodded and his hands replied, "I got it. Go on."

Harper began to move. She was glad to move, wanted her body to catch up to the speed of her thoughts. She ducked through the moss-colored curtain.

Michael was on watch, as he had promised he would be. He had set his *Ranger Rick* aside for once and had his .22 rifle across his knees, was rubbing some oil or polish into the butt with a rag.

"Michael," she said.

"Yes'm?"

"He's awake. Father Storey."

Michael jumped up, grabbing his rifle to keep it from falling on the floor. "You're pulling my leg. No way."

She had to smile, couldn't help it. The simple surprise in his face—the wide-eyed innocence—made him look more of a boy than ever. His guileless expression brought to mind her four-year-old nephew, although in truth they looked nothing alike.

"He is. He's awake and he's talking."

"Does he—" Michael's Adam's apple jogged up and down in his throat. "Does he remember who attacked him?"

"No. But I think it'll come back to him soon enough. He's much keener than I would've expected or hoped for. Listen, he wants me to get John. When John's here, he wants us to bring Carol. And Allie, of course. He wants his whole family around him. And I want you there, too."

"Well—I don't know that I have any place—" he faltered.

"This might be a difficult reunion. I'd like you there in case . . . people get carried away by their emotions."

"You think they might fight about the things Mother Carol has been up to?" he asked.

"You don't have any idea, Michael. It's not what she's done while Father Storey's been unconscious. It's what she did *before* he got his head bashed in. If people knew, she never would've been put in charge of anything. Her or Ben Patchett, either." She thought of Ben Patchett pumping a bullet into Harold Cross and all at once could taste the sweet-acrid flavor of bile in the back of her throat. "Fucking Ben Patchett," she said.

Michael frowned. "I don't think Mr. Patchett is *too* bad a guy. Maybe he got a little carried away once when those outlaws got dragged into camp, but I can kind of understand—"

"He's a criminal," Harper said. "He shot a defenseless boy."

"Harold Cross? Oh, Ms. Willowes, he *had* to do that."

"Did he? Did he really?"

There was such innocence and wonder and bafflement in Michael's expression, she couldn't help herself, had to lean forward and kiss his freckled brow. His shoulders jumped in surprise.

"You remind me of my nephew," she said. "Little Connor Willowes—Connor Jr. I'm not sure why. You both have kind eyes, I guess. Do you think you can be brave a while longer, Michael? Can you do that for me?"

He swallowed. "I hope so."

"Good. Don't let anyone in to see him until I get back. I'm trusting you to look after him."

Michael nodded. He was very pale behind his copper beard. "I know what I have to do. Don't you worry, ma'am. I'll take care of Father Storey."

# 21

She wanted to run, but there was no way. Her stomach, heavy with baby, had assumed a firmness and size that was magnificent, planetary. So she zigged and zagged through the mazy pines in a shambling jog, sweating and breathing hard.

In the dark, with her pulse thumping behind her eyes, it was doubtful she would've seen Michael Lindqvist following at a distance, even if she had looked for him. He went with care, in no hurry, watching for a long time before he moved from one tree to the next. If she *had* seen him, she might've been surprised by his expression, his small tight mouth and narrowed eyes. There was nothing particularly childlike about it at all. He followed her as far as the boathouse, but when she went on toward the dock, he went in, and had soon disappeared among the shadows.

Harper took her time making it down the wooden steps cut into the sandy embankment, grabbing bunches of sea grass to steady her. The ocean was a metal plate dented all over as if it had been battered by a thousand hammer blows. Moonlight blinked silver on the edges of the waves. Looked a little choppy out there. Harper didn't see the man sitting on the end of the dock until she was out on it, halfway to the rowboat.

Don Lewiston jerked his head around to look back over his shoulder. He sat with a steel pail on his right and a fishing pole across his knees.

"Nurse Willowes! What brings you boundin' down the hill?" he asked.

He wasn't fishing alone. Chuck Cargill stood on the pebbly beach, holding a rod of his own, his rifle behind his feet on the rocks. Cargill squinted doubtfully up at them.

"Father Storey is awake. Can you get away? He wants to see John, just as soon as possible."

Don's tangled eyebrows shot up and his mouth opened in an almost comic gape.

"Yar, I think—" He stood, cupped one hand around his mouth. "Chuckie boy! Hold the fort here. I got to row the missus out to see John. She wants to have a look-see at that busted wing of his."

"Mr. Lewiston? Hey, ah—Mr. Lewiston, I don't think—" A tug on his line distracted him. The end of his rod bent toward the water. He gave it an irritated glance, then returned his gaze to Harper and Don Lewiston. "Mr. Lewiston, you better wait before you go anywhere. I should clear it with Mother Carol first."

Don tossed his rod aside, took Harper's arm, and began to help her down into the rowboat. "'S'already cleared or Mama Carol never woulda let the nurse even come down here! Now I ain't gonna let a lady fackin' eight months pregnant try to row herself out there alone in this chop."

"Mr. Lewiston—Mr. Lewiston, you got to hang on—" Cargill said, taking a step toward them, but still holding his rod, which was now curved in a long parabolic arc, the line straining at the end of it.

"You got a hit, Chuckie!" Don cried, stepping into the rowboat himself. "Don't you dare lose this one, that's Ben Patchett's supper you got on your line! I'll be back by the time you reel her in!"

Don bent to the oars and the boat took a herky-jerky jump away from the dock.

As he swept them out across the water, leaning all the way forward and then pitching himself all the way back, the oars banging in their iron rings and plunging into the water, Harper told him what she knew. When she got to the part about Carol setting Harold up, Don made a face like a man who has caught a whiff of something corrupt. Which was more or less the case, she supposed.

"And Ben Patchett was the triggerman for her?"

"It seems."

He shook his head.

"What?"

"I can just about believe Ben would shoot the nasty little fatboy for her. Ben Patchett can talk himself into doin' just about anything in the name of fackin' protecting his people. But I *can't* see him callin' a Cremation Crew on Harold. Too many ways that coulda gone south. What if Harold squawked about Camp Wyndham *before* Ben had a chance to nail him? What if the Cremation Crew was heavily armed and put up a fight? Nope. I *can* see Carol doin' it. She's a hysteric. She don't think through the consequences of her actions. But Ben has a careful mind. He's half cop, half bean counter."

"Maybe Carol called the Cremation Crew first and only told Ben her plan after. Then he was stuck trying to clean up her mess?"

Don nodded glumly.

"You still don't like it."

"Not by half," Don said.

"Why not?"

"Because *she* don't have the fackin' cell phones," Don said. "Ben does. How was she gonna call anyone? How would she even know *who* to call?"

Don took a last heave at the oars and drove the rowboat up into the muck. He hopped out and steadied her as she came to her feet.

"God, you got big alla sudden," he said.

"I like it," she said. "I look silly, I can't run, and I can't wear anything except sweatpants and extra-*extra*-large hoodies. But I like the idea of being so big I can easily trample over lesser beings. I don't want to fight my enemies, I want to squash them beneath my tremendous girth."

Don squinted back in toward shore, but it was too dark for either of them to see what Chuck Cargill was up to. Then he glanced past the shed, up to the top of the ridge. "This camp is about to turn into a fackin' madhouse. I don't think I'll be missed for a few hours. I wanta look over the boat while I'm out here. See how sea-ready she is. Maybe I'll even put 'er in the drink." He cast another glance down at her belly. "If I had my druthers, we'd be on the water by tomorrow afternoon. That baby isn't goin' to wait and we might need a week or two t'get up the coast."

"Go examine the boat. I can paddle back with Mr. Rookwood."

Don walked her to the door of the shed, hand on her elbow, as if she were a recovering invalid. The Fireman answered the knock wearing polka dot pajama bottoms and his black-and-yellow rubber fireman's coat over a grimy undershirt. He was starved, sweaty, needed a shave and a haircut, and he smelled like a campfire. Harper fought down the urge to burrow her face into his chest.

"Lazarus done rose from his fackin' tomb," Don said. He was almost quivering with pleasure, his big craggy face flushed with color. "The Father is awake. He asked for you. He wants to see you . . . and then he wants to see *Carol.* He got a sermon to preach to her, and lemme tell you, Johnny, I think this one might have some fire and brimstone in it."

The Fireman scratched his hairy throat in an absentminded way, looking from Don to Harper. "I better put something on," he said. Harper expected him to shut the door so he could change into a better pair of pants and maybe a sweater. Instead, he looked around in a kind of daze, until he spotted his helmet hanging off a nail by the door. He set it firmly on his head and breathed a sigh of relief. He glanced at himself in the square of mirror nailed up by the door, turned the helmet two imperceptible centimeters to the left, and beamed in delight. "There. Perfect. Shall we go?"

"Don is staying on the island. He's going to put the boat in the water."

The Fireman looked more surprised at this than at the news that Father Storey was conscious.

"Ah. I suppose you'll be going as soon as possible."

"Not *too* soon," Harper said quickly.

"By the end of the week, if I have anything to say about it," Don told him. "That baby isn't going to wait around for when things are more convenient. It's on the way. She ain't got but four weeks at most. Sooner we get Nurse Willowes to Martha Quinn's island and the hospital there, the better I'm goin' to feel. But that isn't the half of it. The nurse reckons Carol Storey might be leavin' with us. After word gets out about what she's done, she might like to take her leave under her own power . . . 'fore they run her out on a rail."

The Fireman turned his gaze back to Harper, fixing her with a stare that had gone from foggy to fascinated in a very short time. "What has she done? I mean, besides using nineteenth-century punishments on her enemies, keeping Harper confined to the infirmary, and threatening to abduct her baby?"

"Two words." Don waggled his overgrown eyebrows. "Harold fackin' Cross."

"I'll tell you in the boat," Harper said.

# 22

He was aghast at the idea that she would row them into shore alone.

"I'll sit on the left," he said. "It doesn't hurt to use my left arm. You sit on the right. We'll row together."

"It'll never work. The two of us will never be in sync. We'll just go around and around in circles together."

"Oh, it won't be so bad. We've been doing that for months."

She glared at him, thought he was having a laugh at her, but then he was bending to the bow of the boat, shoving it into the water, and she had to get beside him to help. A woman eight months pregnant and a man recovering from a chest full of busted ribs. To think Carol was afraid of either of them.

When they were out in the shallows she fell in over the side and then reached across the gunwale to take his hands and pull him in after her. His fireman boots squealed on the hull, grabbing for traction, and he thumped his lousy wrist, and his face went white. He squirmed onto the thwart beside her and she pretended she didn't see him thumbing tears out of his eyes. She reached over and gently straightened his helmet.

They rowed, leaning forward and back, slowly and carefully, shoulders touching. The boat creaked and slid through the water in the night.

"Tell me about Harold Cross," the Fireman said.

He listened with head inclined while she went through it again. When she was done, he said, "Harold didn't have many friends in this camp, but I agree—when word gets out about what Carol did, calling the Cremation Crew on him and all, *well*. That'll be the end for her. Sending her away with you is a great act of mercy, really. It's easy to imagine it could be much worse."

"She'll come with me," Harper said. "And you'll stay here."

"Yes. I'll have to. Father Storey will be too weak to look after camp alone. I expect that's why I'm being summoned to his bedside. I'm being enlisted." His mouth twisted in a sour frown.

"You wouldn't leave anyway. You have to tend your private fire."

"No one else would understand."

"You should let her go out, and come away with me." Harper found she could not look at him when she said this. She had to turn her face toward the ocean. The wind was spooning the foam off the tops of the waves and she could pretend the water on her face was spray. "It isn't safe here. It hasn't been safe for a long time. They're going to find Camp Wyndham. The Marlboro Man and my husband, or men like them. Sooner or later." She thought of the dreams, of Nelson Heinrich in a bloodstained candy-cane-print sweater, grinning out of a skinless face, and shuddered.

She didn't believe in a fixed future, didn't believe in precognition. Didn't even believe in the Marlboro Man's psychic radio station, although it seemed like awfully good luck, him turning up on the exact day she returned home. But she believed in the subconscious and she believed in paying attention when it started waving red flags. She had left Nelson alive—she was almost sure of it now—and that was bad news for all of them. And even if Nelson never recovered to lead the Seacoast Incinerators to camp, then it would be something else. You could hide a small village only for so long.

They drifted, had stopped rowing. After a moment, at some silent, unspoken signal between them, they took up the oars and began to move again.

"I'll be taking Nick and Allie with me," she told him. "No matter how things shake out with Carol. I love that little boy. I'm going to take him someplace safe—safer than here."

"Good."

"Sarah would want you to come with them, you know. She'd want you to look after them."

"You know I can't. The old man is going to need my help around here."

"Then come as soon as he's better."

"We'll see," he said, in a way that meant no.

"John. Her life is over. Yours is not."

"Her life isn't—"

"It is. She told you so herself. You've been keeping her a prisoner. Trapped in a rusted can. You aren't any different than Carol, keeping me locked up in the infirmary all winter."

He turned on her suddenly, his face rippling with pain. "What pestilent, flyblown *bullshit*. I am *nothing* like—and how could Sarah tell me anything? She's a creature of flame. She can't tell me what she wants or feels. She lost her power of speech when she lost her body."

"No she didn't. I don't know what's worse, you lying to me or you lying to yourself. I *heard* you screaming at her. All the way back in the fall. She's already *asked* you to let her go out."

"And how—"

"Sign language. She's at least as fluent as you."

They had both stopped rowing, although the dock was in sight.

John Rookwood was trembling. "You little spy. Listening in on my—"

"Spare me your paranoid insinuations. You were drunk at the time. I could hear it in your voice. Anyone could've heard it in your voice, from half a mile off, the way you were shouting."

Some terrible struggle was taking place in the muscles beneath his face. He kept tightening and untightening his jaw, and breathing strangely.

"It's time to let that fire go out, John. Time to leave your island behind. Allie and Nick are still in this world and they need you. I do, too. I can never be her—I can never be what she meant to you—but I can still try to be worth your time."

*"Shh,"* he said, looking away and blinking at his tears. "That's an awful thing to say. Don't you dare put yourself down. You think I don't love you to pieces, Nurse Willowes? You and your ridiculous, pregnant belly and weird yen for Julie Andrews? I just hate—*hate*—the disloyalty of it. The sickening disloyalty of—of—"

"Being alive when she isn't," Harper said. "Of going on."

"Yes. Exactly," he said and lowered his chin to his chest. Tears dripped off the end of his nose. "Falling in love: what a horrible thing. For what it's worth, I tried to have as little to do with you as possible. To see you as little as possible. Not just because I didn't want to fall in love. I didn't want *you* to fall in love, either. I was aware just how difficult it might be for you to resist my abundant charms."

"You do grow on a girl," Harper said. "Kind of like the spore."

# BOOK EIGHT

# ALL FALL DOWN

# 1

When the rowboat clouted against the side of the dock, Harper scanned the shore, but Cargill was gone. He had left his rod on the rocks. He had taken his rifle.

Probably he had gone to tell Carol something was afoot. That was fine. She was going to know in a few minutes anyway.

It was hard work for a seriously pregnant woman to climb that steep hill, and she was breathing heavily by the time they reached the infirmary. She had a nasty sweat on her face and just as they reached the steps to the front door she was struck with a leg-buckling contraction. She bent, gripping her lower abdomen in one hand, and exhaled a harsh breath through clenched teeth.

"Are you all right?" John asked her.

She nodded and waved him on. She didn't have the air to speak, although already the contraction was subsiding, leaving behind a dull ache and a feeling like she had swallowed a rock.

Harper followed him into the waiting room, which was empty, Michael presumably in the next room. The Fireman held open the moss-colored curtain and ducked into the ward, Harper right behind him.

"Father—" the Fireman said, and a rifle butt shot into the side of his neck with a dull, stomach-turning thud. He went down as if he had been cut in half.

Harper opened her mouth to scream, but Michael had already turned the gun around to point the barrel at Nick. The boy was asleep on his bed, his hands folded neatly across his stomach, his chin almost touching his chest. He frowned, thoughtfully, as if trying to remember something he felt he should know.

"Please, don't. I wouldn't like to have to shoot a kid," Michael said.

Father Storey's head was turned so he seemed to be staring at her, but whatever he was seeing now, it wasn't in the room with them. His face had darkened to a hue that brought to mind summer storm clouds. The IV had toppled over. The needle had come out of his arm. Bright red spots showed on the white sheets.

Michael went on, in an almost apologetic tone, "Here in the next few hours it's gonna come out you murdered Father Storey to keep him quiet. That you were gonna kill Carol and Ben to take over the camp. I got everything I need to make people believe it, but it would *help* if you'd say it's true, ma'am. I know you don't have any reason to trust me right now. But I swear, if you'll do that for me—if you'll admit you and Rookwood were out to finish Carol off—I *swear* I'll keep Allie and Nick from dying with you. I'll look after them."

Harper bent down next to John, who had collapsed on his side. She took his pulse, found it steady and slow. She was trembling. At first she thought it was with grief, but when she spoke, she discovered it was rage.

"You and Carol had Harold Cross murdered."

"I didn't shoot him. Ben Patchett did," Michael said. "I *was* gonna shoot him, then figured it might look better if Ben took the shot. So I handed him the rifle. Besides. The last couple months he was here, I kinda got to liking Harold a little. He was teaching me how to play chess. I got sentimental feelings like anyone else. I didn't really want to be the one who gunned him down."

"You were the one who slipped him out of the infirmary," Harper said. "But in his notebook he called you—" *JR,* she remembered. Harold wrote everything in capitals, like a shout, and so she had naturally assumed those letters stood for John Rookwood. And then she knew why Michael reminded her of her nephew. It had been her subconscious, waving another flag, trying to alert her to the one thing Michael had in common with sweet, innocent-eyed Connor Willowes—"Junior."

"Yep. That was what Harold called me most times: Michael Lindqvist Junior. My daddy never gave me nothing except his name, you want to know the truth. His name and occasionally the back of his hand."

"No one is going to believe I kept Father Storey alive for three months just to kill him now," she said.

"Yes they will. You've tried to kill him on the sly a few times already, sticking him with insulin to bring on seizures. Right between his toes. But then you couldn't do it anymore, 'cause Nick was here, and he had an eye on you all the time. And you were scared, you lost your nerve." He was holding the rifle one-handed, the barrel pointed across the room at Nick. He reached out with his free hand, grabbed her short blond hair, and gave her head a hard snap. "That's important. That part of it. *Don't forget*. You stuck him with insulin. You were hoping he'd die in a way that would look natural. You screwed up the brain surgery, too, stuck the drill in his brain. You did everything you could to finish him off, but he was protected from you."

"Protected how?" Harper asked.

"Protected by the Bright," Michael said, a calm simplicity in his voice. "His mind and soul aren't just in his body anymore. They're in the Dragonscale on his skin. They're stored in the Bright forever and ever, just like files backed up to an external hard drive. He wrote a note, talking about how the Bright kept him safe all these months. I made him write it before I kilt him. I could've written it myself, but I thought it would look better in his handwriting. It's under his pillow. I'll let Carol find it." He reached to the side counter, found a syringe, and held it out to her. "Stick yourself now. Not in your wrist or your neck. Right in your big round ass. I want them to see I snuck up on you."

"I won't."

"Then I guess you fought me for the gun and Nick got shot

in the struggle," Mike told her. "You could've saved me a lot of trouble, you know, if you just got killed a few months back, like you were supposed to. I called the Seacoast Incinerators on you that time you went home looking for medical supplies. I don't know why they didn't find you. I called 'em again the night you went to raid the ambulance. Beats me how you got away from 'em both times."

"How did you call them? I thought Ben took all the phones."

"Who do you think he sent around to collect 'em up? I kept a couple back for myself."

It amazed and appalled her that she had ever for a moment imagined the Marlboro Man really did, perhaps, have some gift for prophecy, some unnatural access to secret knowledge. She felt even the children she had treated as an elementary-school nurse would not have been pulled in by such an absurd notion.

"Enough fucking around," Michael said. "Stick yourself already."

She took the syringe and looked at the clear fluid inside. "What is this?"

"Versed? Is that a good one? You had it in with the other heavy-duty drugs. I don't know much about sedatives. I tranqed Allie once . . . the day we got rid of Harold. I needed to give fatboy a chance to slip out of camp and she was on watch. But back then I had some Lunesta my own mama used to keep in the medicine cabinet, and I knew what I was doing when I slipped some into her decaf."

"Michael, please. I'm eight months pregnant. I don't know what Versed would do to the baby. I don't have any idea."

"It doesn't matter what it will do to the baby. We'll love him even if he's a retard or a cripple. Carol will look after him, make sure he's brought up right. The whole camp will. And don't you worry. I know my beloved. Carol will have the baby cut out of you before we execute you. She'll have the baby yanked out and love it just like it was her own. I found a medical book in the camp library that sort of tells you how to do a C-section. It doesn't seem that hard. I bet me and Don Lewiston can manage it. Don will be lookin' for some way to keep from being slaughtered along with you and the Fireman. Come on now. Stick that needle in. I'm not in the talking business. I'm in the doing business."

"If you try a C-section without any medical training, you will murder me and you will murder my baby."

"Nah. Besides. We'n keep you awake. You can talk us through the procedure. Can't you?"

"Jesus," Harper said, the first tear falling hot down her cheek. "How can you do this to Allie? Kill her grandfather. Threaten her brother. She loves you. I thought you loved her."

"I guess I do, sort of. She ain't no Carol, though. Carol is still a virgin. Thirty years old and she still hasn't bled. She wants *me* to be the one. She says she's been waiting for me her whole life."

He looked like one inspired, his eyes shining strangely. Harper remembered Ben saying he had seen Michael and Allie making out frantically behind the chapel, the same night Father Storey got his head caved in. But of course in the dark it was easy to mistake the niece for the aunt. They almost could've been played by the same actress in the movie version.

"Tom told me his daughter would never hurt him. I can't believe he was so wrong about that," Harper said.

Harper was surprised to see blotches of color break out on Michael's cheeks. He touched a finger to his lips, almost as if he were shushing her. "Oh, I kinda done that on my own. Carol told me Father Storey knew about how we took care of Harold, but she thought when he had time to think about it, he'd accept it had to be done. Only then I met up with all of you to go rescue the convicts. And on the walk to the water, Father Storey pulled me aside and warned me we were going to have to lock Mama Carol up when we got back. Lock her up and send her into exile. He was pretty upset. I figured maybe it would just be easiest if he died for the camp. Tell you what. That son of a gun had a hell of a hard head, though. I hit him with my nightstick hard enough to smash a watermelon into slush and he didn't even go down for almost ten seconds. Just stood there swaying, lookin at me with a puzzled kinda smile on his face."

"When Carol finds out what you did to her father, she'll have you killed. She'll kill you herself."

"She won't find out."

"I'll tell her."

"It'll be a lie. Everything you say will be a lie. And I'll make sure Nick and Allie die with you. Or die later. Whatever. Your only chance to protect those kids is to throw yourself on your sword."

"You can't—"

"Done talkin'," Michael said, and looked at Nick. "One more word out of you, *one more,* and I swear to God, I will spray the little deaf boy's empty head all over his fuckin' pillow. Stick yourself. Do it."

Harper stuck herself.

# 2

Someone slapped her, turned her head halfway around.

"I'n slurry," Harper said, trying to apologize, sure she had done something wrong but unable to remember what it was.

Jamie Close slapped her again. "You aren't yet, but you're going to be. Stand the fuck up. I'm not carrying your fat ass, bitch."

There was someone on either side of her, pulling her to her feet by her arms, but every time they let go, her legs went boneless and folded under her and they'd have to grab her again.

"Be careful," Carol said. "The baby. The baby is an innocent in this. If the baby is harmed, someone will answer for it."

The world was a bad Picasso. Carol's eyes were both on the left side of her face and her mouth was turned sideways. Harper was in the waiting area now, but the room was different, the geometry no longer made sense. The left wall was only about the size of a cupboard, while the right-hand wall was as large as a drive-in movie screen. The floor was so tilted, Harper was surprised anyone could stand upright.

Ben Patchett stood behind Carol. Ben had a mouthful of little ferret teeth and little ferret eyes set in his round, smooth face. Those eyes flashed yellow with fear and fascination.

"Give me four hours with her," Ben said. "She'll tell me everyone who was in it with her. She'll give up the whole conspiracy. I *know* I can make her talk."

"You can also make her miscarry. Didn't you hear what I just said about the baby?"

"I wouldn't hurt her. I just want to talk to her. I want to give her a chance to do the right thing."

"I loved Father Storey," Harper tried to say to Carol—this

seemed an important fact to establish. What came out, though, was, "I luffed other stories."

"No, Ben. I don't want you to question her. I don't want her help and I don't want her information. I don't want to hear her side of the story. I don't want to hear another word out of her lying mouth."

Harper swung her gaze to Ben and for a moment her vision sharpened and things came into focus. Her voice came into focus, too, and she spoke six words, enunciating them with the care and precision of the profoundly drunk. "She and Michael set Harold up."

But reality was too much effort to maintain. When Carol replied, her mouth was on the wrong side of her face again.

"Make her be quiet, Jamie. Please."

Jamie Close grabbed Harper's jaw and forced her mouth open and rammed in a stone. It was too big. It felt like it was the size of a fist. Jamie held her mouth shut while someone else wrapped duct tape around and around her head.

"Everything you want to know you can find out from Renée Gilmonton or Don Lewiston later," Carol said. "We know they were in it, anyway. We've got Gilmonton's notebook. We know they were both candidates to run the show. Only five votes for Gilmonton, that must've hurt her pride."

"And four votes for Allie," Michael said, from somewhere off to Harper's right. "What about that?"

Carol's features floated around her face like flakes of snow drifting dreamily through a snow globe, an effect Harper found nauseating.

"We'll give her a chance," Carol said. "We'll give her a chance once and for all to do the right thing. To show she's with us. If she doesn't take it, then there's no helping her. She gets whatever Renée Gilmonton and Don Lewiston get."

A girl spoke from somewhere behind Harper. "Mother Carol, Chuck Cargill is outside. He's got something to tell you about Don Lewiston. I think it's bad."

Harper was queasy and the thought crossed her mind that if she vomited, she would probably choke to death on it. Rough stone scraped the roof of her mouth and flattened her tongue. Yet something about it—the cold of it, the rough texture—was so real, so concrete, so *there,* she felt it pulling her out of her foggy-headed daze.

The waiting room was crowded: Ben, Carol, Jamie, four or five others, Lookouts with guns. Michael stood in the doorway to the ward. Torchlight flickered—but not within the room, which was lit only by a pair of oil lamps. Harper had, for a long time, been aware of what she thought was a murmur of wind in the trees, a restless sigh and whoosh, but now she determined that sound was the noise of an agitated, restless crowd. She wondered if the whole camp was out there. Probably.

*You are going to be killed in the next few minutes,* she thought. This was her first clear notion since being slapped awake, and no sooner had the idea passed through her mind than she shook her head. No. She wasn't. *John* was. They would kill her later, after they yanked the baby out of her.

"Send him in," Ben Patchett said. "Let's have it."

Soft, nervous voices. The door creaked open on its spring, banged shut. Chuck Cargill stepped around Harper and presented himself to Carol. He looked ill, as if he had just had the wind knocked out of him, his pale face framed by bushy sideburns. His jeans were soaked to the thighs.

"I'm so sorry, Mother Carol," he said. He was shaking, from the cold, or nervousness, or a combination of the two.

"I'm sure you have no reason to be, Cargill," Carol told him, her voice thin with strain.

"I went over to the Fireman's island with Hud Loory, just like Mr. Patchett told us, to get Mr. Lewiston. He had the tarp off the boat and some sails hung over the sides to air them out or something. We thought he was belowdecks. We thought he didn't know we were there. We thought we had the drop on him. There was a rope ladder hanging off the side of the boat and we started climbing up it, quiet as anything. But we had to put our rifles over our shoulders to climb. Hud was up front, and when he pulled himself over the side of the boat, that old—that old basstid thwacked him with an oar. Next thing I knew I was looking up into the barrel of Hud's rifle."

No one spoke and Cargill seemed to have momentarily lost his capacity to continue. The pieces of Carol's face had stopped drifting around, and her features finally stuck more or less where they belonged. Harper could keep them from floating loose through an intense act of concentration, although the effort was giving her a headache. Carol's lips were white.

"Then what happened?" she asked at last.

"We had to do it. We *had* to," Cargill said, and he sank to one knee and took Carol's hand and began to sob. A green bubble of snot swelled in his right nostril. "I'm so sorry, Mother Carol. I'll take a rock. I'll take a rock for a week!"

"Are you saying he's gone?" Carol asked.

Cargill nodded and rubbed his tears and snot on the back of her hand, held her knuckles to his cheek. "We put the boat in the water. He made us. When Hud came around he made us help him launch the boat at gunpoint. He took our guns and—and he went. He just went. There was nothing we could do. He got the sails up like there was nothing to it and we—we threw some rocks, you know, we told him—we told him he'd be *sorry*—we—we—" Another sob broke forth and he shut his eyes. "Mother Carol, I swear to you, I'll take a rock for as long as you want, just don't make me go away!"

Carol let him blot his tears against her hand for another moment, but when he began to kiss her knuckles, she looked sidelong at Ben Patchett. The big cop stepped forward and gripped the boy by the shoulders, prying him free and standing him up.

He said, "You can go over what happened with me another time, Chuck. Mother Carol lost her father tonight. This isn't the moment to blubber all over her. You don't have anything to blubber about anyway. This is a place of mercy, son."

"For some," Jamie Close said, in a low voice.

Harper, though, felt a relief—an easing of pain—not unlike the passing of a contraction. Don was away. Ben wasn't going to use pliers or a dish towel full of rocks on him to make him talk. Jamie Close wasn't going to force a stone into his mouth and stick a noose around his neck. The thought of Don on a boat with the icy breeze whipping his hair back from his brow, and the sail straining and full of wind, made Harper feel a little better. Don would be angry, maybe, cursing and trembling, furious with himself for leaving behind so many good people. She hoped he would make his peace with it. It was stay and die or run while he had a chance. She was glad at least one of them was going to survive the evening.

"Mother Carol," Michael said, from over by the door into the ward. For the first time, Harper heard it: the soft tone of reverence in his voice that suggested not just affection but obsession. "What do you want to do with the Fireman? I can't keep him drugged forever. We're already out of the Versed. I used the last of it."

Carol lowered her head. The flame light of the oil lamp turned the sharp angles of her bare skull to bronze. "It can't be up to me. I can't think. My father always said when you can't think you have to be quiet and still and listen for God's small voice, but the only voice I hear is the one saying, *Make this not true* over and over. *Make this not true. Make my daddy alive.* My father wanted me to love and look after people, and I don't know how to do that now. Whatever we do with the Fireman, it can't be up to me."

"Then it should be up to the camp," Ben said. "You have to say *something* to them, Carol. They're all out there and half of them are witless with fear. People are crying. People are saying this is it, this is the end of us. You *need* to talk to them. Tell them what you know. Put the story in front of them. If you can't hear God's small voice, you can at least hear theirs. All those voices got us through the last nine months and they can get us through tonight."

Carol swayed, staring at the floor. Michael put his hand on her bare arm—she wore a silky pink pajama top with short sleeves, too thin for the cold night—and for a moment his thumb slid gently up her shoulder, a lover's caress that no one seemed to observe but Harper herself.

"All right," she said. "We'll bring them before the camp."

"In church?" Ben asked.

"No!" Carol cried, as if this were a somehow obscene suggestion. "I don't want either of them ever going in there again. Somewhere else. Anywhere else."

"What about Memorial Park?" Michael asked, his thumb moving gently up and down along the back of her arm again.

"Yes," Carol said, her eyes wide and unblinking and unfocused, as if she had had a little hit of Versed herself. "That's where we'll gather. That's where we'll decide."

# 3

In all the time they were talking, Harper felt awfully like she was climbing an endless flight of steps—climbing the steps up into the bell tower above the church, perhaps—rising steadily toward light and fresh air. Only those thousands of steps were in her head, and she was climbing back toward awareness and certainty. It was weary work and it gave her a headache. Her temples were full of splinters and needles. Her mouth was full of rock.

What came to her now was the necessity of holding on to her calm and saving whoever could be saved. Nick and Allie came first; then she would try to protect the rest of them, Renée and everyone else who had put their trust and hopes in the Fireman and Nurse Willowes. She would tell whatever lies made the most sense to limit their suffering. If she was allowed to speak at all, that is.

It was worse, in some ways, knowing that she was going to have to watch John die and she would not be allowed to die with him. They would keep her alive long enough to cut open her stomach and pull her baby slithering and red from her uterus. She would die then. They would let her bleed to death while her baby squalled.

The two Lookouts holding Harper's arm turned her around to face the screen door.

People stood together along the muddy track that led past the cafeteria to the chapel and Memorial Park. Some of them held torches. Harper saw suddenly that the walk across the camp was going to be very bad. She had never been a praying woman—Jakob had ruined God for her—but she said something like a prayer to herself now. She wasn't sure who it was directed to: Father Storey, perhaps. When she closed her eyes for a moment she saw his frowning, creased, loving face. She prayed for the strength to hold on to the best parts of herself, here at the end.

"Get a move on, bitch," Jamie Close said, grabbing the nape of Harper's neck and forcing her forward.

Harper's legs were still loose and wobbling under her, and the Lookouts who clutched her arms half marched, half dragged her out into the crispness of the night. Gail and Gillian Neighbors, Harper saw. They looked as frightened as she felt. Harper wanted to tell them not to be afraid, they were doing fine, but of course she had the stone in her mouth and duct tape wrapped around her head.

The crowd shrank from her, as if she carried some contamination worse than Dragonscale. Children with dirty faces watched with a kind of wondering horror. A silver-haired woman in modish cat's-eye glasses was weeping and shaking her head.

Norma Heald was the first to lunge forward, out of the mass of onlookers, and spit on her.

"Killer's whore!" she screamed in a raggedy voice.

Harper flinched, staggered, and Gail squeezed her arm hard, steadying her. Harper shook her head, reflexively—*no, not me, I didn't*—then made herself stop. For the next half hour she had to be a killer's whore. She didn't know what would happen to Nick after she was dead, but while she was alive, she had to do what she could.

"How could you *do* it!" screamed a beautiful young woman with a blotchy face. Ruth something? She wore a nightgown with little blue flowers on it, under a puffy orange parka. "How could you! He loved you! He would've died for you!"

Another thick, curded wad of spit landed in Harper's short hair.

Ahead, Harper saw the massive, rude stones and that rough

granite bench that she had thought looked like a place of sacrifice—a place where a white queen would slaughter a holy lion. The rest of the camp waited there.

As they came into the outer ring of the circle, Harper's right leg gave completely and she went down on her knees. Gillian leaned over her, as if to whisper some encouragement.

"I don't care if you are pregnant," she said. "I hope you die here." She squeezed Harper's nose, shutting her nostrils. "Far as I'm concerned, you and the baby can both die."

For one terrible moment Harper had no air. Her head was as empty as her lungs. Gillian could kill her as easily as she could flip a light switch. Then Jamie had Harper by the back of the neck again, hoisted her to her feet and shoved her on, smacked her across the ass to get her moving, and Harper could breathe again.

"Giddy-up!" Jamie shouted, and some men cheered.

Harper looked back and saw Michael walking between Ben and Carol. Michael had the Fireman over his shoulder, carrying him the way he might've carried a sack of oats. The Fireman had always seemed an adult and Michael had always seemed a child, but now Harper could see the redheaded boy was bigger than John, broader through the shoulders. It looked like there was something—burlap sacking, perhaps—pulled over the Fireman's head.

Harper was marched to one of those tall, crooked stone plinths. A boy—the kid Harper thought of as Bowie—came forward carrying a yellow mop handle, and Harper wondered if she was about to take a clubbing. No. The Neighbors sisters yanked Harper's arms straight back. The mop handle went across the far side of the stone column, and the girls used more of the duct tape to bind her wrists to it. When they were done, she was trapped, with her back to the jagged stone and her arms wrenched behind her.

Chuck Cargill and some other boys stood the Fireman up against one of the standing stones ten feet away. They pulled his arms back and used the tape to bind his wrists to a shovel braced against the far side of the rock. As soon as they let go, his legs gave out—he wasn't conscious—and he sat down, his feet splayed apart and his chin resting against his chest.

The camp stood back from them, spaced along the outer ring of the stone circle, staring in. In the shifting orange light of the flames, their faces were unfamiliar to her, pale smudges, eyes gleaming dark with fear. Harper looked for someone she knew and her gaze found eleven-year-old Emily Waterman. Harper tried to smile at her with her eyes and Emily cringed as if from the stare of a madwoman.

There was commotion at the back of the crowd, at the bottom of the wide steps leading up to the open doors of the chapel. Harper heard shouts, saw people shoving. Two boys drove Renée Gilmonton ahead of them with rifle butts, striking her in the small of the back and the shoulders. They weren't clobbering her. It wasn't a beating. They were moving her along that way, thudding her now and then to remind her they were there. Harper thought she walked with great dignity, her hands bound behind her back with hairy twine, the sort you might use to tie up a package in brown kraft paper. She was bleeding from a cut along her brow, blinking at the blood that dripped into her left eye, but otherwise her face was calm, her chin raised a little.

Allie was right behind her and she was shouting, her voice hoarse, shaking. "Get the fuck off me! Get your fucking hands off me!"

Her arms were tied behind her back, too, and Jamie Close had her by the elbow. Harper hadn't been aware of Jamie leaving her side, but there she was, herding Allie along. Jamie had plenty of help: there was a boy on either side of Allie, gripping her shoulders, and two more boys crowding in from behind. Blood dripped from Allie's mouth. Her teeth were red. She wore flannel pajama bottoms and a Boston Red Sox hoodie and her feet were bare and dirty.

"Get on your knees," Jamie said as they reached the edge of the circle. "And close your fuckin' trap."

"We have a right to speak in our own defense," Renée Gilmonton said, and a rifle butt shot out and clubbed her in the back of her left leg. Her legs folded and she dropped hard to her knees.

"You have a right to *shut up!*" a woman screamed. "You have a right to shut your *lying* mouth!"

Harper hadn't seen Ben and Michael going off together, but she spotted them now, coming out of the cafeteria. They had Gilbert Cline and the Mazz with them.

Gil's expression was the disinterested look of a seasoned poker player who might be holding a full house or might have a handful of nothing—you just couldn't tell. The Mazz, however, was in a state of high ebullience. Although he was dressed in a denim coat over a stained Bad Company T-shirt, he was practically skipping as he came toward them, walking with the brisk confidence of a man in a tailored suit, on his way to his six-figure job in a Manhattan high-rise.

Gillian helped Carol up onto the stone bench located directly between Harper and the Fireman. Carol stood swaying, her eyes dazed and her face streaked with tears. She did not raise her hands for attention. She didn't need to. The low, fevered murmuring, a mix of urgent whispers and soft sobbing, fell away. In a moment it was so quiet the only sound was the hiss and sputter of the torches.

"My father is dead," Carol said, and a sobbing groan of dismay rose from the crowd of nearly 170. Carol spoke not a word until the silence returned, then continued: "The Fireman tried to kill him three months ago and failed. He tried again tonight and succeeded. He or the nurse injected an air bubble into his bloodstream and induced a fatal heart attack."

"That is a complete fabrication," Renée said, her voice clear and carrying.

One of the boys behind her struck her between the shoulder blades with his rifle butt and Renée fell forward onto her face.

*"Leave her alone!"* Allie screamed.

Jamie hunched down next to Allie and said, "You open that mouth one more time and I'll slice your tongue out and nail it up on the doors of the church." Jamie had a knife in one hand—an ordinary steak knife, it looked like, with a serrated edge—and she held it close to Allie's cheek, turning it so it flashed in the firelight.

Allie cast a wild, furious, frightened look up at her aunt. Carol stared back with eyes that did not seem to recognize her.

"Child," she said, "you may speak when you are called upon and not before. Do as I say or I cannot protect you."

Harper was sure Allie would scream, would say something nasty, and Jamie really would cut her. Instead Allie stared at her aunt in bewilderment—as if she had been slapped—and then burst into tears, her shoulders racked with the force of her sobs.

Carol looked out upon the worshippers, turning her gaze from face to face. The air was damp and cool and smelled of salt. The moon was two-thirds full. The boy in the church tower—the eye in the steeple sees all the people—had his elbows on the railing and was bent forward to watch what was happening below.

Carol said, "I believe the Fireman also killed my sister, Sarah. I think she discovered he meant to murder my father, and he killed her before she could warn us. I can't prove it, but that is what I believe."

"You can't prove *any* of this!" Renée cried out from the ground. She was still in the dirt, in a humiliating position, with her ass in the air and her hands bound behind the small of her back. She had a scrape on her chin where she had come down hard on the mud. "Not one word!"

Carol turned an icy, grieving look upon her. "I can. I can prove the most important parts. I can prove you and the nurse and the Fireman conspired to kill me and Ben Patchett and hoped to set yourselves above everyone else, make this place into a prison camp. I can prove we were next."

She had it so backward, Harper felt light-headed and close to hysterical laughter. Not that she could've laughed.

"They took a vote!" Carol shouted. She held up a sheet of ruled yellow paper torn from a legal-sized notebook. "A fixed vote, maybe, but a vote nonetheless. Over twenty people in this camp voted for Nurse Willowes and the Fireman to do as they liked. Kill who they liked, hurt who they liked, lock up who they liked." She lowered her voice, and then, softly, said, "My niece was among those who voted."

A shuddering sound of misery went through the mass of people crowded around the edges of Memorial Park.

"It's not true," Allie screamed.

Jamie clamped her hand on Allie's jaw, pulled her head back hard, held her knife to the side of Allie's face, and looked up at Carol, waiting to be told what to do. Harper could see an artery thudding in Allie's pale throat.

"I forgive you," Carol said to her niece. "I don't know what lies they told you about me, to turn you against me, but I forgive you entirely. I owe that much to your mother. You're all I have left of her, you know. You and Nick. Maybe they made you *think* I had to die. I hope someday you'll understand that I *am* ready to die for you, Allie. Any day."

"How about today, you manipulative shithead?" Allie said. She said it in a whisper, but it carried throughout the park.

Jamie whickered the knife across Allie's lips, cutting through both of them. Allie shouted and fell forward. She could not stanch the bleeding with her hands bound behind her and she writhed and kicked, smearing blood and dirt across her face.

Carol did not cry out in horror or protest. Instead she stared at her niece for a long, tragic moment, then turned her anguished gaze away, swept it across the crowd. The silence in the park was a fearful, apprehensive thing.

"You see what they did to her?" Carol said. "The Fireman and the nurse? How they twisted her? Turned her against us? Of course Allie is the Fireman's lover, too. Has been for months."

Allie shook her head and groaned, a sound of anger and frustration and denial, but did not speak, perhaps could not, her mouth slashed like it was.

"I think that's why John Rookwood decided to kill my father. Why he stalked him in the woods and crushed his head in. My father found out the Fireman was making a whore of a sixteen-year-old girl and meant to expose him. To drive him from this camp. But the Fireman moved first and struck him down with that weapon of his. You have all seen him with it. The halligan. He never even cleaned it off. You can still see my father's blood and hair on it. Michael, show them."

Michael stepped around the convicts, carrying the long rusted bar of black iron. He carried it past Harper toward the crowd and for a moment Harper had a good look at it. It was slightly dented where, months before, she had struck the Gas-mask Man in the smoke. Now, though, there was what looked like old gummy blood smeared across the bar, and strands of hair that glinted gold and silver in the torchlight.

Michael held the bar up, showing it to the onlookers. Norma Heald reached out with a fat, white, shaking hand and touched it, almost reverently, then looked at her fingertips.

"Blood!" she screamed. "Father Storey's blood is still on it!"

Harper looked away in disgust. She wondered when Michael had crept to the boathouse to get the halligan out of the fire truck and prepare it. She hoped Father Storey had already been dead before he smeared the old man's blood on the rusting iron, pulled the old man's hair from his battered head.

When she turned her gaze from Michael, though, she saw a thing that made her breath catch for a moment. The Fireman's foot flopped to the left, then back to the right. Whether anyone else noticed, she couldn't say. The burlap sack fluttered before his mouth, as if he had sighed.

"You all know how strong my father is. How he fought to come back to us, to recover his poor—his poor—" For a moment Carol was so overwrought with emotion she could not speak.

"He never left us!" a man yelled. "He was always with us in the Bright!"

Carol stiffened, as if stabilized by an invisible hand. "Yes. That's right. He was always with us there and he always will be. I take comfort in that. We can all take comfort in that. We live forever in the Bright. Our voices are never stilled there." She wiped the knuckle of her thumb under one eye. "I know, too, that Nurse Willowes was sure she had destroyed his brain in the course of performing surgery on his broken skull, and that he would never recover, and so there was no reason to see to his death. Keeping him alive was in fact the best way to hide her true intentions toward myself and Ben and the rest of us. Her arrogance was her downfall, though! Soon he began to show signs of recovering anyway, drawing strength from our song, from the Bright. Then she tried to induce seizures by injecting him with insulin. But she only dared try it once or twice. My nephew was there, and I know she felt little Nick had come to spy on her and watch over my father."

She paused again, collecting herself. Her voice was low when she spoke once more, and many in the crowd leaned forward to hear her. "My dad. My dad was so strong. He fought his way back again and again. He began to wake. I think he *willed* himself to wake, against all odds. He knew the danger he was in. He found pen and paper and wrote a message." She flapped one hand up in the air, holding a folded sheet of white paper. Her shoulders shuddered. "It's his handwriting. I've known it since I was old enough to read my letters. It's shaky, but it's his. It says—" She looked upon it, blinking at tears. "It says, 'Dear Carol, I will be dead soon. I hope you find this and not the nurse. Protect yourself. Protect the children. Protect the camp. Protect them all from the Fireman. Remember that Jesus came not to bring peace but the sword. I love you.' "

She lowered the note, shut her eyes, swayed. When she opened them and looked up, Michael was waiting. She handed him the sheet of paper and once more he carried the evidence to the crowd, so they could pass it around, see for themselves.

"None of this proves anything," Renée shouted from where she sprawled in the mud. "There is no court anywhere in America that would accept *any* of this as evidence. Not your father's note, which could've been written under duress, not that halligan bar, which could've been tampered with." She turned her head, staring around at the crowd gathered at the edge of the stone ring. "There was no one planning to kill *anyone.* We talked about leaving! Not about murder. All Harper and John wanted to do was get a small group of us *out* of here and off to Martha Quinn's island . . . which is a *real* place. With a charged cell phone we could prove it to you. Their signal broadcasts on the Internet. No one here—not Carol, not *anyone*—can offer any firsthand evidence of any criminal intention that would stand up in a true court of law."

"I beg to differ," said the Mazz, from the edge of the circle.

When Renée spoke of Martha Quinn's island, there had been an almost immediate murmur of nervous surprise, a low thrum like an amplifier buzzing with feedback. But at this the many went silent again.

"Just a couple nights ago, we all met in a secret conference on the Fireman's island: myself, Gil here, Renée, Don Lewiston, Allie there, the Fireman, and the nurse," the Mazz called out. "Renée asked me if I'd be head of security around camp after the Fireman got rid of Ben Patchett and Carol. And the nurse, she promised me I could have my pick of the girls, anyone over the age of fourteen. All I had to do was keep people in line. What they didn't know was I had already tipped off Mr. Patchett something was up, and promised to work for the camp as a double agent, like. Renée and Allie thought they were so smart, sneaking us out of the meat locker for the meeting. They didn't know Mr. Patchett *let them* break us out. Ben Patchett, Chuck

Cargill, and Michael Lindqvist set the whole thing up so I could collect intel."

"And Cline will confirm all that," Ben Patchett said, and thumped Cline in the back. "Won't you, Cline?"

Gilbert Cline turned his gray, calm eyes on Renée. Renée looked as if she had just caught a rifle butt to the stomach. She looked like she wanted to be sick.

"I can confirm one thing," Gil said. "I can confirm the Mazz is a lying sack of shit who will tell Patchett anything to get out of that meat locker. The rest of it is a crap sandwich and I can't believe any of you are going to eat it."

Ben struck Gil in the back with the butt of his pistol. It made a low knocking sound, like knuckles on wood. Gil dropped to one knee.

"No!" Renée said. "No, don't you hurt him!" Harper doubted if many heard her over the sound of the crowd, which was now making a muted roar of surprise and rage.

Ben stood behind Gil Cline, shaking his head and staring at Carol with a look of outrage.

"He was telling a different story in the basement," Ben said. "He was! He told me he'd back the Mazz up to the hilt, as long as we'd give him the same deal we gave Mazzucchelli. He said—"

"I told you to leave him out of it," the Mazz said. "Why do you think I didn't bring him in from the start? I told you he wouldn't—"

"Enough!" Carol cried, and most of the chatter fell away. Most. Not all. The people of the congregation were restless now, shifting from foot to foot, whispering. "Anyone can see Cline is in love with Gilmonton and will tell any lie to protect her."

"Oh, no doubt!" shouted the Mazz. "They've been screwing for weeks! Her phony little book club was always just a cover story. Reading *Watership Down,* my ass. That was their code word for what they were really up to, which was fuckin' like rabbits, every chance they—"

"Once a perjurer, always a perjurer," Gil said.

"Mr. Mazzucchelli is not our only witness!" Carol cried. "There is another! Ask the nurse herself! Ask her! Is it not true? Did she not watch as the Fireman injected my father with an air bubble and ended his life? Did she herself not drug my nephew, Nick, so they could commit their homicide in peace? Ask her! Is it *true,* Nurse Willowes? Yes or no?"

Harper lifted her head and looked around. A hundred and seventy faces watched, lit an infernal shade of orange by the torches. They watched in fear and rage. Emily Waterman looked stricken. Tears had cut through the lines of dirt on her cheeks. Jamie, on the other hand, seemed almost to quiver with purpose, still gripping Allie by the jaw. At last Harper found Michael, who stood behind the two convicts, just to the right of Ben Patchett. He had recovered his rifle and he held it at waist level, the barrel pointing in the general direction of Allie. He nodded, imperceptibly: *Do it.*

Harper moved her chin up and down. Yes. It was true.

A scream—a bellow of anguished rage—rose all around her, and the darkness itself seemed to quake. Harper had never heard such a sustained howl of noise. It was a chorus of a different sort, and for the first time, Harper saw some of them beginning to shine. Jamie's eyes shone like gold dollars flashing in the direct light of the noonday sun. Norma Heald's exposed arms crawled with Dragonscale, and the Dragonscale crawled with a livid red brightness.

*"Unh,"* the Fireman said through the burlap sack. "What is that? What's wrong? What's happening?"

His heel sliding over the ground, trying to find purchase.

"He's waking up!" Emily Waterman shrieked, in a high, shrill voice. "He'll kill us! He'll burn us all!"

Once again, Norma Heald was the first to break from the crowd. She reared back and threw a rock, a small white pebble not much bigger than a golf ball. There was a sudden instant of silence, as if everyone drew a breath in the same moment. The rock hit the Fireman on the shoulder with a bony *thwock!*

A great and savage roar of satisfaction rose from the crowd.

Not one of them saw the door to the infirmary, three hundred feet away, open and slap shut, as Nick came staggering through it, half awake and half drugged.

Neither did the Lookout in the steeple spy the headlights of the bus, less than a mile away, flashing a frantic warning at the gates of Camp Wyndham. He was looking directly below, watching the action. Watching as the stones began to fly.

# 4

A rock banged off the granite above the Fireman's head. He flinched from the sound. A rock struck his knee with a bony pop.

His left hand erupted into blue flame, melting duct tape, snapping the shovel handle.

A white stone the size of a paperweight struck the burlap bag over his head and his left hand abruptly went out in a poisonous cloud of black smoke. The Fireman's chin dropped against his chest. Rocks thudded off his shoulder, his stomach, the meat of one thigh, banged off the sheer face of the stone behind him.

*No,* Harper thought, *no no no . . .*

She shut her eyes and turned her mind inward and began to chant without words, sing without melody.

# 5

The Zapruder film, the silent color reel that captured the assassination of President John F. Kennedy, lasts less than twenty-seven seconds, and yet entire books have been written in an attempt to adequately explore everything that can be seen happening in the frame. Time must be slowed to a crawl to make sense of any scene of true chaos—to show the flurry of human action and reaction going off like multiple strings of firecrackers, all at once. Every rewatching of the film reveals a new layer of nuance, a fresh set of impressions. Every review of the evidence uncovers a new set of overlapping narratives, suggesting not a single story—the shooting of a great man—but dozens of stories, all caught in frantic medias res.

Harper Willowes didn't have the convenience—not to mention the distance, or safety—of seeing what happened over the next eleven minutes on film. Nor could she rewatch that scene of slaughter later, to see what she might've missed. If such a thing had even been possible, she would've refused, couldn't have stood facing it again, facing all that was lost.

Yet she saw much, much more than anyone else, perhaps, because she didn't panic. It was a curious quirk of Harper's nature that she grew calmer in the moments when others were most inclined to sink into hysterics; that she was habitually at her most observant and clear-eyed in the very times when others could not bear to see what was happening at all. She would've made a fine battlefield nurse.

She opened her eyes as flame leapt from her hands and the duct tape about her wrists shriveled and melted with a filthy stink. Then her arms were free . . . free and crawling with yellow fire almost to her shoulders. There was no pain. Her arms felt blessedly cool, as if she had dipped them in the sea.

There was no need for torches anymore. The camp was all lit up. Harper faced a surging crowd of men and women with eyes that were bright and blind and shining. All of them were scrawled with glowing lines of Dragonscale, the spore casting a crimson light that shone right through sweaters and dresses. Some were outside barefoot and they walked in slippers of bronze.

Norma Heald, her eyes glowing like drops of cherry-colored neon, bent to grab another rock off the ground. Harper lunged and threw her right hand and a crescent of flame the size of a boomerang leapt through the darkness and struck the back of Norma's arm in a liquid spatter of fire. Norma shrieked, stumbled backward, and fell, taking down at least two people who stood behind her.

Harper heard screaming. She was conscious of motion at the edges of her vision, people running, shoving each other down. A rock whickered past her left ear and clattered off the standing stone to which she had been tied.

She turned toward the Fireman and found Gillian Neighbors standing in her way. Harper lifted her left hand and opened her palm, as if to give a high five. Instead she threw a plate of fire, like a pie in the face. Gillian screamed and grabbed at her eyes and fell back and was gone.

A rock struck the small of Harper's back, a sharp momentary pain that quickly faded.

Harper reached up with one hand, found the duct tape around her head, and yanked. It did not tear free so much as slide away in a melted slurry. She opened her mouth and the rock in it fell into her left palm. She squeezed it in her fist and it began to heat, the surface cracking and fissuring and turning white.

Remember the stone in her fist.

Michael reached up to grasp Carol's wrist like Romeo reaching over the side of the balcony to take Juliet's hand, you and me, babe, how 'bout it?

Gilbert Cline was off the ground, turning and sinking his fist into Ben Patchett's stomach. Ben doubled over and seemed to shrink, and Harper thought of a baker pounding risen dough to make it collapse.

Another rock struck Harper in the hip and she staggered. Allie fell in beside her, restoring Harper's balance with a touch of her shoulder. Allie wore a muzzle of blood. She grinned through her split lips. Her wrists, bound in hairy twine, were trapped behind her back. Harper touched them with a hand sheathed in a white glove of fire. The twine fell away in twisting orange worms.

Harper and Allie were at the Fireman's side in three more steps. Harper grabbed him beneath the armpits, buried her hands into the flame-retardant material of his coat. Her gloves of flame went out with a gush of black smoke, to reveal the lace of Dragonscale wound around her forearms. The spore was still lit a feverish reddish-gold. No sooner had the flames gone out than her whole body went thick and strange with goose-flesh and she felt so light-headed she almost toppled over, and Allie had to steady her with a hand on her shoulder.

Blood soaked through the burlap sack over John's head, staining it in two places, one at his mouth, the other on the left side of his head. Allie yanked it off to reveal the face beneath. His cheekbone was split open, and his upper lip was swollen, drawn up in a bloody sneer, but Harper had been braced for worse. His eyes rolled this way and that—and then his gaze found her. Her and Allie.

"Can you get up?" Harper asked. "We're in trouble."

"What elf is new?" he said, blood spitting from his mouth. He glanced from woman to woman with a kind of blurred dismay. "Don't boffer with me. Go."

"Oh, will you shut up," Harper said, yanking him to his feet.

But he wasn't listening anymore. The Fireman squeezed

Harper's shoulder and pointed, his mouth opening wide into a blood-rimmed ring and his eyes straining in his sockets. He pointed into the sky.

"The hand of God!" someone was screaming. "It's the hand of God!"

Harper looked up and saw a great flaming hand, the size of a falling station wagon. It dropped into the center of the ring of stones and fell upon the granite bench where Carol had been standing only a moment before. Now Carol was underneath it and Michael was holding her in his arms.

That enormous burning hand struck the ground hard enough to make the earth shudder. It exploded into vast wings of flame, which billowed up across the inner circle of standing stones and scorched the granite black. Grass sizzled, turned to orange threads, and burned away. A blast of hot air boomed out from the center of the circle, hard enough to knock Harper into John's lap, hard enough to stagger the crowd, to send the front row of people reeling back into the line behind them.

There were screams of anguish and cries of terror. Emily Waterman was knocked down by the scattering, stumbling adults around her, and a 212-pound former plumber named Josh Martingale stepped on her left wrist. Her arm broke with an audible crack.

The burning hand from the sky went out almost the moment it slammed into the ground, leaving behind only burning grass and the smoking stone bench, Carol and Michael cowering beneath it in each other's arms.

"How?" Harper asked. "Who—"

"Nick," the Fireman said.

For a few moments the congregation of Carol Storey had all been shining together, in a bright harmony of rage and triumph, but no one was lit up anymore, and they blundered into one another with all the grace of panicked steers. To the north, looking back toward the infirmary, a gap opened in the crowd. People glanced around, saw what was approaching, and fled. Bill Hetworth, a twenty-two-year-old former engineering student who had been in camp for four months, saw what was marching toward them and his bladder let go, darkening the front of his jeans. Carrie Smalls, a fourteen-year-old who had been in Camp Wyndham for just three weeks, fell to her knees and began babbling to "my Lord in heaving, owls be thy name."

Nick crossed the ground toward them, his head on fire, his eyes like coals, his hands claws of flame, trailing a long black gown of smoke.

# 6

They parted, a human sea before a Moses wrapped in a robe of flame. As he stalked toward them, he was already letting himself go out. The blue corona of fire that surrounded his head guttered, flickered through different hues—emerald, then palest yellow—before dying in a puff of white smoke. His eyes continued to burn, however, remained hot, blind embers.

"Come on," the Fireman said. "Thiff is our cue to go." When he attempted a fricative, his busted lips blew a fine spray of blood.

Harper and Allie pulled the Fireman to his feet, each of them taking one of his hands. He had no balance, no strength in his legs, and almost immediately started to plunge forward. Harper and Allie steadied him and he put his arms over their shoulders.

"Get us behind Nick," the Fireman said. "They're terrified of him. They're at least as terrified of him as they'ff ever been of me."

They only got two steps, though, Harper and Allie helping the Fireman along, when they heard the blast of an air horn, a bellowing *bronk-bronk* that seemed to go right through Harper's chest. She froze and glanced wildly around, staring up the road, toward the crest of the hill.

A pair of headlights came on, bright blue xenon headlights casting an arctic glare above an enormous snow-wing plow.

They shone upon a man, standing eight feet before the truck, a guy in a filthy sweater with reindeer leaping across a green background. This man had a noose around his neck, the hairy rope leading back to the grille beyond the snowplow. His hands were tied behind his back. The headlights turned his wispy white hair to filaments of steel.

Those headlights also fell upon Mark Mazzuchelli. The Mazz was almost fifty yards away, moving up the middle of the dirt road, had apparently decided he had spent enough time luxuriating in the pleasures of Camp Wyndham and was on his way to greener pastures. But when the lights blinked on he took a last staggering step and then went still.

"The fuck is this?" the Mazz said, his voice carrying in the sudden hush.

Another pair of headlights blinked on, and then a third. One set belonged to an open-top Humvee. The other lights blazed from the front of a Chevy Silverado Intimidator, on six jacked-up tires. Blinding floodlights flashed on above the cab. There were at least two other pickup trucks down the road behind them.

Nelson Heinrich, the limping man in the noose, looked over his shoulder into the lights.

*"See!"* he screamed. *"See, I told you! I told you they'd be here! All of 'em! Two hundred infected at least! I told you I could help you! Now you have to let me go! You promised! You promised you'd be done with me!"*

An amplified voice—there were speakers mounted on top of the Intimidator, along with floodlights—boomed into the night. Harper knew it. They all knew it. The Marlboro Man was famous up and down the seacoast.

"A promise is a promise," the Marlboro Man said. "And ain't no one can say the Marlboro Man don't keep his word. Someone cut Mr. Heinrich loose."

A man in fatigues stood up from the passenger seat of the Humvee. He had a Bushmaster and he steadied the barrel on the top edge of the windshield before he began to fire.

# 7

Nelson Heinrich arched his spine, as if he had been struck across the small of the back with a steel rod. Red smoke burst from his chest in puffs, made a crimson mist in the air around him. He tried to run, got two steps, and then the rope circling his neck jerked him off his feet and he hit the dirt.

The Mazz turned and ran, too. He took one step, and a second, and then bullets shredded his legs. Other bullets hit his back with a sound like rain falling on a drum. The last slug caught a shoulder as he fell and spun him around as he dropped into the road, so he landed faceup to the smoky night sky.

The Humvee took off, banging over the rutted road, raising a cloud of white chalk. It accelerated into the darkness between the church and the cafeteria, cutting off the path of escape in that direction. The headlights lurched across the muddy ground and fell upon Nick. The Hummer did not slow, but accelerated, rushing toward him. Harper screamed his name. He didn't hear, of course.

The Humvee went over the Mazz with a crunch and a pop and jolted as if it had slammed into a deep pothole. Nick turned, almost casually, as in a dream. He raised his right hand. Sparks whirled up off it, rising in a funnel into the night, into the stars, a thousand hot stars flying up off his hand. Only instead of winking out as they climbed, in the usual manner of sparks, they brightened and swelled. They rose into a flock of burning sparrows, not one of them any bigger than a golf ball, a hundred darting birds of flame, and then they dived.

They hit the Humvee in a spattering rain of red light when it was still fifty feet away. The burning darts struck in a flurry of wet-sounding smacks and cracked the windshield; hit the men in the front seat and turned them into screaming effigies; lashed the tires and made spinning wheels of fire; pelted a box of ammunition and set it off with a rattling thud and a burst of strobing white lights.

The Humvee swerved to the left. The right edge of the fender clipped Nick on the way by and threw him aside. The Humvee kept going, skewing left. The passenger-side tires struck a half-buried white rock. The Hummer rose up on two wheels, then turned over with a shattering crash. A burning corpse—the driver—vaulted through the night.

Allie screamed Nick's name again and again. She couldn't move. She was stuck in place. She tried to go to him, but the Fireman tightened the arm over her shoulders.

"Ben will get him, *Ben*—" the Fireman said, holding Allie against him for half a moment before she twisted free and began to sprint for her brother.

Ben Patchett was well ahead of her, though. He ran in a shambling waddle, but for all that he was already two-thirds of the way to the boy on the ground. In one hand he held his pistol and he shot blindly at the Freightliner. A bullet hit the plow and threw blue sparks. Ben dropped to one knee, gathered the smoking boy up in his arms, and slung him over his shoulder. He fired again, just once, then began to run back, not so fast this time.

There were men standing behind the snow-wing plow, using it for cover. Muzzles flashed. Guns thudded. Ben stumbled, reeled off course, kept going. Harper couldn't see where the first bullet hit him. The second struck him in the right shoulder and half turned him around. It seemed sure he would go down, or drop Nick. He did neither. He steadied himself and came on, in a sort of exhausted jog, a man at the end of a long run on a hot day. The third bullet to hit him blew off the top of his head. Harper could only think of a wave dashing itself to foam against a rock. His skull came off in a blast of red foam, hair and bone and brain scattering into the darkness.

And still he jogged on, another step, and a second, and by

the time he fell to his knees, Allie was right there, her arms outstretched. Ben passed Nick to her almost gently, settling him into her arms with an unhurried care, as if losing the top half of his skull were a matter of no consequence. Before Ben dropped onto his face, Harper had a last look at his expression. It seemed to her he was smiling.

"Run!" Carol screamed. "Run for the church! Everyone run!" She was standing on the stone bench again, her arms raised out to either side, lit from behind by headlights. Bullets rattled and thwacked on the towering stones all around her and once Harper thought she saw the hem of Carol's robe jerk, as if something had snapped at it. Not a single bullet struck her. Smoke rose from the blackened rock beneath her feet. She looked like an illustration from the Old Testament, a mad prophet in a scene of midnight desolation, calling for God to deliver a stroke of redemptive violence.

The people of Camp Wyndham were already on their way, the whole mass of them. They stampeded for the stairs, 170 of them, shoving and shrieking. Emily Waterman, who was still on the ground, was stepped on by half a dozen people. The last to trample over her, a woman named Sheila Duckworth, a former dentist's assistant, put her foot on the back of Emily's head, driving her face down into the mud, which was where the eleven-year-old suffocated. Her neck was broken by then, and she couldn't lift her face to breathe.

Harper looked around for Renée and saw her at the far corner of the church. Gilbert stood with her, pulling Renée along by one arm. They weren't going into the chapel, but around the side and behind. Renée's eyes were damp and frightened and pleading and it looked like she wanted to stay, but Gil hauled her on, and Harper thought, *Go, just go.* It felt like a deep breath of clean, fresh air to see Renée slip away and out of sight. It was too far to go with John—John could barely stand—but Renée and Gil had already made it, could escape down the hill and into the trees. Maybe they would find their way to a kayak, paddle out to Don Lewiston, if he was out there somewhere, watching from offshore. She hoped they did. She hoped they didn't look back.

Michael was out from under the altar, reaching up to take Carol's hands. She paid him no mind. She stood there screaming for her congregation to run, and when he caught at her wrists, she pulled them free. Michael grabbed her about the waist and lifted her bodily off the stone. He turned and ran with her, much as Ben had run with Nick only a moment before. He ran for the chapel. Most of the rest of camp had already shoved their way in through the red doors.

"Come on," the Fireman said. "The church."

His legs buckled and Harper lugged him back up.

"No," Harper said. "That's a trap—"

"It's shelter, now go."

Her insides tightened, as if being squeezed by a steel brace. Her abdomen hurt so badly it took her breath away and she wondered, wildly, if this was it, if the stress had induced labor a month early.

Then she pushed the thought down and began to make her stumbling way toward the chapel. The Fireman pedaled his feet, mimicking the act of walking, but for all that, she was carrying him. Allie fell in next to them with Nick in her arms. Blood ran from the tip of her chin, but her lips were open in a kind of savage grin.

They thudded up the steps together: Allie carrying Nick, Harper carrying the Fireman, and Michael hauling Carol. No sooner had they reached the top of the steps than the stairs exploded, bullets chewing them up and filling the night with the sweet odor of fresh-sawn wood.

That Chevy Intimidator—a flaming WKLL decal on the passenger-side door—went off-road, booming down the hill, swinging around the outer edge of the ring of stones. It pulled in on the southern side of the chapel, in the narrow strip of open ground between the church and the woods. A fully automatic gun of some sort rattled from the flatbed. Harper didn't know what it was, but it had a flat, plasticky sound that was different from the Bushmasters.

Two other pickups slammed over the open ground to the north, roaring into position to cover the other side of the building. The Freightliner remained at the top of the hill, idling in place, as if Jakob were waiting and watching to see where he might be of the most use.

Gail Neighbors stood just inside the entrance at one of the great red doors. The wispy, elfin boy who looked like young David Bowie was at the other. They were already swinging the doors closed as Harper and the Fireman lurched inside, into dimness, sobbing, shouts, and terror. The doors banged shut behind them—and never opened again.

# 8

Michael bent forward and gently—reverently—set Carol back on her feet in the shadows of the foyer.

"Are you hurt?" he cried, his voice cracking. "Oh, God, please—*please*—don't be shot. I don't know what I'd do."

Her eyes rolled in the way of a panicked horse's. She hardly seemed to know him. "Yes. Unhurt. The Bright. I think it was the Bright! It turned their bullets aside. It was like a force field made of love. I think it protected you, too!"

Harper cleared her throat and nudged Carol gently aside with one elbow. In her left fist was a rock bigger than a golf ball, the rock Jamie Close had shoved in her mouth fifteen impossible minutes before. It was smoking by now, had been heating steadily in her Dragonscale-scrawled hand. She swept it down across Michael Lindqvist Jr.'s jaw, knocking in two of his teeth.

"Nope," Harper said. "No force field on him." As he doubled over and sank down, she brought her knee up into his broken face. At the same time she clubbed him in the shoulder with the molten rock. Sparks flew. The shoulder popped out of its socket with a sound like someone pulling a cork.

She could've kept hitting him. She didn't know herself anymore. Her arm was operating on its own and her arm wanted to kill him. But it would've meant getting down on her knees, and she was having little contractions and that seemed like a lot of effort. Besides, the Fireman had an arm around her, and while he was too weak to pull her back, he was at least trying.

"Wait," she said. "I'm okay. I'm all done."

She thought she was, too, but then he let go of her and she booted Michael in the neck.

"He was a sweet old man," Harper said, as the Fireman

tugged her out of kicking range. "You ought to be ashamed of yourself!"

Carol gave them a bewildered, wondering look. One side of her face was pink and swollen, the skin peeling off her ear. The falling hand of God had given her an instant sunburn on one cheek.

"And you!" Harper said to her. "I guess your force field was never switched on when Mikey was in the mood to finger your pussy."

Carol flinched as if Harper had slapped her. Her left cheek began to turn the same shade as the side of her face that had been burned.

"You can kill me now if you want," Carol said. "You will only be sending me back into the arms of my father. He waits for me in the Bright. Everyone we've lost waits in the Bright. That's our only escape now anyway."

Harper said, "I'm not going to kill you, and I never was. I don't *need* to kill you. The people outside are going to take care of that for me. This place is a box and they've got all the guns. But we might have another five or ten minutes. While it lasts, you think about this. Michael killed your father . . . for *you*. To save *you*. And *himself.* Your father was going to send you away for what you did to Harold Cross. Mikey bashed his head in to keep him from telling the camp about the way you set Harold up and had him shot. When you sent Harold to his grave? You sent your father into the dirt with him. One led naturally to the other. You take that into the Bright with you."

Harper's voice dropped steadily as she spoke, and by the time she had said the last of it, she was trembling, her voice little more than a husky whisper. She was not, after all, really good at being cruel to people, even people who had it coming. Carol's frightened, pale, confused face sickened her. There were dark circles under her eyes and her skin had a gray cast beneath the pink of her burns. Harper thought she finally looked like a grown-up: a washed-out, weary, and not terribly attractive woman who had done some hard living.

Carol turned her baffled gaze toward Allie, who stood there holding Nick in both arms. When she saw her niece, her face shriveled, and she began to weep.

"Allie," she said, and held out her arms. "Let me hold Nick. Let me see him. Please."

Allie spat in Carol's face. Carol blinked, her cheeks and brow dappled in red drops. She held up her hands defensively and Allie spat on them, too, a shower of mucus and stringy blood.

"Fuck I will," Allie said through her slashed mouth. "I don't want you touching him. You got something worse than Dragonscale and I don't want him anywhere near it, in case it's contagious." Blood flew on every other syllable. The gash across her lips was a bad one. Harper thought it would need stitches and was likely to scar badly.

"We don't have time for this," the Fireman said. "We need to get up in the bell tower. We can make a fight of it from up there."

Harper thought this was the most hopeless thing she had ever heard, and opened her mouth to say so, but Jamie spoke first.

"There's at least one rifle up there," she said. Her face was filthy and she was shuddering furiously, although whether from shock or terror, Harper couldn't have said. "And a box of shells. There's always at least one gun there for whoever's on watch up in the steeple."

Jamie Close was a harsh little savage, but she was nobody's fool. She could grasp the situation as well as they could and had shifted her loyalties to the most likely survivors with the businesslike efficiency of a bank teller making change.

The Fireman nodded. "Good. That's good, Jamie. Get up there. We'll follow. We can direct our fire down from the steeple to open up a path, from the basement doors across to—" He paused, eyes straining in his head. He had lost his glasses somewhere. Harper knew he was visualizing the camp, and seeing how the double doors down into the basement opened onto the north field: a vast stretch of bare ground with no cover.

There were two trucks over there full of men and guns. Harper had already thought it through and didn't see a way out.

"Where's Gillian!" Gail was shrieking. "Did anyone see my sister? Did anyone see if my sister made it inside?" She turned away from the double doors and staggered into the nave, where most of the congregation had gathered.

Harper squeezed John's shoulder. "Do you think you can make it up those stairs?"

"Go," he said. "I'll follow."

"I'm not leaving you behind. There's no way. We'll take the steps together."

He nodded, swiped blood away from his cheek. "Come on, then. We'll have a good position on them from up there. I don't care how many of them there are. That's a sniper's nest. We might still be able to shoot and burn our way out. *Somehow.* It's not too late, Willowes."

It was though. The first of the Molotov cocktails hit the south side of the church a moment later, in a crash and rush of blue flame.

# 9

Carol spun on her heel. The high vault of the nave echoed with cries for help, for Jesus, for mercy, for forgiveness. Carol stared into the long and crowded room, her gaze stricken and confused.

Some sprawled on the floor. Some huddled in the pews, holding one another. Many sat at the foot of the altar. Norma sat on the steps leading up to the stage, rocking back and forth, shaking her head.

"What are you *crying* for?" she cried out. "Why are you crying? You think we can't get out of here? You think we're *trapped*? The Bright is *a-waitin'* for us and ain't no one can stop us from flying into it to be free! It ain't time to cry! It's time to *sing*!"

The stained-glass windows that lined the long hall were covered with plywood sheets, nailed up on the outside of the building. One of these plywood sheets was in flames, and the rippling fire cast garish, candy-store colors across the pews.

*"Time to sing!"* Norma screamed again. "Come on! Come on, now!" Her wild gaze found Carol across the full length of the room, through the tumult of the crowd. "Mother Carol! You know what we need to do! You know!"

Carol looked back at her for a long moment, something like incomprehension on her face. But then she drew breath and lifted her voice and began to sing.

*"O come all ye faithful—"* Carol sang. It was hard to hear her, at first, over the moans and shouts.

Bullets drummed against the exterior of the chapel, falling like a hard rain.

*"Joyful and triumphant,"* Carol went on, her voice tragic, and terrified, and sweet. She walked into the nave, stepping around

Michael and holding her hands out to either side of her. Blood dripped from her fingertips.

Gail stood nearby. She seemed to have given up looking for her sister, was just swaying there. Carol took her by the hand. Gail looked down at it in surprise, jumping a little, as if Carol had pinched her.

Carol squeezed her fingers and went on: *"O come ye . . . o come ye . . . to Bethlehem."*

"Yes!" Norma roared. "Yes! To Bethlehem! To the Bright!"

A second voice joined Carol's, someone singing with her in a frightened, off-key lilt.

Someone else was crying out, over and over, "We're going to die! We're going to die in here! Oh God, we're going to die!"

Gail looked at Carol's hand holding hers and began to weep. She wept so hard her shoulders shook. But then she began to sing as well.

Half a dozen of them now, their voices rising together, into the rafters: *"Come and behold him! Born the king of angels!"*

And a silvery rose-hued light raced along the ridges and whorls of Carol's Dragonscale. Harper could see her lighting up through the thin silk of her pajamas.

In a bellowing, grief-choked voice, Norma shouted: *"O come let us adore him! O come let us adore him! O come let us adore him!"* It was more than an exhortation. It sounded almost like a threat.

Another Molotov cocktail crashed against the south side of the church. Flame leapt up a section of wall. Two men ran at it and began to beat at it with coats.

"It's over," Harper said to the Fireman. "It's all over."

Carol walked slowly toward the altar and as she waded into the crowd they rose to their feet and reached for her. Pews shrieked as people pushed them aside. They clambered over and past one another to get closer to Carol.

The worshippers reached for her and sang with her and many gazed upon Carol with adoration. One little boy hurried along in her wake, hopping and clapping his hands in an inexplicable fit of excitement, as if he were being led to the gates of an amusement park he had long dreamed of visiting. Carol squeezed hands as she made her way forward, not unlike a politician making her way through a crowd, sometimes leaning over to brush someone's knuckles with her lips, but going on with her song all the while. She loved them, of course. It was a sick, spoiled sort of love—it was, Harper thought, not so different from the way Jakob had loved her—but it was real and it was all she had left to give them.

Bullets drummed into the wooden doors behind them, snapped Harper out of her trance. She turned the Fireman and half pulled, half carried him into the safety of the stone archway that opened into the stairwell. Bullets zipped and whined, chipping the flagstones on the floor behind them. Allie squeezed in beside them, holding her brother in her arms.

"Any ideas?" she asked, without a trace of panic.

"There might be a way out across the roof," the Fireman said.

Harper knew that once they climbed into the bell tower, there would be no coming back down—not for her, anyway. She would not be escaping across the top of the chapel. It was too high. If she dropped off the steep pitch of the roof she would pulverize her legs and bring on a miscarriage.

But she didn't say this to either of them. The thought was in her mind that Allie, at least—nimble, athletic Allie—might be able to get across the roof and down to a gutter, hang herself off the side and drop. There would be lots of smoke and noise, maybe enough to give her a chance to reach the woods and cover.

"Yes," Harper said, but still she hesitated, stayed where she was, craning her neck to see into the nave.

The voices of all who remained rose in sweet, agonized song. They sang and they shone. Their eyes glowed as blue as blowtorches. A little girl with a shaved head stood on a pew, singing at the top of her lungs. The Dragonscale on her bare arms was glowing so bright it rendered the arms themselves almost translucent, so Harper could see the shadows of bones through her skin.

Norma was the first to ignite. She stood behind the altar, swaying in front of the cross, booming out the words of the song. Her big, homely face was pink and shiny with sweat and she opened her mouth and cried out: *"Sing in exultation!"* The inside of her throat was full of light.

Norma drew a deep breath for the next line. A yellow blast of flame gushed from her mouth. Her head snapped back. Her throat was red and straining as if with some terrible effort. Then her neck began to blacken, while dark smoke boiled from her nostrils. The Dragonscale on the wobbling meat of her bare arms was a livid poisonous shade of deepest red. She wore a black flower-print dress roughly the size of a pup tent. Blue flames raced up the back of it.

Gail choked, stumbled, knocked into the little boy who had been skipping up and down. She waved one hand, back and forth, through the air, as if to clear gnats away from her face. The third time she did it, Harper saw her arm was on fire.

"What's happening to them?" cried Jamie, who had joined them in the wide stone archway.

"It's a chain reaction," the Fireman said. "They're all going down together."

*"Glory in the highest!"* they sang. Some of them, anyway. Others had begun to scream. The ones who weren't burning.

When Carol went up in flames, she was at the center of the throng, dozens of worshippers reaching in to touch her. And all at once she was a white rippling pillar of fire, her head thrown back and her arms spread out as if to embrace an invisible lover. She went up as if she had been doused in kerosene. She did not cry out—it was too fast.

Bullets zinged and whistled through the nave, cutting down people at random on the outer edge of the crowd. Harper saw a teenager, a slender black kid, slap a hand to his brow, as if he had just realized he had forgotten to bring his textbook to class.

When he dropped the hand, she saw a hole through the center of his forehead.

A teenage girl doubled over, grabbing herself, her whole back on fire. The lanky kid who looked like David Bowie had sunk to his knees at the back of the crowd, his head bowed as if in prayer, his hands pressed together. His head was on fire, a black match at the center of a bright yellow flame. A little girl ran up and down the aisle, flapping both of her burning hands in the air and shrieking for her mother. Her ponytail was a blue scarf of flame.

"Oh, John," Harper said and turned her face away. "Oh, John."

He had her by the arm, and he drew her on into the smoky gloom of the stairwell, and they began to climb together, away from shouts, and laughter, and song, but most of all, away from the screams, which rose together in a final wrenching chorus, a last act of harmony.

# 10

Harper had wondered what it must've been like to be in one of the stairwells at the Twin Towers on the day the planes struck, what people felt as they made their way blindly down the steps through the smoke. She had wondered about it all over again the day men and women began to leap from the top of the Space Needle in Seattle, in the first weeks of widespread infection. In those days of conflagration, it happened again and again—the high building in flames, people inside hurrying to escape the fire at their backs, trying to find a way out, knowing all the while that the only exit might be a last jump and the giddy silent rush of falling: a final chance to snatch at a moment of peace.

Most of all, she feared panic. She feared losing possession of herself. But as they made their way up, Harper felt almost businesslike, focused on the next step, then the step after. That, at least, was a reason for gladness. She was less terrified of dying than she was of being stripped of her personality, of turning into an animal in the slaughterhouse, unable to hear her own thoughts over the clanging alarm of desperation.

Harper climbed with the Fireman holding on to her for support, stopping now and then when he got dizzy or when she needed to catch her breath. They climbed like the elderly, going one step, pausing, going another. He was too weak to hurry and she was having contractions. Her womb felt like a stone, a hard block at the center of her.

Jamie Close was already in the tower. She had run past them a minute before. Already, Harper could hear the occasional crack of a rifle from above.

Allie was a little ahead of them, carrying Nick in her arms.

Nick's chin rested on her shoulder, and Harper could see his face quite clearly. He wore a red mask of blood, his scalp torn open where he had been kissed by the Humvee, but his expression was peaceful, drowsing. Once he opened his left eye to peer at her, but then he closed it again.

"Almost there," the Fireman said. "Almost there."

And what would they do when they got there? Wait for the fire to reach them, Harper assumed. Or be shot from below. But she didn't share this thought with him. She was grateful for his closeness, for his arm at her waist and his head on her shoulder.

"I'm glad I fell in love with you, John Rookwood!" she said to him, and kissed his neck.

"Oh, I am, too," he said.

Behind them, the singing went on, although now screams threatened to drown it out. The screams, and the laughter. Someone was laughing very loudly.

The smoke in the steeple was fragrant, smelled of baking pinecones.

"John," she said, seized by a sudden idea. "What if we turned back? What if we tried to go *through* the flames. The Dragonscale would protect us, wouldn't it?"

"Not from gunfire, I'm afraid. Besides, Allie wouldn't come out at all. She doesn't know how to control the 'scale like I do—or like you. And Nick is unconscious, so I don't know—but look, if you want to try it, then let me get upstairs first. We'll see if we can't make you some cover. You might—with all the confusion—" His eyes brightened as he came alive to the idea.

"No," Harper said. "You're right. I wasn't thinking about Allie or Nick. I'm not going anywhere without them."

They were on the uppermost landing now. A door stood half open, looking onto dark, smoke-filled night. He gripped her shoulders and squeezed. "You have a child to think about."

"More than one, Mr. Rookwood," she said.

He stared at her fondly and kissed her and she kissed him back.

"Well," she said, "I suppose we better make a fight of it. Spit spot, out we go."

"Out we go, Nurse Willowes," he said.

The bell tower was an open well, with a catwalk of pine planks going around all four sides of the square hole. The copper bell, stained a dignified green with age, hung over the drop. It bonged whenever it was struck by a bullet from below. White stone balusters supported a waist-high marble rail. Lead cracked off rock, making small clouds of white powder.

Harper did not expect to step over a corpse, but there was a dead boy flung across the last couple of stairs. He was facedown, with a red hole in the back of his chambray shirt. The Lookout who had been on watch in the steeple that night, Harper supposed. He had missed the signal from the bus, down at the end of the road, had been too preoccupied with the stoning in progress below, but he had more than paid for his lack of attention. Harper bent to feel for a pulse. His neck was already cold. She left him, helped John past him, and rose into the night.

Allie sat on the floor, below the railing, with her brother in her arms. Both of them looked as if they had crawled arm over arm through a particularly filthy abattoir.

Jamie was on her knees, the dead sentry's rifle resting on the stone railing. The gun went off with a flat, snapping sound. She cursed, slid back the bolt, grabbed for a bullet in a battered cardboard box at her knee.

Harper had crouched instinctively as she came into the open air. Now she lifted her head to take in a panorama of ruin. From here she could see it all, had a God's-eye view of the camp in its entirety.

The Memorial Park stood just beyond the chapel's front steps. From here, that circle of barbaric standing rocks looked even more like Stonehenge. A half dozen men had fanned out among the boulders and plinths for cover. One of them, a scrawny guy in thick, black-framed Buddy Holly glasses, was crouched behind the blackened altar with what appeared to be an Uzi. He grinned, his face—under a bushy white-boy Afro—filthy with soot.

Some perverse trick of the air currents carried his voice to Harper. She knew his cat screech right away, remembered it well from the afternoon the Marlboro Man had almost found her hiding in her house.

"This is the real shit!" Marty screamed. The gun stammered in his hands. "This is the real commando shit right here!"

To the north was the bare, muddy expanse of the soccer field and the overturned Hummer. A pair of black pickups had parked themselves out there, to cover the double doors that led out of the basement. Through the haze it was hard to tell how many men were in the flatbeds, but Harper saw a steady pop and blink of gunfire, going off like camera flashes. The Freightliner lumbered down the hill, moving to join the others on the north side of the chapel. Maybe Jakob hoped the basement bulkhead would fly open and some folks would make a desperate run for it and he'd have something to do with his plow.

It was harder to see to the south. There was a stretch of grass as wide and even as a two-lane avenue, in the space between the church and the forest. Harper knew the Marlboro Man was down there, in his big silver Intimidator, but she could only barely glimpse the top of the cab by craning her head. It was parked too close to the building to see it well.

A black and filthy smog poured from below, seeping out from under the eaves and boiling through the open hole in the bell tower just exactly the way it would've come streaming out of a chimney. A sickly firelight throbbed within the churning smoke. Harper suspected the tower was only dimly visible from below, maybe the only thing they had going for them.

All that smoke mounted into a soaring cloud bank that spread to the east, back down the hill toward the water. Harper couldn't see most of the sky, the cloud smothering the stars and the moon.

The roof was fifteen feet below the railing of the tower and it was a steeply banked surface of black slate. Harper saw herself leaping, falling, hitting feet-first, her ankles rupturing, crashing to her hip with a glassy crack, sliding straight down the side of the roof, and a tearing inside as her uterus came apart and—

"Fuck that," she said to herself.

She crawled over to be next to Allie.

"How's my mouf?" Allie asked.

"Not too bad," Harper said.

"Fuck you it isn't. I love it. I'm punk rock now. I always wanted to be punk rock." Allie feathered a hand back through Nick's hair. "I tried to do the right thing at the end, Ms. Willowes. Maybe I flunked the exam, but at least I did pretty good with the extra credit."

"Exam in what?"

"Basic humanity," Allie said, blinking at tears. "Will you hold my hand? I'm scared."

Harper took her hand and squeezed.

The Fireman worked his way around the catwalk to the south-facing side of the turret, to be next to Jamie.

"Fuckers in the Silverado," Jamie said. "They're too close to the side of the building. I can't get a bead on them. If we could drive them off, we could hang a rope—"

"What rope?" the Fireman asked.

"I don't know. Maybe we make a rope out of our clothes. We get into the trees. Run for the road. Steal a car." Her voice was hurried and distracted, leaping from one improbability to another. "I know people in Rochester. They'll hide us. But first we need to drive off that truck."

The Fireman nodded, wearily. "I might be able to do something about them."

But when he tried to stand, he swayed, dangerously. Harper saw his eyelids flutter, as if he were an ingénue in a 1940s musical comedy trying to look kissable. For a moment it was all too easy to imagine him dipping backward and falling over the waist-high iron railing around the hole in the center of the tower, dropping away into the smoky dark.

Jamie caught his elbow before he could topple. Harper cried out, let go of Allie's hand, and scrambled around the catwalk toward him. By the time she reached him, he had sunk back to one knee.

She touched his cheek, felt clammy sweat.

"Is the bell droning?" he muttered thickly.

"No," she said. "Not at the moment."

"Christ. That sound must be in my head, then." He pressed the balls of his palms to his temples. "I think I'm going to be sick."

"Don't try to get up."

"We need to drive them back if we're going to have any chance of getting down from here."

"Stay down. Get your wind. You're no good to anyone if you pass out."

She let go of his hands and stood, pouring all her heart into a wordless song. Her right hand was a scimitar of flame. Get a spoonful of this, motherfuckers.

Harper launched a curved blade of blue fire into the darkness. It whizzed, dropping gobbets of blazing light as it flew, and hooked unnaturally just beyond the roof of the chapel, dropped out of sight onto the Silverado Intimidator below. Men shouted as the hood of the truck was blown off in a spout of light.

Bullets spanged and pinged into the bell, hit the railing, flew through the air with an angry whine like lead wasps, and Harper dropped again, her flaming hand fluffing out in a billow of smoke.

One of those bullets struck the rope that held the bell in position, cutting through all but a few strands. The giant bell spun, making a low humming sound. The last few braids of line holding it up popped and broke musically, like guitar strings. The bell fell through the open hole. A moment later it hit the floor of the church below with a resounding *BONG* that shuddered upon the air, visibly shook the smoke around them, and made Harper's eardrums throb.

Nick lifted his head and looked around with muddled eyes. The bell was so loud, Harper thought, it had woken the deaf.

"Oh Christ, what the fuck now—" Jamie shouted, looking north and then scuttling past the Fireman and around to that side of the tower.

Jakob.

The Freightliner had turned to face the broad north side of the church. With a grinding roar it came thundering forward, plow lowered, toward the side of the chapel.

Jamie stood with the rifle socked into her shoulder. She fired. A white spark dinged off one corner of the cab of the truck. She levered back the bolt and the empty cartridge jumped into the air, a bright glitter of brass. She slammed in a fresh bullet and fired again. A blue crack leapt through the windshield. The truck jigged a little to the left, and Harper thought, *Got him*, but then the Freightliner shifted into a higher gear and lunged the last fifty feet and the snow-wing plow buried itself into the side of the chapel.

Harper was thrown into the stone baluster. It felt as if some vast invisible hand had reached down and *adjusted* the entire building, prying it free from its foundation to shift it a few feet back to the south. The rear north corner of the chapel collapsed with a groan and crash of falling slate and smashed wood. A great burning heap of it dropped on the front of the Freightliner, the plow disappearing into curdled smoke and pulverized debris. The jolt rocked the tower. Jamie had been stepping back to open the bolt of her .22 and was thrown onto her heels. Her ass hit the low metal railing over the open hole. She dropped the rifle and grabbed—at air.

"Jamie!" Allie screamed—screaming for the girl who had slashed open her face—but she was beneath Nick and couldn't even stand up, and anyway there was no time.

A moment later, the bell donged softly below when Jamie struck it.

The Fireman looked around in a daze, blood dripping from his face. Harper pushed his hair back from his eyes and then gently, carefully, put her arms around him. It was time to stop fighting, she felt. It was time to just hold each other, the four of them, their fucked-up little family. Five of them, counting the baby. They would cling together and there would be love and closeness at the end. They would have that at least until Jakob backed up and hit the chapel again, closer to the tower this time, and dropped them all into the flames.

The bell below was still echoing. It ding-ding-dinged with a small, piercing, *golden* sound, a noise like a much smaller bell. The Fireman lifted his head and peered out into the smoke, down along the south side of the chapel.

The fire truck—with Gilbert Cline behind the wheel, one hand out the window to ring the brass bell—launched itself through the boiling smoke to the south of the church and hit the Chevy Silverado head-on. The old fire truck with the number 5 on the grille weighed almost three tons. It flattened the front end of the Intimidator like a bootheel coming down on a beer can. The Chevy's engine block came right back through the dash and cut the driver in two. The pickup lifted off the ground, front wheels spinning in the air for a moment, before it turned over on the gunmen in the flatbed.

And still the fire truck pushed the Chevy along, shoving it through the dirt to the very front of the church. The fire engine lurched to a stop with a gasp of its air brakes. A chubby little woman with gray in her cornrows dropped from the passenger seat and hustled around to the chrome step on the back bumper.

Renée climbed to the top of the fire truck and lifted the wooden ladder, turned it on its swivel to face the side of the church. The ends of the ladder banged against the exterior wall. Then Renée stood there, looking to the left and right, as if she had dropped something, an earring perhaps, and was trying to spot it. She bent and opened a compartment on the roof of the truck, looked in at a collection of fire axes and steel poles. She shook her head in frustration.

"It's right at your feet!" the Fireman hollered at her. He seemed to know what she was looking for instinctively. He cupped one hand around his mouth and repeated: *"AT YOUR FEET."*

She squinted up at him, peering into the wafting smoke, and swiped sweat off her cheeks with the back of one arm. She looked down again, between her feet, then nodded and dropped to her knees. There was a rusty iron crank set in a circular depression in the roof. She began, effortfully, to turn it. The wooden ladder vibrated, trembled, and began to bump up the side of the church toward the tower.

In the circle of standing stones, the guy Harper knew as Marty craned his neck to see what was going on past the overturned Chevy. A bullet spanged off the stone bench, right in front of his legs, and he screamed and reeled back and got his feet tangled and fell.

"Damn it," Allie said. She was standing all the way up, the butt of Jamie's rifle resting against her shoulder. She worked the lever and an empty shell casing made a bright leap into the night.

Harper was looking at Allie, not down at the fire truck and the overturned Chevy, so she didn't see a bald man in a blue denim shirt drop out of the Silverado's passenger seat. But she spotted him right away when she glanced back. There was an embroidered American flag on the back of the shirt, the brightest thing in the gloom. He was bleeding from the scalp and staggering a little. He was broad-shouldered and barrel-chested, built like an aging running back who was keeping active in the gym to slow the slide into middle age. He had a gun, a black pistol.

The fire ladder thudded, bumped, and got caught under the eaves, halfway up to them.

The guy with the gun—Harper felt sure it was the Marlboro Man; with that American flag on the back of his shirt, he had to be—began to creep forward toward the driver's side of the fire engine.

"Renée!" Harper screamed. "Renée, watch out! He's coming!" Stabbing a finger and pointing.

Renée Gilmonton stood on the roof of the truck, holding the ladder in both hands, adjusting it somehow, trying to shift it around so it could get up past the eaves. When she had it the way she wanted it, she stepped back and squinted toward the steeple.

"Watch out! Gun!" Harper screamed.

"Guy with a gun! Guy with a gun!" the Fireman yelled.

Renée pointed to her ear and shook her head. She dropped to one knee and began to work the crank again. The ladder whacked against the edge of the roof, rising once more toward the steeple, climbing into the sky a few inches at a time.

The Marlboro Man had crawled all the way around to the cab of the fire engine and crouched beneath the driver's-side door.

Harper rose, thinking, *I will throw fire and strike him down and save my friends.* She began to sing inside once more, singing without words. The Dragonscale scrawled on her palm brightened steadily like an electrical coil heating up. But her hand was thrumming and sore and wouldn't light, and while she was waiting for that first rush of flame, the Marlboro Man stood, planted his foot on the running board, stuck his gun through the window, and fired.

Renée stiffened, lifted her head, looked toward the front of the truck, and then dropped flat on her stomach, spreading out across the roof of the fire engine.

The ladder remained twelve feet out of reach.

Allie's rifle cracked. There were six men with guns in that circle of stones and she was keeping them there, hiding behind rocks. She cursed and loaded a fresh shell.

The Marlboro Man flattened himself against the side of the fire truck and vanished from sight. Harper couldn't see him from her angle. Neither could Renée. But he was down there—working his way along the side of the truck and into a position where he could rise up and shoot Renée Gilmonton.

Harper realized that Nick was standing next to her, staring below with a sleepy, dazed expression. She reached for his shoulder and turned him so his face was pressed to her breast, much as she had done almost a year ago to a boy named Raymond Bly, who wanted to look out a window and see what was happening in the school playground. She didn't want Nick to see what happened next—although she herself could not look away.

Renée held herself flat and very still on the roof of the fire truck. Her right arm was the only thing moving—she was feeling around with one hand. Her fingers found the edge of the compartment she had opened up when she was looking for a way to raise the ladder. She reached inside and grasped the handle of a fire ax.

The Marlboro Man came up like Jack out of his box, his mouth stretched wide in a humorless animal grin, pointing the gun over the roof. Renée brought the ax down on his wrist and he fell back screaming. He left his hand behind on the roof, still squeezed tightly around his pistol. Renée batted it with the blade of the ax, knocking it away from her. The Marlboro Man's right hand skidded over the edge of the roof and out of sight.

The Marlboro Man howled, his voice a low, deep cry of fury and hurt that seemed to echo up from the bottom of a well.

Renée sat on her knees, on the edge of the roof. She turned her head and looked toward the cab. Renée shouted something, but Harper was too far away to hear exactly what she said. Once she thought she heard Renée calling for Gil. Renée sat there for what seemed a long time, although in fact it was only a matter of seconds. Then she turned herself about and began to work the crank once more. Turning it with a kind of dull exhaustion now.

The Marlboro Man screamed and screamed again.

The Freightliner produced a grinding cough and began to

back up. Another shudder ran through the entire church as the plow pulled loose from the hole it had made, and debris came spilling out into the soccer field.

The big truck backed fifty yards from the chapel, then slammed to a stop. Jamie had put a spiderweb fracture in the windshield on the driver's side, and Harper had a sudden thought: Jamie had managed to hurt Jakob, had taken something out of him. Had maybe even come close to killing him.

Allie dropped the rifle and sank to a crouch.

"I'm out!" she yelled. "No more bullets."

The handles of the fire ladder bumped into sight as it made its slow, hitching way up to the railing. The Fireman stood—rocking a little on his heels—reached over the side, and steadied it.

"Go. Down. Now. You first," the Fireman said, nodding at Harper.

"Nick—" she said.

"Allie will have to take him on her back."

"I've got him," Allie said, crawling around the catwalk to Nick.

On the other side of the church, the Freightliner began to move, rumbling toward the base of the bell tower.

Harper didn't like heights, and the thought of putting her leg over the side made her feel dizzy. But she was already straddling the railing, reaching with one bare foot for the first rung.

She glanced over her shoulder, searching for the ladder, and saw the fire engine forty feet below, looking small enough to pick up with one hand, and for a moment it seemed to her the entire bell tower was nodding like a flower, about to dump her. She clenched her hands on the stone railing and shut her eyes.

"You can do this, Harper," the Fireman said, and kissed her cheek.

She nodded. She wanted to say something cute and daring, but she couldn't swallow, let alone speak.

Harper swung her other leg over the side.

She moved her right foot down to the second rung, let go of

the stone railing, grabbed wildly, got her hands on the ladder. The whole thing wobbled unsteadily beneath her.

On the far side of the building, she heard the distinct sound of the Freightliner chunking into a new gear as it sped up.

She had descended not more than five rungs when the Fireman helped Allie over the side, Nick clinging to her back. Allie scrambled after Harper, wearing Nick as lightly as she might've worn a backpack for school.

The Fireman put a leg over the railing, planted one boot on the top rung. His other foot found the second rung. He reached down and put one hand on the ladder itself, stood there clinging to the very, very top of it.

The Freightliner hit the north side of the chapel doing nearly fifty miles an hour. It turned at the last instant, swiping away the entire front corner of the church, throwing enough wood and stone and glass to fill a dump truck.

The steeple lurched, steadied for a moment—and caved in. One moment it was there. The next it wasn't. It dropped in on itself, the stone railing, the balusters, the bell tower roof, the beams, the wooden catwalk. It collapsed with a wrenching boom that Harper felt in her chest, like a throb in the blood. All at once the top of the fire ladder swung in empty air. John Rookwood hung suspended at the pinnacle. A black gush of smoke spun up from the ruin, obscuring him in a whirl of spark-filled darkness.

A blast of cold wind that smelled of the sea carried some of that smoke away a moment later, and the Fireman was gone.

Harper opened her mouth to scream, but then her gaze found him, already ten rungs down from the top and making his way hand over hand toward the earth below. The ladder shook and bounced in the open air. Allie was moving so quickly she was almost stepping on Harper's hands.

Harper made her effortful way toward the engine below. Lower down, the ladder still had some roof to lean against. The southern half of the church remained intact. Harper didn't know she had reached the roof of the truck until she felt metal under her bare feet. She stepped off the ladder on shaking legs and looked around for Renée. She wasn't on top of the engine anymore, had climbed down at some point.

Now Harper felt shivery and weak, cold even in her bones. The shuddering was moving from her legs to the rest of her body. Her first thought was that she was going into shock. Then it occurred to her it might be something else entirely. John had said casting flame used up calories and oxygen and afterward you were dazed and ill and could easily get into trouble if you didn't find a place to rest.

She went unsteadily to the rear of the truck, where there was an old short ladder of rusted iron. She climbed down it to the bumper and stepped off, and her legs collapsed on her without warning. She sat ungracefully in the wet grass. Sparks and smoke whirled slowly above her, like a carousel coming to a halt.

She forced the feeling of weakness back and used the bumper to stand.

*"Oh, you cunt! My hand! My HAND!"*

Harper came around the side of the fire engine, moving toward the screaming. The Marlboro Man was on his back in the grass, arching his spine and digging his heels into the mud. He looked like he was trying to push his way across the dirt on his back. He held his right wrist with his left hand. There was no right hand. There was only a broken bit of pink bone sticking out, where the hand belonged.

Harper stepped over him to get to Renée, who was leaning in the open driver's-side door. When Harper got there, Renée was cradling Gilbert Cline in her arms. Blood still leaked from the bullet wound in his neck, but without much enthusiasm. There was blood all over the front seat.

Harper noticed—almost absently—a severed hand, still clutching a gun, set carefully in on the dash. Renée had thoughtfully picked it up and put it where the Marlboro Man couldn't go after it in an attempt to get his Glock back.

"We were almost to the end of *Watership Down*," Renée said.

"Gil said he never thought he could like a story about talking animals so much. I said life was strange, I never expected to fall in love with a man who stole cars." She was not weeping and spoke with great clarity. "He hot-wired the truck. We couldn't find the keys. While he was doing it, he told me he was just more proof that most criminals went right back to what they knew best as soon as they got out. He said he was sorry to be adding to the recidivism rate. It took me a moment to realize he was joking. He was very dry. He didn't even *smile* at his own jokes, let alone laugh at them. Didn't give you any clues he was being funny. Oh, Harper, I don't want to try and live without him. I feel like I spent my whole life unable to taste food. Then Gil came to camp and suddenly everything had flavor. Everything was delicious. And then that awful man shot him and Gil is dead and I'll have to go back to not being able to taste things again. I don't know if I can do that."

Harper wished there were something to say. Maybe there was, and she was just too wobbly and light-headed to think what. Instead she put her arm around Renée and clumsily kissed her ear. Renée closed her eyes and lowered her head and wept in a very quiet, private way.

The Marlboro Man shrieked.

Harper turned and saw Allie standing over him. Allie had her brother in her arms again. She had paused, Harper thought, to kick the Marlboro Man in the ribs.

"Oh, you fuckin' bitch, you're gonna burn, and I'm gonna jack off on your charred fuckin' tits," the Marlboro Man said.

"You want to jack off," Allie said, "you're going to have to learn how to do it with your left hand, stumpy."

"I don't think he should live," Renée said, wiping her face. "Not when so many other people are dead. It doesn't seem fair."

"Do you want me to kill him?" the Fireman said. Harper hadn't realized he was on the ground, standing behind her. He was swaying himself, and looked as bad—maybe worse—than she felt. Sweat crawled on his wasted, white face. His eyes, though, were as dark as crow feathers, and perfectly serene.

He put a hand on the fire ax that leaned against the side of the truck.

Renée thought it over, then shook her head. "No. I guess not. I suppose I'm very weak and foolish, not to get even while I can."

"It makes you the furthest thing from weak I can imagine," the Fireman said. He looked back at Allie, who had joined them. "You'll have to drive the fire truck, Allie. And you'll have to find somewhere you can hide all of you, somewhere nearby. I'll meet up with you later."

"What are you talking about?" Harper asked him. "You're coming with us."

"Not now. Soon."

"That's crazy. John. You can't be on your own. You can hardly stand."

He waved this notion away, shook his head. "I'm not seeing double anymore. That has to be a sign of progress." And when he saw her expression, he insisted, "I'm *not* abandoning you. *Any* of you. I swear I'll be with you in no more than a day. Two at most."

"How will you find us?" Harper asked.

"Nick will send for me," the Fireman said, looking over Allie's shoulder into Nick's swollen, filthy, dazed face.

The Fireman did something with his hands, moving them here and there. Nick blinked slowly and seemed to nod. Harper thought the Fireman had said something about birds.

Renée said, "We'll have to squeeze in with Gil. I hope that's all right. I won't leave him here."

"No," Harper said. "Of course you won't."

Renée nodded, then climbed up on the running board and gently eased Gilbert aside, making room behind the steering wheel.

The Fireman turned and strode across the matted grass. He crouched over the Marlboro Man.

"You," the Marlboro Man said. "I know who you are. You're going to die. My man Jakob is going to spread your faggot British ass all over the road. He's going to paint the highway with you. Jakob loves killing the burners—he says it's the first thing in his life he's ever done really well. But he's looking forward to doin' *you* most of all. He wants to do it while she watches."

"Jakob likes finishing off burners, does he?" the Fireman asked. He lifted his left hand and a trickle of green flame fluttered like a silk ribbon from the tip of his index finger. The Fireman gazed into it in a sleepy, speculative way, then blew it out, leaving the tip of his finger gray with ash. The Fireman lowered his hand and spread the ash across the Marlboro Man's forehead, drawing a cross. The Marlboro Man flinched. "*Well.* You better get up and get moving then, soon as you can. Because you're one of *us* now, friend. That ash is full of my poison. Maybe, if you're lucky, you'll find a few other people who are infected who will shelter you and look after you, as the folk in this camp once did for us. Maybe—but I doubt it. I think most people will close their doors in your face the moment you open your big mouth to ask for their help. You have a quite recognizable voice."

The Marlboro Man kicked his feet against the ground and slid six inches across the dirt, shaking his head frantically, and began to shriek. "No! No no no, you can't! You can't! Listen to me! *Listen!*"

"Actually," the Fireman said, "I think I've heard more than enough. The only thing worse than listening to men like you on the radio is meeting you in real life. Because out here in the world there's just no simple way to change the station." And he kicked him—lightly, almost humorously—under the jaw. The Marlboro Man's head snapped back and his teeth clapped shut on the tip of his tongue, and his scream became a high, hideous, inchoate keening.

The Fireman started away, staggering a little, his coat flapping about him.

"If I don't see you by tomorrow night," Harper shouted at him, "I'll come looking for you."

He glanced back over his shoulder and gave her a crooked

smile. "Just when I thought I was out of the frying pan. Try not to worry. I'll be with you again soon enough."

"Come on, Ms. Willowes," Allie said. Allie was in the truck now, behind the steering wheel, hand on the door and leaning out to look down at her. "We have to go. There's still men with guns out there. There's still that plow."

Harper jerked her head in a nod, then cast her gaze around for a last look at John. But he wasn't there. The smoke had claimed him.

# 11

The fire truck bashed aside the wreck of the Chevy Intimidator with an almost casual indifference, sent it spinning toward the circle of stones. It struck one of the monoliths with a ringing clang. Marty Casselman was approaching the overturned Chevy when the fire engine struck it. He dived out of the way, but the Uzi in his right hand went off in a chattering blast, and the spray blew off three of his toes.

The big Freightliner was backing from the half-collapsed bonfire that had once been a chapel. The driver saw the fire truck banging up the hill, but by the time Jakob got the Freightliner turned around, his wife, Renée Gilmonton, and the two children with them were long gone.

# 12

Allie pulled the truck to a stop where the dirt lane met Little Harbor Road.

"Where to now?" she asked.

Harper looked out the passenger-side window toward the rusting blue hulk of the school bus. The headlights were on. A skinny girl of about fifteen, with a shaved head, slumped behind the steering wheel. Someone had left a machete in the back of her skull.

Nick reached up to touch Harper's chin, physically turning her head toward him. He was sitting in her lap. He stank of burnt hair, and it looked as if he had gone bobbing for apples in red Kool-Aid, his face was so stained and sticky with blood—but his eyes were more alert now. He spoke with his hands.

"Nick says he knows a place we can go," Harper said, then narrowed her eyes. She replied with some gestures of her own: "What place?"

"Trust me," Nick told her in sign language. "It's safe. No one will find us. It's where I hid everything I stole." He met her gaze with a haunted solemnity. "I'm the thief."

# BOOK NINE

# ENGINE

# 1

In the minutes after midnight—as March became April—the fire engine rushed along Little Harbor Road, following it all the way to where it ended at Sagamore Avenue. Nick gestured for Allie to turn right. They had gone less than a mile before Nick began to signal for her to stop.

Allie turned into the entrance of South Street Cemetery, a graveyard as old as the colonies and half a mile wide. She stopped in front of the black gates, which were held shut by a length of heavy chain and padlock. Nick opened the passenger door and leapt out of Harper's lap.

Nick gripped the chain in one hand and bowed his head. Liquid metal hissed and dripped between his fingers into the dirt. The chain fell apart in two sections and he pushed the gate open, his hand still smoking. Allie drove through and then waited. Nick reached back through the bars, wound the two halves of the chain into a loose knot, and gripped it firmly. There was more smoke and his eyes were as red as coals and when he let go he had welded the links together again.

South Street Cemetery was a kind of city, in which most of the residences were located underground. Nick guided them along its streets and alleys, its winding suburbs and open pastures. They continued until they had reached the dirt road that ran along the back of the cemetery. A second, more modest sort of graveyard awaited in the wet grass and underbrush: a dozen cars in various states of collapse, filthy, burnt out, sitting on their rims. Several were half submerged in weeds, islands of rust in a shallow sea of poison sumac.

To one side of this final resting place for unmourned cars was a squat and ugly cement building with a tin roof. Cobwebbed windows peeked out from under the eaves. At one end of the building was a pair of corrugated aluminum garage doors. The center of operations for the grounds crew, Harper surmised . . . back in the days when South Street Cemetery still had a grounds crew. The knee-high grass growing right up to the front steps suggested it had been a while since anyone had punched his card for work.

Out beyond the wrecks was a wide sandy pit, some kind of debris piled into it, hidden under overlapping brown plastic tarps. Allie parked the truck between the hole and a Pontiac Firebird that had cooked down to the frame. She hunted around under the steering wheel, found a couple of bare wires twisted together, and pulled them apart, with a buzzing snap of electricity. The fire engine chugged, thudded, and died.

They sat in the stillness. Through the oaks at the rear of the park, Harper could see a flat bay, a pebbly strand, and some darkened buildings on the far side of the water. Come to South Street Cemetery. Beachside views available. Quiet neighbors.

"This is only good until the sun comes up. Then this truck will be visible from the air," Renée said.

Harper looked at the garage doors of the building for the grounds crew and wondered if there was enough room in there for an antique fire truck. Nick let himself out of her lap again, throwing open the door. He hopped into blowing mist.

"I don't think this is far enough from Camp Wyndham, either," Renée went on. Her voice had a dull, disinterested quality. She sat on Harper's left, holding Gilbert in her arms. He was between her legs, his head lolling against her shoulder, and her arms were around his waist. "There's a path in the woods. It's only fifteen minutes from here to the archery range. I walked here once or twice myself last summer."

"But it's almost four miles by the road," Allie said. "And they'd expect us to keep driving. No. I think this might do if we can get the truck under—what's he up to?" Unbuckling and letting herself out.

Nick had clambered into the sandy pit. He pulled back one

flap of a tarp to reveal a midden heap of shriveled flowers, blackened wreaths, and mildewed teddy bears. Even grief, it seemed, had an expiration date. Allie caught up to him, found another corner of the tarp, and helped him drag it toward the fire truck. They would only need a couple of them to hide the engine completely.

Harper got down, put her hands in the small of her back, and stretched, popping her spine. She ached as if she were recovering from flu, every muscle sore, every joint achy.

She looked back into the truck at Renée. "We're going to cover the truck and go inside." When Renée didn't reply, Harper added, "I think you should get out now."

Renée lifted her shoulders in a weary sigh. "All right. Will Allie help me carry Gil inside?"

Allie and Nick had by then dragged the tarp to the side of the truck. Allie stiffened and darted an uneasy look at Harper. Harper nodded to her, just slightly.

"Of course I will, Ms. Gilmonton," Allie said, in a tone of insouciance that didn't jibe with her pale look of dismay.

Easing the heavy corpse of Gilbert Cline out of the fire truck was a clumsy bit of business. Renée held him under the armpits and heaved and gasped, nudging him toward the passenger door a few inches at a time. Allie got him by the ankles and they began to shift him out, but Renée bumped her head and lost her grip, and the top half of his body dropped all of a sudden. His head bonged against the step up into the cab. Renée made a shrill yelp of horror and almost fell out after him.

"Oh no!" she said. "Oh no, oh no, oh, Gil, I'm so weak. I'm so useless."

"Hush now," Harper said, moving past Renée and bending to get Gil under the arms herself.

"You can't," Renée said. "Don't, Harper. You're nine months pregnant."

"It's no trouble at all," Harper said, although when she straightened up, her ankles blazed and her back twinged.

They walked Gilbert through high weeds, wet grass shushing against his back. His head lolled. He wore a stoic, almost patient look, his clear, quite blue eyes seeming to watch Harper the whole time.

They had to put the dead man down when they reached the corner of the garage, so Harper could rest and Allie could look for a way in. The door was locked and there was no key under the mat or beneath either of the ceramic flowerpots on the front step (pots full of dirt and a flourishing crop of decorative weeds). But Nick didn't mean to enter through the door. He made his way along the side of the building, peering up under the eaves. At last he stopped and gestured to one of the windows. It was a good five feet over his head, so high up under the eaves it was hard to imagine it let in any daylight. The window was a long, narrow slot, and a triangular piece of glass was missing from one smashed pane. No man could put his hand through the gap, but a child's arm just might fit.

Nick needed Allie to hunch down, so he could climb onto her shoulders. Even when she rose to her full height, he could barely reach the glass. He had to stretch to get a hand in through the window and turn the lock. He pushed it open, grabbed the sill, hoisted himself up, and disappeared headfirst into the darkness.

There must've been something just inside the window to climb down on—some shelving perhaps—because Harper didn't hear him drop. He was gone without a sound.

"I wonder who helped him get in there last time," Harper said, and when Allie gave her a questioning look, she nodded at the high window. "He's obviously done this before, but he's too short to reach the window on his own."

Allie frowned.

The front door popped open and Nick stuck his head out and waved for them to come along, come in, his house was their house.

# 2

When day broke, the engine was completely covered by a pair of tarps, one over the front, another over the rear. Harper had imagined they might be able to put the fire truck inside, but the garage already contained a John Deere and a backhoe. An orderly if cobwebbed collection of rakes and shovels hung from hooks on one wall. An expansive worktable ran the length of the other. That was where they put Gilbert, covering him with a third tarp.

At the back of the garage, a bank of windows looked into a cluttered office: two desks, a corkboard on the wall, an empty water cooler, and a couch the creamy green hue of snot. That was where they slept. Harper took the couch. Allie and Nick slept in each other's arms on the floor, wrapped in a gray blanket that Allie found in a back compartment of the fire truck. Renée didn't join them. She sat on a stool beside the worktable, holding Gilbert's hand. Sometimes she talked to him. Sometimes she laughed, as if he had said something clever. Often she just moved her thumb across his knuckles, or pressed his cold hand to her cheek.

Nick had told Harper he was the thief and promised to take her to where he had stashed the loot. But the Portable Mother was nowhere in sight. The same went for all the other little valuables that had gone missing from camp. Harper assumed Nick would explain when he was ready.

She curled up on her side under a black Windbreaker. The jacket had a print of Death himself on the back, one skeletal hand clutching a scythe . . . and the other raising a lacy bra. GRAVEDIGGERS LOCAL 13—BAD TO THE BONE, it said. The Windbreaker smelled of coffee and menthol and made her think of her father, who was always smearing Bengay on his bad neck. She cried herself to sleep, thinking about her dad, who might be dead now and who she doubted she would ever see again in her life. But she wept quietly, not wanting to disturb anyone else.

When she woke, the children were yet asleep. Was Allie still a child? Looking at her smooth cheek and long eyelashes, Harper wanted to think so. Even in sleep, though, she had a whittled-down quality that made her look very much like a young woman, worn by her cares and worries, too busy to think the things that made children happy.

Harper gazed through one of the picture windows facing the garage and saw Renée had climbed up onto the plywood table and dozed off against Gil, one plump hand resting on his chest. The high windows under the eaves looked out on featureless darkness. Harper had slumbered through the day, and might've slept through much of the next night if she weren't so hungry. They would have to do something about food soon.

The office had a Formica counter with a sink, a microwave, a Mr. Coffee, and a radio that was so old it had a cassette player built into the front. It was plugged into a wall socket, but of course there was no power. There was a fridge, but Harper didn't look inside, didn't want to smell what might be in there. She turned the radio around and found a battery compartment in the back. It required six big D batteries. There was a package of fresh D-cells in the third drawer she tried.

Harper carried the radio out of the office and into the cool, stony quiet of the garage. She paused at the workbench, beside Renée and Gil. The tarp had slipped down to their waists. Gil's shirt was unbuttoned slightly and Renée's hand was curled on his chest, her cheek against his shoulder.

Written in faded blue letters, ornate, almost Gothic, across Gil's chest, were two lines:

It is impossible to go through life without trust:
that is to be imprisoned in the worst cell of all, oneself.
—G. Greene

Harper lifted the tarp up, smoothing it over the two of them, and left them to each other.

She settled on the cement step in a night of surprising, almost liquid warmth, filled with cricket song. She flexed her toes in the damp, gritty loam. When she tipped back her head and looked into the sky, she saw so many stars it made her ache with love for the world. And what a thing: that she still loved the world, even now. The face of the radio glowed a lightning-bug green. What was better than a warm spring night, bare feet in the warm dirt, the smell of budding trees in the air, and a little music on the radio? All she was missing was a cold beer.

She dialed through the FM bands, hoping to hear Martha Quinn and knowing she wouldn't. She didn't. Through a hiss of static she brought in a station playing archival recordings of black gospel, but after a few songs it faded out. Farther down the dial she found a young man—or was it a kid? His voice had the high-pitched, strained quality that Harper associated with incipient puberty—reporting from Red Sox spring training in Fort Myers. She stuck there for a while, pulse thudding heavily, shaken by the thought that baseball was going on somewhere in the world.

But after half an inning she began to suspect the kid of making it all up as he went along. Bill Buckner was playing first base again, over twenty-five years since his last game, and every single ball went between his legs. Vin Diesel was batting as the Red Sox's designated hitter and stroked a ball right at a shortstop named Kermit deFrock. When deFrock caught it, the force of the hit pulled his arm out of its socket. The Sox were playing a team called the Heretics, largely made up of Muppets, monsters, and madmen, who erupted into flames and died on the field whenever they made an error. Harper listened, smiling, for another inning. The Sox were up 3½ to 1 when she changed the station. She wasn't sure how they had scored half a run. The kid doing the announcing sounded about eleven and like he was having the time of his life.

Down at the very bottom of the dial she found a boys' choir singing "O Come All Ye Faithful" and stopped to listen, and at some point she realized she was crying. She had not wanted any of them to die. Not a single one, and it didn't matter how hard it had been to live with them.

When the song faded out, a woman began a report, "Today in Blessings." It was news, of a sort. She said word had come in that J. K. Rowling, author of the godless Harry Potter novels, had been killed by firing squad in Edinburgh. Her execution had been televised on what remained of the Web. She was scribbled all over with the devil's handwriting and had used her money and status to protect and transport others who were sick. When offered the chance to ask forgiveness for her many sins—deluding children, hiding the contaminated—she scorned the opportunity and said she would not apologize for a single adverb. The announcer accounted it a blessing that she would burn eternally in hell, praise Jesus.

In local blessings, the National Guard, supported by the Seacoast Incinerators—a volunteer militia—had discovered six hundred infected sinners hiding on the grounds of Camp Wyndham. A pitched battle ensued, ending when the sick burned to death in a church they had converted to a heavily armed compound, say hallelujah.

Farther north, new fires had started in the south of Maine, but in a sign of the Lord's mercy, the blaze was contained to a mere twenty-mile swath. The New Hampshire Soldiers for Christ had pledged to send more than a hundred men and a dozen fire trucks within the week. Grand Corporal Ian Judaskiller was in close communication with the Maine forest services and stood ready to help any who heard and accepted the truth of his own divine revelations, glory be. Grand corporal? His former title had been governor, but then, his former name had been Ian Judd-Skiller.

The boys' choir returned to sing something in Latin.

When Harper lifted her gaze, Nick sat on the other end of the step, squeezing his knees to his chest.

"Nice out," she said, but with gestures, not her voice. "I love a warm night. Almost like summer."

He nodded, just a little, his chin hovering right above his knees.

"Eat we have to," she said, knowing she wasn't getting it quite right. "I'll find eat. Bring here. Don't worry if me not back soon."

He shook his head.

"I know where there's food," he told her with his eloquent, expressive hands. "Come on."

He pushed himself up and led her into the graveyard.

# 3

For a while they followed the road that ran along the back of the cemetery. Then Nick turned in among the headstones, through the waist-high grass. The boy paused at an old, rough, grayish slab of rock with the name MCDANIELS upon it. He squatted down and touched the edge. Harper saw a dash of bright red paint.

He turned and went on and she followed. At a blue marble slab commemorating the life of one ERNEST GRAPESEED, Nick bent, pointed to another little red line, then looked meaningfully back at her.

Nick finger-spelled: "Nail polish."

Harper remembered, then, one of the first things to go missing: a bottle of red nail polish that had belonged to the Neighbors sisters. Each believed the other had swiped it and there had been a nasty fight.

He led her up and down the rumpled green earth. The grass was growing long throughout the cemetery. Harper thought by mid-June, all but the highest plinths would be sunk deep beneath a riot of wild green. That didn't seem so bad to her. She thought there was more beauty in wildflowers and tufts of beach grass than there was in a whole park of groomed lawn.

They came to a crypt, the walls of white stone buried under vines of ivy and oily green leaves. A captain's wheel had been stamped into the lead door, above the name O'BRIAN. A chunk of rock, with another little dash of fingernail polish on it, held the door slightly ajar.

Nick put a shoulder to. The door slid inward with a grinding shriek.

There was no light to see by and Harper wished she had brought a flashlight—there *had* to be one back in the garage—

but Nick moved quickly around to one of the stone caskets against the wall. His fingertip ignited, spilling a ribbon of bluish-green fire. He touched it to a series of candles, most of which had been melted down to deformed stubs, then shook the flame out.

Harper's carpetbag sat on one of the caskets. Allie's gold locket hung from the handle. Harper felt funny all through her middle, seeing the Portable Mother again. It was like running into someone she had fancied a long time ago—in high school perhaps—and discovering he was just as good-looking as she remembered.

A giant teacup, the size of a soup bowl, sat on another stone coffin lid. Emily Waterman's special cup of stars. The inside was crusted with ancient gobbets of dried meat. Stacked against the wall were three cans of Spam, three cans of condensed milk.

The boy hitched himself up to sit with candles on either side of him. Harper sat across from him, inclined her head, and waited.

"I was trying to catch the cat," he said with his hands. "A big cat with stripes like a tiger. When I stroked him, I could feel him humming, like a small motor. I can't *hear* purring, but I can *feel* it, and nothing feels better. But when I tried to capture him, he always got away. Once I had him trapped in a box and carried him halfway back to camp. But he pushed his head out through the bottom and jumped away."

She nodded to show she was with him so far.

"Michael said he'd help me catch it. It was supposed to be a secret. We'd catch him together and bring him back to camp and I could keep it. Mike told me to sneak Spam and milk out of the cafeteria. He met me with things *he* took out of camp, like soda and candy bars. I asked if we'd get in trouble and he said not if no one found out. I knew we were being bad kids. I felt sorry—*sometimes*."

"But it was nice, too—Michael was paying attention to you," Harper said, moving her hands very deliberately to be sure she said exactly what she meant.

Nick nodded, with an eagerness that broke her heart a little. “Most of the other kids never seemed to even notice I was there. None of them understood sign language—and I can’t follow spoken conversation. I’d sit with them in the cafeteria, but most of the time I couldn’t figure out what they were talking about. If they all laughed, I’d smile, like I knew what was funny, even though I didn’t. They could’ve been making jokes about me, for all I knew.”

He lowered his head, looked at his hands. They twitched, made little motions, and Harper thought, with a flush of surprise and pleasure and sadness, that he was talking to himself, and those little finger-wiggles were his version of a whisper. At last he lifted his chin and met her gaze and began to speak again.

“Mike didn’t know sign language, but we wrote each other notes. He was really good about waiting for me to finish writing when I had a lot to say. He could sit there just swinging his feet for five minutes while I scribbled away. Most people aren’t very patient. He helped me build traps for the cat. Some of our traps were really funny. Right out of comic books. One time we stole a camouflage Windbreaker, and stretched it out over a pit, and covered it with leaves. Like maybe the cat would be stupid enough to fall in.”

Harper remembered the day a camouflage Windbreaker had gone missing. It had belonged to a teenage girl named Nellie Lance, who had been miffed and baffled by its disappearance. *There are literally ten thousand nicer coats she could’ve stolen,* Nellie said.

She. They had always believed the thief was a woman. Everything that disappeared went missing from the kitchens or the girls’ dorm. But of course there was *one* male in the girls’ dorm. Nick had spent the entire autumn there, sharing a bed, at first with his sister, then, later, jumping into Harper’s cot with her.

Nick went on, “Everything we stole from camp we hid here. I used the nail polish to make a trail, so we could always find our way to the stash. Sometimes we broke into the garage for the grounds crew. Mike figured out he could put me up on his shoulders and I could get in through the window."

"People got angry," Harper said. "When you knew people angry, why no tell? You could have explained all and no one mad."

"You're going to think I'm an idiot."

"Try me."

"I didn't know anyone was even *looking* for a thief. Not for a long, *long* time. Everyone was talking about it, but no one was talking to *me*. People made announcements in chapel that I couldn't hear. I asked Mike sometimes what everyone was talking about, but he always said it was nothing. Once, Allie was so angry she was shaking, and I asked her why, and she told me some bitch was stealing from the girls' dorm. I was such a big dummy, I didn't even know she was talking about *me*. I thought someone *else* was stealing things. *Important* things. Stuff that really mattered. I only took nail polish and a stupid teacup and Spam. Everyone hated Spam." He lowered his eyes. "And once I took Allie's locket." Then he looked up, a bright challenge in his eyes. "But only because it was supposed to be *my* locket too. We were *supposed* to share. But Allie said lockets are for girls and so she kept it all to herself and never let me wear it or even look at it."

"What about Portable Mother?" Harper asked.

He rested his chin against his chest and blinked. Tears plopped on his thighs.

"I'm sorry."

"Don't sorry. Tell why."

"Mike said it was big enough to put the cat in it. He said it would be really useful for a trap and we could give it back to you later. I wasn't going to take all the stuff in it, too . . . not at first. I was going to empty it out and just take the bag. But then I remembered my View-Master."

"What?"

He twisted around and popped the carpetbag's gold clasp. He fished around inside and came up with a red plastic View-Master.

"I remember. Carol gave me," Harper said. "For baby."

His face darkened. "It wasn't hers to give. It was *mine*. Aunt Carol told me one day I was too old for it and then she gave it to you. She told me to be a big boy about it. So I took the whole bag. I stole it. Even though you're my friend. And it was really bad." He swiped at his eyes with one hand. The muscles under his face trembled with the force of barely contained emotion. "After I took it, I *wanted* to give it back. I really did. Michael met me here in the tomb and said we couldn't risk it. He said Father Storey had announced that the person who stole the Portable Mother would have to leave camp forever. He said stealing from a pregnant woman was the worst sin this side of murder. Mike told me I couldn't even return it in secret, because Ben Patchett would fingerprint it. And Allie told me whoever took the locket was going to have her hands cut off. Even still I thought I could tell Father Storey what I had done. I was going to. As soon as he got back from rescuing the prisoners with the Fireman. And then—" His hands stopped moving for a bit, while he rubbed the balls of his palms into his eyes. Soon, though, his fingers began to move again. "Mike said maybe it was *lucky* for me Father Storey got smashed in the head. He said he was pretty sure Father Storey *suspected* me. He said before Father Storey got his head crunched, he warned Mike he was going to have to ask me some tough questions about the things that had been stolen, and if I didn't answer them right, he'd probably have to send me and Allie *both* away, forever and ever. Mike said Father Storey would get rid of us both because it was Allie's job to make sure I behaved. And Father Storey also said it was important that the camp knew he wouldn't treat me different just because I was his grandson."

"He lie. Lie bad. Father Storey never hurt you or sister. He never let anyone else hurt you."

She could see Nick didn't want to look at her, didn't want to make eye contact—but it was the curse of the deaf that they could not hide their eyes if they wanted to communicate. He had to keep his gaze on her hands. He blinked at tears and dragged the back of one arm across his nose.

"I know *now.* But I was scared. And that's why I stayed with you in the infirmary. So if Father Storey woke up I could tell him I was sorry and ask him to please not punish Allie for anything I did. And Mike said that was a good idea, and he'd hang around the infirmary, too, as much as he could. That way if Father Storey woke up, he could take most of the blame. Mike said he ought to accept most of the responsibility anyway because he was older."

"Not you fault," Harper told him with her hands. "Michael was a liar. He fooled *all* of us."

Nick's shoulders hitched convulsively. He lifted his hands and dropped them, lifted them and tried again. "I woke up once and got up to go to the bathroom and found Mike bending over Father Storey's feet. He was surprised to see me and stood up really fast and looked scared. And he had a needle in his hand. I asked him what he was doing and he said he had come by to give himself his insulin shot and then he stopped to say a prayer over Father Storey. He was trying to kill Father Storey, wasn't he?"

"Yes. When happen?"

"February."

Harper thought back and nodded. "Father Storey stop having fits in February. That's when he start getting better. After the fits stopped. You saved Father Storey's life. You scared Mike after you caught him with needle. He didn't try poison again."

Nick shook his head. "I didn't save him. Michael still killed him."

Harper leaned forward and put her elbows on her knees. "But not before Father Storey woke and tell you how much he loved you. You understand? You were very love. You are not no bad boy."

Nick looked so disconsolate she had to get up and kiss his head and give him a squeeze.

When she let go of him he was at least not crying anymore. She said, "Do you think that can with meat still good?"

"It was *never* good. But we can probably eat it."

Harper gathered up the Spam and condensed milk in both arms. When she turned around, Nick stood before her, wearing the locket around his neck and holding the Portable Mother open wide. She nodded in approval and dropped the cans inside.

They slid themselves out into the darkness and started back the way they had come. They had not gone more than a hundred feet, though, when Harper heard the whine and roar of a big and familiar engine, a sound that made her insides clump nervously together. She grabbed Nick's shirtsleeve and pulled him down to a crouch behind a Virgin Mary.

The orange plow rumbled past out in the street, spoiling the night with its diesel stink. It moved slowly and a searchlight mounted to the top of the cab dipped and swayed, flashing over the stone wall and into the graveyard. Ten-foot-long shadows of angels and crosses lunged across the grass toward Harper, then retreated. She let out an unsteady breath.

Still out there. Still looking. He knew what they had fled in. Maybe he knew they hadn't gone far. A fire truck was not the world's most discreet getaway car.

She turned to look at Nick—and was surprised to find the boy grinning broadly. He wasn't peering toward the street, but instead was staring intently across the gravel road that bordered the back of the cemetery, watching something in the high, tangled undergrowth. Harper saw ferns twitch as something slipped away.

"What?" she asked him with her hands.

"The cat," he told her. "I just saw the cat. It survived the winter, too."

# 4

Harper was prepared to step between Allie and Nick, was ready for threats, tears, and flying furniture. But Allie did not seem even a little surprised to see the Portable Mother again, or to find Nick wearing her locket. When they reentered the office, Allie sat on the edge of the couch, rubbing her face with both hands. She looked at them with blurred eyes and asked no questions. Harper took a can of Spam out of her carpetbag and hunted in the cupboard for something to spread it on. She discovered a box of saltines and felt a twang of gratitude that approached the spiritual.

Nick planted himself in front of Allie, chin stuck out, waiting for her to say something. She did, at last, finger-spelling only: "I guess you can wear it. I thought it would make you look like a little girl, but at least you're a cute girl."

Harper found a cassette, the Rolling Stones' *Aftermath,* and punched it in the cassette player. Mick Jagger warned his baby, baby, baby that she was out of time. *Just about,* Harper thought.

Harper gave Allie the shorter version of what Nick had told her in the tomb, while she spread gelatinous Spam on crackers. Allie did not interrupt or cross-examine. When Harper had finished and they were all sitting on the couch together, eating pasty meat, Allie used her fingers to say, "I can't believe you fell for Mike's BS about fingerprints. That's pretty dumb even for you."

Nick said, "I know. But by the time I started to think Michael was wrong about fingerprints, there was snow on the ground, and no one could leave camp, so there was no way for me to bring anything back without leaving footprints. Besides. *You* were the dummy who told me when they found the thief, Ben was going to cut off his hands in front of the whole camp."

She nodded. "Don't sweat it. You're just nine. You're *supposed* to be dumb. I'm seventeen. What's my excuse?"

When had Allie turned seventeen, Harper wondered, and then it crossed her mind she had missed her *own* birthday, four weeks before.

"How long will the Spam hold out?" Allie asked. She slurred a little. Her upper lip was ugly, split in two halves where Jamie had slashed her mouth. Harper needed to poke around for a needle and thread.

"We've only got two cans so . . . not long."

"Good. Because it will be sweet mercy when it's gone and we can starve to death in peace."

"I was hoping to avoid that," Harper said, and began to speak to Nick again with her hands. "The Fireman said you can find him and show him where we are."

"If I have to."

"You have to."

"I'd need to throw fire. I don't like to."

"I know you don't."

He gave her a wary, haunted look. "Did John tell you why?"

Harper nodded.

Allie looked slowly back and forth between Harper and Nick.

Harper was going to try and speak to him with her hands, but this time sign language wouldn't do. She got up and hunted in the drawers and came back with a pad of paper and a ball-point pen.

*What happened was not your fault. It takes a minimum of six weeks for the spore to reach the part of the brain that makes controlling it possible. Maybe longer. Your mother wanted to animate fire, the way John does with his Phoenix or you did last night with your little birds. But her brain wasn't ready. What she did was like inducing labor before a baby is prepared to survive outside the womb. Instead of a child, you get a miscarriage. But she didn't know. Neither of you did. THIS IS NOT YOUR FAULT. Or hers. It was a shitty accident. That's all.*

But he shook his head, folded the note once, twice, and pushed it down into his pocket. His face—swollen from crying, pink where he had burned himself, filthy and still bloodstained—had nothing like ease or acceptance in it.

"You don't know," he said with his hands. "You don't have any idea."

Before she could reply, he pushed off the couch with both fists and went to the door out into the garage. He looked back.

"You coming or not?" he asked with his hands.

He led them behind the building. A pulsating harmonic filled the night, seemed to make the air itself vibrate: the shared song of a thousand crickets. Nick moved away from them, into the high grass. He paced in a circle, tramping the grass flat. Wet weeds squealed under his sneakers. He went around and around, going faster and faster, his head swinging back and forth. His fingers danced and played and Harper thought he was singing without a song, listening to a melody that had no sound. Asking for what he wanted without words. It was a little frightening, watching him go about like a figurine in a silent music box lurching along its track. His eyes were closed. Then they weren't. They snapped open, peepholes into a furnace. His fingers trailed orange sparks.

He lifted his left hand and flame trailed off it. Little flames sheared from his fingers, fluttering into the air, but instead of shrinking and vanishing, they took shape, became dainty birds of fire. A burning flock of them fell streaming from his blazing hand and shot this way and that, spinning like rockets into the night. A dozen. Two dozen. A hundred.

"My God," said Renée, who had come to the back door to watch. "How come they don't just burn up and vanish? What are they using for fuel?"

"Him," Allie said and nodded at her brother. "He's the kindling and the firewood both. The lighter fluid and the match."

"No, that isn't right," Harper said. "That doesn't make any sense. I haven't been able to figure this part of it out yet, no matter how much John has tried to—"

But Nick had stopped going about in a circle. He rapidly flailed his hands back and forth and put them under his armpits and the bluish-yellow streamers of flame went out in a whimsical pink gush of smoke. He bent over to blow on his palms, and while he was leaning forward, something gave, and he toppled headlong into the grass.

Allie got to him first, scooping him up in both arms. His head lolled on a neck that didn't seem to have any bones in it. Allie glared.

"He wasn't ready to do that," Allie said. "He's been through too much. We should've waited another night. *You* should've waited."

"But John—"

"John Rookwood can take care of himself," Allie said. "Nick can't."

And she marched past Harper into the garage.

It was what Allie needed, Harper supposed: a chance to stand up for her brother, to reclaim the role of Nick's protector from Harper—or at least reclaim a share of it.

"I really don't understand," Harper said to Renée. "What Allie said just now about Nick being the kindling and the kerosene—that has poetry in it, but it doesn't make a lick of sense."

"That's what poetic speech is for—for the things that are true but don't make sense. For the rough beast and the widening gyre," Renée said, and she lifted her gaze to stare into the night, where a hundred flaming birds turned in a widening gyre of their own before scattering into the stars.

# 5

Harper found fishing line and a hook in a tackle box under the worktable, and used them to put two stitches in Allie's upper lip. Allie sat rigidly while she sewed, gaze pointed toward the ceiling, eyes welling with angry tears. She made not a sound the whole time. Harper wasn't sure if that was the silent treatment or stoicism.

When she was done, Harper worked on Nick. He was deeply asleep and only frowned while Harper put four stitches into his torn forehead. She used the same needle, but she sterilized it by holding it between thumb and forefinger until the steel glowed hot and white.

After, Harper went outside to sit on the stoop and watch the clear night sky. Sometimes it seemed that one of the stars came loose from the firmament and sailed off with dizzying speed to a far corner of the night. In the dark hours before sunrise, constellations came apart and reformed and fell in burning streaks.

At last, in the gray light of dawn, a small sparrow of fire zigged out of the trees behind the graveyard and exhausted itself in a whiff of smoke. A moment later the Fireman followed it, staggering from the forest and into Harper's arms.

The sight of him appalled her. The long gash on his left cheekbone was a ragged line of black gum. The side of his neck was baked red with what looked like an agonizing sunburn. He stank as if he had rolled in the ruin of a campfire.

In his left hand swung a steel bucket full of coals.

"I saved her," he gasped. "We need to put her someplace safe and get her some fresh wood." He gave Harper a frantic look. "She's starving."

He only reluctantly allowed Harper to pull the bucket out of his hand. The tin handle was hot—maybe searing—but Harper's palm lit softly and she felt no pain.

Harper set the pail on the stoop and guided him inside.

He passed out almost as soon as she was done sewing up his slashed cheek. She left him on the couch, where he slept with his own turnout coat as a blanket.

She went outside again, feeling very tired and very pregnant. The small of her back was a continuous shriek and she was experiencing sharp pains of a gynecological nature.

The bucket of glowing coals sat on the rear step, next to the tape deck. Mick Jagger promised he was going home, over a strutting bass line. Those coals swelled with brightness, faded and swelled again, matching the rhythms of the song.

Harper had an urge to kick the bucket over into the grass.

Instead she carried the pail to a big steel drum, standing in the weeds behind the garage, one in a cluster of garbage cans. She poured the coals in on top of old rubbish: splintered boards, rusting beer cans, oily rags. Flames guttered and jumped, the garbage igniting with a soft, hungry *whump*. Harper found some sticks and a rotten log crawling with bugs, fed them to the blaze.

"What's that?" Renée asked. "Cook fire?"

"More like one of these fires you light to remember someone by."

"An eternal flame?"

Harper said, "I hope not."

# 6

They slept on the couch in shifts, ate the Spam, drank the cans of milk. It was hot and close in the garage, stale with the odors of potted meat, concrete, and diesel. They would have to do something about Gil soon. In another day he would begin to spoil.

When the sun was down, Harper slipped out the back door for fresh air. It was better under the stars. The night had a nearly liquid quality, was like sliding into a warm swimming pool, a pool filled with buoyant darkness instead of water. When Harper wasn't paying attention, it had turned full lush spring.

A knot popped in the trash can. Harper turned to look and saw Allie standing over the flames, looking down into the coals with wide, dazed, frightened eyes. She hugged herself tightly, hands squeezing her elbows.

"You okay?" Harper asked.

Allie turned and looked at her blankly.

"No," she said, and went inside.

Harper peeked into the flames herself, but saw only coals.

She sat on the back stoop. She counted how many days till she was due, then counted again to be sure. She made it eighteen if she delivered on time. Sometimes women were late with the first baby.

She listened to *Aftermath* and rested her hands on the hilarious globe of her pregnant belly. But she had to turn the Stones off when it got to "Under My Thumb." She had all her life longed for a world that operated like an early-sixties Disney musical, with spontaneous song-and-dance routines to celebrate important events like sharing a first kiss or getting the kitchen spick-and-span. If she couldn't have *Mary Poppins,* she would settle for *A Hard Day's Night*. But it turned out life was more like the kind of song the Stones wrote: you didn't get any satisfaction, you took one hit to the body after another, if you were a woman you were a bitch who belonged under someone's thumb, and if you wanted mother's little helper from your dear doctor you better have the silver, take it or leave it, and don't come crying for sympathy, that was just for the devil.

She twiddled through the channels. A gospel group clapped their hands for Jesus. The Spring Training boy was back: the Red Sox were having an exhibition game against the Shakespeare All-Stars. Romeo was up to bat. He struck out, broke his bat over his knee, swallowed poison, and died on home plate. Juliet ran over from the on-deck circle, wept for a few moments, then stabbed herself through the heart with the shaft of his Louisville Slugger. The pitcher, Tom Gordon, waited with his hand on his hip while Rosencrantz and Guildenstern dragged the bodies off the field.

Farther down the FM dial, a woman reported that Senior Field Marshal Ian Judaskiller had signed an execution order for the Fireman, who had murdered two New Hampshire Soldiers for Christ in the firefight at Camp Wyndham three days before. In other news, twelve thousand godless Japs had killed themselves in the largest mass suicide ever recorded, in Okinawa. In Iowa, a herd of cows had been photographed from the sky in the formation of a cross. The last days had come and soon the last seal would be opened and the final trumpet would sound.

Something feather-light brushed her knuckles. Harper looked down and found a bushy cat, dark with golden stripes, lifting its chin to sniff at the smell of Spam under her fingernails. Harper studied him for an instant—feeling, somehow, that she had seen this cat before—then reached out to stroke his head. He shrank from her touch, launched himself into a damp green tunnel in the high grass, and was gone.

Harper was still staring after him when John Rookwood stepped out onto the stoop, dressed for duty in his helmet and coat.

"Where do you think you're going?" she asked.

He looked down at himself, as if to remind himself of what he was wearing. "*Well.* I can't go to a funeral dressed like this. And you can't go to one dressed like *that.*" Nodding at her begrimed Boston Red Sox hoodie and sweatpants. The sweatpants had once been blue, but were now mostly black with soot, and smeared with bloody fingerprints. "So I suppose I'm going shopping."

"Are we burying Gil?"

"I think we're burying the whole camp," he said. "In a manner of speaking. Renée needs that."

"We all need it."

He dipped his head in a single nod and began to amble away.

"They're looking for you," she told him. "I heard it on the radio."

"They better be careful," he said, without looking back at her. "They might find me."

# 7

He was back two hours after sunup, pushing a rusted shopping cart through the strangling grass. He bumped it over the back step and into the garage.

The cart was overflowing with suit jackets and ties, dresses and blouses, boots and high-heeled shoes, scarves and hats. Beneath the heap of laundry was enough food to get them by for another week: some canned fruit, a box of instant oatmeal, and a six-pack of soda, an off-brand called Nozz-A-La that Harper hadn't seen since she was a kid. Dropped in among the groceries was an audiocassette. Harper didn't have a chance to look it over. The Fireman plucked the tape up and put it in his coat pocket.

"Memorial this evening. Dress appropriately," he said.

"I get the top hat," Allie said, and delicately set a black stovepipe on her head. "Top hats are metal."

Nick found a pair of opera gloves and pulled them on. They were so long they came to his shoulders.

It was the first time Harper had seen him smile in weeks.

# 8

The mourners crossed the wild grass of the cemetery beneath a star-flooded sky. The Fireman led them, one hand burning blue. Nick walked in the middle, trailing green fire from his fingers. Harper brought up the rear, her own hand a candelabra of gold flame.

The Fireman had converted the shopping cart to a makeshift bier. He had placed two planks across the length of it and secured them with bungee cords. The dead man had been set on top in the tarp that served as his shroud. Renée pushed it along and Allie followed, carrying the tape deck, the music already playing, turned low.

Allie looked good, in her top hat and a black duster that swooshed about her ankles. Nick had ultimately passed on the opera gloves, but he wore a canary yellow tuxedo jacket with tails and his mother's locket. Somewhere the Fireman had come up with an enormous black Patriots hoodie for Harper, an XXXXL. For an enormously pregnant woman, it was the best that could be managed for proper mourning weeds. Renée crossed the graveyard in a midnight blue velvet dress, slit high enough to show the dimples in her knees. She had very sleek, very nice legs. Harper hoped Gilbert had properly appreciated them.

Who knew where the Fireman had got what *he* was wearing: a kilt that showed his bony, hairy legs, a black beret, and a short black suit jacket. Harper didn't believe he was making fun of the occasion. She had an idea this represented his most heartfelt effort to look respectable.

The Fireman pushed open the door of O'Brian's tomb with his burning hand. The flame lit a tidy marble cube, the shadows hovering, seeming to sway to the melody. He had found a copy of Dire Straits' *Making Movies,* and they were listening to "Romeo and Juliet." It sounded good, mixed with cricket-song.

He extinguished his right hand before he walked the shopping cart in. Renée followed, and on the count of three they moved the shroud off the cart and onto one of the stone caskets. Nick lit candles with his fingertip. Allie joined with the tape recorder, but Harper remained just outside, her own hand burning without any sensation of heat at all. It comforted her. That bright blaze seemed to her, that evening, to be her own soul made visible.

The song echoed in the little stone cabinet and in a soft voice, Harper began to sing along. The Fireman joined her, and as he began to sing, he reached back to take one of Renée's hands. Nick took another. The little boy reached for his sister and his sister reached for Harper, joining them in a swaying human chain. Renée lowered her head and shut her eyes, perhaps to cry, perhaps to pray. Only when she looked up at last her irises were threaded with light. The coils of Dragonscale around her bare arms lit a deep shade of plum, traveling down to her wrists. The glow leapt from her hand to the Fireman's and to Nick's. Harper felt her own 'scale respond, a rush of light and warmth.

They glowed in the darkness, all of them: pale shining wisps with rings of light where their eyes belonged, as if *they* were the dead—ghosts risen from their graves—not Gilbert Cline. Harper felt their grief as a slow current of cold water, and herself as a leaf revolving upon it.

As she moved to the music she felt her own self slip away, her own particular Harper-ness. Her identity wouldn't float and was swallowed by the stream flowing through all of them. She was no longer Harper. She was Renée, recollecting Gil's sandpapery cheek against her neck and the sawdust smell of his hair. She recalled the first time Gil had kissed her in a corner of the basement, one hand firmly against the small of her back, as if she had experienced it firsthand. Cobwebs on the bare dead lightbulb overhead. Smell of dust and old brick, the pressure of his dry lips on hers. She was adrift on Renée's memories, rushing along over the surface of them, carried over a drop and into—

—a memory of Carol holding her and rocking her the night her mother died. Carol had held her and rocked her back and forth and been wise enough to say nothing, to offer not a single false word of comfort. Carol was crying, too, and their tears fell together and Harper could taste them right now, standing in the tomb, could taste what Allie had tasted the night Sarah Storey burned. Her perceptions were a leaf, turning rapidly now, spilling again over another fall into—

—a remembrance of being thrown. Gail Neighbors had grabbed her by the ankles and Gillian had held her wrists, and they swung her back and forth like a hammock and chucked her into a giddy silence and she fell soundlessly onto a cot, her lungs convulsing with laughter she couldn't hear. In the awesome quiet of Nick's deafworld, colors seemed to shout. How he had loved the way they tossed him again and again, how he had loved their happiness, and how he missed them and wished he could have them back. But Harper's consciousness was rushing on, plunging over the highest fall yet, into a grief so deep it was almost impossible to see to the bottom of it, cascading into—

—John's head and what thoughts he kept there of Sarah. Harper felt Sarah sitting in her lap, and her nose was in Sarah's hair, savoring the delicate sugar-cookie smell of her. She was working on a crossword, nibbling on her ballpoint pen in thought, and what grace, what confidence it required to do the puzzle in pen! A perfect square of sun was on the curve of her slender brown shoulder. Harper had never been so acutely aware of light and stillness without being high on mushrooms. She thought, with a kind of savage joy, of her father, that brilliant, literary, distant, resentful drunk. *I get to be happy,* Harper thought, in an English accent, *and that means I beat you. That means I won.* Sarah pressed herself back against Harper's bony chest. *Five-letter word for abiding joy,* she asked, and Harper touched her hair, pushing a strand of it behind her pink, delicate ear, and whispered *today.* To have had such contentment and lost it was like a burn that never healed. To think of her was like picking up a hot brand, was being seared afresh.

And on at last into her own smooth pool of hurt, of homesickness for all the good things that had once been hers and were gone now: coffee in Starbucks while the cold drizzle hit the windows, vacuuming in her underwear and singing along to Bruce Springsteen, letting her gaze wander over the spines of books in a little bookstore with high shelves, eating a cold apple in the front yard and raking, hallways full of babbling laughing scuffling children at school, Coca-Cola in a glass bottle. So much of what was best in life went unnoticed in the moments you had it.

The fading current turned her little leaf around and around and slid her away from all memory, away from pain, and on finally to a firm, sandy shore. The cassette player clicked off. The song was over.

# 9

She sat on a sandy bank, her shoulders resting against the grooved stone wall of the tomb. The Fireman sat next to her. Somehow they had wound up holding hands. He had brought the radio outside and it was tuned to the FM. A choir chanted a ringing, mournful plainsong. Stars gritted the night.

Harper had the light, flowing sensation of being just mildly drunk. She was relaxed and it felt good to put her head on his shoulder.

"What's Renée doing?" she asked.

"Still inside. Talking to her man. Going over the things she loved best about him. And what they would've done if they had more time."

"The kids?"

"Walked back to the garage. I found a bag of marshmallows. They're going to roast them, I believe."

"Do you think it's . . . safe? For them to cook marshmallows?"

"*Well,* when you consider all they've been through, I don't think there's much to fear from hot marshmallows. Worst-case scenario, someone burns the roof of their mouth."

"I was thinking of what they might see in the fire."

"Oh." He pursed his lips. "I don't think she'd reveal herself to them casually. And perhaps Sarah would like to see *them.* We aren't the only ones who feel sick about all the good things that are gone now. We aren't the only ones who need to grieve."

She ran her thumb over his knuckles, squeezed his hand.

"I haven't been so drunk on the Bright . . . well, I haven't even been *part* of the Bright in six months." He sighed. "I haven't really needed the protective benefits of harmony since I learned to communicate with the spore directly. I forgot how good it feels. Even when what's being shared is painful, it's a good pain."

Had they really shared memories and thoughts, after all? Harper was of two minds about it. The kids of Camp Wyndham had always believed the spore was a kind of network, a sort of hive mind worn right on the skin, an organic web that anyone who was infected could plug into. There wasn't any doubt that it could carry ideas and feelings. Then again, when one was riding high on the Bright, one was prone to fantasy. The gift of telepathy sounded nice, but Harper thought possessing an imagination was good enough.

A star fell. She wished for him not to move, to stay right where he was, with her head on his shoulder. If time were ever to snag in place, she wished for it to snag there, with John pressed against her and spring breathing in their faces.

He sat up so quickly she almost fell over. He reached across her and fiddled with the volume.

The crazy woman was talking about Grand Panjandrum Ian Judaskiller.

"Oh, this nutty bitch," Harper said. She wouldn't toss around the word *bitch* sober, but she was a lot less prim when she was drunk, which was how she felt now. "You know, every time she mentions this guy Ian Judaskiller, she gives him a different title. One minute he's grand marshal, the next minute he's field general. One of these days she's going to say he's been anointed the mighty muffsucker—"

*"Shh,"* he said, holding up one hand.

She listened. The woman on the radio said His Honor had promised to send twelve fully manned trucks into Maine to fight the resurgent wildfires, with the crews ordered to depart at noon Friday, praise Jesus and the holy host—

"We'll go with them," the Fireman said.

"Go with Jesus and the holy host?" she said. "I thought that's what we were trying to avoid."

"The fire crew," he said, his eyes large in his bony face. "We'll drive right across the bridge and into Maine with them. They'll wave us right through with the others." He turned his head and met her gaze. "They're leaving in two days. We can be on Martha Quinn's island by this time next week."

# 10

When it was time, John woke her with a touch, his knuckles lightly brushing her cheek.

She rubbed her face, sat up on her elbows. "I don't—what? Isn't it too early? I thought they weren't moving out until noon on Friday."

Allie sat up on the floor. Nick was asleep on his side next to her. She yawned hugely into the back of her hand. "Is it noon?"

"Is it Friday?" Harper asked.

"Yes to Friday, no to noon. Only about eight. But if you come outside, you can *hear* them. I told you we'd have plenty of advance warning when they were ready to go. Why do you think so many little boys want to be firemen when they grow up? So they can blast the siren. A dozen trucks were bound to make enough noise to wake the whole city."

He wasn't kidding. Harper heard them even before she stepped out into the smoky, slightly chill morning air: the whoop and shriek of competing sirens, going off less than half a mile away. One would blurp and cry out for a few moments, then go silent, and another would take its place. John had predicted they would mass up at the central fire station, just beyond the town offices, and only a short jog down the road from the cemetery.

"How much of a rush are we in?" she asked the Fireman.

"We don't want to cross the bridge ahead of them, obviously," he said. "But we wouldn't want to be too far behind them, either. Come along. Let's get the kids in the truck." As if they were old hands at parenting and were referring to their own children and a planned drive of some distance to see disagreeable relatives. Harper supposed Allie and Nick *were* their children now.

Renée was already at the back of the truck, opening the wooden cabinets located above the rear fender. The engine had rolled out of a Studebaker factory in 1935, forty-eight feet long, as red as an apple, and as sleek as a rocket in a Buck Rogers strip. It would always look splendidly like the past's idea of the future, and the future's idea of the past. The cabinets were full of filthy fire hose, rows of steel fire extinguishers, heaps of coats, and ranks of boots, extending away into a cavernous darkness. It seemed perfectly possible that Narnia might be found somewhere at the back of one of those compartments. Renée lifted Nick up and he scrambled in.

"Get under the hose," Renée told him, and then *tsk*-ed herself for trying to talk to him. "Harper, will you tell him to bury himself under the hoses?"

Harper didn't need to. He was already at it. Allie leapt up on the chrome bumper, scrambled in beside him, and began to help, artfully arranging coils of hose on top of him.

"This is almost exactly how Gil got out of jail," Renée said.

"Where do you think John got the idea?" Harper asked. "Gil's still helping us, you know."

"Yes," Renée said and squeezed Harper's hand. "I'll get my things, such as they are. And the radio. Don't leave without me."

Harper loaded the Portable Mother in the right rear compartment, setting it behind three rows of chrome fire extinguishers, next to a bag of groceries. There was space back there for Renée and Harper to cuddle together out of sight, beneath a mover's blanket.

And the Fireman—the Fireman would drive.

"I hate that part of the plan," she said to him.

The Fireman was on the running board, next to the passenger side of the cab. He had a bucket of coals in his hands. He set it next to the exhaust pipe, which protruded into the air from a ledge behind the cab. John leaned in and she saw the tip of his pointer finger light up, turning red and transparent—Harper thought inevitably of *E.T.*—brightening until it hurt to look at. Sparks spat as he welded the pail to the outside of the exhaust pipe with his finger.

"What part of it?" he asked, absently.

"The part where you try to drive this thing across the bridge. They're hunting you. There are people who have seen you, who know what you look like."

It had even crossed Harper's mind that the whole thing was only a ploy to draw them out, this well-advertised caravan of fire trucks heading to Maine to fight the fires there. The more she considered it, the more she thought it was quite possible they were driving into a trap and would all be dead by teatime.

In the end, what made up her mind to risk it was a series of contractions that lasted half an hour and made her womb feel like a mass of swiftly hardening concrete. At one point, the pain was so sharp and so rhythmic, and her breath was so fast and short, she was sure the baby was coming. In that precise moment of near-total certainty, the contractions began to abate, and soon they had passed entirely, leaving her in a nasty sweat, with trembling hands. Two weeks—only two weeks till her due date, give or take a few days.

What they were doing now was a desperate lunge, like soldiers in the First World War heaving themselves out of a trench and sprinting into no-man's-land, never mind that the last four waves of soldiers to go over the top had been cut to pieces. But they could not stay, because you could not raise a baby in a trench.

It wasn't just a matter of safely delivering. It was about what happened in the minutes, hours, and days afterward. Especially if the boy didn't have the 'scale. It had been months since she had last seen any data, but back in the days when she still had Internet, there were some numbers to suggest as many as 80 percent of the children of the infected were born healthy. The little guy was going to be pink and clean, and the only way to make sure he remained that way was to find someone healthy who could take him away . . . a thought she refused to give close consideration. First she had to find a place she could bring the baby into the world. Then she would work out the next part, locating a home for her uninfected child. Presumably the doctors on Martha Quinn's island were not carrying 'scale. Perhaps one of them would take the infant. Perhaps her baby could even remain on the island with her!

No. That was probably too much to hope for. She was determined to accept whatever would be best for the child, even though she thought that meant it was likely the day of his birth would be the last time she ever saw him. She had already decided that when the moment came, she would handle it like Mary Poppins. She told herself the child was only hers until the west wind blew . . . and when the gale came, she would calmly open her umbrella and float away, leaving him in the care of someone loving and trustworthy and wise, if such a thing could be managed. She could not have him, but he could have her, in a sense. The Portable Mother would go with him.

"I don't think Nick knows how to handle a vehicle with a standard transmission. Renée has never driven anything this big. Allie is too young. You are too pregnant. Besides—the fuckah they're lookin for talks like Prince fackin' Charles, not like Don fackin' Lewiston," the Fireman told her, his vowels going long, his *R*'s disappearing, so that all at once he sounded as if he were from Manchester in Maine, not Manchester in the United Kingdom. "I can sound like I'm from around here for a few minutes, long enough to get us through the checkpoint."

"What about your wrist?" Harper asked, touching his right arm. The wrist was still bound in filthy tape.

"Oh, it's well enough to use a gearstick. Don't worry yourself, Willowes. I'll get us through the checkpoint. You forget how much I enjoy performing."

But Harper was only half listening to him.

Renée had come to a stop ten paces from the truck and stood bent at the waist, holding her knuckles down so a long-haired cat with golden stripes could sniff at the back of her hand. The cat had come out of the grass with bits of dead leaf stuck in its fur and its tail in the air. He purred so loudly it sounded like someone had started up an electric sewing machine.

Nick had crawled out from under his piles of hoses to stare. He looked back at Allie with sudden excitement and began to gesture with his fingers. She came forward on all fours.

"He says that's the cat he's been feeding since last summer," she said.

When Harper looked back, the big tom was in Renée's arms. It narrowed its eyes in contentment. Renée had set the radio down in the dirt and was gently running her fist down the cat's spine.

"This is *my* cat." Renée looked dazed, as if someone had just woken her up from a deep sleep. "My cat that I let go last May. It's Mr. Truffles. Well, Truffaut, actually, but Truffles to his friends."

The Fireman hopped down off the running board. His face was stony. "You sure of that?"

"Of course I am. I think I know my own cat."

"But he doesn't have a collar or tags. You can't be positive."

Renée flushed. "He came right to me. He jumped into my arms." When John didn't speak, she added, "Why shouldn't it be him? This is my neighborhood. I use to live right on this street, you know. A mile south of here, but still *this* street."

"The cat stays," he told her.

Renée opened her mouth to speak, caught herself, and stared at him—first with incomprehension, and then with a dawning look of acceptance.

"Of course," she said. "It's absurd to think—of course, you're right."

She rubbed her nose against the cat's and set him gently in the dirt.

"No!" Allie cried. "What are you doing? We can take him."

"That's right. I can keep him with me," Harper said.

She was thinking about the expression she had glimpsed on

Renée's face when she recognized her cat. It had been more than a look of pleasure—it was a flash of shock. Harper thought some part of Renée had given up on happiness—had left it behind in the tomb with Gilbert—and the possibility of delight had blindsided her. Nick, too, had already jumped down out of the truck and dropped to his knees in the dust, was carefully creeping toward it with an intent, almost mesmerized expression. The cat twined between Renée's ankles and watched the boy with wary jade eyes.

"And if they look in the rear cupboards and discover him?" the Fireman asked.

"They'll think a cat stowed away in your truck. They'll laugh over it."

"No. They'll start digging around, is what they'll do."

"Let's vote," Harper said.

"No fucking vote! It isn't safe. The cat stays."

Harper said, "Mr. Rookwood, I have had my fill of people claiming the unique authority to decide what is and isn't best for others. I tried marriage, and had five years of being told the things that made me feel like a human being were no good for me. I tried religion—the scared church of the holy sing-along, temple of the Bright—and got more of the same. We're on to democracy now and we're going to vote. Don't pout, you get one, too."

"Three cheers for the electoral process!" Allie cried.

The Fireman swept a hostile glare across her and her brother. "Most societies recognize that children are not well enough informed to participate in public debate."

"Most children haven't saved your scrawny and ungrateful ass from a public stoning. We vote. All of us. And I vote cat," Harper said.

"I vote for a feline-free future," the Fireman said, and stabbed a finger at Renée. "And so does she. Because unlike you, Renée Gilmonton is a woman of reason, logic, and caution, *aren't* you, Renée?"

Renée wiped the back of her hand against a wet cheek. "He's

right. If anything happened to the kids because we brought the cat along, I couldn't bear it. It's an unconscionable risk. And besides I—I suppose it might not be my cat after all."

"You are lying, Renée, and I see right through you," Harper said. She turned her head and glared with a righteous fury at the two children. "How do you vote?"

"I vote cat," Allie said.

Nick put his thumb in the air.

"You are both outvoted!" Harper cried. "Mr. Truffles comes with us!"

Renée shivered. "Harper. *No. Really*. You don't—we can't—"

"We can," Harper said. "We will. Democracy, motherfuckers. Get used to it."

Mr. Truffles rubbed his spine up against Renée's ankle and looked at Harper with an expression that suggested the matter had never been in doubt.

# 11

Harper stretched out in the dark beside Renée with the cat nestled between them, in the space behind three rows of fire extinguishers. Allie and Nick had settled under the hoses in the other compartment. Harper's face was buried in Mr. Truffle's fur and with each inhalation she smelled the last nine months of his secret cat life: must, dust, grave dirt, basements and tall grass, beach and drainpipe, Dumpster and dandelions.

The truck droned and thudded. They were on South Street now, Harper could tell by their slow progress and all the swaying. There were a lot of curves on South Street. They hit a pothole and her teeth banged together.

"It used to be five hours to Machias. How long do you think it takes now?" Renée asked softly.

"We don't know what the interstate is like. The fire last fall burned from Boothbay Harbor to the border. Thousands and thousands of acres. Who knows if we'll be able to drive the whole way. If we have to walk some or most of it, it could take us—well, a long time."

Mr. Truffles's purrs echoed in the wooden cabinet, a rhythmic rattling that made Harper think of someone playing a washboard in a bluegrass band.

"But if the road is clear, we *could* be on the island tonight."

"We don't know how long they'll need to process us. Or how often they send over the boats."

"Wouldn't it be something to take a shower in hot water?"

"That's crazy talk. Next you'll be daydreaming about food that doesn't come from a can."

"Have you slept with him?" Renée asked, out of the blue.

The fire truck shifted gears and began to accelerate. They

were off South Street now and on Middle Road. The blacktop was newer under the tires, Harper could tell from the smoothness of the ride.

"No," Harper said. "I mean—we've been in bed together, but we've only ever just held each other. His ribs. His bad arm." She didn't know how to explain about the other woman who was always in the room with them, the one in the flames. "More recently, I've been very pregnant."

"I guess you can straighten that out when you're on the island." The fire truck rocked and clattered. "I wish Gil and I had that. I wish there had been a way—but the Mazz was always watching, always in the room with us. I know I'm not so much to look at. I mean, I'm fat and I'm almost fifty. But he had been in prison a long time, and—"

"Renée, you are adorably fuckable," Harper said. "You would've rocked his world."

Renée clapped a hand over her mouth and quivered helplessly.

The fire extinguishers clattered and rang, chiming against one another.

When Renée had control of herself again, she said, "You've kissed him, though? And used the L-word?"

"Yes."

"Good. Gil never said it to me, so I never said it to him. I didn't want to say it and have him feel like he was obliged. I wish I had now. Risked it, I mean. I don't care if he said it back to me. I just wish he had heard it from me."

"He knew," Harper said.

The sound under the tires changed, became deeper and hollow somehow. Harper thought they might be on the ramp, climbing to I-95 now. *Any minute,* she thought. *Any minute. Any minute.* When they went up onto the bridge, it would make a steely, rushing roar. There would be no mistaking it. The checkpoint was located a third of the way across the bridge.

"I wish I had said it to *him* this morning. If they stop us and find us, I might not get a chance," Harper said. Her pulse quickened as the truck sped up. "I do very much love *you,* Renée Gilmonton. You are the most thoughtful person I know. I hope I can be like you when I grow up."

"Oh, Harper. Don't ever be anyone but yourself, please. You are perfect just as you are."

The bridge began to ring under the tires and the truck was slowing.

With her eyes closed, Harper could visualize it: the bridge was six lanes wide, three going south and three going north, with a concrete island separating the two. In the old days one swept right across into Maine without pause, but the governor had thrown up a security checkpoint back in the fall. There would be something blocking two of the three lanes headed north: police cruisers, or Humvees, or a concrete barrier. How many men? How many guns? The air brakes squealed. The fire engine rocked to a halt.

Boots clanged. She heard muted conversation, followed by an unexpected outburst of laughter—John's, Harper thought. More chatter. Harper noticed she wasn't breathing and forced herself to exhale a long, slow breath.

"Can I hold your hand?" Renée whispered.

Harper reached blindly through the dark and found Renée's warm, soft palm.

The door at the rear of the compartment opened a quarter inch.

Harper caught her breath. She thought: *Now. Now they look in.* She and Renée were completely still under their blanket, in the space behind the fire extinguishers. Harper figured it was simple. If they looked behind the fire extinguishers, everyone died. If they didn't, they would all survive the morning.

The cabinet door crept open another quarter inch, and Harper wondered—with a kind of irritation—why the fuck the dude didn't just throw it wide.

"Oh God," Renée said, understanding before Harper by a fraction of an instant.

Harper sat up on her elbows, her pulse jumping in her throat.

It wasn't someone outside opening the door at all. The door was being opened from the inside. Mr. Truffles stuck his head out and stared into the bright morning. He brought his shoulders forward, nudging the door open another six inches, and hopped down. *Thanks for the ride, kids, this is where I get off.*

Renée was squeezing Harper's hand so hard, Harper's fingers ached.

"Oh Jesus," Renée whispered. "Oh God."

Harper pried her hand free and sat up on her knees to look over the tops of the fire extinguishers. She saw a slice of glorious blue sky, fading to white in the distance, and the gray curve of the bridge bending back down to New Hampshire soil.

Wrecks lined the breakdown lane, stretching all the way to the foot of the bridge and beyond. There were maybe a hundred empty vehicles back there: all the cars that had tried to run the blockade and failed. Bullet holes cobwebbed windshields, punctured hoods and doors.

Voices drifted back to them from the front of the truck. Someone was saying, "You're kidding me. When was the last time it saw service?"

Harper gently lifted one of the fire extinguishers and moved it aside. It clinked softly.

"No, Harper," Renée whispered, but Harper wasn't taking a vote on this one. If the cat stepped into view it would draw attention to the rear of the truck.

She moved another fire extinguisher. *Clink.*

"Oh, we usually bring it out t'garage every Fourth of July. We blast the kiddies with the hose, knock 'em right off their feet, they think it's a scream." A laconic Down Easter was speaking toward the front of the truck. His voice was vaguely familiar. "They wouldn't think it was such a scream if we put it on full pressure. There'd be six-year-olds flyin' up into the fackin' trees."

This was met with a ragged bellow of appreciative laughter, half a dozen men at least. It came to Harper in that instant who was doing the talking. The droll old salt running his yap was the Fireman, putting on his Don Lewiston voice.

She pushed open the door and stuck her head into the day.

The air smelled of the river, a sweet mineral scent with a just slightly rotten odor beneath it. No one was in the road behind the truck. The sentries were standing up by the cab. A white booth with dusty Plexiglas windows stood empty to the immediate right. A CB mounted to the Formica desk crackled and spat.

"Your front end looks pretty banged up. You hit something with it?" asked one of the sentries.

"Oh, that was a couple months ago. I struck what I thought was a fackin' pothole. Turned out I went over a Prius with a couple burners in it. Oops!"

More laughter and louder this time.

Mr. Truffles looked up from the road at Harper, narrowed his eyes, yawned, then lifted a rear leg and began to lick his furry balls.

"I don't see you on my checklist," one of the sentries said. He didn't sound unfriendly, but his voice wasn't exactly quaking with laughter, either. "I got a list of all the approved trucks headed north. I don't see your plates."

"Can I look?" asked the Fireman.

Papers ruffled.

Harper put a foot down on the blacktop, eased herself out over the bumper.

The line of shot-up wrecks went on and on, following the edge of the road all the way down the bridge and out of sight. Harper saw a station wagon with half a dozen bullet holes in the sagging windshield. There was a child seat buckled in back.

"Ah, there," said the Fireman. "This one. There's my love."

Harper thought his accent had slipped for a moment, wondered if anyone else had noticed.

"The 1963 Studebaker? I'm no expert, but this fire truck doesn't look like something from 1963."

"No, it sure doesn't. It's not a '63. It's a '36. They flipped around two of their numbers. Wrong fackin' license plate, too. What you've got here was probably the old plates. They were swapped out for antique plates three—fuck, four? At least four fackin' years ago."

The guy sighed. "Someone's going to eat shit over this."

"Yeah. You can count on *that,*" said the Fireman. "Ah, fuck it. If *someone* has to get in trouble, it might as well be *me.* How they going to yell at me? If someone wants to bitch me out, they're gonna have to come north to Maine and find me. Give me your pen. I'll write in the correct license plate."

"Would you do that?"

"Yep. I'll even initial it."

"Hey, Glen? You want me to call it in on the CB?" someone else asked. He sounded young, his voice almost cracking. "I could clear this up in five minutes with the town office."

Harper picked Mr. Truffles up in both hands. He mewed softly. She started to pivot back toward the fire engine, then froze, staring into the empty booth.

A video camera, mounted under the eaves, pointed back at her. She could see herself, a little out of focus, on a blue-tinted TV screen on the counter inside the booth.

She was still gaping at herself on the security monitor when one of the guards walked into view, stepping into the space between herself and the dusty kiosk. He was barely more than a kid, with close-cropped, carrot-colored hair and an M16 on one shoulder. His back was to her. If he had looked over his shoulder he would've been staring right at her. If he glanced into the booth, he would see her image on the monitor. But he did neither. The sentry was gazing toward the front of the fire truck. He gestured with one thumb at the booth.

"I know all the guys in Public Works," he said. "They've got a list of all the approved vehicles and there's always someone in the office—Alvin Whipple, maybe, or Jakob Grayson. They could tell us what to do."

Harper pushed Mr. Truffles up into the cabinet. She lifted her foot carefully, stretching her leg as high as she could, and pulled herself into the back.

"Good idea! Do that," the Fireman called out. "No, wait—shit, come back here. You're going to want your clipboard so you can call in the correct plate."

Harper peered out through the cabinet door, still open a crack, and watched the redheaded boy jog back toward the front of the truck. In a moment he had trotted out of sight.

Harper eased the door shut.

She handed Mr. Truffles to Renée and rearranged the fire extinguishers to hide them . . . an unnecessary task, as no one ever opened the back compartments, and in another moment they were moving. Harper laid herself flat. A muscle twitched nervously in her left leg.

Mr. Truffles purred softly. Renée ran her fingers through the fur on the crown of his head.

"You want to know something, Harper?" Renée asked softly.

"What?" Harper asked.

"I don't think this *is* my cat," Renée told her.

# 12

The fire truck hitched, seemed to roll back a foot or two, then lurched forward, almost reluctantly. The metal grooves in the asphalt began to sing under the tires again. Harper distantly heard the ding-ding of the brass bell, the Fireman ringing it *adios*.

The truck picked up speed, running north.

"We made it," Renée said. She sat up on her elbow. "I think we're safe."

Harper didn't reply. She lifted her head slightly and banged it back down against the steel floor, thinking of the camera.

"What?" Renée asked.

Harper shook her head.

The truck went on for a while. Harper thought John had it all the way up to sixty or seventy, had a feeling of smooth, fast riding. She thought with enough time, the rock and sway of the truck and that sensation of rushing along might put her to sleep.

After ten minutes, though, he downshifted. The truck rolled softly to a stop, gravel crunching under the tires and stones pinging the undercarriage.

Harper was on her knees by the time the Fireman opened the back cabinet door.

"We're in trouble, aren't we?" she said.

"No." He had a bad habit—when he was lying, he always looked you right in the eye. "I thought I'd see if you wanted to sit up front with me."

The other compartment opened and Allie put her head out, rubbing a hand over the honey-colored bristle growing back on her skull. "Take Nick too. His feet stink."

"All right, then," he said.

"I don't think you should've pulled over here," Harper said. "We're too close to the border."

"I have to feed the pail," he said.

All of them climbed down and out to stretch. Harper pushed her knuckles into the small of her back, and popped the joints of her spine. A breeze, silted with fine grit, blew her hair back from her brow.

They were north of Cape Neddick, in what had once been a nature preserve. On the Cape Neddick side of the road, it still was. Heavy oaks, splendid with new green leaves, waved their branches. Bees thrummed in the tawny grass.

On the other side of the road was a moonscape of charred sticks and blackened rock, standing in drifts of ash. The blasted remains of the trees looked like shadows sketched against a background of pale grime. A building of corrugated tin stood a hundred feet off the road, the sides buckled from exposure to heat, so deformed it resembled a five-year-old's drawing of a house. Those acres of desolation went on and on for as far as Harper could see.

"Is it all like this?" Renée asked, shading her eyes with one hand

"The state of Maine? Based on what I've heard, no. Farther north it should be much worse." He looked back the way they had come. "I don't have any idea what the roads ahead might be like. The fire crew we're pretending to be part of was only going up 95 as far as York, then were branching off to take a state highway directly north. We're a bit beyond York now, out in the great unknown."

Harper followed him off the road, into the weeds. He foraged around, collecting old, dry tree branches. Nick stood at the tree line, his back to them, taking a leak into the ferns.

"It won't take them long to figure out they shouldn't have let us through," Harper said.

"It won't matter. When they realize their mistake, I imagine they'll just keep their mouths shut. After all, it's much easier to make an example out of *them* than *us*. The higher ups don't have to catch *them*. No, I think we'll be—"

"I don't think you really understand. Something happened on the bridge. There was a fuckup. The cat jumped out. I was scared someone would see him and they'd decide to do a thorough search of the truck. So I got out to grab him and there was a camera in the booth. They have video that *proves* you were carrying stowaways."

"If they even watch it," he said. Then he looked back at her and said, "I told you that cat was a mistake!"

"Is there anything in all the world you like better than saying 'I told you so'?" Those words had been favorites of Jakob. She didn't like the idea that John resembled Jakob in any way at all. Just the thought made her want to punch him, *hard*.

The Fireman turned with his armload of exhausted-looking wood and wrestled his way back through the weeds.

"They won't send anyone after us," he said, finally. "New Hampshire is sealed off—a police state. They *can't* send anyone after us. They can't risk it. Anyone they send might decide not to come back. This is the problem with police states. The prison guards are prisoners, too, and most of them know it."

But he looked her in the eye the whole time he was lecturing her, which is how she knew he didn't believe it himself.

He climbed on the running board and began to push sticks into the smoking pail. He was still feeding the flames when Nick wandered back from the pines.

"Why is there a bucket full of coals on the truck?" Nick asked with his hands.

She needed to do some finger-spelling to explain. "It's a souvenir of his favorite fire."

"He's as crazy as a shithouse rat," Nick said. "Sometimes I forget."

"Watch your language or I'll wash your filthy hands with soap, young man."

"Ha ha," he told her. "I get it. Very funny. Everyone loves a good deaf joke. Hey, why did God make farts stink? So deaf people could enjoy them, too."

When they pulled back onto I-95, the Fireman leaned out the window and rang his bell again into the emptiness.

# 13

The farther north they went, the less it seemed they were driving on the Earth. Dunes of gray ash had drifted across the road, sometimes so high and so wide—islands of pale fluffy grime—it seemed wisest to slow down and steer around them. The landscape was the color of concrete. Carbonized trees stood on either side of the road, shining with a mineral gleam under a sky that was steadily turning pale and pink. Nothing grew. Harper had heard that weeds and grass recovered swiftly after a wildfire, but the soil was buried under the caked ash, a whitish clay that permitted no trace of green upon it.

The breeze gusted, grit fluttered across the windshield, and the Fireman turned on the wipers, which smeared long streaks of gray across the glass.

They had been on the road for perhaps twenty minutes when Harper saw houses, a line of mobile homes, on a ridge to the east of the car. There was nothing left of them. They were black shells, windows smashed out, roofs collapsed in. They flickered past, a line of warped aluminum shoe boxes, open to the sky.

By then they were only doing twenty miles an hour, the Fireman weaving in and around mounds of ash and the occasional tree across the road. They passed above a stream. The water was a trough of gray sludge. Debris was tugged reluctantly along in the filthy drink: Harper saw a tire, a twisted bicycle, and what looked like a bloated pig in denim overalls, its ripe, spoiled flesh swarming with flies. Then Harper saw it wasn't a pig and reached over to cover Nick's eyes.

They went down into Biddeford. It looked as if it had been shelled. Black chimneys stood amid collapsed brick walls. A line of baked telephone poles stood in a long file, looking for all the world like crosses awaiting sacrifice. Southern Maine Medical rose above it all, a stack of blocks the color of obsidian, smoke still fuming from the interior. Biddeford was an empire of ruin.

In sign, Nick asked, "Do you think most of the people who lived here got away?"

"Yes," Harper told him. "Most of them got away." It was easier to tell a lie with your hands than when you had to actually say a thing.

They left Biddeford behind.

"I thought we'd see refugees," Harper said. "Or patrols."

"As we head north, I suspect the smoke will intensify, and other toxins in the air. Not to mention all the ash. The air could turn poisonous very quickly. Not for us, mind you. I think the Dragonscale in our lungs will look after us. But for normals." He smiled faintly. "Humankind may be on the way out, but we have the good fortune to be part of whatever is next."

"Yay," Harper said, looking at the acres of waste. "Look at our good fortune. The meek shall inherit the Earth. Not that anyone would want what's left of it."

The Fireman popped on the FM band and twiddled through a haze of static, past muted, distant voices, a boys choir reaching for a high note in an echoing cathedral, and then—through the haze—the sound of a leaping, almost goofy bass line, and a man bemoaning that his lover was determined to *run away, run away*. The signal was faint and came through a maddening crackle and pop, but the Fireman leaned forward, listening with wide eyes, then looking at Harper.

Harper stared back, then nodded.

"Do I hear what I think I hear?" the Fireman asked.

"Sure sounds like the English Beat to me," Harper replied. "Keep driving, Mr. Rookwood. Our future awaits us. We'll get there sooner or later."

"Who knew the future was going to sound so much like the past?" he said.

# 14

A couple of miles north of Biddeford, the Fireman took his foot off the gas, and the truck began to slow.

"To be fair," he said, "we had almost forty miles of smooth sailing, which was more than I ever expected to get."

An eighteen-wheeler was parked across the northbound lanes. Like everything they had seen for the last hour, it looked as if a bomb had gone off near it. The cab was a baked shell, burnt down to the frame. The container on back was blacked with soot, but through the filth, Harper could dimly see the word WALMART.

Above the corporate logo, someone had wiped away the grit and spray-painted a message in dull red letters:

PORTLAND GONE

ROAD WIPED OUT NO THRUWAY

HEALTHY? REPORT TO DEKE HAWKINS IN PROUTS NECK

INFECTED WILL BE SHOT ON SITE

GOD FORGIVE US, GOD SAVE YOU

The Fireman opened the door and stepped onto the running board. "I have a tow chain. I may be able to tug that lorry aside. Doesn't look like we'd need much room to get around it. Maybe we should feed the pail, while we're stopped."

Nick followed Harper around to the rear of the fire truck, to check on Allie and Renée. Allie was in the road, reaching up to help Renée down over the bumper. Renée looked almost as gray as the landscape. She clutched her cat to her breast with one arm.

"How are you holding up, old woman?" Harper asked.

"You won't hear me complain," she said.

"No shit," Allie said. "Who could hear anything over that cat yowling?"

"Our little hitchhiker has decided he doesn't like riding in coach," Renée said.

"He can sit up front, then," Harper said. "And you can sit with him."

Renée looked battered and fatigued, but she smiled at this. "Not on your life."

"You aren't riding in back, Ms. Willowes," Allie said. "We hit one of those deep potholes, your baby will probably come flying out. Projectile delivery."

Renée blanched. "That's delicious imagery."

"Isn't it? Who wants to eat?" Allie said, reaching into one of the back compartments for the bag of groceries.

Harper carried a can of peaches and a plastic spoon around to the front of the truck, thinking John would want to share with her. She found him standing on the hood of the big eighteen-wheeler, shading his eyes with one hand and gazing up the highway.

"How does it look up ahead?" she asked.

He sat and slid off the hood. "Not good. Big chunks of the road are missing and I see an absolutely massive tree across it half a mile away. Also, things are still smoking."

"That's crazy. This fire is—what? Eight months old? Nine?"

"It won't die out as long as there's anything still to burn. All that ash is a protective blanket for the coals beneath." He had slipped out of his turnout jacket and stood in a stained undershirt. It was midday and heat wobbled off the blacktop. "We'll drive until we can't drive anymore. Then we leave the truck and go on foot." He looked at her belly for a moment. "I won't pretty it up for you. It's going to be hot, and we could be limping along for days."

She had tried not to allow herself fantasies of reaching Martha Quinn's island that night—had tried not to imagine a bed made up with fresh sheets or a hot shower or the smell of soap—but hadn't entirely been able to help herself. It dispirited her, to hear it was going to be longer and harder to get there than she had hoped, than they had all hoped. But no sooner had she registered her own disappointment than she decided to set it aside. They were on their way and they were out of New Hampshire. That was good enough for today.

"What?" she said. "You think I'm the first pregnant lady who had to do some walking? Here. Eat a peach. It'll give you something to do with that mouth of yours besides make dour speeches and grim predictions. Do you know you are drop-dead sexy until the minute you start to talk? Then you turn into a colossal ass."

He opened his mouth for a plastic spoonful of peach. She followed it with a long kiss that tasted of golden syrup. When she broke away from him he was smiling.

Nick, Renée, and Allie began to clap, standing in a line behind them. Harper showed them her middle finger and kissed him again.

# 15

John and Allie strapped a tow chain to the hitch at the front of the fire engine and led the other end to the eighteen-wheeler. While they were hooking the line to the rear of the semi, Harper had a look inside the long Walmart container. The interior smelled of burnt metal and burnt hair, but there was a stack of wooden pallets against the back wall. Harper dragged one out, to see if she could break it up and feed pieces to the bucket of coals.

Renée brought her a crowbar and an ax. Harper leaned the pallet against the fire-blanched guardrail and began to whack at it. Chunks of pine splintered and flew.

Renée squinted into the bright afternoon at the bucket welded behind the cab.

"I've been meaning to ask—" she said.

"Probably just as well not to."

"Okay."

Harper carried an armful of shattered wood to the truck, climbed on the running board, and looked inside the pail. Coals pulsed. Harper fed pieces of wood, one by one. Each stick ignited in a fluttering hiss of white fire as it went in. Harper had jammed in four or five sticks, then paused, holding another stick over the pail, trying to figure out where to put it.

A deformed red banner of flame, shaped like a child's hand, reached up and snatched at it. Harper let go with a soft cry and jumped off the running board. Her legs felt watery and loose beneath her. Renée put a hand on her elbow to steady her.

"I've heard of tongues of flame," Renée said mildly. "But not arms."

Harper shook her head, couldn't find her voice.

The Fireman slammed the driver's-side door and put the fire engine into reverse. The towline was yanked taut with a snap. The fire truck's tires spun, smoked, found purchase, and dragged the rear of the eighteen-wheeler aside with a shriek of metal.

When the big rig was out of the way, Harper could see up the road for the first time. Less than twenty feet beyond the semi, a crater the size of a compact car had swallowed one lane. Not far after that was *another* crater, but in the passing lane. Half a mile down the highway, Harper saw an enormous tree across the interstate, a vast larch that had somehow been crystallized by fire. It looked as if it were made of burnt sugar. The road was long and straight, and heat distortion climbed off the softened, buckled ruin of the blacktop.

"We'll have to take it slow from here on out," the Fireman said.

He had that one wrong.

# 16

The Fireman steered the truck around the great crumbled pits in the road, rolled along to the fallen larch, and stopped again. Harper and the others didn't even bother riding with him in the truck but followed along on foot. The sky hazed over as if it were going to rain, only it wasn't going to rain, and the color of the clouds was wrong. Those clouds were salmon-colored, as if lit by sunset, and never mind it was midday. The air had the staticky feel that sometimes warned of thunderheads. The pressure tickled Harper's eardrums unpleasantly.

The Fireman strapped the tow to the downed tree and ran the truck back. There was a loud crack. He cursed artistically.

"Did you hear what he said? *No* woman could really do that," Renée said. "It's anatomically impossible."

He jumped down from behind the wheel. The towline had yanked a ten-foot branch right off the tree.

"You have to get the chain around the trunk," Allie said. "Or it'll break into pieces."

Nick sat on the rear bumper of the fire truck with Renée and Harper, while Allie and the Fireman ran the tow around the center mass of the tree.

"Let's play a game," Renée said. "Twenty Questions. Who wants to go first?"

Harper translated. Nick replied in sign.

"He wants to know if it's animal, vegetable, or mineral."

"Mineral. Sort of. Oh boy. We're off to a bad start."

They went back and forth, Harper serving as their conversational go-between.

"Is it yellow?" Harper asked for him.

"Yes, but also sort of orange."

"Now he wants to know if it's bigger than a car."

"Yes. Much bigger."

Nick spoke rapidly with his hands.

"He says 'It's a truck,'" Harper said.

"No!" Renée said cheerfully.

Nick hopped off the rear bumper, his hands flying, arms waving.

"He says 'It's a big orange truck,'" Harper said.

"*No!*" Renée told her again, frowning. "Tell him *no*. He's wasting his questions."

But by then Harper was off the fender herself, staring back down the interstate.

"We have to go," she said.

Nick was already running toward the front of the truck. Harper jogged after him, shouting the whole way, her voice rising from a yell to something that wavered at the ragged edge of a scream.

"John! We have to go! We have to go. *Right! NOW!*"

John was half in the cab, one hand on the steering wheel and one foot on the running board. He leaned out of the fire engine to shout instructions to Allie, who straddled the larch, adjusting the towline around the trunk. When he heard Harper hollering, he glanced around, then narrowed his eyes and squinted past her.

On the far rise, a mile away, an orange truck winked in the sun. Harper could distantly hear the building roar of its engine as the Freightliner barreled toward them.

"Allie, get off the tree!" John shouted.

Allie cupped a hand to her ear and shook her head. *Can't hear you.* Harper could barely hear John herself over the fire truck's idling engine.

Harper jumped up on the running board beside the Fireman and rang the brass bell, hard and loud as she could. Allie read Harper's face, leapt off the tree, and came running.

"In the truck, in the truck!" John shouted. "Quick, now, I need to back up."

Allie snatched Nick off the ground, arms around his thighs, lifted him off the road, and hustled for the rear of the fire truck.

John gave them perhaps ten seconds to climb in and then he threw the fire truck into reverse, gunned the engine. The tree caught the truck and anchored it in place. The tires spun. Harper stood on the running board, clutching the open door with one hand and John's arm with the other.

Jakob's Freightliner was less than a mile away, sun glaring bleakly off the splintered windshield. Harper could hear the thin whine as it accelerated.

John applied more pressure and the tree rocked, turned over, and began to slide through the ash. Branches snapped and broke, littering the road.

A half mile away, Jakob's snow-wing plow clipped the back end of the Walmart truck and tore the trailer to shreds, launched it up and out of his way with a metallic crash.

The tree caught on a fissure in the road, wouldn't budge. John cursed. He put the truck in drive, rolled forward ten feet, and slammed it into reverse again. He ran straight back, tires shrieking. Harper held on, clenching her teeth, her pulse sick and fast, bracing herself for the jolt. The larch tree jounced up in the air and crashed back down, boughs shattering and flying, rolling far enough to one side to clear a lane.

"I'll unhook us," Harper said. She jumped down and ran around to the front of the truck.

"Hurry, Willowes," the Fireman called to her. The sound of the Freightliner rose to a bellowing roar. "Get in, *get in*."

Harper slipped the towline free from the front hitch and ran for the passenger side.

"Go!" she yelled, grabbing the passenger-side door and stepping onto the running board.

The fire truck lumbered forward. Thick branches cracked and shattered under the tires. By the time Harper pulled herself part of the way up into the passenger seat, he was doing nearly twenty miles per hour. He swung around the larch, building speed slowly but surely on a straight stretch of road that climbed to the top of a little rise.

The snow-wing plow struck the tree. The larch wasn't swatted clear so much as pulverized, branches shattering in a cloud of gray powder and black fragments. The Freightliner screamed. Harper felt she was hearing Jakob's true voice for the first time.

She had one knee up on the passenger seat when the Freightliner slammed into the rear of the truck. The impact dropped her. Her legs fell back out the open door, hung over the road. She got one arm through the open passenger-side window, hanging on to the door. Her other hand grabbed the seat.

"Harp!" the Fireman yelled. "Oh God, Harp, get in, get in!"

"Faster," she told him. "Don't you dare slow down, Rookwood."

She kicked her feet but couldn't seem to pull herself up into the seat. Too much of her was hanging out the passenger-side door and her center of gravity was too low, all her mass and weight dangling over the road.

Harper turned her head to see where the Freightliner was and in the same moment Jakob hit them again. Harper *saw* him then, behind the wheel: Jakob's starved, bristly, scarred face. He did not smile or look angry. His head rolled on his neck as if he were dosed up with some heavy anesthetic.

"Will you for God's sake get in the truck," the Fireman said. He had one hand on the wheel but wasn't looking out the windshield anymore. He had stretched all the way across the passenger seat to grab for her, extending his right hand with its taped wrist.

She swatted wildly for his arm, caught his fingers. He hauled at her, straining against the slipstream that wanted to vacuum her right out of the front seat. Her feet kicked in the air and then her knee found the footwell and she was in the cab.

The fire truck had been drifting while he dragged her up.

They clipped a baked Honda Civic parked on the left-hand margin of the interstate. The Honda's back end flipped into the air as if a mine had exploded under the rear tires. They sped past it, left it behind.

The Honda came down across the turnpike behind them with a rattling thud. The snowplow hit it an instant later and knocked it aside with a shriek, a sound of almost human fury, mingled with the crunch of imploding glass.

She scrambled into her seat, the passenger door still open and waving back and forth. Harper grabbed the black leather strap hanging above the door and stuck her head out, looking back.

"The fuck are you—" the Fireman asked.

She was full of song, a song of outrage and grief that had no words and no melody, and her hand ignited like a rag soaked in gasoline when touched with a match. Blue flame roared from it and she threw it, threw a softball of fire. It struck the windshield of the Freightliner, sprayed across the glass in a liquid fan of flame—and went out.

Harper threw fire again and again. A blast of blue flame snapped off the passenger-side mirror on the plow. A bolt struck the plow itself, briefly turning the snow-wing into a shallow trough filled with crackling white flame. The fourth time she cast flame, it hooked, like a curveball or a knuckler, and struck the front passenger-side tire. The wheel became a blazing hoop.

"Can you blind him?" the Fireman asked.

"What?" Harper asked.

"Blind him. Just blind him for ten seconds. *Now,* if you please. And for God's sake put your seat belt on."

The tendons stood out in John's neck. His lips were drawn back in an appalled grimace. They were rushing up a hill toward some kind of overpass. The front of the fire truck thwacked aside a diamond-shaped orange sign, a warning. Harper didn't have time to see what it said before the Fireman sent it spinning.

Harper didn't bother with the belt. She couldn't buckle in and still lean far enough out the door to throw flame directly at Jakob behind the steering wheel. She stuck her head into the boiling afternoon air and looked at the Freightliner. Jakob stared back through his cobwebbed windshield, the cracks running from a single bullet hole, just to the right of where he sat. Harper thought Jamie Close had come very close to shooting him through a lung that night in the church tower.

She took a deep breath and threw a fistful of fire. It hit the windshield at the bullet hole. Flame squirted outward, following the cracks, making a web of flame. A little fire spattered through the hole and Jakob flinched, turned his head away. Harper thought, for a moment, he shut his eyes.

Harper turned to see what lay ahead and saw the overpass was gone. BRIDGE OUT—that was what the orange safety sign had said. The overpass had collapsed in the center, leaving a chasm thirty feet across, rebar sticking out of shattered concrete. At the last instant it came to her that she still didn't have her seat belt on.

John hammered his foot onto the brake and wrenched the wheel to the side, veering suddenly and sharply away from the drop.

It was almost too much, too hard. The fire truck slewed sideways, tires whining, a high ragged whine of blistering rubber. Blue smoke poured from the undercarriage. Harper could feel how the truck wanted to topple over. John had his whole body across the steering wheel, pulling against it. The truck slid sideways, shuddering with the force of a jackhammer. *I am going to lose this baby,* Harper thought.

The Freightliner clipped the rear end in passing The fire engine spun like a revolving door. For an instant they were staring back the way they had come and still sliding backward. Centrifugal force slung Harper against her door. If she had not closed it the moment before, she would've been hurled out. The steering wheel whirled so quickly in the Fireman's hands that he let go of it with a cry of pain.

They were looking back in the direction of New Hampshire, still skating over the blacktop, so Harper didn't see when the Freightliner blew past them and over the drop, fell thirty feet and hit the road below with a concussive crash that seemed to shake the world. It felt as if a bomb had gone off beneath them.

She still felt a little as if they were spinning, even after the fire truck stopped moving. She looked at John. He stared back at her with wide, bewildered eyes. He moved his lips. She believed he was saying her name, but wasn't sure, couldn't hear over the drone in her ears. Nick was right. Reading lips was hard.

He gestured with his hands, a little shooing motion. Get out. He was fighting with his seat belt.

She nodded, stepped down through the open door on trembling legs, climbed onto the running board, then lowered herself to the road. She let go of the door and looked toward the gap in the overpass and felt all the wind go out of her.

The back half of the fire engine hung over the edge of the chasm. It was tipping. As Harper watched, it seesawed back, the front tires rising into the air.

Harper just had time to catch her breath. She was getting ready to scream John's name when the fire truck tilted over the side, into the gap, and took the Fireman with it.

# 17

Harper ran to the edge of the missing overpass and stared down past twisted rebar and crumbled concrete. The fire engine had dropped straight back and turned onto its passenger side. She had the wrong angle, couldn't see into the cab, couldn't see John. The Freightliner was upside down. Something was burning down there; Harper could smell the stink of scorched rubber.

It was only shock that held her where she was, a great tingling throb of emotion that she could feel in her nerve endings, in her fingertips. *All dead,* she thought. *All dead, all dead, John and Nick and Allie and Renée and John and Nick and Allie and Renée and John and Nick and Allie and Renée.*

Her throat hurt and she realized she was screaming, had been screaming for almost a full minute, and she made herself be quiet. The thing to do was to get down there. Get down there and see what she could do.

She turned—and almost ran right into Allie. Her face was aglow with sweat and she was gasping from her run.

"Where did you come from?" Harper asked. "How did you get out?"

Harper gazed blankly past her. Half a mile away she saw Nick trotting along the margin of the road, leading Renée by the hand.

"Never got in," Allie said. "Never had a chance. Renée shoved us into a ditch as soon as I reached the back end of the truck with Nick. The next thing I knew, you and John were driving off without us. Where's John? Where—"

As Allie spoke, she was creeping past Harper to look over the drop. Harper grabbed her arm and drew her away before she could reach the edge.

"Don't look. I don't want Nick to see and I don't want you to see, either. You stay here and don't come unless I call for you."

Harper wanted to run, but her days of running had ended several weeks before. She did a funny sort of pregnant-lady trot, holding her stomach. She climbed over a guardrail, and slid down the bank on her big pregnant rump, grabbing fistfuls of brush to slow her descent.

The road below was a divided highway, running east and west. The fire truck lay across the eastbound lanes. A lake of fire sputtered and gushed across the blacktop and Harper thought, wildly, *Gasoline, it's spilling burning gasoline, it's going to explode.* She skipped over the flames and reached the front of the engine.

She could see in through the windshield. It was smashed and sagging inward from the frame. John hung sideways, still buckled in his seat, his head on his right shoulder, and blood dripping from under his hairline and nose. But: not dead. Harper could see the rise and fall of his chest.

What she couldn't see was how to get him out. She was too pregnant to climb up to the driver's-side door, which currently faced the sky. She couldn't smash in what was left of the windshield without a tool, and was afraid to spray him with broken glass.

*A ladder,* Harper thought. Not the big ladder mounted to the roof, but one of the smaller ones packed into the rear cabinets.

She hopped back over that long ribbon of fire (what exactly was burning? it didn't smell like gasoline) and made her way to the rear of the truck. Compartments all along the fire engine had been torn open and she stepped carefully through a Lincoln Log tangle of ax handles and crowbars. She was in a hurry and almost stepped on the cat, recoiled when it yowled at her in alarm.

Harper caught herself, took a step back. Mr. Truffles gazed

up at her, his jade-colored eyes glazed with shock, his fur ruffled up. Renée had got all of them away from the truck except for him, it seemed.

"Oh, you," Harper said, crouching down and reaching toward him. "My God, how did *you* survive? I wonder how many of your nine lives you just used up."

"All of 'em," Jakob said and a shovel swiped down through the smoke and struck the cat like a croquet mallet impacting the ball.

Mr. Truffles flew, broken-necked and dead, through the air and into the brush. Harper screamed and went straight back, falling on her butt. Jakob lifted the shovel over his head in both hands. She pushed herself back with her heels and the blade of the shovel came down in the soft blacktop between her feet.

She dragged herself away from him, pulling herself along on her bottom, through broken glass and loose rock. He had to wiggle the handle of the shovel back and forth to loosen the blade before he could step forward and she had time to get a good look at him. His right hand was blackened and burned to the texture of fried chicken skin. The flesh had fissured to show ripe, pink meat beneath, glistening with pus. The right side of his face was charred too, and the hair on that side of his head was still smoking. An old black burn in the shape of a man's hand mottled the loose flesh of his throat.

He came forward, flat-footed and slow, with nothing of his former dancing grace. When he spoke, his voice was thick and slurred. His lips had fused together at one corner of his mouth.

"I was right when I said you made me sick, babygirl," he said. "It's true you didn't contaminate me with Dragonscale, but you made me sick in a different way. A worse way. Being around you was like having a low-grade fever. A woman like you is a kind of infection. You were living off me like a bacteria. You don't know how badly I want to be well. To be cured of you."

He took another swipe, but she pushed back on her heels. The shovel blade sliced through the haze, dragging silky shreds of smoke behind it.

"I thought you would be my muse, once," he said, and laughed, a strange, discordant sound. "I thought you'd inspire me! Well. In the end, you sure did. In the end, you led me to my real calling: putting out fires. I'm such a good little fireman, I put them out before they even start. You see? In a way, you *were* my muse!"

She was no more a muse than he had ever been a writer, Harper thought, and she wasn't sorry, not for that. Jakob could only see her in terms of blame or inspiration, but either way it reduced her to a kind of fuel. Either way, she had always just been something for him to burn up.

"Is your boyfriend still alive?" Jakob asked, nodding back toward the truck. "I want him to be alive. I want to slice off your head and put it in his lap before I kill him. I want him to look into your face one last time and say your name. I want him to know that he couldn't keep what he took away from me."

In her mind, Harper began to sing without words. Her left hand sputtered, smoked, glowed, and began to flicker with firelight. She lifted it and Jakob smashed it with the shovel and the flame went out. Harper shouted at the pain of it.

"Did he teach you a little trick?" Jakob asked. "Besides how to suck his cock? Too bad he didn't teach you not to play with fire. A woman your age ought to know how that ends, babygirl. Little girls who play with fire get burnt in the end. They get burnt all up gone."

But Harper wasn't listening. Harper was looking past him. She felt a sick rush of blood to her heart and was having trouble finding her breath.

*"Pay attention to me,"* Jakob said. He put the point of the shovel under her chin and used it to lift her head, forcing her to look up into his eyes. "I'm *talking* to you, babygirl. Did you even hear what I just said? Did you listen to me at all? Little girls shouldn't play with fire. That's how people get hurt."

"Yes," Harper whispered. "You're right. I'm so sorry, Jakob."

He narrowed his eyes in a question, then started to turn his head.

By then, the woman of flame had crossed half the distance between him and the truck. She was Jakob's very height, and her hair flowed for yards behind her, yellow and red. She was nude, in a sense, although her shifting, wavering shape seemed more like a form made out of crimson silks. Her eyes alone burnt hot blue, like the flame of a blowtorch. She left footprints behind her—footprints of red flame.

"Mom?" Allie said, from thirty feet away. She had made her way down the incline after all, and stood there holding Nick's hand. Her voice was small and bewildered.

The woman of fire threw a hatchet of flame. It wasn't there until the instant she drew back her hand. It struck Jakob in the face and he screamed, flame splattering across his features, up into his hair. She cocked back her hand and a new hatchet of fire appeared in it, leaping into her fist out of nowhere. She threw again, coming toward him. The second hatchet struck him in the chest and the filthy, oil-stained ruin of his white T-shirt ignited. He took a staggering step toward her, but he couldn't see through the black smoke engulfing his head. She stepped aside like a bullfighter. He stumbled and fell to one knee.

She sank down beside him and took him gently into her blazing arms.

# 18

Allie crouched at the bottom of the embankment with Nick in her arms. She clutched her brother's face to her chest and buried her own head in his shoulder, the pair of them squeezed together like the two halves of a walnut.

The flame that had once been a woman rose from the black and smoking corpse of Jakob Grayson. She left her kill and walked toward the children. Her heels left bubbling footprints. liquefying the asphalt beneath them.

When she was ten feet from Nick and Allie, she lowered herself with an exquisite grace, hooking her ankles and sinking down to sit cross-legged. Allie lifted her head and peered at her, then squeezed Nick's shoulder to let him know it was okay to look.

Her golden hair flowed and crackled. The road beneath her was melting, turning to a puddle of tar.

Nick spoke with his hands. He said, "Mom?"

She nodded and said, "I was once," moving her hands in swirls of fire. "Most of who I was has burned away."

"I've missed you," he said, and Allie finger-spelled, "Me, too. So much."

Sarah nodded again. The top of her head was an open chalice of flame. Whatever she was burning to stay with them—the air and a million whirling grains of spore—she was using it up fast now, cooling out, cooling off. When the breeze gusted, she rippled like a reflection in unsettled waters.

"It was all my fault," Nick told her with his hands.

"You don't blame a match for starting a fire," the Sarah flame said. "You blame the person who strikes it. You were just a match."

"You'd still be with us if I hadn't tried to teach you how to cast fire."

With her hands, she said, "I *am* still with you." With gestures, she said, "I am always with you. Love never burns away. It just keeps on and on."

They were crying again. Perhaps she wept as well. Flame dripped from her face and spattered in the road.

The children spoke to her with their hands and she nodded and replied in kind, but Harper turned away from them and did not see the end of their conversation. What they said to each other was for them alone.

Harper came unsteadily to her feet and looked around. Jakob's charred and withered corpse poured filthy black smoke. Harper walked to the rear of the wreck and dug through dirty coils of hose. She excavated a fire blanket and flapped it over Jakob's head and shoulder, then backed away, waving the smoke from her face. It smelled like a trash fire.

She bumped into someone standing behind her. Renée put a steadying hand on her shoulder. Renée had made her way down the embankment to join them at last.

"Have you seen the cat?" Renée asked, her voice strained and stunned.

"He—he didn't make it, Renée," Harper said. "He was—thrown clear in the accident. I'm sorry."

"Oh," Renée said and blinked. "What about—"

"John. Is alive. But hurt. I need help to get him out of the truck."

"Yes. Of course." Renée looked back at Allie and Nick and the burning woman. "That—what is that?"

"She came with John," Harper explained.

"She's—" Renée began, then swallowed, licked her lips, tried again. "She's—" Her voice caught in her throat again.

"An old flame," Harper said.

# 19

Renée wedged a crowbar under one corner of the windshield and pried it free. It flopped into the road all in one piece, a jingling blanket of blue safety glass with a thousand fissures in it, impossibly holding together. Harper and Renée squeezed into the cab together and stood below John, who hung suspended above them, strapped in by his seat belt. A drop of blood fell into Harper's right eye, and for a moment she was seeing the world through red-stained glass.

The two of them did their best to get him down to the ground without jostling him, but when his right foot struck the blacktop, his eyes flew open and he cried out in a thin voice. They dragged him from the wreck of the truck. Renée went to get something to put under his head and came back with the Portable Mother, which served well enough as a pillow.

"Oh," he said. "Oh, my leg. It's bad, isn't it? I can't look."

Harper moved her hands over his thigh, feeling the break in his femur through the thick rubber of his fireman pants. She didn't think it had punched through the skin and was certain it hadn't nicked a major artery. If it had, he wouldn't be asking her about his leg. He'd be unconscious from blood loss, or dead.

"I can deal with it. I'll have to set it and splint it, and without painkillers, that's going to hurt." She probed his chest. Once he gasped and shut his eyes and pressed his head hard back into the carpetbag beneath it. "I'm more worried about the ribs. They're broken again. I'll have to scratch around, see what I have to set your leg." She felt a heat at her back and knew who was standing behind her. "There's someone here to keep you company while I'm rummaging around."

She kissed him on the cheek, rose, and stepped aside.

Sarah stood blazing over him. She lowered herself to one knee and looked into his face, and Harper thought she was smiling. It was hard to tell. Her face was little more than rags of flame. When Sarah had first appeared she had been a shroud of white fire with a core of almost blinding heat at her very center. Now, though, her dominant hue was a dull, deep red, and she had diminished to childlike proportions, was about the size of Nick.

"Oh. *Sarah.* Oh, look at you," John said. "Just hold on. We'll collect up some wood. We'll keep you going." He lifted his hands, trying to say it in gestures.

She shook her head. Harper was sure now she was smiling. The lady of fire lifted her chin, the breeze gently blowing the last tatters of her hair, and she seemed to stare right into Harper—to stare at her in the dreamy way Harper herself had often stared into moving flames. At the last, Harper thought Sarah winked at her.

When she went out, it happened all at once. The girl of flame collapsed into herself in a rattling drizzle of cinders. A thousand green sparks whirled up into the afternoon. Harper raised one hand to protect her eyes and was stung all over—gently stung—as they rained into her, touching her bare arms and brow and neck and cheeks. She flinched, but the light prickling was gone in a moment. She wiped at her cheeks and came away with a palm of smeared ash.

Harper rubbed it between thumb and finger, watching the pale grime drift off on the light breeze, thinking of what they said at funerals, the bit about ashes to ashes, which went along with something about the certainty of resurrection.

# 20

John's eyes were scared, his face pebbled with sweat and soot. His pants were off. The right thigh was black and bloated, twice as thick as his left. Renée's chubby palms rested below the break, while Harper's gripped the leg just above it.

"Are you ready?" Harper asked.

John gave her a tight, frightened nod. "Let's get this Dark Ages medical procedure over with."

Allie was standing thirty feet away, but when the Fireman began to scream, she turned her back on them and clapped her hands over her ears. The bone made a grinding sound as the two broken parts settled back together, a noise that reminded Harper of someone dragging a rock across a chalkboard.

# 21

Allie was the one who figured out how to make a travois by folding blankets across a segment of fire ladder. They lashed him down to it, running bungee lines across his shins and hip bones. A final cord went around his forehead. Those were the only places they could put the cables without crossing a broken bone.

He was, by then, unconscious but restless, blowing air from his lips and trying to shake his head. He looked very old, Harper thought, his cheeks and temples sunken, his brow creased. He also had a flustered, dim-witted expression that made her heartsick.

Renée disappeared for a while, but when she returned she had a road map of New England, which she had discovered in the glove compartment of Jakob's Freightliner. Harper sat with it across her knees for a while, then told them it was two hundred miles to Machias.

"If we set a pace of twenty miles a day," Harper said, "we can be there in a little over a week."

Harper waited for someone to ask if she was kidding.

Instead, Allie crouched, took the ends of the homemade travois, and stood. John's head rose into the air until it was about level with the small of her back. Allie's face was a grim, stoic mask.

"Better get going, then," Allie said. "If we start right now we can make ten miles before we lose the light. I don't see any good reason to waste the day. Do you?"

She glared around at them, as if she expected a challenge. She didn't get one.

"Ten days on your feet," Renée mused. She looked at Harper's distended belly. "When's the due date?"

Harper showed her a tight smile. "Plenty of time."

She had lost track, but was pretty sure it was down to less than two weeks.

Renée salvaged a bag of groceries from the wreck and Harper picked the Portable Mother out of the road. They had struggled their way back up the slope to I-95 before Harper noticed Nick was carrying a fire ax. He was a practical child.

Where it wasn't shattered, the road was blanketed with ash. There was nothing to see, all the way to the horizon, except cinder-colored hills and the charred spears of the pines.

A few hours before dusk they reached a place where the interstate caved away into what had once been a creek. The water was choked with ash, had become a magnesium-colored sludge. A '79 Mercury floated down it, up to its headlights, looking like a giant robot crocodile patrolling a toxic canal.

Allie set the travois down by the side of the road. "I'll go upstream, see if there's another way across."

"I don't like the idea of you taking off alone," Harper said. "We don't know who might be out there. I can't lose one more person I love, Allie."

It blindsided Allie, hearing Harper tell her she loved her. She looked around at Harper with an expression of shock and pleasure and embarrassment that made her seem much younger than she was: twelve, not seventeen.

"I'm coming back," Allie said. "Promise. Besides." She tugged the fire ax out of Nick's hands. "My mom isn't the only one who knows how to sling one of these around."

She went down the steep slope at the side of the road, sweeping the blade back and forth to clear her way through the shoulder-high grass.

She was back just as it turned twilight, the sky curdling a sickly shade of yellow. When Harper asked if she had found anything, she only wearily wagged her head and didn't speak.

They camped on the banks of the river, under the overhang of the collapsed bridge. In the night, the Fireman began to rave.

*"Chim chiminee, chim chiminee, chim chim che-ride, find me some water, 'fore I burn up inside! Chim chiminee, chim chiminee, chim chim cha-red! If I was on fire, would you piss on my head?"*

*"Shh,"* Harper told him, one hand across his waist, clasping herself to him to keep him warm. The day had been sullen and hot, but after dark the air was so cold and sharp they might've been on an exposed mountain ridge. His face was drenched with an icy, sick sweat, yet he kept grabbing the collar of his shirt and pulling at it, as if he were roasting. "*Shh.* Try and sleep."

His eyelids fluttered and he gave her a wild, distracted look. "Is Jakob still after us?"

"No. He's all gone."

"I thought I heard his truck. I thought I heard him coming."

"No, my love."

He patted her hand and nodded, relieved, and slept again for a while.

# 22

They spent most of the next morning doubling back, retracing their steps to an off-ramp, which led them down past the napalmed ruin of a Pizza Hut. The Fireman slept most of the way. When he did wake, his eyes were stunned and uncomprehending.

He didn't have much to say—at first—and sometimes it was necessary to ask him a question a few times before he'd hear it. His replies, however, were coherent and sensible. Yes, he *would* like some water. Yes, his leg hurt, but it was all right, he was managing. His chest didn't hurt so much, but it felt *heavy,* it felt *tight.* He asked Allie several times to loosen the strap across his chest. At first she told him there *wasn't* a strap across his chest, but the third time he asked, she said sure, no problem, and he thanked her and dropped the subject.

Only once did the Fireman do anything particularly troubling. He moved his hands, speaking to Nick. Nick's reply was easy to understand: he shook his head *no.* Then he hurried to catch up to Harper and walked along beside her, where he could avoid eye contact with the Fireman.

"What did he say?" Harper asked.

"He said he was pretty sure the truck was still behind us. The big plow. I told him it wasn't, but he said he could *hear* it. He said it was still coming and if it got any closer we'd have to leave him."

"He's sick. Don't worry. He's mixed up."

"I know," Nick said. "Your sign language is getting pretty good."

Harper was going to say, "Maybe I'll teach my son," and then she remembered if everything went according to plan, she would never know her own son. She would be giving him up to someone healthy. She put her hands in the pockets of her hoodie and left them there, all done talking for a while.

They stopped for lunch in an improbable stand of birch trees, located in a center island between two lanes of a country highway. The hills to either side of the road were crowded with blackened trees, but in the small teardrop-shaped island, there was a place that had been untouched by fire, a zone of green, ferny cool.

They drank bottled water and ate pretzels. At some point a soft, dry hail began to spatter down around them, striking their shoulders and the trees, the leaves and the ferns. Harper found a ladybug crawling on the back of her hand and another on her wrist. She brushed a hand through her hair and swept half a dozen ladybugs into the grass.

When she lifted her head she could see hundreds of them, crawling on the trunks of the trees, or opening their shells to glide on the breeze. No: *thousands*. Ladybugs soared on the updrafts, hundreds of feet above, a slow floating storm of them. Renée stood up wearing hundreds of ladybugs on her arms, like elbow-length gloves. She dusted them off and they fell pitter-patter into the ferns. John wore them like a blanket until Allie gently dusted him with a fern.

They camped that night in the ruin of a cottage by the side of the road. The west-facing wall of the house had been swept by fire and collapsed, burying the living room and kitchen in charred sticks and burnt shingle. But the east-facing wing was mysteriously untouched: white siding, black shutters, blinds drawn behind the windows. They settled in what had once been a guest bedroom, where they found a queen bed, neatly made. A dried, withered bundle of white viburnum rested on the pillow. A former guest had written a message on the wall: THE CROWTHER FAMILY STAYED HERE ON OUR WAY TO SEE MARTHA QUINN, followed by a date from the previous fall.

By the time they lost the daylight, John was shivering uncontrollably, and his body only relaxed when Harper curled against him under the quilt. He glowed with heat, and it wasn't Dragonscale, either. It scared her, the dry, steady blaze of his fever. She carefully put her ear to his chest, listening to his lungs, and heard a sound like someone pulling a boot out of mud. Pneumonia, then. Pneumonia all over again, and worse than before.

Nick stretched out on John's other side. He had discovered a copy of the *Peterson Field Guide to Birds* on an end table and was leafing through the pages, studying the pictures by the light of one burning finger.

"What are you thinking?" Harper asked him.

"I'm wondering how many of these have gone extinct," Nick told her.

The next day the Fireman was gummy with sweat.

"He's burning up," Renée said, putting her knuckles to his cheek.

"Be funny if I cooked to death," he muttered, and everyone jumped. He didn't speak again all day.

# 23

They splashed through a soupy, Dijon-colored fog, beneath trees festooned with streamers of dirty mist. They walked north into it, and by midmorning the sun was no more than a faint brown disk burning a rusty hole through the pall. It was impossible to see more than a few yards into the miasma. Harper spotted what she thought was a hulking motorcycle leaning against the ruin of a barbed-wire fence. It turned out to be a dead cow, its blackened skin fissured to show the ripe, spoiled flesh beneath, its empty eye sockets buzzing with flies. Renée staggered past it, coughing, holding her throat, trying not to gag.

It was the first and last time Harper heard anyone cough all day. Even the Fireman's breathing was long and slow and regular. Although her eyes and nostrils burned, she might've been breathing fresh alpine air for all that the roiling smoke bothered her.

The idea occurred to her that they were breathing poison, had crossed into an environment roughly as hospitable to human life as Venus. But it didn't drop them, and Harper turned that thought over in her mind. It was the Dragonscale, of course, doing its thing. She had known for a while that it converted the toxins in smoke to oxygen. This, though, led to another notion, and she called for Allie to stop.

Allie held up, flushed and filthy. Harper knelt beside the drag sled, unbuttoned John's shirt, and put her ear to his chest.

She still heard a dry and gritty rasp she didn't like, but if it was no better, it was also no worse. He was smiling and, in sleep, almost looked his old, calm, wry self. The smoke around them was as good as an oxygen tent. It wouldn't make his pneumonia go away—the best chance for him now was a course of antibiotics—but it might buy him time.

In the early afternoon, though, they dragged him clear of the haze and went on beneath a clear, cloudless, hateful blue sky, the sun throwing blinding flashes off every piece of metal and every sooty fragment of glass. By the time they finally got off the road, John was worse than Harper had ever seen him. His fever returned, a sweat springing up on his cheeks and in his gray, depressed temples. His tongue kept flicking out of his mouth, looking swollen and colorless. His teeth chattered. He spoke to people who weren't there.

"The Incas were right to worship the sun, Father," the Fireman said to Father Storey. "God *is* fire. Combustion is the one inarguable blessing. A tree, oil, coal, a man, a civilization, a soul. They've all got to burn sometime. The warmth made by their passing may be the salvation of others. The ultimate value of the Bible, or the Constitution, or any work of literature, really, is that they all burn very well, and for a while they keep back the cold."

They settled in an airplane hangar beside a small private landing strip. The hangar, a blue metal building with a curved roof, didn't have any planes in it, but there was a black leather couch in one office. Harper decided they ought to bungee him down to it, so he didn't fall off in the night.

As she was binding him down, his rolling, baffled eyes locked in on her face. "The truck. I saw the truck this afternoon. You ought to leave me. I'm slowing you down and the plow is coming."

"There's no way," Harper said, and brushed his sweaty hair back from his brow. "I'm not going anywhere without you. It's you and me, babe."

"You and me, babe," he repeated, and flashed a heartbreaking smile. "How 'bout it?"

After he drifted off into fitful slumber, they collected together by the open hangar doors. Allie broke up a bookshelf with a hammer and Nick made a campfire from the shelves and piles of flight manuals. He ignited the whole mess with one pass of his burning right hand. Renée turned up some Dasanis and dried pasta in a cupboard. Harper held a pot over the flames, waiting for the water to boil. Harper's hand extended straight into their cook fire, the blaze licking around her knuckles. Once you had mastered Dragonscale, you could skip the oven mitts.

"If he dies," Allie said, "I quit. I don't care about Martha Quinn's island. I don't even like eighties music."

The fire snapped and popped.

"Here's the part where you promise me he won't die," Allie said.

Harper didn't say a word for ten minutes, and then all she told them was, "Pasta's done."

# 24

Late the next morning the small party of pilgrims came around a bend and drifted to a shuffling, weary halt.

What stopped them initially was a shock of color. On the left side of the road was the sort of scenery they were used to: blasted trees and a long slope of burnt sticks and ruin. But on the right was a gray-green forest of pine. The branches of the firs were caked in ash, but the trees beneath were healthy, undamaged, and the grass growing below them was rich and lush. Through the evergreens they saw a gleam of black water.

A billboard stood on the green side of the road. Originally it had featured an ad for GEICO insurance. A dainty little gecko suggested that fifteen minutes or less could save a buck or two. Spray-painted directly under this helpful suggestion was a message in black:

NEW MAINE FREE ZONE
INFECTED TAKE GLOVES + COAT
STAY ON ROAD CONTINUE NORTH
TO MACHIAS FOR MARTHA QUINN ISLE
INFECTED WEAR ORANGE SAFETY
GARMENTS AT ALL TIMES!

An elderly pickup was parked alongside the billboard. The flatbed contained milk cartons crammed with bright orange work gloves. A pile of orange rain slickers had been heaped beside them. Nick climbed up to root around, lifted one of the slickers, and turned it so they could see.

A biohazard symbol had been stenciled on the back in black.

"What now?" Renée asked.

"Looks like we get dressed," Harper said. "Will you be a hon and find me a coat? I don't want to try and climb up there."

Ten minutes later they walked on, all of them in the orange slickers and orange gloves that marked them as sick. They hadn't tried to pull a coat on the Fireman, had only tossed one over his chest.

The pond they had glimpsed through the trees turned out to be a nasty body of water indeed. Masses of dead fish rotted on the stones at the edge of the water, and the shallows were hidden beneath a floating blanket of ash, although the center of the little pool was clear and black. There were a few undamaged and empty cottages built alongside the water, from the days before there were setback rules on construction. Notices had been nailed to the front doors, above more black biohazard symbols.

"Hang on," Harper said and left them in the road.

She climbed the steps of the first cottage and read the notice.

THIS HOUSE HAS BEEN DESIGNATED A TEMPORARY OVERNIGHT SHELTER FOR THOSE INFECTED WITH DRACO INCENDIA TRYCHOPHYTON A/K/A DRAGONSCALE. IF YOU ARE HEALTHY DO NOT ENTER.

DO NOT DRINK THE WATER OR USE THE TOILETS. THERE IS BOTTLED WATER IN THE FRIDGE AND CANNED GOODS. DO NOT TAKE MORE THAN YOU NEED. THERE IS ABSOLUTELY NO SQUATTING. VISITORS MUST DEPART WITHIN 12 HOURS. THIS RESIDENCE IS MONITORED BY LOCAL LAW ENFORCEMENT.

WEAR YOUR ORANGE SAFETY GARMENTS AT ALL TIMES. IN-

FECTED FOUND NOT WEARING CLOTHING THAT MARKS THEM AS SICK WILL BE CONSIDERED HOSTILE AND MAY BE SHOT.

YOU ARE 131 MILES FROM MACHIAS, WHERE YOU MAY BE PROVIDED WITH TRANSPORT TO THE FREE WOLF ISLAND D.I.T. CARE UNIT. OUR PRAYERS ARE WITH YOU.

"What's it say?" Allie shouted.

"It says we can stay here overnight if we need to," Harper said, but she already knew they weren't going to. It was too early in the day to stop.

She let herself in, pushing back the door and stepping into the front hall. The cottage had a pipe-smoke and dusty-book smell that Harper associated with the aged. The phone on the wall had a rotary dial.

Harper found her way to a kitchen with a view of the pond. A 1950s-era Coldspot refrigerator the color of a banana milk shake stood against one wall. A picture of Smokey Bear in a rustic wooden frame hung next to the back screen door. ONLY YOU CAN PREVENT FOREST FIRES.

The light switches didn't work. She peeked into the fridge and found pallets of room-temperature bottled water. The bathroom was as dark as a closet, and Harper had to fumble around for a while before she found the catch on the medicine cabinet.

When she came out of the lake house five minutes later, Harper had a case of water under her left arm and a bottle of Bayer aspirin in her right hand. She squatted on the flagstone path and used a rock to crush four aspirin tablets into a fine powder. She spoonfed the smashed pills to John, mixed in with little sips of water.

"Will that make him better?" Allie asked.

"It'll bring down his fever," Harper said. *For a while,* she thought. If they didn't get antibiotics into him soon, all the aspirin in the world wouldn't keep his infected respiratory system going. He'd suffocate on his own fluids.

*"Chim chim cher-ee,"* John muttered. *"Chim chim cher-uck. Here comes Jakob in his truck. Chim chim cher-ee, chim chim cher-all. Desolation's plow sweeps away all."*

Harper kissed his sweaty, damp cheek, stood, and nodded to Allie. Allie bent and took the handles of the ladder.

"Let's go," Harper said.

# 25

They left the lake behind and soon crossed back into another burn zone. Low clouds of smoke smothered the sky, and they were hot and sticky in their slickers. A wind came in spasms, blowing grit. Harper had ash in her mouth, ash in her eyes. Allie collected ash in her long eyelashes and eyebrows and short, bristly hair. With her pink, dust-irritated eyes, she very much looked like an albino. When they stopped to rest, Harper took John's pulse. It was shallow and erratic. She crushed four more aspirin and force-fed them to him.

Late in the afternoon they came over a hill and looked down into more green, and this time it was on both sides of the road. On the right were swaying evergreens. On the left was a meadow of russet straw, bordered by blueberry bushes that were months from bearing fruit. A mile away they saw a white farmhouse, a barn, a gleaming steel silo.

As they neared the farmhouse, Harper saw a woman standing in the dooryard, shading her eyes with one hand and peering back at them. A screen door slapped shut. A dog barked.

They arrived at a fence of stripped, shining logs, with the farm buildings on the other side. A black retriever ran back and forth on a chain, flinging himself in their general direction and barking without cessation. His eyes shone with a jolly lunacy.

A white bedsheet hung over the fence, one corner flapping in the breeze. Words had been written on it in Sharpie.

WE ARE HEALTHY. PLEASE GO
ON. MACHIAS, 126 MI.

GOD LOVE AND KEEP YOU. HELP AHEAD.

"These fucking people," Allie whispered.

"These fucking people might have children," Harper said. "And maybe they don't want them to burn to death."

"Burn to death!" John Rookwood shouted, cawing like a crow. He began to hack, a dry, wrenching cough, twisting violently on his stretcher.

The woman continued to watch them from her front step. She looked like she had walked out of another century, in her ankle-length dress and blue denim blouse, a kerchief holding back her graying brown hair.

Paper cups had been set along the fencepost. They contained what looked like orange Gatorade.

Nick picked it up, sniffed at it, glanced at Harper for permission. She nodded that it was all right to drink.

"What if it's poison?" Allie asked.

"There's easier ways to kill us," Harper said. "They could just shoot us. Who wants to bet that man watching from the second floor has a gun?"

Allie darted a surprised look back at the farmhouse. A lantern-jawed man with raven-black hair—graying at the temples, swept back from his high brow—regarded them from a window above and to the right of the front door. His gaze was dispassionate and unblinking. Sniper eyes.

The woman watched them drink but didn't speak. Harper thought the orange stuff might be Tang. Whatever it was, it was sweet and clean and made her feel almost human.

"Thank you," Harper said.

The woman nodded.

Harper was about to go on, then paused and leaned over the fence. "Our friend is sick. *Very* sick. He needs antibiotics. Do you have antibiotics?"

The woman's forehead wrinkled in thought. She looked at the Fireman, strapped to the travois, and back at Harper. She took a step toward the fence and opened her mouth to speak and the window on the second floor banged open.

"Keep walkin'," the man called, and Harper was right. He had a rifle, although he didn't point it at them, just cradled it to his chest. "You take one step our side of the fence, you won't take another. There's a place for people like you up north."

"One of them is sick," the woman called up.

Her husband laughed. "All of them is sick."

# 26

All through the following morning, Harper was conscious of being observed, sometimes surreptitiously, sometimes openly. An old man in a wifebeater glared at them from behind the screen door of his cottage. Three small and nearly identical boys with running noses studied them from the window of their ranch house. Nick waved. They didn't wave back.

Another time, a black car followed them, hanging about a quarter mile back, gravel grinding under its tires. It stopped when they stopped, and when they proceeded it rolled on in their wake. Four men in it, two in front, two in back, men in flannel hunting coats and porkpie hats.

"I think they have guns," Renée said. "Do you think we're safe? No, don't answer that. They say there's no such thing as a stupid question, but I believe that qualifies. We haven't been safe in months."

The black car kept pace with them for over an hour before suddenly accelerating, then lurching off the highway onto a narrow side road, tires throwing stones. One of the passengers hurled an empty beer can out the window, but Harper wasn't sure he was throwing it at them. She didn't see any weapons, but as they took the corner, a fat, ruddy-faced man in the backseat made a pistol with his hand, pointed his finger at Nick, and pulled an imaginary trigger. Pow.

Very late in the day they reached the Bucksport Trading Post, which had the look of a former stable, with a hitching post out front and window frames of wormy, untreated pine. Antlers rose above the front door. A nonfunctional Coke machine from the forties collected dust on the board porch. The dirt lot was empty, a chain hung across the entrance. A white sheet had been draped over the chain, words slapped on in black paint:

ALL HEALTHY HERE SICK GO ON

But a folding table had been set up on their side of the rusty, swinging chain. On it were paper bowls of chicken noodle soup. Paper cups of water had been arranged in a row.

The smell of the soup was enough to get Harper's saliva glands working and her stomach tightening with hunger, but that wasn't what really excited her. Over on one corner of the table was a bottle of some kind of pink syrup and a little plastic syringe. It was the sort of syringe you might use to orally administer medicine to a dog or a small child. The label on the bottle said ERYTHROMYCIN and gave a dosage for someone named Lucky. It had expired over a year ago and was only half full, the outside of the bottle tacky with dried syrup. Pinned beneath the bottle was a ruled sheet of notebook paper:

*heard you are with invalid will this help?*

Harper took the bottle in one hand and peered up at the Bucksport Trading Post. A black man in a flannel shirt, with gold spectacles resting on the end of his nose, peered back from behind a window crowded with knickknacks: a carved wooden moose, a lamp with a driftwood base. Harper lifted a hand in a gesture of thanks. He nodded, his glasses flashing, and retreated into dimness.

She gave John his first dose, squirting it into the back of his mouth, and followed with aspirin, while the others sat on the side of the road, tipping their paper bowls to their mouths to drink lukewarm soup.

An orange DETOUR FOR SICK sign pointed them west, along a winding country road, away from the town of Bucksport itself. But they paused at a wooden sawhorse (SICK DO NOT CROSS) to peer along a lane that led into town and down toward the sea. The street was shaded with big leafy oaks and lined with two- and three-story Colonials. It was late in the day and Harper could see lights on in the houses—electric lights—and a streetlamp casting a steely blue glow.

"My God," Renée said. "We're back in a part of the world that has power."

"No we aren't," Allie told her. "That part of the world is on the other side of this sawhorse. What do you think would happen if we tried to cross?"

"I don't know, and we're not going to find out. We're going to follow the signs and do what we're told," Harper said.

"Walk right this way," Allie said. "Up the ramp and into the slaughterhouse. Single file, please. No shoving."

"If they wanted to kill us, they've had plenty of opportunities," Renée noted.

"Never mind me," Allie said. "I'm just your typical jaded teenage leper."

# 27

They spent the night in a public campground that had been marked specifically for the use of the infected. The dirt road in was flanked by a pair of enormous wooden heads, carved to look like noble Indian chieftains, complete with sad, wise eyes and feathered headdresses. Hung above the entrance was a banner that proclaimed SICK STAY HERE WATER FOOD TOILETS.

They slept under picnic tables, rain plopping on the wooden planks and dripping down on top of them. But there were port-a-potties, an inconceivable luxury after over a week of using rags to wipe, and John surprised Harper by sleeping through the night, his chest rising and falling deeply and his lean, lined face set in an expression of dreaming calm. He woke just once, when she put the syringe in his mouth to give him another squirt of the antibiotic, and even then he only made a small sound, an amused sort of snort, and slipped away again.

They stayed in the campground most of the morning, waiting for the rain to pass. It quit around lunch and the afternoon was fine for walking. A cool breeze shushed in the big-leafed oaks. The daylight glittered on every wet surface, made spiderwebs into nets studded with diamonds.

They followed THIS WAY SICK signs north and east—mostly north—past forest and lake. Once they passed a folding table by the side of the road where someone had set out a bowl filled with individually wrapped Oreo cookies, a steel jug with blessedly cold milk in it, and Dixie cups. There were no houses in sight. The table stood alone at the end of a dirt lane that led back into trees.

"This is fresh," Harper said. She shut her eyes to savor an icy swallow. "It can't have been sitting outside for long."

"No. 'Course not. They know we're coming," the Fireman croaked from his stretcher.

Harper almost coughed milk up her nose.

In the next moment they were all on their knees around the travois. John looked at them from half-shut eyes, his chin bristly and his cheeks caved in from all the weight he had lost. His color was ghastly. His smile was fond but weak.

"I wouldn't say no to some of that milk myself, Nurse Willowes," he said. "If it won't interfere with my recovery."

"Not at all. But I want you to take some aspirin with it."

She put a hand behind his head, propping it up, and gave him slow sips from her own cup. She didn't say a thing. For the next ten minutes, Allie and Renée were talking over each other while Nick gestured furiously with his hands, all of them trying to tell the story of the last week and a half at the same time. The Fireman looked this way and that and nodded sometimes, making a drowsy effort to attend to each of them. Harper wasn't sure how much he was getting, although his brow furrowed when Allie told him they had left Bucksport behind that morning.

"The four of you carried me all the way to Bucksport?"

"No," Harper said. "Just Allie."

"Lucky your bony English ass is light," Allie said.

"Lucky you don't know how to quit," John said to her. "Lucky for me. Thank you, Allie. I love you, girl."

Allie wasn't good at the emotional stuff. She looked away into the trees, clenching her jaw and clamping down on some intense upswell of feeling.

"Try not to get nearly killed again," she said, when she was able to speak.

They all seemed to run out of things to say at the same time, and then there was a pleasant silence, no sound except for the swish of the cool wind in the trees and the twittering of the birds. Harper found herself holding John's hand.

"Perhaps we can procure me a crutch," he said. "Or fashion one. I wouldn't like to burden you all any longer."

"Let's not get ahead of ourselves," Harper said. "Yesterday this time, I wasn't sure you'd live to see another morning."

"That bad?"

"Buddy," Harper said, "I thought you were smoked."

"Ha ha," he said. "Good one, Willowes."

# 28

He slept through most of the next twenty-four hours, waking only to eat meals. Dinner was cold beef stew, left out on the side of the road in a deep steel pot. There were no bowls, so they took turns drinking right from the ladle.

It was rich—so rich it made Harper a little light-headed—and salty and gluey in consistency. Big carrots and buttery pieces of beef and a smoky undertaste of bourbon. Harper didn't care that it was cold. She could not remember a better meal in all her life. John couldn't manage the big pieces, but he was able to get down some peas and a few of the smaller bits of beef, and when he dozed off again, Harper thought his color was better.

Early on the afternoon of the following day, they found themselves at the bottom of a long rise, the sides of the road crowded with leafy oaks, so that the two-lane blacktop passed beneath a canopy of pale green. Sunlight flashed and winked through the waving branches and a dappled brightness danced across the road. It was a long, sweaty trudge to the top of the hill, but the climb was worth it. At the top, the trees parted to the right, to reveal a view that went for miles, across meadows and dense bands of forest. Harper saw grazing cows and the roofs of a few farmhouses. And beyond it all was a dark blue reach of ocean. When Harper breathed deeply, she thought she could almost smell it.

John had missed their glimpse of the sea when they crossed through Bucksport and asked Allie to turn him so he could admire the scenery. She held him tilted almost upright in the drag sled while he stared out across the fields, drenched in golden midafternoon light, and on to the deep blue water. The wind whisked his hair back from his smooth brow. Every time Harper looked at his forehead she wanted to kiss it.

"Is that a sailboat?" John said, narrowing his eyes. "Does anyone else see a sail?"

All of them stood there squinting.

"I don't see anything," Renée said.

"Me neither," Harper said.

Allie pointed. "Yeah. There."

John said, "Do you see something *on* the sail? A little splash of red?"

Allie peered into the distance. "*Nnnoooo*. Why?"

But John had turned his head and asked Nick with a few gestures what he saw. Nick nodded and replied. Harper didn't catch it.

"What'd he say?"

"Nick's eyes are best," John replied, in a slightly irritating tone of satisfaction. "He sees the little splash of red too."

"So what?" Harper asked.

"You never saw the *Bobbie Shaw* out on the water," he told her. "The boat. But I did. I was out in it a time or two, the year I was a counselor at Camp Wyndham. There's a picture of a large red crab on the sail."

"No," Renée said. "I know what you're saying, John, but it can't be Don Lewiston. It can't. It's been four weeks. I don't know how long it would take to get from Portsmouth, New Hampshire, to Machias by sail, but not almost a month."

"We ran into a few setbacks along the way," he said mildly. "Maybe Don did, too."

They stood there a while longer and then without a word Allie turned the travois and began to tramp on. One by one the others fell in behind her, until only Harper remained. Squinting hard into the distance.

There. On the very line of the horizon. A tiny white splinter against all that blue.

With a little red fleck upon it.

# 29

They were perhaps fifty miles from Machias the morning they found the crutch.

It was, by then, two days since John had woken and asked for a glass of milk. Allie had gone on hauling the drag sled—there was no other reasonable option—and John had rediscovered his voice, which he used to complain about being shaken and bumped. He kvetched about itches he couldn't reach, a sore back, and the sun in his eyes.

"I liked it better when you were dying," Allie said. "You didn't bitch so much."

"Look sharp, Allie. I think you missed a pothole back there. You don't want to break up your streak of dragging me over every one."

Allie slowed, straightened up, and stretched her back. "You want a break from me? Be careful what you wish for, smartass. You just might get one. Is that what I think it is?"

It leaned against the trunk of a great old oak, with a red bandanna tied around it so it would catch their eye: a stainless steel crutch with a yellow foam armpit pad. No note, no explanation. A white cottage stood behind a picket fence nearby, but the windows were dark. If they were being watched—Harper felt sure they were—she couldn't tell from where.

Nick undid the bungee cords that held John to the travois and helped him up. Allie supported him while he fitted the crutch under one arm. He was testing it out, hobbling in little circles, when Harper noticed Renée blinking at tears.

"So much kindness," Renée said. "So many people looking after us. They don't know a thing about us except we're in need. I read a Cormac McCarthy novel once, about the end of the world. People hunting dogs and each other and frying up babies, and it was awful. But we need kindness like we need to eat. It satisfies something in us we can't do without."

"Or maybe they just want us to hurry up," Allie said. "The sooner we go on our way, the safer they are."

"It's hard to imagine a sinister agenda behind the food they've left out for us. The soup, the pitchers of milk. I just can't imagine a secret wicked purpose behind supplying us with endless goodies."

"Neither could Hansel and Gretel," the Fireman said. "Shall we limp on? I think I'll stretch my one good leg for a while."

# 30

He lasted all of five minutes before he sat on the curb, white and sweaty and shaking, and agreed to climb on the stretcher again. All the talk seemed to go out of him and he bore every thump and bump with gritted teeth.

The next day, though, he crutched along with them for half an hour in the morning and another twenty minutes in the afternoon. He was better still the day after that and kept up with them for most of the A.M.

On the fourth day after they found the crutch, he hobbled along on his own power from breakfast until they broke for lunch, only resting when Harper insisted. Lunch was a selection of mushy brown cupcakes and some bologna sandwiches wrapped in wax paper. Someone had dropped them in a plastic shopping bag and left them dangling from a mailbox at the end of a gravel driveway. Harper unwrapped one of the sandwiches and took a whiff. It had a faintly corrupt odor, like the inside of a sneaker.

They stuck with the cupcakes—at first. But Harper carried the bag, and at some point, late in the day, found herself tucking into one of the sandwiches in spite of herself.

"I hope that doesn't make you sick," Renée said. "You *are* nine months pregnant."

"Nine months and a week. And that's why I'm eating it," Harper said. "I can't help myself."

After the third bite, though, she was finally able to *taste* it, and knew it was spoiled. At first she had missed the slimy texture of the meat, and a faint but definite sour flavor that brought to mind sepsis. She spat it out and tossed what was left of the sandwich in the grass with a revulsion that approached moral horror.

She was guiltily licking bright yellow mustard off her fingertips when the Fireman said, "Hold up."

Harper lifted her head to see what had caught his attention and saw a pair of jeeps, parked in such a way as to block both lanes of the highway, nose to nose. Two men stood in yellow rubber overalls and yellow masks with clear faceplates. Yellow booties and yellow gloves. Harper recognized it as the same outfit she had worn during her weeks as a nurse in Portsmouth Hospital. The sentinels carried assault rifles. One of them stepped forward, hand raised, palm outward. Harper wasn't sure if this gesture meant for them to halt, or if he was simply waving hello.

Allie stopped walking, took Nick's hand, and squeezed it to indicate he should stop as well. Renée walked past them without missing a step.

"You really think we ought to just hand ourselves over?" Allie asked.

Renée tossed a casual glance back. "Oh, Allie, we've been in their hands for days."

A third man sat in one of the jeeps. He wore yellow, too, although he had his hood off, so Harper could see a full head of white hair and a big, craggy face. He had a knee on the steering wheel and a slender paperback open across his thigh. It looked like he was working a crossword.

"Five on the road, Jim," said one of the armed men, his voice muffled by his mask.

Jim looked up from his book and gazed mildly around. He had a big, humorous beak of a nose, and pale eyes, and overgrown eyebrows. He dropped his crossword puzzle and hopped out. He squeezed between the gunmen, and as he did, he reached out absentmindedly and put his hand on the barrel of one of the machine guns, nudging it so it pointed down at the blacktop. Harper took this as a promising gesture.

"Welcome to Machias!" called the one named Jim, slowing as he walked toward them. "You've had quite a walk. Dorothy didn't have to go half as far with Toto."

"Are you going to take us to Oz?" Renée Gilmonton asked.

"It's not exactly the Emerald City," Jim said. "But they've got hot water and power out on the island." His gaze drifted to Harper's stomach, and for a moment his smile faltered, and he looked thoughtful and a little sad. "Doctors, too, although their head researcher, Professor Huston, died in the big fire back in January."

"Big fire?" Renée asked. "Does that mean what I think it means?"

"No cure, I'm afraid," Jim said. "And more than a few setbacks. Including one mishap that was, well, pretty awful. No way around it. A whole control group of thirty infected had some kind of reaction to a drug they were testing. They all went up within a few hours of each other. The fire slipped out of control and burnt down the central medical facility, although the remaining staff has set up shop in a farmhouse. Now, don't you worry. We sent word one of you was pregnant and looked to be pretty far along. When are you expecting?"

"I believe I'm a few days overdue, actually," Harper said.

Jim shook his head. "At least you didn't have to deliver on the road. The medical folk out on the island are aware of your condition. They've got a bed all made up for you."

Harper was surprised by the intensity of her relief. For a moment her legs felt wobbly beneath her. Something, some muscular ache, a cramped tightness, seemed to let go behind her chest . . . some part of her that had been clenched up, perhaps for months.

"If we move we can have you there by midnight," Jim said. "It's a three-hour ride in the boat, and we have to pass you through processing before we can depart. The good news is we knew you were coming. Boat is already loaded, prepped to go."

"What's he saying?" Nick asked with his hands.

Harper explained. The man named Jim watched, his bushy eyebrows knitted together, half smile on his face.

"Deaf?" he asked, and when she nodded he shook his head. "Deaf *and* infected. Some kids get all the luck." He crouched down, hands on his knees, to look into Nick's face, and in a very loud voice, moving his lips slowly, he said, *"There's plenty! Of kids! Where you're going! Lots of little guys! To play with!"*

Nick looked at Harper and she explained with her hands, standing to one side. Nick's reply required no translation at all. He gave a thumbs-up.

Jim nodded, satisfied, and slopped his mask onto his head. "Come on. Jump in the jeep."

Harper walked beside the Fireman. She held his elbow with one hand and carried the Portable Mother in the other. She raised her voice to be heard over a sudden gusting wind. "I have only two questions: When do we get to meet Martha Quinn, and does she take requests?"

Jim glanced back at them as he got behind the wheel. Through the plastic window in his mask, he smiled. "You'll be with her before you know it."

He didn't answer the second question.

# 31

After twenty days of walking, Harper found the rush of moving at high speed in a jeep a little alarming. She sat up front, next to Jim. Renée and the Fireman sat in back, Allie squeezed between them and Nick perched on Renée's lap. One of the gunmen traveled with them, too, although he sat on the very back of the jeep, holding on to the roll bar, his feet dangling over the rear fender and his gun swinging carelessly from a strap around his neck.

It didn't help Harper's troubled stomach any when Jim turned the jeep around and drove it up onto a wide gravel path, not a road at all. They jounced over ruts and potholes, the branches of fir trees whipping past above them. Jim said they were on something called the Sunrise Trail.

"This thing was intended for bicycles," he said, by way of apology. "And hikers. But it's the best route to the processing center without bringing you through town."

The Fireman leaned forward. "I'm surprised you're wearing all that gear. They must thoroughly understand how transmission works by now, after, what, a year of study? If *we* understand it, *they* must. Your experts out on the island."

Jim listened but didn't reply.

"It's the ash!" the Fireman yelled to be heard over the roar of the slipstream. "If you don't come in contact with the ash, there's nothing to worry about!"

"That's one theory," Jim said.

"It's not one theory. It's the fact!" the Fireman said.

"You some kind of biologist?"

"I used to teach at UNH."

"I'm sure they'll be glad to have your expertise," Jim called back. "Put you right to work."

The way he said it, Harper wasn't sure if he was making fun or being serious.

Back on the highway, it had been a dim, rose-tinted dusk. Beneath the trees it was already full splendid night, the pines whipping by in a warm blast of darkness. Through gaps in the trees, Harper glimpsed an estuary, a broad plate of black glass under a blushing sky. She spotted a scattering of electric lights, the town over there somewhere.

The Fireman leaned forward again. "You still have power. Do you have cell phone coverage as well? I'm curious how folks were able to pass word up the road that we were coming."

"We're very grateful to everyone who put food out for us!" Renée called.

Harper was grateful to everyone who had put out food except for whoever decided to get rid of their rancid bologna by dumping it on the pregnant lady. Her stomach was a knot of worms.

"Yeah, power in some places. Though it's spotty and it goes out quite a bit. No cell phone coverage, but we've got a working landline system in Machias—the governor saw to that—and we can communicate with people farther away by CB." Jim thought for a moment, the steering wheel rocking gently in his hand, then said, "We don't get too many coming from the south anymore. Not across the wastelands. We don't get many at *all* these days, but when we do have new arrivals, they're usually from the north. Across from Canada."

"How many have you saved?" Harper yelled. She thought talking might help take her mind off her building nausea.

"Six hundred and ninety-four men, women, and children," Jim proclaimed. "And with you it'll be six hundred and ninety-nine. No, make it seven hundred on the dot, counting baby! Can't forget baby!"

"We need to talk about that," Harper said. "About who will take him, assuming he's born without contamination."

"What do you mean?"

"It's been a while since I've read the medical literature, but last I heard, there was a hypothesis that the children of mothers with Dragonscale are unlikely to carry the infection themselves."

"I'm afraid my medical expertise pretty much ends at putting on Band-Aids when my eight-year-old scrapes her knee."

"But there must've been children born on the island, with almost seven hundred people there. Maybe?"

"Above my pay grade!" he said cheerfully.

The trees began to break up, and to the right of the jeep, Harper saw high grass, a stretch of wet sand, and distant water. Out across a bay stood a lighthouse, sweeping the ocean. It did actually resemble a candle on the water, a thick white one, lit to mark a child's first birthday, perhaps.

"If the baby is born uncontaminated," Harper tried again, "I'd like to have some say over the foster family."

"I don't know anything about that. I haven't heard of anyone adopting sick babies."

"He *won't* be sick," she said, feeling he was missing the crucial point.

Jim's smile broadened behind his clear plastic faceplate. "It's a boy? You know that for certain?"

"Yes," Harper said. It felt certain to her.

She waited for him to comment, but Jim fell quiet again. She decided to leave it, supposed she could coordinate with the medical staff on the island. The trees fell away and they went on and on. To the right was a shabby tilting fence of pickets and wire. Harper saw, in the distance, a striped yellow-and-white tent, brightly aglow, a sight that made her think of small-town fairs. There would be a bucket to bob for apples under there, and a place to buy caramel corn.

As they approached the pavilion, the grass thinned out on their left, and Harper saw a narrow road running parallel to their trail. Up ahead was a parking lot, off to one side of the big striped tent, a few cars parked there. Harper smelled the boat before she saw it, a sickening stench of cheap diesel. Her stomach flopped. As they rolled the last few hundred feet to the processing area, she saw a dock at the end of a spit and a dirty fishing trawler, THE MAGGIE ATWOOD written in cheery cursive across the back. Men in full-body biohazard outfits carried cardboard boxes down the ramp and onto the deck.

Beneath the pavilion were a few long folding tables. Christmas lights had been strung along the steel pipes overhead, creating a weirdly festive air. It was almost crowded, nine or ten people in yellow rubber suits moving around behind the tables. A steel pot steamed on a camp gas burner in one corner.

"They've got cocoa," said Jim. "And gingerbread cookies. And a pretty good turkey stew. Everyone gets fed before they go across the water."

Harper turned in her seat and moved her hands, passing along the good news to Nick.

He grinned and signed back to her: "Look at all the lights! It's like where Santa lives! It's like we walked all the way to Christmasland!"

Harper signed, "I think you mean the North Pole," but Nick wasn't paying attention anymore, craning his head to see into the pavilion.

Jim turned the jeep into a place where the grass was flattened down and switched off the engine. They followed him into the tent, under the festive lights.

"Come meet the volunteers," he said.

The volunteers were all women, most middle-aged or older. They reminded Harper of the sort of cheerful, efficient old dolls who organized baked-bean socials for their church. Jim led the refugees to the folding tables, where the first of the women waited for them with forms on a clipboard. Through the clear window in her rubber mask, she showed an eager grin, and seemed especially delighted to see a little boy with them.

"Hello! And haven't *you* come a long way on foot! You must

be *ex*-hausted. My name is Vivian, I'm going to take your information. Then we'll get a picture of each of you for the Web site and give you your housing assignments and some supplies for your trip."

"And some of that soup, I hope," Renée said. "Smells so good it's making me light-headed."

Harper could smell it herself, an odor of chicken broth and stewed carrots, mixed with the black stink of the boat. It made her feel very close to retching. It appalled her that she had been stupid enough to have even a single bite of that rotten sandwich. She should've had some sense, if not some self-restraint. She had let pregnancy turn her into a foul pig and now she was getting what she deserved. She knew she was going to puke, she just didn't know when.

"You bet!" Vivian cried. "Soup and fresh milk and coffee for the grown-ups and we'll get you on your way! We'll make this as quick and painless as we can. Let's just begin with the basics—*who* are you?"

Harper opened her mouth to speak, but Renée got there first. "We're what's left of the Camp Wyndham Conspiracy. These are our evil leaders, Mr. Rookwood and Nurse Harper. We come in peace."

Jim, who had moved behind the folding tables to join the grannies, threw back his head and barked a laugh at this.

"Whoo!" Vivian said. "An evil conspiracy! Haven't had one of those yet."

"Well, we're a democratic conspiracy. Everyone gets a vote. Even the kids."

"I don't know how I feel about that one. *My* kids would probably vote for ice cream for dinner and no bedtime. Did you get to vote on your bedtime?" she asked Nick, bending down to look into his face.

"I'm afraid he's deaf," said the Fireman.

"You're British!"

"All the best evil masterminds are. And if my son did get

a vote, he would probably vote for chicken stew before filling out forms." Harper almost missed him saying *my son*, but she didn't miss it when John put his arm around her waist and added, "My wife, too."

Vivian put them down just as he said: husband and wife, Mr. and Mrs. Rookwood. Harper didn't object. She felt that, in many ways, John had told the truth. She put her head on his shoulder while Vivian asked her questions and scratched down the answers.

Vivian wanted to know how far they had come and where they had set out from. She asked when they got sick and where they had traveled since their infection. She wanted details on their symptoms, if they were prone to hot flashes, charring, smoking.

"Not at all!" Renée said. "We have a technique for pacifying the infection: daily sing-alongs. Keeps it from going critical. You can bring the spore under control with almost any kind of group activity that gives pleasure. Something to do with a hormone your brain releases, oxytocin? Nurse Harper can explain it best."

But Nurse Harper didn't need to explain anything. Vivian smiled. "I understand group therapies are very popular on the island and are still the most successful treatment. They have eighties sing-alongs after breakfast. Toto and Hall & Oates."

"In that case," the Fireman said, "I think I'd rather burn alive."

There were a lot of questions about the impending baby. All of the women were excited, and the plump old woman who took their photos told Harper at length about her own first grandchild, little Kelly, who had been born three weeks before, and who she said sounded just like a sheep when she cried.

*"Baa! Baa!"* said the older woman, laughing.

But when Harper said she was hoping to talk to someone about adoption for the baby, assuming it was healthy, the newly minted grandmother began to fiddle with her camera and looked vexed. "This thing!" she said, and wandered away.

Farther down the table, the Portable Mother was opened and searched for weapons by a thin, indifferent woman with a sharp, narrow face and nothing to say. Yet another lady handed them blue folders, a thick stapled packet inside each. Harper saw a photocopied thirty-page document, *Free Wolf Island: A Guide to Health and Safety,* published by the CDC.

Each folder also had a real estate listing in it. Harper and John and the kids had been offered a two-bedroom, two-bathroom cottage at 3 Longbay Road. A smeary black-and-white photo showed a small white cottage and a leaf-strewn backyard with a child's play set in it. Renée was offered a bedroom at 18 Longbay, in the Longbay Bed & Breakfast, which was a kind of dorm for half a dozen others. Some color photocopies showed the island from above, on a fall day, the trees dressed out in their autumn colors, a patchwork of rusty oranges and buttery yellows. A map of town marked out the clinic, the communal greenhouses, the town library, a former general store that was now serving as a supply-distribution center, and other points of interest.

At the end of the line of tables a beaming Asian granny dished out paper bowls of stew and paper cups of milk, and they were directed to sit and rest their feet on a stack of hay bales just outside the pavilion. Harper couldn't eat. By the time they had made their way through processing, she was having contractions—bad ones—and her stomach was boiling with sickness. She sat on the edge of one of the bales and clutched her abdomen in both hands, grimacing. Her distress unsettled John, who skipped his meal as well and sat beside her, rubbing her back in circles.

"I haven't seen you like this," he said. "Do you think you're going into labor?"

Her stomach cramped and she made a small sound of unhappiness, then shook her head. "Get something to eat, John. You need your strength."

"Maybe in a minute, Harper," he said, but he never did get up, although Nick brought him a creamy, sugared coffee.

They sat on the bales, on the outer edge of the light, John stroking Harper's back and Harper waiting for her contractions to pass. They did—eventually—but the nasty slick feeling in her belly and intestines remained. Filthy clouds of black smoke rolled back up the beach from the boat and when she caught a whiff of the stink, it took all her will not to gag.

Before they departed, the woman named Vivian approached, holding a little shoe box. She brought it to Nick and held it out to him, then spoke to the Fireman, so he could translate.

"These are all my *Doctor Who* episodes," she said. "There's a boy who went over to the island three months ago. He's a few years older than Nick here, about fourteen, and I happen to know he's a science-fiction fan. I promised I'd get him my collection so he'd have something to watch. Will you tell Nick to give these to Jared Morris? And please tell Nick he can watch them, too. I think Jared would like that. I think Jared would also like a smart friend who can teach him sign language."

"You're too kind," John Rookwood said, and explained to Nick, who solemnly took the shoe box full of DVDs.

When Vivian stood, her eyes glittered with tears. "You people. I can't imagine what you've been through. I pray every night you'll be healed. A lot of us do. Someday you'll be back and you'll be well, and what stories you'll have."

"Thanks for everything you've done," Harper managed.

"I wish it was more," Vivian said. "Turkey stew and old DVDs for people who have been through hell."

"Turkey stew and old episodes of *Doctor Who* comes pretty close to my idea of heaven," Renée said.

Vivian nodded. She couldn't speak, was obviously overcome with emotion. She held her gloved fingertips to her faceplate and mimed kissing them and then reached out and touched Nick's cheek. "Tell Jared his aunt loves him."

She raised her hand in a last wave and turned away, blinking at damp eyes.

"Did you like the stew?" Renée asked Allie.

Allie gave her a blank look. " 'S'okay. Can we get this show on the road?"

"Yes!" Jim said, walking over to them. "Let's. Your yacht awaits."

# 32

The boat beat its way down a wide inlet, into the hard slap of the waves. Harper threw up over the side before the lights of the pavilion were out of sight. John stroked her neck while she gasped and spat.

"Want some of my coffee?" he said. "I've still got half. It'll get the taste out of your mouth."

She shook her head. He tossed the rest of his coffee over the side and the paper cup, too.

"It wasn't very good anyway," he said.

The ship was grimy, the deck slopping with a quarter inch of nasty water. An exhaust pipe protruded from the rear of the little captain's cabin and the wind blew the smoke back down on them, where they sat in the open on the stern. They huddled on cushioned seats along the sides, squeezed into their orange life vests. Nick's vest was so big on him, most of him had disappeared behind it: there was nothing left to see of him except his head poking through the collar and his feet sticking out below.

"Is it raining?" Harper asked. Cold, salty spray drizzled down on them.

"That's coming off the chop," John said.

"I think I hate the open ocean," Harper said.

They banged through a wave and Harper turned her head and vomited into their wake again.

There were three men in biohazard suits in the pilot's cabin: Jim, one of the gunmen from the checkpoint, and whoever was steering. The captain, Harper imagined. They hadn't been introduced.

"You told them we're married," Harper said, when she had recovered herself and wiped her lips. "I was wondering about that. Remember you said that a fireman could grant divorces? What about marriages?"

"I'll tell you a secret. I'm not a real fireman. But the man steering the ship is a real captain, and they can marry people." He looked at her with a sudden luminous gleam of inspiration. "Ms. Harper Willowes! I think I should ask you something."

*"No,"* she said. "No, *don't.* Please. I was just kidding, John."

His head sank and his expression took on a glum, downcast look.

"But only because my answer might involve kissing. And I can't kiss you now, that would be gross. Not with the taste of vomit in my mouth." Although now that she had been good and sick her stomach felt better—or would've, she thought, if the goddamn contractions hadn't started up once more.

His face lit back up. She took his wet, cold hand and squeezed it, and his grin made his ears jut from the side of his head.

Waves hit the boat and came over the rail in an icy, drenching spray.

"Thank God for the rain slickers," Harper said as they crashed into another trough. "This is miserable."

"It isn't bothering Nick." Nudging her with his elbow. "I think he was out before they untied us from the dock."

"He's done a lot of walking," Harper agreed.

The boat pitched. She looked through the drizzle for the lighthouse she had seen earlier, but they were already too far out to see it.

John yawned into the back of his hand. "Maybe I'll catch a few minutes of shut-eye myself."

"How can you sleep in this?"

"I don't know," he said. "Renée managed it, though."

Harper looked across the stern. Nick dreamed with his cheek against Renée's bosom. She slept with her chin on his head. Allie was awake, though, clutching her life preserver in both hands, and staring darkly into the captain's cabin.

"John," Harper said. "John, why is Renée sleeping? *Who* could sleep in this?"

"*Well*. You said it yourself. We walked at least fifteen miles today, and—"

"Wake her up," Harper said.

"I don't want to wake her up."

"Try. Please."

The Fireman gave her a sidelong look—his gaze hooded and questioning—and then he rose on his crutch and leaned across the deck and shook Renée's knee.

"Renée. Renée, wake up."

The boat slammed over another wave and unbalanced him. He managed to heave himself back onto his seat before he could fall down.

Renée smiled in her sleep and showed no reaction.

"What's wrong with them?" Allie asked.

John's chin had sunk a little. Harper thought his eyes were just slightly unfocused.

"Goddamn it," John said. "Can't *something* work out? Just for once?"

Allie shook Nick's shoulder. He slumped over, fell face-first into Renée's lap.

"The stew," John said.

"The coffee," Harper said.

"But Allie is fine."

"I didn't have any," Allie said. "I didn't trust them. I just pretended to have some and I poured it out when no one was looking."

"I wish you hadn't," Jim shouted to be heard over the engine and the wind.

He had opened the door to the pilot's cabin and leaned in it, staring out at them through his clear plastic faceplate. He had a .45 in one hand, but he wasn't pointing it at them, just casually holding it down by his leg.

"We try and make it peaceful," Jim said. "No fear, no pain. A little something to put you to sleep and then over the side."

"No," Harper said. "No, no, no, *no*. You *can't*. *Please*. This doesn't make any sense. *Why?* Why would you go through this big charade? Why didn't you just fucking shoot us? Anyone could have shot us anytime. Why put on a big act for us?"

"But it *isn't* for us," the Fireman said. "Is it?"

Jim shrugged. "I like to think it's nice for you folks to go out on a high note. To fall asleep dreaming of a place where you'll be safe. Where you'll be looked after. Christ. We're human beings, not *monsters*. We don't want anyone to suffer. But—no. No, we do it for the community. People like Vivian believe in the island, too, most of them. You don't know how important it is for morale, to believe they're saving people. *Helping* people. If they thought we were sailing out here just to throw people over the side, there'd be a lot of broken hearts. A lot of discontentment, too." He paused while the boat crashed over another wave and steadied himself against the doorframe. "You have to understand. You folks said you're—what? The last remnant of a little democracy? You *voted* to come here? Well, we've got a democracy, too. Our own private leadership council. Just the governor and twelve others, including myself. You aren't the only ones who took a vote. So did we. And this is what we voted for."

"There's no island," Allie said.

"There is! Or there was. The CDC abandoned the place in November. There was a revolt. They were using some experimental drugs that had killed some people and the ungrateful sons of bitches seized control of the hospital. They said they didn't *want* a cure anymore. They were raving about how they had made their *own* cure, were learning how to control fire. They were holding the medical staff hostage to deter military action. But they don't know our governor. He doesn't cut deals with terrorists. He commandeered a B-17 out of Bangor and dropped daisy cutters from one end of the island to the other. It's just a black rock now. They could see the smoke from Machias. That's when we made up the story about some burners having a bad reaction to one of the new medicines and the hospital burning up."

"But we heard Martha Quinn on the radio," Harper pled. "We *heard* her."

"Yeah. We've got a hundred hours of her on old recordings. We just replay them on a loop. The governor's argument has always been that this is the fastest way to wipe the epidemic out in the Northeast. Bring all the sick to one processing center and then humanely dispose of them. Drop them in the North Atlantic Current, where there's no chance of the bodies washing back up in Machias. I am really, *truly* sorry."

"You can't," Harper said. "Please. My baby might be healthy."

At this, his face hardened. She could see his jaw tighten behind his mask. "That's a lie. If you're sick, he's sick."

"That's not true. You can't know that. There are studies."

"I don't know what studies you've been looking at. It's true a lot of women who are sick will deliver babies without *visible* Dragonscale. But blood tests show it lurking in the DNA, waiting to emerge. And I don't mind saying: I don't think much of a woman in your condition carrying a baby to term. You were a nurse. You had access to pills. You should've taken something a long time ago. Put yourself to sleep. The thought of you gestating a little guy loaded with disease—that makes *me* want to throw up over the side." He cast a glance into the blackness, then looked back at them. "Look. I don't want to shoot you. It's better in the water. More peaceful. It doesn't matter you didn't get dosed up. The cold will put you to sleep inside ten minutes. It's like the end of *Titanic* out there. Besides, if I have to shoot you I might put a hole in the boat. It's inconvenient, you know? Help a fella out. Take off your vests. Pull the little boy out of his."

"Either we get out of our life vests," John Rookwood said, "or you shoot us. Is that right?" He was tugging at the fingers of the glove on his left hand.

Jim nodded.

"How about a third option," John said, yanking his glove free, throwing it over the side. His palm crawled with threads of gold light.

"How about not," Jim said and shot him in the stomach.

# 33

John touched his navel. His hand was still aglow and it seemed he was bleeding light, that his palm was a saucer filling with gold. He was full of gold and now it was coming out of him. A wave struck the side of the boat—it felt like they had slammed into a rock, it jolted them so hard—and John dropped ungracefully to the deck.

Allie was trying to scream. Harper could see her at the edge of her vision, Allie's mouth open, the tendons standing in her neck, so it looked like she was choking. If she was actually making a sound, Harper didn't know, couldn't tell. She couldn't hear anything except the deep, hard wallop of her own pulse in her ears.

Harper sank to one knee, gripping John's shoulder, turning him a little. The dirty water slopping around the deck was already turning red while his blood pumped into it. His face was white with anguish and shock. She felt for the wound, thinking *Pressure, stop the bleeding first, then try and assess the damage.*

"Oh," he said, his voice a faint gasp. "Oh! I've been shot right through."

"Goddamn it," Jim said. "Now there's blood all over the deck."

"John," she said. "Oh, John. John, my love. Please stay here. Stay with me. Please don't go."

"Get away from him. Stand up and take your vest off or I'll shoot you, too. I'd rather not. Please. It's better in the water. Easier," Jim said, but she wasn't listening.

The blood dripped into John's palm, sizzled, and smoked, smelled like a burning frying pan. Harper wasn't crying, but he was.

"I'm sorry," he said. "I was so self-important. So full of myself. So fucking smug. I'm seeing it all and I was so—so desperate for attention—so desperate to impress you. Oh, Harper. I'm sorry I wasn't a better man. I wish I was better."

"You are perfect. You are the most perfect thing. You make me happy. You make me laugh. I never laughed in all my life like I laughed with you. You don't have to apologize for anything."

A weak smile twitched at the corners of his mouth. "Maybe one thing. I apologize I didn't cook that half-wit with the gun before he shot me. But better late than never." Gold rings flashed in his irises, his eyes brightening like steel coils with an electric current passing through them.

The hand, hidden under his body, began to leap with red flame.

"Do me one favor," he said. "Please. Promise me one thing."

"Yes, my love. Anything. Anything for you, John."

"Live," he said.

Harper shoved herself away from him. He lifted his chin and opened his mouth and Jim screamed *"What the fuck!"* and a jet of yellow flame poured in a great hot blast from the Fireman's open mouth. Jim raised one arm. Flame spattered over the yellow rubber of his suit, blistering the material. He reached to steady himself against the doorframe. The boat lunged over another swell and Jim staggered and waved his gun wildly, pointing it into the cabin. It went off with a harsh blam. The skipper ducked. A window shattered.

The armed sentry shouldered past Jim, lifting his assault rifle. Harper was already rising from her knee. The boat took another lurch and flung her into the soft, warm mass of Renée Gilmonton.

The Fireman ignited, all at once, with a soft, deep *whump,* as if someone had thrown a match on a pile of leaves soaked in lighter fluid. He was a roaring bed of flame, a nest, and a bird began to rise from it. A great red prehistoric thing with vast and spreading wings. The assault rifle thundered, splintering the deck.

The boat slewed across a high wave. Allie grabbed Nick by the vest and stepped onto the cushioned seat and leapt. Harper had her arms around Renée and carried her over the side and as she lifted she had a sense of something tearing in her groin, in her abdomen. A man was screaming behind her. A yellow light was rising.

She hit black water, so cold it burned, it was like dying, it was like spontaneous combustion. A hundred thousand silver bubbles spun around her in a frantic whirl. She came up gasping, caught a mouthful of salt water and began to choke.

A blazing bird of fire, with eyes of blowtorch blue and the wingspan of a single-engine airplane, opened its terrible beak and seemed to scream. A man who wore a shroud of flame twisted madly before it. The pilot's cabin was full of fire. Gray smoke boiled from the destruction. The boat was still moving, leaving them behind, already almost a hundred feet away.

Another wave slapped Harper in the face, blinding her, deafening her. Her vest carried her up and down in the tormented water. She rubbed her hands in her eyes and cleared her vision just in time to see *The Maggie Atwood* shatter, as the flames reached what must've been a propane tank. There was a flash of white light and a blast of concussive sound that struck Harper like a blow, knocking her head back. She would discover her nose bleeding a few moments later.

A blinding tower of fire rose into the sky from the immolated wreck of the boat, and a bird was hatched from that column of fire, a bird as big as God. It spread its wings and lifted into a sky of roiling black cloud, drew a great red circle of light in the sky, spinning above them. To Harper, it seemed magnificent and dreadful, a thing barbaric and triumphant.

It circled once, and again, and although it was high above them, Harper could feel its heat on her upturned face. Then it banked—banked and began to sail away, giving its wings one slow, dreadful flap, leaving them and the sinking, burning, hissing wreck.

Harper was watching it go when she noticed her thighs weren't as cold as they should've been. There was a sticky, unnatural warmth around them.

Her water had broken.

# Delivery

The water seemed less choppy once she was in it. Her vest lifted her gently to the top of each wave and dropped her back down over the side. The motion was almost soothing, didn't make her feel seasick at all. Or maybe she was too numb, too frozen through, to care. She already couldn't feel her hands, her feet. Her teeth were chattering.

Renée blinked and sputtered, shaking her head. She peered around in a frightened, shortsighted sort of way. She had lost her glasses. "What? Did we capsize? Did we—" A wave caught her in the side of the face and she swallowed some, coughed and choked.

Harper struggled toward her and took her hand. "Allie!" she screamed. "Allie, where are you?"

"Over here!" Allie cried, from somewhere behind Harper.

Harper kicked and waved her arms feebly and got turned around. Allie was making her clumsy way to her, towing her brother by the back of his vest. He was still asleep, his plump, smooth face turned to the sky.

"*G-G-G-God,*" Renée said when she could speak again. "*S-s-so c-c-c-cold.* What—what?"

"You were d-d-drugged. The stew. They were going to kill us. John. John." Harper had to stop and catch her breath.

Instead of trying to explain, she pointed at the wreck. The prow of the boat had already dived into the water, the stern lifting into the air. The big rusted blades of the motor, snaggled with seaweed and algae, revolved slowly in the dark. The flames sputtered and seethed as *The Maggie Atwood* slid into the water. A great black oily bank of smoke mounted into the night. Harper moved her finger from the blazing ruin to the Phoenix, which was now no more than a distant bright glare of yellow in the night sky, like a remote passenger jet.

Renée looked at her without any understanding at all. She was still half doped, Harper thought, incapable of following any complicated chain of cause and effect.

Allie caught up to them and took Harper's other hand. They were strung out in a line now, the four of them, kicking feebly in the black and icy water. Harper could see her breath. Or maybe that was smoke.

"We'll die," Allie panted. "We're g-g-going to freeze to death."

"S-sing," Harper said.

Allie looked at her incredulously.

Harper lifted her voice and called out, ""*In every j-job that must be done, there is an element of fun! Find the f-f-fun and, snap! The job is a game!*"

"Why?" Allie said. "Why? This is s-s-*stupid*! It's over. Does it matter if we die in t-t-ten minutes or in t-t-ten *hours*? We're going to drown out here."

Harper kept singing. *"And every task you undertake, becomes a piece of cake, so sing! I'm not going to fucking argue with you!"* She sang this last part right in key.

Renée, blinking and rubbing at her face with her pudgy hands, joined her voice to Harper's.

They kicked together in the water, their wavering voices rising and falling as their bodies rose and fell in the waves.

Allie's hands, scrawled with Dragonscale, began to shine, a yellow light spreading up her wrists and under her soaked shirt. A warm brilliance shone from within the hood of her orange rain slicker. Her eyes brimmed with gold.

The light seemed to race across her thin white fingers and up Harper's hand. Harper felt warmth, a deep, cozy warmth, rushing up her arm and across her torso, as if she were easing sideways into a hot shower.

Their bodies smoked in the freezing water. When Harper looked at Renée, the older woman's eyes were alight. Her blouse was torn at the collar and her throat wore a pretty choker of glowing gold wires.

"What about Nick?" Allie shouted when they had sung through the whole of "A Spoonful of Sugar."

"Keep singing," Harper said. "He doesn't have to be awake. He won't hear us anyway. We're singing for the Dragonscale, not for him. Sing, goddamn it."

"This is pointless!"

"Are you alive?"

"Yes!"

"Then there's a point," Harper told her and then couldn't say anymore. She was having contractions, hard ones. Her insides seized up, relaxed, and then seized up again. She had always wanted a water delivery. That had been all the rage not so long ago.

They were singing "A Spoonful of Sugar" a second time when *The Maggie Atwood* was sucked underwater with a last loud hiss, a blast of gray smoke, and a noisy roil of bubbles.

They sang "Chim Chim Cher-ee." When they forgot the words, they made them up.

*"Chim chim-a-nee, chim chim-a-nee, chim-chim-a-chick, paddling in the water sucks a big dick,"* Allie shouted.

*"Blow me a kiss and you can blow it out your ass,"* Renée sang.

"Look," Harper said.

Nick was glowing right through his sweater. Blue lights swarmed beneath his hoodie. The water steamed where it touched his pink, warm, sleeping face.

They started "A Spoonful of Sugar" again. Harper was in too much pain to join them, though. She clenched her teeth together and shut her eyes, weathering another series of contractions. When she opened her eyes, she saw the Portable Mother, her enormous black carpetbag, floating past them. The wide mouth of the bag was open and filling with water. As Harper watched, it revolved in a slow, dreamy circle and sank out of sight, carrying everything she had meant to give her child with it.

She wished the Phoenix had not soared away. For a long time she had been able to find it against the dark horizon, an intense, brassy gleam, but at some point—around the third run through "Candle on the Water"—she lost sight of it. Losing sight of it felt very much like losing hope. She could not imagine why it would go. Why John would leave them. That vast, monstrous bird—that was John, somehow. It was maybe more essentially John Rookwood even than the man who had gone down with the *Atwood*. It was the *true* John: immense, larger than life, a little silly, somehow invincible.

Harper could not tell Allie that she was going to continue singing for as long as she could because John had asked her to live. She wanted to try to do that much for him.

There had been lots of things she had wanted for both of them, simple domestic pleasures that she had started to imagine, in spite of herself. She had wanted a lazy Sunday morning in bed, with the sunlight falling in on them. She had wanted to put her hands on his bony hips and see what that felt like. She had wanted to watch some old sad movies with him. She had wanted to take some walks together in the fall and smell the autumn leaves crunching underfoot. She had wanted to see him hold the baby, and never mind that the more realistic part of her mind had always meant to give the child away. She had a theory John Rookwood would be fantastic with the baby. She had wanted him to have some fresh air and some happiness and to be free of his guilt and sorrow and loss. She had wanted a few thousand mornings of waking up next to him. They weren't going to have any of it, but *he* had wanted her to live—he had loved them and wanted them *all* to live—and she thought he ought to get something for all his trouble.

They sang "Romeo and Juliet" and they sang "Over the Rainbow." Allie sang the chorus of "Stayin' Alive" while Renée rested her voice, and then Renée sang "Hey Jude" while Allie rested hers.

When Renée had finished, she shot a frightened look at Allie. "Why is Harper making that face?"

"I think she's having the baby," Allie said.

It had been a long time since Harper was able to sing. She jerked her head up and down in a wretched nod. She felt the baby—a dense, slippery, unbearably painful mass—shoving his way down through her. It felt like her guts were being pulled out, hand over hand.

"Oh, Christ, no," Renée said, her voice a sickened hush.

Harper was in so much pain, she was seeing flashing lights. Black dots and silver flecks swarmed through her vision. She had an especially painful glare at the corner of her right eye, a persistent gold flickering. She shook her head to clear it, but it wouldn't go away.

"Look," Allie said, and grabbed Harper's shoulder and squeezed. "Look!"

Harper turned her head to see what Allie was on about.

First she thought Allie was excited because Nick was awake. Nick waved his puffy hands this way and that, gazing blearily about, wiping at his streaming face. But Allie was pointing past him into the east.

Then Harper thought Allie was excited because it was dawn. A line of shimmering copper light lit the horizon. The sky in the east was crowded with fat masses of clouds, tinted in hues of cranberry and lemon.

Harper caught a splash of water in the face, blinked her burning eyes. For a moment she was seeing everything in double, and there were two bright, golden points of light in the distance. Then her vision collapsed back together into a single image and she could see a hot, dazzling glow, high in the clouds, growing steadily. She couldn't help it. At the sight of the Phoenix returning, her heart lifted, and she felt a warmth that had nothing to do with Dragonscale. For a moment even the sharp, steely cramps in her abdomen seemed to fade. She blinked at salt water that might have been ocean or might've been tears.

But Allie wasn't pointing at the Phoenix, either.

She was pointing at the sail.

A great white triangular sail, with a stylized red crab printed on it. When the boat crossed in front of the rising sun, that sail became a shimmering veil of gold.

The boat had the wind coming hard off its starboard quarter and was canted over at a forty-five-degree angle, foam frothing over the bow. It came on toward them as if riding on a rail just out of sight under the waterline. Harper thought she had never seen anything glide along with such effortless grace.

The Phoenix dived low as it roared past them, less than eight feet over their heads. It had lost mass in the hours it was away, had shrunk to no more than the size of a condor, yet still it tore past with a blasting sound like a passing truck. A gush of chemical heat, smelling faintly like brimstone, washed over them. It was so close for a moment, Harper could've reached up and touched it. With its long hooked beak and flowing comb of red fire, it looked for all the world like a proud and ridiculous rooster, somehow given the power of flight.

Don Lewiston backed the sail and his long white craft slid the last hundred feet toward them on sheer momentum, the boom swinging loose and the canvas sagging and wrinkling. He threw a chain ladder over the stern, and when Nick began to climb, he reached a bony hand over to help him up. His blue eyes shone with something that was neither terror nor wonder, but both and more . . . an emotion Harper took for awe.

They fell in, sopping and shivering helplessly, one after another. None of them were shining anymore. They had each ceased to glow almost as soon as they caught sight of the sail, the Dragonscale giving out as if exhausted. The last ten minutes had been the hardest. The cold burned as if they were up to their necks in acid—and then it didn't burn, and the numbness was even worse than the pain, killing the sensation in Harper's feet and hands, creeping up her legs. By the time Don hauled her in—an unlikely catch indeed—she couldn't even feel her own contractions.

Don left, came back with towels, with blankets, with baggy sweatshirts, with cups of coffee for Renée and Allie. He had lost weight, was gaunt and cold-looking, the only color in his face the deep red of his nose.

Harper had water in her ears and was distracted by contractions, coming rapidly now, so she didn't get much of what anyone was saying. Renée asked questions, and Don answered them in a low, shaken voice, but Harper only caught pieces. Renée asked him how he happened to be there, close enough to fish them out of the drink, and he said he had been off the coast waiting for days. He knew they were walking into Machias because he had heard all about it on the ham. Harper imagined Don Lewiston holding a ripe roast ham to his face, like a meat telephone, and came very close to laughing, bit down on a hysterical quaver of mirth. "The ham?" Renée asked. "Yes'm," he said. He had a ham radio that got CB. He could pick up signals all along the coast, and he knew all about the woman who was enormously pregnant, walking north with a black woman, a teenager with a shaved head, a little boy, and a desperately ill man who raved in a British accent. The pack of them were making their slow way to Machias, where they would be processed and sent to Martha Quinn's island.

Only Don had been out to Martha Quinn's island, sailed around it and walked on it, and had seen nothing but blasted dirt and blackened skeletons. He had heard ol' Martha on the radio—several times—talking about the pizza parlor and the one-room schoolhouse and the town library, but the place she was describing had not existed for months. Had been leveled.

If Martha Quinn's Island wasn't a refuge, then it was a trap, but Don couldn't see how to keep them from walking into it. He had vague notions of hovering close to the bay, and maybe—*maybe*—sailing in under cover of dark when Harper and company were close to Machias, trying to intercept them, warn them. But then, in the last couple days, people had stopped broadcasting about them and he hadn't known where they were or what was happening. He had been anchored near the ruin of Martha Quinn's island when he saw the Phoenix sink from the clouds like fackin' Lucifer falling from heaven. Don said he wasn't sure if he had been led here, or chased here.

Harper only distantly heard this last part. She felt her insides were being turned inside out.

"What's happening?" Don Lewiston asked. "The fack is happenin'? Oh shit. Oh shit, don't tell me."

"Breathe, Harper!" Renée cried. "In and out. Baby coming. All done in a minute."

Allie was between her legs. Somehow Harper's sweatpants had come off and from the waist down she was wet and naked to the day.

"I see his head!" Allie shouted. "Oh, holy fuck! Keep pushing, bitch! You're doing it! You're making this shit happen, right now."

Nick ran and hid his face in Don Lewiston's stomach. Harper shut her eyes and pushed, felt she was shoving her intestines out onto the deck. She could smell a sharp, briny tang that might've been the sea or might've been placenta. When she opened her eyes for a moment, she saw the Phoenix again, now no larger than an ostrich, floating on the peaceful water beside the boat, wings drawn against its sides. He watched her with calm, knowing, humorous eyes of fire, a burning slick of oil on the sea.

She pushed. Something gave. She was torn open, her crotch a ragged seam of flame that made her sob with pain and deliverance.

The baby waved fat arms and squalled. Her head made Harper think of a misshapen coconut, slicked with blood: a dense thatch of brown hair, smoothed down to a lumpy skull. A fatty red cord dangled from her stomach, coiling on the deck and winding back into Harper herself.

It was a girl, of course. Allie put the child in her arms. Allie was shaking all over, and not from the cold.

The boat rocked at ease and the baby rocked in her arms. In a voice pitched just above a whisper, Harper sang a few lines of "Romeo and Juliet" to her daughter. The infant opened her eyes and looked at her with irises that were bright, shining rings of gold, the Dragonscale already deep inside her, wound right around the core. Harper was pleased. Now she didn't have to give her up. All she had to do now was sing to her.

Sunlight glinted off the steely blue edges of the waves. When Harper looked for the Phoenix, there was nothing left except a few tongues of flame flapping off the water. Sparks and flakes of ash drifted in the still, cool air, pattering down into Harper's hair, onto her arms. Some of the feathers of ash fell on her daughter, a smear of it across the little girl's forehead. Harper bent forward and kissed her there.

"What will you name her, Harper?" Renée asked. Renée's teeth were clicking together. She was shivering, but her eyes were shining with tears, with laughter.

Harper rubbed her thumb on her daughter's forehead, spreading a little of the ash around. She hoped some of John was in it. She hoped he was all over her, all over both of them, keeping them still. She felt he was.

"Ash," Harper said softly.

"Ashley?" Allie asked. "That's a good name."

"Yes," Harper said. "It is. Ashley. Ashley Rookwood."

Renée was telling Don about Machias, about their final boat ride and the men who shot John.

Don wiped his mouth with the back of a hand. "They'll be after us. But maybe not for a while. We could have a twelve-hour head start on 'em. We might like to use that time to make ourselves scarce."

"Where?" Allie asked.

Don had sunk down on one knee to be next to Harper. He slipped a hand out of his pocket with a small knife in it, unfolded the blade, shot her a questioning glance. She nodded. He made a loop with the umbilical cord and sawed through it in two strokes. A weak gout of blood and amniotic fluid pumped over his knuckles.

"An Tra," he said.

"Gesundheit," Renée told him.

One corner of his mouth turned up in a weary smile. "It's on Inisheer. Heard about that on the BBC World Service. I'n pull in about thirty different nations on a good clear night. Inisheer is an island off Ireland, An Tra is the town. Eight thousand sick. Full support of the gov'nment."

"Another island," Allie said. "How do we know that's not bullshit, too?"

"We don't," Don said. "And this boat ain't equipped for a transatlantic sail. We'd be damn lucky to make it. *Damn* lucky. But it's the best I got."

Allie nodded, turned her head, squinted into the rising sun. "Well. I guess we don't have anything else to do today."

For herself, Harper felt no alarm it all. She was sore, but content. Those fat clouds were breaking up, and the sky to the east was an almost perfect, serene shade of blue. She thought it seemed a nice enough day for a sail, and she recalled that John's mother had been Irish. She had always wanted to see Ireland.

Nick had crouched down on his knees to be next to her. He looked at the baby with a sweet, plain curiosity and then moved his hands, writing on the air. Harper smiled and nodded, and then bent close and put her nose to Ashley's.

"Hey. Your big brother has something to say to you," Harper told her. "He says hello. He says it's a pleasure to meet you and welcome to Earth. He says get ready to have some fun, little girl, because it's a big bright morning, and this is where the story begins."

BEGUN ON DECEMBER 30TH, 2010
COMPLETED ON OCTOBER 9TH, 2014
JOE HILL, EXETER, NEW HAMPSHIRE

# Credits



**CODA**

"What if There was Just a Bit More Story?" by Joe Hill. Copyright © 2016 by Joe Hill. Because there is. A boy saw it first, a serious little boy of six named Caius, who was walking home with his mother. He tugged her hand and said, "Look at the falling star, mama," and pointed. The woman, Elaina, held up, shaded her eyes against the bright of the day, peered out to the southeast and saw: a trim white boat, sail swollen full, the stylized image of a red crab stamped upon it. At first glance it seemed it was pursued by a red blast of flame, a comet-flare that rose and swooped and dove. As the craft clipped swiftly through the water, though, Elaina saw it was not running from a ball of fire at all, but was instead accompanied by a great blazing bird. That falcon of flame was using its heat to drive hot air into the sail, speeding the boat to a giddy, almost dangerous clip. Elaina spied a woman with yellow hair, standing on the pulpit at the tip of the bow. The faraway woman raised a hand in greeting, a hand that glowed as if it wore a glove of pure light. Caius waved in return, his own hand blazing up like a torch, green ribbons of flame trailing from his fingertips. "No one loves a show-off, Caius," Elaina warned him, but her smile suggested she didn't mean it.

# Acknowledgments

If you drive to the end of Little Harbor Road, in Portsmouth, New Hampshire, it will take you to the ocean, but you won't find the sandy lane to Camp Wyndham. I made the place up. Many other features of the area, however, are much as I presented them: South Street Cemetery, South Mill Pond, the Piscataqua Bridge. Here and there I have changed features to suit the needs of the story.

One danger of writing an acknowledgments page is the great likelihood of leaving out someone who made important contributions. When I was expressing my thanks at the end of the last novel, *NOS4A2*, I neglected to mention how grateful I am for my occasional conversations with Dr. Derek Stern. Talk therapy has been out of fashion for a while now. Who wants to talk when they could just pop a pill, am I right? But psychopharmacology has its limits; no one can write you a prescription for a sense of perspective. I'm not sure I ever would've finished that last novel (or this one) if not for Doc Stern's wry, literate support.

When you work on a book for four years, you get useful information from a lot of quarters. My thanks to Dr. Marc Sopher, Dr. Andy Singh, and Dr. Brian Knab for answering so many of my medical questions. Where I got it wrong, don't blame them—when I had a choice between serving the story or serving medical truth, I chose the story. To put it another way, you can't pop a dislocated lunate back into someone's wrist by squeezing, although it's a nice fantasy. Kids, if this ever happens to you, proceed to the emergency room, and prepare for surgery. That said, most of Harper's medical procedures are within the realm of possibility . . . including relieving the pressure on Father Storey's brain with a Home Depot hand drill.

A number of friends read some or all of this book in the early stages and provided helpful feedback: Chris Ryall, Jason Ciaramella, C. Robert Cargill, Lauren Buekes, Shane Leonard, and Liberty Hardy. My screen agent, Sean Daily, and his wife, Sarah, offered support and good advice, and then Sean turned around and sold the film rights to 21st Century Fox and Temple Hill. My deepest thanks to Steve Asbell, Isaac Klausner, and Wyck Godfrey for placing a bet on Harper and John, and to Sean's boss, Jody Hotchkiss, for placing a bet on me.

My editor at William Morrow, Jennifer Brehl, and my UK editor at Gollancz, Gillian Redfearn, are a seamless creative yin-and-yang. Every single page of this book is better because of their diligent attentions. Kelly Rudolph and Sophie Calder plotted world-beating publicity campaigns. HarperCollins/Morrow has a murderer's row of professionals, who worked tirelessly to make every aspect of *The Fireman* shine. They include Kelly O'Connor, Tavia Kowalchuk, Aryana Hendrawan, Andrea Molitor, Maureen Sugden, Amanda Kain, Leah Carlson-Stanisic, Mary Ann Petyak, Katie Ostrowka, Doug Jones, Carla Parker, Mary Beth Thomas, an incredibly hard-working sales team, and publisher Liate Stehlik. The UK squad is no less formidable, beginning with David Shelley, and including Kate Espiner, Jon Wood, Jen McMenemy and the whole marketing team, Sophie Calder, Craig Leyenaar, Paul Hussey, my pal Mark Stay, and the rest of the Orion sales crew. Kate Mulgrew read this book on audio, instantly making me sound at least five times cooler than I really am. She is owed a nice bottle of wine. My thanks to Laurel Choate at the Choate Agency for looking after business so I could stay focused on the creative end (i.e., the fun stuff).

Love and thanks to Christina Terry, who made sure I occasionally got away from the office to have some fun while I worked on this thing. All the love in the world to the King-Braffet compound, to Naomi, and to my parents, who as a group, in a thousand ways, made this book possible, and make my days a joy. Above all, thanks to my three sons, who make me so happy—I love you boys. I'm so grateful for our life together.

Finally: shortly after I completed the third draft of this novel, my friend and agent of twenty years, Mickey Choate—Laurel's beloved husband—passed away of lung cancer, at the age of fifty-three. I didn't know he was sick. He kept it to himself. The first I learned of his illness was when Laurel called me up to tell me he had died. He never smoked and he ran every day and it all seems very unfair. In our last conversation he had just finished reading *The Fireman* and he told me he thought it was a damn fine book. His approval meant the world to me; at the same time, I hate that so many of our conversations were about me and my writing. I wish we had talked about him a bit more. Mickey loved to get a good meal at an exciting new restaurant, and I wish we had had a last dinner together, so I could've told him I thought he was a damn fine friend. Maybe turnabout is fair play, though. Mickey represented me for almost a decade before I told him Hill wasn't really my last name. We each of us managed to spring at least one truly jolting surprise on the other.

I love you, Mickey. Thank you for letting me have a place in your life.

# About the Author

Joe Hill is the author of the *New York Times* bestsellers *NOS4R2, Horns,* and *Heart-Shaped Box,* and the prize-winning story collection *20th Century Ghosts.* He is also the Eisner Award-winning writer of a six-volume comic book series, *Locke & Key.* He lives in New Hampshire.